Bridie tramped into the Bow Road at eight o'clock that evening, badly footsore and sweating in the skirt and jumper that were too heavy for the warm day. The case felt fit to break her arms and she longed to stop and put it down. She didn't dare. As she'd moved steadily eastwards, away from Euston and through the great City, the grand buildings had tailed off. For a long way now houses and people became poorer and rougher with every street she passed. On and on she walked. When the sole fell off her shoe where Bow Road turns to Stratford High Street, she began to cry. Tears made tracks in her dirty face as she slumped in a heap at the edge of the road, put her head into her aching arms and wept.

Recent Titles by Christine Thomas

BRIDIE

Christine Thomas

This first hardcover edition published in Great Britain 1997 by
SEVERN HOUSE PUBLISHERS LTD of
9–15 High Street, Sutton, Surrey SM1 1DF,
by arrangement with Headline Book Publishing PLC.
This title first published in the U.S.A. by
SEVERN HOUSE PUBLISHERS INC of
595 Madison Avenue, New York, N.Y. 10022.

British Library Cataloguing in Publication Data

A CIP record for this title is held at the British Library.

ISBN 0 7278 5281 7

Typeset by Palimpsest Book Production Limited
Polmont, Stirlingshire, Scotland.
Printed and Bound in Great Britain By
Hartnolls Ltd, Bodmin, Cornwall.

For Hilary
With Love

Prologue

'Theresa O'Neill 1882–1918. May her soul rest in the peace of the Lord.'

Bridie knelt on sharp, prickly grass, churned round the edge of her mother's grave. It stung her bare knees as she carefully held her skirt out of the dirt. Her mother would have scolded if she had got grass stains. She gazed intently at the words on the plain headstone, put in place only yesterday. Leaning forward across freshly heaped soil she traced letters with her finger on pale grey stone warm with early summer sun. The newly chiselled shapes still had their first sharp edges. They'd slowly wear away with rain and frost until the words mellowed into a mossy little memorial like most of those on graves surrounding it. That would suit her mother better, thought Bridie. She'd been a gentle, soft-voiced woman, always with a kind word and loving touch for children. Bridie, sixteen years old and her eldest child, loved her dearly.

As she stroked her fingers over the letters a light breeze touched her, and Bridie thought for a moment that she felt her mother's hand rest tenderly on her unruly red hair. In longing, she bowed her head on her

1

knees and began to to weep. For the first time since the village priest left, solemn-faced, and her father had come lumbering down the narrow cottage stairs to tell her brusquely that Mam and the baby were passed away, she realised that it was true. Tears came at last.

Doubled over with sudden pain, she crouched on her elbows in dry, rough clay, rocking back and forth until her clothes were stained and her face was streaked with mud. She shook her fists towards the empty blue sky. With swollen eyes Bridie searched its high pale brilliance and found nothing. No angels, no God, no spirits. Nothing. Rage and betrayal shook her so, her teeth chattered, until at last exhaustion began to steal over her, loosening her fists, hanging her head, calming the painful sobbing.

Beside the small wooden hut where the gravedigger kept his spades, Father Robert, the parish priest, paused on his way out of the churchyard to look at the little figure sitting motionless on the ground. His lined face softened as he watched. He was fond of Bridie. He'd christened her, taken her first communion and supposed he'd marry her one day. He'd been to the cottage many a time and found her helping her mother when she should have been at school. Mrs O'Neill had looked anxiously at her husband when the priest told him bluntly that he was breaking the law, but she depended on her daughter and so mostly Bridie stayed at home, looking after the three little ones. Now, he supposed, she'd take her mother's place. He sighed, knowing that wisdom didn't always come best from books. His hand strayed automatically into the sign of the cross, and, respecting her need to be alone, he turned on his heel and went on his way.

The sun grew warmer, and from all sides birds sang and called from the dense yellow-green May foliage. They hopped and squabbled and busied above paths white with early daisies. Bees hummed. Clover grew in pink and white clumps along the bottom of the grey stone wall enclosing the church and its graveyard. Pale grass as fine as hair covered a recent grave; a child had died of scarlet fever. Many did. Bridie brushed listlessly at her skirt. It only made things worse so she gave up and, cupping her chin in her fists, sat gazing at the quiet place until she felt quite empty inside. Quite scoured out.

It was noon when she got stiffly to her feet, stretched, and tried to run her fingers through her hair, to separate the tangled mass glued to her face by tears. She turned back to the grave and was at last able to do what she'd come to do hours earlier. She began to repeat her favourite psalm, under her breath. 'The Lord is my shepherd, I shall not want,' she whispered. When she'd said it through she crossed herself and half lifted her hand as if to wave goodbye, then walked slowly along the grassy path to the church gate. It always squeaked. Pushing her way through, Bridie ran her hand up and down the smooth wood, full of memories of long Sunday Masses listened to drowsily from tall pews bathed in shifting shafts of red, blue and gold sunlight as it shone through high

3

stained windows. Bridie had thought the light came from Heaven; God's candles. She half smiled at her childish idea and let the gate swing slowly shut behind her. On her way back along the lane to the village, she vowed to herself that she'd do her very best to look after them all, Maire, MaryEllen and May, because her mother would want her to. So would her Dad.

Sean O'Neill was as rough and ready as his wife had been gentle. They'd married when both were just sixteen and had loved each other despite poverty and sickness, just as their wedding vows had said they should. Sean had been stoical about the many stillborn babies, and even about his four daughters and no sons. Theresa, who'd actually had to bear all the pain and loss, was not so much stoical as resigned to suffering. Often she looked at her four daughters and her eyes were full of sadness.

Watching them around the tea table, Mam had wondered how Bridie could be so different. Maire, MaryEllen and Little May had dark hair and pale cheeks, black curls and deep, deep blue eyes. Their faces never tanned, even when they worked the fields in high summer. Alabaster faces, smooth, delicate and round. Most of the village girls looked like the O'Neill girls; it was the local genes. Bridie stood out like a flame in darkness. In church, of a Sunday, the priest's eye would be drawn again and again to her bright head glowing coppery above the highbacked pews. In the rows of dark heads, Bridie's was startling. Her red curls grew in a mass and no amount of brushing or hairpins would make the wiry hair lie flat.

4

'Botticelli,' they'd have said, if they'd known. Her long, fine-featured face was as fair as the others', except for freckles which faded and darkened with the seasons.

'Don't know where she gets it from,' Sean would growl. 'I never heard of no colouring like that in my family.'

Theresa felt accused. 'I don't know, either, I'm sure,' she'd say, looking again at her unlikely daughter.

'Well, now,' Aunty Aileen who lived in Dublin said, 'that's Kerry features she's got. Down round Dingle Bay you'll see ever so many of the young women with our Bridie's looks. There's Kerry blood there, to be sure.'

'Must be way back, then,' Theresa had answered, 'None of my relatives ever said anything about Kerry.'

'I don't know of none, either,' agreed the old woman, 'but you can take my word that's what it is.'

Bridie would look at herself in the tiny mirror above the scullery sink. She liked the way she looked. Her freckles crinkled together on her nose when she laughed. Sometimes she pulled a face into the mirror, just to watch them. Light could change the colour of her eyes from grey to green to the whitish sheen of a stone on a dull winter day. Bridie liked being different.

Her mother's sudden death brought changes that meant much less time for peeping in mirrors. Cleaning, washing and cooking saw to that.

'I know we always helped her,' she told her sisters, 'but sure and I didn't know how hard she worked. How she did it with all them babbies as well. . . .' She shrugged.

But she took over cheerfully and chased her sisters into doing their chores so that they got on good-naturedly instead of grumbling. Little May, though, got away with murder. She was everyone's favourite, including Sean's. She wound him round her finger, Theresa used to say. He didn't spend a lot of time with his girls, as he called them. Never had done. So long as they helped out, and got in no trouble, Sean was content to leave the girls to their mother.

'Woman's work,' he'd say to the other men leaning on the bar in O'Donnell's, down in the centre of the village. 'They're best left to it.'

The men nodded agreement, and ordered fresh pints of dark, nutty-flavoured Guinness. Women were for leaving at home, except on holidays and Saturdays when the fiddles and squeeze boxes and penny whistles would come out and the bar burst with joyous playing and singing and banging of beer mugs until one o'clock in the morning. Since his wife's death, Sean had been spending more time than usual with his elbows on the bar. O'Donnell's open, generous face sobered in sympathy and he was ready and willing to advance a few pennies of credit to a fellow in distress. Sean O'Neill was a bit of a layabout, but no one held that against him since it was generally agreed that most of the village men were tarred with a touch of the same brush. Women clicked their tongues when they went into the main street in mid-afternoon, and heard their men's voices murmuring deeply from O'Donnell's. But it had always been that way and they had always been poor. And tomorrow didn't always come. Almost every man in the bar had lost more than one child. They knew about death, so they watched with understanding when Sean's big stubbly face would get redder and redder from unshed tears and Irish whiskey; by the end of the evening he would be snoring on the pitted, scratched wooden bar top until someone going that way propped him up and half carried him home to his front door.

One Saturday evening, about six weeks after Theresa died, Sean was waxing maudlin around midnight. O'Donnell had chalked up a lot more than usual, and he was still going strong.

'God save us, she's gone. God rest her. T'resha. Know?' He raised a watery, bloodshot eye to the room. 'God rest her shoul, buried shix weeks. My T'resha.' Sean began to mumble and a tear dripped into his beer glass. He hiccoughed several times, then started to cry loudly.

O'Donnell cast an experienced eye over his customer.

'Be better off at home, I reckon,' he said to several of the drinkers who were watching Sean's maudlin tears with interest. 'Anyone goin' his way?'

Two men sitting at a small table put down their dominoes.

'We can leave it and finish the game later. Don't no one interfere. We'll carry him between us. Reckon he deserves it, poor feller. Give 'im here.'

7

Between them they hoisted his weakly resisting frame between them. He was a tall, heavily built man with a belly bulged by years of beer. Taking his dead weight, the two men staggered as they hitched his arms up, one over each of their shoulders.

'Come on,' they said, impatient voices rough with sympathy. 'Let's get yer home.'

Feet dragging between his two minders, Sean's voice could be heard fading into the distance, singing disjointedly about Irish Eyes and hiccoughing steadily until the listeners in the bar could hear no more. With customary discretion, he was propped against his front door and left. He slid down the door-jamb and sat, stupefied, on the ground. He mumbled incoherently and the word 'Theresha' was audible from time to time. Half sitting, half lying, on the warm earth, he alternately talked to himself and dribbled tears that smelled of ale.

Upstairs Bridie started to worry. It was the first time her father hadn't come in and gone to sleep almost at once. She wondered what Mam would have done; he hadn't usually got as drunk as this when she was alive. Bridie bit a fingernail and listened to the sounds outside. When he started crying again she felt tears rise, stinging, to the back of her nose.

'Oh, poor Dad,' she said aloud. The jagged, drunken sobbing brought back her own grief in the churchyard and her heart ached. She slipped off the bed she shared with Little May and put her fingers to her lips for the small girl to be quiet. May's dark eyes watched her sleepily over the thick blanket of knitted

8

squares Theresa had made. Maire and MaryEllen were silent in the tiny third room, fast asleep. Going quietly down the stairs in bare feet, Bridie opened the door at the bottom that led into the main room. Light from a full moon poured through the uncurtained window and the white walls gleamed dully. Her father's voice sounded even louder. She opened the door carefully, in case he was propped against it, and found him lying on his back staring up at the brilliant stars, his face working as tears welled over stubble unshaven for several days. He looked ghastly in the bright moonlight, his eyes watery holes above blotched patches that the moon made stains. Bridie caught her breath and stood staring at him.

'Come on, Dad,' she said eventually.

She bent to help him sit up, and suddenly Sean noticed her.

'Eh?' he said out of a mouth that hung slack.

'It's me, Dad. Bridie.'

'Terry.'

'No, it's not Mam. It's me. Come on, Dad.' Bridie's voice began to have an edge to it as she verged on panic. It wasn't clear she'd be able to get him inside the house at all.

He rolled back, stargazing. 'Oh, God help us,' his daughter muttered. She put her hands under his armpits and began to pull. He didn't move. She dropped him and his head hit the ground with a thud. He let out a roar of pain and surprise. Bridie bent again and took a firm grasp on the coarse stuff of his jacket.

'Come on, help me,' she said crossly, and pulled

harder. The sleeves began to ride up round his neck but he didn't move an inch. Exasperated, Bridie deliberately let his head bang again. Sean clutched his churning skull and moaned.

'Jaysus, girl, you'll kill me.'

'You've no call to get so drunk you can't get inside your own house,' snapped his daughter. Her sympathy evaporated and she waved a hand to dispel the fumes that rose in waves every time he moved. She'd just have to get help. In the distance, towards the village, doors banged and men's voices shouted goodnights. O'Donnell's was shutting up at last. Bridie leant against the edge of the door and watched the lane that ran past the front of the cottage. It was light enough to see anything that moved. After about ten minutes she heard slow footsteps crunching along the gravel at the edge of the lane. She screwed up her eyes and saw a new labourer from one of the farms further outside the village trudge past, humming to himself.

'Mister.'

The man stopped and looked around.

'Mister. Can you lend me a hand getting me Dad inside? I can't move him.'

The farmworker came to the low gate that led straight into the lane. He leant over the gate, thin as a hayrake, his nose a sharp spike in the shadows. 'Oh, it's O'Neill. Yes, he's the worse for wear. I saw him earlier, down O'Donnells. You got your hands full, darlin'.'

'Will you help me drag him in?' Bridie repeated.

The young man opened the gate and came down the path.

'You take his feet so they don't drag too much, and I'll pull him this way.'

Between them they hauled a semi-conscious Sean over the threshold into the whitewashed room. The labourer looked round and nodded towards the space in front of the blackleaded range that took up most of the longest wall in the room.

'Put him there?' he asked, raising an eyebrow in the gloom.

Bridie couldn't see anywhere else where there'd be enough room for her father to stretch out on the floor, and he was beyond being put up to bed.

'Yes,' she whispered. They half carried his inert body across the floor and dropped him, spread-eagled, on to the rag mat before the range.

'It's not cold at night, this time of year. He'll be warm enough,' remarked the young man.

'You've been real kind, Mister.' Bridie looked critically down at her father. 'I know he'll be grateful to you in the morning, though he's in no state to thank you now.' She giggled, suddenly seeing the funny side of it, and put her hand over her mouth apologetically.

The young labourer grinned and put his hands in his pockets. 'Glad to help you. Let him sleep it off, and he'll be all right tomorrow. Can you manage now?'

She nodded, and he thought how pretty she was in the dim light. He felt sorry about her father, it was hard on her.

'I'll be off, then.' He turned and ducked out of the low door.

Bridie watched him vanish into the night air, and went to put down the latch after him. She looked at her father, who was snoring massively, and shook her head at his inert body. Closing the stair door quietly behind her, she crept back upstairs and into bed with Little May.

Silence fell again, that dense, pressing hush that brings the rushing blood loudly to the ears. Bridie, tired after the struggle with her father, slept deeply and when a touch came on her hair she dreamed again the loving touch in the graveyard. Her mother had come. Bridie smiled and turned her face to the gentle kiss. Mam stroked back the thick hair and bent to kiss the dreaming lips. The touch grew bolder and the kiss hurt. Mam's mouth became scratchy and menacing. The dream began to change. A nightmare, a hand pulling her head roughly backwards so that she half woke in fear. The hand buried itself in her hair, turning her head, and as she fought to wake up she found her father standing over her, one hand pulling at his trousers and the other pulling her mouth towards his.

Bridie lay paralysed. Staring, she watched Dad finally get his belt and trousers undone and dropped round his knees.

'T'resha. Darlin',' he whispered.

Bridie shook her head wordlessly.

'Come here.' Dad began to pull her towards the edge of the bed. The clumsy movement helped Bridie find her tongue.

'No, Dad. No, no! I'm not Mam. Dad, what are you doing?' Her voice rose in terror as her father took no notice, and slid his hand under her back and down, clutching her buttocks. He began to pull her night-gown clumsily from under her.

'Stop it,' she cried.

She opened her mouth and took a deep breath, to shout at him, but his mouth was on hers, tongue thrusting violently, stinking of whiskey. Her stomach heaved. She struggled to drag her face away, to draw breath. He lurched, knocking Little May sideways, so that she woke with a violent start and began to cry. Her tears stopped abruptly and she held her breath as she took in what was happening a few inches away. Dad and Bridie were having a fight. Little May froze. She crept backwards to the very edge of the bed and lay clutching the coarse grey sheet to her with both hands. Eyes round and unblinking as saucers stared at the shadowy heap of bodies writhing, thrashing and very nearly knocking her to the floor. Bridie's strength was of sheer terror. She pushed her father away and clawed his face.

'No, Dad! NO. Please, don't. NO.' The plea came out in a voice so thin and shrill it cut into his throbbing head. He shook her off and, with a grunt of effort, put his leg across so that she was pinned beneath him. Bridie began to moan. Her lips drew back in a snarl and, raising her head with an effort that made the tendons stand out in her neck, she bit her father hard. The girl heard a hoarse gasp of surprise and rage and felt him raise himself on one hand. He pulled himself right up, drew back one arm and struck her full across the mouth. Bridie half screamed and Little May whimpered. Then the kissing started again. Helplessly, Bridie mewed in the back of her throat while her father forced her knees apart and was in her. A sharp pain came again and again, and then, with a sort of coughing noise, he pushed in her slowly once or twice, and fell forwards. His face slid limply down into her neck, and soon after he began to grunt as he sank into a dead sleep.

Little May took her hands off her ears when the bed stopped bouncing up and down and opened her eyes, which she'd kept squeezed tight shut after her Dad had hit Bridie. Her mind was still repeating HolyMaryMotherofGod like a frantic talisman while her eyes, adjusted to the darkness, took in the sight of her father lying quite still on top of Bridie, who was hidden underneath him, not making a sound. She wondered what Bridie would do, and lay holding her breath until something more happened. Nothing did. Bridie lay quite silent and still. Her father snored as usual.

After a while May lifted her head cautiously and whispered into the darkness, which was now dense as the moonlight faded. 'Bridie?' There was no answer. May went cold with fear. What if Bridie were dead? Her mother had lain in bed all still and silent when she was dead. Little May felt trembly. She didn't want Bridie to go away like Mam. She stuck her thumb in her mouth and sucked hard as she decided that Bridie couldn't be dead, because if she was her father would know. He wouldn't let Bridie lie there dead. Just before dawn the little girl fell asleep, thumb in mouth, curled up against her father's warm, comfortable back. Lulled by his presence and his rhythmic snoring, she slept an uneasy, fearful sleep.

Bridie heard Little May call to her as if from some faraway place. She lay very still and wide-eyed, staring into the dark. She tried not to blink because each tiny moment that her eyes closed, the horror flashed before her. All of it. Blink. The touch on her hair; the kissing; the awful pain.

Blink.

She swallowed and her throat hurt. Her lip was aching and stiffening as it swelled. She felt sore, bruised all over, but numbed by Dad's weight. Cold and squashed, she couldn't move, and it wasn't just because of Dad. She had a strange, awful feeling that went through and through her mind as she lay in the cold wet misery of her bed. She somehow wasn't inside herself like she had been only a few hours earlier, when she stood with the young labourer and they'd smiled at each other over Dad's sad, drunken body. Blink. Oh dear God. Blink.

Bridie knew when it was dawn, even though the first faint patches of grey had not yet tinged the horizon. With the most delicate care, she rolled Dad off on to his back. She slid her cramped, aching legs from beneath his, and gently unclasped his arms from around her. He lay right up against Little May, who did not move. Bridie put her feet carefully over the side of her bed on to the chilly floor. Even in high summer the cottage got damp and chilled in the dewy mornings. Her thighs were slippery and her night-gown clung to her, sodden with her blood. She screwed up her nose in disgust then stood up quickly. There was only one thought in her mind: to get to the water tap in the scullery and wash. Wash. She must wash. And wash. And wash.

She tiptoed to the bedroom door and opened it just enough to slide through. The hinge grated if it was opened all the way. Creeping down the narrow stairs, she began to shiver wildly as she opened the door at the bottom. The cottage suddenly seemed full of doors, creaking, squeaking hazards to bring Dad roaring after her. She lifted the wooden latch on the scullery door silently and stood bemused by shock and fear in the earthen-floored lean-to where they did their washing. A single tap stuck out from the wall. Below it a wide, shallow sink and above, the tiny mirror that had once reflected a girl who seemed now to belong to another lifetime.

Under the sink stood what she wanted. Moving like a sleepwalker, she bent down and lifted the metal bucket up to the tap. Using both hands, she put it gently into the brown crock sink. It filled slowly as she ran the cold water in dribbles that wouldn't make too much noise. As the tinny sound of running water plinked in her ears, she listened, stiff with dread, for any movement from upstairs. Commonsense would have told her that once her father went to sleep after drinking, the Apocalypse itself wouldn't waken him. But commonsense and the Dad she loved had vanished in the night, bringing God knew what along with the beginning of a new day. With the bucket half full she lifted it down and set it in the middle of the tiny room. She looked at the cold clear water uncertainly, then decided to bathe her face first. She put her head under the tap so the water wouldn't make such a noise running straight into the sink, and turned it on. She was lucky it was summertime; in midwinter the water, if it ran at all, would have been nearly ice.

She gasped nonetheless as it ran over her head and down her face, pouring off her nose into the bowl of the sink. Her long hair hung in a sodden solid mass over her face; the darkening bruise on her mouth stung. She turned her head to one side and caught several mouthfuls, rinsing and spitting. Finally, she reached up blindly and fumbled for the tap. When it was off, she wrung her long hair out like a sheet and twisted it into a tight coil. It was wet enough to stay put, more or less, while she prepared to wash. The puddle she'd lain in so long had made her night-gown stick to her. She took it by the hem and carefully rolled it up until she could pull it over her head without having to let it touch her face. Naked, she trembled as she straddled the cold bucket. Squatting as best she could, she began to splash water over her legs. When all trace of blood was gone, she emptied the bucket down the sink and refilled it. This time she took a piece of rag from a collection under the sink and, standing over the bucket again, scrubbed and scrubbed and scrubbed where her father had soiled her, until her skin, white and chilled, began to break

17

and bleed. Half sobbing, she still dipped and rubbed, dipped and rubbed, until the pain broke through her trance. It was enough.

Once more Bridie emptied and refilled the bucket. This time, with fresh rags, she washed, then dried herself from top to toe. She made another effort to wring out her dripping hair and rummaged in a basket that lay on the floor. It held dirty clothes waiting for washday when she'd scrub them on the bleached wooden washboard, in hot water from the range. She managed to find enough of her own clothes and borrowed a woollen jumper of Maire's which was a bit tight, but she was so cold she had to wear something. Creeping into the other room, she fetched the comb from the shelf above the range. It stuck and dragged in her wet hair but she persevered until it hung in strands round her shoulders and could be tucked back behind her ears.

Bridie stacked the bucket and rags back under the sink. She opened the scullery door and walked down the path with its bright geraniums and phlox to the little gate. She didn't care now if it squeaked. Pushing it open, she turned into the lane and walked towards the village.

The early rays of sun shone white gold above sparkling fields. The first birdsong had shrilled into the soft air when Bridie was filling her bucket. Now the dawn chorus had faded into daytime chattering and shrilling. Birds rustled and started in the hedgerow as she passed and a mouse caught up late ran across the lane ahead of her. Bridie was dully aware of

18

creatures around her. She wanted to run, hurry hurry hurry. But pain slowed her and she hobbled slowly, as if prematurely aged. The sun rose higher by the minute. It dried her hair and its warmth seeped through and comforted her. She felt Maire's jumper grow warm on her back and with that, the deep inner shivering was calmed.

Morning voices drifted from the village. A door banged and a woman's voice called something and laughed. At the crossroads just before the village really began, she turned right. Not wanting to walk down the main street like she was, she took the long way round. A track led through hedgerows thick with nettles, buttercups and heavy, sweet heads of cow parsley which made her sneeze. The little lane wound ahead. Bridie didn't see it. Her eyes didn't leave the path in front of her. She plodded awkwardly, hurting.

At last she came to the church. Resting her hand on the gate to the churchyard, she stood and looked across to her mother's grave. The flowers were still fresh from yesterday. Bridie closed her eyes.

'I'm sorry, Ma. I didn't mean it. Please know I'm sorry.'

The words fell emptily. Her mother had gone. She couldn't be reached. Bridie's heart ached worse than the rest of her. She went up to the heavy church door. It was never locked, and swung open smoothly as she pulled the big iron ring of a handle and went in.

It was a small village church with a tower but it always seemed vast to Bridie and the village children. She loved the holy feeling of the still air hanging under the high roof. At Mass voices rose up and up until they reached the fairytale cloud city of Heaven, where God listened and knew if you were singing or not, and could see you if you'd played about, giggling with the O'Donnell boys instead of paying attention. Bridie had long since outgrown her childhood ideas of Heaven, but she loved the church for its peacefulness. She breathed in the scent of dust and lavender polish. Stale incense hung in corners; dusty spirals lazily danced in sunlight reflected off the high polish of rows of old, blackened pews. Bridie held on to the curved, carved back of the first pew while she genuflected painfully to the altar. Then she walked slowly down the aisle to the very front pew where the priest's very very old mother sat when she visited, all alone in her worn widow's black. Her feet trod indifferently the polished brass set into the floor to mark the graves of two former British landlords. Village women took it in turns to come each week with cloths and a bottle of Brasso, to polish the brasses until they shone like pure gold. Bridie sometimes wondered how rich you'd be if it was real gold, and you could prise it away and keep it. This morning she didn't wonder anything. She slid silently into the pew and sat with her head bowed. She didn't pray. She didn't do anything. She just waited.

Father Robert came in by the side door. He genuflected in the direction of the altar and strode briskly down the side aisle to the vestry. He carried a pile of new catechisms under one arm and was tucking a packet of Players into his trouser pocket with his free hand. He enjoyed his first smoke of the day on the short walk from the presbytery to the church. He bustled about for five minutes and then emerged into the front of his church to check the candles. Small white ones were kept on a shelf above the branching metal holder where there were usually at least half a dozen burning at any time. The day Bridie's mother had been buried all the little holders had been full the whole day.

The stout little priest's black gown rustled round his ankles. His boots had steel tips to make them last longer, so whenever he stepped off the carpet, he clattered loudly. Bridie listened unseen. She heard him cough and blow his nose on a big linen handkerchief before he opened a fresh box of white candles and began to stack them on the narrow shelf just to one side above the candleholder. He was balancing the last three carefully on the top of a pyramid of white tallow when a movement caught his eye. He turned to look and recognised the crown of the red head bent almost out of sight in his mother's pew.

'Bridie O'Neill?' he called quietly. 'Is it you, Bridie?'

The head raised itself and a very pale face appeared out of the shadow.

'Yes, Father.'

He stuck the last of his candles, which wouldn't fit on to the pyramid at all, into one of the holders and came over to the pew. As he came closer and could see the girl more clearly, his heart sank. She'd been beaten.

21

'What is it, Bridie? Why are you here so early? What has happened?'

Bridie shook her head dumbly.

'Your face is bruised. Has someone hit you?'

'Yes, Father.'

There was silence.

Bridie dropped her eyes and stared at the hassock hanging on a nail in front of her. It was embroidered with lots of tiny red crosses in thick wool that prickled your knees when you knelt on it for the prayers. She made up her mind.

'I'd like to make my confession, Father. If you wouldn't mind. It's early, I mean. I could wait here. . . .' Her courage began to fail her.

The grey-haired man nodded. 'Surely you can. Go on in. I'll be a few moments.'

The steel tips rang across in front of the altar, paused as he turned to bow and stopped as he walked on to the carpet in the vestry. When he came out he had the blue and white stole over his shoulders that he always wore when he heard confession. Bridie heard him sit down in the other side of the tall black box where he listened to the day to day sins of the whole community. A bit of stealing, quite a lot of fornication and lust, sometimes adultery and a great many people feeling guilty that they didn't even try to be very good. He opened his worn black book and began to read aloud, inviting Bridie to confess her sins and ask God for His forgiveness. They both knew the words by heart. There was a long pause.

'It was Dad.' The words came out finally in a

whisper so low that Father Robert had to strain to hear them. He was helped by the fact that he'd guessed already what had happened to Bridie in the course of that dark night. He'd looked at her pallor, the spreading bruise and the unconsciously twisting hands, and knew that, in all likelihood, she would tell the story she was about to utter through dry, white lips.

'I couldn't stop him, Father. I would have but he was too strong.'

'All right, Bridie.'

'Father?'

'Yes?'

'I think I'd have killed him if I could have. Is that a mortal sin? Will I go to hell for that? I wouldn't want to have hurt me dad, but when he . . . he . . . I would've killed him.'

Anger stopped Father Robert answering at once. He rubbed a weary hand over his face and turned towards the grille through which he could faintly make out the shape of Bridie's head.

'Bridie, listen to me carefully. You have done wrong through no fault of your own. You are your father's victim. He has done you the wrong. You have sinned, Bridie, but you are not responsible. But you will want me to give you a penance for the things you have felt and thought.'

There was a long silence while Bridie felt the words hang in her mind. She couldn't make anything of them.

The elderly priest stifled a deep sigh. He knew she

would carry the guilt and also knew from experience how futile it would be to say more.

'Me penance, Father?' Bridie prompted.

'Ah, yes. Let us see. Which psalm do you know best?'

'The one hundred,' she answered without hesitation.

'I want you to repeat it each day before you go to sleep, and think about what it means. For one week. Will you do that?'

'Yes, Father.'

'Good.'

There followed the lovely ritual of the absolution – for a sin, reflected the priest wryly, it flew in the face of commonsense to say she had committed. He left the confessional quickly, discreetly leaving her to take her time. He pottered in the vestry, then went out to see what she was doing.

Bridie was sitting on the steps of the altar with her chin in her hands. He stood in front of her, hands behind his back. After a bit she said apologetically, 'I'm sorry, Father, but I can't go back. I can't go home, because he . . . he's there, and. . . .'

The priest stared at her. 'Have you any idea what you can do instead?'

This was a matter that had occupied Bridie in the night. She'd made a plan.

'I'll go to England, Father.'

Robert looked surprised. He knew his parishioners well, and he'd not heard of the O'Neills having kin on the mainland.

'Have you family over there?'

'No, Father.'

'Ah.'

'I can get work. I'm old enough to go into service or something like that.'

He looked at her gravely.

'Fifteen?'

'Sixteen.'

The priest swung round on his heel and marched slowly halfway up the aisle and then back down again.

'I've an idea. I have an old friend, Francis Holmes, who lives in London. He's a good man, and kind. If I call him, he might help you find a position in service and keep an eye on you when you arrive. Its not like the village, Bridie, London is like nowhere you've ever been. Do you think that would be of help?'

Her face looked all eyes.

'Yes, Father. Thank you, Father. Oh, yes, please.'

'We will do that, then. Is there any other way in which I can help you?'

Bridie hesitated.

'I'm ever so sorry, Father, to be a nuisance, but I'd be so glad if you could ask Maire to bring me my clothes and things.'

The priest realised that he'd overlooked the most important question. What was she to do for money?

'How will you buy your ticket?'

Bridie had thought of this.

'I've me mother's ring. I don't want to, but I'll pawn it.'

The priest nodded again. She was sensible. She'd survive.

'I've to go down to your end of the village later, and I'll see Maire.' I'll see your father, too, he thought grimly, but said nothing of that to her. 'Just now, will you go up to the presbytery and ask Mrs O'Sullivan for some tea and jam. Tell her you've been on an errand for me and I told you to come. Tell her I said you were to lend her a hand with the kitchen until I come in. Will you do that, Bridie?'

For the first time a small, lop-sided smile brightened her face.

'Be off with you, now,' he answered sternly.

She walked stiffly away up to the church door and across to the priest's home, where his housekeeper clucked with disapproval when she saw the girl's bruises, but held her tongue and expressed herself instead by way of hot sweet tea and a large plate of bread and greengage jam. Bridie had to eat slowly, though she was ravenous. She was saving the last deliciously jammy soft bit from the middle of the bread for last, while topping and tailing gooseberries for Mrs O'Sullivan, when there was the ringing sound of metal on the flagstones in the hall, and the priest came back from the village. Father Robert smiled at Mrs O'Sullivan.

'I'm afraid I have to take your helper away,' he said across the big scrubbed table, helping himself to a ripe gooseberry.

He beckoned to Bridie, who followed him down the hall to his study. He gestured to her to sit down and, hitching up his cassock, perched on his desk in front of her.

'I've seen Maire and MaryEllen,' he began. 'They are putting your belongings together and will bring them up here as soon as they can. They are, of course, completely puzzled and upset by the idea of your going away. They really do need you, Bridie,' he raised his eyebrows at her, 'now your mother's gone. Would you not be able to stay if you were quite certain that your father would never touch you again? I believe that if I spoke to him in the strongest possible words about what has happened, he would be very contrite indeed. You said he'd been down in O'Donnell's drinking unusually hard. I doubt he may even remember what he did. He'd not a bad man, your father, Bridie, and I believe he was probably too drunk to know what he was doing.'

Bridie stared at him, appalled. Was he changing his mind? He'd seemed all understanding and sympathy in confession, and now he was talking as though it had all been just a bit of a mistake. She shook her head speechlessly.

'You're bent on going to England?'

She found her voice as anger overcame her disappointment.

'Yes, Father. I couldn't stay, no matter what. I know the others will be upset, and it upsets me to leave them. But I have to go. I think Maire would understand if ever she knew what's happened.' Her voice sounded stronger, more decided. The priest realised that he was dealing with a young woman, not a child. He looked at her thoughtfully and finally nodded.

'Very well. What are we to tell them? They have to have a reason, and I doubt you want to give the truth?'

Bridie felt astonished. Father Robert was inviting her to lie? The world had indeed turned upside down since yesterday. She thought rapidly.

'Well,' she said at last, 'there's no easy explanation comes to mind. Would it sound all right if I just said I wanted to go away to find work? I know it won't make them feel happy, but it's a kind of reason.'

The priest pursed his lips doubtfully.

'It'll have to do,' he said, 'because I can't come up with anything better. It's what I'll tell Frank Holmes as well, all right?'

'Yes, please. Nothing about the . . . the . . . you know?'

'That's confession, Bridie. It can never be repeated. Now then,' he continued, 'you'll be needing money, and tickets and instructions where to go and how to get there. It's a long way you're going, young woman, and on your own. Think you'll manage?'

'I'll just have to, won't I?'

The priest looked at her seriously.

'I think that is just what you're going to have to do. The Good Lord will watch over you, you know.'

'He didn't last night.' Bridie put the bad thought into words before she could stop herself. In front of Father Robert, too. She flushed with shame and picked at her skirt nervously. The priest went round to open a drawer of his desk, taking out an envelope which he handed to Bridie. 'Here. I've put Mr Holmes's address in this, and some money. That is for your ticket.' He raised a hand at Bridie's protest. 'I don't like the idea of your pawning your mother's ring. It belongs to you and you should keep it. This is from the fund I have for helping people in trouble; the poor box, if you like.'

Bridie took the envelope. The priest saw her turn it over before stuffing it into her pocket. Ah, the Parish daughters, he thought sadly. If the Good Lord doesn't take better care of them, then the poor box must, I'm afraid.

He knew all too well how many village girls could tell tales not much different to Bridie's. Mostly they stayed, though, not saying much. Few had the kind of outraged determination that the little O'Neill girl was showing. The money was partly a gesture of respect. The elderly man liked people who stood on their own two feet; he met too many altogether of the other kind in his line of business.

'The first step is to go to the train station in Dublin,' he began to explain the journey. 'I heard old Barney say he was taking a sheep over to a fellow just outside the city, and he's willing to let you ride on the cart. He'll see you get there. Then from Dublin you take the train to Dun Laoghaire. There you take the steam packet to Holyhead on the other side of the water. You buy your ticket straight through to London from Dublin. That way you needn't spend time looking for one ticket office after another. All right? One ticket, Dublin to London. Then in Holyhead you'll have to find your way to the train station again, and ask for the train to Euston. Then you just sit tight until you get to the end of the line. At Euston the train stops. Goes no further. So you can't go wrong. Dublin, Dun Laoghaire, Holyhead to Euston. Got that?'

It might just as well have been Jerusalem to Istanbul. Bridie, who'd only been to Dublin two or three times in her life, nodded and clutched the envelope in her pocket tightly.

'And I've telephoned Frank Holmes on your behalf. He tells me you are welcome, and he will do everything he can to find you some work. He has very generously offered to let you stay in his house until you've come to some arrangement about a job. You're lucky to have such an offer, and I hope you do his kindness justice, Bridie.'

'I will, Father. Oh, I will.' She was so relieved to have somewhere to go that she'd have promised anything.

'Time is going to be tight,' the priest went on. 'There's a night ferry goes, I think, around ten o'clock. If you can get the train at five, that should give you time enough. Old Barney wants to go at midday. Can you be ready to leave then, if Maire and the others bring your things over here?'

Bewildered by the speed with which it was happening, Bridie nodded. What had been a plan born of a nightmare was now being calmly discussed in terms of timetables and train stations.

'All right, that's how we'll do it then. I'll ask Mrs O'Sullivan if she'll be good enough to put some sandwiches together.' He went towards the kitchen, but turned back as the doorbell rang. Outside stood Bridie's three sisters, with a suitcase on the step in front of them. Little May, seeing Bridie in the study doorway down the hall, ran forward with a cry and flung her arms round her sister's waist. She held on tightly while Maire and MaryEllen came in with the case. They all stood uneasily in the hallway looking at Bridie, waiting for her to say something. She did her best, making up the story she'd suggested to the priest. They all looked blank.

'What on earth do you mean?' asked Maire. 'We manage well enough. There's no call for you to go away to work. Who'll look after us? It'll have to be me, won't it, and I'm not sure I could manage without you.' She looked round for help from her younger sisters. 'We need you much more than we need more money, Bridie. Please don't go away.'

Bridie felt as if she were being steadily torn in two. She shook her head. 'I know. I really do know, but I have to go anyway,' she said in a low voice.

Maire put her face close to her sister's and looked at her hard.

'Why?' she demanded. 'I don't believe what you are saying.'

Trapped, Bridie looked furtively at the priest, who took no part in the discussion.

'Who give you that lip?' The question wouldn't

31

brook evasion. Maire confronted her sister angrily, demanding to understand.

Little May suddenly gave a shriek and buried her head in Bridie's skirt.

'What's she on about?' Maire was getting more baffled by the minute.

'I dunno,' muttered Bridie, who could feel the situation sliding completely beyond her control.

'You do. You do, so.' May pulled her head out of its hiding place and looked up desperately at the big girl's face. 'I'm going to tell if . . . if you don't.'

'Tell what?' Maire's voice was shrill with frustration and curiosity.

Bridie, harassed and hopeless, gave up. 'Dad gave me the lip,' she said, and hoped they'd leave it at that.

Maire looked sceptical. 'You planning to go away because of that? It's not the first black eye or whatever we've had, and you never wanted to go away on account of nothing thing like that before. Tell the truth.'

Bridie shook her head in misery.

'I can't.'

'Bridie O'Neill, you're lying to your own sisters. You should be ashamed.' Maire was hopping mad.

Then May shocked them all into horrified silence.

'It was Dad. He came last night and had a fight with Bridie. And he hit her and made her cry and cry. He lied right on top and squashed her.'

Three pairs of eyes swivelled downwards to the little girl's pinched, furious small face.

'He hurt Bridie something bad. Didn't he?' she

turned to Bridie fiercely, demanding honesty.

'Oh my Lord,' whispered Maire, in spite of the parish priest standing there. 'Is that it, Bridie?'

Shamed beyond any words, Bridie nodded numbly.

Her sister gazed at her with fascinated pity. She was way more precocious than the older girl and had a good enough idea of what May was describing.

MaryEllen, always shy and diffident, began to cry quietly.

'Shut up, MaryEllen,' snapped Maire impatiently. 'There's nothing wrong with you. It's Bridie.'

Chastened by the lack of sympathy, MaryEllen subsided into silence again.

Maire pushed the case with her foot, edging it towards Bridie.

'Here. I think you'd best go after all, though I'll miss you badly, I really will. I wish you could stay at home, but I don't believe you can, can you?'

With the terrible feeling that her boats had just been burnt so there'd be no turning back, Bridie looked her sister straight in the eye.

'No, Maire love, I can't stay at home again. I'm glad you've found out why, because now I don't have to go away feeling I left you with lies. I never wanted to do that, but I didn't know what to say.'

Maire suddenly pushed Little May aside and threw her arm's around her elder sister.

'Oh, Bridie, it's awful. I'm sorry. I'll kill Dad.'

'No!' cried Bridie, alarmed. 'You mustn't talk like that. He probably doesn't even know what he did, he was too drunk.'

The priest intervened for the first time.

'Leave your father to me, Maire. I'll talk to him, and he will know exactly what he did, and he will grieve for the rest of his life for it. You might come and see me later on, when Bridie has gone. Would you like to do that?'

Maire looked around at the other two. 'We'll all come, Father.'

Mrs O'Sullivan opened the kitchen door and stuck her head into the hall.

'Old Barney's coming up the path. His cart's outside the gate.'

The priest looked at Bridie.

'Are you ready?'

'Yes, Father.'

Little May, realising what was about to happen, began to shriek. A tantrum erupted that forced the others to put their hands to their ears. Bridie prised May's fingers off her skirt only to have the little fingers clutch tightly at her hair. They hurt enough to bring tears to Bridie's eyes. Maire went to pull her away, but May kicked and struggled and screamed. Her hair torn almost from its roots, Bridie pushed her small sister desperately at Maire. 'Take her, for Heaven's sake,' she gasped.

The priest stepped forward, and picking up the howling child, held her away from him at arm's-length. May fought furiously to be put down, but he held her easily and in a few moments the yells diminished into sobs and she put out her arms to Bridie in appeal.

'You won't start screaming again?'

May shook her head.

Bridie took the little girl into her arms and kissed her. 'I love you, little one,' she whispered, 'and I will come back and see you one day. Perhaps you'll come to see me. Be a good girl and do as Maire tells you.'

The small dark head nodded. Bridie turned to Maire and MaryEllen.

'I love you, too, and I won't forget you. I'll think of you all the time and I'll miss you so much.' Her voice began to shake. She hugged them, first MaryEllen and then Maire, swallowing back tears. She gave a passive May into Maire's arms and picked up the case.

'Is Barney wanting to go?' she asked.

Father Robert nodded. She carried the case through the kitchen and out of the back door.

'Goodbye, Mrs O'Sullivan,' she said.

The housekeeper thrust a packet at her.

'Here. I've made you some sandwiches. You take care and be a good girl now.'

Case in one hand, packet in the other, Bridie pulled herself on to the back of Barney's cart, along with a large unshorn sheep that shied away from her. The wizened old man grinned at her toothlessly, his faded brown eyes quizzical as he asked was she ready to go. Bridie nodded.

Barney settled himself at the reins and gave them a jerk. The cart jolted forward. Bridie waved and waved until the cart rounded a bend, and then sat watching the road slowly unfold beneath her dangling feet.

The dirt track turned to stones, the stones to paving and finally they were on the streets of Dublin. 'Here we are, coming up now,' said Barney. It was the only time he'd spoken throughout the drive. 'Station's along there.' He gestured with the end of the reins. 'Let you off here then?' he suggested.

'Yes. This'll do nicely, thank you, Barney.'

She heaved the suitcase down and stuffed the sandwiches in her pocket. ' 'Bye Barney. Thanks.'

The old man grunted and jerked his reins again. He and the cart lumbered off down the road and Bridie, completely alone, turned into Dublin Station to begin her long journey, to leave everything and everyone she loved and with a place she didn't know for her journey's end.

Chapter One

Bridie had lost all sense of time as, by the blind walls of the Bank of England, she came to a halt. The great intersection – Cheapside, Cornhill, Threadneedle Street, King William Street, with Princes Street and Victoria Street – bemused her completely.

'I can't follow me nose in a circle,' she said under her breath, echoing the advice of the policeman who had given her directions earlier, and looked round for likely help. The heavy buildings closed in on her, a frightening foreign country. It was all so grey and black, bricks and stones crusty with soot and dirt. Pigeons, whole flocks of them, scavenged and squawked on the sills and in the street, their droppings making whitish smears against the soot. Fearless, arrogant birds. Bridie tried to skirt round them, alarmed by the quick, poking beaks. She bit her lip agitatedly and the pigeons suddenly scattered.

One of the biggest of the doors across the way swung open. A bucket and mop were followed down the steps by an impressive figure. Encased in a floral pinny and firmly rooted in carpet slippers, it wheezed its way to the gutter, where the woman wrung out the greasy strands of the mophead before chucking the filthy contents of the bucket into the road. As she straightened up she met Bridie's eyes. The girl smiled and two button black eyes almost vanished as the City cleaning woman beamed back.

'All right, duck?' she asked companionably.

Bridie shook her head slightly.

'I'm lost.'

'Where did you want to get to, love?'

'Stratford.'

'Yes? I'm from Bethnal Green meself. Out the same way.' She clanged the bucket down and pointed a red, chapped hand down the road.

'Over there, see? Down Cornhill and Leadenhall. Straight over Aldgate until you come into Whitechapel. Then it's just straight on until you see Stratford High Street. You're there, then. T'ra then, love,' she called cheerily as Bridie turned to go. 'Take care.'

The carpet slippers slopped their way back up the steps and the bright pinny disappeared into the high gloom of the interior as the door swung shut behind her.

Bridie tramped into the Bow Road at eight o'clock that evening, badly footsore and sweating in the skirt and jumper that were too heavy for the warm day. The case felt fit to break her arms and she longed to stop and put it down. She didn't dare. As she'd moved steadily eastwards, away from Euston and through the great City, the grand buildings had tailed off. For a long way now houses and people became poorer and rougher with every street she passed. On and on she walked. When the sole fell off her shoe where Bow

Road turns to Stratford High Street, she began to cry. Tears made tracks in her dirty face as she slumped in a heap at the edge of the road, put her head into her aching arms and wept.

She'd stopped near a crossroads. On the corner of four mean streets stood a public house whose double doors gave directly on to the road. Although it was hardly dusk, the gaslights had been lit, and the lighted windows looked cosy. Bridie wiped her nose, runny with tears, on the hem of her skirt as the doors opened on a gust of good-natured laughter, and the familiar smell of beer and tobacco spilled out. A young woman in a green cotton dress had started to turn up the road away from Bridie when she stopped and looked back.

'You in trouble, love?' she asked.

Bridie, embarrassed, bent as if to show her foot.

'I've broken me shoe. Me feet are all over blisters,' she complained, poking at her toes, half to show the blisters, half to avoid looking up.

The girl was used to seeing children run barefoot. 'Oh, yes,'she said vaguely.

She went to move on when Bridie, in desperation, said, 'Miss, can you tell me how far I've still to walk? To Stratford?'

Miss looked round.

'You're nearly there. Up the road, at the top, and you're in the High Street.'

'Oh, thank God,' Bridie cried in relief.

The girl looked at her curiously. 'You going anywhere I know?'

'Tredegar Square.'

A surprised expression came over the girl's face. 'Really?'

Bridie was nonplussed. 'Yes, I'm going to a friend of a friend. I want to go into service, and he's helping me.' She felt so low, the urge to confide overcame discretion.

'Oh, I see.' The young woman pointed the other way. 'Well, you've come past it, then.'

Bridie felt tears brim over at the very idea of going back again.

'You go back, about halfway down Bow Road. Tredegar Square is on your left, going that way.'

Bridie looked back and shook her head in despair.

'Look, it ain't far. I'm going that way meself. Want me to show you?'

'Oh, yes.' That was different. Bridie bounced to her feet, blisters forgotten. Hastily dragging off the other shoe she left it lying in the road and hurried barefoot after the green dress in case it wouldn't wait. Hopping and and skipping to avoid stones, she caught the girl up.

'I know some of the people in the Square, 'cos me sister's in service near there. You going to anyone in particular?'

'Yes. A man called Mr Holmes.'

'Mr Holmes? Are you – honest?'

'Why?' asked Bridie anxiously. 'Do you know him?'

'Oh, not personal like. But everyone round here knows about him.'

Bridie felt dismayed. Was this good or bad? The girl chattered on.

' 'e's on the Council, or works for the Council, or summat. Anyway, 'e gets things done . . . like water taps. It was partly him that made them give us taps with clean water. He's always on about dirt, and tries to make 'em clean up, like. And scarlet fever, and the diphtheria, and the consumption. That kind of thing. He tries to do something to stop it. I think that's what he does, anyway.'

She looked at Bridie with new respect. 'If you're going to work for him, all I can say is, you're lucky. By all accounts he's a lovely man.'

Bridie digested this news in silence. 'Is he old?' she asked at last.

'Well.' The girl waggled a hand back and forth. 'So-so. Not old exactly.' She laughed. 'But 'e ain't no spring chicken neither.'

'Has he got a wife?'

'He did have. She died quite a long time ago. I've heard that that was what got him going on his work. She died of the consumption, come to think of it. I think me nan said that's what happened.'

'Oh,' said Bridie. Mr Holmes was turning out fascinating.

'This is your turning,' said the girl suddenly.

Bridie looked down the tree-lined street. Plane trees rustled lazily in the summer dusk. At the far end the little street opened out into a square filled almost completely by a green and overgrown garden. Black iron railings barely contained the rambling roses that, covered with tight buds, climbed everywhere. Rhododendrons made a dark mass at one end, and beneath a spreading magnolia tree a long wooden bench sheltered a sleeping cat. Tall houses stood round the sides of the square, their windows open to the soft air.

'Oh my,' said Bridie softly.

'Nice, ain't it? A lot of nobs live round here. I told you you was lucky. Anyway, I'll love you and leave you. What did you say your name was?' The girl had half turned to go, and asked the question as an afterthought.

'Bridie O'Neill.'

'Mine's Daisy Davids. Might see you again. T'ra then.'

'T'ra,' echoed Bridie.

She walked beneath the plane trees to the end of the little road and looked round the square. The cat looked up lazily as she perched on the edge of its bench, dragging a comb through her hair. Tugging at her curls as best she could, until the comb went through them, she hoped she looked a little neater. She bent down and hastily wiped her face with the edge of her skirt, and ran her hands down her sides to try to get off the worst of the dirt. She knew she probably looked like a tramp, but making the effort was something.

'Bridie's such a sensible girl.' Her mother's voice seemed to come from nowhere. She sighed and pocketed the bit of comb.

'Number twelve,' she said aloud, and picked up the case for the last time. Scanning the front doors in the gathering gloom, she found number twelve at the far end, in one corner of the square. A garden ran round the front and side of the house, tree-lined and private. Heavy curtains not yet drawn let the glow of gaslight, recently lit, spill on to the area and steps. Bridie could see a brown, booklined room with a high white ceiling. She squared her shoulders, clenched her fists and climbed the steps. Lifting the heavy brass doorknocker, she let it fall.

Footsteps approached, the brown-painted door opened and a spare man of middle years, with a thin, lined face and penetrating grey eyes, smiled at her.

'You must be Miss O'Neill. Come in, my dear, I've been expecting you.'

He bent to take her case and welcomed her in so warmly that Bridie burst into tears. Hot with shame she turned away but he reached towards her and touched her arm. They stood awkwardly in the doorway.

'Please, Miss O'Neill, please do come in. It doesn't matter at all.'

As he spoke there was a furious yowl and a large tabby flew over a garden wall two doors down and tore up the front steps of number twelve. The cat dodged frantically around Bridie's feet and sent her stumbling. Tripping over herself in agitation, she sat down heavily on her suitcase.

'Vermin!' exclaimed Mr Holmes.

Bridie looked up, startled, and both hands flew to her hair.

'Oh goodness, no!' cried Mr Holmes. 'I meant the cat. Vermin Ermin. He was christened that as a kitten.

43

He was so flea ridden, you see, and because of his markings. Ermin, you understand. Oh dear, it's not what it seemed.'

The gesture dismayed him dreadfully and Bridie stared at him distractedly. Her will to go anywhere ebbed away. This London was a mad place. Sniffing, she let herself be helped up and led down the hall to a room at the back of the house. In front of an open kitchen window a table for two was laid and ready. Fragrant bread, a big chunk of yellow cheese, a small bowl with pats of butter, and two covered dishes in the middle holding something that steamed.

Bridie's mouth began to water.

'I was just about to eat myself, not knowing when you might arrive. This is excellent, we can eat together now.'

She looked longingly at the food as he beckoned her through the door.

'Come with me, and I'll show you where you can wash. You must be so tired and hungry. Mrs Goode has got things ready for you. You'll see her in the morning. She's my housekeeper.'

Talking all the way, he took Bridie upstairs to a small room at the back. It overlooked the garden and here again the window stood open. A small bunch of flowers had been placed on the washstand, and folded towels lay on the counterpane of a high wooden bed.

'The bathroom is there.' He indicated along the landing, where a door stood open.

Bridie's face dropped in astonishment. A bathroom!

'If you take your towel, you'll find soap and water there. Come downstairs when you've finished. The door to the kitchen will be open.'

He left her standing there, and went back to make a pot of tea. The girl was filthy but for all that he had been struck by how pretty she was. Mrs Goode would have her scrubbed in no time. Tonight, the poor child must be close to exhaustion. Francis Holmes sat down, poured himself a cup of tea, and waited. He waited so long that he put the hot dishes back in the range to keep warm, and after a while brewed a fresh pot of tea. He began to wonder if he shouldn't go up and see what his guest was doing, but, being patient by nature, he picked up the evening paper and let Bridie take her time.

Upstairs, his guest was paralysed. She stood rooted to the spot where he'd left her. The room she stared at was tall and square. The long window, by now quite dark, was framed by deep blue velvet curtains reaching all the way to the floor. Varnished boards made a narrow edge round a patterned carpet, soft under Bridie's bare toes. Looking down, she stepped hastily off into the bare space by the door. A bowl with fluted edges and tiny forget-me-nots around the edge stood on a marble-topped washstand. There was a mirror above the washstand and by the wooden bedhead hung a crucifix carved in pale wood.

Poor Bridie had never in all her life felt so utterly out of place. Overcome by misery and embarrassment, for two pins she'd have fled and never, ever, come back. Staring at the towels folded on the end of the bed, she suddenly knew what to do. Straining her ears to try to tell if Mr Holmes was anywhere near, she could hear nothing but the sigh of leaves outside. Slowly she undid her skirt and stepped out of it, unbuttoned her blouse and screwed the two into a bundle.

She tiptoed on the carpet until she could reach the towels. The largest fell open into a big oblong that would wrap round her. She took the other and cautiously opened the door a crack. No sound. No movement. Her heart beating painfully with fright, she crept to the open bathroom door and looked in. A great white bath tub stood on curly legs, inviting her. Closing and locking the door, she first pulled the blind down over the window, then took off all her clothes. Teeth clenched with desperation, she took the first bath of her life. Plug in, taps on full, cold water and soap. Grey scum. Fingering it with disgust she pulled the plug and began again. The next bathful wasn't so bad, and the third stayed quite clear. At last she felt clean.

Looking in the mirror, she saw her face was drawn and wan. The swelling round her lip had blackened and the flat wet hair clung to her head. Her heart began to bang again as she faced the return journey. Sliding round her bedroom door, she jumped. Vermin Ermin gazed at her from the middle of the counterpane. He stretched a languid paw and picked at his claws with sharp yellow teeth, watching her with great black, dilated eyes. Bridie stared back. He was a huge tabby with white whiskers.

'Vermin?' she asked.

The dark ears pricked forward.

'You arrived filthy, too, by all accounts. Friends?'

The cat turned and began to wash his tail.

'All right. You can keep me company.' Opening the suitcase she'd carried such a very long way, she squatted down and considered. None of its contents were suitable for this grand house, but they'd have to do. She took out the dress she'd wear to go to Mass of a Sunday. With fingers that trembled clumsily she buttoned the dark blue bodice fitted close to the waist. It gathered into the long folds of skirt that fell almost to her ankles. Her mother had been a skilful needlewoman. Fully dressed, Bridie scrabbled in her discarded heap for the bit of comb. Her curls would spring back round her head as they dried. She had no shoes. Anxious to leave the room tidy she stuffed the filthy things she'd taken off behind the washstand and the closed case underneath the bed. Downstairs, a door opened and closed. He was still there. Her throat tight with nerves, she tiptoed out of the little blue bedroom and went down.

Francis, who was getting very hungry, was glad she'd come down at last. He looked up to greet her and his eyes widened slightly with surprise. He'd listened to the activity in the bathroom but it hadn't prepared him for her transformation. He'd noticed she was pretty when she first arrived, but now he saw she was like some medieval painting of a woman – burnished crinkly hair, long features, prominent eyes. The awkward moment passed.

'Did you find everything you needed?' he asked, to break the tension.

'Yes, thank you, sir.'

'Good, good. Now let's have our supper. I think we're both hungry.'

Guilt suffused Bridie's face again.

'Oh, I'm sorry, sir. I've kept you waiting. I didn't think.'

Francis saw the girl was beside herself with nerves.

'Look,' he said in his very kindest voice 'it's quite all right, and you must stop worrying. I'm very glad you've come to see me, and I'm hoping that over supper you'll tell me about my old friend Robert. I haven't seen him for several years, though we've kept in touch. You can tell me all about yourself, and what's brought you all this way. Now come and sit here. You'll feel better when you've had some of Mrs Goode's lamb stew. She's a wonderful cook.'

As he filled her plate and asked her one question after another about Father Robert and her journey, Bridie forgot her fright and began to chatter. She grew warm inside. Her skin glowed from cold water and scrubbing. Colour came back into her cheeks and her eyes sparkled. Much of the sparkle was the shine of exhaustion. Her eyes began to droop and, embarrassed, she struggled not to fall asleep.

'Right, Miss O'Neill, I think it's time to clear this away. I'll see to it. I want you to go up to bed.'

She began to protest that she'd see to the dishes, but there was no heart in it and Francis wouldn't hear of it. They bade each other good night and she once more climbed the stairs. The gaslamp burned at the side of her bed. She hung her clothes carefully over the back of a chair and dragged out her case to find her night-gown. Then, pulling back cold, stiff sheets that felt luxurious beyond belief, she turned off the gas and sank into bed.

Despite her weariness, sleep did not come. Her legs ached and stung. Behind closed eyes images began to unreel, a disjointed parade. She tossed and turned, half asleep, half awake, until she remembered Little May's woeful crying as Bridie pulled her arms from round her neck and walked away. Then tears came.

Francis heard the low sobbing go on into the night, until in the early hours the sound died away. He wondered what it was that made for such grief, but supposed it was a young, frightened girl's first, painful homesickness. He wondered again, though, how she got that discoloured swelling on her mouth.

Then finally the whole square slept. Vermin Ermin curled cosily in the warm hollow by Bridie's knees, until a blackbird woke him very early, and he crept secretly out of the open window into the summer dawn. Disturbed by his going, Bridie stretched in the space he had left, and slept on until the sun was high in the sky, and the grandfather clock in the hall downstairs gave out its sonorous chimes at midday.

Chapter Two

Earlier that sunny morning, Francis summoned his Mrs Goode to his study.

'I think we could do with the help,' he told her. 'Your arthritis isn't getting any better, I can see that for myself, and you could give her some of the heavy work that you shouldn't really be doing any more. She'll need showing, of course, but I think she'd learn quickly and be willing.'

Dora Goode, who had run his household for him, and his wife when she'd been alive, pursed her mouth thoughtfully. She stood nearly as tall as him, a wiry woman. Pernickety ways and a stern expression hid a kind heart full of fierce loyalty. Devoted to Francis, her upright and principled nature matched his. Her back was ramrod straight, and so was her sense of right and wrong.

Goode by name and Goode by nature, people said, sometimes admiringly but as often as not half afraid of her. If you were on the right side of the house-keeper, you had a friend indeed, but if she caught you out doing something that you oughtn't – 'Gawd 'elp yer,' as the coalman said, when she ran after his cart the time he'd not bothered to sweep up round the coalhole. Even Francis avoided her when he knew she'd taken badly to something. 'Do as you would be done by,' was one of her favourite sayings, delivered with a birdlike stare and a slight gathering of the lips. Now, this morning, considering the suggestion he'd put before her, she suggested giving Bridie a chance but no promises.

'I could give her a try and see how she comes along,' she offered. 'A lot of girls these days are lazy and don't know what work is. Out dancing and flapping or whatever they call it, and no good to anyone. I'd rather do the work myself than be chasing some idle good for nothing.'

Francis smiled. 'I have a feeling you'll get on well together,' he said. 'And it would be useful for me to have someone in the house when you go home. I've been thinking about it for some time, and since she's been sent by an old friend of mine, it seems an excellent time to put the idea to the test.'

Hearing the hint of a criticism, Dora took umbrage. 'If I don't work enough hours, sir, then I'm sure I think you might tell me so. I thought we had a satisfactory agreement on that matter.'

Oh dear, she would take offence. 'No, no, no.' He shook his head. 'It's not that at all. You do more than enough. It's a question of needing another pair of hands, and someone who can run errands for me, or be here when you cannot.'

He rubbed his hands together worriedly. 'Dear Dora, don't look so cross. Neither of us is getting any younger, and I think this girl could be a godsend.

You wait until you've seen her. She's been well brought up.'

He appealed to her sense of fairness. 'You wouldn't want to dismiss her before you've even met her. That's not like you at all, Dora.'

Mrs Goode was mollified. 'Well, so long as you're not saying you're dissatisfied,' she began.

Francis shook his head emphatically. 'You know me better than that. I'd have called you in and told you straight if that had been the case.'

She nodded. 'All right then, sir, I'll see how she does.' Her face lost its righteous air and broke into a surprisingly sweet smile.

Francis stifled a sigh of relief. Mrs Goode on her high horse was a trial that he bore with goodwill because most of the time she was one of the most sensible women you could ask for.

'Thank you,' he said. 'She arrived filthy and exhausted last evening. She spent a pretty long time in the bathroom, but she'll need showing one or two things about how we go on here. She comes from a poor family who will have had none of our modern luxuries.' He grinned at her, knowing that the bathroom upstairs was her pride and joy, scoured and scrubbed and polished until she could stand in the doorway and straighten her back in deep satisfaction that there was no cleaner bathroom, not even in Buckingham Palace, God bless them. She frowned suddenly, and Francis, who teased her sometimes about her perfectionism, knew what was passing through her mind.

'The bathroom'll be needing a going over and a half after her, I'll be bound.'

'Now then, Dora. The poor girl had travelled non-stop for more than two days. And she'll need clothes if she's to work here. Can I leave you to see to that in the next day or two?'

Mrs Goode brightened. It seemed she was to have the girl to mould properly.

'Yes, sir, I'll get her what she needs.'

'I think that's all then. When you hear she's woken, would you kindly give her some tea and breakfast and then send her here?'

'Yes, sir. Was there anything else, sir?'

'No.' He watched her black-clad figure march across the Indian carpet to the study door, closing it quietly behind her. He wondered why she always wore black. She had a wardrobe of pinafores and aprons, but the dress underneath, winter and summer, was black. He'd sometimes thought to ask her, but it seemed vaguely improper, so he never had.

Francis went behind his desk and sat down. Reaching down beside his chair, he lifted up a shabby leather briefcase and took out a pile of papers. Spreading them before him on the broad mahogany surface, he was soon absorbed in long columns of statistics that told a dismal story. Hidden in neutral numbers was a picture of misery, suffering and death that Francis painted in dry tones in Council offices all over London, and even to Westminster. (Rumour had it that the story had been told at the Palace, too, but that had never been confirmed.) Francis was a brilliant statistician and epidemiologist. An expert in the incidence of disease, he had come to devote his life to pleading, persuading and convincing those who had power, that the streets and sewers and water supplies of East London bred disease and should be cleaned up. He described conditions of filth, disorder, carelessness and indifference; poverty, overcrowding and dirt. He preached a gospel of cleanliness and possessed the immense patience to keep on with such a crusade. The politicians must in the end take note. Bent over his papers, he sighed. It showed no sign of happening yet. There was a knock at his door. Lifting his head he called, 'Come.'

Bridie stood in the doorway. As she crossed the room to stand in front of him, he saw that the long sleep had done her good. The bruised lip was less swollen, and although she looked serious and slightly apprehensive, her grey eyes met his directly and there was colour in her cheeks.

'Good morning, Miss O'Neill. You slept well?'

'Oh yes, sir.'

'Has Mrs Goode given you breakfast?'

'Yes, sir.'

'She and I have a suggestion that you might like. Would you care to stay and go into service here; help Mrs Goode and take charge when she cannot be here? She is agreeable, and I've been thinking for some time that I need someone to live in, as well as my housekeeper. She lives not far away, but she has her family and a good many other calls on her time. What do you think? She'll show you what to do.'

He smiled at Bridie. 'She can be a bit of a Tartar at times, but she's kind and you couldn't find a more careful housekeeper. You would have an excellent training if you work with her.'

A slow smile crinkled Bridie's freckled nose and her eyes widened with delight. 'Oh yes, please, sir. I'd like that. I'll do my best, sir.'

'I'm sure you will. Good. That's settled then. Your wages will be thirty pounds a year and all found, which is quite generous, I believe. You can stay in the room you are in now. Will that suit you?'

Bridie was overjoyed. She'd woken in the little blue room and, pulling back the curtains, looked around in the midday light. It was even prettier in the bright sunlight than it had been under the gaslamp. She wondered what to do about the smelly rags stuffed under the bed. They were horribly out of place, an embarrassing reminder of the state she'd arrived in.

Down in the kitchen she'd met Mrs Goode, who'd looked her over and noted the bare feet and creased dress, but said nothing. The girl needed taking in hand all right. Dora started happily planning a shopping expedition for sober cotton skirts and crossover overalls. Boots, stockings and a good stout shawl were added to the mental list. It was May so she wouldn't need a coat. Something had to be done about that hair, too. She'd show Bridie how to make a neat bun. Hairpins and ribbon went on the list.

Mrs Goode laid a plate of bread and jam and a pot of tea in front of her, and asked her about her travels. Bridie told her about the high wind that tossed and buffeted the old grey steam packet across the water, and how everyone had been sick. She said how friendly and helpful the copper had been in Euston station, how the cleaning woman in the City had shown her the way, and she told the housekeeper about the kindness of Daisy Davids, who'd shown her the square.

'Oh, so you bumped into Daisy, did you? Well, you want to stay well away from the likes of her.' Mrs Goode sniffed disapprovingly.

Bridie looked up in surprise, her mouth full. She swallowed and said curiously, 'Why? She seemed very kind. I'd have got much more lost without her.'

'Never mind now. Just mark my words, and you'll come to no harm.'

Bridie was puzzled, but the housekeeper clearly wasn't going to explain. For some reason she remembered the laughter that had burst from the open public house doors as Daisy had come out. She gave a little shrug and forgot about it as Mrs Goode told her that if she'd finished she was to go down the hall and knock on Mr Holmes' door. He wanted to see her.

Having settled matters with his domestic help, early that afternoon Francis took his briefcase and went off to the Town Hall in Stratford, where he had an office. Mrs Goode lent Bridie a pair of boots that were too big, but had to do, and together they walked down to the market in Roman Road. It wasn't far and Bridie could hear the hoarse voices of market traders shouting their wares soon after they'd left the house. They made their way slowly through the throng of shoppers, idlers, stall keepers and darting children. Dogs scavenged underfoot and snarled over titbits pulled from piles of waste mounting, as the day went by, at the sides of the street. Slimy puddles shone evilly in the sunlight and a stench caught at the back of Bridie's throat. Mrs Goode noticed.

'Foul, isn't it?' she agreed. 'It's worst in summer, when it's hot and the flies are bad.'

But Bridie was enchanted by the colourful stalls and the variety of goods on sale. Pallets heaped with vegetables stood cheek by jowl with carts piled high with bright fabrics, cheap imitation jewellery and racks of skirts, dresses and blouses. There was strange fruit, filling the air with ripe, exotic fragrance, as well as homely apples, pears and plums.

'We're near the Docks and Covent Garden here,' explained Mrs Goode, 'so we're lucky. There's always a lot of choice, and things you can't get so easy elsewhere.'

She stopped at a stall and bought a single orange. 'Here, you can eat it while we go,' she said, handing it to Bridie. The sweet juice ran over her fingers and she sucked them with enjoyment, following the housekeeper's narrow back until they came to the stall she had in mind.

Bridie stood patiently while Mrs Goode held one dress and skirt after another up against her, considering. Between them they picked out two dresses, two skirts and four blouses. Mrs Goode and the woman in charge of the stall knew each other well. They haggled briefly over the price until Mrs Goode nodded in agreement and a deal was struck. Bridie carried her new wardrobe over her arms, longing to get back and try it all on.

'Cardigan next,' announced the housekeeper, and dragged Bridie further down the market. Suddenly, behind them, there was a spate of shouting and then an uproar of protesting voices. Two children raced past, pushing their way violently through the shoppers. Twisting and ducking round crowded stalls, they vanished in opposite directions into side streets.

'Bloody varmints!' roared the man who'd lost a fur jacket to the thieves. 'If I get my hands on those . . . those . . .' He choked with rage and frustration. The crowd moved on. Children thieving was common enough. The luckless stallholder complained bitterly and colourfully, to anyone who would listen, for the rest of the day. Bridie meanwhile became the owner of three cardigans in plain dark colours that buttoned from the neck right down to her hips.

'It's expensive, buying them like this,' grumbled Mrs Goode.' You'll have to learn to knit your own.'

'I can knit. Mam taught me. We all could,' cried Bridie indignantly.

Mrs Goode looked taken aback. 'You can knit?' Her prejudices betrayed her.

' 'course I can. I'm good at it. You should have asked and I'd have told you.'

'Oh, well,' muttered the Englishwoman. 'Another time we'll get the wool.'

She felt uncomfortable. She would have to explain the expenses to Francis, and didn't relish the prospect of admitting that she'd taken for granted that Bridie, being Irish, was stupid. It was a bit of mean spiritedness that shamed her. Her black brows drew themselves together in a frown and she looked sideways at the ground while she digested the unpalatable fact. She'd not really given the girl a chance, she admitted to herself, not in her heart. After all, what did either of them know about each other? That soft, musical Irish voice was really quite lovely, and the girl had been so eager to please.

'Dora, do as you would be done by,' she admonished herself sternly, and decided that in a day or two, when Bridie had settled down, she'd buy her some needles and wool, and see what she could get her doing by way of making things for the three of them.

With a quieter conscience, she led the way to the boot and shoe stall where she always went for her own family. 'One boots, one indoor shoes, and one slippers. For this girl here,' she reeled off.

Florence, a small, thin woman with a nose that gathered dewdrops in slow, unstoppable progression, until they were absent-mindedly wiped off on the edge of her sleeve, ducked under the back of her stall and came up with several newspaper packets. She put her rough hand on Mrs Goode's sleeve.

' 'ere, Dora, 'ave a look at these.' She parked the bundles on the edge of the stall, and unwrapped the first. A small pair of sheepskin slippers lay fluffy and creamy in the sun. 'What yer think of them?' said Flo proudly. 'I reckin they'd fit your Sammy a treat.'

Dora's eldest grandson was seven years old, and the apple of her eye.

'Where'd you get them?' she asked suspiciously. They were real quality goods.

'I were given them,' cried Flo triumphantly. 'Down Bethnal Green. You know back of Northiam Street, nearly down in Cambridge Heath? Old Czopor the shoemaker? His place. He were throwing them out. 'e'd had an order from some place up the West End for the best quality, and the 'prentice did the stitching wrong, so he wanted shot of them. So he give them to me, seeing as I looked after 'is missus when she were took bad last winter.'

Flo stroked the sheepskin. 'Thruppence to you, Dora,' she offered.

Mrs Goode picked up one of the little slippers. 'You'll have them back if they won't fit?'

' 'course I will.'

'And what's in the other packets?'

'Two more slippers and two boots. But the boots don't match proper. The lad got the leathers mixed up. Silly sod.'

She unrolled the newspaper. The boots were for a woman, and were of fine leather. They'd small heels, and buttons all up the front, with a tiny leather bow stitched on the back. They would have been perfect, but the shoemaker had been dozing, and had stitched dark blue in with the black, so that they didn't look right at all.

'Someone'll be glad of those, but we'll not take them, ta all the same,' said Mrs Goode.

She tipped her head at Bridie. 'Needs slippers, shoes and boots, like I said.'

They began to rummage among the heap on the stall, comparing, trying on and considering, their heads on one side, until Bridie was fitted. Money changed hands, and calling, 'T'ra, duck,' Mrs Goode shepherded her charge to the last two or three stalls, where they picked up underwear, stockings and hairnets, pins, brushes and ribbons.

'That'll do you for now, I think,' she said finally to Bridie, who had so many things piled in her arms her chin rested on the top, and she couldn't even nod. On the way back Mrs Goode filled a string bag with onions and potatoes and carrots and crisp spring greens whose leaves squeaked as the vegetable seller stuffed them into the top of the net.

'I'll pick up a bit of cheese from Mac at the far end,' she told Bridie, 'and then we'll go back for a cup of tea and get off our feet.' Bridie, weighed down by precariously balanced bundles of clothes, struggled after Dora, through the crowds, back to the square and home, where she dropped the whole pile on to the kitchen table. Mrs Goode went to put the kettle on and called to Bridie over her shoulder to start unpacking it all.

With a fat brown teapot steaming on the table, they became happily absorbed in looking over their purchases. Mrs Goode told Bridie to strip to her drawers and bodice, then she buttoned and smoothed and tugged as Bridie tried it all on.

'Good thing you're nice and slim,' she remarked.

'It's easy to fit a figure like yours.'

The skirts needed taking in round the waist, just a little, and two of the blouses were on the generous side across the shoulders, but Bridie was happy. After more than an hour she stood in front of the house-keeper, neatly brushed and combed and with every button and tuck in place. The wild red hair had been scraped back and stuffed into a net that held it on the nape of her neck. Tendrils were already pulling free and making ringlets by her ears but, as Mrs Goode remarked, in the end you can only do your best with what you're given. An apron with its strings tied in a bow finished the effect, and, transformed into the very picture of a demure housemaid, Bridie was sent upstairs where there was a mirror. She looked at her-self in delighted amazement until Mrs Goode's voice told her to stop primping and come down and do some work. Swishing her new skirts round her legs as she went down the stairs, Bridie obeyed, and went willingly to work in the kitchen under the scrutiny of Mrs Goode's sharp eyes.

When Francis came home in the early evening, he smiled to hear the steady chatter of voices in the back room. All was going to be well.

Chapter Three

Mrs Goode turned out to be a demanding teacher. 'You mind, now,' she said sharply one day to Bridie, who'd been delegated to iron the linen.

Bridie glowered. Mrs Goode shook out the bright white sheet and examined it critically.

'Look here. Like this. You fold it in half, and half again this lengthways, not like you've done it. Then turn it. Take that end and we'll do it properly.'

Bridie grabbed the proffered sheet and tugged crossly. She'd spent ages with the heavy irons, one in use, one on the range to heat, and her arms were tired of pushing them over the sheets that lay spread out on the big deal table in the back room. Folded blankets covered the table underneath and made sure the iron didn't burn marks into its well-scrubbed surface. She shook the sheet straight so hard the linen made a cracking sound. Mrs Goode frowned at her.

Bridie lowered her eyes and silently called her a silly old bat. Pernickety Goodie Two Shoes, complaining about the stupid folds being in the wrong place. Daft, daffy, dippy, dopey, dotty Dora. The song of abuse ran delightedly through Bridie's head as she folded the linen obediently.

'That'll do, young woman.' Mrs Goode stared suspiciously at the bowed head that somehow didn't look meek at all.

'Why does it have to be folded like that, anyway? It only gets crumpled again on the bed,' demanded Bridie sulkily.

'Because Mr Holmes is particular, and so am I. You've done well, Bridie, but you've a thing or two yet to learn about running a big house, and you'd do even better to change your attitude, my girl.'

Bridie heaved a sigh that was just exaggerated enough to bring a tight-lipped glare from the housekeeper. 'You be careful,' she warned icily.

Suddenly Bridie's face crumpled and she started to laugh. She leant on the table, creasing the sheet in both hands. Giggling helplessly until her cheeks were red, she put her hand over her mouth and tried to stifle her snorts of merriment. 'Oh, Mrs Goode, you are funny. You look so cross, and your mouth makes a little round, like this. . . .' And she imitated the housekeeper's *moue* of disapproval to perfection.

Dora found herself, as always when Bridie behaved this way, nonplussed. The girl was impossible. How did you discipline someone who laughed in your face, and made you feel slightly pompous, even a little ridiculous, even though two moments ago you'd been absolutely right? Eighteen months had made Mrs Goode very fond of Bridie, whom she found a hard worker and honest. But she still couldn't make her out, sometimes, and when she did this, well. . . . Mrs Goode felt a smile begin to work its way up her own face, and hastily straightened her lips; before you knew where you were, there'd be no discipline at all. Briskly she picked up the cooling iron and put it to heat.

'Here. Get on with it, do. That's enough of your nonsense. I don't know, I'm sure.'

Bridie rubbed her apron where her chest ached from laughter.

'Yes, Mrs Goode. Here we go again. All folded and correct.'

The iron rose and fell, making a swishing sound as it steamed over the damp linen for the second time. Five minutes later Bridie held out a folded white oblong with mock solemnity.

'Madam's folds, neatly presented in a sheet for Madam's inspection.'

Mrs Goode slapped the newly pressed linen on top of the pile on the sideboard without comment. That verged on cheek, but she wanted to avoid a repeat of the giggles, so ignored it. She glanced at the wooden clockface on the wall.

'Time for a pot of tea. How much longer are you going to take?'

Bridie became serious, and looked at the linen basket with a practised eye.

'Ah, well now, about twenty minutes? Half an hour at the most, if you count clearing all the ironing stuff away.'

'All right, I'll put the kettle on and we'll sit down for five minutes when you're done. Then I have to go down to the market, and I want you to do the scullery

floor. And sort out the cupboard under the sink, will
you? It could do with a scrub inside and out.'

'Yes, Mrs Goode,' sighed Bridie. You'd think
floors were for eating off, the way she carried on with
the scrubbing brush. Born with one in her hand,
Bridie reckoned.

'Jaysus save us,' she'd remark to the young women
she met in the church porch after Mass on a Sunday
morning. 'She's never satisfied, that Mrs Goode. You
can scrub your fingers to the bone, and she'll find a
fault somewhere.' Her grey eyes would widen to make
her point, and they'd all move off down the path to
the church gate, a shrill, gossiping little crowd, bright
and sharp like East End sparrows.

Bridie's best friend, Lizzie Symonds, was learning
to be a nurse at the London Hospital, about a mile
away towards the City. Lizzie was clever and had been
to the grammar school. After months of seeing each
other at church, and then sometimes meeting for tea
and a bagel in old Mrs Wisniewski's eel pie and mash
shop just off the Roman Road, they'd become best
friends. One day Bridie had diffidently asked Lizzie
to help her take up reading and writing again, which
had been so neglected while she was kept from school
to help her Mam. 'Only if you've got time, though,'
she said anxiously, 'because I know you've got your
studies and everything.'

Lizzie, who was a free thinker and an independent
spirit but still turned up at Mass most weeks, was
delighted. She told Bridie that she had a duty to learn,
and brought her some paper books with simple

stories, used in schools. They pored over them together, sitting in the window of old Widow Wisniewski's. The wizened little Jewess watched them over the shiny grey metal top of her counter, where tin trays of steaming pies lay next to a bigger tray of live eels. Bridie and Lizzie would hang over the counter and watch them squirm malignantly, coiling and uncoiling in shallow water. 'Ugh, look at them!' they'd shrieked to each other the first time they'd ventured into the shop together, drawn by the fragrant smell of fresh bagels just brought round from the Jewish bakers in the next road.

'You want I should kill one for you, eh?' asked the old woman. She came along the counter to peer at the eels, and prodded them with one fat wrinkled finger. The eels suddenly came to life and Bridie drew back, revolted.

'Do people really eat them?' she asked the woman, who nodded.

'Eel pie. Very nourishing,' she said, in a heavy Austrian accent. 'You eat it one day, maybe.'

By the time her first Christmas in London had come and gone, Bridie was reading Lizzie's books faster and faster and going on to more interesting things. She took to reading bits of *The Times* when she was supposed to be rolling it up for firelighters. She didn't tell Mrs Goode what she was doing, but the house-keeper's observant eyes didn't miss much that went on in her kitchen, and she noticed Bridie's finger travelling slowly along the smudged print. She had made steady progress, and now, not long before her second Christmas, could read quite well, and write to a very passable standard.

'Why don't you go to evening classes?' suggested Lizzie. 'You're getting too good just to go on like this. And I've got exams coming up, so I'll be too busy to come over.'

'Oh, I don't know. I'm not too sure what they'd say.'

'Who? Why should anyone say anything?' asked Lizzie, puzzled.

Bridie shrugged. 'Dunno,' she said truthfully. 'They just might.'

In fact, the idea of classes frightened her. Having spent so little time inside one, Bridie had hazy and alarming notions of schools, and of nuns and teachers. Lizzie was different, being a friend. Mrs Goode could read and write well, but then she'd had schooling. Most people did in the East End, because most children, however poor they might be, went to school. Mr Holmes had been heard demanding wryly what was the good of money spent on children's minds if their bodies went and died before they could make any use of it. But then, Mr Holmes was known to feel strongly about such matters, and not to mince his words. Bridie had once seen him raise his fist in anger and say something about a long word that sounded like 'philanthropists'. He was angry with them for some reason to do with consumption. The rest was lost on Bridie, who'd been sent to fetch his new packet of cigars from the drawer underneath the coatstand in the hall.

My word, she thought to herself, to be sure he can get worked up about things.

Bridie was thinking about that as she dragged the tin bucket out from under the sink. Blink. A peculiar swimmy feeling went through her arms and legs. Memory of another bucket rose, ghostly, in the back of her mind and she shook her head, frightened. Her skin crawled all of a sudden as though her body wanted to remind her of a cruel, cold scrubbing inflicted in the midst of some distant nightmare. Bridie picked up the heavy wooden scrubbing brush and lifted the bucket to fill it with hot water from the range.

She swallowed hard and the sense of another time began to fade. She rubbed sweat from her brow with the back of her arm, and concentrated on swishing the bar of coarse soap around in the water to make suds. Then she carried the heavy pail to the cupboard beneath the sink, which she'd already cleared out, stacking the cleaning stuff on top of the copper. She crouched down on her knees, tucking her skirt and apron well under her, out of the way, and taking a brushful of suds, began to scrub.

She felt the cold air on her back as the front door opened and let in a draught that blew straight through the house. She half turned her head in the small space in the cupboard, expecting to see Mrs Goode's feet appear.

'Hullo,' she called, 'you forgotten something?'

'Hullo, Bridie.' Her employer's voice came from the hallway, where he stood taking off his muffler and overcoat. Blowing on his hands, he came into the kitchen and looked into the scullery.

'You look busy,' he remarked, 'but I wonder if you could bring me some tea into the study. It's cold out. In fact I believe we could have snow later on; the sky looks heavy with it. I'd be glad of a cup of tea, if you please.'

' 'course, sir. I'll be along with it as soon as the water boils.' Bridie's voice was muffled by the cupboard and he watched her back moving as she mopped the soapy water from a corner of the floor. She drew her head out to wring the cloth into the pail and looked up at him.

'I won't be a moment, sir.'

He smiled at her, and her head disappeared back into the cupboard.

'I'll put the water on myself,' he said to her back. He picked up the kettle and leant across her to fill it at the tap above her head. As he turned the water off, his leg brushed against her side, and for a moment his eyes closed and, unseen, he swallowed and looked down at her. His eyes were full of longing, but he put the kettle to heat on the range and went to his study. Pulling his armchair up before the fire that Bridie had lit that morning, he passed a thin hand over his face.

His mouth turned down in a self-deprecating expression and he shook his head slowly. The long straight nose and kindly, quirky mouth were overshadowed by piercing grey eyes that looked out under fair, bushy brows. The whole face was thin and lined and rather sharp. He stretched his legs out to the fender and staightened his waistcoat. He found himself slightly ridiculous, mooning over an Irish servant who was the age his daughters would have been, had he and Emma had any.

The object of his attention wrung her rag out and slopped it over the edge of the pail. Done. The kettle was singing on the fire, so she made tea quickly and put a dish of Mr Holmes's favourite biscuits next to the cup. Then, taking off her thick apron, she exchanged it for the white pinafore Mrs Goode had taught her to wear whenever she served her employer. Balancing the tray, she opened the morning room door and took it along to the study.

'Come in,' called Francis, when he heard her knock.

'Here you are, sir,' she said. 'Where would you like me to put it?'

'On here, please, Bridie,' He patted the footstool that stood to one side of his outstretched legs. He bent forward and half took the tray, to help her set it down, and his hands covered hers. They placed the teatray on the stool between them, but he did not take his hands away. Bridie, bending right down over the tray, face averted, froze. Francis's hands moved up her arms and tightened.

'Dear Bridie,' he murmured.

He lifted her hands away from the tray and pulled her gently upright until he could see her scarlet face, eyes lowered in profound embarrassment.

He dropped her hands as though he'd been struck. She looked terrified. 'Oh, my dear,' he said in distress,

'I didn't mean to harm you. I mean, I . . . oh, Bridie, don't look like that.'

'No, sir,' she whispered.

She raised her eyes. Francis was dismayed to see tears in them.

'Oh please, Bridie, I didn't mean to upset you so.' He didn't know what to say; the situation seemed to have turned to disaster.

'Upset me, sir?'

'Yes, clearly I've embarrassed and frightened you, and I wouldn't have done that for the world.'

Her deepening blush told him that not all was lost.

'No, you've not really frightened me, sir. Surprised me, more like.' Bridie was not entirely astonished at what he'd done. She'd seen the way he looked at her when he thought himself unnoticed, and had often felt his eyes on her. She'd almost known his mind before he did, but the moment itself came out of the blue. She put out a hand to him and held it there, with all its suggestions and implications and future unknowns, until very slowly, unable to stop himself, he took it in his and drew her to him. He gently wiped away the tear that spilled and ran down her cheek.

'Don't cry, dear Bridie.'

She sniffed and wiped her nose on the back of her hand.

'Here.' He pulled a crisp white handkerchief from his pocket.

Bridie blew her nose and stuffed it into her apron. They lapsed into an awkward silence. Then, as the strain began to tell, they simultaneously turned, as if with one mind, to pick up the teapot.

'Shall I pour . . .?' they chorused, and both began to laugh.

'Come here,' said Francis. He put one arm around her waist and pulled her close to the armchair, and then, before either of them had a moment to think about it, she was sitting in his lap with her head resting tenderly just beneath his chin. Francis held her very carefully, and they stayed quite still, each looking into the fire while they longed to look at each other.

Then, with a deep sigh, Francis slipped one hand up her back and began to stroke her hair. Gradually the pins came out and were placed on the teatray. At last the glorious hair tumbled free, and, as in a thousand dreams, he ran his fingers luxuriously through the soft, glossy curls. Breathing more heavily, he gently turned Bridie's face towards his and kissed her. Her mouth was sweet and warm and soft, and she turned against him, reaching her arms around his neck and pulling him close. She made no move to stop him as his hands moved over her neck, down to her breast, and brushed over the soft fabric of her dress. He took his mouth from hers and murmured, half smiling, 'I can't be doing with the buttons, Bridie. Can you help me?'

She blushed richly and began to fumble with the long row of tiny buttons that did up the bodice of the dress. Their hands tangled together in mounting haste and excitement. Francis almost tore the last stubborn buttons open, and the dress at last fell half off her shoulders. He pushed the teatray and stool impatiently to one side, and they slid in a laughing heap on to the rug that lay, as if in readiness just for them, in front of the blazing coals in the fireplace. Bridie felt the flames warm on her face as she lay gazing up into his intense grey eyes.

'Bridie, I want you. I've wanted you for so long.' He kissed her long and hard so that she felt he'd bruise her lip. Blink. With a cry she drew away and turned her head wildly. He misunderstood, and instantly pulled away.

'No? Have I mistaken . . .? Do you mean you don't want me?' His voice was hoarse and filled with dismay.

She shook her head against his chest and her voice sounded like a little girl's. 'No, no. It's not that. I thought. . . . Oh, sir, you've been so kind, so very, very kind.'

She turned a flushed and eager face to his, and reassured he put his lips to hers once more. They drew closer and closer until, with her help, he drew the long skirt up round her waist and was in her, holding his breath to prolong the delicious moment. The flames leaped and cast a red glow over their delight. Bridie gave little sobs of pleasure and then at last he let go with a groan of release and joy.

They lay in each other's arms, eyes half closed and mouths part open with rapid breathing. Lulled by the warmth and the cosy sound of shifting coals and occasional popping of the flames, they dozed, Bridie held close in Francis's arms. After a while he stirred and kissed her neck. Thin, ink-stained fingers lay on her damp breast, and she looked down at them and saw how the light from the fire caught the fair hairs on the backs of his hands, making them glint a reddish gold. Light grey eyes gazed into dark grey, so close they had to draw their heads back to see each other.

'Oh, Bridie. Oh, Bridie O'Neill, who would have thought . . .?' Francis shook his head in wonder, quite captivated.

Bridie smiled up at him. His face, softened by pleasure, didn't look so old after all. He bent to kiss her but she turned her face away.

'Mrs Goode will be back, sir.'

'Ah, indeed she will. What a shame.'

He stroked her hair, which clung to her temples and tangled on the floor.

'Yes,' he sighed. 'You must go before she's back.'

He sat up and began to pull his clothes straight. Bridie felt languid, and got slowly to her feet. When she was dressed and had smoothed most of the crumples out of her skirt as best she could, she stood before him. Demurely she cast her eyes down, and with every appearance of innocence asked, 'Will you be wanting anything else, sir? Your tea, maybe?'

Francis laughed out loud.

'Bridie, you're a wonder. Go and brush your hair. Look, all your hairpins are here. Take the tray, and yes, I'll take my tea now, if you'll be good enough to bring me a fresh pot.'

They shared the gentle teasing with soft looks and shy glances. As the door closed on Bridie's departure with the tray, he leant back in his armchair and pure contentment stole over him.

'Emma,' he said after a while, to the portrait of his wife that hung above the mantelpiece, 'she reminds me so much of you. Will you forgive me, Emma?'

The dark eyes in the portrait seemed to look into his with a question in them. Francis felt his conscience stir uneasily and glanced back at his wife's painted face. 'I'll care for her, Emma,' he said defensively.

The painting simply gazed at him. Bridie came in with the tea.

By the time Mrs Goode came in from the market, bringing a great gust of icy air with her, Bridie had only half finished the scullery. The housekeeper dumped her load of string bags on the deal table and looked round in outrage.

'What on earth have you been doing, girl?' she cried. 'I've been gone an age, and you've done nothing.'

Bridie bent over her work and stifled a grin.

'You bin up to something, Miss?' Mrs Goode's voice was heavy with suspicion.

Bridie sat back on her haunches and looked up at the angry housekeeper. 'I've been helping Mr Holmes move some books in his study. He come home early, so's he could work in his study, and he called me in to lend him a hand.'

Mrs Goode looked doubtful. 'He never said nothing to me about moving books. I s'pose if that's what he wanted you to do, then it's your job to get on with it. But look at this mess.' She surveyed the wet scullery floor, arms akimbo. 'Hurry up and get it done. Then put the vegetables away in the larder. We'll be late starting cooking because of you.'

She grumbled her way round the morning room, banging cupboard doors irritably as she tidied away the groceries that were stocked in the tall shelves either side of the fireplace. Vermin ambled round the door in search of food, and mewed hopefully. Mrs Goode pushed him away irritably with her foot.

'Take yourself off, you mangy animal,' she said crossly. Vermin, sensing the atmosphere, scarpered hurriedly.

'Dratted cat!' muttered the housekeeper. When only the things that went in the cold larder, and the vegetables, were left, she poked her head round the scullery door and let the rest of her annoyance vent itself in the direction of Bridie's back.

'And another thing, my girl. If you haven't got them coal scuttles filled in double quick time, before we end up with all the fires going out, I'm going to ask Mr Holmes to have a word with you. He don't like to employ lazy workers, no more than I do, so you watch out, young woman.'

Bridie raised her eyes to the ceiling and stuck her tongue out in a gesture that Mrs Goode felt rather than saw. 'All right, you go and ask Mr Holmes for a word. Let him say I wasn't doing errands for him. You go right along and ask him.'

Bridie's thoughts made her shoulders twitch with laughter. The housekeeper, outraged, flounced through the morning room and along to the study.

Francis saw her tight-lipped expression and raised an eyebrow enquiringly.

'Trouble, Mrs Goode?'

Her lips tightened further. 'It's that girl. She's cheeky and now she's turning lazy. I've warned her, sir, but she don't listen.'

'I thought you were very satisfied with her,' Francis said mildly. 'Whenever I see her, she seems to be busy.' He turned the page of his book. Mrs Goode stood and waited.

'Is there something in particular that has brought you to complain?' Francis asked her after a pause.

'Yes, sir. I left her to do the scullery and cupboards while I was out, and when I reprimanded her for having done almost nothing, she was insolent.'

'Insolent, eh. That's not to be borne, Mrs Goode. But, you see, I wanted her to help me in here, so it was me who took her away from her work. You must blame me, not her.'

Mrs Goode felt flustered. 'Oh, well, if that's the case, we'll say no more, sir. But she can be insolent, and I've been quite firm with her that if it continues, you'll be wanting to have a word with her.'

'My word, Dora, she has upset you.' Francis glanced at her under his brows.

Mrs Goode stared back, mortified. He wasn't taking her seriously. She sniffed. 'Very well, sir. If that's all, I'll be back to the kitchen.'

'Very well, Dora.' He didn't even look up as she marched out of the study, and for the rest of the day she carped at poor Bridie resentfully, sensing that in some way she couldn't fathom, she was being made a fool of. Bridie did her best to soothe her ruffled feathers, and by the time Mrs Goode pulled on her shawl to hurry home, head bent against the bitter wind that was already gusting little flurries of snow, they had almost made it up. She answered the housekeeper's grudging 'Goodnight' with a cheerful 'Cheerio, Mrs Goode,' and the older woman was gone.

Bridie hummed carols to herself as she tidied away for the night. She pulled aside the curtains to look outside and see if it was snowing. It was. Fat white flakes whirled past on the wind and splashed on the warm windowpane. She closed the curtains with a small shiver and put the guard in front of the dying fire. Then she went upstairs to her cosy blue room. The velvet curtains were tight closed and the fire glowed in the darkness. She reached up and put a match to the gas. Night-dress and books on the counterpane, all ready, Bridie hurried to the icy bathroom to splash in freezing water. Running back on feet numb with cold, she huddled in her night-dress in front of the fire. Warm again, she read until the fire died down, then climbed into bed.

Much, much later, as she drowsed in the delicious warmth of a feather mattress and piles of thick woollen blankets, there was a hesitant tap at her door. Turning her head on the pillow, she could just make out in the dark the spare figure standing in the doorway. Neither moved until Bridie slid one warm hand from under the sheet and pushed the covers back a few inches. Francis closed the door and came towards her. She opened the covers wider and, wordlessly, they turned to each other in the narrow bed.

In the small hours of the morning, Francis went silently across the wide, square landing to his room. He fell asleep instantly and Bridie listened from the edge of sleep to the howling of the wind as it hurled snow in drifts and banks across the mean streets of London.

The grandfather clock in the hall ticked the hours away, its solemn sound falling into the icy air and beating like a steady heart against the wild shriek of the gale. In the morning, dawn came early, because of the brilliant glare of snow. The gale died away. Bridie, drawing back her curtains, gave a cry of delight and ran to dress and go downstairs, to open the door and throw crusts into the pure, perfect white blanket, pockmarked near the windowsill by the impatient red robin waiting for his breakfast.

He flew at the crusts and grabbed, wary of Vermin. Bridie clapped her hands with wonder and excitement, and, startled, the robin shot into the safety of a climbing rose-bush, bringing down a shower of glittering ice all around. It was a perfect winter's day!

Chapter Four

Outside in the square, snow had drifted deeply at one end, while the fierce wind had left the other nearly bare. The ground looked scoured by ice and air. Birds squabbled over crumbs and bits of bacon rind thrown by one of the women from halfway down the other side of the square. A flock of starlings, sharp-eyed, had wheeled in mid flight and landed gracelessly on top of the scattered crumbs. A sparrow landed, but the starlings screamed angrily and ran it off in a flash of blue-green wings. Standing legs astraddle on the back of the bench, Bridie's robin turned one beady eye on the marauders. He watched unblinking, with his head on one side.

Nearby, a front door opened, and two children, whooping and shouting with excitement, ran through the powdery snow, knocking it in glittering showers off the bushes as they went. The starlings screeched and flew up to a chimneystack above, pushing and shoving. The robin hopped down. Snatching a crust, he took it into the cover of some evergreen, away from running feet. One child slipped, fell, and got up laughing, white from head to foot. Their faces glowed in the bitter air and the harsh white light of sun on snow.

Bridie paused in her dusting and watched them from the window in the front parlour. Harsh-smelling whitish smoke curled up the back of the chimney as the coals spat and were slow to catch. She ran the duster round the fender in a desultory manner, and then did it again. If Mrs Goode saw dust there'd be trouble and Bridie was anxious to stay on the right side of the housekeeper, and be friends. When she'd done, she picked up the empty coal scuttle to take it down and fill it from the bunker in the cellar. Holding it in one hand, she looked out of the window again. Mrs Cotteslow from number three was rounding the corner on her way to the shops, a shawl clutched warmly over her coat and a bundle of bags under one arm. The children had started to build a snowman. It was half done when several others arrived, so wrapped up in woollies and coats and hats and boots and shawls and mittens that all you could see of them were red noses, and bright, excited eyes. A dark figure entered the square at the far end and stood watching. The copper slapped his arms round himself to warm up and got moving again.

'Bleedin' weather,' he muttered to himself as he followed his beat down the side street that led through to the Roman. Above him, in the window of the house on the corner, Bridie caught a movement across the way. The maid in number eleven was watching too. Bridie grinned and waved. The other girl lifted her hand and then disappeared, called by someone within the room. Behind Bridie the fire began to crackle and flames to lick round the damp coal. It would warm up soon. There was still a thin film of ice at the bottom of the window, on the inside. She listened to make sure no-one was coming, then scratched a little heart shape with her finger-nail. The ice melted on her hand, and she hastily rubbed the heart away with her warm palm. Guiltily she grabbed her duster and ran downstairs to do the coal. She wasn't exactly frightened of the cellar, but she didn't like it either.

Wooden steps led down into a gloomy space that led off into smaller, earth-floored rooms with entrances that were no more than holes in brick walls. It was kept tidy and the earth smooth, but little was stored down there expect for the coal, which arrived through a coalhole in the path outside. Sack after sack, the coalman would tip, until the pile below reached right up, against the wall, to the coalhole itself. Bridie would stand on the pavement, counting the sacks and stroking the patient brown horse that pulled the cart.

She pulled a face as the strong smell of coal met her on the cellar stairs. Lizzie had once described the symptoms of consumption to her, with grisly relish, and for some reason the smell always reminded her of that. Hastily she shovelled the scuttle full and hauled it out of the cellar. The parlour was only one flight of stairs, if you didn't count the cellar, but the bedrooms meant a real long climb that nearly had Bridie's arms out of their sockets.

She was just putting the scuttle beside the fireplace

in the parlour, when Francis came into the room. 'Good morning, Bridie,' he said cheerfully.

Her cheeks, rosy from cold air, darkened to a deep blush. 'Good morning, sir.'

He stood looking out of the window. 'Snow, eh. The children make a pretty sight down there. Do you like cold weather, Bridie?'

She felt astonished. Everything had changed, and nothing. He was just as usual. Then, in confusion, she wondered just what sort of change she'd expected, and felt foolish.

'Tell Mrs Goode when she comes in that I'm out until about nine o'clock. There's a meeting. Please have my supper ready then.'

'Yes, sir.'

He seemed to notice her properly for the first time, and smiled. 'How are you this morning?'

She flushed again. 'Very well, sir, thank you.'

'So am I,' he said heartily. 'So am I.' He pulled on his gloves and picked up the briefcase that stood ready. 'Don't forget, supper will be late.'

He opened the front door and cold air stung their faces. Francis's feet spoiled the pillows of snow still lying on the steps. He looked back up at Bridie.

'These need clearing, please. First thing, before they become dangerous.'

'I'll do it right away, sir.' Mrs Goode's arthritis was worse in the cold weather, and she could no longer manage things like steps. Bridie stood and watched Francis walk round the square, raising a hand in greeting to the neighbours. He spoke to the milkman briefly, who was delivering frozen bottles in hands so cold he couldn't feel anything. Bridie wondered how it was that heat, in summer, made things smell stronger, like flowers, or dust, but in winter you could smell the cold itself.

Francis enjoyed cold weather. He felt alive and cheerful this morning, striding briskly along, dodging round piles of snow thrown to the edge of the pavement by householders clearing their paths. Outside the grey stone façade of Stratford Town Hall he met up with Angus Hamilton, the District Doctor, his good friend. They saw eye to eye on many public health issues.

' 'morning, Angus.'

His light voice was answered by the Scotsman's deep rumbling tones. 'Cold enough for you?'

Francis put a friendly hand on Angus's back as they went through the door together.

'I like it. I think it agrees with me.'

'Something agrees with you,' said the doctor, 'you look very chipper this morning.'

Francis picked up a *Times* from a pile on a table in the entrance lobby, and grinned.

'Let's have a look.' He shook out the paper. 'What's His Majesty's Government up to just now?'

Angus tucked his own copy under his elbow and looked over Francis's shoulder.

'Aha! Tories planning to field five women candidates at the next election. Oh my, what is the world coming to? Women in Parliament, whatever next?

Shall we see a woman Prime Minister in our time, do you think?'

Francis laughed. 'We may yet. And who's to say it would be a bad thing? What with our ludicrous wars and nonsensical policies, they could hardly do worse, now could they, Angus?'

The Scot decided to take the bait. 'That's practically Pankhurst talk. Are you really that converted to feminist views?' He looked at his friend curiously.

Francis shook his head. 'No, of course not. Not really. But sometimes I look round, and I see so much foolishness and greed and downright wickedness that it makes my heart go cold. And that's the truth, Angus. Have you seen any of the rehabilitation wards recently, where they've got the gas chaps? Every one of the poor blighters blind. But the worst are those who just stare, or talk to themselves. Do you know the chaps I mean? Out of their minds with shock, or some kind of thing. Some medical men, and even some of the Brass put it down to bombardment, shell bursts and what have you. We've given ourselves some terrible problems for the future.'

They turned a corner and climbed a flight of wide grey stairs. 'Of course I've seen them. But cheer up, old chap. You were looking bright when we came in, and now you're doing a grand job of depressing yourself.'

Angus turned bright blue eyes on his friend. 'You can't take on the world, you know. Sometimes I think you want to fight everyone's battles.'

They arrived outside Francis's office. 'Come on

in; I want to show you something. No, you're right. But this isn't the world – it's the problem of isolation at our local level.'

He sorted through two piles of paper and grunted with satisfaction when he found what he was looking for. 'See these?' he said, pushing them across the desk to Angus. 'Figures for beds occupied in isolation hospitals by scarlet fever patients. We're chock-a-block, Angus. They've beds in the corridors and the whole thing makes a nonsense of nursing procedures.'

He pushed across two more sheets of paper. 'Now look at the figures for admissions with diphtheria and typhus.'

Angus looked at the statistics and his brows drew together in a heavy frown.

'Quite,' said Francis.

There was silence for a while. 'So scarlet fever is at epidemic proportions, and we're admitting very few other cases.'

'And the result,' Francis finished for him, 'is that we're inviting an explosion of typhus and diphtheria, because without hospitalisation, the cross-infection in the community will go unchecked. We're on course for typhus and diphtheria epidemics in the new year, Angus.'

He nodded, eyes still on the papers.

'And the government is claiming there's no epidemic,' Francis went on remorselessly. 'They say the hospitals are coping. And if that weren't enough, we are desperately short of nurses because they're sent to the casualty wards to nurse soldiers. No-one wants to know about Mrs So-and-So's kiddies, dying at home because there's nowhere else for them to go. We're going to be at our wits' end, and damned Westminster sits on its hands and looks the other way.'

Angus looked up, his deep-set eyes sad and angry. 'A quick dose of typhus in the Commons drinking water would do the trick,' he remarked acidly. 'An epidemic in the West End would work marvels, I've no doubt.'

'I'm due in Limehouse this afternoon,' said Francis. 'I'll talk to Clem Atlee while I'm there, and see if I can persuade him to make a call or two in the Westminster direction. He has friends who may be of some use. I'll brief him before tonight's policy meeting, anyway.'

'Verra well,' the kindly doctor agreed. 'I'll back you all I can at the meeting, laddie, but expect no miracles.'

'Miracles!' Francis snorted.

Angus put on his thickest Scottish accent. 'D'ye often wonder whether presairrrrving the human race is wurrrth it?' he asked.

Francis grinned. 'It's my crusade you're blaspheming, man. Don't mock the faithful.'

Angus heaved his long length out of the wooden chair. He rested his hands for a moment on the desktop. 'It's a fanatic ye are,' he said half seriously. 'They can be the worst.'

Francis indicated the door. 'I'm busy,' he said.

'See you later when I've talked to Clem.'

'Right you are,' the doctor answered amiably. He was so tall he had to duck his head under the door lintel as he vanished into the grimy passages that represented the East End corridors of power. Francis pushed his sleeves up a bit, and bent back to work.

Chapter Five

That winter dragged on into a late, drizzly spring. Mrs Goode's fingers got a little more bent, and she complained sometimes of pain. In early May they were still putting the gaslamps on early, because the dreary weather brought dull grey evenings. Then, without warning, the sun broke through, and it was summertime. Pretty frocks brightened the streets and by the time the last blossom had dropped from the late flowering of the magnolia tree, Bridie's face was pale brown with being out in the sun. She and Mrs Goode took their work outside and sat on the bench by the kitchen wall. One day the previous year Francis had come across Bridie stoning cherries, sitting on the seat beneath the branches of the magnolia. A few weeks later a stout bench was carried round through the corner gate and placed on the paving stones outside the kitchen window.

'There,' he said to the delighted girl. 'You can sit here in privacy. There's no need for you to go out in the square.'

So they took to sitting outside to peel the vegetables, exchanging gossip with the man who came to do the garden several times a week. It reminded Bridie of

93

a convent garden she'd once seen as a young girl. Enclosed and quiet, high ivy-covered walls shutting out the world. Here, on warm days, she would sit with her face turned to the sun, day-dreaming. Intoxicated bees droned in the rose bushes, so laden with pollen they lurched clumsily from flowerhead to flowerhead. Bumble bees' deep hum could be heard right from the other end of the lawn. Cabbage whites fluttered over the walls.

'Pests, they are, even if they are pretty,' Mrs Goode said as Bridie tried to persuade one to crawl on to her finger. It flew away.

Lupins and foxgloves, hollyhocks and pinks, bloomed in the flowerbeds. The gardener knelt with the shears and cut the edges of the lawn in straight, sharp lines every week. Immaculate, it was, like a bit of Mrs Goode's ironing.

Summer drifted past. The three of them, Francis as well, went on an outing to Brighton, and Mrs Goode had a week's holiday, which she spent with her daughter and grandchildren. They went to Epping Forest for a picnic, and her face glowed as she told Bridie how the children ran and played in the trees and dropped icecreams down their best frocks. Bridie was given a week, too, but she stayed at home. Lizzie had asked for some off-duty at the hospital at the same time, and they went walking together out along the leafy banks of the River Lee. One weekday they walked the towpath that followed the canal down to the docks at Limehouse.

Bridie followed Lizzie reluctantly as she explored

the maze of streets that ran, narrow and sinister, between the high walls of warehouses. Chinese faces looked out at the girls and curiosity flickered deep in slanting sloe-black eyes. Bridie took Lizzie by the elbow and begged to turn round and go. The place had an unhealthy, creepy feel, and Lizzie, seeing that Bridie really was frightened, agreed to leave.

Long, summer walks brought them home tired and flushed with sun and laughter. Lizzie's homely round face caught the sun and tanned deeply, so that under her pale hair she looked almost pretty.

Some evenings they sat under the magnolia, reading. Lizzie was nearly qualified and had only one more set of exams. She'd started walking out seriously with one of the young doctors at St Bartholomew's. Bridie, seeing the stars in her friend's eyes when she described him, hoped that if she must get married, that she'd not move too far away. When Lizzie teased her, and asked when was she going to find a young man of her own so they could go out in a foursome, Bridie just smiled behind her hand and shrugged her shoulders.

Francis, whose desk was near the window, sometimes watched them, and had been touched and surprised the first time he'd realised that Lizzie was helping Bridie with reading. Afterwards, he'd offered Bridie his own books, and suggested that she might browse in the study to see if anything caught her eye.

'It's dull stuff, mostly, for you, I suppose, but there are some novels and travel books you may enjoy.'

She'd looked when he was out of the way, but

preferred the paper-covered romances Lizzie lent her, much passed round among the nurses and dog-eared from use.

Apples were ripening in mid-October, and the rosehips had turned a deep glossy red, when Bridie realised she was pregnant. She was more annoyed than dismayed. Francis tapped on her door once or twice a week, late in the evening, and they still loved with passion and tenderness. Sometimes he would kiss her hair in passing, if Mrs Goode was nowhere to be seen. But their unspoken agreement about discretion kept them circumspect, and even after ten months, no one but them knew their secret. A baby would soon change that. Unsure what to do, Bridie did nothing, until one day Mrs Goode caught her leaning against the kitchen table, clutching her stomach and white with nausea.

Pulling herself upright, with hands planted firmly on her hips, the housekeeper prepared to speak her mind.

'Not showin' yet.' She pursed her lips and looked Bridie up and down, by way of opening the topic.

Bridie screwed up her face and moaned.

'Gettin' what you've asked for, if you want my opinion,' said Mrs Goode sourly. 'Stupid girl! Fancy going and getting yourself in the family way. How long do you reckon you've been expectin'?'

Bridie shook her head, a sheen of perspiration on her forehead. 'Not long. Maybe two months.'

'You've bin out there throwing up in the morning several weeks. I've heard you, young woman, don't think I haven't.'

Bridie took a series of deep breaths and some colour began to come back into her face. 'Don't scold, Mrs Goode, I don't feel well.'

'Huh!' snorted the housekeeper. 'You're a fool to yourself.'

'My mother used to be sick, I remember, and it didn't last much after the first three months, she always said. So maybe I'll feel better by then.'

'You're getting no more than you deserve.'

Bridie ignored the jibe. 'Could you let me have a glass of water, please, Mrs Goode?'

The housekeeper couldn't help but feel sorry for her, she looked wretched. Running the tap until it was good and cold, she drew the water and gave the glass to Bridie.

'Here, this'll help. And you'd best sit down.'

'It won't last long, now. Thank you,' said Bridie.

'It's you'll not last long, the way you're going on,' retorted Mrs Goode piously.

Bridie ran her fingers through the front of her hair and said nothing.

'You said anything to anyone?' demanded Mrs Goode with no attempt at delicacy.

Bridie shook her head. 'No.'

'Well, what will you do?'

Bridie shrugged her shoulders. 'I've hardly had time to think. I've been so sick . . .' she tailed off vaguely.

Mrs Goode, frustrated by the girl's apparent indifference to her situation, clucked her tongue in concern and anger.

'You realise you could end up in the workhouse? You lost all reason? Don't you know what you've gone an' done?'

Bridie stared at her. Ah yes, the workhouse.

'You'll have to tell Mr Holmes, and my advice to you is to do it soon. If there's one thing he can't abide after stupidity, it's deceit. You wait for him to see for himself, and you'll be asking to go to the workhouse. He's bin so good to you, and this is how you repay him? I'm sure I don't know.'

Moral indignation fired Mrs Goode's eyes, and she flashed scorn at the top of Bridie's bent head. The girl was so worn out with sickness and the fright of being found out, that hysteria began to make her voice tremble.

'I'll tell him, I will. Just let me do it my way. After all,' and her voice began to shake dangerously close to desperate laughter, 'this is my business if ever anything was. If he wants to see me in the workhouse, that's between me and him.'

Mrs Goode had to admit the truth of that.

'And another thing,' she said, beside herself with curiosity, 'who is it?'

'Who's what?' asked Bridie obtusely.

Exasperated, Mrs Goode tried again.

'The baby. Whose baby is it?'

'Mine,' said Bridie, and looked her straight in the eye with such an expression that even Mrs Goode didn't dare go on. Then an even more scandalous thought hit her.

'Don't you know?' she gasped.

Bridie's fists clenched.

'How dare you?' she shouted. 'How dare you poke your nose in my business? I don't have to tell you anything, and I'd be obliged if you'd hold your tongue, Mrs Goode. I'll tell you, *if* I tell you, when I'm good and ready, and not before.'

Mrs Goode was speechless.

'That's a slander,' went on Bridie. 'How dare you suggest I wouldn't know who my baby's father is? That's a dirty, ugly, horrible thing to say.'

Bridie's fists clenched and unclenched and tears of rage and humiliation filled her eyes.

Mrs Goode, all prepared to shout back, suddenly felt ashamed. She couldn't help wanting to know. Unused to apologising, she fumbled for something to say that might begin to mend the situation.

'Shall I make us a pot of tea?' she offered finally, by way of an olive branch.

Bridie began to laugh weakly. 'You're a one, you really are,' she said to the housekeeper. 'Yes, please, a pot of tea.'

'How about a bit of toast?' suggested the housekeeper as she filled the kettle. 'I used to swear by that for morning sickness when I was expecting. You have it dry, and it seems to do the trick, somehow.'

'Yes please. I'll give anything a try if it'll stop me feeling so bad.'

They took the tray outside and sat at either end of the bench. It was a day when the gardener didn't come, and they had the place to themselves except for the pigeons calling softly from the roof.

'I owe you an apology,' said Mrs Goode eventually. 'There was no call for me to poke my nose in, as you say. I did it because I'm fond of you, Bridie, and I couldn't bear to see you end up in the workhouse, duckie, I really couldn't.'

'Do you think he'd really throw me out?' The question had been burning in Bridie's head ever since Mrs Goode had suggested it. Was Francis really a hard, cruel man like that?

'Well,' Mrs Goode considered, 'it would be very tricky, wouldn't it? Your place here is to work. How could you with a new baby? It's not his fault you've gone and got yourself in trouble.'

Bridie looked at the housekeeper solemnly. Indeed! She twisted her mouth in a wry gesture. Yes, it would be tricky, she had to agree.

They sipped their tea thoughtfully.

'I could pay a woman to look after it, out of my wages,' suggested Bridie.

'Maybe, but you'd have nothing left, and you'd still be lucky to find an employer who'd have a baby in the house what didn't belong.'

'I'd have nothing left in the workhouse, neither,' Bridie pointed out ruefully.

She could see that her position would be desperate if the baby hadn't been Francis's own, and apprehension was beginning to blossom on that score, too. She couldn't take it for granted that he'd look after her; she could see that now. He might throw her out and not think twice about it. Bridie took a gulp of cooling tea and tried to shrug off her mounting dread. She'd coped before, and she'd cope again. You didn't have to go in the workhouse.

A vision of Daisy Davids in her pretty green dress rose before her. Daisy had got her face carved up in a drunken brawl between two impatient clients one evening, while cruising the labyrinth of horrible streets behind the Limehouse waterfront. Rumour had it one of them had been Chinese. Bridie shuddered. They'd stitched her features back together in the London Hospital, and Lizzie, who'd had a friend working on Women's Surgical at the time, said it gave you the shivers to look at her afterwards, when the scars began to heal. By all accounts she was practically what you'd call a freak now, and it was rumoured that when she went back to work they were queuing up for her. Things like that made you wonder, Lizzie'd said. It was ghoulish. Bridie got nervous just thinking about it; too many girls stayed out of the workhouse like Daisy had done.

'Oh, well,' she said in a more optimistic tone as she piled the dirty cups into each other, 'it's no use cryin' over spilt milk. Better get on.'

Indoors Mrs Goode covered the deal table with oilcloth and newspaper. Between them they carried the heavy trays of silver cutlery from the drawer in the morning-room sideboard, and settled down with silver polish and soft cloths to clean it. Mrs Goode impulsively leant across the table after a while, and put a stained hand on Bridie's.

'You'll be all right, my dear,' she said gruffly. 'And I'm here if you need me.'

Tears sprang to Bridie's eyes, and scraping back her chair, she ran to the housekeeper and threw her arms round her neck.

'There, there. Don't take on.' Mrs Goode patted her head. 'Here, come on, you start slacking and we'll be here all night.'

She pushed the girl away, and, smiling shakily, Bridie got on with her work.

In the event, it was Francis who raised the subject. He'd worked late, and Bridie was reading in front of the small fire in her room when he'd stopped at her door and knocked. Smiling, she opened the door wide for him to come in. He sank into the armchair by her little fender and looked at her through half-closed eyes.

'You look very tired,' Bridie told him.

'I am. I spend so much time trying to bring mountains to Mahomet that I sometimes think my back will break.'

Bridie leant her head on his knee.

'Did you enjoy going to the fine restaurant, anyway?'

The dinner had been mediocre and the company pompous, but he said yes to please her. He gazed into the fire and stroked her head, feeling the tension begin to seep away.

'May I stay?'

She smiled up at him. 'I'd like you to.'

She stood up and began to undress. It was late November and she was already wearing heavy winter clothes. As she drew her dress over her head, Francis saw her in outline against the blue curtains and was startled. He watched her thoughtfully as she slipped the long white night-gown over her shoulders and came to sit on the floor near him again.

'Bridie?' he asked after a long, companionable silence.

She looked up.

'You've gained weight.'

In the gaslight, her face went pale.

'Are you . . . er . . .?' He made a gesture with one hand, embarrassed at the suggestion he was making. She took a deep breath. At last.

'Yes,' she said simply. 'I'm going to have a baby.'

'Ah.' Francis was at a loss. He and Emma had had no children, and long ago he'd stopped thinking of fatherhood. He rubbed the bridge of his nose with two fingers, and realised he'd things to think through in his own mind.

That night, he lay smoothing Bridie's curls until she slept. Uncertainty lay between them like a bedfellow and they didn't make love, but lay quietly together. When he was sure she was asleep, he left her very carefully and lay awake for a long time in his own room, remembering the promise he'd made to Emma's portrait many months earlier, and staring into the dark.

Chapter Six

Two weeks later, as December brought preparations for Christmas and the market sprouted with holly, ivy and fir trees brought down by the cartload from the Norfolk forests, Francis made up his mind. There was tension in the atmosphere these days, and he was uncomfortable. He found himself evading Mrs Goode's eyes. It wouldn't do at all, he decided.

'Very well, Emma,' he said to the portrait. 'I know it's what you'd want of me.'

The following day was his fiftieth birthday. It seemed an appropriate time for new beginnings, so he asked Bridie to come to his study.

She stood with her hands clasped loosely over her thick skirt and apron. It was still hard to tell, thought Francis, as he tried to think of a good way to start. He realised that sitting behind his desk with her standing before him felt like an interview. He rose and went round to the fire.

'Come over here and sit down.'

They faced each other on the sofa, he well back with his legs crossed comfortably, she perched on the edge, afraid of what was to come. There was silence, and Bridie couldn't bear it any longer.

'Are you going to send me away?' she asked in a voice that was breathless with anxiety.

'Send you away?' Francis was astonished. 'Where to?'

Bridie's hands fluttered.

'I dunno. The workhouse?'

'Good God, no. Though I had wondered about your family. Would you be thinking of going home? To Dublin, that is.'

Bridie spoke with no consciousness of the irony.

'No, sir. Me Dad would beat the livin' daylights out of me if I went home now.'

'Your sisters could help you with the baby, though?' Francis pressed her.

'Sure, they would. They'd love a baby. But there's no work there, sir.'

Bridie knew that wild horses wouldn't get her back to Ireland, but she couldn't and wouldn't tell him that.

Francis stroked his chin thoughtfully.

'I'd been thinking that you might want to go, not of sending you away. That hasn't been my intention at all. Not at all,' he repeated.

Bridie felt her knees go quivery with relief. She smoothed her skirt anxiously with fingers that trembled.

'Do you mean I can stay here, sir?' she whispered.

'But of course,' said Francis, for the first time becoming aware of the depth of her fear. 'Do you think me a monster, Bridie? That's a poor opinion after all this time, I must say. Have I given you cause to believe so badly of me?'

Bridie looked down in shame. 'No, sir.'

'Well then.'

She chewed her lip. Francis waved a hand at the picture over the fireplace.

'Emma and I had no children, as you know,' he began, 'and I'm fifty today. That's a little late in life to begin a family, but I'm quite beginning to like the idea. However, I've no wish to have my son born with the stigma of illegitimacy, and I think we should be married.'

Bridie's heart shrank. When she finally spoke, it was with all the pride and defiance of a humiliated woman. 'No, thank you, sir.'

Francis was astounded. 'Pardon?' he said foolishly.

'I said, thank you, sir, but I'd rather not marry you.'

'Good God!' It had never crossed his mind that she might turn him down. 'What *do* you want, then?'

'I'd appreciate it if I could stay here, like we just said, and carry on the same as before. I'll go on working for you. Mrs Goode knows about the baby, but she don't know about you bein' its father. Do you want me to tell her?'

Francis was completely taken aback. 'Oh, well, I suppose she'll have to know sooner or later. Yes. But for Heaven's sake, Bridie, why won't you marry me? It seems to me the only sensible thing to do, in the circumstances.'

Bridie couldn't look at him. 'I don't know, sir. It doesn't seem so right to me, I suppose.'

'Well, think it over and we'll talk about it again,' he suggested. She was just surprised and unprepared, he told himself, and she'd be sensible when she'd had a bit of time.

'Did you want anything else, sir?' she asked after a lengthy silence.

'What?' He started out of his wandering thoughts. 'Oh, no, thank you. I wish you'd consider this matter carefully, Bridie. There's the child to think of, you must surely see that?'

'Yes, I do, sir. Can I go now?'

He nodded slowly, and watched her leave the room, hardly able to believe what had happened.

Mrs Goode couldn't believe it either. 'Have you taken leave of your senses?' she gasped, in utter astonishment.

'No,' said Bridie.

The housekeeper felt mortified and furious at the idea of all that carry on, all going on behind her back. She'd been made a complete fool of, and was beside herself with outrage. Only a fear in the back of her mind that it might anger Francis stopped her from boxing Bridie's ears.

'How could you?' she appealed for some kind of explanation. 'How could you behave so deceitfully?'

'I haven't. We was just . . . just discreet, that's all. You seem to think that everyone should tell you their business, but I don't want to go blabbing everything I do. You don't have no rights over what I do.'

'You're glad enough of my help, though, when your sinfulness comes home to roost.' Mrs Goode mixed her metaphors agitatedly. The barb shot home. Bridie was having trouble squaring her conscience about confession. She worried that she should be full of guilt and contrition, and since she wasn't, she couldn't really confess. So she'd avoided the parish priest, and wandered into old Mother Wisniewski's on Sunday mornings, instead of going to church. Sooner or later Father Eric was going to turn up to find out what was keeping her away, and she was dreading the visit.

'Anyway,' Bridie pointed out, 'we was both going behind your back, if you want to put it that way, not just me.'

Mrs Goode was scandalized by the direct reference to her employer's philandering.

' 'E 's a man,' she said loftily. 'It's different.'

Bridie had to admit that it was different for a man. That had become painfully clear earlier that morning. It was all right for him, sitting there cool as you please, wanting to get everything sorted so that his son wouldn't have that awful 'ILLEGITIMATE' stamped all over his birth certificate. Bridie didn't like the thought much, either, but it was no way to go and get married. Not to a man who only wanted to be married for a piece of paper. Bridie didn't reckon she could live with that. What about loving each other? What about all that tender sharing, and the loveliness? He hadn't said anything; he hadn't looked as though he'd thought, even, about that.

Under Mrs Goode's enraged eyes, she burst into tears, put her head in her arms and howled.

'Oh give over,' said the older woman angrily. 'Shut the water works, Bridie, you'll get no sympathy that way.'

Bridie looked up, scarlet-faced and streaming. She wiped her nose miserably on her knuckles. 'He asked me to marry him,' she admitted at last.

The housekeeper's expression changed from rage to righteousness. 'Well I never! There, didn't I just tell you he was a good man.'

Bridie quailed. 'And I said I wouldn't.'

Words failed Mrs Goode. She simply stood opening and shutting her mouth, like a fish. Bridie took a bit of rag out of the cupboard behind her head and blew her nose and wiped her eyes. The housekeeper continued to stare at her as though she'd suddenly sprouted a second head.

'What?' she squeaked finally.

Bridie, relieved that all her secrets were out, started feeling a bit braver. 'Mr Holmes said he'd marry me, on account of the baby, and I said I didn't want to,' she repeated.

'You're mad. You must be. They ought to take you away.'

'No, I'm not. I don't want to marry him for the baby. If I hadn't fallen for the baby I don't think it would have entered his head to marry me, nor me him, I suppose. If he wanted to marry me because he loved me an' wanted me, then I would and be glad. But not this way. No, not this way.'

Indignation covered the wound in Bridie's heart, and made her voice strong.

'Well, I never did,' said the housekeeper again. 'You're a wilful one, and no mistake. There's girls would give anything for the chance you've got, and you turn it down. You'll likely live to regret this, my girl.'

'Maybe I will, but I'll cross that bridge when I come to it.'

'What are you going to do, then?' Mrs Goode had calmed down enough for her natural inquisitiveness to re-assert itself.

'Carry on here the same as usual, at least until I have the baby. Then I'll see.'

'Mr Holmes agree with that?'

'Except for the marrying bit, yes.'

'Good gracious.'

Mrs Goode looked at the clock on the wall. 'Oh, my goodness, look at the time.' As she spoke they heard the front door open and bang shut. 'He's home already, and we've done nothing. It's your fault.' In a fine state of agitation, the housekeeper jumped as Francis put his head round the morning-room door.

'I'm in,' he said.

He looked from one embarrassed face to the other, and could well imagine that acrimonious words had been exchanged between the two of them. Something would have to be said to Dora, or she'd persecute Bridie out of mistaken good intentions. Francis felt his well-ordered life begin to slide towards confusion. What with the tension between his little household, Bridie's astonishing behaviour, and the fact that her pregnancy must soon be obvious to everyone, Francis wondered what his friends and neighbours would say.

'It's really none of their business,' he murmured to himself as he hung up his overcoat and propped his galoshes by the umbrella stand. It was raining cats and dogs outside; he'd got soaked coming home.

The following evening, after she'd finished the chores, Bridie lifted down her own coat, and taking a big black umbrella because it was still pouring down, walked up to Stratford High Street. Looking out from under the shelter of the brolly, she watched people hurry past, splashed and muddy and cold. Faces that were pinched and pallid on account of not enough to eat and horrible damp houses where people coughed all the time. Nits and lice and dirt. Smells you couldn't always put a name to, and others that had names as foul as the stench itself. Children with impetigo running over their faces. Sick children. Dead children. Mothers with tired, lined faces yelling at the bigger ones to look after the babies.

Bridie's feet slowed on the streaming path. Was this what she wanted for her baby? This ugliness, this awful, frightening world where girls like Daisy lost their souls and bodies in the back streets.

She'd arranged to meet Lizzie by the library, and because of the downpour they went in. They stood whispering in Adult Fiction, moving up and down the stacks pulling out books so that the librarian wouldn't catch them and tell them to be silent.

'So I said I couldn't,' she explained in a very low voice at the end of her story.

Lizzie had had her suspicions for a long time, but

112

had been much too tactful to say anything to Bridie until she saw fit to bring it up herself.

'I think you're right,' she whispered back, 'but how will you manage?'

Bridie shook her head at her friend.

'I'll take it one thing at a time. I don't know what will happen in the future. I've nothing to plan for, so what's the use of worrying about it. Take it as it comes.'

Lizzie turned a professional eye on Bridie's stomach. 'May, you said?'

Bridie nodded.

'D'you know Mrs MacDonald, down Stepney High Street, just by St Dunstan's? She's lovely, and she's the best person to go to if you need a midwife. I've heard she's really good. I've met a few women who've had her look after them, and they speak very well of her.'

'Oh, I'd not really thought that far ahead.'

'Well, you'd better,' whispered Lizzie sternly, 'because she's busy and you need to be sure she'll come when you need her.'

The librarian stopped on silent feet at the end of the shelves. 'This is a library, not a public meeting place. If you wish to stay, would you kindly not talk.' She pointed to the SILENCE notice at the end of the stack.

They burst into giggles as she stalked away.

'Come on, if it's stopped raining we'll walk back.' Lizzie grabbed her friend by the arm.

They loitered in the green-painted library entrance. Beyond the door the rain fell in sheets.

'Oh, bother!' Lizzie's fair hair was still stuck to her

head from the walk she had earlier. Hazel eyes screwed up in thought, she wondered what to do on such a horrid evening. It was pitch dark as well. Behind them, the library was light and warm; some-one coughed quietly and turned a page.

'Oh, come on. Can I share the brolly?'

They plunged into the miserable darkness, huddled close together in the shelter of the umbrella, and began to pick their way as best they could among the rain-pocked puddles.

'Can't see a thing. We're going to get drenched,' grumbled Lizzie.

'Never mind. We'll have cocoa and biscuits when we get back, and you can give your hair a rub.'

Lizzie had been paid the honour of being invited into Mrs Goode's kitchen some months earlier. Satisfied that she was a nice young woman, with decent manners, Mrs Goode had let it be known that she was welcome any time. In winter it was cosy to sit by the stoked-up range, toasting their feet and faces in the red glow. Turning into the square, they gave up all pretence of staying dry, and ran through the dripping garden to the back gate. Bridie fumbled in the dark to open the door into the scullery, and rain ran in cold trickles all down her neck.

'There,' she gasped, and they pushed through the door, making puddles on the scullery floor. The brolly dripped rivulets that ran under the sink.

Bridie sucked her wet fingers. 'Perishin', isn't it? Here.'

They spread their coats over the top of the copper

to dry off a bit, and Bridie lit the gas. She was just fetching milk from the larder for cocoa when Francis surprised them both.

'Good evening,' he said pleasantly to Lizzie. 'Bridie, do you know if there's any more brandy? The bottle in the parlour is finished.'

'Oh, yes, there's some in the sideboard.' Bridie went through and opened the cupboard. She took out two dark bottles. 'There's this kind, and this one. Which did you want, sir?'

'The French, please.' He smiled at her. 'It's Dr Hamilton. He's partial to this brand.' He disappeared with the bottle.

'He's ever so much older than you. Don't you mind?' Lizzie asked curiously.

'I never thought much about it,' Bridie answered honestly. 'He's so . . . interesting, I suppose. More than boys. Well, the ones I meet, anyway. Its different for you, Lizzie. You've got all those doctors and students and things to go round with. Me, I'm just a housemaid. You and me get on nicely, but I wouldn't know what to say to some of your lot.'

'Don't you say that.' Lizzie's voice was indignant. She shook an admonitory finger at Bridie. 'Don't you put yourself down like that, not to me, anyway. I won't listen. You're as just as good as anyone else, and don't you think otherwise. You're good fun, you are, and look how fast you learn things. I think you're cleverer by half than some of those doctors, and you've a mind of your own . . . a kind of truthfulness, and I don't mean just not telling fibs. Just look at the

way you won't be bullied into marrying. You've got
. . . what's the word? Integrity, that's it.'

Bridie looked at her friend's passionate little face.
'You're the best friend I ever had, except for my sisters.
I'm glad.'

'So am I,' said Lizzie, and they smiled at each
other over the cocoa mugs. 'Do you miss them – your
sisters?'

'Yes. 'course I do.'

'Wouldn't Mr Holmes let you go and visit?'

The open smile disappeared from Bridie's face. 'I've
not asked him.'

'And what about your Dad. Aren't you going to tell
him about the baby. It's his first grandchild, isn't it?'

'Yes,' said Bridie shortly.

Lizzie looked at her curiously and wisely decided to
say no more. She had a feeling there was more to the
O'Neills than met the eye. 'Can I come and help, when
the baby's born?' she asked, changing the subject.

'Of course you can. Why didn't I think of it myself?'

'You'll see Mrs MacDonald anyway, won't you?
She's got the experience. But I could lend a hand. Fetch
hot water or something.'

'Oh, yes,' cried Bridie, delightedly.

'Maytime. That's a good time of year for a baby.
Nice and warm.'

Bridie patted her stomach gently. 'I didn't exactly
ask this little one to come, but he seems to have
organised himself pretty well so far.'

'Might be a girl, you know.'

'He or she. Francis thinks it's bound to be a boy. To

116

hear him, you wouldn't know there's such things as girl babies.'

'What you goin' to call it?'

'I haven't thought yet. Maybe Lizzie – well, Elizabeth – if it's a girl. After you.'

Lizzie grinned. 'If it's like me, you'll be in for a handful. My mother still shakes her head when she talks about some of the wild things I did.'

'Get along. You? Wild? The pillar of the London Hospital.'

'I'm reformed,' said Lizzie virtuously. 'And with that baby, you'd best reform and get plenty of early nights. That's professional advice for free.'

She stood to go and collected her wet things from the scullery. 'Ugh! Sopping,' she said.

Bridie saw her to the garden gate. Lizzie kissed her cheek as she said goodnight.

'You take care walking back,' said Bridie.

'And you. See you next week.'

Lizzie walked quickly into the dark, and, turning back beneath a shower of raindrops from the over-hanging bushes, Bridie looked up at the stars, shining in a sky washed clear of clouds, and thought that it might not be so bad, having a baby, after all.

Chapter Seven

Bridie's son was born on May Day, 1921. The pains started on the Tuesday afternoon. Bridie put on her shawl, took up the basket of baby clothes and the bundle of her own night-gowns, and walked slowly over to Mrs MacDonald's house in Stepney. Several times she stopped to lean on a wall, breathing deeply as the pain came and went.

'You all right, ducks?' asked a woman, passing by with two small children.

Bridie waited for the pain to pass. 'Yes, ta,' she said. Now the time had come, she was quite calm.

She arrived at Mrs MacDonald's small house at teatime. The midwife took the bundles from her, and showed her upstairs to the clean, whitewashed little room at the back where she'd offered to look after Bridie when the time came.

'I just don't,' was all she'd say in answer to Francis's questions as to why she didn't want to have the baby in her own room. Mrs MacDonald had asked no questions and had promised Bridie that she could stay with her as long as she liked.

By nightfall the pains were coming stronger and more often. Mrs MacDonald popped in and out and sat for a while with her knitting at Bridie's side. As she felt the baby sometime near midnight, with cool, firm hands, she told Bridie she thought it most probably would be morning before he arrived.

'You're as bad as Francis,' joked Bridie, between pains. 'He always says it's a he, never a she.'

Mrs MacDonald clucked her tongue. 'There's many as thinks it's better to be born a boy,' she said, smoothing her grey hair back after bending over Bridie. 'I'm afraid there's truth in it, too, my dear.' When Mrs MacDonald smiled you could tell from the way her eyes crinkled that she smiled a lot.

The night passed slowly. Soon after dawn Bridie began to groan and clutch the edge of the sheet with white fingers.

'I think I'm nearly there,' she called in a squeaky, breathless voice, hearing the midwife's footsteps coming up the stairs.

'Indeed you are.' Mrs MacDonald's thin, kind face disappeared behind Bridie's raised knees.

'Yes, my dear. You can push when you feel you want to.'

A fierce pain came and seemed to last forever.

'Lizzie,' she gasped. 'Has anyone told her?'

'Yes, our Jimmy was going by the hospital on the way to Spitalfields, first thing. If she can come, she will.'

Bridie's face screwed up and the pain tore a shriek out of her. The midwife spoke soothingly.

'There, there, my dear. That's it, push now. And again. Another one.'

The room was silent except for Bridie's panting breathing.

'One more, dear.'

And it was over.

Mrs MacDonald bundled the baby in a clean towel and handed him to Bridie.

'Here we are, lovie, a perfect little boy.'

Bridie scarcely noticed as the midwife busied herself with the final stages of the birth and began to clear up. Pulling herself half upright, she gazed at the baby. He didn't cry. Two bright, alert blue eyes stared unwaveringly back at her. The tiny red face was intense and serious, and the drooping little mouth opened and closed as if he were silently talking to her. Bridie was enchanted. She carefully stroked the little wrinkled cheek. The baby's head turned to grope for the finger, and he began to cry.

'You put him to the breast,' advised Mrs MacDonald. He suckled eagerly.

'Oh look, Mrs MacDonald. Look at his little ears. Did you ever see anything so sweet?'

'He's a lovely baby, my dear.' Mrs MacDonald nodded approvingly. The baby fell asleep on Bridie's breast, and when all else was done the midwife lifted him gently away.

'Let's freshen you up, too, my love,' she said, bringing a bowl of cool water to the bedside. Gently she washed and dried Bridie's face and arms, helping her into one of the fresh night-gowns she'd brought with her the day before.

'There we are.' She brushed the tangles out of the

121

red hair and stood back to survey her patient. 'How about a nice cup of tea?' she suggested, tucking the baby into Bridie's arms under the sheet.

Easing her baby so they were both comfortable, Bridie laid her head back on the pillow and nodded.

'Yes, please.'

The window stood open and a slight breeze billowed the pale green curtains lazily against the white wall. It moved deliciously over Bridie's face, and she closed her eyes in utter contentment. When Mrs MacDonald climbed the stairs a little later, she found mother and baby fast asleep. Smiling to herself, she took the tea back down again, and quietly got on with her work.

The afternoon turned to evening. Outside, shadows began to lengthen in the slanting sunlight. The street bustled with homecoming workers and women called from their doorsteps to children to come in for their tea. Bridie stirred and woke, and her movement woke the baby. He promptly started to cry. Mrs MacDonald hurried upstairs.

'He's hungry,' she said.

'So am I,' said Bridie, as the baby settled down to suckle. 'In fact, I'm starving.'

'Well, you would be, after all that hard work,' the midwife said briskly.

'Could I have some toast, Mrs MacDonald? And a huge pot of tea?'

' 'course you can.' Mrs MacDonald went off to make toast by the range, and Bridie looked down at her son. His eyes were half closed in contentment and

122

even when he finished feeding, he made little sucking movements with his mouth.

'Oh, you are beautiful,' Bridie whispered to him. 'You're the most beautiful thing I ever saw. You're mine. It's just you and me, baby. And I'll love you forever and ever.'

The baby turned his head and snuffled.

'Here you are,' said Mrs MacDonald, as she put the tray of hot toast and steaming tea on the end of the bed.

She took the sleepy baby from Bridie.

'I'll see to him, and you get that down you.'

Bridie ate hungrily, and had nearly finished when there was knock at the front door downstairs. Lizzie burst in, half hidden behind a bunch of flowers, bought from the stall outside the hospital.

'Oh, my goodness! Did you ever see such a gorgeous baby?' she cried, as Mrs MacDonald stood holding him while Bridie pushed away the tray and Lizzie stooped to hug her. 'Was it all right?' she asked.

'She had an easy time,' answered the midwife. 'You was no trouble, was you?' she added, looking at the baby.

Lizzie put her finger into the tiny fist. 'Did you ever . . .' she marvelled.

Bridie lay on her pillows and watched. Lizzie turned to her. 'You got a name for him yet?'

Bridie nodded. 'David.'

Lizzie and Mrs MacDonald exchanged approving nods. 'That's nice,' they agreed.

Bridie held out her arms for her baby. 'David O'Neill, come here,' she said quietly.

Lizzie sat on the end of the bed. 'I couldn't come earlier,' she said. 'I was on duty, and Matron was in one of her moods, so I didn't dare ask for time off. But you're all right, and he's so lovely, and I'm here now.'

Mrs MacDonald left her chattering, and went to put the flowers in water. When she came up, Lizzie was standing preparing to go. 'I bet you're tired out,' she said to Bridie, who nodded, because she was.

'If this young man lets her get some sleep, she'll be as right as rain,' said the midwife.

And so it was. David woke Bridie several times, with mewling little cries. She fed him sleepily, and felt such joy that she held her breath in wonder. They were both wide awake at six o'clock and the midwife, shaking the night's ashes from the grate in the range, heard the soft murmur of Bridie's voice talking to her son. She smiled into the raked embers. Bridie was going to make a lovely mother.

Four days later the euphoria passed. Outside it had turned chilly and a thin drizzle misted the window. The weather seemed to echo Bridie's mood. She told Mrs MacDonald that she didn't want visitors, meaning Francis, but the midwife remarked bluntly that a father ought to see his baby if he wanted to, and never mind the circumstances.

'I don't approve,' she said, when Bridie pouted and

held the baby so tightly to her he began to cry.

So they agreed that Francis would come on the fourth day, and maybe Mrs Goode the day after. Saturday afternoon, and Francis was shown upstairs by Mrs MacDonald. He seemed to fill the room in his dark, damp overcoat.

'I'll be downstairs if you want me,' the midwife said, and, closing the door discreetly behind her, left the three of them together.

Francis found Bridie in a distracted mood. All her delight and joy at the baby's birth seemed to have vanished, leaving her fretful and edgy. She turned her cheek for him to kiss in an offhand sort of fashion. Francis's heart sank; it wasn't going to be easy. He bent over to look at the baby, almost hidden beneath the cover, held close in Bridie's arms.

'Can I see him?' he asked in a hushed voice.

'You don't have to whisper,' answered Bridie crossly. 'He's dead asleep and won't wake up until he's hungry again.'

She pulled the blanket back. The tiny boy was flushed with warmth and sleep and the fine, fair fuzz on his head was slightly streaked with sweat. He snuffled rhythmically and stirred as Bridie moved him a little, for his father to see him better. Francis was awe-struck. His mouth opened and closed several times, and Bridie was amazed to see tears gather in his eyes.

'Oh Bridie, oh dear. . . .' He couldn't find words. He fumbled in his coat pocket and tugged out a handkerchief, then brew his nose discreetly, so as not to wake the baby.

'Yes, well . . .' Bridie said uncomfortably, wishing he'd sit down and stop mithering.

'Mrs MacDonald tells me he's to be called David.' Francis scratched at his sidewhiskers as he spoke. 'I wish you had talked to me about his name first, before you decided, but David is a good name. There's been no Davids in my family as far as I know, but it'll do well.'

They sat in uneasy silence for a while, and then Bridie, with no warning at all, burst into tears. She wailed aloud and rocked to and fro, knuckles pressed against her mouth to check the sobs.

'Oh dear,' cried Francis distractedly, 'you mustn't carry on like this. Bridie, when are you and David going to come home?'

He rubbed his hands together anxiously, wishing she'd stop. Bridie wept harder. The baby woke at the uproar and his thin, shrill cries added to the sounds of distress reaching the midwife's ears below.

'This won't do at all,' said Francis agitatedly to the room in general. 'They've got to come home.'

Mrs MacDonald poked her head round the stair-corner to see what all the fuss was about. 'Ah, Mrs MacDonald.' Francis turned to her in relief and appealed for help. 'Can you do something for her?'

As Bridie's hysteria showed no sign of abating. Francis threw all caution to the winds. 'Tell her to come home,' he said loudly to the midwife. 'For God's sake, this can't go on. Bring my son home, Bridie.' His voice rose and cut across the din. He took the howling girl by the shoulders and gave her a shake. 'Do you hear me?'

Bridie opened her eyes and looked at him bleakly. Then she looked down at the baby, gave a sob that shook the bed, and said, 'Yes,' in such a small voice he hardly heard her.

'That's better,' said Francis, looking at Mrs MacDonald, who nodded. Bridie hiccoughed quietly for some while after, but the worst was over. The baby, amazed at the disturbance, settled down to suckle, and calm descended once more on the small white room. Downstairs, Francis arranged with the midwife that she'd see Bridie home at the soonest possible moment after her lying-in had safely passed. Upstairs, he was firm with Bridie, who was reduced to meek reasonableness.

'We'll be married as soon as you are able,' he told her. 'My son can and must be properly cared for, and you can only do that as my wife.'

If only you'd say you *want* me as your wife, thought Bridie, but she merely nodded at all his instructions, and kept her thoughts to herself. Many years later, when she was in a reflective mood and recalling the past, she'd complain he took advantage of her when she was weak.

'Everyone knows your nerves are low after a baby,' she'd remark, 'and he took advantage. Lots of things might have turned out different if he hadn't done that.'

Chapter Eight

Mrs Goode lifted the heavy grey silk dress over Bridie's head. Its smooth cold folds slid down her body and made her catch her breath. The bodice was boned and stretched glossily round her midriff. She tugged at it and wriggled to get comfortable.

'Stand straight,' instructed Mrs Goode, 'so's I can do the hooks up properly.'

'I'm too fat,' complained Bridie.

'Nonsense!' retorted the housekeeper. 'What do you expect, anyway, hardly five minutes after you've had a baby? You just wait and see. The work of him will have you trim in no time.'

'Hm.' Bridie sounded unconvinced.

'Hold your breath in a minute.' Mrs Goode pulled hard at the hooks in the small of Bridie's back. She did as she was told, and pulled her shoulders back as the housekeeper rapidly threaded hooks into eyes all the way up the back of the dress.

Bridie let out a sigh as the last one, at the base of her neck, snapped into place. She put down the thick shining plait of hair gathered into a knot with a white ribbon and stood back to look at herself in the long mirror they'd wheeled from Francis's room into hers that morning. She tilted her head on one side and considered. She saw a young girl, straight and square, with direct, grey eyes set in a rather tired, freckled face that was a little plumper than it used to be.

The high-necked dress of plain, pale grey silk fell in straight folds to the floor, the perfect complement to the bright hair and its ribbon.

'Oh, it's lovely.' Bridie half turned, and lifted her skirts to show the matching grey slippers that had delighted her more than anything.

She looked at Mrs Goode in the mirror and her face lit up with a slow smile. 'It really is lovely.'

Delighted, she turned and threw her arms round the beaming housekeeper's narrow shoulders. 'You've been ever so good to me. Me and David, we wouldn't have got along so well without you. Thank you for everything.'

Mrs Goode set her shoulders back and blinked with pleasure. 'Get along with you,' she said briskly, to cover her embarrassment.

She held Bridie away from her. 'The veil, now,' she said.

It lay in a box on Bridie's bed. The housekeeper took it out carefully and held it up. The bright June sunlight poured through the window and the plane tree threw shadows on the bright, white lace that draped between the housekeeper's hands. Bridie stared at it. For her, more than anything else, the veil told her that she was about to be wed. A sudden chill shivered through her.

* * *

'Have what you need,' Francis had said. They'd sat together in the parlour, that rainy day four weeks ago. Bridie, tired after getting up to feed David several times a night, had drowsily watched raindrops running down the glass, resting her cheek on the smooth velvet of the big armchair, curled up cosy enough to drop asleep only Francis insisted on making arrangements.

With eyes half closed she watched him take money from the strongbox that lay in front of him. Francis's long fingers counted out the big white bank notes. Bridie had never seen so much money all at once. She wondered if he was rich – really rich.

It was strange, she suddenly thought, that you could be so close to someone but not know something like that about them. She wished that Little May could come, she thought sadly. Lizzie and Mrs Goode were to be witnesses at the wedding, but it wasn't quite the same. She studied her future husband's face. The mouth that could be so loving was set in a stern, straight line as he counted banknotes. He looked austere, yet she knew how generous he could be. Bridie sighed. She'd never really make him out.

'There.' He finished folding bank notes. 'You must go with Mrs Goode to the West End and buy what you need. I have asked her to be sure that you have everything.'

'Yes,' said Bridie.

'I've spoken to Father Eric,' he went on remorselessly, 'and he says he can offer us the last Saturday in June. I said that it would suit us quite well.'

Bridie's mind went far back to her village church and the lined face of the priest who knew her well. She tried hard to hold back tears. An image formed slowly in her mind. She saw herself standing at a familiar altar, shimmering in white, with Little May behind her and flowers all around. A tall stranger stood beside her, in his good dark suit . . . a young man from a farm outside the village. . . .

'Bridie, you're not listening.'

Francis's voice broke in and dissolved the vision. Bridie let it go, sadly because it was strangely familiar, and made herself attend to what he was saying.

'He suggests two o'clock. We'll be back here at about half-past three. Mrs MacDonald has kindly said she'll come and take care of David, so you needn't worry about him. Lizzie will come back and have a glass of champagne with us, but I asked Mrs Goode to prepare supper for just you and me. We'll be very quiet.'

No, thought Bridie, you'd not want anyone else, seeing as you're marrying the servant.

'Yes,' she said again.

Francis frowned. 'Don't the arrangements please you, Bridie?' he asked. Her indifference puzzled and upset him.

She sat up straight in the armchair. 'Oh yes, yes of course they do.' She spoke more energetically. 'I'll love to go shopping in the West End. Just fancy, me going to the big shops for my wedding dress. It takes a bit of getting used to, all this does, sir. That's all.'

Francis rose from his seat at the table and wandered to the window. 'It's still pouring. You'd never think it was summer,' he remarked.

He pulled the dark brocade curtain aside and peered out. Beyond the railings at the front of the tall house, at the edge of a flower bed, a gardener stood, leaning on his fork, gazing at something he'd turned up in the soil. Rain drip-dripped off his sou'wester. An old man, he moved very slowly. Old men had plenty of work these days; there were few young men left. Feeling Francis's eyes on him, the fellow looked up and raised a hand in a gesture of salute. Francis nodded at him. He turned back to Bridie.

'Old Tom is getting soaked out there. I trust it won't rain for us like this,' he said more lightly. 'That would be a disappointment.'

'I can't wear a white dress,' said Bridie suddenly.

'Ah, no, I suppose not.' Francis was taken aback. He was not used to thinking of dresses, and this situation was proving trickier than he had foreseen. 'Does that matter very much?' he enquired cautiously.

Bridie spread her hands in a dismissive gesture. 'No, I suppose not. I just thought you'd best know that I wouldn't be buying white. I'll look to see what else might do. Mrs Goode agrees, because I've asked her about it, and she says, with David and all, that it wouldn't do at all to wear white.'

It was a kind of protest. Bridie had a feeling that this wedding was a kind of half-truth. There was something not quite right about it which made her uneasy.

'Getting wed for appearances isn't a real wedding, to my mind,' she'd said to Lizzie angrily, when the demands of the baby left her tired and low-spirited. Then she'd remembered how sweetly Francis cared for her, and felt badly. 'Oh blow it all,' Bridie muttered under her breath, dismissing all the doubts that went round and round in circles until her head ached. 'Just get on with it, do.'

She stood up and, crossing the room to where Francis stood with his back to the window, kissed him lightly on his cheek. 'I'll see Mrs Goode directly, about going to get the things in the West End. Maybe we can go the day after tomorrow, if Mrs MacDonald could look after David. I'll send and ask her.' She stroked his face very gently. 'You have been dear to me.'

Francis's expression softened. 'Will you be happy, Bridie?' he asked. 'Sometimes you are so distant, I wonder.'

Bridie kissed him again silently. She smiled at him. 'I'll find Mrs Goode now, and then go up to David.'

Francis watched her leave the room; a vague unease weighed on his heart. Something about her eluded him; she was open as a book, and yet . . . yet there was something secretive. It puzzled and bothered him. Often he sat alone in his study, urgent papers spread before him, and yet these days, he realised, he often caught himself gazing with unfocussed eyes, day-dreaming.

His heart ached sometimes, but he could not have said why. He was well aware that theirs was an odd affair, looked at askance by a good many people, but for the elusive sadness between them, he could find neither reason nor solace. The middle-aged man sighed to himself and started to lock up his strong-box. He tried to picture Bridie in a wedding dress, bought with the money he had just taken from it, but for some reason the picture wavered and blurred until the dress became a shroud. Horrified, he shook his head until the evil image vanished.

Shaken, Francis busied himself with putting the box away, and turned for comfort to his neglected paperwork. He became absorbed in reports about the incidence of infant death in East London, and didn't lift his head again until Mrs Goode came in to see if he wanted a fire lit in the early evening, as the rain was still falling and the air was cool.

On this, her wedding day, the rain had gone, and the sun shone for Bridie. Mrs Goode shook out the beautiful square of French lace and said admiringly, 'It's just exactly right. You've a good eye for what suits you, my duck, indeed you have. You'll take Mr Holmes's breath away, I don't doubt.'

Bridie's mind lingered on that cool May evening and the shopping expeditions that followed. They'd walked themselves weary round the great shops, Bridie wide-eyed at the smart dresses and haughty shopgirls who brought out box upon box of lace, silk and velvet. She'd picked the grey silk the moment she saw it. Their heads together, the grey and the red almost touching, she and Mrs Goode had fingered and stroked the fabric, excitedly nodding to each other that here was just the very thing.

'I fancy it quite plain,' Bridie had exclaimed. 'But with a long veil that should be lacy so as to set off the way the dress is simple.'

Mrs Goode said she could picture it well, and so they'd agreed the cut and style, and ordered the first fitting. Then they'd wandered around and around the displays of lace and trimmings, looking for ribbons and a length of lace that would be right for Bridie's wedding veil. They'd come away empty handed that first time, but when they made their third, last journey westwards for the final trying on of the completed dress, they'd passed the lace counter and there it was, lying in a small bolt on the counter, waiting to be put on display.

'Look!' Bridie had cried. 'Isn't that just lovely?'

Mrs Goode looked. The shopgirl, seeing their interest, had held up one end and unrolled a yard for Bridie to see.

'It's newly in from Lyons, France,' she said.

Bridie stroked it gently. 'It's for my wedding,' she confided. 'It's the prettiest I've seen.'

And so the veil was bought, followed by dainty grey slippers to match the dress. 'I shall look quite the lady,' Bridie exclaimed to Mrs Goode, laughing. 'Who'da thought it? Me, with a fancy wedding like this.'

'You'd best get used to it,' answered Mrs Goode acidly. 'Because you're wedding a gentleman, young woman, regardless.'

'Regardless? Regardless of what, I'd like to know.' Bridie's expression darkened.

Mrs Goode looked at her squarely. 'Don't you take that tone to me, young woman. You may be marrying that man, but it don't make you no better than you was before unless you become a lady by your own efforts. I'll speak my mind to you whether you like to listen or not. And I'll thank you to remember that you being wed won't make no difference to that. I speak my mind, and I ain't doing no different.'

Mrs Goode held up her head defiantly. The question of the change in their respective positions had been much on her mind of late, and she'd resolved to get it clear with Bridie before the wedding day.

Bridie looked astonished, then chastened. 'Oh, I never did think about that. I thought you meant David. Not being able to have a white dress, an' all.'

She giggled suddenly. 'My lady won't get above herself, I don't think.' She hugged the box with her dress in it to her. 'I'm just so excited. I never had nothing like this before.'

Mrs Goode softened. 'Just so long as we've got an understanding, then.'

'Oh, I 'spect I'll still scrub the kitchen and you'll still go on about the cupboards and tidying. He said we'd get some more help, anyway. He's talking of a nursemaid and another girl to come in for cleaning. We'll do nicely, you and me, Mrs Goode.'

'That's all right then. It won't really do for you to scrub, not now. I just wanted to be plain with you.'

They skirted round the milling crowds and headed for the tram stop, clutching their purchases. A newsboy shouted above the roar of trams and the hubbub of chatter from jostling shoppers. Bridie breathed deeply of the dusty air and hurried after Mrs Goode's black-shawled back, thrilled by the noise and excitement of the great city. She gave a little skip of pure joy and ran on ahead for the tram.

Now, after all the preparation, the moment had come to wear the veil. Bridie bowed her head as the housekeeper placed it carefully over her hair and fastened it with two tortoiseshell clips. Bridie turned back to the mirror and slowly drew it down over her face. Then she turned.

'I'm ready.'

Mrs Goode opened the door of the room with the plane tree at the window which had so often whispered to Bridie in the dark of the night. A last backward look at the bed where she and Francis had loved for so long, and, straightening her back, she marched across the familiar landing and down the stairs, head held high, to meet her future. He stood, frock-coated and grave-faced, at the foot of the stairs.

'Why, Bridie, you are beautiful,' he said as she came down towards him. 'You truly are beautiful.'

She tucked her hand under his arm, turned a smiling, half-hidden face towards him, and said, 'Let us go, then.'

They went, accompanied by Mrs Goode. Lizzie met

them at the door of the church. They made their vows almost in solitude before the young priest. As Bridie lifted the veil from her face and kissed her husband before the altar, she felt solemn, as though something was given to her alone, to have and to hold, from her innermost strength, from that day on. Unsmiling, she gave her flowers to Lizzie.

They left the church in a small, quiet group and, with her veil floating gently behind her in the warm air, Bridie in her dainty grey slippers walked slowly home with her husband.

Chapter Nine

The wind howled dismally round the streets and whipped at the long dark skirts of women trudging home from market, carrying string bags of vegetables in red, chilblained hands. In the warmth of the parlour at the front of the house in Tredegar Square Bridie paused, heavy red curtains half drawn to shut out the wintry scene. She looked up and down the road in the half light, but there was no sign of her husband. It was early for him yet, she thought.

She pulled the curtains together and looked round the room with satisfaction. It was warm and inviting. Flames flickered in the grate, blacked by the maid that morning until the metal shone. Number twelve had not changed much from the bachelor house it had been, but she'd re-covered some of the parlour furniture, and here and there her touch was beginning to turn a residence into a family home.

Kneeling to brush fallen ash back under the grate she stayed there, gazing into the coals. Through the half-open door she could just hear Mrs Goode chattering away to the baby as she fed him before taking him up to his nursery. Susan, the nursemaid, would put him into his little flannel night-gown and call Bridie to say goodnight when he was ready. Bridie put her arms round her knees and hugged herself in contentment. Sitting on the thick carpet she thought of the red and blue Indian rug in the study where she and Francis had made love for the first time, almost two years earlier.

She smiled at the memory, unconsciously turning the wedding ring around and around on her finger. Enjoying the warmth of the firelight on her face, she ran her hand over the slight swell of her belly. It wouldn't be long before everyone would be able to see they were expecting their second child. Francis wanted to announce it at once, but Bridie was enjoying her secret and had persuaded him to wait and say nothing. This time, they talked delightedly of sons and daughters, names and futures. Bridie sometimes looked at David, more like his father every day, and wondered if babies could possibly know if they started out not completely wanted. It would be a terrible thing, because you could never put the clock back, never start again, to take the feeling away.

Lizzie said that books and doctors didn't think babies knew much about anything, and that it didn't matter. But Lizzie hadn't had any babies, and Bridie privately doubted if what she said was true, even though she hoped that it was right.

Mrs Goode, a little greyer than when she and Bridie had shopped for wedding dresses, stuck her head round the door. 'David's going up. Will you be coming now?'

Bridie got to her feet and smoothed down her dress. 'I'll come up directly. Will you tell Susan to put another blanket on his cot, please? It's getting so cold.'

The housekeeper nodded and disappeared. Bridie heard her going upstairs, humming under her breath as she so often did. It was a habit she sometimes apologised for, only to walk away humming again, quite unaware.

She went to the window again, just to see if Francis was anywhere in view, hoping that he might be home in time to say prayers with David. The bleak street was quite dark, and as far as Bridie could see, deserted. She closed the curtains again and left the room. Outside, the hallway was cold after the warm parlour and she shivered.

Climbing the stairs, the smooth wood of the banister was chill to her touch; the thick walls of the house kept the heat inside the rooms while the hall and landing could be freezing. You had to be brave, sometimes, to go from one room to another, when the real wintry weather came, putting frost on the inside of windows and freezing the chamber pots under the beds. Bridie loved winter. It made her feel like an animal, curled up in a snug nest, half asleep, while the winds and snows roared outside and devoured the unwary and unprepared.

Upstairs, David's shrill little voice came babbling from the nursery. Susan, the fourteen-year-old nursemaid, chattered to him in her rough, Cockney voice. Every day the baby learned something new. Bridie said he was clever, like his father. Francis, pleased, would smile and shake his head. He sometimes looked in on his sleeping son, when he came home late, and wonderingly touched the fine, silvery hair. Francis didn't say anything to Bridie, for he knew he'd get the sharp end of her tongue for it, but he longed for a daughter. Each night he silently prayed that this second child would be a healthy girl. He pictured a small girl, another Bridie, as flame-headed as her mother, and felt that she would be the most perfect gift that life could give him.

When Bridie went into the nursery, David was sitting in his cot with Susan beside him. They both looked up. The baby face broke into beams of delight. His mother picked him up and, holding him under one arm, checked the blankets and sheets.

'I've put on an extra, like Mrs Goode said to,' said the girl.

Bridie felt the weight of the blankets with one hand. 'Even that may not be enough. It's very cold, and getting colder, I think, so maybe you'd best fetch another.'

Susan went to get the bedding and Bridie sat down with David on her knee. She put her cheek against the baby hair, then brushed her lips to and fro across the little head. He chuckled and clutched at her hair.

'Ouch!' said Bridie in mock pain. The child tugged harder until Bridie disentangled the small fingers because he began to hurt. Placing the little hands together between her own, she began to repeat the simple prayers her own mother had said with her in just such a fashion when she herself was tiny. Bridie remembered her mother each evening, as she, in her turn, began to repeat the lessons of her own babyhood. 'God bless Mama. God bless Papa. God bless Mrs Goode, and Susan . . . Keep Grandpa safe and watch over Maire, MaryEllen and May. God bless all the poor people. . . .'

The little boy watched her with serious eyes. Downstairs the front door banged.

'Papa,' cried Bridie. 'Here's Papa home. Papa to say goodnight to David.'

Francis, still in his overcoat, came round the door. 'Davey.' He held out his arms to the child and Bridie lifted him across. Her husband bent to kiss her and then turned to his boy. 'What have you done today?' he enquired.

'Mama,' said the small boy, wriggling because the touch of the coat was rough and icy.

'Mama indeed,' replied his father. 'Papa has been busy today. Papa has in fact been very busy,' he repeated, looking over the child's head at Bridie.

'It looks as though we are making progress on the sewerage extension problem,' he said, his face lit up with unusual excitement. 'Clem Attlee is to go to the Minister in a week's time, to see what might be done about making a special case for parts of the East End. If they'd agree to spend the money, we could have work start almost immediately. That's real progress, Bridie, to gain the ear of the Minister.'

'To be sure that's a thing to be proud of,' she answered. 'Will you be going with Clem to see this Minister?'

'No, he'll go and present the case, and if there are

more discussions to follow, then I may become involved in them. My main task has been to prepare the brief that he'll take with him.'

'Maybe you'll now stop working 'til past midnight,' suggested Bridie.

He shook his head. 'If this goes through, it'll be more work, not less.'

Bridie threw up her hands in pretend dismay. 'And where would you be without it?' she asked. 'You and your paperwork.'

'Why don't you do some?' he suggested. 'You could go much further with the studying, go to night classes up in Stratford. You've done so well at what you've taken up so far.'

'Lizzie suggested that, ages ago.'

'Well, why not, then?'

She was silent. She'd had the same thought herself, but had dismissed it, even though Mrs Goode had urged her on. She felt irritable and upset at the suggestion coming from Francis.

I was good enough the way I am before we was wed, and I count myself good enough now, so he can leave his lessons out of it. The thoughts came unwillingly and guiltily because she knew the suggestion was well-intentioned.

'I don't know,' she answered vaguely when the subject was brought up again, 'I'll perhaps think about it when the baby is born. Not before, though.'

'Very well, dear.' Francis knew better than to try to force the issue. Maybe one bookish person in the family was enough. He put his son in his cot and, pulling off his overcoat, went downstairs. Bridie kissed a sleepy David goodnight and left him, seeing Susan place the nightlight on the mantelpiece and tiptoe round clearing up the last little bits of baby clothing that lay discarded on the nursery table.

Bridie went into the morning room, where they took their meals, and began to lay out the silver cutlery that she and Mrs Goode polished together each week. The housemaid clattered pots in the scullery and the smell of boiling vegetables was strong. Bridie pulled a face and her hand went to her stomach. She wasn't tormented this time by the violent nausea she'd suffered with David, but strong smells brought back queasiness.

'Ellen,' she called to the girl in the scullery.

'Yes, Missis?'

'Can we do without cabbage and sprouts for the time being? I can't be doing with the smell of them just now.'

Ellen put down the pan of potatoes she'd been about to empty and came to the door.

'Them's the cheapest this time of year, Missis. That's why Mrs Goode said to get them. And there's plenty of fresh down the market, so she thought. . . .'

'Oh yes,' Bridie interrupted impatiently, 'usually they're what we have, but just for now, don't get any more. Choose something else.'

'Yes, Missis.' Ellen's head disappeared back into the steam.

I surely don't have to have cabbage if it makes me

147

sick, Bridie thought rebelliously. The poor ain't going to notice one way or the other for a bit of cabbage.

She had got to know all too well how quickly her husband's kindness could turn to cold disapproval if she failed in some way to match his inflexible standards. If criticised unjustly, she'd stand her ground, but inwardly she was sometimes afraid of him.

'Never mind, Ellen,' she called finally. 'I'll talk to Mrs Goode tomorrow.'

Over dinner they talked about Christmas. Francis enthusiastically raised his idea for the holiday.

'Bridie, why don't you arrange for your family to come and see us? It doesn't seem right that you've been away from them so long and never tried to visit them. You can hardly make the journey on your own now, but I've been thinking what a good idea it would be for them to come to stay with us. Not for Christmas this year, it's too late now, but what about in the spring? It'd be easier travelling then. I'd like to meet them, and after all David has a grandpa he doesn't know!'

It was not the first time the question had been brought up. 'Christmas is a time for families,' he'd said as autumn brought the first mild frosts and the end of the year seemed to be approaching fast. 'I've no one, but you shouldn't be so neglectful of yours.'

Bridie chewed her food and stayed silent. Her husband looked at her curiously. 'Why do you avoid it like this?'

'I don't avoid it. I just don't think anything about it now.'

'But you told me once how you miss your sisters, and the youngest one 'specially. Would you not like to see her?'

'No,' said Bridie flatly.

Francis was at a loss. He could hardly believe her; he was sure she wasn't telling the truth.

'Why do you never write to each other?'

Bridie shifted impatiently. Her lips clamped together, she shook her head and refused to discuss the subject any further. Baffled and mystified, Francis had the dishonest thought of writing to Robert himself, to enquire discreetly into the circumstances of Bridie's family. Her stubbornness only served to sharpen his curiosity. For the time being, he decided to let the matter rest.

'We'll fetch the tree from the greengrocer's next week,' said Bridie, by way of changing the subject on to safer ground.

'How many days is it now?' Francis smiled his acceptance of her change of tack.

'Only ten. David's first Christmas, just think. This year has flown by so fast.'

You're making talk, thought her husband suddenly. As if you're nervous.

Bridie saw his sharp look and became agitated. 'I don't feel so well, with the baby an' all. You'll excuse me.' She left the room hastily. In the cold air of the hall she felt she could breathe more easily. Blink. Oh dear. Please, not again. Don't let the panic come. Blink. Blink. No, please, I'll do anything if you'll just go away.

Rubbing her forehead with the back of her hand, she could feel the cold sweat that had broken out at the mention of going home. If only he'd realise that she couldn't even think of it – not even think. She sat down abruptly on the stairs. Trembling, she pressed her hands to her face.

'Stop it,' she whispered fiercely to herself. 'Just stop this, do you hear? Take no notice. Think only about what's right now. There's nothing, nothing else at all.' She clung to the polished banisters, leaning on their solidity. Peculiar feelings racked her limbs and for a moment she thought she'd fall into bits like a broken doll, but they passed.

A painful effort of will brought her laboured breathing back to normal. She stayed on the stairs, too weak to move, praying that Francis wouldn't leave the morning room and find her before she'd got herself in hand. After a little while she was able to pull herself on to her feet and make her way, still trembling, into the study. There the warm fire brought colour back into her cheeks. She rubbed her hands together; they'd gone numb. By the time Francis came in with his paper and a fresh packet of cigars, followed closely by Vermin, she was busy with her sewing. She looked up with a smile as he settled down opposite her.

'Are you unwell, Bridie?'

She shook her head. 'It's probably me being silly, because of the baby.'

The explanation didn't satisfy Francis; the same thing had happened before when there'd been no baby. But he said no more.

He began to open his cigar case. Outside, in the black December night, a bitter gale lashed at the windowpane. The thick, lined curtains swayed very slightly as the wind forced its way between every slender entrance it could find. A draught slid like a knife across the room and Bridie felt the cold touch her ankles. She drew them beneath the hem of her long skirt. An inner chill touched her heart and she sensed a darkness in the depths of her being that howled as desolately as the winter winds. An invisible shudder ran through her. Picking up her sewing, she pricked her fingers clumsily as she struggled to banish the sense that some unnameable threat hung over her, a darkness that lurked just at the edge of consciousness, waiting to engulf her.

Vermin Ermin raised his big head sleepily and looked at her with knowing yellow eyes. He stared at her, unblinking, for a very long time.

Chapter Ten

Christmas Day in the year 1921 was nearly over. The small wax candles in their holders had gone out one by one against the dark green needles of the fir tree standing in the corner of the parlour. Thin trails of smoke hung on the air and spiralled lazily in and out of the twinkling, shining decorations that Bridie had hung three days earlier. The little family had enjoyed the last carol service of the year on the wireless, Bridie humming along cheerfully with her favourite hymns.

She sat on the floor with David. She held his fat wrists and rocked him back and forth, clapping his hands together and shaking her head at him. The baby laughed so hard his eyes disappeared behind his plump, pink cheeks.

'Clap hands!' cried Bridie and the baby chuckled all over.

Francis watched them over the top of his book, smiling. 'Gently, dear,' he advised.

Bridie sat back on her heels and raised a flushed face to her husband. 'He loves it,' she replied. 'He likes rough and tumble.' 'Don't you, then?' she asked the baby. 'Aren't you a proper little fellow?'

David rolled over and began to crawl rapidly over the carpet. Bridie reached to catch his feet and pull him back, but he was too quick for her.

She caught her breath, coughed, then coughed again, quite painfully.

'I've got a bit of a sore throat,' she remarked. 'I hope it's no more than too much singing. I don't want a cold, not at Christmas.'

She beckoned the baby. 'Come on back, Davey. Look at you, Mischief.'

'Honey and lemon might do some good,' suggested her husband.

'Oh, it's probably nothing. A catch in the throat.'

'You'd be well advised to take care anyway,' replied Francis. 'It's a bad time of year to take chances. There's so much sickness, it's in the air everywhere.'

'Very well,' she said, to please him. 'I'll take some before I go to bed.'

She caught David's bare foot in her hand and played idly with his small toes. Then, for a moment, she was quite still. 'Francis?'

He looked up.

'I felt it move, the baby. I'm sure I did.'

Francis gazed at her. These were mysteries. For want of knowing what to say, he nodded.

'It's a fluttering, like a trapped moth.' She faltered as she saw his blank look.

Moths. Francis was bemused by the idea and picked up his book from where it lay beside his chair. 'Remember to take the honey and lemon,' he remarked as he turned his page.

154

Bridie grimaced behind the book. He was hopeless sometimes. She picked up David and cuddled him close. The warm little body wriggled away from her and reached to be put down. All he wanted to do these days was crawl and get into everything. Bridie watched him set off for the far end of the room where a small pile of bright wrapping paper waited to be put away and kept for next year. David seized it with interest and began experimentally stuffing some into his mouth.

'No.' Bridie got to her feet and took the paper away. 'Come on, if you're that hungry you'd best go to Susan for your tea.'

Susan had shared their Christmas and would go to visit her mother for a couple of days when Mrs Goode was back. 'I'd stay,' the housekeeper had apologised, 'but I promised my married daughter that I'd go to her this year, and I can't let her down.'

'Her daughter has four children including a son who is a cripple,' Francis had explained to Bridie. 'Mr Goode seldom says anything about it, but I know she feels an obligation, and goes and helps her daughter quite a lot when she's not here.'

The story saddened Bridie, who regarded Mrs Goode with renewed respect after what she'd heard.

'You never know what people keep to themselves like that,' she'd remarked thoughtfully to Susan, who, being born and brought up not a stone's throw from Mrs Goode's daughter's household, knew far more about it than Francis.

'She's a close one, that's certain,' Susan had

155

agreed. 'But the little un's got a head that's too big for his body and they take him around in a pushcart. Give's you the creeps to see it, it does. I 'spect that's why she don't like to say much.'

The tale reminded Bridie of the stillborn lambs her father used to bring home, sometimes, to burn. It upset and unsettled her.

'Sure and it's horrible to see such things,' she said, frowning, 'I don't know how a person would be able to bear a burden like that. I'm sure I couldn't.'

'What else can you do?' asked Susan. 'No one's going to take the babby for you, and you can't just leave it. Anyway,' she added matter-of-factly, 'that kind of babby don't live long, usually.'

'No, I suppose not, though it would depend, wouldn't it?' Bridie answered after a pause.

'Well, David's fine and bonny so you don't need to go fretting about it.' Susan was unaware of the new baby, or she'd have spoken more carefully.

Bridie gave her young nursemaid's blunt, round face a sideways look as she folded David's small clothes into a tidy pile.

'Hm,' she said, half to herself, 'but I still don't know how they can bear it, though if it's your own, perhaps it might be different.'

She'd intended to ask Lizzie about it, but it had been driven from her mind the next time they met when her friend, shyly radiant, had shown her the small diamond ring on her finger. Jonathan, her long, lanky doctor, whose good-natured, intelligent face was as homely as her own, had asked her to marry him. Overcome with excitement and delight, Bridie threw her arms round Lizzie's neck and hugged her tight. Francis and Bridie invited them both to tea the following Thursday, when Lizzie had a day off. They'd sat close together on the settee, delighted with each other, and finding it so hard not to hold hands that Bridie's face ached from the big smile she could feel just refusing to fade.

Lizzie held her cup and saucer so that the little ring sparkled in the bright light from the window. She tried not to look at it too often, but her eyes kept lingering on it until she'd catch herself with embarrassment, and turn her finger away again. Bridie was so joyful for them that all mention of crippled babies flew out of her head. The conversation came back to her, for some reason, as she bent to pick up David and take him to the kitchen.

'You're getting heavy, young fellow,' she told him. As she put him into his baby chair her arms felt tired. He really was getting to be a weight for her now. Leaving Susan to feed him, she went back to the parlour. Sitting in the armchair opposite Francis, she turned her thoughts to the following day. They'd agreed that Christmas Day would be quiet but on Boxing Day they were to entertain several of Francis's colleagues, and Bridie was anxious that the afternoon should go smoothly. She knew very well that some of Francis's friends looked with real disapproval at what they regarded as an ill-advised marriage. She'd been frightened, at first. The intrusion into her home of possibly hostile observers had made her quail, but she had given herself a talking to.

'Stupid girl,' she said aloud to herself. 'It's them that's ignorant. I'll show them whose an Irish peasant.' She'd cracked eggs into the cake she was baking and stirred the mixture energetically; they'd find no fault with her baking, that was sure. She'd planned carefully for the tea she'd offer them, and had rolled up her sleeves and ironed the table linen herself until she was satisfied that even Mrs Goode at her most picky wouldn't be able to fault it. The silver spoons were polished to brilliance, and the glass cake dishes buffed with a soft tea towel until there was no trace of a smear however much you held them up to the light and looked. The afternoon was to be Bridie's declaration of respectability, and she had determined to match the best of them. The tiredness was probably all that hard work, along with Christmas.

'I think I'll go to bed early, even though it is Christmas night,' she murmured in the direction of Francis's book.

He looked up. 'You've a busy day tomorrow,' he agreed. 'Leave Susan to see to David, and ask her to bring you up a hot drink. A good sleep will see you right in the morning.'

Bridie rose with an effort and kissed the top of his head as he bent back to his reading. She hesitantly put out her hand and touched the back of his neck.

'It's been a lovely day. Our first real Christmas. Thank you.' She spoke quietly. If Francis had looked up, he'd have seen the unshed tears in her eyes.

But he just put his book face down on his lap and took her hand from where it lay on his shoulder. 'I have you to thank, my dear.' He fumbled for words. 'I'd not expected so much. I have been fortunate, dear, you make me so happy. . . .' He patted her hand awkwardly.

The stilted words came from his heart, Bridie knew, and she bent and kissed him again.

'You go up, my dear, and have an early night.'

She determined more than ever to make him proud of her the next day, and, bidding him goodnight, left the room to climb the two flights of stairs to their bedroom above.

An hour later Bridie lay propped against her feather pillows, sipping the last of the honey and lemon that Susan had brought up from the kitchen. An unaccountable lethargy crept over her, and yet she found herself fidgeting, unable to get comfortable.

I must have caught a chill, she thought with frustration. Fancy getting it now, today of all days. Oh, bother it!

She lay back and closed her eyes. Her head swam slightly and she sat up again. She pressed her forearm against her brow and wondered what to do. A cold cloth. She'd put one on her forehead and that would ease the dizziness. Pushing the covers back, she swung her legs out of bed. Her knees buckled under her and she slid to the carpet in an ungainly heap.

Astonished and frightened, she lay there, all tangled up in her long white night-gown. Moments passed and she began to get cold. Little by little, she dragged herself up again and determinedly crawled back into bed. She lay still, exhausted. She opened her mouth to call for Susan, but realised that she'd gone to her room, out of earshot, after bringing up the lemon toddy. She considered calling as loudly as she could for Francis, but all that came out when she tried was a hoarse whisper. She daren't call again. She dreaded disappointing him with her illness, for she knew that tomorrow was important to him as well as to her. So she lay alone and afraid, in the big mahogany bed, watching as the glow of the fire in the grate opposite slowly died away until all that was left was pale grey ash.

Long past midnight, Francis put down his book. He sat contemplating what he had been reading until the great grandfather clock chimed one o'clock.

'Time to go up,' he murmured to himself. The room was deathly silent save for the occasional shifting of a coal in the grate. He stretched out and pulled the fireguard into place then stood and began to turn off the gaslamps. Closing the parlour door quietly behind him, he silently climbed the stairs. The house was still as the grave except for the sound of the clock.

Francis opened the door of the bedroom, trying not to make a sound. Emerging ten minutes later from his dressing room, he bent over Bridie and looked at her sleeping face in the soft gaslight that spilled from the half-open door behind him.

He smoothed the damp curls from her brow and frowned. She felt hot. He bent lower to kiss her half-open lips and stiffened from head to foot. He sniffed cautiously at her breath and his heart went cold as stone.

He shook her by the shoulder. 'Bridie. Bridie, wake up,' he whispered urgently. 'Wake up, Bridie, will you?'

She stirred and opened her eyes. They were shiny with sleep. Blinking, she lifted her arms to put them round his neck as he bent over her, but they sank slowly back to the counterpane.

'Francis? I feel so strange.' Her voice was hoarse.

'Dear God, Bridie, you're sick! I shall call the doctor directly. You are to stay quite still. I'll wake Susan. She can stay with you until I get hold of Dr Hamilton. Do you understand me?' Fear made his voice sharp and Bridie shrank back.

'No, no, my dear. Don't be afraid. I'll call Susan now.'

Trying to calm the dread that made a vice around his heart, he ran upstairs and banged on Susan's door. Her sleepy, good-natured face eventually appeared, topped by a crown of curlers in her straight brown hair.

'Susan, you are to put a gown over your night-dress and come down at once. My wife is sick, and I want you to stay with her while I telephone Dr Hamilton. Pray God he's in tonight. Take a bowl of lukewarm water and sponge her face and arms. Keep doing that even if she tells you to stop.'

Susan's dark eyes grew round. 'What is it, sir?'

'Never mind that now.' The startled girl went back into her dark room to fetch her gown, and Francis hurried downstairs to the telephone. He fumbled with the gas tap in agitation, and when it flared at last, turned with relief to the black telephone standing on the hall table.

Angus, for Heaven's sake be in, he prayed silently.

The bell at the other end rang for what seemed a long, long time. Francis tapped the cold, polished surface of the table impatiently. 'Come on,' he said to the sound of the ringing.

At last the phone at the other end was taken off the hook. 'Hello? Yes?' said the unmistakable deep voice of the Scottish doctor.

'Angus, thank God you're there! This is Frank Holmes. Bridie is taken ill. Would you come? I'd not wish to disturb you tonight, but I believe I must.'

'I'm here to be disturbed,' said the doctor shortly. 'What's wrong?'

'Bridie has a fever if the touch of her is anything to go by, and she's complained of tiredness. Angus, I think it's diphtheria,' Francis blurted in his anxiety.

'Hold your horses a moment, Frank,' the doctor protested. 'She may have nothing but a chill. What makes you think it's something more?'

'Smell of it,' said Francis succinctly.

'Ah.' The doctor's voice became grave. 'I'll come as fast as I can. If she's quite feverish you could help by sponging her with tepid water. Try starting that at once.'

As he put the earpiece back on its hook, Angus reflected that Francis was unlikely to be mistaken. He and diphtheria were old acquaintances. Angus knew he'd know that smell, the unmistakable musty stench that gave sinister warning of the fast-spreading membrane on the back of the throat. The killer web that could choke its victims – and if it didn't, thought the doctor wryly, was liable to kill them weeks later from heart failure and paralysis. Angus took the stairs back to his bedroom two at a time.

'Must you go out?' his wife asked sleepily.

'It's Frank. Bridie's unwell.'

Elsie Hamilton digested the information and raised her head. 'Nothing serious, is it?' she called through the door to where her husband was pulling on his boots.

'Well, Frank says he thinks it may be diphtheria, but he may be mistaken. Let us hope he is.'

'Oh dear,' said Elsie. 'That's bad.'

Angus came out with his black bag in his hand. He kissed his wife quickly and hurried out of the room.

The doctor slammed his front door behind him and began to walk rapidly through the streets towards the house in Tredegar Square. The Christmas festivities were almost over. Here and there a lighted window still shone in the early morning darkness, and distant voices called from somewhere eastwards, towards the river. The sky was sprinkled with stars and frost crunched underfoot.

It had been an unseasonably cold snap, thought

the doctor, which made his work all the harder. His breath streamed white as he walked faster, to warm himself up. A quarter of a mile and, turning a corner, he was in the square. The lovely façade of the terrace of tall houses loomed blackly to his right, and he could make out a slight glow on the third floor of the end one. He knew that behind that window Bridie could be beginning to fight for her life. He bounded up the steps to the front door and lifted the heavy knocker. Its dull clang echoed loudly in the silence. A shadow moved on the edge of his vision. Narrowing his eyes he could just make out the stealthy shape of Vermin. The cat slunk up the steps and mewed round his knees.

'Too cold for you, out here, is it?' Angus said amiably. 'Wait a minute and you'll get yourself let in.' He knocked once more, waiting on the steps until the door opened. Francis stood there, as he had three years and more earlier when Bridie had first crossed his threshold, and gestured the doctor inside. Vermin shot indoors before anyone could grab him and throw him out again. Francis dodged him and swore.

'Blasted cat. Come on in,' he said, now as then, and took the other man's overcoat. 'I'm glad you're here. Come straight up.'

The doctor followed his friend upstairs, silently offering a brief prayer that he would not have to confirm Francis's diagnosis of the deadly disease.

Susan stood up as the doctor approached the bed. She removed the bowl in which she'd been wringing out a piece of rag. Standing to one side, she watched the doctor feel for Bridie's pulse. Bridie opened her eyes again and laid her hand on the doctor's arm.

'My throat,' she rasped. The doctor nodded at her.

'I know,' he said very gently. 'I'll look in a moment. I know it is hurting you.'

He slipped his watch back into his pocket and took a little flashlight from his big bag. 'Can you open your mouth, Bridie, so that I can see?'

She pushed her head back into the pillow and raised her chin. The doctor peered into her open mouth and saw what he had hoped would not be there. A greyish mass covered her tonsils and spread down the back of her throat. He clicked off the little light and looked up with a sombre face. Francis did not need to ask; the doctor's expression told all.

'We have a chance,' said Angus. 'We've caught it very early. Come now, let's fight this thing with everything we've got. I've the serum here and she can have that immediately. Susan, will you get fresh water and several cloths? The fever is quite high and I want you to continue to sponge Mrs Holmes to try and bring it down. It will make her more comfortable.'

He busied himself with a large ampoule of clear fluid and a syringe then looked over at Francis, who stood gazing at Bridie as if transfixed.

'Man, you'll be no help to her unless you put your fears aside, and do as I tell you. You know that. You know the nature of this thing, and you know it can be beaten. Go downstairs and give yourself a stiff brandy, then come back up and we'll get to work.'

Francis turned a dazed look on him.

'I'm ordering you to do it, as your doctor.'

Francis nodded. He went with a heavy step out of the room while the doctor prepared Bridie's arm with alcohol, ready for the injection.

Angus heard him speak to Susan, who was hastily bringing to life the banked fire in the kitchen range for all the warm water she'd be needing. The big doctor turned back to his patient. His face was very grave and he talked to her as he gave the injection.

'This is excellent. You've had the serum early enough to make a real difference to how ill you may get. Tonight, Susan will keep trying to lower your fever. You won't get much sleep, I fear, but that can't be helped. Tomorrow is Boxing Day. It'll be the devil of a job to get you into hospital on that day of all days, but I'll try to send an ambulance as soon after breakfast as I can get someone moving. There's no point in even trying to move you tonight.'

Bridie's eyes glittered as she listened.

'What about David?' she whispered.

'Once you've gone, he should be in no danger.'

Bridie tried to nod, and winced.

'Stay still,' ordered the doctor. 'Don't try to do anything. If you want anything, ask someone else to do it.'

Francis came back, looking more himself. Angus repeated what he'd told Bridie.

'I'll contact St Leonard's first thing and let you know,' he said.

Francis agreed that he and Susan could manage between them until the morning. Angus put a reassuring arm round Francis's shoulders.

'Chin up, old chap,' he said gruffly. 'She's young and strong.'

Francis ran a hand over his face and made no response. He was grateful to the doctor for his kindness, but each man knew as well as the other that in truth Bridie's life was in danger, and for all her youth and health, they were all about to engage in a battle that no one could promise they would win.

Chapter Eleven

Boxing Day dawned cold and bright, with a pale, wintry sun low in the blue sky. Angus rubbed his eyes and stretched. He'd returned at half-past five, and had been sitting at Bridie's bedside for nearly three hours. He pulled out his watch and felt for her pulse. Then he checked her breathing, and noted that the colour of her lips was as usual. Satisfied, he rose and left the room.

Francis met him at the foot of the stairs. 'Susan will bring us some tea in a moment. Come on into the study.'

The curtains were pulled back, and Angus walked to the window, enjoying the cheerful winter's scene outside. A group of children played with skipping ropes in the corner just by the garden wall. Shouts and shrill laughter alternated with chanted rhymes as they turned the ropes for each other. Heavy rope thwacked at the paving stones. One little girl tripped and fell. The others gleefully pushed in her place, and she stood to one side, thumb in mouth and face solemn with the effort not to cry. A clock chimed the half hour somewhere in the distance, the sound carrying clear on the chill air. Angus's breath condensed on the windowpane as he leant to watch the children. He rubbed it off with his hand, then turned to Francis.

'The hospital lab will be working normally again tomorrow; there's no point in trying to send in a swab until then, but I think the diagnosis is certain from the clinical signs.'

Francis nodded agreement. 'Faucial?' he asked.

'By the look of it, yes.'

It was the commonest, and most virulent, form of diphtheria.

'I'm a little puzzled by the fever,' the doctor continued. 'It's higher than I'd expect. Occasionally there is an unusual fever, but Bridie is very hot. Has she been unwell apart from the last twenty-four hours?'

'She's complained of being tired, and of having a sore throat, but those were presumably the onset of diphtheria.'

'Hm,' said the doctor thoughtfully. 'She's maybe hiding tonsillitis behind the diphtheria. She's very sick, Frank.'

Francis sank into his armchair and ran his fingers through his untidy hair. 'I know. When can you get her to hospital, Angus?'

'I'll send her in as soon as I can.' The doctor tried to sound reassuring. 'For now, though,' he continued, 'you must keep on with the sponging. I'm hoping the serum will prove effective; it should, as we caught it so early on.'

Angus looked at his friend pityingly. He was well aware that Francis already knew every word that he was saying. Angus and his wife had shaken their heads disapprovingly over the Bridie affair; Angus had even considered approaching Francis, unasked, and advising him that the general feeling was that he was making a fool of himself. Now, he was glad he'd done no such thing. The peculiar marriage was obviously working.

The door opened and Susan, rings under her eyes from having been up all night but with her curlers out, brought in a steaming pot of tea and a pile of toast.

' 'ere you are,' she said as she put the tray down. 'What do you want me to do about David, sir?'

'Do?' Francis looked at her blankly.

'I've bin working all night, sir, and I'm very tired.'

'Of course.' He thought for a minute. 'Can you first run down to Mrs MacDonald and ask her if she would do me the greatest of favours and take David while you come back and get some sleep? Can you manage that?'

'Oh yes, sir. I'll do it as soon as I can. Is Mrs MacDonald to come 'ere, or is she to take David to 'er 'ouse?'

'Not here, with infection in the house. Ask her if she can just do me the kindness of having him for today.'

'I 'spect she'll 'ave 'im, sir, she's ever so fond of 'im.'

'Yes, Susan, she is. When you've done that, you may go and sleep for as long as you need.'

'Ta,' said the girl, and went humming back to the kitchen to finish giving the little boy his breakfast.

171

Then she wrapped him up very warm, put him in his carriage, and prepared to push him over to the midwife's house, where she knew he'd be welcomed like one of the family and spoiled all Boxing Day long.

Pouring tea, the two men discovered that they were hungry. The toast disappeared in no time, and over their tea they agreed on what was to be done for the rest of the day.

'My word, that's better,' said the doctor as he pushed his cup aside. 'I'll go up and see Bridie again, and then I'll be off to see to all the necessary. I'll do my best to get her into hospital by midday.'

He stood to go upstairs again, then paused and looked at Francis. 'Frank,' he said, 'Bridie needs you to take care of yourself. You can't look after her or David if you're exhausted yourself, so my advice to you is to take yourself to another room and go to sleep as soon as Bridie leaves. Let me and the ambulance crew take over; it's our job and what they're trained to do. David will need you, for Bridie won't be up and about for several weeks at best, and even then she'll face quite a convalescence. Susan's good with him, but you'll still need to keep an eye on things.'

'Mrs Goode will be back in a day's time.' Francis clutched at straws.

'Well, you have my advice. I suggest you take it.'

Francis turned a haggard face up to the doctor. 'I hear you, my friend,' he said. 'I merely meant that Mrs Goode's return will make what you say easier to do.'

'Fine,' the doctor said in a mollified tone.

'You speak of convalescence. Do you believe that Bridie can recover?'

Angus began to feel angry. 'Look here,' he said very sharply, 'if you sit around feeling sorry for yourself you'll do no one any good. Your young wife is a strong, healthy woman, and she's got every chance of recovery, if we help her. Pull yourself together and remember you've a family to be responsible for.'

Francis did not respond, and the doctor thought he'd gone too far. After a pause, though, the older man sat forward in his chair and heaved a great sigh.

'You are right, of course. I thank you for your bluntness, Angus, and I will do what I can. Now we'll go up to Bridie.'

Once more they climbed the stairs. Bridie was awake and turned her neck painfully towards the door as they came into the room. She tried to smile at her husband, but the movement made her wince.

'You'll have a very painful neck for a little while,' Angus told her.

She made a tiny face.

'Yes, I know,' he replied, 'but I tell you now so you won't be too frightened if it gets worse. You might get some swelling, too, which is one of this disease's horrid symptoms. It's not nice, I'm afraid, Bridie. You are going to be very poorly for a while, but I believe you'll get better quite fast.'

Her eyes were very serious as she followed what he was saying. She swallowed, and it was an obvious effort.

'Doctor,' she whispered, 'what about the baby? Will the baby be all right?'

Angus had been prepared for this question, and scratched his ear as he considered it. 'Are you brave, Bridie?' he asked.

She shut her eyes for a moment, then opened them and said hoarsely: 'Yes. I'd rather know.'

'There's a chance the baby will come through. It really depends on whether the diphtheria leads to any complications. If it does, we can help you, but it's not so easy to help the baby. I can't promise. You're fine and strong, and there will be other babies later, I'm sure.'

Bridie stared past him at the ceiling. That's what she'd thought, lying there alone with time to remember what she'd heard about this illness. She knew a lot of children died of it, but she hadn't heard of any adults who'd had it. Under the covers her hands strayed to her stomach. Poor baby. She felt helpless sadness creep over her; she couldn't do anything to protect it, only love it and hope for it, and for herself. Tears spilled out of the corners of her eyes and ran down past her ears. Angus pulled out his handkerchief and gently wiped them away.

'We'll just have to wait and see, Bridie, my dear. There's no other way.'

'Yes,' she murmured in that harsh whisper.

He took her hand and held it firmly. 'It's you who matters most. The better we look after you, the better chance your baby has. While you are in hospital, Susan and Mrs Goode between them will take care of

David. All you have to do is try to get well again.'

He squeezed her hand in encouragement and smiled at her. Downstairs he took his leave at the door.

'Try to keep her spirits up,' he told Francis, and ran down the steps. Back in his surgery he began to make telephone calls. Call after call. His face grew grimmer each time he hung up the earpiece to dial again. There was no bed for Bridie.

In Clayhill Isolation Hospital an overworked nurse answered the ringing telephone.

'Yes?' she said, and listened for a moment or two.

'We've not a bed to spare. We've got patients practically two to a bed – well, not literally, but it's so crowded they might just as well be.'

A heavily accented voice roared down the earpiece. The nurse held the instrument away from her ear.

'No, I don't think I caught the name,' she answered cautiously.

'Mrs Holmes. Wife of Mr Frank Holmes. And you say you've no bed?'

The nurse began to get nervous. Mrs Holmes was someone. 'I'll see if I can find the physician superintendent,' she said. 'Can you hold the line, sir?'

'Certainly.' This, at least, was progress.

Angus waited, rearranging his pens in their ebony holder.

'Dr Hamilton?' A new voice came down the telephone.

'Yes.'

'We can offer Mrs Holmes a bed, but I'm afraid that, as my nurse has explained to you, we are well over capacity already. Mr Holmes is, I've no doubt, one of the few people who is actually aware of the kind of pressure we're under. It's most unfortunate that his wife should be needing us. I can't offer you the best, I fear, but I have one room. But I have to say, sir, that it may not suit. . . .'

'Thank you,' Angus's voice cut in. 'Mrs Holmes will be arriving as soon as I can arrange the ambulance.'

He put the black telephone back on his desk, tired and irritated. Clayhill was way out in Essex, miles from anywhere. But then they all were, the isolation places. He picked up the telephone again and arranged for an ambulance. Then, taking his overcoat and case, he left his consulting room and made the ten-minute walk to Tredegar Square once more.

The ambulance attracted a small crowd from around the square. Women stood, arms folded, shivering with cold and nervous excitement.

' 'oo's took bad?' demanded Mrs Cottesloe of her next-door neighbour.

'Number twelve.'

They gazed in fascination at the ambulance. The back doors stood open, and the two drivers had taken a stretcher and three red blankets into the house, but no one had been seen to come out as yet.

'Ooh, there's Dr 'amilton. My Sid says 'e's bin in an' out all night.'

'And what would your Sid be doin', watchin' out the winders at night?' asked Mrs Cottesloe's neighbour suspiciously. 'Nosey Parkerin', if you ask me.'

'Huh, you can talk, Alice Higgins. Look at you, eyes out like organ stops.'

Alice sniffed.

Milly Savage from the other end stopped at their gate. 'Trouble, then,' she remarked.

The three women moved in a little group to stand next to the empty ambulance. A housemaid from Number four was chattering to three or four other women, still holding her broom.

'Do we know who's ill?' asked Milly.

The housemaid gestured with her broomhandle. 'Bridie, I think. I'm sure I heard one of the men say Mrs.'

Mrs Cottesloe's little black eyes lit up.

'There you are,' she cried triumphantly. 'Didn't I say she'd come to no good, the madam! Pride goes before a fall, I always say.'

Opinion was deeply divided among the inhabitants of the square as to the goings on in the Holmes household. The older women clucked their tongues and muttered about his being old enough to be her grandfather. Well, almost. The younger women, in a world that had buried their brothers and fiancés, were more charitable. If they weren't, it was more out of envy that Bridie had her man at all. Bitter words had been said on occasion by both camps.

'You always say too bloody much,' retorted Milly

Savage. 'You want to wash your mouth, talking like that. It's a disgrace.'

'*She's* a disgrace, carrying on like she done,' cried Mrs Cottesloe.

Milly grabbed the broom off the housemaid and waved it threateningly two inches from Mrs Cottesloe's outraged face.

'Don't you dare!' yelled Milly. 'Another word about Bridie outta you and I'll see your nose broke.'

Alice Higgins decided to put in her ha'porth. 'Look who's talkin', any road. What about your girl's Maisie, then? I 'eard she's in the family way an' all. What does your girl think about that? Yer own granddaughter.'

'Yes,' shrilled Milly. 'You old hypocrite! You shut your mouth.'

Mrs Cottesloe's eyes narrowed. 'You'll not speak to me like that, Milly Savage.'

'Oh no?' Milly shook the brushhandle. The women drew back to give the antagonists space to swing the broom. Then a sigh went up, and all their heads turned. The dour-faced ambulance crew had come through the front door, and were easing the stretcher down the front steps. Vermin appeared from the end of the garden wall and jumped down. He ambled over to the group of legs and began to purr round Milly's ankles. She kicked him hard. He squawked and, tail held high, wandered off in dudgeon and sat down to wash on the pavement, a bit further up.

'It's Bridie,' they murmured as her face appeared, just visible above the red blankets. Each woman's right hand crept up to touch her collar in superstitious dread. To ward off the plague. Please God, take her, not me.

'Come on, ain't yer got no 'omes ter go to?' a crewman said sourly to the gawping women.

Bridie's eyes were closed. She could hear the murmuring voices of the women and longed to be safely away, out of sight. She felt the men slot the stretcher into its rack, and the vehicle tipped as Angus climbed in.

'All ready?' he said to the crew. 'You both go in front, and I'll stay here.'

They nodded, and the group of watchers moved back as the ambulance men swung themselves into their seats.

'Where're you taking her?' called Alice.

'Clayhill, if it's any business of yours,' said the driver.

The women exchanged glances. Clayhill was for isolation cases. Collars were furtively touched again. She must be bad.

The driver's mate climbed out again with the starting handle. He puffed, red in the face, as the engine turned and turned, then finally caught. He climbed back in and slammed the door. Angus braced himself with his long legs as they turned in a circle and chugged smartly out of the square, into Bow Road, where they turned east, and began the long drive to Clayhill.

*　　*　　*

The Essex countryside was flat and barren. Bare trees made lacy patterns against the horizon. A grey river crawled between muddy banks and gulls swooped, screaming, over a rubbish tip nearby. The steely sky turned from blue to white in the distance. Angus peered out of the windows in the doors and thought how dreary the English landscape could be when it tried. He pressed Bridie's hand, where it lay curled in his big palm.

'It's not far, now, lassie. We'll have you tucked up in no time.'

She tried to smile 'My head aches so,' she whispered.

'Aye, it would,' said the doctor.

The driver swung the wheel hard left and they passed through some high iron gates. The ambulance went slowly up a drive that was bordered on one side by bushes and on the other by a wide, sweeping expanse of grass. The hospital was the only sign of human habitation in sight.

It's a bit like a leper colony, thought Angus. Tuck 'em away, miles from anywhere. It makes medical sense, but it's unpleasant all the same.

They came to a stop in front of a long, low building with wide green doors.

'Here we are, mate,' said the driver.

Angus got out of their way, and waited while they carried the stretcher out and up the steps to the green door. Inside, a porter sat in a little cubicle, drinking a mug of tea. Angus had to bend down to speak to him.

'Could you call the physician superintendent for me. He's expecting us.'

'What name?' enquired the man.

'Holmes. That's the patient's name.'

The man got slowly off his stool and opened his cubicle door. 'Right you are. Wait here.' He disappeared through a pair of swing doors that led to some stairs.

The arrivals waited in silence. Eventually the swing doors opened again. The physician superintendent was remarkable for nothing so much as his resemblance to a toad. He waddled forward on short squat legs as he stretched out a hand to shake Angus's. He was completely round; a spade-shaped head with no neck and bulbous eyes.

'Dr Hamilton. How d'you do.'

'Sir.' Angus ducked his head at him. He was fascinated; man or reptile?

The superintendent looked over at Bridie. 'If you'd care to bring Mrs Holmes this way,' he said to the crew. He waddled off along a corridor, and Angus watched that amazing shape lead the way past long yellow walls with windows inset every few feet. Beyond the glass they could see beds, crowded so close together they almost touched. Children – forty-odd in a ward intended for twenty-five. The acutely ill lay listlessly in bed, or tossed and turned feverishly.

Convalescents played in groups, and a few ran up and down in a game of tag, banging carelessly in and out of beds where the sick ones lay. A hubbub of voices penetrated the glass. Angus stared, shocked. A child sat in a bed in the far corner, rocking fast, to and fro, to and fro, to and fro. No-one took any notice. Another cried steadily, with its thumb in its mouth and a dirty bit of rag pressed against its face by way of comforter. Many of the children had peeling skin on their faces and bodies, with the raw flesh underneath exposed, unprotected and untreated. Peeling was an unavoidable symptom of scarlet fever, but to leave it like this, on children who could end up disfigured. . . . The Toad saw his expression of horror. 'Oh yes, it's bad all right. I can show you wards worse than this. Would you like me to take you round?'

Angus nodded reluctantly. 'While I'm here,' he said, with no enthusiasm at the prospect.

The Toad stopped outside a green door. All the doors in this place were green, noticed Angus. 'Dr Hamilton,' he began, 'I tried to warn you on the telephone that I had nothing suitable for this patient, but would offer her all I had, which is this.'

He swung the door back on what Angus saw was little more than a broom cupboard. It was windowless, and contained a single, high hospital bed which had had a pile of linen dumped on it, presumably by way of preparation for Bridie's arrival. A single gaslight stood out of the peeling yellow walls. It smelt stuffy and dusty. As Angus stared, a nurse hurried down the corridor towards them. Her wide starched cap made wings on either side of her anxious face. They flapped as she walked.

'I'm sorry, sir,' she said to Toad, 'but Matron called me away before I had time to finish making the bed.'

The spade-shaped head swivelled towards her. 'I want it done immediately.' The oily voice was cold.

Angus came to life. 'No, nurse. Don't bother.'

The Toad looked at him without surprise. 'I warned you,' he repeated, with a shrug of the massive shoulders.

'She can't stay here,' said Angus. 'It's impossible.'

The ambulance crew shifted their hold on the stretcher. It was starting to get heavy. Angus looked up and down the ugly corridor. 'What about one of the wards?' he asked. 'Do you not have an Adult Diphtheria at all?'

He knew the hospital was overcrowded, but surely . . .

'No. We're not getting diphtheria. It's all this.' He gestured at the scarlet fever patients behind yet another row of windows just a few feet further up the passage.

'I can't put diphtheria in with a ward full of scarlet fever.' The Toad was adamant. 'We'd have the lot of them catching it from each other. It's here or nothing. It's all I've got.'

'Yes, yes. I realise that, doctor.' Angus began to accept the unavoidable.

Bridie lay looking from one to the other. She wished they'd just let her get into bed, and go away. Angus thrust his hands into his coat pocket and looked at his feet, considering. One of the crew coughed meaningfully.

'Back home.' Angus spoke to no one in particular. Toad opened his mouth. 'I'm sorry to have taken your time for no purpose,' Angus said before the other man could speak. 'It was good of you to take the trouble. You are indeed overwhelmed with patients, I can see. Thank you for your kind offer, but I really don't think Mrs Holmes can stay here.'

Toad's face went a purplish colour. 'I warned you,' he said again. 'I told you.'

'Yes, yes. The fault is entirely mine.' Angus didn't want the odious creature upset. 'I owe you a full apology. You shall have it in writing. Tomorrow.'

Toad glared at him. 'So long as it's understood. We can't do the impossible, Doctor.'

'No, of course. One might say you already do the impossible, Doctor. Working in such conditions . . .'

Damn Toad, he was making him grovel! Angus nodded at the crew, who were watching his discomfort with amusement.

'Back down, please.'

The little party trailed back the way it had come. Inside the ambulance, Angus took Bridie's hand again. 'Oh, my dear, I'm so sorry. I had an idea it would be dreadful, but I have an obligation to try to take you to hospital. I have to make my best efforts, or there'd be real trouble. I think now that I have pulled every rabbit out of the bag that I could hope to find, and all we can do is take you home.'

They jolted as the engine puttered into life again. 'Here we go,' murmured Angus. 'It'll be getting dark before we're back.'

He sat, head bent, weighed down by a feeling of hopeless anger. Such conditions were unthinkable, yet they were happening in every hospital within reach of London. Not a bed to be had. The very crisis that he and Francis had foreseen eighteen months earlier was now well and truly and intractably upon them. Diphtheria had a firm hold in the slums of East London, and there was nowhere to send their patients. Those children weren't being properly nursed. It was a scandal.

Angus leant uncomfortably against the side of the ambulance, and his head bumped back and forth as they made their way back towards London. Eventually he dozed, and Bridie, watching his head droop slowly forward until he was doubled up, with his head resting on the red blanket not far from hers, put out one hot hand and held him carefully so that he slept the rest of the way back and didn't fall.

The ambulance lights disappeared out of Tredegar Square several hours later. Angus ran a hand over the stubble on his cheeks and said to Francis, 'I'll arrange for nursing. She'll have to stay here until there's a bed free, and God knows when that'll be. I'll get on to the agency at once. Then you'll just have to leave her in the nurses' hands, and I'll take the case myself for as long as is necessary.'

He shook his head at Francis's offer of a whisky. 'I'll go and get it arranged, then I'm going to ask Dr Patton to take my calls, and sleep like a dead man,' he said cheerfully. 'Elsie can take messages if you need anyone. I'll see Bridie again tomorrow.'

He shrugged on his coat and opened the front door. 'Just give the nurse a free hand. She'll know what to do,' he repeated, then went briskly off into the frosty evening. Francis closed the door and the square fell silent once more.

'Come on, Vermin Ermin.' Francis picked up the cat, and went upstairs to wait with Bridie for the nurse's knock at the door.

Chapter Twelve

Angus did his work well. Two hours later Francis hurried down to answer a knock at the door. On the steps, bag in hand, stood a young woman.

'Good evening,' she said cheerfully. 'I'm the nurse, Emmy Dobson. Dr Hamilton sent me. You must be Mr Holmes.'

'I'm so glad you've come,' Francis told her as she hung up her long blue cloak in the hall. 'My wife is upstairs.' He looked over his shoulder at her as they went up. 'Has Dr Hamilton told you what has to be done?'

'Oh, yes,' she answered. 'Your wife is sick with faucial diphtheria. He's explained it all to me.'

They stood outside the bedroom door. 'Have you experience of nursing diphtheria patients at all?' Francis was too anxious to be tactful.

'Oh yes, sir. I did my training at Bart's and I've been doing private nursing for two years. I've looked after seven cases of diphtheria on my own, and I've worked for Dr Hamilton before.'

Francis heaved a sigh of relief. He should have trusted Angus more. The little nurse put her hand gently on his arm. Her eyes were steady and intelligent and she spoke in an unhurried voice.

'It's very worrying, sir, I know. I've seen others go through it, but I do know what I'm doing.'

Francis hesitated. Then, 'Tell me something,' he said in a low voice, 'did any of the other seven survive?'

She looked him straight in the eye. 'Yes, sir, one. The other six were small children, and they all died.'

'Thank you,' he said, and led the way into the bedroom.

At lunchtime the following day Angus arrived to find the bedroom rearranged into a sick-room. He put the two shiny metal bedpans he'd brought on the top of the bureau and looked round with approval. The little nurse was rubbing Bridie's ankles briskly.

'Bedsores,' she'd said to Bridie. 'They're horrid, and we don't want you getting them, so several times a day I'll rub you and turn you, so you don't lie in one position all the time. You just stay still and let me do everything.'

Bridie, who felt lightheaded and in dreadful pain, wasn't inclined to argue. She simply watched the nurse through glazed eyes, passively letting her lift and turn and sponge. Sometimes the nurse seemed to float before her. The pain became agony.

'Hm,' said Angus when he examined her.

To the nurse he expressed concern. 'She's too hot,' he said worriedly. 'She shouldn't have such a fever.'

'I'm worried about that, too,' said the girl in her calm manner. 'It's not usual, though I have seen patients who've been quite feverish with diphtheria.'

Angus asked Bridie to open her mouth so that he could look at her throat again. Crying openly, she did her best. He peered at the grey mass he'd seen the night before.

'I could try to remove it,' he said to the nurse,' but I don't think it would come away easily, and might make things worse. I'm concerned that there's an additional infection there.'

The nurse nodded. Her reddish hair caught the light and the doctor's eye. 'I've been wondering about that.'

Angus stood up and paced to the window. 'No,' he said decisively, 'we won't touch it. We'll proceed by constant observation, try to lower the fever as we've been doing, and pray there are no complications.'

He took Bridie's pulse once more. 'Slightly fast. Not significantly,' he said to the nurse. 'That's a very good sign,' he added to Bridie. 'You carry on the way you are, and you'll be just splendid.'

Francis had been immensely relieved to hand the sick-room over to the capable hands of the nurse. He'd spent a good deal of time on the telephone, letting people know that Boxing Day tea had been overtaken by illness. Their sympathy and anxiety came as a surprise. The withdrawn, self-absorbed man had cocooned his little family and his private life inside the walls of his tall house. The telephone calls left him feeling vaguely betrayed. His child bride had become a woman, and he'd scarcely noticed. Other people had.

Late that afternoon, Francis heard his name being called from outside the study door. He found the nurse standing in the hall, looking for him.

'Did you want me?'

'Yes, sir. I'd like to use your telephone.'

'Help yourself. Use it when you wish. There's no need to ask each time.'

'Thank you.' She hesitated 'I'm going to ask Dr Hamilton to visit.'

'Why?' Francis looked at her, suddenly anxious. 'Is something wrong?'

'There's a change, really, and I wondered. . . . Mrs Holmes has come out in a rash, and I'd like Dr Hamilton to look at her. To my mind, she's got the scarlet fever, but of course it's not really for me to diagnose.'

Francis's face brightened unexpectedly. 'The fever. It would explain it, wouldn't it?'

The nurse nodded her head. 'It would, sir.'

Francis counted on his fingers. 'Let's see. Two, going on three, really. It's the right number of days. Let's go up and see her.'

He took a mask from the pile outside Bridie's door and pulled a face at the overpowering smell of carbolic inside. A sheet that was wrung out in the stuff every two hours hung, sodden, across the doorway. Feeling that any germ that could survive the stink deserved to live, Francis pushed it to one side with a finger and ducked into the room. His eyes watered with the fumes. Blinking the tears away, he peered at his wife. Pulling the sheet away from her body he saw that she was covered in a bright red rash. Her face was flushed, except for around her mouth, which was ringed with a bluish tinge.

'That's scarlet fever, all right,' said Francis. 'As clear a case as ever I saw.'

'That's what I thought,' agreed the nurse.

He stood, his breath damp inside the thick mask, and considered. For a patient as ill as Bridie, anything like this was bad news. But – and here Francis felt more cheerful – it was a diagnosis. They now knew the fever would go quite quickly.

'Yes I'm sure of it, but you'd better ring Angus anyway.'

The doctor confirmed their diagnosis. 'The lassie has hit the jackpot,' he said sardonically. 'Two in one. No wonder she's hot. I wonder if she didn't pick it up from that hell-hole at Clayhill.'

'She couldn't have,' Francis said.

'I know, I know. But if you'd seen it there, Frank, you'd believe anything was possible in this worst of all worlds.'

They edged round the horrible curtain again and pulled off their masks.

'Well, it's a case of carry on as before,' continued Angus. 'At least now we know we're doing all the right things for both diseases. That's some comfort.'

Bridie lay in a fog of carbolic, windows carefully

closed against draughts. The air in the sick-room grew fetid – bedpans, carbolic and vomit. Unable to do anything for herself, she simply lay, sometimes barely conscious and at others wandering in and out of delirious dreams. If she so much as tried to turn in bed, the nurse tut-tutted a warning and lifted her skilfully into another position. Bridie got thinner, easier to lift. Her face began to look gaunt. The fever still persisted.

'Three days,' noted Dr Hamilton that evening. 'I'd hope to see it go down soon.'

He eyed her uneasily, though the signs were still good. On the fourth day the swelling on her neck became grotesque.

'It gets in the way,' Emmy complained as she tried to tidy Bridie's long thick hair out of the way. 'I'd like to cut it.'

Bridie listened. It might ease the pain if the nurse had to turn her less. 'Cut it off,' she croaked.

The young nurse raised her pale eyebrows. 'It would be a help, but would you mind dreadfully?'

'Yes, but just do it.' She spoke with a terrible effort. 'Please cut it.'

Emmy fetched a pair of sharp surgical scissors. 'It's such beautiful hair, it's a shame, but it'll grow again, and I do think you'll be more comfortable with it shorter.'

Bridie tried to move her head to one side so that the nurse could get at it with the shears. The pain raged. A thin trickle of bloodstained pus ran out of Bridie's ear and down her neck. The nurse wiped it away with a piece of wet cottonwool.

'It must be agony,' she said in a low voice to Bridie. 'But if the boils in your ears burst, it'll relieve the pain wonderfully.'

She placed a hot towel, from in front of the fire that burned night and day, under Bridie's other ear. 'There. Let's encourage the other one to burst. You'll be so much better when they've started to clear.'

Carefully, the girl started to cut off the long, curling tresses of bright hair. 'There we are,' she said as she finished. 'It's not the best haircut you ever saw, but short hair suits you, I think, and just now it's ever so fashionable. You never know, you might want to keep it that way when you're better.'

She put the hair into a twist of paper, in case Bridie wanted to keep it. Half an hour later Francis put his head round the sheeted doorway. He looked taken aback when he saw Bridie's shorn head.

'I look horrible,' Bridie whispered.

Francis couldn't say anything. She did indeed look frightful; the loss of her hair accentuated her swollen neck, the horrible 'bull-neck' of diphtheria. A yellowish mess was running down her cheek. His throat went tight and and he tried push away his shame at his sudden revulsion. He sat down by her bedside and looked at Emmy.

'Is she still as feverish?'

The nurse nodded.

Gently, he touched Bridie's cheek. It was burning.

'She's as hot as ever,' he said.

'I know.'

'Horrible,' cackled Bridie again.

Shocked, the others turned their heads to stare at her. She lay, swollen and hideous, with great shining eyes. Blood ran from the same ear. The nurse hurried to fetch the bowl of water she kept for sponging Bridie, and began to lay a wet cloth on the poor disfigured face.

'I think you'd better telephone for the doctor,' she said quietly to Francis.

He almost ran from the room, swearing furiously as in his haste he caught his face on the cold sodden sheet over the door. He swore again in frustration when he could not trace the doctor directly, but had to be satisfied with leaving messages for him to come with the utmost urgency. Entering the room again, he found Bridie with wet towels on her body. After lying still and passive for several days, she was now twitching from head to foot.

'Dear God, what's happening?' asked Francis helplessly.

'Fever,' said the nurse. 'She's delirious.'

'It's horrible.' The voice was dry as bone.

'No, Bridie!' cried Francis in distress.

'No? No, Bridie? No? No!' Bridie's painful croaking got louder and her hands beat at the air in front of her. Her body began to rock from side to side.

'Help me hold her,' said the nurse. 'It's dangerous for her to carry on like this.'

They pulled the sheets tighter round the thin, thrashing body. Francis tried to restrain her by putting his arms round her. Bridie let out a hideous shriek and fought him like an animal. Horrified, and frightened of her astonishing strength, he pulled away from her.

'No,' she hissed. 'Get away, Dad. You hear, Dad? Get off, get away from me.' Broken screams began to tear out of her agonised throat.

'No Dad, no Dad. No no no.' Her hands plucked in a frenzy at her stomach and legs and her whole body arched off the bed, in a shocking gesture of desperate refusal. One hand suddenly flew to her mouth and she began to cry with horrible, hoarse tearing sobs as she sank back into the mattress and shrank into herself like a creature mortally wounded. Above the desolate mouth that stretched in an awful silent scream, her eyes stared at something only she could see, but which was dawning with the most appalling clarity on the watching pair.

The little nurse had her hands to her mouth in horror, her eyes quite round. As the ghastly cries faded and Bridie collapsed, breathing raggedly, she came towards the bed almost unwillingly.

'I'm sorry, sir,' she whispered to Francis, 'but I've never seen the like. It's awful, sir.'

He stood as though turned to stone. The nurse looked at him and realised she'd get no support there.

'He's in shock. We're both in shock,' she muttered to herself. She wiped a trembling hand over her brow and began to wring out the sheets that now lay in tepid disorder around Bridie's still form. She worked frantically to get her patient back in some kind of order. Clean linen replaced the sweat-sodden mess, and, fetching a bowl of warm water from downstairs, she forced herself to stop shaking and bath Bridie in a blanket. It took her twice as long as usual, but eventually Bridie lay fresh and cool in an immaculate bed. The nurse was clearing up the great pile of discarded bedlinen when Francis finally came to himself, and stirred. A pair of tired, dazed eyes sought out the little nurse and registered what she had done.

'Oh, thank you. That's better now.'

She looked at him, and young though she was, she drew away from him, afraid of what he might say. 'I think she'll sleep for a while, sir,' she said, to break the silence.

'Unspeakable,' said Francis to himself.

'Yes, sir, it was.'

He raised his head; she averted her eyes from his, overcome with embarrassment at the knowledge they had unwittingly shared. 'You must never speak of this,' he said to her.

She remained silent. She was duty bound to report her patient's crisis to Dr Hamilton, but she wasn't sure it was necessary to give the details of the nightmare.

Francis looked back at his wife and with a long groan laid his head on the side of her bed and wept. The nurse crept out of the room. She went downstairs into the parlour and found the brandy in its decanter in the cabinet Bridie had so recently polished for her guests. Pouring two glasses with hands that still shook, she took them back to the bedroom.

'Here, take this, sir,' she said. She steadied his hand for him as he raised the glass. He tasted his own tears on the rim as he drank.

Emmy sipped at her own, pulling a face at the strong taste. 'There we are, sir,' she said as she put the glasses on the bureau, ready to take away. 'You'll feel a bit stronger in a minute.'

They stood together like conspirators, uneasily wondering what might come next. Downstairs there was a loud banging on the front door. Mrs Goode, who had returned from her daughter's to find her employer's house upside down and Bridie half dying, hurried to open it. She'd been calming the indignation of Ellen, the scullery maid.

'What do they think I am?' she shouted. 'A bleedin' washerwoman? If I've lit that copper once this week, I've lit it every day.'

Francis had heard the shrill voices from upstairs. Mrs Goode's voice had been raised in reply.

'You'll do what's needed, my girl. There's poor Bridie so sick upstairs and you complaining about the washing. You should be ashamed.'

Ellen poked sullenly at the huge pile of sodden bedlinen. 'It's so bleedin' 'eavy,' she whined.

Mrs Goode could see her point. 'Come on now, I'll lend you a hand.' She was just putting on her apron when the doorbell sounded and she opened it to an anxious Dr Hamilton.

'Hello, Mrs Goode,' he said as she stood aside to let him in. 'I believe I'm needed.'

'There was some commotion upstairs, sir,' she answered. She'd heard Bridie shriek and had stopped her work to stand with one ear tilted in the direction from which the sound came. She registered the turmoil coming faintly from the bedroom, but had not heard the words clearly enough to understand what had happened. Even if she had, wild horses could not have dragged out of the housekeeper anything of a private matter between members of the household. Irrepressibly inquisitive herself, she was discretion itself when it came to outsiders knowing their business, and she held the doctor as being no exception.

'She's real bad, isn't she, sir?' she asked as she hung up his coat.

'Let me go up and see her first,' he answered.

The two already up there turned almost guiltily when he came into the bedroom.

'Thank God you've come!' said Francis. He gestured at the sleeping form on the bed. 'She's had some kind of turn, a crisis.'

The doctor looked enquiringly at his nurse. She felt Francis's silent gaze on her and it seemed to her, in her heart, that there were things that could not be put into words, and sometimes a person shouldn't even try.

'Yes,' she told the doctor, 'there's been a crisis. Mrs Holmes went into delirium and it was as though she had a nightmare. Delirious ravings. But she's quiet now, as you can see. Her pulse is good and respiration's rather fast – but I'd expect that after what happened.'

She looked at Francis. 'Mr Holmes was here to help me cope, fortunately, and between us we managed.'

Angus went over to Bridie and gently pulled back the cover. Her face was grey and sunken, but her breathing was indeed reassuring. He felt for the hundredth time the vital regularity of her heartbeat.

'She's incredibly resilient,' he observed. 'No recent vomiting, either. She'll pull through yet.'

'I think the fever is going down, too,' said the nurse, looking at the thermometer that she'd taken from her patient's mouth.

'Yes, that as well,' agreed the doctor. He smiled at Francis and remarked lightly that Bridie would be fashionable with her cropped hair. Francis smiled back weakly and rocked on his heels, for once at a loss for words.

'Should she not be taking more fluid?' he asked, more to break the silence than to interfere with the doctor's handling of his patient.

Angus glanced at him from under heavy brows. 'We'll see how she is when she wakes. If she can take glucose by mouth, we'll let her. Otherwise I may put in a tube, but I prefer to do that as a bit of a last resort since it only adds to the poor lassie's discomfort.' He replaced the covers over Bridie's arms. 'I think we have good cause to be optimistic.'

He repeated his cheerful prognosis as he left. Mrs Goode hovered in the background, and her face went all crooked with relief as she heard him say: 'I'll look in on her tomorrow, Frank, but I believe we'll win this one. I can't be pessimistic about a patient who puts up the kind of fight Bridie has. She's got an extraordinary will to live, and that kind of patient often pulls through against the longest odds. So cheer up, man, your wife is doing splendidly.'

Yes indeed, thought Francis as he closed the door

on his departing friend. Bridie is a survivor, that is certain. But, dear Lord, what is it that she has survived that I did not know? I hardly dare understand things that made no sense before. Her refusal to see her family, to go back to Ireland. . . .

Reluctantly he began to consider what he and the little nurse had witnessed. Nausea crept over him as he let his mind touch cautiously on the edges of understanding. He went into his study, closed and locked the door, and, sitting in solitude, stared fixedly into space while his mind filled with images that could drive a mad mad.

Chapter Thirteen

New Year had come and gone. The clear, cold weather of the last days of the old year had given way to a dismal shroud of grey rain that fell ceaselessly beyond Bridie's window. Night seemed to run into brief, dull days, and then long before teatime the faint light faded into night again. The gaslights were on all the time in the sick-room, and Emmy was glad to draw the curtains on the dreary scene outside when Mrs Goode brought up her pot of afternoon tea.

'There's some seed cake, fresh from the oven,' she remarked as she put the tray down on top of a chest of drawers.

Emmy pulled a chair out at Bridie's bedside for Mrs Goode and smoothed the cover with a sweep of her hand as she came to get the teatray.

'I expect Mrs Holmes could do with some of that,' she said conversationally to the housekeeper. 'I imagine she's sick of glucose and pap by now, poor thing.'

They both looked at Bridie, who lay with closed eyes, half asleep. The ugly swelling that had so upset Francis several weeks earlier had disappeared, and beneath the cropped hair Bridie's white, freckled skin stretched taut over bones that were almost visible, so skeletal had she become. The nineteen-year-old girl had become like a wizened old woman on the verge of death.

And yet, Bridie had not died. By some extraordinary effort of will she had survived an illness the ferocity of which had had no parallel in Angus's experience. The double infection she'd suffered had taken her so close to death that Francis had called the priest.

She'd lain, so weakened that she was barely conscious, as the young Father from the presbytery intoned the last rites over her motionless body. Unable to hear confession from the dying woman, he'd prayed for forgiveness for sins which, he said, God would know about whether Bridie was able to tell them or not. Francis had turned away, unable to endure the words. Emmy Dobson had watched him, the only one of the group around the bed who knew what was passing through his mind. She lowered her head and prayed silently and passionately for her patient, and her awful secret.

Angus had stayed behind after the priest and the rest of the little household had gone. He'd taken Bridie's pulse, frowned, then dropping her hand back on to the covers he walked to the window, whistling tunelessly through his teeth. He waited with his hands in his pockets for several minutes then, still whistling, went back to the bed and took her pulse again. Twice more he did the same, then heaved a sigh and shook his head. Bridie's heartbeat, which had remained miraculously steady throughout the long weeks of sickness, was soft and slightly irregular.

'It's the end,' murmured Angus to himself. 'She's so weak that heart failure will kill her almost immediately.'

He sat at the side of the bed, and held her hand in both of his. He could feel the bones limp in his fingers. Francis, his back to the window, made a dark figure against the light, watching.

'Bridie,' said the doctor softly. He bent his head so close that his mouth was only an inch from her ear. 'Bridie,' he said again. 'Do you hear me? Can you hold on, Bridie? You've fought so hard, and so well, don't give up now. For me, for David, for Francis, can you cling on? Live, Bridie. A little more effort, and you can live. I know you can. Bridie, live.'

He stroked the transparent hand so gently. 'Come on, lassie, you're a true fighter. Don't give up now.'

Bridie, who was sliding further and further away into a blessed light that was so peaceful, heard the plea with some part of herself that stopped and half turned at the sound of Angus's words.

There was a pause. With terrible reluctance, her soul turned from the beckoning peace of death and looked backwards. To come back again? Her exhausted body protested that it could not be, that enough had been done. But she was alert now, and the decision made despite herself. Bridie began to struggle back to consciousness, to life and all the pain that still remained for her. Watching, Angus saw her eyelids twitch and a small sigh escape her. His heart leaped with excitement and hope; he was sure that she could will herself back if she could be helped to make this one final effort.

'Good girl,' he said quietly. 'You are hearing me, Bridie. I'll stay here with you, lassie, and we'll bring you back together.'

Francis came from his post at the window. He pulled up another chair at the opposite side of the bed, and took Bridie's other hand. The doctor continued to talk to the girl in a deep, slow voice. Sending the night nurse away to busy herself in the kitchen as best she could, the three of them fought for Bridie's life long into the night, refusing by sheer willpower to let her die. Her heart remained irregular, but no worse. Towards the dawn Bridie's eyelids slowly opened and she looked at Angus as though she'd drowned and then risen from some depths that lay beyond his living experience. He smiled at her and ran his finger along her thin cheek.

'We're here, lassie.'

Bridie gave a look of assent and her eyes closed once more, but this time she slept in the land of the living.

Since that long night she had steadily gained strength. She still slept a great deal, and Angus knew that she was by no means out of the woods, for some of the complications of the illness did not usually appear for many weeks after the patient began to feel better. But he was hopeful that the damage to her heart was minimal, and that she would come through without permanent disabilities.

As Emmy poured out her tea, Bridie's voice came from the bed. 'Sure and I would love some tea, if I may.'

The nurse put down the teapot and turned a beaming smile on her patient.

' 'course you can.'

Mrs Goode bustled downstairs to fetch another cup. The housekeeper helped Emmy prop Bridie up against her pillows and held the cup to her lips when the tea had cooled a little.

'There, my duck,' she said happily 'Oh, it's a real pleasure to see you asking for tea again. You'll be wanting cake next! It's a real sign you're getting properly well again.'

'That's nice,' said Bridie, as she pushed away the half-empty cup, 'but it's enough for now, thank you.'

The nurse helped herself to a second slice of seed cake. 'Your cooking's delicious,' she said to Mrs Goode.

The housekeeper was pleased by the compliment. 'That's one of Mrs Beaton's,' she explained, 'and I don't reckon you can do better for cake recipes than hers.'

'Where's David today?' asked Bridie.

'Mrs MacDonald's,' said Mrs Goode.

'It is good of her,' said Bridie, 'to have him for all this time.'

'It was the best thing for him,' said Emmy. 'We didn't want him catching anything off you. She's so nice, that Mrs MacDonald, to have a child from a house with diphtheria. It's very good of her, to my way of thinking.' Her small, capable hands crumbled seedcake onto the plate in her lap.

'She's always had a soft spot for Davey,' replied

Bridie, in a voice already weak from the effort of conversation. 'She saw him born, and she took to him almost as strong as I did. I wonder if he's missed me. Between Susan and Mrs MacDonald, he's probably been spoiled so he won't want to come home.'

It was seven weeks before Angus pronounced Bridie well enough for a visit from David. The carbolic curtain had long since been discarded, and Emmy said no-one coming in need wear masks any more. Three weeks earlier, Bridie had been carried out of the bedroom, and tucked up on the settee downstairs in front of a roaring fire. Emmy stayed with her, while upstairs Mrs Goode and Ellen went to work. Lizzie turned up on the second day, and rolling up her sleeves, borrowed an apron and mucked in with a will. The bedroom was stripped. Linen taken out to the end of the garden and burned. Books, too. The windows were thrown wide and at last fresh air streamed in, banishing the stink of sickness. Rugs were taken up and beaten outside 'til dust flew everywhere and made Ellen cough badly. The long green curtains that had shrouded them from the outside world for so long were unthreaded from their poles and thrown on the bonfire after the linen. Bridie said she fancied a warmer colour to replace them, and Mrs Goode brought home samples for her to finger. They chose a very beautiful textured velvet in deep crimson. Francis agreed that it was expensive, but told Mrs Goode to go ahead and have it made up anyway.

It took the three of them as many days before the room, scrubbed and fumigated and aired in every nook and cranny, was ready for redecoration. Workmen arrived at seven in the morning and the scraping and painting and papering and varnishing went on for almost a week. Then the women took over again, and everything was put in its proper place. Furniture shone with polish and reflected the gorgeous heavy folds of the new curtains. The impedimenta of the sick-room had shrunk to two bedpans and a neatly folded pile of blankets used at bathtime. Flames flickered cheerily in the grate, and Bridie settled back between fresh, starched sheets.

She was so light that Francis, carrying her upstairs, felt he could break her just by tightening his arms. All her night-clothes had had to be replaced. Mrs Goode, grieving over the skeletal little body, had been extravagant. Lace and fine cambric lay soft on Bridie's skin. It had taken a long time to heal from the peeling of the scarlet fever, but amazingly there were no scars. No scars on her body at all. Extreme weakness. A porcelain, doll-like fragility. But no visible scars.

'You're a miracle, d'ye know?' Angus told her. 'No room at the inn, two deadly sicknesses, and all you have to show for it is a wee bit of weight loss. Mind you, from what I saw at the hospital, it's probably just as well they'd nowhere for you. They'd take one look at a case like you, and. . . .' He jerked his thumb down.

Mrs Goode popped her head round the door. 'Can I come in?' she asked.

'Come on, Dora,' Angus said heartily.

She placed a paper bag on the side of Bridie's bed. 'Here, I brought you something. It's to help give you something to do. Sitting there all this time, you'll soon be well enough to be bored, I thought. Have a look.' She pushed the bag towards Bridie.

With hands that were weakened by the effort, Bridie slowly pulled out the contents. Several bright hanks of lambswool tumbled out, and Bridie drew out two pairs of bone knitting needles. A pattern book was discovered, folded at the bottom.

'Oh, Mrs Goode, you are such a dear. Thank you.'

'You won't get much done to start with, 'cos I expect you'll get tired easily, but I remembered when you said your Mum taught you to knit, and I thought that that would be the very thing.'

'It's lovely.' Bridie chuckled. 'And I remember you thinking I was too stupid.'

Mrs Goode patted her hand as if to say, 'We won't say no more about that.'

Bridie raised a face that was all eyes, to ask Angus: 'Is that all right. Can I do some knitting?'

'Certainly,' said the doctor. 'From now on, you'll get a little stronger each day, and may do what you feel like doing. And eat – little and often – as much as you can.'

Bridie's eyes met the doctor's. She must eat for two. Despite her illness, she had not lost the baby. It had preyed constantly on her attendants' minds that she might do so. Angus had briefed the nurse on what she should do if Bridie started to haemorrhage.

'The aim is to save her, not the baby,' he spelled out very clearly.

Throughout her sickness, Angus had worked for Bridie's life first. It was true to form, he thought when he examined her, that she'd hang on to her baby, just as she'd hung on to life. Eventually, as she began to recover, she'd asked the inevitable question.

'Can it possibly be all right, Dr Hamilton? I've got so thin, I don't see how it can be. Are you sure it's still alive? I haven't felt anything.'

Angus re-examined her. 'Your baby is without a doubt alive and growing. I can hear the heartbeat. Its growth may well have been slowed down, though.'

Bridie voiced her real fear. 'What if it's been harmed. Might I have a baby with something wrong with it?'

Angus was equivocal. 'That's a risk in any pregnancy. There's no knowing at this stage whether your illness has increased that risk, or by how much. It's one of those situations where I have no answers, I'm afraid, Bridie. We have to wait and see.'

Emmy found she didn't have to coax much for Bridie to eat. The baby needed food, so Bridie ate. The baby needed her to get strong, so Bridie sat up one day, got up the next, and was soon hobbling weakly round the room on legs as thin as matchsticks. Determined to be back on her feet as soon as she could, she was the most willing and helpful patient Angus ever had. Lizzie, who was staff nurse on a surgical ward at the time, suggested some exercises that she'd seen the physiotherapists do with patients after they'd lain in bed a long time on account of operations. Bridie co-operatively wiggled her feet and legs and did cautious sit-ups and arm swings. It all helped and at last they told her that David could come to see her, and if all continued to go so well, could come home for good a day or two later.

Bridie sat in the chair by the bedroom fire, tense with expectation. She'd decided to ask Lizzie to bob her hair properly. It was too curly to go into a fashionable sleek line, but the result was pretty nonetheless. With her thin cheeks and short hair, she wondered if David would recognise her. Doors banged downstairs, and there was the sound of voices on the stairs. The bedroom door opened and Mrs MacDonald's excited face peeped round.

'Look who's here,' she exclaimed, and opened the door wide. David stood, shyly holding on to her skirt, one finger in his mouth. Bridie's mouth fell open in astonishment. He was walking! She held out her arms.

'Davey! Oh David, darling. Come and see me.'

He shrank closer to Mrs MacDonald.

'Come on,' begged Bridie.

Mrs MacDonald took his hand and began to urge him into the room. He turned to grab her skirt in both fists and started to cry. The midwife picked him up and brought him over.

'Don't let it upset you,' she said, seeing Bridie look as if she wanted to cry as well. 'It's only 'cos he's been away for a long time. He'll be as right as ninepence in no time, you'll see.'

She plonked the child firmly in Bridie's lap. 'Now

you be a good boy and say 'ullo to your mum,' she ordered.

David kicked angrily and reached for the midwife, who backed away. 'No,' she said sternly. 'You're to stay with your mum, and give her a nice kiss.'

David scowled and hid his head from Bridie.

'My word, we're cross,' observed Mrs MacDonald.

David scowled harder. Bridie stroked the little boy's head.

'Are you angry that I've been ill so long?' she asked him in a low voice. 'I'm sorry. I've missed you terribly, Davey.'

David's lip stuck out and he wriggled.

'If you won't give me a kiss, then I'll just give you one.' Bridie put her lips to his round, red little cheek, and he swung a fat arm up and knocked her right on the nose. She gasped with shock and pain.

Mrs MacDonald took a hold on the two small waving arms and said loudly: 'David O'Neill, don't you dare. You wicked boy.'

David, surrounded, looked up at his mother. She rubbed her nose. 'This is a fine welcome, I'm sure,' she said to her son. 'What a temper.'

He suddenly got to his knees on her lap, and pulling himself up willy nilly by her clothes and hair, put his baby arms round her neck and hugged her so tight she could hardly breathe.

'There,' said Mrs MacDonald. 'What did I tell you?'

Bridie ached, she loved the little boy so. Keeping him close, she looked at the midwife.

'I don't know how we'll ever thank you, Mrs MacDonald. There's no way to repay kindness like yours, except to say . . . well, I can't find words. We owe you such a debt.'

'Nonsense,' said the midwife brusquely. 'It's just nice to see you lookin' better, is all.'

David started to slide off Bridie's lap. Lizzie caught him as he set off on two quite steady legs to explore the room. She let him go again when he struggled. 'He's strong, isn't he?' she remarked.

'Oh my, yes. A real little lad, that one. A mind of 'is own, like 'is mum.'

Mrs Goode arrived with a tray of teacups.

'Stay and have yours with us,' Bridie told her.

Perching the tray on the top of the bureau, the housekeeper poured milk into a glass for David and tea for the rest of them. The child, a half-eaten biscuit going soggy in his hand, leant against his mother's knee and patted her gown with one fat fist. He crammed biscuit into his mouth and held up his arms to be lifted. Lizzie hastily leant over and helped Bridie pick him up. She watched their faces, each so different, and each so loved, over the top of her son's small head. Resting her chin gently on it, she thought how strange it was that being so close to death somehow brought you closer to life. As if you discovered in some odd way that life and death were but one.

She bent her head to hide tears. Maybe the price of her life would be the death of her baby. Only time would tell.

Chapter Fourteen

Bridie's baby didn't die, though the few people who ever saw her agreed that it would have been better if she had. Bridie had known immediately. The labour had been very long and difficult. Angus and Mrs MacDonald had been with her for hours before the baby was finally born. Looking at their faces over the mound of her stomach, Bridie saw them go white. They glanced at each other and then at her.

'What is it?' she cried anxiously. 'Something's wrong, isn't it?'

She struggled to sit up and look. Mrs MacDonald pulled herself together hastily and ran round the bed. She went to push Bridie back down, and leant across to block her view. Bridie, weak after almost two days of labour, sank back under the midwife's hand.

'Tell me what's wrong. It's the baby. What's wrong with my baby?'

Between Bridie's raised legs, Angus forced himself to stay calm, and helped the tiny body into the world. His deep voice came from behind Mrs MacDonald.

'Ye've a wee girl, my dear.'

'Why won't you let me see her?'

The doctor didn't answer. He was staring at the

baby. Such a one shouldn't live – wouldn't surely live? But even as he watched, the baby's skin began to turn a healthy pink and she gave tiny, mewling cries. Angus cut the cord and very gently wrapped the baby in a soft white towel that had been warming by the fire.

Mrs MacDonald stroked Bridie's hair off her face. 'Now don't take on. There, there,' she soothed. The midwife's worn, kindly face creased with concern. She looked enquiringly at Angus, who reluctantly picked up the baby and nodded. All Bridie could see was a white bundle. The baby cried louder. Mrs MacDonald pulled away from Bridie, her face was grim. Angus stood, holding the baby, not giving her to Bridie.

'My dear,' he began painfully, 'do you remember that we talked a long time ago, when you'd been so ill, about whether your sickness might have affected the baby?'

Terror filled Bridie's heart. 'It has, hasn't it. She's not right, is she.'

Angus slowly shook his head. 'No, my dear. She's not at all right. I don't know how to say this without giving you the most dreadful shock, Bridie, but. . . .' He sat down on the edge of the bed and bent forward. 'Look,' he said in a voice that trembled slightly, and pulled back the edge of the towel.

The blood drained from Bridie's face. Mrs MacDonald got a bowl to her lips just before she was sick.

The tiny girl was beautiful. Fuzzy red hair promised

that she would fulfil Francis's dream, and be just like her mother. The little mouth was the image of Bridie's and as she stopped crying, with Angus's movement, her baby blue eyes met Bridie's, which, glassy with horror, wandered from the angelic little face to the baby's featureless second head.

No one could say a word.

After a bit, Angus laid the baby on the side of the bed, and got on with clearing up. He moved stiffly, as if he had to force himself. When he and the midwife had completed their work, they discreetly left Bridie alone with her child.

'I can't believe it's alive,' the doctor muttered. 'By all that's holy, it should die quickly. It's unthinkable it should live.'

'Whatever will she do?' asked Mrs MacDonald.

'I've no idea. I can't imagine.' The doctor shook his head. 'And there's Frank, as well. Someone's got to tell him.'

He looked hopefully at Mrs MacDonald. 'That would be best coming from you,' she said. 'You'll be able to help him through it. . . .'

'Oh, aye. Help him through.' The doctor's voice was sardonic. 'How d'ye help a man come to terms with, with . . . that?' He raised his hands and let them fall hopelessly. 'As if they haven't had enough. Poor wee bairn.'

Mrs MacDonald wasn't sure whether he meant Bridie or the baby. Probably both.

*   *   *

215

The baby cried harder. The little white bundle kicked and began to unroll itself. The tiny face screwed itself up and yelled. Bridie stared, transfixed, but didn't touch the baby. She felt numb, dead, frozen. The baby yelled louder. She worked herself into a rhythmic screaming. Bridie watched. Then, suddenly, the noise stopped. The small mouth gave a pathetic sob and the baby lay quiet, her eyes beginning to close. As if in a trance, through no will of her own, Bridie's cold hands reached out and picked up the bundle. Startled, the baby's eyes flew open and gazed at her mother. They looked at each other with that peculiar kind of intimacy which can bind executioner and victim.

The baby's gaze questioned Bridie, who finally nodded, as if they'd reached some sort of truce. After a bit, Bridie began to unbutton her night-gown.

When Angus told Francis, he fainted.

Bridie didn't leave the house while her baby lived. She hardly left the room where the child had been born. She asked Francis, through the door, to get the priest to come, and she alone was present when the infant was christened. She called her Rosa, for Dolorosa – sadness. Francis saw his daughter once. He emerged from the room ten minutes later, his face a frozen mask, and never went up there again. He took to spending much of his time in his study, with the door locked. Even David found himself locked out, out of his parents' presence and it seemed his parents' hearts.

Rosa lived four months. Angus, who alone was

allowed to see her, was relieved when he signed the death certificate. The small coffin stood in the room for two days, and then Bridie and Francis went silently together to the graveyard and watched the priest bury the child. As the gravedigger began to throw the first shovels of earth into the hole, Bridie turned away.

'It's over,' she said dully.

They walked, unable to speak any comfort to each other, back to the square.

Outwardly life returned to normality of a sort. Bridie tidied away every trace of little Rosa's brief life, then closed the door on the room and never entered it again. She didn't cry. Angus wished she would, but she seemed bent on burying the memory of the child as silently as she'd buried the sad little body. Francis said not a word about the child. It was as if Rosa had never existed.

Bridie took up her household duties again, and Francis spent less time in his study, but more time at work. He took to leaving early in the morning, returning late to solitary suppers in the morning room, while Bridie sat alone in the parlour. David, growing fast, loved to be out of doors, so Bridie walked for hours in streets and open spaces, pushing his carriage when he tired of all his running and climbing, and was ready to go to sleep.

The exercise did her good. Four months shut up indoors had left her wan and thin. Walking and walking in the open air brought colour back to her cheeks. She began to feel hungry and her gaunt look softened as her face rounded out once more. She was still lovely, but no longer a young girl. Experience had aged her. Lines round her eyes and mouth were the indelible effects of what she had suffered.

Lizzie felt her heart ache as she looked at her friend. Bridie had sent a message of congratulations on her wedding day, but had said through the closed door that she could not attend. Lizzie had first begged, then suggested putting the wedding off, Bridie's absence upset her so much, but Jonathan pointed out that no one knew how long this would go on, and it wasn't fair on either of them to wait indefinitely. So they'd married, both conscious of the empty space where Bridie should have been. Francis sent his apologies.

One evening, weeks after, he came home at midnight. Bridie heard the front door close and looked at the clock. He got later and later. She hesitated, then slipped out of bed and put on her robe. She found Francis standing in the hall, head bent, rubbing his eyes wearily as he undid his coat.

'Dear? You're home very late? Is everything all right?'

Francis didn't meet her eyes. 'Oh yes,' he said vaguely, 'there's a lot to do at work.'

'Have you had anything to eat?'

'Yes. Thank you.'

She followed him down the passage to the morning room. 'Can I get you anything?'

'No, thank you. I don't want to keep you up, Bridie.'

'It's worry about you that's keeping me up,' she said after a pause. 'I worry because I hardly see you, and because we never seem to talk to each other.'

Francis gave a humourless smile. 'It's difficult to talk to someone who locks themselves up,' he agreed.

Bridie stared at him in disbelief. His eyes on hers were hurt and cold. 'What else would you have had me do?'

'You could've sent it away. Angus offered.'

'It? Is that how you think of her? Never!' Bridie's voice was hard and flat. 'I couldn't. I tried, and I did talk to Dr Hamilton about it, but in the end he saw how it was. He understood that I couldn't ever have sent her away. Not if she'd lived four years. He understood, even if you can't.'

'I understand that she took everything. I didn't matter. Nor David. How much time did you have for him?'

'Please, Francis. Please try to understand. I didn't mean to shut you and David out, but I didn't know what else to do. I did the only thing that seemed right. I thought and thought about it, but there wasn't any other way.'

'You kept that . . . that . . . monster. You didn't have to.'

'Don't you dare,' hissed Bridie. 'Don't you ever call her that again. Do you hear? Ever.'

'You pretend it wasn't?' asked Francis icily.

'I'm not pretending anything. I'm telling you never

219

to call her that wicked word again. Her name was Rosa. She was yours and mine and I looked after her. I'm glad she's dead, poor mite, but I could never have done one single thing to make her life shorter, or not to make it as happy as it possibly could be.'

'I didn't mean that,' said Francis defensively.

'I think I know what you mean. I couldn't do it. And it sounds strange, hearing this kind of thing from you. You come home at midnight because you are too busy working for them, out there,' she waved a hand that shook with anger, 'to want to see your own family. We need you more than they do. It's been an awful time for all of us. I'd never want to have to go through a time like this again. But you're making it push us apart.'

'No.'

'Yes.' Her voice dropped. 'Look at us. We've never quarrelled before.'

Francis's eyes looked hunted. Bridie put her hand on his arm.

'Please let's love each other again. I do love you.' She went to put her arms around his neck, and he stepped backwards.

'Please? I want to be close again, try to put this terrible thing behind us.' She put her hands out to him in appeal.

'No. I can't.'

She shook her head, not believing the words. 'But why? What do you mean? Darling?'

The rare endearment made him look painfully at her. 'No, Bridie,' he repeated. 'I can't.'

'Can't what?'

'Anything. Touch you.'

She recoiled. 'What do you mean?' she whispered, shocked.

'Bridie, you are forcing me to say things we may both regret. I'd rather go up now, and we can talk in the morning if you wish.'

'No.' She spat the word at him. 'You can't do this. I have a right to know what you mean when you say you can't touch me.' She barred his way to the door. 'Tell me.'

'You may wish I hadn't,' he warned.

'You've no choice. I won't give you one. Not now.'

Francis spoke in a level, cold voice about what had happened in her sick-room, many months earlier. He might have been reading statistics.

'The nurse saw you, too. It was only too clear what had happened. You were raped, weren't you? After all this time, to discover that my wife was raped by her own father! Now do you see, Bridie? Every time I even think of touching you, that memory comes back, so clear and so – so –' he groped for words – 'filthy. I can't bear it.'

Bridie was white as a sheet. Blink. Blink. Then like the slow sharpening of a photograph on paper that was already full of pictures while seeming blank, it came back. She felt her head spin wildly and then come to a sudden stop. It all came back.

'Yes,' she whispered.

Francis looked at her with pity. 'You see?'

'Yes.'

'That's why you came to London, isn't it?'

'Yes.'

'Lies! All this time.'

She shook her head despairingly. 'No, not lies. I forgot, I truly did.'

'More lies?'

Mrs Goode's voice rang hollowly in her ears. 'If there's one thing he can't abide more than stupidity, it's deceit.'

'No,' she said in a dreary voice, 'it wasn't lies. I did forget. It was like a dream. You know you've been dreaming, but you can't remember what. Sometimes there are flashes, funny feelings, and then it's gone again. I did forget, and I never told no lies. If you'd asked me outright, I don't think I could have told you, not until now. There were things I didn't understand myself. Now I will.'

Francis didn't believe her. Out of the blue, after all these years, the anger finally came as she saw bitter rejection in his face.

'It was not my fault,' she cried fiercely. 'I was young, and I knew nothing. He was drunk out of his head because Mam had just died. He thought I was her, and I fought him, but I couldn't stop him.'

She shook with fury and distress. 'I never lied to you, but dear Lord, how I've paid! I've paid and paid and paid. Rosa – she was part of the paying, too. I don't owe nothing, no more. I knew when I didn't die after the fever, there'd be paying, and there has been. A death for a life.'

Her grey eyes blazed at Francis. 'Well, I'm done

paying, now. No more. Not to you, nor no-one else.'

Francis listened silently.

'I'm goin' up now, Francis,' she spoke more calmly, 'and in the morning I'll take what's mine, and go. I wouldn't stay another day in the same house as you, not if you begged on your bended knees.'

He looked at her bleakly. 'Very well, if that's what you want.'

'It is.' The coldness of her tone matched his.

The door closed behind her. Francis suddenly looked haggard and old. He fumbled in the cupboard until he found an unopened bottle of brandy. Sitting by the cold grate, he quietly set about blotting out the pain that threatened to knife his heart in two. He was fast asleep in the chair, an almost empty bottle on the floor beside him, when Bridie, after a sleepless night, came down early the next morning. She propped a cushion under his head, put a blanket over the rest of him, and cautioned Mrs Goode to leave him alone. He still slept when, some hours later, she picked up her case, and, taking David firmly by his small hand, left the house for the last time.

Chapter Fifteen

Three women sat toasting their toes by the fire. They were considering Bridie's future.

'I could go back into service. Mrs MacDonald might agree to have David for me.' Bridie's voice wasn't very sure. It didn't sound a practical idea.

'Anyroad,' said Ethel DuCane, Susan's mum, 'who round here would give you a job? No offence, ducks, but everyone knows your husband, and I don't think any of 'em would want to put 'im out, if you see what I mean.'

Bridie saw very well what she meant. 'It's David. I've got to find some way of looking after him, at least until he's much bigger.'

Susan's mum nodded sympathetically. 'Everything's trickier when there's kiddies, no mistake.'

'Well, I'm without work, now, ain't I?' said Susan. 'If David's here, Mr Holmes won't be wanting me no more. Until I find meself another position, I'll 'ave David, as usual, while you sort yourself out.'

Her round young face broke into a generous grin.

'Yes, how about that?' cried Ethel. 'See how you go, anyroad.'

Bridie began to brighten up. 'You sure?' she asked.

'Go on with yer. 'course.'

'Oh, Ethel, you're kind. And David will be happier with Susan than with anyone else.'

Bridie's face fell again. 'We've still got to think what I can do, though. It's not much use Susan looking after David, if I'm not doing anything to earn some money to pay her.'

There was silence while they all considered the problem.

'You never worked before you come to London?' enquired Ethel.

'Only at home. I never had a job. And I'd help Dad about the place, but nothing that's any use here.'

'Could you work in a shop?'

'They wouldn't have me, with a child and all. The big ones, you have to live in and not be married. They wouldn't look at me.'

Ethel pursed her lips and nodded. 'Buggers, they are. Minute a girl gets married – out. It's wicked.'

'Well, it's no help to me.'

'What can you do? Let's look at it that way.'

Bridie turned to her and ticked things off on her fingers. 'Cook, clean, look after babies, run a house, bake, do accounts.' She hesitated, then added, 'I can read and write, and I'm quite good with figures. Dora Goode an' me, we always did the accounts, and I liked it. I used to enjoy it.'

Susan said, 'Well, most of them things aren't no use, but the reading and figures might be. What can you do with them? It could be shop work again, only we know that's out.'

There was silence again. Ethel broke it.

'It's probably not the kind of thing you'd think of, but what about something like behind the counter in a betting shop? That's money and accounts and things. Or Old Finkelstein has women in the office to keep his books.' She slapped her knees and laughed at the idea.

Susan chuckled. 'I can just see you and that skinflint getting along. Evil old beggar, 'e is.'

An idea dawned at the back of Bridie's mind. She shook her head, it was too bold. But having arrived, it wouldn't go away again.

It sat there, beckoning for attention, while they prepared their supper and ate when Ted DuCane, Ethel's old man, got in from Billingsgate, where he worked as a porter.

' 'e stinks but the money's good, so you can't complain,' said Ethel to Bridie over the washing up. 'An' talking of money, it's been on my mind to ask you summat.'

Bridie looked round from the soapsuds. 'Go on, then.'

'Well,' said Ethel slowly, 'I know if it were my Susan in your position, I'd want her home here, where she belongs, regardless. I might think she'd made a fool of herself, or I might not, depending. But here's where she'd come. Now, I can't help wondering why you aren't goin' to your family. Blood's thicker than water, I always think, and if you can't rely on your own family, who can you?'

Bridie sighed inwardly. It seemed that this question

227

was going to haunt her wherever she went. She fished in the suds for knives and forks, and made up her mind.

'I know Ted's asleep in there, but would you mind shutting the door? Being more private.'

Full of curiosity, Ethel closed the door on her husband, his bald head just visible over the top of the chair where he dozed by the fire.

Bridie told her tale, briefly and without emotion. 'So that's what finished Francis and me, and now I 'spect you can see why I can't go back to him, not to me Dad neither. I've got to manage on my own this time.'

'Oh, you poor girl,' said Ethel quietly. 'I'd never have guessed. Oh my word, what you've been through. Oh my lor'.'

She put two beefy arms round Bridie, soapsuds and all, and hugged her tight against her big, none too scented, bosom. The sharp smell of sweat stung Bridie's nose, as she returned the hug warmly.

'Now don't you fret, ducks, you can stay 'ere and welcome until you've got going,' soothed Ethel, still overcome by the story she'd just heard.

Bridie decided to let the idea loose and see what happened. 'You know you mentioned Old Finkelstein, and his loanshark office?'

Ethel nodded. 'Goin' to ask him?' she asked.

Bridie shook her head. 'No, but it gave me another idea. I don't know whether it would work or not, but it might be exciting to give it a try. I've got a bit of savings from the last two years. Not a huge lot, but a little bit put by out of housekeeping with Mrs Goode. We were so careful, there was often some left over so I saved it. What if I put it into a business? I could lend out myself. Small amounts. A personal sort of business, for small borrowers.' The idea sounded more and more exciting. 'What d'yer think, Ethel?'

She mused on this novel suggestion, pleating and unpleating the drying-up cloth in her big rough hands.

'Well,' she said finally, 'it's not exactly what you'd call a woman's job, is it? Anyroad, I never heard of no woman moneylender. It's usually them Jews, an' all the ones I know of are men.'

Bridie drew a pound sign in the suds. 'That's not to say a woman couldn't do it,' she answered.

Ethel dried a bundle of knives and spoons. 'No, p'raps not. You thought how you'd start, then? How do you get going in a thing like that?'

Bridie shrugged. 'I only thought about it at all this afternoon. But it's the first thing that's come into my mind that I really think I could do. And it's independent. I wouldn't be asking no man to help me out. I don't want to do that. I've had enough of that carry on.'

'Well, if you feel that way, you should give it a try, I reckon,' said Ethel. ' 'ave you thought, though, that you might put their noses out? Old Finkelstein, an' Sam Saul – them lot. They ain't nice people to offend, Bridie. You'd need to be real careful.'

'The way I see it is, they're big. They deal in a lot of money. What I'm thinking of is small amounts – stuff they wouldn't be interested in.'

'Well, p'raps,' said Ethel doubtfully. 'You'd have to be ever so careful, though, not to get on the wrong side of 'em.'

Bridie pulled the plug in the sink. 'All done,' she said.

Ethel had another thought. 'And there's another thing,' she said. 'You look at Sam Saul's place, for instance, and you'll see it's all over barbed wire. You noticed? Windows blocked off, and all that. It's not a safe thing to be, a shark. You get yourself hated without even trying. And all that money. It's asking for trouble. What would you do about that?'

'I wouldn't be a shark,' said Bridie. 'I'd help people out.'

'I don't doubt that's what Old Finkelstein would say he does,' said Ethel sourly, 'but there's not a soul does business with him, and still has a good word for him.'

'You don't sound like you think it's a good idea.'

'I never said that. I'm wondering if you know what you'd be taking on, is all.'

'Well, beggars can't be choosers, can they? And I've no intention of going begging, so I have to find something that'll keep me and David going. I've a feeling I could do it if I tried, and I could be different from that other lot.'

'All right then, dearie,' said Ethel comfortably, 'you give it a try, and count us behind you. You're welcome to the room upstairs as long as you want it. Six shillin' a week and all found. That fair by you?'

'That'll be very fair. Me and David will do nicely, thank you, Ethel.'

Ethel's back-to-back was in one of the many long sooty rows of squalid houses in Plaistow. A sour, sunless back garden led to the privy at the end.

Bridie cupped her face in her hand and leant on the windowsill of the back room she and David would share. Outside in the November halflight, she saw windows lighting up, and the smell of a hundred cooking pots temporarily drowned the odours from the end of the gardens. It was a far cry from Tredegar Square. One small room held a bed she'd share with David, a chair, and a cupboard built into the corner took her clothes. She had a washstand and basin, but water had to be carried from downstairs. If she wanted a bath, Ethel had said, she was welcome to take down the tin tub, and have a washdown in front of the fire, provided no one was about.

'You'll find the clothes horses out the back, and if you put towels over them, it keeps the draughts out,' Ethel advised her, 'but if you don't want a public bath, do it when Ted's at work.' She grinned. 'Not as he'd mind, but you might not want 'im walking in on you.' Meals, offered Ethel, could be taken with them downstairs. All in at six shillings, plus extra for coal in winter.

Bridie knew she was lucky. They were a decent, friendly family, and the rent was more than fair. Ethel was a happy-go-lucky housekeeper, though, and the place was none too clean. Bridie felt a pang of guilt. She was comparing this with Mrs Goode's impeccable standards, and if she went about doing that, they'd feel she was looking down her nose, and that was the quickest way to end up out on the street.

'Anyway,' she said to herself, 'who are you to talk? Back home, you shared a bed and washed under the tap. You've left the grand living behind, my girl, and don't you forget it. It's up to you to make the best of it, now. Ain't no one going to bale you out.'

There was a set of small flags pinned on one wall. They made a colourful splash against the drabness. Bridie could pick out the Union Jack, but the others were all foreign.

She decided to ask Ethel about them after she'd put David to bed. He took a long time to settle, and was grizzly and bad-tempered about his new surroundings.

'Where Papa?' he cried at bedtime. 'Where Papa?'

'Papa's at home,' answered Bridie, 'but we are going to live here now, you and me, David.'

The little boy looked around him with big, bewildered eyes. Bridie took him in her arms and rocked him to and fro, smoothing his hair and whispering in his ear until his eyelids drooped shut. She laid him carefully in the middle of the double bed, and pulled the shawl he'd had from a tiny baby, round his shoulders. Then she put the rough blanket over him. As she turned away to tiptoe out, there was a series of bangs from next door, and through the thin walls she heard a man and woman start shouting at each other. Someone else slammed a door and ran down the street, steel-tipped boots ringing noisily on the cobbles. Ethel's voice said something audibly downstairs. David started awake and looked round, frightened, for his mother. She turned in the doorway at his cry. He was sitting up, looking at the wall, where more bangs resounded, his small face bluish with weariness and fear.

'Bumps, Mama, bumps,' he quavered, pointing at the wall.

'Yes, bumps,' agreed Bridie, sitting back down on the bed. 'I'm afraid I think we're going to have to get used to them, Davey. They won't do you any harm. Lie back down again, or you'll get cold.'

The child obediently sank back. 'Stay here, Mama,' he begged.

It was more than half an hour, after the racket had subsided, before David went to sleep again, holding tight to Bridie's hand. In the dark room, feeling the warm little fingers hanging so fearfully on to hers, her shoulders slumped. She felt tired and lonely.

'Oh, David,' she whispered to the sleeping child, 'I'm sorry. What are we to do, you and me?'

She pushed off her shoes with her toes, and curling up under the blankets, put her face against his soft little head. Fully dressed, she let weariness and sadness carry her into sleep. She dreamed of great fish swimming after her in a small pool. She went round and round and round, but they got nearer and nearer. She woke, sweating with panic, her chest aching from holding her breath. David slept on his back a little way away from her, and the night was pitch dark.

She'd fallen asleep, and now everyone in the house had gone to bed. She lay wakeful in the strange place, turning plans over in her head, trying to find ways round the multitude of problems she could solve only by using her wits. Time dragged. Nearby a clock chimed and she counted. Three o'clock. David would wake her by seven at the latest. She seemed more wakeful than ever, but when the clock chimed the half hour she was dozing fitfully, and by four o'clock was once more fast asleep.

'Oh, them flags, yes,' said Ethel the next morning. 'They're Edward's.'

'Of course,' cried Bridie. 'I forgot. How stupid of me.'

'Edward's me eldest,' said Ethel proudly.

'I know, Susan often talked about him. It's his room I've got.'

'Yes, but it don't matter,' Ethel answered. 'I'd have let it any road, seeing as he's away such a lot. We need the money, and he can always kip down somewhere else when he's at home.'

'He's in the Navy, isn't he?' said Bridie.

'Yes. Joined two years ago. Engineer, 'e wants to be. He were clever at school, and the Navy gives a first-rate training, so 'e reckons. If he stops long enough, and does well, he might make officer. So he says, anyroad.' Her plain features crumpled in a broad smile.

'I'm real proud of him. His dad is, an' all. He

234

comes home on leave, all togged up in his sailor uniform, an' he's so handsome you wouldn't believe. All the girls run after him, but he's too busy getting on, he says, to tie hisself down to anyone. You'll see, next time he comes home.'

'Is that often?' asked Bridie.

'Well, depends where his ship is. If it's in dock fer repairs or summat, he stays a while. But they're at sea for long stretches, and then we don't see him for months on end. The first year he joined, well, it was seven months he stayed away, then he had a month at home. It was grand to hear him talking about all the places he'd been. The things he sees!'

It was plain that Edward was the apple of his Mum's eye. That's lovely, thought Bridie. I hope I talk like that about Davey when he's a man. I hope he's as good a son as Edward.

'Susan's a good 'un, as well,' said her mum. 'I'm real lucky with my kiddies. They're both a credit, I reckon.'

Bridie smiled and nodded. 'They are, they really are,' she agreed.

A real credit.

Which was more than David was over those first few weeks. He missed his old life sorely, and let everyone know it.

'David, for goodness' sake, shut up!' hissed Bridie, near the end of her patience one afternoon. 'You get us thrown out, and you'll really have something to moan about.'

He whined and stamped and yelled and rolled on the

floor, until the palm of Bridie's hand itched to smack him.

'Why don't yer?' asked Ethel affably, when Bridie confessed to feeling like hitting him. 'Spare the rod an' spoil the child, I reckon. You let him get the upper hand, an' you've made a rod to beat your own back. You'll regret it, mark my words if you don't.'

Bridie thought back to the black eyes she'd had from Dad, and doubted whether hitting did much good, but when David continued to play up so much that she feared he'd try Ted and Ethel's patience too far, she smacked him. Shocked, David turned frantic eyes on his mother. He began to cry, a thin, lost wretched sound that tore Bridie's heart in pieces. She held him to her, and rocked him.

'I'm sorry. Oh, I'm sorry. I didn't mean it.' Anxiety about smacking the child was added to her anxiety about keeping the room.

'He'll get over it. You fret too much,' observed Ethel.

'But he's making such a nuisance of himself. I can't think you'll want us to stay if he carries on,' cried Bridie in despair.

'Oh, you goose! He's only little. What do you expect?' exclaimed Ethel, half exasperated. 'Give him a chance and he'll settle. I wouldn't want you out of the room just for that.'

Bridie felt overcome with relief that Ethel had said it at last.

'But just the same,' she said, 'the sooner I can get rooms of my own, the better. It's good of you, Ethel, but it gets on my nerves, and I feel I ought to keep him quiet, and he just won't.'

'P'raps if you was to get out and working, and let Susan have 'im, he might settle quicker than with you fussing around him. No offence, dearie, but you do.'

Bridie thought over what had been said that night, lying awake only ten days before Christmas. Ethel was right. She was too cooped up with David, and too worried to take a balanced view of things. And Susan would get another job before she knew it, and her chance would be gone.

'Yes,' said Bridie to herself into the blackness, 'it's time I got going. Tomorrow I'll start. Bridie O'Neill is going into business – tomorrow. It's a promise.'

She reached over and drew David's warm little body close. 'It's a promise,' she whispered. 'For us both.'

Chapter Sixteen

Halfway down Vallance Road Bridie knocked on her hundredth door. There was no response. She banged again, and was about to turn away when it opened a crack and a suspicious eye looked her up and down.

'Whatcher want?' a short-tempered voice demanded.

'I'm Mrs O'Neill,' began Bridie once more, 'and I make loans. Small to medium, but nothing over ten pounds, and that only with security. Up to five pounds, no security. Decent interest. No loan too small.'

The eye sharpened with interest. The door opened a bit wider. 'Never seen you before,' said the voice truculently. 'You new round 'ere?'

'In business, yes,' said Bridie truthfully.

'What interest you charge?'

'Four per cent. Nothing compared to some.'

'That's right.' The voice had become thoughtful. The door swung wide. The voice's owner was a bent little woman whose face was lined and tired. Hair still unmarked with grey was wound tight round curlers and hidden under a scarf. Her eyes were young.

'Me 'usband's bin off with the fever. The doctor's bin, and said he's through the worst, but 'e won't be back at work a whiles yet. We're skint fer Christmas. You ready to lend us money?' The voice was flat with disbelief.

'How much do you need, and again, how much can you repay when he's back to work?'

The voice rose incredulously. 'You'll lend us?'

'What's he do, your old man?'

'Not a bad job, when 'e's fit. He's a baker, down Commercial Road way.'

'All right. How much?'

'Fer coal, and food, 'is fags and summat fer Christmas dinner.' The woman began to do rapid calculations on her fingers. 'Would three pound— no, make it four pound – be all right?'

'Yes,' said Bridie. 'To repay plus interest the end of his first week back. Interest only, and it goes up to ten per cent.'

The woman's eyes narrowed. 'Steep, innit?'

'Not really. Sharks can charge fifty.' Bridie shrugged. 'Even a hundred per cent if you get unlucky. I do small loans, and the interest is low if you repay it all. It's fair and reasonable.'

The woman grunted. Bridie took out a notebook from under her thick shawl.

'Name?'

'Grundy.'

Bridie looked at the door.

'Number Fifty-two. Mrs Grundy. Four pound.'

The woman signed her name. Bridie unclipped the

heavy moneybelt that was tied round her waist, and counted out four pound notes into the woman's outstretched hand.

'There you are.'

The woman, unable to believe her luck, grabbed it. 'Ta, Missus, you've saved us.'

She folded the precious notes into her bodice. 'Week after he goes back. Guaranteed.'

'Right you are.' Bridie stepped away from the door and went to move on to the next.

'Missus?'

Bridie turned back.

'You doin' this regular?'

'If there's enough custom, yes.'

'T'ra then.'

Bridie nodded her head, unsmiling, at the bent woman. 'T'ra.'

She banged on the next door. Business was better than she had dreamed possible. And her fears had been vivid. Closed doors and angry, hostile faces. Jeers and menaces. Instead, she met suspicion, then caution, then a reticent, concealed relief at the small sums she'd loan, and the unheard-of low interest rates.

'It bein' Christmas, we're real pushed,' they said, one after another. The moneybelt was getting lighter and lighter as coins changed hands, and the notebook's pages were filling fast. As early winter night set in, Bridie made a note of the next address, for tomorrow, and turned to retrace her footsteps back to Ethel's house. She felt tired, shaky after all that bottled-up apprehension and tension, which had gradually seeped away as the day wore on and she'd begun to realise that she'd fallen, by sheer good chance, into something for which there was a great need. She could hardly believe her success, and, tightening the moneybelt, loosened from good business, hurried home to count up the profits that should start making her a living of sorts from the start of the following week.

When she let herself in through Ethel's front door, she heard Lizzie's voice out the back, where Ethel was getting supper. Hanging her heavy shawl up on the nail by the door, she slowly untied the moneybelt and walked through to the scullery.

'Hello, Lizzie.'

Her friend spun round from peeling potatoes over a colander in the sink. 'Bridie!' She dropped the peeler and ran, wet hands and all, to hug her.

'How long have you been here?' asked Bridie, still holding the moneybelt.

'A couple of hours. Ethel kindly said I could wait. I wanted to see you, and I've been trying to find you everywhere. Bridie, what on earth has happened? Why are you here? What's going on? Why haven't you told me?'

Bridie put out her hands to stem the flood of questions. 'Wait a minute.' She raised her eyebrows 'Have you seen anyone back at the square?'

'Yes, Mrs Goode. She said Francis wasn't seeing anyone, and that you'd gone but she didn't know where, and that so far as she knew you wouldn't be back. Oh, Bridie, she'd been crying, I could tell, and I've been so worried.'

'How'd you find me, then?'

'I bumped into Susan over in the High Street, and she told me.'

'What else did she say?'

'Nothing. Please, Bridie, what has happened?'

'Ethel, is David with Susan?'

'Yes,' said Ethel. 'She took him over the Roman to do a bit o' shoppin'.'

'Come on up with me, then,' said Bridie to Lizzie, 'and I'll tell you.'

The two women climbed the stairs, Bridie groaning softly that her feet ached fit to kill. She sat on the edge of her chair and began to unbutton her boots, while Lizzie perched on the side of the bed and watched her, agog with curiosity.

'Well?' she demanded, when Bridie showed no sign of saying anything.

'Oh, Lizzie, I don't know what to say, or where to start. It's a pickle an' I'm doing my best to get out of it. Francis and me, we fell out over something that happened a long time ago. He's an unforgiving man, Lizzie. He sees things good or bad, black or white, but not much in between. And there was something between us that he couldn't ever let go, that's what he said, and I knew it was true, so I came away for good. It wasn't any use stopping there. Even for David. It would just have been a misery for everyone.'

She looked at Lizzie for the first time. 'So here we are. Ethel's being very kind, and giving me a chance to pull myself together. Her and Susan, they've been such a help. I don't know what I'd do without them. Even Ted's good to us.'

Lizzie looked upset. 'Why didn't you tell me? Why do all this in secret?'

'I haven't. It all happened too quickly, and I've had so little time, and so much on my mind. I was going to come and see you, of course I was.'

'Whatever it was happened suddenly? It wasn't Rosa, was it?'

'Well,' said Bridie hesitantly, 'Rosa didn't make things easy, and the way Francis spoke of her, it did upset me. But by itself that wouldn't have driven us apart. It was this other old thing, and it's done and gone as far as I'm concerned, but it never will be for him.'

Lizzie was desperately curious, but didn't like to ask any more questions. 'Oh,' was all she said.

'Any road, as Ethel says. . . .' Bridie smiled. 'How's things with you?'

Lizzie beamed. 'The house is lovely. I walk round it when no one else is there, and hug myself. It's like having a doll's house to play with, only it's real. Jonathan walks to Bart's every morning, and it only takes him ten minutes.'

They'd rented a house in a small turning by St Bartholomew's, their first real home.

'But I do feel badly. It seems all wrong that you've lost your lovely home at the very time when I'm nesting away like mad. Why don't you and David come and stay with us?'

Bridie had a moment of sore temptation. Then she shook her head. 'Thank you, Lizzie, but no. I'm going to stay here. Here, Susan will look after David for me, and today I started work. I can manage here, although it's not luxurious, without imposing on anyone. And I would be imposing on you and Jonathan, even if you were kind enough to pretend I wasn't.'

They sat quietly while Lizzie thought that over.

'You can understand if anyone can,' said Bridie into the silence. 'You're independent. You always have been. You've got a real job, a real training, and if anything happened to you and Jonathan, you can look after yourself. That's what I want—independence. I want to live . . . how can I say what I mean? . . . for myself.'

Lizzie nodded. 'I think I understand,' she said slowly, 'but you're making it hard on yourself, doing it this way.'

'Well, it is hard. That's a fact. and I won't pretend it ain't. But I'm doing it the way I want to.'

'Ethel said you're going out moneylending. Isn't that dangerous?'

Bridie drew her nail over her skirt thoughtfully. 'Yes, I 'spect it could be. But I haven't got what you've got by way of schooling and things, so I have to use what I can do, and I decided to try going into business. I don't know yet whether it'll work, but what matters is that I decided to try, and I am.'

Lizzie eyed her with respect. ' 'course, you could try applying for something like nurse training?' she suggested.

Bridie shook her head stubbornly. 'Lizzie, shut up. I've said what I'm doing, and that's it.'

Lizzie laughed out loud. 'And you say Francis is stubborn! There's nothing to choose between the two of you. Stubborn as mules, the both of you.'

Bridie grinned. 'Come on, let's go and give Ethel a hand. You stopping for supper?'

'If I may. I'd like to see David.'

When Susan arrived, pink-cheeked with cold, the three women were busy setting and serving stew and vegetables, edging round each other in the cramped space. Susan and David added to the crowd, and David was put to sit at the table, out of the way. They were just ready when Ted came in, stamping frozen feet and his big ears all red with cold, saying he was hungry as a horse. Steam rose in mouthwatering clouds from the pan on the table, and the chatter of women's voices became subdued as they all picked up knives and forks, eagerly attacking their piled plates. The clatter of cutlery stopped conversation altogether for a while, as they sat elbow to elbow round the table. One by one, they pushed their chairs back a bit and wiped their mouths. David wanted a drink of water, and Bridie squeezed between chairs and the wall to get to the scullery. On the way she put her hands on Lizzie's shoulders. As she got behind the chair, she bent and planted a kiss on her friend's cheek.

'Thanks for coming tonight.'

Lizzie smiled up at her.

'She'll do all right, ducks, you see if she doesn't,' said Ethel from across the table.

Looking round the steamy little room at the circle of good-natured faces, Lizzie's heart was warmed for her friend. She would be all right here, indeed she would.

Three days before Christmas business had been so good that Bridie's moneybelt was empty by early afternoon. She was glad to turn homewards. An unexpected warm spell had brought fog, which had been getting denser as the day went on. Passers-by coughed and cursed. The streets were hazardous enough when you could see what you were walking in, but horrible when you were fumbling blindly along in what promised to be a real pea-souper. She was almost at Ethel's front door, when she heard a voice calling her cautiously from above. Looking up, the fog stinging her eyes and nostrils, she could just make out Ethel's round anxious face, hanging out of the upstairs window.

'Oi, Bridie?' she called.

'What you got the window open for, in this?' Bridie called back.

'I bin watching out fer yer. You got a visitor. In the front room.'

Bridie peered up through the murk. 'Who?'

'Mr 'olmes. Yer 'usband, ducks.'

'Oh.' Bridie paused, then asked: 'Is David there, too?'

'Yes. It's too foggy for 'im to go out. Anyroad, I didn't want fer you to get a shock. So I come up 'ere to see if I could spot you comin'.'

'Thank you, Ethel,' said Bridie, coughing into mittened hands. 'I'll go in and see him.'

She found Francis sitting in the parlour, looking ill at ease, with David on his knee. They avoided one another's eyes. Bridie hung her shawl on its nail.

'Hullo, Francis,' she said, with her back to him.

'Bridie.' Unseen, Francis ducked his head in greeting.

She sat down on a chair opposite him and smoothed her skirt over her knees. Damp clung to the fabric. It smelled of fog.

'Did you want something, comin' here?' she asked after a bit.

Francis made a thing of transferring David to his other knee. The child wriggled and slid off, running to Bridie. Sitting on his mother's lap, he stuck his fingers in his mouth and solemnly stared at his father.

'I came to see my son,' started Francis, 'and to try to talk to you.' He folded his hands round one knee and leant forward earnestly. 'I believe we are making a mistake, Bridie. I don't think you should go on like this.'

'Why not?'

He gestured round the room. 'It's not right for you and David.'

'What *is* right for me an' David?'

'I think you should come back to the house, and we'll work something out.'

'No,' said Bridie flatly.

Francis took a deep breath. 'Look, my dear, please try to be reasonable. We must think of David. Bridie?'

A dull flush reddened her cheeks. 'You got a nerve,'

she said in a quiet voice. 'You come 'ere, telling me what's right and wrong. "Should this, and should that"—just like when we got married. It's all "my son" and what everyone else oughter do. I don't want to come back and be worked out. You hear?' Her voice was rising.

Francis was shocked. Bridie had always been respectful. He dismissed the memory of the last time she'd shouted. She'd been under strain. Upset. That baby had been a terrible thing for them both.

'You don't mean this,' he began. 'I'm sure if you consider. . . .'

Bridie's temper erupted. 'Who do you think you are to tell me what I mean? I mean what I say. No, Francis, David an' me are stopping here. Is that simple enough for you to understand? We're stopping 'ere.'

Her rudeness shook him. 'I don't recognise you,' he muttered.

They sat, each shaking from the anger that hung round their heads, thick as the fog outside. Francis rubbed his eyes with finger and thumb, then sat, head bowed, pinching the bridge of his nose.

'I cannot believe that this is what you want.'

'Since when did you ever ask me what I wanted?'

'Weren't you happy, then? Was that all a sham?'

'It was you that talked about sham!' she cried. 'You! I couldn't stay after what you said to me, and I ain't never comin' back. So you might as well go now, because nothing you can say is goin' to make any difference.'

Francis got up stiffly. 'I shall make some financial arrangements for my son,' he said coldly, 'and will inform you of them.'

'He's not legally yours. You can arrange what you like, but he's mine when it comes to it.'

White-faced, Francis faced her. 'His illegitimacy,' the word was cruelly stressed, 'is on your head. You refused to listen to reason, then as now. I shall not try to talk to you again.' He slammed the front door behind his departing figure, and vanished immediately into the fog.

Ethel stuck her head round the door. 'You all right, ducks?' she asked.

Bridie began to laugh and half cry at the same time. 'Oh, Ethel! If you could have seen it. He's so . . . so . . . what is it? Pompous. I don't know how I stood it. He wants me to go back, and he's no idea how to ask. I couldn't.'

'Well,' said Ethel, 'I can understand after what you told me, but it do seem an awful lot to give up.'

Bridie sobered down. 'It is,' she agreed, 'but I'd be miserable, however much comfort money would give us. It'd never be worth it, Ethel. You've got a lovely man in Ted. You don't know what it's like to have a man speak to you like Francis does to me. I ain't desperate enough to put up with that.'

'Well, least said, soonest mended. There's enough bin said already, I reckon,' said Ethel briskly. 'Let's make a pot of tea, and I'll be quiet while you go over your books. If all that writin' in your little book is anythin' to go by, you're thrivin'.'

Bridie, carrying David, who had watched the whole episode in silence, went down the dark little hall to the back room, and setting the child to play with an old pan and some wooden bricks, spread her elbows on the kitchen table. She was soon absorbed in rows of figures, and simple interest sums. Ethel sat sipping hot, sweet tea, and threaded cotton reels on to string to make a pullalong toy for David. The room was cosily busy.

I feel that comfortable with them two, it's like 'avin' another daughter, thought Ethel, looking at Bridie's bent head. I'm sorry on account of the little un, but fer meself, I'm glad she ain't going.

Chapter Seventeen

They were shelling peas in Ethel's kitchen when Susan made her announcement.

'I'm ever so sorry, Bridie,' she said, 'but I 'ad a message to go see that Mrs Anderson that lives over near St Dunstan's. They've got a big house near the vicarage, if you know the one I mean. Her husband's a businessman in the City, she told me. Anyway, she's expecting next month, and wants a nurserymaid. She's offered it to me, and it's live-in and ever such good wages. So I said I would.'

Susan didn't say that it had been Angus Hamilton who'd recommended her, unaware of Bridie's dependence. After all, she said to herself when the question first came up, you have to take your chances in life, however they come up. And Mrs Anderson spoke to her so nice, she couldn't turn down an offer like that. All the same, she'd dreaded telling Bridie.

She needn't have worried. Bridie had noticed that Susan had been restless of late, and sympathised with her wanting to move away from home and Ethel once more.

'It's all right, Susan,' she said. 'Don't take on. I

253

expected it. It's been real kind of you to take David as long as you have. I don't take no offence.'

Susan broke into a happy smile. 'You really don't mind? I was worried to death about it.'

'Of course I mind,' said Bridie, 'but only because there's no one as good as you with David. He's known you since he was a new baby, and he'll miss you.'

'What'll you do?' asked Ethel.

'Look after him myself. Not much else I can do, is there?'

Angus would have been more than upset if he'd known.

The morning Bridie left him, Francis slept so long that in the end Mrs Goode panicked and asked Dr Hamilton if he'd step round to have a look at him. Angus had taken in the scene at a glance.

'What's happened?' he asked the housekeeper. 'He's drunk as a lord. That's not like Frank.'

Dora hesitated.

'Come now,' said Angus, 'you've called me in, so you'd better spill the beans as to why this house feels like a funeral parlour this afternoon.'

He folded his arms across his chest, and waited for an explanation.

'She's gone and left,' Dora said.

'Who's left? Bridie?' Angus sounded astonished. 'What do you mean?'

Dora's hauteur collapsed suddenly, and she sat down abruptly on a kitchen chair. 'Have a seat,

Doctor.' She waved at the chair at the end of the table.

'All right. From the beginning,' said Angus.

'I don't rightly know what's brought it to a head,' explained the housekeeper, 'but they've been very standoffish and silent with each other ever since Rosa was born.'

Angus nodded. 'I know that caused a great strain. But I hoped they'd come to terms with it and, not get over it, exactly, but at least put some of the bitterness behind them.'

'They wasn't very forgiving, either of 'em, if you ask me,' said Mrs Goode. 'Then this morning I come in, and there's Bridie packing her bag and putting David's coat on. She just said not to disturb Mr Holmes, and never said where she was going, just that she'd be off, and not to expect her back. She didn't look as if she'd slept a wink. I thought they must have had a to-do, and that she'd be back, but she never. I ain't seen her since. I feel all cut up about it, Doctor, I can tell you. And I'm worried about him.' She jerked her head at Francis.

Angus pulled one of Francis's eyelids up. 'Nothing there that aspirin and black coffee won't cure,' he said.

Francis, disturbed by the cursory examination, stirred and groaned.

'Hello, old chap,' said Angus heartily, as Francis painfully opened the same eye. Then the other one. He winced at the loud voice.

Angus grinned maliciously. 'Head hurt, does it?'

Francis raised a hand and cautiously touched his forehead. 'Oh my,' he muttered, 'it's agony.'

'You've indulged yourself rather freely, by the look of you,' said Angus. He saw the brandy bottle rolled under the chair and bent to pick it up. 'Aha! The best stuff. Seventy per cent proof. You'll be having a splendid hangover for a while yet.'

'Shhh,' begged Francis.

'Medication, please, Mrs Goode,' ordered Angus, ignoring the plea. While Dora went into the scullery to fill the kettle, Angus looked sternly at his wretched patient. 'What on earth brought this about?' he asked.

Francis started to shake his head, and his eyes glassed over.

'I'd keep rather still, if I were you,' said his medical adviser.

'She's left me,' Francis admitted in a low voice.

'Good Lord, has she really? Do you want to tell me what's happened?'

'No.' The one word had a bleak and final sound about it.

'Verra well,' conceded the doctor. 'It's not my business. But for her to take off, it must have been bad. She's a loyal little lassie, one of the best. You've lost a treasure, there, Frank.' He shook his head at his friend. 'And it's no good carrying on like this. If ye can't make it up, then at least accept it with a bit of dignity.'

'Make up?' asked Francis, holding his head. 'She said she was going for good.'

'Where?'

'She didn't say.'

'Well, man, ye've to find her, and maybe, if you ask her, she'll come back again.'

'Thank you for your advice,' said Francis as Mrs Goode came through the door, preceded by the fragrance of boiling coffee. Francis pulled a face as she clattered cups and saucers on to the table.

'And the doctor says these as well,' she said, putting two aspirin into Francis's shaky hand. He sipped cautiously at the scalding drink.

'That's getting better, though my head still goes round.'

'Aye, it will for a while. Fresh air and some exercise when you feel fit enough. That's the best cure.'

Angus stood up to leave. 'I'd try to find her, and talk to her,' he repeated his counsel as he left the room.

So Francis asked Mrs Goode to make enquiries, and it was only a matter of hours before the news came down the prolific East End grapevine that Bridie was staying at Ethel's. The outcome of the advice was that Francis eventually found her that foggy, clammy afternoon, and returned, still alone, sourly reflecting that Angus didn't know as much about women as he liked to think.

Now Angus had put a spoke in her wheel for sure. Bridie gave the matter some thought, then asked Susan a favour.

'Could you nip over and get David's carriage?' she asked the nurserymaid. 'Mrs Goode will let you in, I'm sure. And they've no use for it. There's not much space for it here, but we'll just have to manage.'

She obliged, and was eagerly offered tea by the housekeeper, all agog for news. 'She sends her regards,' Susan said on her return, 'and says to tell you she misses you an' David.'

'I miss her, too,' said Bridie absently. She was examining the inside of the carriage. 'It's a little dusty, but it'll do the trick nicely. With some blankets and a cushion, he'll be able to sleep even though it'll be a bit small.'

She turned to Susan. 'I'll look after him meself. We'll go round together. It's good quality, not hard to push, and it won't likely do him no harm to be out in the air. Not so good when it's foggy or pourin' with rain, but we'll cross them bridges when we come to them.'

And so Susan went off the following week to Mrs Anderson, and, bundling an excited David into the baby carriage, Bridie left Ethel's house at seven in the morning, moneybelt full and paperwork tucked down at the end of the carriage, by the child's feet.

'Off we go to work,' chirruped Bridie cheerily as she began to push. David clapped his hands, and looked over the side at the uneven cobbled street.

'Off we go, off we go,' the high little voice sang back.

Bridie's back ached after an hour or two, but having David with her gave an unexpected turn to her doorstep negotiations.

'That your son?' asked one housewife after another.

Bridie said he was her son.

'Well, I never!' was the general response. Her regular customers smiled benignly at the carriage, and seemed rather pleased that the moneylender had a child. The slums of Plaistow, which made up Bridie's business territory for the most part, were sufficiently removed from Tredegar Square, in every respect, for Bridie to go unremarked as anything other than the Irish woman what lent out at decent rates.

She took to hiding her hair, and so to some extent her youth, under a headscarf which she tied tightly under her chin and round the back of her neck. Men looked speculatively after her sometimes, but she had a no-nonsense way, and a ready tongue for them as got cheeky, so that for the most part they merely looked and gave her a wide berth. Women found her honest and straight. Not generous. She was never generous. If you couldn't pay, you was in trouble, and the interest promptly mounted up something alarming. But if she treated her clients with unsentimental manners, she treated 'em fair. They agreed on that.

So she became a familiar figure, pushing her carriage, trudging from door to door in a pair of black men's boots and long skirts in drab colours. Always the headscarf to disguise the glorious hair underneath, and deepening frown lines on her forehead as she wore down stub after stub of pencil, noting, lending, collecting, calculating. Weary, footsore, often soaked and chilled to the bone, Bridie went her rounds, month after month after month, until the months began to turn into years. Business flourished and David grew.

One spring morning, just after David's fourth birthday, Bridie was on her way to collect a debt that had been outstanding for too long. She was in a determined mood. The woman who owed the money made excuses. Bridie occasionally encountered bad debts, but her personal appearance on the doorstep, regular as clockwork, and the fact that she didn't lend more than she reckoned the borrower could afford, meant that usually her accounts balanced pretty well. David dawdled behind her. He'd found a bit of stick in the gutter, and was dragging it in the dirt to make patterns.

'Come along,' called his mother, leaning on the well-worn carriage. She hitched up her moneybelt which was so full, it sagged. Fridays were usually busy, with people needing more of everything because the men were at home all day of a Sunday.

David ignored her.

'Oh, come on, do,' she repeated. Leaving the carriage, she went back to get him. 'Come on, get in. I haven't got all day.' She picked up the child and popped him inside. As she pushed him, protesting, round the next corner, she came face to face with two men.

'Hello darlin',' said the bigger of the two. 'We bin waitin' fer you.'

Bridie looked from one to the other. 'What d'you want?' she demanded brusquely.

'That,' said the big man, pointing to the moneybelt.

Bridie glanced up and down the street. A few front doors stood open, and a dog rooted hopefully in a heap of rubbish fifty yards away. Otherwise it was empty.

'There's no one about,' sneered the smaller one, a fat creature with tattoos on the back of his pudgy hands.

'Let's be having it quick,' said the first one. He started to move towards her.

'Shove off! I'll have the law on you,' shouted Bridie, standing her ground.

'Aw, give it 'ere,' called Podge, following his partner nearer. He raised a clenched fist. 'Don't want yer nose broke, do yer, love?'

The taller, bearded thief glanced up and down the street. 'Cut the cackle,' he ordered. 'Take it off.'

'No,' said Bridie.

They moved in. One fist landed on her cheek, and the shaggy man's rough hands scrabbled at her clothes, trying to find the fastening to undo the belt. Bridie screamed with shock and fury. She lashed out ferociously with clawed fingers, and drew two long red scratches down Podge's face. He roared and stepped back, shaking his head. The tall man had an arm round her neck, trying to hold her still, while with his other hand he pulled clumsily at the belt.

'Give me an 'and,' he shouted at Podge, who was wiping blood off his cheek.

Bridie fought and twisted away from his grasp, and, feeling Podge coming at her a second time, made a last desperate effort. She jabbed the tall man viciously in the midriff with her elbow.

'Ouff!' he gasped. His face darkened with pain and rage as he let her go. 'You've asked for it, now, you bloody cow!' he snarled. He raised a huge fist. Bridie swung at him and her skirt swirled up round her knees with the force of the movement. The beard split open into a howl of agony as the steel toe of her man's boot dislodged his kneecap.

An incoherent string of obscenities rolled frantically off his tongue as he hopped, staggered and finally fell, rolling into the gutter.

Podge stood with his mouth open. 'Gawd!' he said finally.

The commotion brought people to their doorsteps. A row of faces up and down the street watched the progress of the fight with detached interest. No one would have dreamed of interfering.

' 'ere, you all right?' Podge asked his partner, voice querulous with fright. 'I'm off, or we'll 'ave the Law turnin' up.'

Bridie glared at him. 'I'll break *your* knees an' all, if I ever set eyes on you again. Push off, yer fat bastard.'

Podge fled.

Bridie went over to where the injured man sat holding his leg, tears running down into his whiskers. She drew back her foot. He let out a howl of terror.

'You bloody hellcat! Gerroff,' he yelled, shrinking from her in panic.

Bridie put her foot down again, slowly. 'You come near me again, an' I'll cripple you. You hear?'

He nodded, too agonised to speak.

262

She swung on her heel and, grabbing the carriage, wheeled a frightened and fascinated David in a defiant march straight up the middle of the street. On either side, people watched her.

'Be a while afore anyone tangles with her again,' they murmured to each other.

When Bridie had long disappeared in the direction of Stepney and her defaulting customer, Podge crept back to his cursing would-be partner in crime.

'You want an' 'and down the London?' he enquired.

'Took you bleedin' long enough to come an' ask, dinnit?' replied his friend ungraciously. He allowed Podge to haul him to his feet, and leaning heavily against the little man, he hobbled and scraped off down the street, cursing women at every excruciating step. He emerged some hours later from the Accident Department, knee in plaster and propped on a pair of wooden crutches.

Word soon got round that Bridie had put a bloke in plaster, and the fight was described in ever more dramatic and spectacular terms in public houses from the far end of Stratford to the other side of the Commercial Road.

Bridie herself had had to sit down when she got out of sight. Her legs simply gave way. David clamoured to be let out of the carriage, so she let him out, stick and all, to play in the gutter while she sat, head on her arms, and waited for the trembling and sick feeling to pass.

'It was strange,' she said, when peacable Ted,

intrigued, asked her if the rumours were true, 'I never even hit anyone before, but when they threatened me, I was so scared, and so furious, that I'd have done anything to stop them. They might have hurt David an' all. It was like I was another person, I was that mad.'

It was several days later that another man stopped her in the street and said he had a message for her.

'Sam Saul told me to tell you he wants to see you.'

'What for?' asked Bridie.

'I dunno. Business between you an' him, I suppose.'

'I don't have business with Sam Saul,' she said.

'If you've any sense, you'll not ignore him,' said the man. 'I'd not cross Sam if I was you.'

'Ta, anyway,' said Bridie. It wasn't wholly unexpected. Her business was doing well, and she guessed she must be having some effect on the loansharks whose territory she worked.

'Tell Sam Friday afternoon, I'll stop by and see him then.'

'Righto,' said the messenger agreeably. 'Friday. I'll tell him.'

Friday came. It was nearly midsummer. Bridie asked Ethel if she'd mind her taking down the tin bath early and having a good scrub. Ethel helped heat the water, then stood guard in case of anyone dropping in. Bridie washed and dried and brushed her hair until it shone. Working out of doors had turned her naturally pale complexion a dusky, glowing rose. She presented herself to Ethel and said, 'What d'you think?'

Ethel turned her round and said, 'Very nice. You'll bowl 'im over.'

Bridie laughed. 'That's just what I mean to do.'

She'd exchanged her steel-tipped boots for fashionably heeled leather shoes. Her bare ankles were slender and her hips in the low-waisted yellow dress were slim. Constant exercise had fined her down, and from the chrysalis of the dowdy workaday drudge emerged an elegant, confident woman. Only her hands betrayed her. Surveying her broken nails and the stains from ceaseless handling of coins, she sighed. Rubbing glycerine in, to soften them, she had to concede that they were no lady's hands.

'Ah, well,' she remarked to Ethel. 'Sam will probably see them as signs of success. All that money they've handled!' she gave a mock leer and rubbed her fingers together greedily.

'You be careful with that Sam Saul,' cautioned Ethel.

Bridie grinned in reply. 'Got a reputation, ain't he?'

'Yes. And not just for meanness, neither. You watch your step there.'

Bridie twirled an ankle, kissed David goodbye and said, 'Be good for Ethel, now.'

Out on the street, men stared. She walked carefully in the unaccustomed heels, head down against the appraising looks. It took her almost an hour to walk across to Stepney, to the corner shop above which she saw the familiar boarded and wired windows of the loanshark's offices. She sniffed derisively. They were hated, the big boys, and went in fear of their lives, avoiding ever setting foot in the back streets where there wasn't a soul what wouldn't look the other way if one of them them was to be found in the gutter. They'd be left there for dead. She found the door round the back, barred and bolted, with a small steel grille in the top. She pushed the bell and waited. The grille squeaked as it was pulled back, and a woman peered out.

'Yes?'

'I've got an appointment,' said Bridie. 'Mrs O'Neill.'

The grille squeaked shut and moments later the door was pulled half open. The woman gestured her in. 'Hurry up.' she said, anxious to throw the bolts again, just in case.

Bridie climbed the narrow stairs behind the woman's fat, tired legs. A small anteroom held several filing cabinets and a desk with a huge diary open on top. It was covered in tiny, regular handwriting, and down each page, at the edge, ran columns of figures. The woman saw Bridie glance at it, and hurried round the desk to close the book.

'Ain't your business,' she said, rheumy eyes staring up at Bridie. A door behind her swung open.

'Mrs Holmes? Come in.'

The man who stood smiling in the doorway was so tall his head brushed the door jamb. He had beautifully groomed glossy black hair, and a neatly trimmed beard. Elegant eyebrows rose as his black eyes took in every detail of the woman standing before him. They widened appreciatively. Handsome, rich and suave, he was used to drawing attention from women, but this one was unusual. An expensive education had removed all but a trace of his Yiddish accent.

'Come in, Mrs Holmes,' he repeated.

Bridie walked round the desk under the hostile stare of the receptionist and followed Sam Saul's gesture to the chair beneath the window, to the side of his desk. There were more filing cabinets, tops were piled high with ledgers. Gaslamps burned at each end of the narrow room, as the windows let in only a suggestion of light. Bridie felt it was a place where it might get hard to breathe.

'You asked for me to come and see you,' she opened the conversation. 'Why did you do that?'

Sam Saul spread his hands. 'We are in the same business, and it has come to my attention that you are proving remarkably successful. I like success, and I wanted to meet you.'

'I get by,' acknowledged Bridie.

'You more than get by, I think,' replied Sam. 'According to my accounts you are doing much better than that.'

'I make a small profit.'

'Mrs Holmes, let us not beat about the bush. You are proving a little expensive to my own operations. You have encroached on the small loans market, and you have done it so successfully that you are affecting my profits. I have asked you here to discuss what we might do to remedy the situation.'

Bridie smiled sweetly. 'You run a real big empire. How can someone like me affect you?'

'I have just told you. You are taking my customers.'

'We all have to earn a living, Mr Saul.'

'Sam.'

'We all have to work, Sam.'

'I work for profit, Mrs Holmes, and you are taking some that rightly belongs to me.'

'Well, what do you want, then?'

Sam Saul hesitated. When he'd sent for her, he'd seen her in the distance a couple of times, and had remembered with indifference a drab figure in large men's boots. Now she was in front of him, he felt far from indifferent. He admired the combination of beauty, toughness and high spirits. It appealed to a man who was himself ruthlessly greedy under the smooth, urbane manner. He contemplated her through half-closed eyes, wondering how much she'd give.

'Is it true you broke a man's knee?' he asked at last.

'He attacked me. I kicked him. I never meant to hurt him bad.'

He looked at the slim figure, and shook his head wonderingly. 'You are a very determined lady, Mrs Holmes. Or may I call you Bridie?'

'You've been checking up on me, haven't you?' she asked calmly.

'Well, I was curious,' he admitted.

'Then you know I've got what you might call connections.'

'That is true,' he agreed. 'One might say you are not entirely what you seem.'

Bridie crossed her legs, and Sam's eyes followed the movement. 'How about a partnership?' she suggested bluntly.

Sam felt the interview beginning to slip away from him. *He* was supposed to be doing the bargaining. *He'd* called *her*. He was the aggrieved party. He gazed at her, surprised and discomfited.

Bridie crossed her legs again, and her skirt slipped accidentally over her knees. She straightened it. Sam, mesmerised, cleared his throat.

'A partnership? What sort?'

The grey eyes looked straight into his. 'You'll fund me for larger deals. Not often, because I don't get much call for that kind of money. But I'd like to be able to if I want. And at a quarter the rates you charge. In return I'll pay you a percentage on my everyday business of one quarter of one per cent.'

Sam threw back his head and roared with laughter. Bridie folded her hands in her lap demurely. 'You mean it?' Sam stopped laughing.

'Yes.'

'Many deals like that, and I'd be out of business.'

'A deal like that, and we can both stay in business and help each other.' Bridie's voice was amiable.

'Whatever makes you think I need help?' Sam spoke in astonishment.

'You can't just run me off the streets,' said Bridie composedly, 'because if you tried I'd have the law on you. I ain't ignorant. I listen to a lot of people in a lot of places, and I hear things, Sam Saul, that could put you in prison.'

His mouth went grim. 'You trying to blackmail me?'

'Isn't that what you called me here to do?' retorted

Bridie. She rose from her chair and, walking elegantly across the room, perched herself on the edge of his desk. He found he couldn't think straight.

'So I thought a deal that made it easier for both of us?' she suggested.

His black eyes stared unwaveringly back at her. This close, he could see all the tiny freckles on her nose.

For the first time in his life, Sam Saul gave in. 'You got a deal,' he agreed. What he wouldn't do to have this woman! Reading his mind precisely, Bridie slipped off the desk.

'That's that, then,' she said briskly.

'I'll have to see you again, go over details. Paper-work,' he said quickly.

She nodded. 'You know where I live. You're welcome to stop by and we can go over it.'

She watched him struggle with his feelings. He lost.

'Very well.' He pushed himself out of his chair, hands on his desk.

'I'll see myself out,' she said, opening the door to the tiny outer office. 'If this lady will kindly unlock the front door.'

Sam waved a hand at the receptionist, defeated. 'Go ahead,' he said. 'Whatever you like.'

It was a meeting he never forgot. Bridie giggled herself almost into hysterics, so that she tottered in her heels and had to take them off, walking barefoot on the baked earth at the road's edge, laughing out loud to the amazement of passers by.

Chapter Eighteen

Ethel gave a cry of delight and waved a sheet of notepaper at Bridie.

'He's comin' home,' she declared happily. 'Our Edward's got leave.'

'When?' asked Bridie.

Ethel consulted the letter again. 'He says he'll be docked at Portsmouth from the first week in September. Ooh, that's not long, is it? It's only another ten days. And they're stopping for six weeks. Ooh, ain't it lovely.'

Bridie agreed it was, but it gave her something to think about. She'd paid Ethel extra and had Susan's room for David, except for when Susan came home for a rare night away from the Anderson nursery. Edward would no doubt want his room back, and it would make for a very squashed household, especially if Ethel's son was built on the same scale as his mum.

Pushing the carriage round dried-up pot-holes, while David chased pigeons, Bridie decided that she'd have to move. Sam Saul had been right. She was doing well, and the profits in the heavy steel box under her bed were mounting. She could, if she was careful, afford a place of her own. But it meant moving out of Ethel's friendly, homely house, and she loved it there. She'd been in two minds about it for a long time, but now, with Edward coming back, it seemed she would have to get on with it and take a decision.

That Saturday she hung up her working clothes and put on the same silky yellow frock she'd worn to go and see Sam Saul. The sun was warm on her bare arms as she went down the High Street in Plaistow, studying the advertisements in agents' windows. Reaching the end of the parade of shops, she turned back and resolutely opened the first one's door. The woman inside was kind, and went through her property list for Bridie, but there was nothing in the right place, at the right rent.

'Sorry, dearie,' she said affably. 'You could come and try again next week.'

Bridie smiled and nodded and went out of the gloom into the brilliant sunshine. She screwed her eyes up against the glare, and saw the next agents a little further up. The man in there was helpful, too.

'I tell you what,' he suggested, when he'd listened to what she wanted, 'there's something a bit different that might interest you. Depends how you feel about graves.' He grinned.

Bridie raised her eyebrows.

'Corner of Hermit and Grange Roads. On the corner by the entrance to the Cemetery. There's an end of terrace house. It's standard – two up, two down, privy outside. It's goin' a bit cheap on account of

being so close to the graveyard. Lot of funerals, you
see. Some people mind.'

'How much?' asked Bridie.

'Well,' drawled the young man, 'round there you'd
expect to pay ten shillin' a week, but for you, this
one's nine and six.'

Bridie was silent. A house of her own. Alone for the
first time in her life. What a wonderful idea!

'Can I go and see it?' she asked.

' 'course,' nodded the agent. He fetched his hat
and together they walked the length of Upper Street,
and down to the huge graveyard gates.

'Get a good view of all the best buryin's,' joked the
agent, as they turned into the weedy little front
garden. Two upstairs windows and one by the front
door, all peeling brown paint. Bridie could smell the
soot on the bricks. The agent went round the side and
unlocked the back door. Inside was as unprepossessing
as outside. Peeling green and brown walls flanked a
range thick with cold, dirt-encrusted grease. Nothing
had been cleaned, ever. Bridie went into the front
room. Dark, as well as filthy, because the windows let
in only smeary grey light.

'You expecting nine and six for this?' she
demanded sarcastically. 'Pigs might fly! It's gloomy
as the grave in here, never mind over the way.'

She didn't say anything about the view out of the
back bedroom, straight into the leafy branches of a
great old apple tree standing in waist-deep grass.

'Well,' said the agent hopefully, 'an adjustment
might be possible. It does need a bit of paint. Not,' he

added hastily, 'as there's anything wrong with the structure. Sound as a bell.'

Bridie stared at him derisively until his eyes dropped.

'Six shillin'?' she offered.

'Not a chance. You'll lose me my job,' retorted the young man.

Bridie wandered to the grimy window and looked round. She had a vision. Fresh brown paint on the walls, the range scoured and blackleaded 'til it shone, reflecting its own cosy glow of an evening. Cotton curtains at windows polished bright, two big armchairs, a box of knitting by the hearth. . . .

'You interested or what?' demanded the agent, getting impatient.

'Seven and six.' Bridie spoke in her take-it-or-leave-it voice.

'Oh, all right. Good thing I don't get many of you.' He hid his relief. The place had been on the books ages.

'I'll come back with you and pay the rent in advance now,' said Bridie, making up her mind on the spot.

'Won't your old man want to see it first?' enquired the agent cautiously.

'It's for me,' said Bridie. 'And my son.'

'Oh.' The man was taken aback. 'We don't usually rent to ladies, it's generally their husbands.'

'Rent's rent, and if it's paid regular what's it matter to you?' asked Bridie defiantly.

The man shrugged. He'd noted the wedding ring. War widow? He eyed her doubtfully.

'Don't be daft. Take the rent, and be glad you've let this stinking place.'

He saw her half-smile, and knew he was beaten. 'Go on, then, we'll say no more. Rent's two weeks in advance, Tuesdays,' he grumbled.

He chatted amiably all the way back, but Bridie listened with less than half an ear. She was planning her decorating campaign.

Bridie broke the news to Ethel when she came in from shopping. Ethel dumped her string bag crossly on the table and said: 'What for? Why do you want to move out?'

'It's not that,' Bridie explained, 'but with Edward home, you and Ted need the room. Don't take offence, Ethel love. Living here, it's been like having a second mum, and I'll miss you. It's time for a change, that's all.'

Ethel was upset, though, there was no pretending she wasn't.

'All right ducks,' she said at last, 'it's not far anyway if it's this end of the cemetery.'

'Ten minutes if you dawdle, five if you hurry,' said Bridie. That didn't sound so bad. 'It's in an 'orrible state, Eth. It needs cleaning and painting before it's fit for man or beast to move into.'

'I'll be glad to lend a hand,' cried Ethel, as Bridie had hoped she would, 'and Ted'll come an' all. He's handy and willing when he's not dozy.' She laughed and pinched Bridie's cheek.

That weekend, a small crocodile made its way to Hermit Road. Bridie led the way, followed by Ethel,

275

Ted, Lizzie and Jonathan – like Snow White and her Dwarves. They carried buckets and pails, brushes and brooms, rags and scouring powder, polish, paint and blacklead for the range. Jonathan had borrowed a pair of stepladders from the porters at Bart's, swearing to have them back in their cupboard by Monday morning. David carried the picnic. Food, Lizzie said, for the workers. Herself expecting, she said she wouldn't do the strenuous stuff, but would look after David.

Bridie stood aside to let Lizzie go in first. She stood looking round with the practised eye of a housewife.

'It's pretty,' she cried. 'Underneath all that muck, it's lovely. What a find. You have been lucky.'

Ethel, still smarting from Bridie's desertion, conceded that it would be a dear little house, looked after proper.

Jonathan and Ted exchanged meaningful looks. Women! They rolled up their sleeves, wrapped themselves in old aprons it wouldn't matter if they ruined, and settled down to stripping old paint and paper. Bridie drew a bucket of cold water and started on the horrid job of cleaning the range. Ethel began on the windows. Seeing everyone busy, Lizzie took David out into the garden at the back.

He gave a whoop of joy and raced into the jungle that flourished between the back wall of the house and the broken wooden fence some eighty yards away. Brambles, thistles and columbine grew densely among the tall grasses. A prickly thicket of gooseberry bushes made an impenetrable wall down one

side. The apple tree was covered in tiny green fruit
that would ripen and fall in the autumn. David found
a stick and sent thistle fairies spinning in the air.
Lizzie sneezed and brushed seeds from her skirt. A
movement under the gooseberries caught her eye.

'What's this, David?' she called to the little boy.

He stopped decapitating plants and came to look.
Hidden in the undergrowth was a nest. Safe beneath
the prickles a mother cat bared her teeth uneasily at
them. Curled by her side were two very tiny, new
kittens. David put out his hand and the cat snarled.

'Careful! Don't touch her, she's quite wild,'
warned Lizzie. 'She's worried you might touch her
kittens, and so she might bite if you went too near.'

David looked solemnly at the mother cat, who
stared back with unblinking green eyes. One of the
babies stretched and David saw the tiniest red mouth
yawn wide with contentment, then close with a little
snap.

'Ooh, babies,' he said, awed. He sat on his
haunches, keeping quite still, and watched.

'Would you like to give her some milk?' asked
Lizzie. 'The mother might like some, and we can put it
in a saucer just a little way away, so she doesn't get
frightened.'

'Yes, let's,' said David, jumping up eagerly. They
fetched a bottle of milk from the picnic basket, and
one of Ethel's saucers.

'Do you want to pour it?' asked Lizzie. 'Carefully,
now.'

Carefully, the tip of his tongue sticking out as he

concentrated, David poured milk into the saucer and pushed it towards the cat. She stiffened and nudged at her kittens to get behind her, then the smell of milk tempted her. She crept forward until she could lap at the edge of the saucer, and the milk disappeared in no time.

'Shall I get her some more?' asked David.

'Later on,' said Lizzie. 'Wait until she gets thirsty again or the milk will go off in the sun.'

'Babies like milk,' remarked David.

'They get their milk from their mother, like you did when you were a baby,' said Lizzie.

David put his hand carefully on Lizzie's big belly. 'This one too?' he asked.

Lizzie smiled down at his serious little face. 'Yes, my baby, too. Let's go and see how they're getting on indoors.'

The house was a hive of activity. Damp, mouldy paper lay in drifts on the floors. Ted was scrubbing down paintwork. He paused and looked over at Jonathan. 'Fancy a beer, mate?'

Jonathan grinned and nodded. 'Lizzie, love, what about taking David down to the pub, and fetching us a jug of ale?'

Lizzie took a shilling from Jonathan's shirt and she and David walked hand-in-hand to the nearest public house. She told the landlord they were just moving in, so he lent her a jug with a lid on it, to carry the ale.

'Hungry?' she called, unpacking the picnic basket. One by one they put down their tools, rinsed their hands under the tap and sat down, leaning against the walls, munching bread, cheese and Ethel's home-made mustard pickle.

'There's kittens in the garden,' announced David with his mouth full. 'Me and Lizzie saw them.'

'How many?' asked Ted.

'Two,' said David. 'And mother cat.'

'We gave her some milk. If you feed her regularly, she might tame,' said Lizzie.

David jumped up. 'I'll show you.' He pulled at Bridie's hand.

Outside, he pointed. 'There,' Bridie squatted down and peered into the prickles. The mother had retreated a little further back, but the two little ones were there to be seen.

'Oh, tabbies,' said Bridie. 'They'll be pretty later on.' She pulled herself upright. 'Come on, we've lots more work to do. Will you help Lizzie put the food away?' David nodded and trotted back inside.

Ted and Jonathan made heavy footsteps overhead. They'd made a start on the bedrooms. Every window was thrown wide. Loose plaster and dust hung in the air. Lizzie took a broom and began to tidy damp wall-paper into heaps. She and Ethel carried armfuls down to the end of the garden, where it could be burned later.

'She's got a job and a half on her hands,' observed Ethel, looking round.

'She'll do all right,' replied Lizzie. 'I bet you don't recognise this place in a few months' time.'

They kept going until the light faded so that indoors

you couldn't see your own hand. Ted reported the bedrooms ready for painting, and they all exclaimed over the miracle cold water and determination had wrought on the range.

'It's not that bad, actually,' said Jonathan to Bridie. 'I must say that at first I wondered what you'd got yourself into, but really it's just dirt and neglect. The house itself seems sound. I've kept an eye open for rot and what have you, but I haven't found any.'

Lizzie heaved a sigh of relief. It really was all right. Bridie grinned from ear to ear. She'd never doubted.

The tired little crocodile wound its way back to Ethel's house, where all the tools were laid ready for the next day. Lizzie and Jonathan called goodbye and goodnight from the darkness as they went home.

At first light, Bridie was up and ready, chivvying the others as they grumbled and groaned. Back in Hermit Road by six, the other two joined them at nine o'clock and the small house resounded once more to the banging and scraping and sweeping.

Late that evening six very tired people and one sleepy child looked round in triumph. Fresh flowered paper hung on walls, paint glistened in the gloom as it began to dry and the smell was thick on the air. Windows shone, letting moonlight fall on bare, scrubbed boards and gleam dully on the blackleaded range in the kitchen. Bridie's home was ready. Ethel stood, arms akimbo, surveying the scene in the dark.

'Ready when you are,' she announced to Bridie. 'We done a good job here. We should be proud of ourselves.'

Bridie hugged her, wet apron and all. 'I couldn't have done any of it without you.' She kept her arms tight around Ethel. 'Thank you,' she said, to everyone.

On Monday morning, Bridie was out first thing, round the second-hand furniture shops. A lot came from the pawnbroker, too. When she added sheets and blankets to her great heap of goods, he blessed this as his lucky day and offered her a cup of tea. Young lads came and went up the weedy front path, humping chairs and beds and carpets, cooking things and curtains, while the neighbours stared and Next Door offered tea and a piece of cake in the afternoon. The coal merchant arrived to fill the bunker at the back, and Bridie was just putting a match to the range for the first time when Ethel turned up with David in tow. She dumped a suit-case by the front door.

'That's the last of your things,' she told Bridie, who was blowing on her fire to help it catch. She wandered into the front room and saw how homely it looked. Bridie had filled a milk bottle with wildflowers from her garden and it stood before the still-drying front window, on the newly delivered oak table.

'It's lovely,' she said to Bridie, who was still trying to get the range to go. Bridie stood up at last and said she thought she'd got it going and could make tea later. The two women stood together, listening to David run around upstairs.

'It'll be good for him, you having a place of your own,' remarked Ethel generously.

'Yes,' said Bridie. 'I think it will.'

'I'd best be going along then. Let you get on.'

Bridie smiled at her. 'I'll see you every day,' she said. 'You'll hardly notice the difference.'

Ethel nodded. Then she was gone.

Late that night, as David slept in his own bed and Bridie leaned on her bedroom windowsill, she gazed at the dark shape of the apple tree, so close she could almost reach out and touch the tips of its branches. Below, in her tangled territory of gooseberries, two golden eyes stared up at the head in the window. The cat's nose snuffled and twitched at new scents on the cooling night air. People had come to stay.

Chapter Nineteen

Ethel's broad face beamed with joy as she threw her arms round Edward's broad shoulders and gave him a great big smacker, right on the mouth.

' 'ere,' she cried, holding him away from her, 'let's be lookin' at you.'

She surveyed her bearlike son from top to toe. He stood still tolerantly while she exclaimed that she thought he might, just might have got even taller since last time. He nodded good-naturedly, both of them knowing that at twenty-six he wasn't going to change much in either direction. They were so alike, mother and son. Both were tall, broad, with big, kindly features. Edward's nose was blunt and wide, just like Ethel's. But where she had brown eyes, Edward had inherited Ted's, bright blue and humorous. They lifted his features from being plain to almost handsome. The mouth, so ready to smile, grinned now at his mother.

'Come on, Mum, it's only me.'

'Only, indeed,' protested Ethel. 'You hear that, Ted? After all this time away, he says only me!'

Ted gazed at his son affectionately. He was proud

of him, standing so straight, in his blue and white uniform, on the dockside at Portsmouth.

'Come on, Eth, put him down, 'e's a big lad now,' he advised mildly.

The three of them walked slowly across the cobbles, under the shadow of the great ship that towered above them. Around them, groups of young seamen loitered, canvas bags at their feet. Mothers and fathers, sisters and brothers, gave little shrieks of delight, and everywhere there was a hugging and a kissing and a few tears wiped away on the edges of sleeves. Young wives handed bemused children into their father's stranger's arms, and older children stood aside and stared. Officers in white and gold watched from the rail high above. Two policemen sauntered past, nodding affably at the sailors.

Edward pushed his mother gently away and picked up his bag. 'Come on Mum, Dad. I've been looking forward to being home for weeks, an' all you can do is stand and stare.' He put a beefy arm round Ted's shoulders, and hoisted his bag over his own shoulder. 'Let's go.'

During the train journey back to Waterloo they chattered eagerly about his months at sea, about Susan, about Ted's promotion to foreman at Billingsgate, about this and that, and how they'd had a lodger who they'd been ever so fond of, but she'd moved out to a place of her own near the Cemetery, just in nice time for him to come home.

Edward listened to their excited voices, and the wonderful warmth of them flowed over him. His rolling stride began to quicken as they got off the tram. Within a few yards of their door, it flew open and Susan came running down the road to throw herself at Edward, who dropped his bag and caught her, swinging her round so her dress flew up and her shoes were two feet off the ground.

'Mrs Anderson said I could have the afternoon off,' she gasped, answering her mother's unspoken question. 'So here I am. Welcome home.'

She tucked her arm into her brother's, asking teasingly what he'd brought back for her this time as she led him into the house. Ethel went to put on the kettle, and there was a hubbub of voices in the small back room as they all talked at once. Edward, trying to answer a dozen questions, fished at the same time in the top of his bag for the presents that always came out to 'Oohs' and 'Aahs' of excitement and curiosity. Susan unwrapped a tiny twist of paper and found in the palm of her hand a small, pale heap of gold – a delicately engraved head of a sun god with crooked rays depicting sunlight instead of hair. There was a fine gold chain from which to hang the figure. 'I got that in Thailand,' said Edward. 'I thought it would look pretty on you.'

She held it up against her neck. 'Oh, it's beautiful. Put it on for me.' His huge hands opened and closed the tiny clasp with delicate care. 'I'll wear it always, it's so lovely,' she said, bright-eyed with delight.

For Ethel there was a shawl of Indian cotton, brilliant colours for a summer day. Ted fingered a pair of Turkish slippers, intrigued but doubtful that he'd ever quite put them on his feet. They were of soft leather, sewn with fine thread and embroidered with layers of intricate stitching.

Edward, seeing his face, laughed. 'They actually wear those in Turkey, Dad. And fezzes with tassels, and great baggy trousers. The women are veiled, and all in black robes. You can only see their eyes. It's all another world.' He shook his head. 'Things you see out there, you wouldn't believe.' There was a knock at the front door.

'See who that is, Ted,' Ethel called, busying herself with the teapot in the scullery.

They heard Ted's voice say, 'Come on in, love.' Footsteps across the front room, and Bridie appeared in the backroom doorway with David in front of her. Edward looked up from delving in his bag for more goodies, and stopped.

The girl in the doorway was the one in his dream. It came repeatedly when he was far away at the other end of the world. When he turned restlessly, hot and sweaty in tropical nights, as the ship rolled under him and cramped, sleeping men muttered and grunted around him, Edward would have a dream. It was always the same. A lovely, fiery-haired girl called him from across a river but as he waded in to go to her, the riverbed sloped steeply. Water rose over his head and turned to ice. It froze him, trapping and cutting with cruel spikes and shards, until pain woke him and he'd lie still until, as always, he dreamed again.

This time, his soul floated high above a frozen river, looking down at his body, trapped in ice. Light

286

filled the air. A hand in his pulled up and up and up, until the earth was left far beneath them. In every dream, he turned to find the glowing face of the girl by the river, who led him ever higher. The dream ended as the earth became a pin-point in the infinite blackness of space. Gripped by panic he strove to keep the earth in sight, to make it out from all the myriad stars that filled his vision, and he'd wake again, trembling, afraid of something nameless in the darkness. The nights he dreamed those dreams, he always slept like the dead afterwards, no matter what the rolling of the ship, nor the human sounds around him.

He realised that everyone was staring at him as he sat, wide-eyed, gazing at Bridie. He lowered his head and fumbled in his bag, shaking off the peculiar sensation of something seen before.

'Meet Bridie,' said Ethel, drying her hands on her apron as she came from the scullery. 'She's bin renting your room while you was away, like we told you.'

Edward stood up and held out a hand. 'Pleased to meet you.'

He wondered if she felt like him, that this was not the first time they'd met. Her hand felt long familiar, as a mother's hand to a child. He looked at her face, curious to see if she gave any sign. Then Ted started pulling out the table, and gave Edward the knives to lay, and Ethel brought in a steaming teapot followed by plate after plate of sandwiches, biscuits and cakes until they laughingly protested that they'd never be able to eat another bite after this.

The homecoming lengthened into drowsiness. Edward told stories of far-off people and places, funny tales about his shipmates until, tired by excitement and laughter, the pauses became longer and longer and Ethel began to brush crumbs into a pile on the table-cloth.

'I'll be clearing away,' she announced. 'No, you've got David,' she added to Bridie's offer of doing the washing up.

The little party began to break up. Bridie and David kissed Ethel goodbye in the scullery, and calling goodnights to all, made their way home. Bridie put David to bed and, taking a shiny new pair of shears she'd got down at the ironmonger's, went out in the garden. Kneeling on an old mat, she began to cut the long grass in tall swathes. The cat watched indignantly while her protective wall of grass and weeds fell away. Bridie put the shears down and fetched a drop of milk to soothe her.

By the time her arms began to ache, more than half the garden was just rough stubble. Ruefully inspecting the red patches on her hands that would be blisters tomorrow, Bridie started to plan her garden: phlox and hollyhocks, roses and marigolds. At the bottom a small vegetable patch. String beans fresh from the poles in early summer. Transplant the raspberry canes, and prune the gooseberries. Here was something that Ireland had taught her, gardening and growing things. The ironmonger had racks of seeds outside.

She wiped the green stains off the blades of the

shears and stored them up on a nail in the scullery, where David couldn't reach them. And all the time, at the very back of her mind, she wondered about Edward.

He took to popping round to see Bridie of an evening. Ethel noticed, and was pleased. In fact a good deal of his time he was over in Bridie's direction on one pretext or another. When David was tucked up in bed, they'd work in the garden together, sometimes talking, sometimes not. He found Bridie cutting the undergrowth at the far end of her patch one evening, and offered to help. It had become a delightful habit, to plan and potter together. He brought over Ted's spade and fork, and began on the vegetable patch.

'It needs leaving, turned over, all winter. Then the frost breaks the clay and it gets the air to it, and it's easier to break up fine in the spring,' explained Bridie, when they were wondering which jobs to do first.

Sometimes Ethel and Ted strolled over, after Ted had had his supper. He brought her a wooden box of wallflowers.

'Put them in now, and you'll have blooms next year, love,' he told her.

Bridie collected windfall apples, and they ate sour applecake, sitting on a rug on the shorn grass. September passed, fine and dry. October began golden, but went rapidly downhill into autumnal damp. The day came for Edward to rejoin his ship.

The morning he was to leave was soft and drizzly. Tiny droplets of mist clung to the thick serge of his uniform and shone on his hair as they all stood to bid him farewell on the station platform. Ethel pretended she wasn't crying. David hung round his knees, begging to go too. Edward, tall enough to look over his mother's head at Bridie, smiled. Susan clung on his other arm and blew her nose loudly.

'Would you mind if I wrote to you sometimes?' he asked Bridie across the tearful women. She smiled back.

'No, I'd like that.'

He grinned broadly. 'I will, then. You'll hear from me. And you, nipper,' he said to David, ruffling his hair.

Bridie watched him kiss his family one last time, then, saluting her solemnly with his blue eyes steady on hers, he turned and hefted his bag across his shoulders and climbed into the waiting train. For a while he disappeared, then they saw him, one face in a long line, all pressed against windows and hanging out above closed doors. A forest of hands waved and waved. The train rounded the far end of the platform and drew slowly out of sight. The disconsolate crowd of relatives and friends took one last look and trailed off the platform with lagging feet. Edward was gone.

Life returned to normal. Bridie continued to push the carriage, by now decrepit with bumping and humping round pot-holes and puddles and the onslaughts of bad weather. It really only served as a shelter these days. If David whined he could sit in it and doze with his head propped on a blanket against the side. Bridie was looking forward to the spring. David would be five years old then and she could enrol him in school. She was determined that he should have all the schooling she'd missed.

'I'm not having 'im do it the way I had to,' she told Lizzie firmly.

Lizzie felt her own baby turn in her belly, and agreed. She asked Bridie if she'd heard from Edward.

'No, not yet. Maybe he's changed his mind. When you get that far away, I expect your mind gets filled with other things.'

Bridie was busy, what with traipsing the streets and keeping up her accounts, but each day the absence of a letter was a small disappointment. Which made it all the more exciting when the postman knocked at the front door early one morning and delivered a small packet, all covered with brightly coloured foreign stamps. Bridie's name and address were printed in bold black ink on the brown cover.

'That looks interesting. Got a boyfriend?' remarked Bert the postman.

Bridie took the little parcel and turned it over. On the other side it had Edward's name, and the name of his ship, printed in much smaller letters.

'It's from a friend,' she said sharply, shutting the door on the postman's nosey look.

All day she kept the packet, unopened, in her skirt pocket. She could feel it as she did her rounds. Her doorstep transactions were not usually sociable. Often children would spot her coming, and run to call their mothers. They came to the doorstep, pennies in hand, and the exchange of money was brief. Occasionally someone would query the interest, or ask Bridie for more time to pay. She was invited to step inside the doorway only in the worst of weather, when the women themselves didn't want to shiver. She made no attempt to make friends. But this morning, her step was light and she had a pleasant word for her borrowers. When David fell in a puddle, despite being warned a dozen times, she merely picked him up and said, 'Silly child,' instead of pulling him up to his feet with a jerk and an angry smack on the bottom.

That evening she cooked their dinner of Irish stew, thick with mutton and potatoes and leeks, humming happily around the warmth of the range. When she'd set David to play on the floor with a box of picture books and some plywood puzzles, she pulled out her packet and opened it. Half a dozen letters fell out. Each had been carefully dated on the outside fold, so that she could sort them into order. She unfolded the first. Edward had written the week he left England. He started by explaining that he could only post letters when they went into port, so he'd write regularly, and post each voyage's letters together.

That explains it, thought Bridie, delighted that he should be thinking so much of her.

His letters were just like Edward. Full of lively descriptions of life on board, his fellow crew members, his success in his engineering training, and how he hoped to get promotion if all went well. Then there was a colourful account of a stop in Hong Kong before going due south into Malaya and then on into Indonesia.

Bridie sat with dreams in her eyes, seeing it all, the hustle and bustle, the queer smells and sights. She tasted salt spray on her lips, felt the glare in her eyes as the early morning sun rose red over the horizon, dazzling straight into the wheelhouse, making the skin prickle with sweat.

At the end of the last letter there was a box number and address for Bridie to write to, care of the Port of Singapore.

'We go south, through the South China Sea, calling at Brunei in Borneo, and then on to Malaya and Singapore,' he had written. 'Please do write, because I would so much like to hear from you. How is the nipper? Truly yours, Edward.'

Writing back was a business. Bridie went up to the High Street and came back with two packets each of pink envelopes and paper. She bought a fresh supply of black ink, like Edward's, and called on Lizzie, whose baby was due any moment. She came to open the door and, when she saw them, pulled a face.

'Come on in, if you don't mind me moaning and groaning. I feel so enormous I wish this baby would come, before my tum sags to my knees. I'm turning into a human elephant.'

She ruffled David's hair and kissed the top of his head. 'D'you want a biscuit?' she asked. 'If you do, they're in the tin on the dresser.'

While David ate fig rolls, Bridie and Lizzie talked

babies. When the topic was not exactly exhausted but thoroughly explored, Bridie said she wanted some help.

'What with?' asked Lizzie. 'I'll be upstairs with my legs in the air, having a baby any minute now, so it'd better be quick help.'

Bridie took a book out of her basket. 'I need to know how to use this,' she said. It was the Oxford English Dictionary.

'Righto. Come here and I'll show you.'

Together the two women pored over the blue bound volume, Lizzie turning pages, running her finger down the columns and columns of words. Long words, short words, a whole language that Bridie had never heard before.

'It's all a matter of the alphabet,' explained Lizzie. 'First letter, second letter, and so on. Look.'

She looked up several words, then asked Bridie to try for herself. After a false start and some embarrassment, Bridie got the hang of it. 'That's marvellous,' she cried. 'I can write proper now.'

Lizzie raised an inquisitive eyebrow.

'Oh, Edward's written me such lovely letters. They all came the other day, together in a bunch. I'm going to write back, but I wanted to do it right. So I got this.' She stroked the cover of the dictionary.

Lizzie clutched her swollen stomach and groaned. 'They keep coming, but I don't think I've really started yet. It's just those practice ones, you know?'

Bridie nodded. She certainly did.

'So the great Edward has written? That's nice. He's

one of this world's truly decent people, Bridie. You're lucky.'

Bridie shook her head. 'We're only friends,' she demurred.

'So?' demanded Lizzie. 'To have a friend like that is lucky, is what I meant. Why, you got something else in mind?'

Bridie flushed. 'No, not really. It's just that the letters were so . . . like they was to an old friend, like we'd known each other a long time.' She broke off, confused. 'Don't you start teasing, Lizzie Norris.'

Lizzie shifted uncomfortably and groaned again.

'Here!' cried Bridie. 'You sure you aren't on your way? Them pains seem pretty regular to me.' Lizzie's face stayed screwed up at least a minute, then she let her breath out again.

'You think this might be it?'

'Lizzie Norris, here's you supposed to be all educated and expert at people's bodies, and you don't even know if you're in labour! You get upstairs quick and into bed, and I'll run over for Mrs MacDonald. Where's Jonathan?'

'He's on duty. He might be home at five o'clock, he said, but he often doesn't get off when he's supposed to.'

'David, you stay there like a good boy. I'll be back in a tick,' said Bridie.

As Lizzie lumbered upstairs, stopping halfway to hold tight on to the banisters as another pain came and went, Bridie picked up her skirts and ran for the midwife. Mrs MacDonald took one look at her hot, panting face and reached for her shawl and bag. They hurried back, Bridie holding her hand to the stitch in her side while she explained that she reckoned Lizzie was well advanced in labour. They ran into the house, and before they were in the front door could hear Lizzie crying out upstairs. Mrs MacDonald ran up, while Bridie hastily put pans of water on the hob and opened the vent to make the fire roar in the range. She told David to stay in the back room and play, while she popped upstairs to see if she could help.

Lizzie, propped on pillows, was panting hard while Mrs MacDonald's voice called, 'Don't push, dearie, don't push.'

Lizzie turned despairing eyes on Bridie and moaned, 'I have to.'

'Go on then.'

Two minutes later Mrs MacDonald held up a very tiny baby boy for Lizzie's inspection.

'He's a small one, but he's fine. A grand little boy.' Mrs MacDonald asked Bridie to fetch up some water while she wrapped the new infant in a clean white shawl.

'He'll make a mess of the shawl, I'm afraid, but if you will leave everything until the last possible moment, young woman, you have to make do. I'll give him a little washover when Bridie fetches the warm water.'

Lizzie held out her arms eagerly for her baby, and let out another great groan.

'Goodness me,' observed the midwife, 'the after-birth doesn't usually hurt much.'

'I want to push again,' gasped Lizzie, her face straining.

'Oh, my word.' cried Mrs MacDonald. She hastily put the baby boy into the crib standing ready by the bed, and ran back to Lizzie. A tiny head appeared. The midwife pushed Lizzie's legs apart, and said, 'There's another one. Push!'

In no time at all Lizzie's and Jonathan's daughter was born, yelling thinly and thrashing her arms.

'My word, she's goin' to be a madam, if she's started like she's going to go on,' remarked Mrs MacDonald. Both babies cried, and Lizzie too with joy and shock.

'Twins! Oh my word,' she said feebly to the midwife.

'And both fine babies,' said Mrs MacDonald reassuringly.

Bridie helped bathe the twins and their stunned mother, and into all the commotion walked Jonathan, who sat down very suddenly on the linen chest at the far side of the room when he looked at the two women, each busy with a different baby.

'Good God,' he said in a faint voice. 'It's twins.'

'No wonder you felt like an elephant,' remarked Bridie.

Lizzie laughed, hysteria not far away. 'Oh my word, yes,' she said.

A small hand pushed the bedroom door open, and David peeped round.

'Let him come in,' said Mrs MacDonald fondly. 'We're nearly done here.'

'I wondered where you were,' said David timidly. 'You didn't come back.'

'No, because I was helping Lizzie. Look, David, Lizzie's babies. She's got two new babies. Twins. Isn't that wonderful?'

David eyed the crumpled red faces dubiously. 'They'll cry,' he announced.

Lizzie laughed hollowly. 'I'm sure they will,' she murmured.

Tall Jonathan bent over the crib, with its two little bundles, who were defying David's prediction for the moment and not crying at all. 'Amazing,' he muttered to himself, and drew back the shawls slightly, to examine their faces and hands. 'Lizzie, you must look as soon as you can sit up. They're amazing. Like nothing you ever saw. You're so clever!'

Mrs MacDonald was bathing his wife's face and combing her hair. 'She'll be right as ninepence in a moment, Dr Norris, but she's ever so tired, and if you don't mind, I think she should sleep a while.'

As if in agreement, the twins' faces too relaxed into sleep and their father carefully put the shawls down. Bridie fetched another cover and laid it over the sleeping pair. 'Have to keep them warm, they're small,' she said to Jonathan.

'Yes.' He still gazed at them, unable to believe his eyes.

'Come on,' ordered Mrs MacDonald, 'downstairs, all of you.' She turned to Lizzie, pale and exhausted. 'You get your sleep now, my duck,' she said, 'and we'll be up again as soon as they wake.'

Downstairs Jonathan poured glasses of wine for all of them with a none too steady hand. 'Twins! Wait 'til my colleagues hear. There'll be no end of ribbing.'

'You don't sound like you mind,' said Bridie.

He shook his head in wonder. 'I'd never have guessed. Never entered my mind, nor Lizzie's as far as I know.'

Bridie drank down her wine, and rose to go.

'Bless you for your help,' said Jonathan, having been assured by the midwife that if she had arrived a moment later, things might have gone decidedly less well.

Bridie grinned. 'Congratulations,' she said, and kissed his cheek. 'You've got two lovely babies, though I've no doubt you've got some hard work ahead of you. I'll go and leave you in peace now.'

Mrs MacDonald gave David a resounding series of kisses and a mint humbug from her pocket. 'Come and see me soon,' she ordered. 'I don't see you half often enough.'

'We've been ever so busy, Mrs MacDonald. But we'll call round soon. Tell Lizzie from me to take care.'

As Bridie and David hurried round the end of the road, they could hear in the distance the shrill, demanding wailing of Lizzie's two tiny, hungry babies. Bridie shook her head and laughed into her hand.

'Oh, my,' she said to David,' 'what a turn-up for the books. Twins, indeed. Did you ever!'

It made the perfect first letter to Edward, first

written in pencil and checked with the dictionary. Then neatly copied in ink onto the pink paper. It ran to eight pages, the most Bridie had ever written in her life. She'd set it down so eagerly, and with such a sense of talking to Edward and hearing his deep chuckling voice answer, that it hadn't even seemed like hard work. She folded it in three, like he'd folded his, and tucked it into its envelope. Then she wrote the date on the outside. The 14th January 1926. The first letter.

Chapter Twenty

The time had come round for one of Sam Saul and Bridie's impromptu business meetings. Sam parked his elegant legs on Bridie's brass fender and considered the proposition she'd just put to him.

'How about a broader partnership?' he suggested, a wicked glint in his gleaming black eyes.

'Broader? With the likes of you? I wouldn't get mixed up with you,' Bridie retorted.

'My dear, you *are* one of the likes of me, you just have a different – ah – style. Why do you think I enjoy doing business with you if we are not, as you put it so delightfully . . . mixed up?'

'You know very well what I mean,' she said crossly.

'I know I'd heartily enjoy a partner such as yourself.' He flickered a glance at her to see how she responded. If only, he thought, he could dismiss her as common. But she was one of the most uncommon women he'd ever met, damn it! He looked at her again hopefully, hiding the expression under his eyebrows.

Bridie was getting nervous. This was the most direct proposition he'd made, although there had been plenty of hints and jokes.

'You hold your tongue,' she snapped at him. 'I'm a married woman, remember?'

He spread his hands apologetically.

'Forgive me. Your husband's presence being notable by its absence, I took liberties,' he pronounced pompously. Then he laughed aloud. 'Come on, Bridie, we're two of a kind, you and me. I know you. We could have a wonderful time together.'

'I 'spect your wife would like that,' she replied acidly.

'My wife is my business, and your husband is yours.'

'You're rotten right through, you know, Sam Saul? A real bastard.'

'So they say, my dear,' he said comfortably, 'but you see, it doesn't worry me in the least.'

'Well, it would worry me,' said Bridie firmly. 'I know we could have fun, but it would be the sort of fun that hurts other people, and would get us in the end, too. I don't care much for that kind of fun, Sam.'

He shrugged, disappointed.

'I'll do business with you, provided it's honest, but I'll not have the other, if you don't mind. I couldn't start anything like that.'

'Very well,' he said irritably. 'But don't you ever look round you and think "killjoy" to yourself? Don't you fancy any men after that aged husband of yours?'

His malice went too far. Bridie rose from her chair behind the table and her stack of papers and slapped his face hard. 'You talk like that again, and you won't set foot in this house again, ever.'

He rubbed his stinging cheek and glared back. 'All right, all right, keep your hair on,' he muttered resentfully. No other woman on earth would get away with it but her, and the more she turned him down, the stronger the fascination got. He swung his feet off the fender and reached over for a bit of paper.

'Let's get on with it,' he said with abrupt bad temper.

They discussed and agreed figures, and then returned to the proposition that had led to the argument in the first place.

'Why here? That's the obvious question. It's a crummy area, to be candid. You could do better somewhere else, say up towards Mile End, or even over in Hackney.'

' 'cos I don't fancy moving. An' this is where I work. An' there's Ethel easy to walk to. An' I live here already, an' I like it.' She ticked the reasons off on her fingers.

He shrugged again. Once she made her mind up about something, he was blowed if he could ever change it. He studied the calculations on the scrap of paper again.

'Next question. Why not go to the bank or a Friendly Society?'

'Don't be stupid, Sam. They wouldn't deal with me except I take Francis along, and I won't do that.'

Sam glanced at her in agreement. Banks wouldn't lend to a woman on her own. She was right.

'And because you'll charge me two per cent and the

bank will be nearer four. So will the Society charge me four, only they won't lend me, neither.'

He suddenly lost his cool manner. 'What?' he shouted, unable to believe his ears. 'Two per cent! Are you mad?'

Bridie looked at the ceiling and waited.

'All right, how can you explain a deal that is on the face of it daylight robbery?'

'It's part of our original agreement,' she said calmly, 'that if I wanted larger sums, I'd come to you and you'd take a quarter your usual percentage in return for some of my regular earnings. Well, you've bin gettin' your part of the deal ever so nice and regular. Now I want to borrow off of you to buy this house. You'll have it as security.'

Sam swallowed hard. 'You expect me to lend you one hundred and forty pounds.'

Bridie smiled sweetly. 'No, I don't expect you to, I know you're goin' to.'

'At two per cent?'

'That's it.'

'And I don't get anything by way of recognition that it's criminal generosity? Ludicrous? Extortion?'

Bridie giggled. 'You sure know all about them things, Sam Saul,' she agreed.

Sam felt his blood pressure near boiling point. 'No recognition?' he said with emphasis.

'Yes, I'll give you a nice cup of tea afore you leave,' she said cheerily, and went to put the kettle on. Sam groaned and banged his fist on the chair arm.

'You're the hardest woman I know. God preserve

me from any more like you,' he called.

'Yes,' came back the light answer, 'but you see, my dear, I don't mind.'

He laughed ruefully.

Bridie came to the doorway. 'We'll draw the papers up tomorrow, then. I've got a lawyer who will do it.'

Sam groaned again. 'It's legal, yet. Oi yoi yoi.' Distress brought the Yiddish lilt back to his voice.

'Don't be a fool,' said Bridie. ' 'course it's got to be legal and proper. It's property.'

Drinking hot sweet tea gave them both a few moments of companionable silence. 'Well,' she said, putting down her cup, 'you'd best be getting home to that patient wife of yours. How she puts up with you, I don't know.'

'She's nothing like you, that's for sure,' said Sam dourly. He gave a little snort of laughter. 'Just as well, isn't it? I'd soon be bankrupt.'

Bridie just grinned. He bent down and kissed her cheek. 'You're my *bête noire*,' he whispered in her ear. 'You know it, don't you?'

Bridie had never heard of a *bête noire*, but she got the drift. She gave him a little push.

'Go on, get along home where you should be,' she said, and leaned on her front door to watch his tall figure stride off down the road. She hugged herself with nervous delight. She was really going to buy her house. The lawyer had seen no problems, the agent had said the landlord would be willing to sell and Sam Saul, against all his better judgement, was going to lend her the balance of the money.

Bridie pressed her hands against hot cheeks, and said, 'Oh my word, it's really going to happen.'

She went inside and sat down to consider the other matter that was pressing for a decision. She pulled out the letter in its stiff white envelope and slowly made her way through the complicated, verbose sentences again. She understood the main part of it, but was uncertain about all the fancy language that might be hiding things she ought to know. Francis wanted David, or at least to see him. At first, when it became clear what the letter meant, Bridie had been outraged. What a thing to do, to make some fat-assed lawyer ask to see her son! If Francis had come round and asked nicely, Bridie would have been agreeable enough, but to do it this way made her so angry she felt like saying no.

The letter acknowledged that since she and Francis had got married after David was born, he was still illegitimate, and that in law he was hers. But, it pointed out, Francis had in every respect been a father to his son, until the separation, and had a moral right to see him, or even to have him live in his house. Bridie shivered when she got to that bit.

Never. Over my dead body, she thought furiously. All this time, an' all he does is pay money into the bank. He hasn't been to see us, an' he hasn't sent any presents on birthdays, not nothing. An' now he comes marching in with 'is lawyers and his long words. Oh damn!

A tear trickled down her cheek, a tear of fear and loss and being alone with only David. No one could take him away. She'd given up Rosa without complaint, had stoically accepted what had to be. But David . . . she'd fight tooth and nail anyone who tried to take him from her. She wiped her eyes. Just the threat of it threw her into turmoil. She didn't sleep well that night, and was troubled by dreams and nightmares. The following day she called in at her lawyer's office and told him to go ahead with the purchase of her house, she'd got the money.

Then she said, 'There's another thing. My husband has written me this.' She handed over the letter.

The lawyer read it carefully, then looked at her over his glasses. 'Do you want my advice as a lawyer, or as an old man who has seen a lot of life?'

'What do you think, yourself?' asked Bridie.

'My dear Mrs Holmes, you are a remarkable and resourceful woman, but I do not have the impression that you have a taste for malice or unpleasantness. Am I right?'

Bridie nodded.

'Then my advice to you is, avoid the law at all costs because it only ever serves to make things like this worse. Take your little boy, in his best clothes, to see his father. Swallow your understandable feeling that the thing is offensive, and be as charming as I'm sure you know very well how. That way, you son will not suffer, your husband won't have a leg to stand on in any argument, and you will have merely the passing inconvenience of a little hurt pride. That is my advice. It is what I would endeavour to do myself if it were my child.'

Bridie sat with head bowed. Hurt pride, she thought, *hurt*. But he was right.

'Thank you,' she said, raising her head. 'That's not the advice I thought I wanted, but it's what me and David needed. I'll do it.'

The old lawyer smiled compassionately. 'That's the brave way, you know,' he said. 'The other – the fighting and the arguing – that's the real coward's way, for those who cannot endure their own feelings and have no respect for the feelings of others. A lifetime in the law, and I have been more sure of that with every passing day.'

Bridie stood up and shook his hand warmly. 'Thank you,' she said again. 'I'll wait to hear from you about the next step on the house.'

'Yes,' replied the old man, smiling at her. 'It's an excellent thing, this house buying. Property is the best investment, always has been.'

Bridie went down the dark, narrow stairs to the butcher's shop below the lawyer's office. The smell of meat hung round the entrance, and sawdust from the butcher's floor lay in little drifts in the lawyer's doorway. She bought two chops for their dinner, and then made a decision. There was a tobacconist's three shops down. Waiting to be served, Bridie sniffed the fragrance coming from the rows and rows of packets and tins, all neatly stacked on shelves the length of the shop. A mahogany pipe holder stood on the glass counter, with pipes of every size, colour and wood sitting in glossy rows. She bought a packet of Francis's favourite cigars. She'd go one better than her lawyer's advice, and take David to see his father carrying a gift.

Collecting him from a long looked forward to afternoon with Mrs MacDonald, she confided in the midwife what she had done.

'He's right, in my view,' said Mrs MacDonald. 'Do you recall, when David was born? You didn't want his father in then, and I disagreed with you at the time. Well, I'd say the same today. You heed what you was told.'

'I am,' said Bridie meekly.

It took two weeks to make satisfactory arrangements for David to visit Francis, who had been taken aback by the friendly answer his letter had received. The first week in June, Bridie's letter to Edward was all about the visit, and how it had gone. It hadn't started too well.

It had been unseasonably chilly that week, so Bridie had put a woolly over David's grey cut-downs. He looked every inch the East End kid, though better turned out than many. Bridie wiped his nose and gave him the handkerchief to put in his pocket. She put a knitted shawl over her own light dress, and wore a fashionable new pair of brown leather shoes with a strap across the front. A spot of powder on her nose, and they were ready.

They went up to Manor Road, and caught a tram that took them into Abbey Lane, past the school in Three Mills and up on to Stratford High Street. Bridie gazed around at the familiar places as it took them down into Bow Road and they jumped off at Maplin Street, just opposite the Tredegar Square turning. The square gardens were in the full bloom of spring, the magnolia tree just beginning to shed its waxy pink blossoms and open its leaves.

Bridie bravely led David up the front steps of number twelve and banged on the door. Mrs Goode answered. Bridie impulsively went to hug her, as in days of old, but the housekeeper drew back.

'Good afternoon,' said Dora formally. 'Hello, David.'

'Hello, Mrs Goode.' Hearing David's high voice, Francis could wait no longer, and emerged from his study into the hall. He nodded stiffly to Bridie, and squatted down in front of his son. 'Hello, young man,' he said. 'Would you like to come in?'

David looked up at his mother questioningly. She nodded. 'Yes, go on.'

Francis took the child's hand to draw him in. His eyes met Bridie's. 'Do you wish to stay?' he asked.

Bridie had thought about what she would feel, and say, at this moment, but now it was upon her, it was easier than she had expected. She shook her head.

'No. You and him, you'll get on better if I'm not there watching. You and Mrs Goode have him for a while, and I'll take myself down the Roman and do some shopping. I'll fetch him again after tea.'

Relief flooded Francis's lined face. 'Yes. That will do us very well. Thank you, Bridie.'

David ran forward anxiously. 'Don't go, Mum.' He plucked at her hand.

Bridie picked him up and put him firmly on the hall floor. 'I'll be back after tea,' she said calmly, 'and you'll be a good boy and stay with your dad. I bet Mrs

310

Goode's got a big biscuit tin in her kitchen. I remember
it. If you go along and ask her, she might let you have
something out of it.'

In the background, Dora nodded. 'There might
even be chocolate,' she remarked, as if to no one in
particular.

David's head turned. The housekeeper beckoned.
He turned back and allowed his mother to kiss him,
then followed the housekeeper down the passage, to be
fed biscuits and milk until he felt sick. Afterwards he
and Francis sat outside on the weathered wooden
bench by the kitchen door, and Francis asked so many
questions that David chattered nineteen to the dozen
and climbed excitedly on and off the bench, until he
ventured further and further away, to explore the
whole garden. It was much bigger than his own, but
had the same slugs and snails and spiders.

Francis wandered after him, hands folded behind
his back. He was pleased with the child's bright interest, found him clean if shabby, and his speech not completely uncivilised. With a pang, Francis looked into
the small face and saw himself. But here, at least,
whatever the regrettable past, was a child whose mind
could be educated. Francis resolved to ask Bridie what
she had in mind in the way of schools. David was ready
to start after the summer. That was how they ran into
trouble.

Francis invited her in, when she came to get David,
and she sat once more in the same old chair opposite his
desk. David sat on her knee, sucking his thumb.

'I wanted to ask you about schooling,' began
Francis.

'He's going to Falcon Street. It's Catholic, and near to where we live,' said Bridie.

'He'll be taught by nuns?'

'Yes. Any objection?'

Francis decided not to make an issue of it. 'No. They provide a good education. What did you have in mind for when he's eight?'

'Oh my,' said Bridie, 'he's barely five. I'll worry about when he's eight when the time comes.'

Francis sighed in a way familiar to Bridie, and disturbing. It was a critical, dismissive sort of sigh. 'If he's to go to preparatory school, his name must go down immediately. It should have gone down at birth.'

Bridie stiffened. Francis had been plotting. 'What's that? Preparatory school?'

'It prepares boys for public school. They go as boarders when they are eight, then to public school at eleven. If they get in, that is. It's all been left very late for David. I shall have to get in touch and pull a string or two.'

Bridie passed a hand across her brow. This was the very thing from which she had fled. Here it was again, unchanged, ruthless.

'No,' she said, feeling her knees begin to tremble. 'David is going to an ordinary school – The Falcon. Then I hope he'll go to the grammar school, if he passes the examinations. I've talked to Mother Superior at The Falcon, and she's explained it all to me. Me not having been to school as much as I should have, I made a point of finding out. And I wouldn't send him away on no account.'

'You would deny him a decent start in life?' asked Francis.

'He'll get as good a start as I can give, and it'll have to do, because he's not going away to some fancy place with posh accents. He belongs here, and he ain't going nowhere else.'

Francis winced. 'You'd have him illiterate? Crippled in life by poverty and a coarse environment?'

Bridie felt rage beginning to boil, then abruptly it vanished, leaving pity for this lined old man whose life, devoted to others, was a sham.

'I'm sorry, Francis. You haven't ever been to see us, so you don't know that we don't live in no slum. I have a nice house of my own. We're not grand, it's true, but we get by, and David don't go without. And we got lots of friends who love him, and I couldn't think of sending him away, ever.'

'Then if you are intransigent, you leave me powerless. All I can do is place money in his bank account, and hope that it will be used wisely later on. I shall ensure that there is enough for him to stay on at school after thirteen if he wishes, and for university later. I hope you take this with the seriousness it is due, Bridie.'

'As one who had no learning, I respect it more'n you, probably,' she cried, stung by the implication.

'I doubt it, somehow,' replied Francis, 'but let us not argue. Money there will be.'

'That's David's. I don't touch it,' she said. 'That's for him to decide when he gets old enough.'

'And . . .' Francis started again. Bridie closed her eyes. She'd had enough. 'I wondered if we could

313

repeat this visit?' Francis thawed for the first time. 'It's been such a joy to see him, Bridie. Could you bring him again, please?'

At last they were on safe ground.

'Yes, I'll gladly bring him. I'd be pleased. Or you can come and see us. You'd be welcome. How often?'

Francis, anticipating resistance, hadn't thought that far. 'Oh, er . . . would twice a month be possible? Every other Saturday, maybe?'

Bridie smiled at him. 'Yes, if he wants to. 'course, I wouldn't make him come if he didn't like to. I'll bring him in the morning, and you can have him for the day, if you like?'

They looked at each other with a faint trace of the old affection.

'Thank you,' said Francis gently, 'you really are being very generous.'

'I'll be off then.' Bridie spoke briskly and put David down, brushing crumbs off his woolly.

'You'll bring him a fortnight today?' asked Francis anxiously.

She nodded. 'Don't worry, I will. And if there's anything goes wrong, like he gets took bad or something, I'll send you a note.'

They parted, not touching, at the doorstep. David, tired but excited, fidgeted and sucked his thumb in the tram until Bridie felt exasperatedly that if visits were going to end like this, then maybe they weren't a good thing after all. Shortly before they got to their stop he fell heavily asleep, and she had to carry him all the way home.

Chapter Twenty-One

Ethel and Ted were talking about going hop picking in Kent in the early autumn. They'd done it several years running. Ethel, who went for a full three weeks, always came back brown as a berry and with hands torn and stained. She loved it. Bridie thought about having a week down with them, then had another idea. It was Francis going on about education that put it in her mind. She asked him what he thought when she delivered David to him one hot Saturday in July.

'I'd like to take him to the seaside,' she explained. 'For a week. It would be good for his health, and set him up before he starts school after the summer. And it would teach him things. He's never seen countryside and sea. He could go in the water and try swimming. It would be so good for him.'

'It would,' Francis agreed. 'So what do you want?'

'For you to pay his way, if I pay mine? Since I took on buying my house I'm pushed. I can run to it for one of us, but not for two. I've never asked you for money before, but it's for David, not me.'

Francis thought it was a splendid idea. Of course he'd help out. 'Where will you go?' he asked.

'There's a place in Kent called Romney. Romney

Marsh. It has wonderful beaches, by all accounts. It's safe, and there are plenty of guest houses that put you up comfortable, and don't charge the earth.'

She wasn't going to let on to Francis that the source of all this information was Sam Saul. He'd been round one evening to collect her house loan repayment, and to spend time sitting in her back garden under the apple tree, trying, half joking, half seriously, to suggest that she needed a holiday – with him. He'd painted a lewd and vivid picture of their elopement to the seaside, while his wife went to stay with her elderly parents in Golder's Green. His black eyes flashed with suggestive good humour, and he gave an exaggerated gesture of despondency when she giggled and said, 'Give over, Sam Saul. You're a caution!'

'You won't make me a happy man, then?'

'Yes, I'll bring you out a glass of lemonade. I made it fresh this evening.'

'If at a loss, feed the beast,' groaned Sam, and rolled on his back in the crushed grass. He came eye to eye with one of the kittens, now grown into a graceful tabby cat. She mewed, showing small, perfectly white teeth.

'What do you do with women?' he asked her. She hitched up a hind leg and started to wash, turning her back indifferently. 'Yeah,' said Sam to her busy head, 'you're just like the rest.'

He raised himself on his elbow, and watched Bridie and David carry out a plate of cakes and a big brown jug of lemonade.

'Aren't you going to bed, young man?' he asked David.

'The nights are so light, there's no point. He only plays, so he stays up later for the moment. When he goes to school he'll need his sleep.'

'He ought to have a holiday, too,' remarked Sam idly. He had no children, a fact which was the cause of much wailing and throwing up of hands in his wife's parents' home, but didn't bother Sam himself in the slightest.

It was a whole new thought. Hop picking was hop picking, but a real holiday was something few East Enders would have entertained. A day out, yes, but to stop away . . . out of the question.

'Bridie . . .' Sam implored.

'Shut up,' she said. 'I'm thinking.'

Miffed, Sam popped a cake in his mouth and turned his back on her. 'You get some cards, and I'll teach you some games,' he said to David with his mouth full.

'You leave him be,' said Bridie, 'I don't want him learning gambling games off of you.'

Sam looked hurt. 'I only meant snap, or things like that. Can't you give me any credit, you harsh woman?'

'Only the sort that comes as bank notes,' snapped Bridie. 'Listen, where's a good place to go? On holiday?'

'You've changed your mind!' cried Sam.

'You are getting dull, Sam. I mean for me an' David.'

'Ah. . . . Well, now, I'd say down in Romney, on the Kent coast. Big flat beaches. Can be windy, though.'

Open spaces, the fresh sweet air in your face, a horizon that stretches the eyes. Bridie suddenly felt a rare pang of homesickness for the uncrowded, lazy Irish countryside. The little garden she loved so much felt cramped and seedy all of a sudden. She'd made up her mind at that moment, and now Francis was agreeing. A wide smile of delight lit her face. Francis, despite all that had gone wrong between them, still found himself gazing at that face with an ache in his heart. The passing years had brought depth, an inner strength, to her expression. She was apparently quite unaware of it, but, he thought sadly, she had become beautiful since Rosa's death.

'Would you do something for me, as well?' he asked.

Bridie looked up at him enquiringly. 'You remember the small room at the back, that you had when you were here?'

Puzzled, she nodded.

'It's being redecorated throughout, and I'd very much like David to feel that it's his. Would you let him stay overnight sometimes?'

'Yes,' she said promptly. 'It's the same as always – if David wants to, he can.'

It had actually come in quite handy to have David stay a whole weekend with Francis. Sam Saul had done some telephoning for Bridie, and had booked a room for her in a small guest house next to the beach. It was Tuesday to Tuesday, so she spent her weekend without David washing and ironing and bathing. It was, she discovered, a luxurious feeling, time on her own. She didn't even feel inclined to rush round to Lizzie, who was so overcome by babies that she hardly came out of the house these days. She was looking tired and drawn, and Bridie, remembering Rosa, felt sorry for her. But it wasn't enough to make Bridie give up her newfound freedom, and by the time she fetched David home on Sunday afternoon, their clothes lay in two carefully folded piles, ready to go in the case. Sam came over on the Monday, and took away with him, on the passenger seat of his shiny new motor car, Bridie's strongbox. It had proved a good time to persuade her to do something he'd been urging for a long time.

'You're asking to get done over,' he'd cried in exasperation, time and again. 'I know you've got a reputation round here for standing no nonsense, but if a couple of really determined men came after you, you could get badly hurt.'

It was clearly out of the question to leave the house for a week with money inside, so at last Sam had his way. The box was safely stored inside his own safe that evening. Bridie had given him a very old-fashioned look when he'd first brought up the idea of her money in his safe.

'How do I know I can trust you?' she'd demanded bluntly.

Sam looked pained. 'Would I cheat on a friend?' he asked plaintively.

'Probably. Given the chance.'

He was genuinely hurt. 'I'll make money any way I can. I love money, and the more I have the more I love it. But I love you, too.' The words were out before he realised they were on his tongue. They were both equally astonished. Sam hastily tried to put things right.

'That is,' he said, in his best, urbane manner, 'I esteem you highly as a friend and colleague. I wouldn't want to harm you, Bridie, and I swear I'm straight with you,' he finished lamely.

'You're a strange man,' said Bridie softly. 'And I'm fond of you in a funny kind of way, but it can't be any more than that.'

'I know.' Sam looked cast down, then brightened up. 'But I can still try, can't I?' He gave an irrepressible grin and pretended to leer.

Since that time, Bridie had accepted Sam's gestures of friendship, and even protectiveness. She let him arrange the holiday for her, and was overcome to be offered a ride to the station in his new motor car. The Tuesday morning of the journey dawned fine and clear. Bridie and David were up ridiculously early, and ready to go long before Sam puttered up to their front gate and hooted. Neighbours came to their doorsteps and watched as the three of them settled on to the high polished leather seats. Several small boys sidled over to gasp at the wonderful sight. One put out a hand to touch the elegant trim of the high back, and his mother called him sharply away. Bridie was accepted. Sam Saul was a different matter. He had a bad reputation and people drew aside from him. Gossip wondered at the strange relationship between him and Bridie, who had an equally strong reputation for honesty.

Ted and Ethel at first looked askance when Bridie mentioned Sam's name in a friendly sort of way, but, having met him at Bridie's on occasion, when he'd put himself out to charm and entertain, they had to admit that he was an appealing rogue.

'But you watch that man,' Ethel had advised. 'He's dangerous.'

'I know,' said Bridie. 'And I do take care.'

Looking at his dark, handsome face close to hers as he solicitously tucked a rug around her knees, she sat up very straight and let excitement wash through her. Oh, to be off to the seaside, and in such a fine car! David knelt on the back seat and waved to his friends as they set off down the road. Bridie imagined herself resplendent in furs, veiled hat, and tiny satin shoes. Oh, she felt grand. They chugged smoothly along, Sam hooting and waving at drivers in passing vehicles and mockingly doffing his hat at pedestrians. Utterly enchanted, Bridie looked here, there and everywhere, storing away all she saw for a letter to Edward.

They bowled along through the City and across the river. A light breeze ruffled their hair and they sniffed at the river air. It was in full tide, long strings of barges up and down. A river police boat idled in the middle and watched a cruiser coming down fast from its mooring further up at Hampton Court. Gulls swooped and screamed harshly. London Bridge station came into view all too soon. Sam drew up smoothly outside, leapt out and hurried round to open her door and hand her down. Bridie chuckled.

'I'm quite the lady today, ain't I?'

He raised her hand to his lips and kissed it.

'For me, always,' he said gallantly, and lifted out their case, then David, who said he felt sick.

'Don't you dare, it's just excitement,' warned Bridie.

In the station, Sam went off to buy the tickets, leaving the other two to sit on a bench with their luggage. It reminded Bridie of that afternoon, seven years ago, when she arrived in Euston with no knowledge of what would become of her. Sam came back, and, handing the tickets to Bridie, escorted them on to the platform. He settled them into seats with their backs to the engine, and stowed the case underneath the seat so that she wouldn't have to lift it down. With a flourish, he produced a bag of assorted sweeties, several comic books, and two magazines. David grabbed the sweets and immediately began sorting them through. Whistles blew, the sound of the steam from the engine turned to a straining chuff, chuff, chuff, and Sam leapt for the carriage door. It was already moving as his feet touched the platform. Bridie pulled down the window and hung out. He walked, then ran alongside, waving first to her, then to David, then her again, and all the time calling orders.

'Take care. Have a wonderful time. Teach the nipper to swim. Don't get sunburn. Look after yourselves now. . . .'

The words were torn from his mouth as the train picked up speed and he fell back, almost at the end of the long platform. Bridie gave one last wave, and turned to David, who was counting green and red and yellow fruit drops.

'Can I have a purple one? They're my favourites,' she asked.

David nodded and picked one out of his little bag. Her cheek bulging with the tart-tasting sweet, Bridie settled down and picked up her magazines. Through the slightly open window steam and smuts flew in on the wind, and this time the singing rails told her, 'Sunshine and sea, sunshine and sea, sunshine and sea,' as they tore through the quiet Kent countryside. Oast houses built of warm red brick raised their odd circular roofs among fields of high-strung young hops. Sheep grazed peacefully on green slopes that were formed as deliciously as the curve of a child's cheek. David knelt up on the seat and pressed his nose to the window, his eyes quite round. He kept turning to his mother and plucking at her, crying, 'Look, Mum, look. . . .' The sweeties and comics were forgotten.

In a little over an hour, they slowed for the umpteenth time and drew into their destination.

'Folkestone. This is Folkestone,' shouted the guard up and down the train.

'Come on,' ordered Bridie, helping David down the high step to the platform. She told him to put his sweets in his pocket and carry the unread comics for later. They had their tickets clipped, and Bridie asked the inspector the way to the bus station.

'Where are you going?' he asked.

'Dymchurch,' answered Bridie.

'That's easy, then,' he said. 'There's a stop just across from the station. It's frequent. You shouldn't have to wait long.'

They found it at once, and within fifteen minutes were sitting on top of an omnibus, trying to see the sea as they whizzed along the coast road, through the tolls to Hythe. David stared and stared.

Bridie soon found herself in a village with a wide main street leading directly down to golden sands at the end. While David tugged at her skirt and begged to go and play right now, Bridie asked directions. Their guest house, as Sam had promised, overlooked the beach itself. A stout little woman welcomed them in and said she was Mabel, the owner.

Two flights of stairs up she showed them to a room with cool green walls. There was a big bed for Bridie and a truckle bed to one side, for David. Mabel offered Bridie a cup of tea and a bite of lunch, but David clung and begged to go out, so she shook her head and said she'd like some tea later on, if Mabel didn't mind. Wise in the ways of children, Mabel didn't mind at all, and offered to make up a sandwich for when they came back. Leaving their case on the floor between the beds, they hurried outside. David went to run off, but Bridie pulled him back.

'Here. Take off your shoes and socks.' Then she gave him a little shove, and the child ran delightedly down the beach. It was wide and flat. When he finally reached the edge of the sea, he stopped and looked. It went on forever and ever. Small waves hissed at his toes and made bubbles in the sand, ridged and

324

sculpted by the eddying water. David jumped and shrieked. A crab the size of his thumbnail emerged from the sand and hurried into the sea. David fled back to Bridie, overcome by it all. She had taken off her own sandals and was nearly at the water's edge.

'What?' she asked, laughing, to his jabber of explanation. 'Crabs won't hurt you. They're more scared of you than you are of them. Was it a big one? I once saw a huge one the time I went to Dublin Bay.'

'Yes,' said David, 'like this.' And he made a circle of his finger and thumb. His mother laughed again.

'Huge,' she agreed. 'Would you be wanting to go and find a bucket and spade?'

They set off, hand in hand, along the waterline to where they could see a shack at the top of the beach, displaying buckets, spades, balls, and windbreaks. They reached it just as its owner was shutting up for lunch.

'All right, dearie, I'll serve you,' she said, seeing Bridie's look of disappointment. 'What colour did you fancy?' They chose matching red buckets and spades, a windbreak and a white beachball. David ran off, joyously banging his bucket with his spade, and settled down by the water's edge. Bridie, rolling his cut-downs up as far as they would go, planted the windbreak, although there was no wind, and lay on her side on the warm sand, watching him.

The small blond head was bent in concentration, filling and emptying his bucket more times than Bridie could count. She got up, and taking her own, showed him how to pat the wet sand down, turn the bucket over and bang the top before lifting it off a perfect sandpie. Soon there was a line of wobbly sandpies between her and the sea. The quiet plash of the waves made her drowsy, so she got up and paddled, not wanting to fall asleep with David near the water. The sun reddened their faces and beat on their arms.

Eventually, hunger drove them indoors again. Mabel took their sandy things into a lobby already full of beach items, and in the dining room served a brown pot of boiling tea, and two platefuls of sardine, cheese and pickle, and cucumber sandwiches. A jug of milk for David, and fruit cake for afters.

'Now you just call out if you want anything. I'm out back getting ready for dinner.' She fussed and bustled around them, her rosy, motherly face eager to see them pleased. 'It's any time between seven o'clock and nine this evening. So you finish up as much as you can, and you can have a good hot meal inside you tonight.'

Bridie felt like she'd ended up inside Buckingham Palace by mistake, but she didn't want to let on so she just nodded her head and thanked Mabel for her kindness. David grabbed at the food. Bridie caught his hand and held it.

'Manners,' she said sternly. 'Here, you use manners. You don't reach and grab. You say excuse me, and I'll give you what you want.'

David, starving, opened his mouth to argue, but seeing how determined his mother looked, desisted. He knew that look. It meant she was serious and he'd better watch out.

'I want a sandwich.'

'No. Can I have a sandwich, please.'

David sighed. She was being difficult and he was oh so hungry.

'Can I have it, please.'

Bridie handed him the plate.

'Here, take two. An' I want you behaving yourself like a gent, you hear? Please, and thank you, and sit still at table.'

'Yes.' Too hungry to argue, David accepted the conditions.

They wolfed down the meal in silence. Afterwards Bridie sat back and stretched. She felt like going for a walk. They piled up the plates for Mabel, and went back down to the beach. Strolling along, watching holiday-makers basking in the sunshine, Bridie felt contentment steal over her like a soft shawl warms on a cool day. Heads bobbed far out in the cold sea as the braver ones went shrieking and gasping, knitted swimsuits water-logged and sagging, in and out of the blue expanse. Showers of droplets caught the sunlight as a fast swimmer back-stroked dramatically out to a yellow buoy that floated lazily on the incoming tide. Bridie decided to buy swimming costumes for them both, tomorrow. She couldn't swim, but she felt that here, in this magical place, she might do anything.

By seven o'clock the sun was fading. They dragged the windbreak through the sand back to Mabel's guest house. The dining room was full of chattering children and parents. A mouthwatering smell of roast chicken caught at their noses, and suddenly the pile of sandwiches might never have been.

There was a big bathroom upstairs. Bridie sighed with pleasure, and occupied it for the next half an hour. She and David emerged scrubbed from top to toe and smelling of coal tar soap. Wearing their best clothes, they sat down to platters of chicken, mashed potatoes, cabbage and carrots, placed before them by Mabel's two daughters.

Bridie caught the eye of a woman at a table opposite. She nodded amiably and lit a cigarette with a lighter. It was a Trench. Bridie's gaze turned to her husband. He must have fought in the War. Later, when the family rose to leave the dining room, Bridie saw the man had a pronounced limp as he made his way to the door among the cluster of tables. He moved awkwardly, as if his wounds had left him disjointed in some strange fashion. His wife turned to ask him something but he shook his head, and she offered him her arm in such a loving gesture that for the first time Bridie felt a pang of loneliness. But it didn't spoil the moment.

She and David sat together, gazing out of the wide window at the view over the sea as the sun began its slow descent to the horizon. Long before dark, David was curled up, rosy with sun and fresh air, fast asleep. Bridie lay on her bed, reading Sam's magazines, until dusk passed into dark and the whole house slept.

That was the pattern for seven idyllic days. They rose early, eager not to miss a moment. They made a habit of sandwiches in the early afternoon, and avoided the crowded dining room at lunchtime. Evenings, they had 'their' table, a very small one under the window, because there was only Bridie and a child. In the evenings, they feasted on the view, until David made friends with the soldier's three children. Then they all ran off to play hopscotch and grandmother's footsteps in Mabel's backyard until it was time for bed, and the two mothers reluctantly called their children in.

'Seems a shame to bring them in,' admitted the soldier's wife, 'but if I let them stay up 'til all hours they get fretful in the day, and I get no peace then.'

She lit a Players and leaned on the doorjamb, watching a skipping game. 'Been here before?' she asked.

'No. It's lovely, isn't it?'

The soldier's wife blew out a thin stream of smoke. 'Mabel's a dear. We've been coming for four years. My husband was wounded in the Somme, and at first he found it really hard to get about, but Mabel never minded. She gave us a room on the ground floor, 'specially, and fetched and carried for us like a mother. She's a darling.'

'A friend recommended her to me,' said Bridie. 'I think she's lovely. She's been ever so kind with David.'

'You lost your old man in the War?' asked the other woman. 'I noticed you're on your own.'

Bridie gazed at the children in the yard. 'Yes, I'm on my own,' she said.

The soldier's wife squashed out her cigarette with

her heel. 'There's ever such a lot of women having to manage like you. I've been real lucky, myself. Come on in!' she shouted to the children. Like a troop of chickens they followed her obediently upstairs and Bridie heard the chirruping of their voices quickly fade into silence as they were put into bed.

It would be wonderful to live here always, she thought as she and David climbed the stairs to their room. If only this could go on and on and on, and never end.

But later, as she sat downstairs in the sitting room, absently turning the pages of a magazine and listening to soft music on the wireless on a dresser at the far end of the room, she remembered Edward, and the letter she'd written on the beach while David built an elaborate sandcastle, and she smiled, shaking her head to herself. No, she didn't really want it to go on forever for then she'd lose Edward, Sam Saul, Ted and Ethel and Susan, Lizzie, Jonathan, twins Oliver and Bridget, and dear Mrs MacDonald. All the people she loved. It would soon be time to go back to them, to where she belonged.

'Well, my dears, you've had the best week of the summer, it looks like,' said Mabel cheerfully as they licked the last vestiges of marmalade off their fingers. Breakfast was over. Their case lay waiting in the hall, buckets and spades washed free of sand and salt, ready to take back to London. Outside a warm drizzle fell on the beach, empty except for a few hardy souls, walking dogs up towards the dunes.

'It's been a wonderful week. Look at him, a picture

of health,' said Bridie, nodding at her son. 'He's even started to learn to swim. Well, we both did. It wasn't very warm, but at least we both got wet all over!'

They'd ventured bravely out in bathing costumes, and had sat in the shallows, shrieking as the waves broke over them. David had danced like a dervish, throwing up swirling, whirling waterfalls of spray with flailing arms and feet. He'd make a good swimmer, thought Bridie, showing no fear of the water at all.

'Perhaps we'll see you again next year,' went on Mabel. 'You'd be welcome any time, my dear.'

Bridie smiled at the friendly little woman who'd made them so welcome. 'If we can, we will,' she said.

Then it was time to go. Their bill was paid, farewells said to the soldier's family, who were staying a second week, and a kiss from Mabel sent them on their way.

Walking over London Bridge to find a 'bus to take them home, Bridie breathed in a great gulp of sooty air. It smelled lovely – like home.

It was early evening before they were properly back in their little house again. The range had to be lit and fresh food bought from the corner shop up the road. Bridie grumbled at the expense compared to the market, but for now it had to do. David gobbled his tea and ran up the road to play with the gang of five, six and seven year olds who roamed the street, kicking an old football and swapping boasts. Swimming in the waves – David really had something to boast about, and was bursting to tell stories.

Bridie cleared the table, and sat down to open the packet from Edward that had been waiting. It had been one of the things to look forward to, that had made the end of the holiday happy. She was just sorting the letters when there was a bang on her front door. Sam stood on the doorstep.

'Hello,' she said, resigned to the fact that she'd have to wait for her letters now.

'I wanted to assure myself that you were both back safely.'

'We are, and we had the best week you could imagine. Come on in, and I'll show you the picture postcards I bought.'

Sam installed himself at the table and eyed the pile of letters jealously. Bridie swept them up without a word and stuffed them into the dresser drawer. She pulled out a handful of cards instead. They sat side by side, Sam nodding in a familiar kind of way as she explained and described the walks they'd taken along country lanes behind the beach. She told him about swimming and sun-bathing and eating so much they thought they'd burst.

'Nipper behave himself?' asked Sam.

'It did him good. He had to behave, and the other children there had ever such nice manners, so it was a good example to him.'

'Good. I've missed you. It's been a long week. But my wife came home today.' He pulled a face. 'So life returns to normal. I'm glad you enjoyed yourself, and the nipper. But I'm glad you're back, as well.'

He leant forward and kissed her cheek. 'Welcome home.'

Abruptly he got up and pushed his chair away. 'I'll leave you to read your letters from loverboy,' he said, then regretted his tone. 'Didn't mean to sound spiteful. I just sometimes wish his ship would sink.'

Bridie knew it was useless to protest.

'I'll need my strongbox tomorrow,' she said instead. 'Can I come by and get it?'

'You could, but why take it away? You can leave it, if you want, like I keep telling you. There's nearly always someone in the office so you can treat it as your own. I've told Miriam to give you access to the safe. You see,' he said pointedly, 'I trust you.'

'All right,' decided Bridie, 'it does make sense. I'll come over first thing and take out what I need.' She eyed the moneybelt, hanging empty over the back of a chair. Work as usual tomorrow.

Sam got up to go. 'I'll be in the office early, so I'll see you.'

He'd make sure he was there whether he needed to be or not. Bridie stifled a sigh. He got worse and worse. She just hoped he'd get tired of the frustration of unrequited love and start behaving normally again. Sam hopped into his motor car, singing under his breath. They were back again, and that was all that really mattered.

Bridie got out her letters and smoothed the creases out. She was absorbed in the fifth of the pile when David ran in.

'Mum, can I go down with Cissie and get chips?'

333

Bridie fished in her pocket for two ha'pennies. 'Here, get us some as well, will you?'

David took the money and nodded. The fish and chip shop at the far end of Hermit Road sold delicious crisp, vinegar-soaked chips. A big twist of newspaperful for a ha'penny. A lot of kids didn't eat much else. Bridie returned to the letters. Edward wrote that they'd had yellow fever on board and that several of the men had been taken off. He himself was well, though. In letter eight, he had splendid news.

The Captain had asked to see him, to say that his application for officer training would be favourably considered at the end of this voyage. And letter number eleven, the last, gave the news Bridie had been looking forward to. They were returning to base in August, and would once again have six weeks of shore leave.

Bridie gave a little jump for joy. Ethel would have had her letters, too, and now they could plot all manner of treats for when Edward came home. The back door banged and a strong smell of malt vinegar wafted into the house.

'Here's yours,' called David, his own mouth bulging. He ran off back to Cissie's backyard, where seven or eight small boys were squabbling over extra vinegar out of a brown bottle. Popping the hot, fat chips into her mouth, Bridie sat and imagined Edward's homecoming. She could hardly wait.

Chapter Twenty-Two

There was the most awful noise from downstairs. Bridie struggled awake and raised her head. Someone was banging and banging on her front door. She had no idea of the time, just that it was the early hours, and the banging on her door sounded urgent and insistent.

David's frightened voice came from the next room. 'Mum? What's that, Mum?'

'Someone at the door. I'm going to see, don't worry,' his mother called back, and hurried into her dressing gown. Still pulling it round her she ran downstairs and called, 'All right, all right, I'm coming.'

The banging stopped. Bridie fumbled with the lock and opened the door a crack, on the chain. She peered into darkness, then realised that she was looking at the policeman who patrolled her part of the streets. He was a familiar sight, sometimes on foot, sometimes on a pushbike. Tonight, Bridie saw out of the corner of her eye, he had his bicycle propped against her wall while he made enough noise to waken the dead. She shut the door and released the chain, then opened it wide and said: 'What on earth . . .?'

'Mrs Holmes, I've got some bad news for you. Can I come in?'

Bridie clutched her dressing gown tighter to her neck and a thin tendril of fear worked its way coldly round her heart.

'What? What's happened?'

She showed him in with one hand. Oh please God, don't let it be Edward!

'Your husband has been took very bad. Heart attack, the doctor said. He wants to see you and the boy, if you please.'

Bridie shook her head, at a loss. 'How? At this time of night . . .? Oh yes, of course we must go.'

She began to turn to go to the stairs when the copper's voice went on: 'Seein' as it's three o'clock in the mornin' I took the liberty, and I hope you won't mind, of asking that gentleman friend of yours to take you over in his motor car. He was very obliging and will be round directly.'

Bridie stared at him. 'Sam Saul?' she asked finally.

'Mr Saul, yes.'

'Well, I never! What else don't you know about me?' she said, angry and suddenly afraid of him.

'It's a small patch, round here. We know pretty much who knows who. I said it was a liberty, but in the circumstances . . . Only Mrs Saul seemed at all put out.' The policeman spoke stolidly, without a trace of irony.

'It certainly was a liberty. But thank you, anyway.'

They turned their heads as the putt putt putt of Sam's car came round the corner and down the sleeping street.

'There he is now,' said the copper unnecessarily.

Outside in the ghostly light filtering through the high wrought iron gates of the cemetery, Sam clambered out of his motor and ran to Bridie's door. He and the policeman met with a bump. Apologising to each other, they drew back and the copper said, 'I'm glad you're here, sir. Mrs Holmes is upstairs getting dressed. She'll not be long.'

'Is she all right?' asked Sam anxiously.

'Oh, I think so, sir. She's quite calm.'

The copper was right. Outwardly Bridie was calm. Inwardly she was in turmoil. Pulling a woolly over David's protesting head, she wondered what was about to happen. A heart attack. That sounded so serious. Was Francis going to die? Her confused and frightened mind tried to turn over this new and shocking idea, to get to grips with it, but it was too sudden. David was pale with sleep and fright underneath the seaside tan.

'Come on, lovey,' she whispered, scooping him out of his warm bed. 'We are going to see Dad. In Sam's car, I think.'

'In the night?' asked David in bewilderment.

'Dad is not well. He wants us to go to see him. Now, in the night.'

The little boy, so like his dad, surveyed her face anxiously. 'Sam's coming too?' This was unheard of.

'To take us. In the car. Come on, now.'

She carried him downstairs. The policeman and Sam waited in silence. 'Here, take him for me,' ordered Bridie, giving David into Sam's arms, 'while I brush my hair. I can't go looking like this.'

She fumbled agitatedly in the dresser and brought out a brush and comb. Going into the scullery, she brushed her long hair and quickly twisted it into a knot. Speaking through hairpins, she said, 'Do you know how bad he is?'

The policeman looked warningly at Sam and shook his head slightly. 'No,' he called back, 'just that the doctor is with him, and he's expressed a wish to see you.'

'Is that Dr Hamilton?' asked Bridie, coming in looking wider awake and more composed.

'Yes, that's him,' said the copper.

Sam shifted David to his other arm and put his free arm round Bridie's shoulders. He gave her an encouraging squeeze.

'Come on, I'll take you there now,' he told her very gently, seeing with a lover's eyes the real depth of her shock and fear.

They shivered in the early morning chill. Dew had fallen on the seats of the car, and Sam wiped Bridie's front seat with his handkerchief before allowing her to climb in. 'Here, you take him,' he said, lifting David on to her lap. He shook out the blanket and tucked it well round them both.

'Thanks, chum,' he said to the policeman, who stood watching.

'Hope he's all right, Mr Holmes,' said the copper sombrely. 'They need the likes o' him around here.' He looked at Bridie, wondering once again what had brought her, the wife of such a man, to these mean streets. He shrugged. None of his business, but he hoped the old gent pulled through. He pushed his bike slowly down the pavement as the red lamps at the rear of Sam's car disappeared round the corner, heading for the High Street and Tredegar Square.

Bridie half saw the streets go by through unfocussed eyes. She saw the years of her married life pass disjointedly through her thoughts. David put his thumb in his mouth. He hadn't sucked it for months, now, Bridie thought distractedly. Then, before she had realised quite where she was, Sam turned the corner into the square and parked a few houses from number twelve.

'Listen,' he whispered to Bridie, 'I can see the doctor's motor here, and with that many lights on, there's a lot happening. You go on in, and I'll tuck myself up here and wait. Don't worry about me, I'll wait as long as needs be.'

He slid down his side of the motor and helped Bridie out, with David clinging round her neck. He kissed her briefly.

'Hope he's all right,' he said gruffly, then gave her a tiny push towards the house. He saw Mrs Goode open the door to her, and they all went inside. The door closed behind them. Sam got back into his motor and putting the rug round his long body, settled down to wait.

Upstairs Angus heard the motor car draw up, and the door open and close. He looked at the figure on the bed and murmured, 'Thank God, they're here,' under his breath. Francis's breathing was heavy and loud and laboured. Angus, checking the rapid, thready pulse, was surprised he was holding on as long as this. It was almost as though he refused to die until Bridie and David had come. He crossed the room with long strides and met them coming upstairs. He opened the door of another bedroom, and said, 'Please come in here first, my dear. I want to talk to you.'

Bridie looked from Angus to Mrs Goode's serious face and back again. 'He's really bad?' she asked in a low voice.

'He's been asking for you constantly, my dear,' replied the doctor. 'He had a major heart attack early this evening. My colleague Dr Potter was here earlier, and we agreed that we'd not move the poor man to hospital, but make him comfortable here. I don't think he has long to go, Bridie, but he seems to be holding on until he sees you. I'm desperately sorry to have to give you such news, my dear, but you'll see for yourself in a moment. You can take the wee boy in, as well. Come.'

He led her gently by the arm into the room where Francis lay dying. Mrs Goode had placed an oil lamp at the foot of the bed, with its wick turned low so as not to glare in the sick man's eyes. Bridie approached the bed slowly, leading David by the hand. She knelt down until her head was on a level with her husband's and said very quietly, 'Francis? We are here.'

She leant forward and kissed him very gently. The lined face, stony in semi coma, softened. Francis opened his eyes and looked at her. It was a long, long look, as of a man going on a far journey, who longs to imprint a memory of a beloved thing he cannot take with him.

'David?' he asked at last. The normally sharp, incisive voice was blurred by pain and approaching death.

'Here,' whispered Bridie, and lifted the little boy up on to his father's bed. Francis made a tremendous effort of will and put up his hand to touch his son's fair hair. 'Take care of your mother,' he murmured.

He turned his eyes back to Bridie. 'I have tried to take care of you. I was at fault. I'm sorry, Bridie.' There were long pauses between each word, as he struggled to stay with her. 'Will you forgive me? I can die at peace then. Rosa. Everything. Forgive me.' He moved his head in a gesture of humility.

A movement disturbed Bridie and David. They had not noticed the priest standing in the shadows of the room. The black figure moved silently towards the bed.

'He refused confession and the last rites until you had been here,' he murmured to Bridie. 'I would like, now . . .' He gestured.

Bridie nodded slightly and turned back to the sick man. She put her face against his and her arms crept round to hold the thin shoulders. 'Of course I do. You always had that, although I never said. 'course I do. I never blamed you. Oh, don't think that.'

The priest's voice began to murmur in the background.

Francis's eyes opened again, painfully. 'God bless

341

you,' he whispered to her. 'Now I shall have peace. I have provided . . . for David.'

His eyes closed once more, and as the priest repeated the words of the last rites, the final farewell, Francis sighed and the awful breathing stopped.

Bridie lay with her head buried in his shoulder while the onlookers prayed for the soul of the man who had been Francis.

'Mum?' David looked at his father, lying so quietly after making that horrible noise, and saw that his mother was crying silently. He was frightened, and shook her arm.

'Mum, why are you crying?'

Angus stepped forward and lifted the boy out of her reach. He wriggled and tried to get down.

'Listen,' said the doctor gravely, 'your mummy is crying because your daddy has died, and has gone to Heaven.'

Round-eyed, David looked back at the still figure on the bed. He knew what death meant. The mother cat had been found stiff under the raspberry canes one day, and while they buried her at the very end of the garden, Bridie had explained that the cat had been very old, and that when you died you went away to Heaven. She wasn't sure whether cats went to Heaven, but she thought they probably did. Now his dad was dead, like the mother cat.

David, suddenly terribly frightened, burst into noisy tears. He struggled free of Angus's grip and slid to the floor. Running to Bridie, he threw himself against her. Automatically, she turned and held him close against her. They sobbed, the three of them together for the last time in this world.

When the first storm lessened, Angus gently helped her to her feet. He took the white sheet and carefully ensuring that Francis's eyes were fully closed, pulled it up, and led Bridie and David from the room. The priest stood with bowed head at the foot of the bed, praying silently.

Mrs Goode stood in the doorway. 'He's gone?' she whispered to Angus.

'Aye, the poor man's gone.' She put a handkerchief to her eyes and sniffed loudly.

In the bedroom, the priest gathered up his book and beads and with a last nod of respect to the corpse, emerged blinking on to the brightly lit landing.

Bridie, white with hectic cheeks, looked at him. 'Thank you, Father,' she said automatically.

'Shall we all go downstairs?' the man suggested.

Bridie brushed a hand across her brow. 'Oh, yes,' she said, and led the way down. David was already in the parlour with Mrs Goode, still with her handkerchief dabbing at her eyes.

The curtains had not been drawn, and the sky was tinged with the dawn light. Birds chirped intermittently in the trees and the dawn chorus would soon be in full swing. Bridie seeing the world unchanged, felt bleakly disorientated. Nothing was different, yet she and her life had been changed irrevocably. Her head swam, and she staggered. Angus caught her and helped her into an armchair. He poured a glass of brandy and gave it to her.

'It's shock,' he said kindly. 'Drink this.'

The strong fumes made her cough and cleared her head. She rubbed her eyes and heard the birds singing with all their might and main outside. Was Sam still there? What was she to do with him? And David? She had somehow to go on with all these people, all these . . . things, situations. She handed the glass back to Angus.

'There'll have to be a funeral. What do I have to do?'

He shook his head kindly. 'Nothing much, unless you want to. Mrs Goode knows which funeral parlour to call, and will do that now. Usually they do all the organising, at least until you feel stronger. I shall sign the death certificate and do that side of things. Then there's Frank's Will. That will have to be read. But there's no necessity for you to be much involved, unless of course you want to,' he repeated.

'I'll go to the funeral, of course. And David,' she said.

'Naturally.'

She gave an unnatural, high-pitched laugh. ' 'course, it's funny, because I live right next to the cemetery. I see lots of funerals. We're quite used to them, in fact.'

'I know you do, my dear.' Angus looked with concern at her feverish excitement. 'Look,' he said, making up his mind, and taking a small bottle from his bag, 'I'd like you to go home, now, and go to bed, and take two of these. I think you are very shocked, and it might be the best thing to help your poor mind accept

344

what has happened. Would you do that?'

Bridie closed her eyes. 'I don't know,' she said in a small voice. 'I'll take the bottle and see, if you don't mind.'

She did feel exhausted, it was true. But there was David. He sat, pale and quiet on a chair by the window. Bridie suddenly wanted to go home more than anything else in the world. She nodded at Angus.

'All right.'

'Would you mind if I called round to see you this evening?' he asked as he fetched her shawl. 'I'd like to make sure you are all right.'

She smiled wanly. 'You'll be welcome. You know where the house is?'

He nodded. 'Yes.'

It seemed everyone knew everything about her, from the police to Angus. It was somehow disquieting, but Bridie pushed the thought from her head. From the top of the front door steps she could see Sam Saul, muffled in his rug, fast asleep at the steering wheel of his lovely motor car. Suddenly she wanted nothing more than to lean on his arm and have him take care of her, with his funny, sardonic poses and his fierce, sarcastic love.

She took David's hand and turned to Angus. 'I'll be seeing you tonight. Thank you for all you've done. I can't seem to think properly just now, but I know I have to thank you for making Francis's death right for him.'

Tears spilled again. She hurried down the steps, avoiding looking up in case neighbours were already peering from surrounding windows. She felt like an animal must when it flees for its burrow. At the car, she shook Sam's arm gently.

'Sam,' she said.

His head flew up out of his arms. 'Ah! Just forty winks,' he explained, taking in immediately what her face told him.

He leant down and put an arm round her shoulders. 'It's over, then?' he said gently. She nodded and her lip trembled. He got out of the car and lifted David into the back. Then he stopped and lifted Bridie like a baby, and placed her tenderly in the passenger seat. Out came the rug once more. He put her unresisting arms inside his own jacket, and in shirtsleeves and braces, he drove her back home, taking every corner with unusual care, so that she wasn't swayed or jolted.

Disregarding the stares of both passers-by and neighbours, he carried Bridie into her house, David tagging behind. Up the stairs he took her, and laying her on her bed, he began to loosen her clothes and take off her shoes. The covers were pulled up, the curtains drawn on the waving tips of the apple tree. He told David to stay with his mum, and went down to brew a pot of tea. With a hot, very sweet cup in one hand, and Angus's bottle in the other, he went back up. Propping Bridie up against his strong chest, he let her sip the tea until it was cool enough to swallow two of the pills. Her eyelids began to droop.

'David and me will spend the day together,' he reassured her. 'We'll not be far away, so if you wake and need us, we'll be near.'

A dizzy feeling started to fill Bridie's head, then a worry pushed its way forward. 'Your wife,' she said, in a slightly slurred voice. 'What will she say?'

'My wife will take care of herself. She's a kind woman, for all I'm cruel about her. She wouldn't like it, but she'd understand if she knew what's just happened.'

Bridie nodded drowsily. 'You stay, then. I want you to, please.' She was already half dreaming.

Sam sat beside the bed, watching her slide deep into drugged sleep. David came and leaned on his knee, his own eyes drooping. Sam felt that if he lived for ever and a day, he would never love anyone like he loved this woman. He took her sleepy son into his own room, and tucked him into his bed. Then he went downstairs, and, taking the garden tools that Bridie stored in the scullery, he rolled up his sleeves and started to dig a new flower bed along the fence that separated her garden from next door's. He'd plant flowers in abundance for Bridie, some for every month of the year, living, beautiful things, like the love that lived in his heart.

When Angus kept his word and arrived to see Bridie at six o'clock that evening, he found Sam and David busily digging flowerbeds. The chatter of voices had led him round the back. He stopped to watch them, unseen. The tall Jew who cared nothing for children was listening seriously as David explained in a breathless voice that you shouldn't chop worms in half because they were good for the garden, and grew new heads like magic.

'My dad told me that,' said the small boy proudly.

They carefully removed the worm that was clinging to Sam's forkful of earth.

'You keep the edge straight when you start that bit,' ordered Sam, and the two of them squatted down and began to mark out the next section.

Angus shook his head in wonder. He knew of Sam Saul by reputation, and could hardly believe with his own eyes the gentle patience he was showing with David. Yet. . . . He coughed and both heads turned.

'Dr Hamilton, come on in,' said Sam, rising from his knees and brushing loose soil from his grey trousers.

Angus held out a hand and, Sam glancing apologetically at his dirty fingers, the two men shook hands.

'How is Mrs Holmes?' enquired Angus, smiling at David.

'She's slept all day,' said Sam. 'So's the young man here. He only got up a couple of hours ago, and came to help me here.' He gestured at the new flowerbed.

'I'll pop upstairs, if I may, and have a look in on her.'

'By all means. I'll show you.'

The two tall men had to duck their heads through the back doorway, then Sam showed Angus upstairs. Bridie stirred and their entrance woke her. For a moment she was confused, then it all came back. Francis – he was dead. She sat up and pulled the covers up under her chin.

'Hello, Dr Hamilton,' she greeted him. 'It's kind of

you to call. I'm afraid I'm still half asleep.'

'Good. It was the best thing.' He turned to Sam. 'May I have a wee word with Mrs Holmes, if you please.'

'Of course.' Sam obligingly started back down the stairs. 'I'll look in the larder to see what I can do about something to eat.' His black head disappeared from view.

Angus perched himself on the end of the bed. 'Do you feel able to talk?' he asked.

'Oh, yes.'

'Mrs Goode has asked the funeral director to make the arrangements that are necessary. They would like to arrange for Frank's funeral to be held next Tuesday. Would that be all right with you?'

'Yes,' said Bridie in a whisper.

'Are there any special wishes you'd like me to tell them to observe?'

'No, I don't think so. I shall be there with David, of course.'

The doctor nodded. 'I'll have a motor car sent to fetch you to the house, and the funeral will go from there. You must let me know if there is anything you want, Bridie.'

She shook her head, puzzled. 'I haven't got used to the idea of it. My head feels funny.'

'It will take time. Like Rosa.'

'No,' said Bridie, 'this isn't like Rosa at all. We have been apart a long time, Dr Hamilton. I feel strange that Francis isn't there any more, but it isn't like Rosa. Nor Mam. We wasn't close at all, not for a

349

long time. Not since I got used to what had happened, and made my own way.'

Angus wondered once again what had happened. 'And there's another thing,' he said, into the pause that followed. 'Frank asked me to be his executor, and there is of course his Will to be read. I imagine it will be a matter of me, you and Mrs Goode getting together. Would you care to do that after the funeral? Do it all in one day, as it were?'

Bridie nodded. 'Funny. I never thought about Wills,' she remarked. 'He did say he'd provided for David. So maybe it'll be mostly him in the Will.'

'One never knows,' cautioned Angus. 'Though as far as I know Frank had no other family.' He stood up. 'No point in speculating, anyway,' he observed. 'We'll read it on Tuesday.'

'What did he want?' Sam enquired nosily, when Angus had gone.

'To see how I am. And to talk about the funeral and the Will,' said Bridie.

Sam suddenly looked thoughtful. 'That's a point. You may come into a lot of money.'

'I don't know that he had a lot of money. He was always very careful. It was odd, it was one of those things I never got to know, whether Francis was rich or not. It never seemed to matter.'

Sam gave an evil grin. 'That's why you'll never make a real fortune in business. You do good business, but underneath you don't really love money. Not enough.'

Bridie glanced at him. 'You're probably right,' she

said indifferently. 'So long as I have what I need, it's enough. What's David doing?'

'Digging.'

'Where?'

'Come and see.'

He took her arm and led her into the garden. They'd dug about ten feet along the edge of the fence, and the border was three feet deep. It was untidy, but a start had been made.

Bridie looked up at Sam. 'Whatever is it for?'

'A border of flowers. You've got vegetables, and apples and fruit bushes, but not many flowers. So I thought we'd make a bed along here, and plant a variety of things that would always have something blooming, even in winter, like Christmas roses.'

Bridie squeezed his arm. 'What a kind thought. That's you all over, Sam, a horror one minute and a real romantic the next.'

He looked at the face turned up to his and considered kissing it, but decided against it.

'You get us dinner, and me and David'll get this cleared up.' He bent down and started to gather handfuls of grass lumps and weeds. 'This lot can go on the compost heap,' he directed David to help.

Bridie rubbed the last traces of sleep from her eyes, and, still smiling at the idea of the year-round flower-bed, went indoors to cook dinner.

Sam eventually went home late that evening. His long-suffering wife wailed as soon as he walked in.

'Where have you been? Oy yoi yoi, I sit and I wait, and I wait, and I think – he's come to no good, he's done something and been caught. And still there's no word. You want I should suffer?'

'Woman,' roared Sam, 'be quiet. I have a friend in trouble, so I stayed. A good Jew should help a friend, no?'

'Friend?' shrilled his wife suspiciously. 'You got no friend. Money you got plenty. Friend, you got none.'

'That's all you know,' said Sam angrily. 'I got a friend. Now hold your tongue.'

Muttering under her breath, and with swift suspicious glances, Mrs Saul subsided and did as she was bid. But she wondered about it for a long time, even though Sam, being disinclined for trouble at home, was diplomatically present and charming for the rest of the week.

Bridie and David went alone to the funeral. Sam had offered to accompany them, but Bridie thought it best he did not. They arrived first at Tredegar Square, and then at the church, in the promised motor car, driven by a chauffeur. It was a slow and dreary ride. Back they came the way they'd gone, to the cemetery gates. Down long wide avenues to a corner where the newly dug grave lay waiting.

There had been a large congregation of mourners, many of whom had followed the coffin to its resting place. Bridie, dry-eyed, accepted condolences and curious stares indiscriminately. Angus hovered. The priest's voice came to an end. Out of respect for the widow, people stood back and waited for Bridie and David to leave first. Glad it was over, Bridie, David and Angus, with a silent, red-eyed Dora, were driven back to the house. Dora opened a bottle of sherry and fetched three glasses, while Angus sat down behind Francis's desk and prepared to read the Will. It was very brief and to the point.

Francis left Mrs Goode an annuity of one hundred pounds, at which Dora gasped and burst into suppressed tears. He left his books to his old friend Angus Hamilton. The rest of his estate in its entirety was left to Bridie, with the proviso that she look after his son with every possible care and there was a request that David should receive the estate in his turn if Bridie herself so willed. Angus continued to read the details of her inheritance. The freehold property in Tredegar Square and all its contents, Francis's pension and the holding in the bank after Dora's annuity had been deducted. Stocks and shares and investments amounting, according to their value at the time of writing, to about twenty-five thousand pounds.

Bridie went very pale. Her head swam for the second time in this room. Francis had been wealthy. Now she was wealthy. She was stunned by the size of it all. Dora and Angus watched her, waiting for her to say something.

'Oh,' was all that came out.

'Well,' said Angus finally, 'ye're a woman of means now, Bridie.'

She nodded slightly. 'I . . . I had no idea,' she stumbled. 'I never thought . . .'

'I think ye'd better go and have a wee talk with Frank's solicitor. And soon,' suggested Angus. 'Ye'll be needing to make some decisions about where you are going to live, and how to manage the house and so on.'

'Yes, I will. I'll have to think. Would you arrange for me to see him tomorrow, please?'

Angus smiled. 'The telephone downstairs is yours now,' he pointed out. 'You'll be able to do such things for yourself.'

Bridie put her hand to her mouth in astonishment. So it was! She looked round the familiar room. To live here again? A little shiver ran down her back. She didn't know if she could. There were memories here that might be best left to rest in peace. It would need thinking about. Meanwhile she wanted to get away, see what had happened from a bit of distance.

'Dr Hamilton, thank you for everything you've done. Mrs Goode, thank you, too. If you wouldn't mind asking the driver to bring the motor, I'd like to take David home.'

Angus gathered up the pages of the Will that lay on Francis's desk. 'I'll go and see the lawyer tomorrow, I promise.' She nodded at Mrs Goode reassuringly as well. Angus took one of her hands in his big fists and gave her an encouraging squeeze.

'I'm glad Frank has done this. It seems quite right to me,' he told her.

Bridie half smiled. 'I can talk to you on the telephone when I have talked to the lawyer.'

'Aye, that you can,' answered Angus. 'I'll look to hear from you tomorrow, then.' Bridie nodded agreement.

The three of them went to the front door, where the driver waited patiently. He drove her in silence back to Plaistow, his stiff back betraying distaste for the narrow streets and huddled houses. People turned to stare after the woman, dressed all in black, who rode next to the child in his black suit and cap.

Bridie was relieved beyond words to shut her front door on the rest of the world. She took off her black bonnet with its heavy veil, and sat down by her unlit fire.

'My goodness gracious me,' she said to David, stroking his head as he leant on her knee, 'what are we going to do with it all?' She looked tenderly at the fair hair. His future was assured. She could give him the world now, if she wanted to. The thought lightened her heart, and she picked the child up. Putting him in her lap, she kissed his soft cheek and sat rocking him quietly, imagining . . . dreaming . . . wondering . . . what in the world they would do.

Chapter Twenty-Three

Ten days later a very tall, very broad figure dressed in white strode round the corner of Hermit Road, and, quickening its pace, turned into the little front path that led to Bridie's door. It knocked several times. The door opened, and there was a moment's stillness before Bridie put out her hands, to be swept up into a great bear hug that left her breathless and laughing.

'Oh, Edward! I didn't expect you 'til tomorrow. In your letter, you said tomorrow.'

'I got discharged early so I thought I'd surprise you. I haven't even seen Mum yet.'

'Oh, what a surprise! And you look so grand. My word. Just look, all starch and braid. How do you keep clean!'

Edward laughed. 'We don't. It's overalls most of the time.' He grinned at her. 'I've been looking forward so much to seeing you. How's the nipper?'

'At school!'

' 'course. Time's gone so fast.'

He placed his cap on the kitchen table. 'Not fast enough, though, for me. To get back, I mean.'

Bridie smiled shyly. 'Yes. I've been longing for you to come home. So many things have happened since I last wrote, I hardly know whether I'm coming or going. Oh, Edward, Francis died a couple of weeks ago. It was so sudden and it's changed everything. One minute I knew where I was, but now – oh, it's all of a heap.'

'Whoa, slow down,' cried Edward. 'Francis dead?'

Bridie nodded. 'Of a heart attack. It was all over in a few hours. I saw him, an' he said goodbye. Then he was gone.'

Edward digested the news in silence. 'Two weeks ago?'

'Yes.'

'So the funeral and everything's all over.' He might have been speaking to himself. Bridie watched him. He raised his head thoughtfully. 'How's he left you?'

Bridie knew exactly what he meant, and had been dreading the effect of the answer. 'There's the house in Tredegar Square, and some money.'

There was a long silence between them. Finally Edward spoke calmly.

'It's not too bad, a junior officer's pay, though of course I'd be away for long spells. I was thinking that we could manage on my wages, once I'd been made an officer. This puts a different light on it, though.'

Bridie shook her head. 'A different light on what?' she asked, her heart tight.

'You and me. I was going to ask you to marry me, one day in the future. When you were free. I'd have waited and waited for you, Bridie. But now you're a rich woman, by the sound of it. . . .'

Bridie sprang to her feet and stopped him by

putting a hand over his bearded mouth.

'No, don't say that,' she begged.

Edward's bright blue eyes looked into hers very seriously.

'I was waiting, too, Edward,' she promised him. She took her hand away. 'I've waited for you, too,' she said again, a blush rising from the neck of her dress and travelling all the way up to her hair.

Edward held the hand that she'd taken from his mouth. 'Do you really mean that?' he asked, trying to stop the overwhelming flood of joy that threatened to burst out in a roar of delight.

'Yes. I've meant it, I think, since the first time I saw you, in Ethel's back room. I think I knew then.'

With a great whoop of happiness he swept her on to his knee and held her tightly. He gazed at her for what seemed like a long time, then, lifting her as easily as a doll, set her on her feet. Standing up so that he towered over her, he took her hand in both his.

'Will you marry me, Bridie?' he asked formally. 'And please say yes, or something terrible will happen to my heart that won't be very repairable.'

'Oh, yes, I will, dear Edward. Oh, yes, of course I will, as soon as some time has gone past. That's only decent.'

Understanding, Edward nodded. She could smell the salt tang of the sea on his face as he kissed her, the thick brown beard soft on her mouth. They clung to each other, holding each other and not wanting ever, ever, to let go. Bridie felt as though, after an endless wandering, she had at last truly come home.

When the clock ticking away on the mantelpiece chimed softly, Edward lifted his mouth from hers and said, 'Nipper?'

She nodded.

'Let's go and get him together.' He kissed her again because he couldn't bear not to.

'What about Ethel? She'll be ever so put out if anyone sees you before she does. Even seeing me first might upset her.'

Edward smiled, the most loving smile she ever saw. 'Not when I take my future wife home to see her. She thinks the world of you, Bridie. She's always thought of you as a daughter, just like our Susan. She'll be over the moon.'

Tucking her hand in the crook of his arm, he walked with her round to the convent school where David went every day. 'House and money, eh?' he remarked as they went. 'Do you know what you're going to do with it all?'

Bridie smiled up at him. 'That depended on you,' she confessed. 'I'd thought ever such a lot about it. I don't want to go and live in Tredegar Square. It wouldn't feel right. So I think I'll sell the house and sell this one, too, and buy another one somewhere else. There's enough money to start up a proper business, though I'm not sure what just yet. But if you hadn't asked me, and if we weren't going to be married, I'd have just sold Tredegar Square, and stayed where I am. But I'd love to go somewhere new with you, to start afresh in a home that's only been ours. That's why it depended on you.'

Edward put up a hand. 'I don't fancy living on my wife's earnings or property,' he said, with a serious look at her. 'You keep what's yours, and it'll see the nipper right later on, but I wouldn't like to live way above my own means because it would make me uncomfortable, Bridie. I wanted to look after you myself.'

'We could maybe look after each other, instead?' she offered. 'I've been on my own a long while, Edward, and I'm used to seeing to myself. And you'll still be away so much, I'll need something to keep me busy. What about a house we put equal money into, and the rest held for David through a business? The lawyers are clever at working out how to invest money, and how to keep it in trust for someone.'

Edward thought it over as they strolled along. Just before they got to the school gates, he nodded, satisfied.

'So long as its fifty-fifty on our house, and you have the rest for your business. We'll use what you earn, and what I earn, but keep the capital. How would that be?'

To the fascination of several mothers waiting for their children outside the gates, Bridie put her arms round Edward's neck and hugged him close.

'That would be just splendid,' she whispered.

He bent down to murmur in her ear. 'I love you so much, Bridie. I don't know how to say it.'

She drew back and smiled. 'You do already. And I know, because I love you too.'

The whispered conversation was interrupted by the

shrieking of children let out of school. David came bounding down the school steps, swinging his bag and jumping the last three steps. He looked round for his mother, and, seeing her standing with a familiar figure, gave a cry of excitement and rushed through the jostling crowd of children to hurl himself at Edward. The big man caught him and swung him high in the air.

' 'lo, nipper!' he shouted, swinging the boy round in a hug.

' 'lo,' answered David, all out of breath. He planted a kiss on Edward's ear and slid down to the ground again.

Bridie took one hand, Edward the other, and, by unspoken consent, the three of them walked slowly round to Ethel's house, to break the good news to all and sundry.

Chapter Twenty-Four

Things didn't go altogether as they'd expected. Ethel had reservations which, in their delight with each other, they had not foreseen. She didn't beat around the bush.

'You're Catholic, love,' she pointed out to Bridie, 'an' he's bin brought up Church of England.'

'Oh, Mum,' protested Edward. 'I go to the service on board sometimes, and if the men have problems there's always the ship's chaplain to talk to, but I wouldn't say I minded very much one way or the other. And you and Dad aren't exactly regulars, are you?'

'That ain't the point,' said Ethel firmly.

'Then what is?'

'It's things like . . . the kiddies. You'd have Catholic kiddies. Wouldn't you?' she appealed to Bridie for confirmation.

'Well, me being a Catholic, my priest would say I should bring the children to church. But does it matter so much? David goes to a Catholic school, an' I go to church some Sundays, but it never seemed to make no problems either way. I don't see as it matters.'

'And what about the wedding?' Ethel went on to

her next worry. 'You'd have to be wed in your place, wouldn't you?'

Bridie took Edward's hand in the shelter of the hanging table-cloth. She was starting to feel anxious. Ethel's broad features had lost their usual beaming good nature and were creased up with doubt and uncertainty.

'Well,' began Bridie, 'there might be ways round it. I'd have to go and ask. Perhaps we could go to the register office, and then have a blessing or something.'

'Blessing!' squawked Ethel. 'Me only son get wed in the register office, and then 'ave a blessing. I never heard the like.'

'We're looking for a way round it, Mum. Don't get all upset.'

Ethel turned her gaze from Bridie to him. Love and hurt fought a battle over her plain features.

'I am upset,' she told him, 'and I ain't pretending otherwise. It's not you, ducks,' she explained to Bridie's unhappy face, 'goodness knows I couldn't ask for a better daughter-in-law. I'd be real pleased. But there is a problem, and I can't make out there ain't.'

Edward turned to Bridie. 'What about getting married in the register office, and leaving it at that?'

'I'd be livin' in sin,' said Bridie miserably.

'Here's your father, at last,' Ethel said, hearing the door bang.

'Sorry I'm late. There was overtime going so I took it,' explained Ted as he came through the door.

'Hullo Dad,' said Edward.

Ted stopped unbuttoning his coat, surprised. 'Thought you was coming tomorrow,' he said.

'I got off earlier than I thought.'

'It's good to see you, lad,' said Ted, clapping him on the shoulder. Then he looked round the circle of serious faces. 'What's 'appened?' he asked.

Ethel put him in the picture. 'Our Edward wants to marry Bridie.'

A huge grin spread over Ted's face. His long, kind face lit with delight. 'But that's wonderful news. What you lot looking so glum for?'

'She's Catholic,' said Ethel, outlining the problem succinctly.

'Ah.'

Ted knew his Ethel, and he instantly appreciated the glumness. He fell silent and scratched his chin, wondering how to steer around this one. Eth was a good soul, but when it came to Family and Sticking Together, she could be stubborn as a mule. Ted realised that Ethel would find this very hard to bear.

'Can you imagine our Dan and Dot, or Bert and 'is stuck-up wife Clara, grinnin' all over their faces at me in a Catholic church? Ooh, it don't bear thinkin' about.'

'Why should they mind?' asked Ted mildly.

'Yes, Mum,' Edward broke in, 'why should they? If I'm marrying the woman I love, why should anyone give tuppence about where I do it? And if they are going to feel offended – well, why invite them?'

Ted nodded, but he knew it wouldn't work.

'What?' Ethel was scandalized. 'Not invite them?

365

My only son, and not invite the family to 'is wedding. What an idea! 'course I'd have to invite them. I'd be a laughing stock, else.'

There was silence. Bridie picked at the edge of the table-cloth, wishing she was anywhere but here.

Ted spoke first. 'It seems to me, we have a choice. They can get married in the register office, and the relations can be invited there, and then go an' do whatever has to be done in church afterwards. Or they can be wed in church, with only a few family, who wouldn't make you feel badly.'

'What about the kiddies?' persisted Ethel.

'That's for them to decide, Ethel love. It ain't our business, and that's a fact.'

For a moment Ted thought his wife was going to cry.

'Mum, what's really more important? Me and Bridie doing what is right for us, or a bunch of aunts and cousins who probably don't care much anyway?'

'Don't you say that, son,' said Ted reproachfully. 'There's not one in the family who wouldn't put theirselves out for you if you was in trouble.'

'I didn't mean it that way,' said Edward. 'I meant they are fond of us, what we are, regardless. I bet if you asked them, they'd mostly say it didn't really matter, so long as we're happy with each other.'

'Ooh, the shame of it,' whimpered Ethel again.

'No, Mum. You're wrong. You just see.' He put his arm round Bridie. 'Look at us, Mum. Do you see anything to be ashamed of?'

Ethel was forced to shake her head.

'Imagine it, Mum,' said Edward, who had a fair idea of what his wedding meant to Ethel, 'there'll be me, in my best Whites. I can have a Guard of Honour. Can't you see it? Bridie in a pretty dress, me in my Whites, and eight others lining the way from the church. Oh, come on, Mum, it'll be one of the grandest weddings the family's had in years!'

Ethel began to feel a little bit better. Maybe it wouldn't be a disaster after all. A Guard of Honour, eh? That'd make Clara green with envy.

'All right,' she said reluctantly. 'I'll think about it. I'm not saying as it's sorted,' she added, 'but it might be. I'll have to see.'

Unseen by Ethel, Ted winked at Edward. He leant over the table and patted Bridie's hand.

'I'm real pleased for you, love,' he said. 'Our Edward's a lucky man.'

Bridie looked at Edward. 'I'm lucky, too.'

Ted nodded. 'You two will do well together, I reckon,' he said with satisfaction.

David came running in from the street. 'I've fallen over,' he cried, showing a scraped knee.

Ethel and Bridie took him into the scullery and lifted him up to sit on the draining board while they washed the dirt off with cold water. Ethel touched Bridie's arm.

'I 'ope you don't take no offence,' she said apologetically, 'but I must speak my mind because he is my son, after all.'

Bridie hugged her future mother-in-law's stout frame. 'Ethel, he's so like you. That's what I love, the straightforwardness. I know I can trust Edward 'til the day I die, and it's you an' Ted has made him that way, because that's how you are, too. I'd never take offence, and I know you didn't mean none.'

They put a scrap of sticking plaster on David's knee.

'I suppose that convent don't do him no harm,' remarked Ethel grudgingly. 'It's improved his manners, I've noticed, and there's not a lot of kiddies you can say that for, round here.'

'That and his dad,' agreed Bridie.

Ethel looked at her questioningly.

'Talkin' of his dad,' she went on, 'when did you have in mind for this wedding? I mean, it's a bit early days yet, ain't it? ' she finished delicately.

'It's strange,' answered Bridie. 'Although we were apart so long, I still feel . . . I don't know what to say . . . like a widow, I suppose. As though Francis and me not being together didn't mean he wasn't my husband. I even miss him, in a peculiar sort of way. And David hardly knows he's gone, yet. Edward and me haven't had time to talk about it, but I don't think I'd feel ready to get married just yet. A decent time has to pass, though I couldn't rightly say why exactly. It just does.'

Ethel sighed with relief. It was what she'd hoped they'd do, and not rush into anything indecently soon.

'That's right, my duck.' She gave Bridie's cheek a smacking kiss. 'Why don't you leave me to keep an eye on David, and you two go for a walk? You've got such a lot to talk about, and he'll be gone again in a few weeks.'

And so they did. They walked arm in arm down the little byways that led to the River Lee, winding its way down to Canning Town and the East India Docks. They came to a scrubby bit of land that overlooked the wharves and cranes half a mile away at the edge of the water. In the midst of the thistles and coarse grass, there was a wooden seat facing the river. They sat down and Bridie snuggled warmly up against Edward's jacket. They talked of Ethel and her reluctance to go to a Catholic church, then of this and that, and when they'd get married, and who would come. Bridie pressed tighter against Edward's side when he asked the question she knew must come, and had been wondering how to answer. As with Ethel, she decided honesty was the only choice.

'What about your family?' asked Edward. 'You never mention them. I wondered about them, and I was going to ask you next time I wrote to you. Where are they?'

'Your mum knows about my family,' she answered after such a long pause that Edward turned and looked hard into her face with puzzled eyes. 'I told Ethel when I went to live in your house. She asked me, just like you have. So I knew I'd have to tell you, too.'

'What are you on about?' asked Edward, mystified.

'If you'd have asked me in one of your letters, I

would have told you everything, and it might have been better that way. But here we are now, and it's not a letter. Oh, Edward, I hope this isn't going to make you hate me, like it did Francis.'

Edward took her by the shoulders and turned her white face to his. 'Tell me,' he ordered. 'Stop beating around the bush and driving me mad. Tell me.'

She did. Everything.

'That's a terrible story,' said Edward at last.

'Yes,' whispered Bridie. She could feel hot tears at the back of her throat.

'What did Mum say when you told her?'

'She said something like, "Oh, you poor duck",' answered Bridie, not knowing whether to laugh or cry.

'Good,' said Edward brusquely, ' 'cause if she'd said any different, she and me would have had words.'

Bridie's pinched face lifted to his, which was deep in thought. 'Do you mean, it won't make a difference, to us? Will it still be all right?'

'All right? All right?' bellowed Edward. 'Anyone ever hurt you again, and I'll kill them with my bare hands, so help me.' His big knuckles worked at each other, white with fury.

A tear ran down Bridie's cheek and she swallowed the rest hard. 'I was so dreadfully afraid,' she admitted at last. 'It's done so much harm, and I knew I had to tell, and I didn't know what would happen after that. I thought you might hate me.'

Edward pulled her closer. 'I don't believe we could

hate each other ever, not even if one of us did do something bad. And you didn't do anything bad – the other people did. Francis sounds a monster.'

'Oh, no,' cried Bridie in distress, 'he wasn't that at all. He . . . he felt sort of deceived and he couldn't get over that. We didn't understand each other.'

'I love you enough to want to understand. Will you always tell me everything, so that nothing like that can happen to us?'

Suddenly bone weary, Bridie gave a small smile. 'Yes,' she promised. 'No secrets.'

'Then I have something to tell you.'

'A girl in every port?' asked Bridie, half anxious, half teasing.

'One or two,' admitted Edward, 'but hardly in every port, and never serious. No, it's that I used to dream about you. I had a dream that came quite often, for years. It was always the same, and I used to wake up from it sweating and shaking and afraid. When I first saw you, I couldn't believe it because there you were, the girl in the dream. I've never had it from that day to this. A kind of fear got lifted away, though I couldn't say what I was afraid of.'

'We both had something to be afraid of then,' said Bridie.

'Not any more.' Edward's warm lips on hers drove away the fears and doubts for the last time. He smoothed that unruly red hair, and vowed in his heart that he would protect her and care for her. They sat, quietly looking out over the grey river landscape, the dust making little eddies round their feet, each lost in their own thoughts.

They agreed to wait about six months. By then, Edward expected to be back again.

'If not,' he said, 'I'll apply for special leave to get married. So either way, it'll be an early spring wedding. March?'

Bridie imagined a bright crisp day, with an east wind blowing in cold sunshine. She'd have a fur wrap. She could afford it now!

'March,' she agreed.

Ethel had either overcome her objections, or was keeping them to herself. Her eyes lit up with excitement when they announced their plans. A March wedding in St Saviour's up in Stratford, and a move to Hackney.

'We thought Hackney because there's the park, and the market nearby, and a school for David, and lots of space. It's healthy down there,' Edward told Ted, who nodded agreement.

'I think it's a wise move. Property pricey down that way?'

Ted, who'd rented his small home ever since he and Ethel had married thirty years earlier, felt a bit awed at his son going out and buying a house. He swelled with pride when he told his mates over at the Market. He felt he'd taken on a whole new status. Having a property-owning son was almost as good as owning something himself.

'Yes. More than in Plaistow, because it's a much better area. I know Bridie will be sad to move away, she's ever so fond of that house of hers.'

But in the end Bridie was overjoyed with the house they found on the edge of the canal, directly overlooking Victoria Park. From the back windows, she could hear the water tumbling and sliding under the great wooden sluice gates, a hundred yards downstream. The towpath on the far side of the canal was a riot of wild flowers. Patient horses dragged barges down to the Docks, three miles away, and then back up again to the factories over in West London, towards Windsor and Slough. The park was green. Grassy spaces lay beneath great banks of almond trees, and tall, massive chestnuts.

'It's like being in the country,' cried Bridie when the agent first showed them round. 'Oh, it's lovely, Edward.'

The house had three storeys, and all the rooms were much bigger than the ones she had at present. It was like a more modest version of Tredegar Square, which had sold in a flash for a very good price. Angus had heartily approved the sale, and had done everything he could to make it go through quickly.

'I'm delighted for you, lassie,' he told Bridie, when she introduced Edward and outlined her plans for her possessions. Her old lawyer, who had advised her so wisely, peered at her over his half-moon glasses and smiled gently.

'You see?' he said, and needed to say no more.

He handled the sale of her little house in Plaistow, and five days before Edward was due to leave for Dartmouth, and his officers' training, they stood in their own house, tired after all the rushing about and signing of forms, but completely content.

'There's just one thing missing,' remarked Edward, as they stood, arms entwined, surveying their castle.

'What's that?' Bridie asked, looking round.

'This,' he answered.

He fished in his pocket and pulled out a tiny leather box. On a velvet cushion glinted a thin gold ring with a single ruby.

'You can't be properly engaged without a ring,' Edward said solemnly, and, lifting her hand, he slipped it gently on to her ringless finger. She'd put away Francis's ring now she was to marry another man.

'There,' he said, in satisfaction. 'Now it's official!'

David, running round excitedly exploring all the rooms, wondered why his mother suddenly threw her arms round Edward's neck like that. He sighed.

Grown ups, he thought dismissively, and ran upstairs to investigate the bathroom, something he'd never remembered having before.

The days had flown by. So absorbed in each other, and with so much to do, they'd hardly seen anyone except Ted and Ethel, and Susan when she could get away from Mrs Anderson's fourth baby. So Ethel went the rounds two days before Edward was due to leave. He and Bridie and David arrived at the station platform to find not only his family, but a whole farewell party gathered together. Lizzie and Jonathan each had a twin in their arms. They were growing into bonny babies, having been a real handful for their first year. Angus stood head and shoulders above everyone else except Edward, his whiskered face alight with pleasure at the turn of events. Mrs MacDonald had a pocketful of sweets for the babies and David, and, sloping unhappily in the background but unable to stay away, was Sam Saul.

When he'd first heard the news a pain like a knife had gone through his heart. It was so many years since Sam had known tears that he hadn't recognised the stinging feeling in his nose. Then, telling Miriam that he wasn't in the office – to anyone, anyone at all – he locked his door and opened his safe. He stubbornly and systematically counted his way through its contents, and noted each amount on a sheet of accounting paper. It was past midnight, and Miriam had long gone home, by the time he finished. Red-eyed and exhausted, he sat quite still in front of the last pile of securities and listened for the pain. A faint echo of terrible loss called out of some deep part of himself. When he got home, he stopped his wife's wailing in mid sentence by saying, 'You want to go for a cruise?'

Mrs Saul's mouth worked silently. For the first time in her life she was at a loss for words.

'What?' she finally got out.

Sam gave her one of his patient looks.

'A cruise. I asked you if you'd like to go on one.'

Mrs Saul, not trusting her voice, nodded vigorously.

'All right. That's settled.'

375

Leaving his astounded wife, never to be any wiser, Sam took himself off to sleep in his dressing room. With his affairs in the hands of a willing but equally bemused Miriam, he departed a month later and healed his broken heart in the fresh air of the seas around Bermuda. In the second month they were away, Mrs Saul became pregnant. Her son, David Saul, was born eight months later after a difficult time, and Sam, viewing the minute scrap of a baby boy lying in his arms, at last found something else to love.

But that afternoon on the grey platform he only knew that he'd become a stranger where before he'd been a friend. It was nothing anyone said or did, it just was.

There were tears and kisses and hugs and promises of letters. Bridie and Edward wandered a little way from the others, to say their farewells.

'Go safely,' she said, smiling and dry-eyed.

'And you. Take care of everything for me.' He lifted her hand and kissed the little ring. 'I'll be back. I'll send you a telegram as soon as I know when.'

'We'll be waiting for you.'

They had one long, last kiss, then, to catcalls from the train doors where his fellow cadets had gathered in a curious bunch, craning their necks to see Bridie, he turned and laughed back at them. One last hug for David, one last gruff pat on the shoulder from Ted and a weepy wave from Ethel, and he ran to join the long train, radiating the joyful energy of a man completely happy and content with his lot.

Chapter Twenty-Five

Bridie set about taking care of everything, as Edward had instructed her. She enrolled David at the Catholic school in Victoria Park Road, a green and grassy walk away, across the heart of the park. Then, though still having to make trips to Plaistow twice a week to wind down her business there, she had time on her hands. One morning, after taking David to school, she called in at Hemmingway's, the local builder's. After a good deal of discussion, an arrangement was made for Mr Hemmingway himself to call round at the house by the canal. Together he and Bridie went over every inch of it. Mr Hemmingway went away, to return two weeks later with a sheaf of drawings under his arm. They spread the sheets out on the kitchen table and pored over the elegantly penned blueprints. On paper, the house had been transformed. Scullery and kitchen had been made one, with space for the centre-piece of the new kitchen – a gas cooker. Mr Hemmingway had been more than pleased to be asked to install one of the new type of cooker.

'It's still mostly ranges round here,' he explained to Bridie, 'though some of the big houses across the park are putting in the gas. Not many, though. We don't get much chance to install these, and it'll be good for the lads to have the experience, though the gasmen will be responsible for the pipes, of course.'

Then there was to be a boiler for hot water, which could be piped upstairs. Mr Hemmingway raised his eyebrows. Luxury standards. Redecoration throughout, and the building of a glass conservatory overlooking the water and trees opposite. Ambitious plans, to be completed without fail by the end of February. Mr Hemmingway sucked the end of his pencil. It was the wrong time of year to start major alterations. Weather got bad. Workmen got sick. The lady was adamant. February. Mr Hemmingway chewed his stub of pencil and decided that customers like this didn't grow on trees.

'All right, we'll have it done February. It'll put you to some inconvenience, mind.'

'As much as you like,' accepted Bridie. 'So long as it's done.'

'Right you are.'

Mr Hemmingway stomped off in his wellington boots to get his paperwork started, and Bridie got out her magazines again. She'd bought a whole armful, all telling the reader how to run, look after and decorate their homes. Brown and green were popular. For the kitchen, a lovely brown, similar to the one in Plaistow. For the back room and the hall, green. But for the rest of the house, Bridie decided she wanted something brighter and lighter, and, taking her cue from the watery colours and wild flowers outside, she

378

chose blues and golds and greens and pinks for the other rooms.

'Unusual, very different . . . but pleasing,' was Mr Hemmingway's verdict.

While her home was in uproar, with workmen in and out and cups of tea permanently on the go, Bridie sorted out her affairs with Francis's solicitor. She wished she could transfer the whole lot to her own lawyer, whom she had come to trust completely. But Francis had left so much, and some of the investments were so complicated, that it seemed wise to stay with the man who had been in on the arrangements from the start.

'The money is mostly in stocks and shares. Some in other property, such as three small cottages down at Mile End. You have the residue – substantial, I may say – of the sale of your two houses and purchase of your present property. What do you intend to do with it?'

'What's best?' asked Bridie.

'More of the same. Stocks, bonds and property.'

'Should I leave it all where it is?'

'Your husband was a very conservative man. He liked to play safe. You could do worse than follow his example.'

'And I'd have an income from that?'

'A very substantial one, Mrs Holmes.'

Bridie leaned forward. 'I'd like to leave the capital untouched, then, but with the income I'd want to start up afresh with the moneylending business and expand – but honestly. There's them as say you can't succeed in business unless you cheat, but I know that's not true.'

The solicitor looked at her from under his eyebrows.

'I know what I can do, and I do it well. There's always a call at this side of London for that kind of trade. Not loansharking. Honest loaning. From an office where people can come easily.'

Whatever would this woman do next? The solicitor ran a hand over his hair.

'Very well. I'll continue to administer the main part of the inheritance for you. How would you like to receive the income?'

'Quarterly, in the bank.'

'A bank account?'

'Yes, Lloyds.'

'You would like me to deal with all tax issues?'

'Yes.'

'It's most unusual, what you are planning to do. Most, for a woman. My dear Mrs Holmes, you do realise you don't need to work?'

'But that's not true! I do. I love working, and I love business. I thought of all sorts of other things to do – not lending – but it's what I like to do. And I enjoy the way people need it. It may be a bit different, Mr Brown, but that don't make it wrong.'

'No, no, no. Of course not. Now, unless we have anything else to go over, will that be all for today?' He did find Bridie a little overpowering. Himself, he liked his women more retiring, not bold and blunt like this one.

Bridie got up to go, and then had another thought. 'Oh yes, there was one thing.'

Mr Brown suppressed a certain irritation.

'I want you to make a separate investment of some sort that will make sure that David has enough money to go to university, or wherever else he wants to, when he's eighteen. His teachers tell me he's clever enough, and I think he'll go to the grammar school when he's ten. I want that money to be foolproof. Invested in something that never goes wrong. Can you do that?'

'You know yourself that nothing is one hundred per cent foolproof,' replied Mr Brown, 'but some things, like property, don't make the big killings but are very sound. Very sound indeed. Or there's gold, even. That's as near as you'll get to certainty.'

'Then make it gold. Yes,' instructed Bridie, 'that's a very good idea. Please buy that.'

Mr Brown nodded. Perhaps she'd go, now.

'I'll be off then. Thanks, Mr Brown.'

He said goodbye and heaved a sigh of relief. She was not his cup of tea at all, he feared, not at all.

Chapter Twenty-Six

Edward found his front door ajar. Swinging his kit bag down off his shoulder he looked round the hallway. The house was still and silent.

'Bridie,' he called.

Nothing.

He propped his bag against the wall, which he noticed had been freshly painted a light shade of green, and walked along into the back room. What had been the back room. He stared. The wall between back room and scullery had gone. Along one side of the large room were wooden cabinets and fitted shelves, laden with neatly arranged pots and pans, plates, cups, saucers and all the paraphernalia of cooking and eating. New brown lino fitted snugly over the floor. Edward's eye ran over the new drop-leaf table and matching chairs. A stove of some kind glowed over in a far corner and, resplendent in pride of place, a brand new, shiny white gas cooker faced a metal sink and draining board, installed underneath a window that had not been there when Edward last stood here. Taking it all in, he shook his head slowly.

A thought struck him. He raised his eyes to the ceiling with some reluctance, and then, shrugging slightly to himself, he left the kitchen and went along the passage to the stairs. To the right he found the door to the front room. Pressing his lips together, he walked in. His face became expressionless. Walls painted a pale gold reflected wintry sunlight as clouds broke and scudded away. It slanted in, catching on the brown shiny fabric covering a curvaceous three-piece suite. Dark red carpet lay thick on the floor.

Upstairs Edward's face first darkened, then grew thunderous. He marched from room to room. Pink and green and gold bedrooms. Pink curtains. Carpets. Fancy furniture all over the place. At the back he found the conservatory. He had to admit, even in his by now towering rage, that it was sunny and bright. The house had been changed beyond recognition. *His* house!

'Bridie,' Edward roared. He stamped downstairs, and, finding that staying in any of the rooms simply fuelled his rage, sat down at the bottom of the stairs to wait. It was only about fifteen minutes, but with nothing to vent his rage on, it seemed forever. Finally Bridie, with an armful of early daffodils and a bag of food, pushed open the door. Dropping her shopping with a cry of surprised delight, she turned to Edward with outstretched arms. He put up a hand. She stopped and took a step back. Puzzled, she scanned his face and for the first time saw the barely contained rage, the blue eyes, usually sparkling with good humour, now sparking fire. His nostrils pinched above a jaw where she could see the muscles clenched.

'What is it, Edward?' She faltered, shaking her head in confusion.

'What the bloody hell have you been doing?' he demanded.

'What do you mean?' she put a hand to her cheek as if to ward off a blow.

'What do you think I mean, woman? What in the world have you done to my house?'

'Oh.' That was all. 'Well, I renovated it. Me and Mr Hemmingway, we . . .'

His roar of rage cut across and drowned out her words.

'Renovated.' He repeated the word with savage sarcasm. 'Renovated. Is that what you call turning my home into a whorehouse?'

'What?'

'Look at it.' He shook a furious hand at the ceiling. 'Fit for whores and queers. You'll make me a laughing stock. How could I bring my mates here now? It's a damned boudoir you've gone and made. Good God, Bridie, I'll never hold my head up in the Navy again if anyone comes here and sees this.' Out of breath, he glared at her.

'But I thought. . . .'

'No, you didn't!' he bellowed at her, so that her ears rang. 'One thing you never did was think. I'm a plain workin' man. I get my hands dirty. I have grease in my nails. Half the time I stink. I'd feel more at home in a tart's parlour in Shanghai than here in my own house.' He thrust a fist under her nose.

'Go on, look properly. They're a workin' bloke's

hands. What did you think I was else? Think? Fat lot of thinkin' you've been doin',' he finished with a humourless smile.

'What do you know about whores?'

'None of your business! I'm a sailor. I never claimed to be no angel. Grow up, for God's sake.'

Bridie whimpered.

Edward grabbed her by the elbow and half pushed, half pulled her up the stairs. 'Look at that.' He pushed her into the sitting room she had furnished so tastefully and with such love. 'What the devil's that supposed to be? For drinking tea with your pinkie waving in the air and a lot of mealy-mouthed women gossiping? Is that your idea of living round here?'

'No!' protested Bridie. 'I wanted it to be . . . oh, a bit classy, nice to live in. Different.'

Edward let out a whistling breath of exasperation. 'It's different all right. It's an 'orrible disaster. A joke.'

He pushed her away from him in frustration and she stumbled across one of the armchairs.

'If this is the kind of living you want, then you'd better look for it somewhere else. It's not me. I'm an ordinary bloke, Bridie. If you want a bloke as likes this sort of carry on, you better go out and find him. It's not me you want.'

'I wanted to give you a surprise. I would have written, but I wanted to surprise you.' Tears of dismay gathered in her eyes.

'Oh, you have. I'm astonished in fact. I never thought you could be this selfish, this . . . ignorant.'

The word hurt dreadfully.

386

'And whose money did you use?' The rage in his voice lashed her.

'Mine,' she whispered.

'So much for agreements. We had one, and the minute I'm away, it's out the window, is it?'

'I never meant to. You aren't being fair,' cried Bridie hotly, her own temper rising at the accusations.

'I suppose you call turning my home into a bordello being fair?'

'It ain't a bordello, it's been done up nice, that's all. I like it, an' you don't. You weren't here to ask.'

'Woman, do I have to tell you again? I'm a sailor. I'll never be here much, and if I can't trust you while I'm away, we'd better forget the whole thing.'

Bridie's face was ashen with fury.

'Well, I'd have you remember as *I* am here all the time, so I want to live in a house I like, too. You don't have no right coming along here and yelling and shouting about whorehouses. If you feel that way, and you know so much about them, you'd best get back there, where you'll feel comfortable.'

His hand shot out and caught her on the side of her jaw.

'You bastard!' she screamed, and slapped his face so ferociously that blood trickled from his nose. Edward dabbed at it with the back of his hand, amazed.

'Bloody hellcat, you are,' he remarked, almost conversationally.

'Don't you call me names.' She raised her fist again and swung it at him. The huge man, on his guard this time, caught it in one hand and laughed. Wiping his bloody nose again, he said, 'Oh no you don't,' and jerked her towards him, out of range.

She tripped and put out a hand to save herself, catching his jacket. Sobbing with rage, she tugged his jacket button off, fighting like a wildcat to get free enough to hit him. Frustrated to the point she was beside herself, she threw her head back to spit at him and suddenly his mouth was on hers, crushing her lips against her teeth. He kissed her frenziedly, picked her up with one arm and carried her through into the despised bedroom, tearing the buttons off her dress with the other hand.

Bridie's rage, in full flood, turned to excitement. She pulled his shirt free of his white officer's trousers and tried to tug at the belt. He drew his face back from hers and laughed aloud.

'You made us a whorehouse . . .' he whispered at her, grinning.

She raised an arm, but he caught it and bent it above her head.

'Would you?' he mocked, undoing his belt skilfully with one hand.

She kicked, but only to egg him on. Still holding one arm above her head, strong fist looking incongruous on the silky pillow slip, he stretched her beneath him and lowered himself over her. Bridie gave a shriek that died away to a moan of pleasure. Edward, lying still, kissed her lips, then ran his mouth down her chin and into the damp place where her neck curved sweetly down to the top of her breasts. Pushing the ruined dress gently aside, he took one hard nipple in his mouth, and caressed the other. Bridie pushed against him hard, breath coming short and fast. Edward, lifting her under him, stroked her teasingly until she begged him with little sobs, 'Oh please, oh please.'

Edward lifted his head from her breast and said, 'Say, "Sorry, next time I'll ask you first, Edward." ' Bridie shook her head violently. He lifted slowly out of her.

'No, no,' cried Bridie.

'Say sorry . . .' he stroked her neck with fingers that were trembling. 'Go on.' He stroked her again. Bridie shook her head with closed eyes. He drew a finger down, over the taut nipples, down her stomach, and raising himself slightly, down to where he lay in her. 'Say sorry.' She groaned and tried to move under him, but he was too heavy for her. He moved very very slowly in and out of her. Pleasure so intense it was like a sweet agony lay just beyond, just beyond . . . and he was holding her on the very edge, and she had to let go, let go. . . .

A long cry of surrender broke out of her, and through teeth clenched with frustration, she wailed, 'I'm sorry.'

Edward kissed her. 'And?' he asked relentlessly.

'I'll ask you another time. Now please, Edward, love me, please, please. . . .'

Edward crushed his mouth to hers and felt rather than heard her high-pitched scream of pleasure and the rapid convulsions of her body as she came to him. With a groan, he let go in ecstasy that brought blackness behind his eyes and stupor to his limbs. They lay, breathless, in a jumble of torn clothes and rumpled sheets.

Edward didn't move. He wound her hair round and round his finger, letting it go, then winding it round again. Slowly his mouth found hers, and they began to kiss, long exploring, questioning kisses. Bridie held his head between her two hands, feeling his coarse hair springy under her fingers. She felt him grow again inside her, and she stroked his broad, muscled back with hands that tensed as he began to move. This time he was demanding. He leant on his elbows, looking down at her, his eyes never leaving hers, until with whimpers and little cries, Bridie's eyes glazed and he watched her mouth draw back as he thrust faster and faster until it was over, and they held each other loosely, bodies aching and satiated and breathing as one.

Languidly Edward drew his head away from her neck and looked at her with soft, sleepy eyes.

'We'll have to fight a lot,' he said contentedly.

Bridie poked her tongue out at him and turned away hastily as she caught the look in his eye.

'I could quite get to like the whorehouse,' he remarked, 'but the rest has to go.'

She drew breath to argue, but he laid a finger on her lips. 'You said sorry, so that's that part done with. But the rest has to go,' he repeated.

Her grey eyes met his, and for a long moment they faced each other. Then she dropped her gaze, and he sighed. The issue was settled. He moved her gently from under him and put his arms around her from behind.

'You can see Hemmingway later on, and tell him to re-do all downstairs except the kitchen, and the sitting room upstairs, by the time we get married.'

'But . . .' said Bridie.

'Haven't you learned yet?' he said sleepily.

On the other side of the silken pillow a red head nodded very slightly. Yes, she'd learned.

They slept, curled up against each other, for an hour. Bridie woke to find Edward leaning on one elbow, gazing at her. As he bent towards her, she pushed him away, half laughing.

'Oh no,' she said, shaking her head at him, while her eyes belied the words. This time they made love in a slow, companionable way, high passion spent. When they finally sat up, side by side, on the bed, Edward kissed the lobe of her ear and announced that he was starving.

'What have you got to eat in this ridiculous place?' he demanded.

Bridie pushed him so that he had to grab at the sheets to stay upright. 'I'd just brought back a load of shopping when you started yelling at me.'

He remembered the bag she'd dropped in the hall-way. 'Go on, then, go and cook. I fancy a plate of eggs and. . . .' His voice was drowned in an earsplitting roar from beneath them. The floor shook and little puffs of dust rose from the bottom of the skirting board. Edward, trained to react fast to emergencies, leapt from the bed and, throwing a towel round his waist, ran for the stairs.

Bridie, shocked and bewildered, sat transfixed, eyes staring at the doorway through which he had disappeared.

'Edward?' she quavered. 'Can you see what it was?'

She heard his voice say something in answer but couldn't make out the words. A lot of noise came from below. Water splashed and objects scraped and banged in a way that made no sense. Bridie hastily got out of bed, and, dragging a gown around her, went to the top of the stairs and peered down. Clouds of black smoke were rising slowly up the stairwell. She coughed, half choking. 'Edward?' she called again, beginning to be frightened for him.

'Come and give me a hand,' he called.

She went downstairs. Holding a hand over her nose and mouth against the dense smoke, she found Edward opening doors and windows in the kitchen, coughing and cursing. Water lay in puddles where he'd thrown it at the fires that had started at several points in the room. A pile of linen waiting to be washed still smouldered. 'Got a set of spanners?' he asked, standing in the doorway breathing fresh air. Bridie nodded speechlessly. She ran to the dresser and pulled out a case of spanners from the bottom.

She handed them to Edward, who knelt down in front of the blackened heap of twisted metal that had been her gas cooker, and busied himself turning off the screw that controlled the flow of gas. The kitchen was so full of smoke they could hardly see each other. 'Turn off the gaslight,' he ordered.

Glancing at Bridie, he saw her hesitate. 'It's been blown out by the blast, but it's still pouring gas,' he said patiently. 'So turn it off, quick.'

They brought the gas under control and stood in the open doorway, breathing carefully, to survey the damage. It was a disaster. The whole room was black, and smoke filled the ground floor with dense fumes.

'What happened?' asked Bridie, awe-struck at the scale of the mess.

'Gas blew up. Must have been a faulty installation. We were lucky not to go with it. It can't have been leaking long, or the whole house would have gone up like a bomb.'

Bridie's mouth hung open silently. Her beautiful house was a ruin. They looked at each other. Edward began to grin.

'What are you finding funny?' she demanded, feeling her own tears brimming at the sorry sight around her.

Edward bent down and kissed her.

'My darling,' he murmured, 'I'm smiling at the sight of my future wife with a black face, hair on end, and the look of a small girl who's had her toy snatched away.'

Bridie wiped the filth more evenly over her face with the back of one hand and tightened her grip on her gown.

'I don't see nothing funny,' she retorted crossly. 'It's an 'orrible mess.'

'It's poetic justice,' said Edward amiably.

'What?'

'Hemmingway will have to re-do it now, won't he? The whorehouse has stayed in one piece, but, oh my word, just look at the rest!'

Bridie's eyes were round. 'You're pleased, aren't you?' she cried.

Edward shrugged. 'We'd agreed to have some redecoration, hadn't we?' he answered cheerfully. 'This just makes it a little more . . . ah . . . urgent. And,' he continued more seriously, 'that ass of a builder had better come in immediately to check for structural damage.'

Bridie looked woeful. 'My lovely kitchen,' she said tearfully.

'Come on, it's not the end of everything,' cried Edward, putting his arm round her shaky shoulders. 'You can get another kitchen, and even another gas cooker, only this time I'll make sure it's put in properly. Heaven knows what that idiot Hemmingway did. It's a new technology, gas, and you have to be careful with it . . . know what you're doing, or you get this kind of thing.'

Bridie sobbed, to be drowned out by the clamour of bells and shouts as the local Fire Brigade rounded the end of the road at high speed and clanged to a halt outside. A tremendous banging on the front door announced the arrival of a red-helmeted figure who stopped and took in the scene with practised eyes. Bridie, unnerved by yet another shock, clung to Edward and babbled in near hysteria.

'It's my fault, I didn't think, and I let Hemmingway do it all, and I never knew what a lot could go wrong. I am sorry, Edward, truly I am, and I'm sorry you don't like any of it. I'll never leave you out again.'

He laughed heartily. 'Oh, you goose,' he said, in a loving voice, and kissed her blackened lips.

The fireman coughed irritably. 'If you two love-birds could see your way to 'elpin' us check that you ain't about to get blown up fer good any minute now, I'd be glad of your co-operation, sir.' His gaze took in their state of undress and the 'sir' was said with suppressed amusement. Bridie looked up guiltily.

'Better get your men in.' Edward nodded apologetically. Four firemen picked their way through the wreckage, checking carefully for any sign of fire and making safe the gas inlets.

'I'll get over to Hemmingway right away,' said Edward as they went upstairs again.

Bridie fingered the patches of greasy black on her bedroom floor and tried to take in what had happened while Edward scrubbed himself clean in the bathroom.

'You clear up here as best you can, and I'll come back with Hemmingway, if I can find him. In fact, I won't come back until I've got him with me,' ordered Edward. 'And on no account touch anything connected to the gas, will you?'

Bridie shook her head.

Pulling on his jacket, Edward leant across the bed to kiss her. 'Never mind, it'll all get put right,' he reassured her unhappy face. 'You see, it'll look even better.'

She gave a little nod.

Edward became serious.

'Bridie?'

She looked up.

'Its as though you are my wife, now. I'd love you even if we lived in a hovel and had never heard of pink walls and gas stoves. They aren't what matter. Only you matter, for me. I don't think anything could change that, not even the whorehouse.' A smile broke out despite himself. 'And that was beautiful. The most beautiful thing. I'm half glad that Hell broke out downstairs, or I might have found it hard to come down from Heaven.'

He grinned and pulled a curl back from her cheek.

'So cheer up and get dressed. I'll be back directly, and you don't want Hemmingway gossiping, do you?'

He winked cheerfully at her and went off to look for the builder. As if the whole neighbourhood wouldn't gossip, never mind the Fire Brigade!

Bridie gazed at her ruined home, and wondered, despite Edward's cheerful words, how they'd ever get straight in time for their wedding, which had to be soon if they weren't to run out of time. Edward only had six weeks before he went back to Dartmouth, and that, sitting in what felt like a battlefield, didn't seem much to the bride-to-be. She retreated into the bathroom and emerged a long time later, pink and composed, to dress and wait anxiously for Edward to come home with the builder.

Chapter Twenty-Seven

There were a lot of sidelong glances, whispers in corners and significant little nods of the head. Bridie noticed them vaguely, immersed as she was in the job of clearing up after the explosion, and overseeing Mr Hemmingway's apologetic efforts to put things right. This time, two men in overalls came from the Gas Board to inspect the installation of new pipes. A splendid new stove replaced the one that had been nothing but a mangled heap, pulled out of the general wreckage to be added to the pile outside the back door, waiting for the dump. Next to the rubbish was a stack of bricks, for the side wall of the house had been blown out and made unstable by the blast.

Hemmingway had put up scaffolding, right up to the roof, and explained that bad weather or no, the wall would have to come down to be rebuilt from the ground up. Standing among the dust and chaos, Bridie wailed that she'd never see how they could cope with a wedding on top of it all, and finally dissolved into tears.

David added to her distress by running excitedly in and out of the ruins, helping the workmen, and showing every sign of having a thoroughly wonderful time.

Each evening his mother took down the old tin bath that had been brought back from retirement to cover the emergency created by the lack of water pipes in the house. David contentedly soaked in front of the fire in his bedroom, while Bridie distractedly tried to find a way around the problem of Edward's ever-dwindling leave. He was unforthcoming about the wedding arrangements, frustrating her with his vague 'Leave it to me, it'll be all right' remarks when she pressed him for help. He was staying at Ethel's, and came over only during the day.

Bridie started to feel miserably that everything had gone awry, and even confided to Lizzie, in a rare moment of disloyalty, that she wondered whether Edward was trying to avoid getting married, and perhaps it had all been her fault for the high-handed way she'd behaved over the house. Though, she added, the fresh decorations were being done in a colour scheme that they'd agreed on, and at the time she'd thought Edward had seemed delighted with the new plans. Lizzie looked up from spooning porridge into Oliver's mouth and gave Bridie a funny look.

'Oh,' she said, 'I should think it'll be all right. You've got a week or two yet.'

It was the same sort of unsatisfactory reply she got from Edward, and everyone else for that matter. Ethel was uncharacteristically non-committal as well. Bridie began to worry in earnest. Noticing this, Edward called a family meeting at Ethel's when Bridie was busy with the builders. It was unanimously agreed that the plan should be brought forward, even though preparations were not perfect.

Four days later Edward found Bridie listlessly putting away folded clothes in the whorehouse. He put his arms round her from behind and leant his chin on top of her head.

'You look like you could do with cheering up,' he told her reflection in the mirror.

'I'd cheer up if I knew whether I was coming or going. I'm beginning to think that you'll go away and that'll be it. I'm all muddled about what's going to happen, Edward, and you are so little help, I'm wondering if you've changed your mind.'

'It is trying, and I'm doing my best to make the arrangements,' said Edward solemnly. 'But, you know, what with here out of action, and Mum fussing about having the reception there, well, it's not easy and that's a fact.'

Bridie looked sceptical. To her ears, he sounded like a man evading the issue. She twisted the little ruby ring around her finger and eyed him doubtfully.

'Look,' cried Edward as if inspired, 'I brought you this.' He groped in his pocket and brought out a scrap of white card. It had black letters engraved on it.

'It's an invitation to visit *The Stalwart*. Cadets' Day. We bring our families on board as guests. They usually lay on a good spread, and you can see almost all over the ship. It's the day after tomorrow. Shall we go, Bridie? My Captain likes to meet Cadets' wives – and wives to be,' he added quickly. 'It'd do you good. Get a bit of colour into your cheeks. Ever since the explosion you've been looking peaky.' He looked eagerly at her, holding the white card by its corner. Bridie took it and looked at it.

'Yes, all right. I'd like to go. And David would be thrilled to bits. What should I wear for a thing like this?'

Edward appeared to consider.

'Well,' he said at last, 'it's a pretty formal sort of occasion, and the wives and girl friends all sort of try to outdo each other. It's sort of showing off. A bit silly really, but everyone has a good time.' He narrowed his eyes and grinned at her. 'I think you should dress up to the nines. Knock 'em all out. The most glamorous outfit you've got.'

'The only glamorous thing I've got is what I'm going to – or was going to – wear to be married,' said Bridie in a flat tone.

'Tell you what, then,' cried Edward, 'wear that.'

Bridie was scandalized. 'I can't do that.'

'Why not?' demanded Edward.

'You just don't. A wedding dress is a wedding dress, no matter what.'

'Ah.' Edward looked downcast. 'I suppose you'll have to come in something more ordinary, then. It's a pity, because the impression you make can mean promotion comes quicker for me. A man's family sort of reflects on him, and if you meet my Captain for the first time looking absolutely stunning, well, it sort of lingers in his mind when promotion comes up.' Behind his back Edward crossed his fingers like he used to do as a small boy.

'Really?'

'Really.' Edward nodded seriously. 'It's most important.'

'It's a stupid way to promote people,' said Bridie, considering the idea.

'Probably is,' agreed Edward cheerfully, 'but that's the way of the world. It's a pretty stupid place in more ways than one.'

Bridie gave in. 'All right, I'll wear my lovely cream silk suit, but you keep me a mile away from grease and dirt and all them bits and pieces you leave lying all over ships. I've seen them on the ferry from Dublin. A right mucky place that was.'

'A Royal Navy destroyer can hardly be compared to something that's not much more than a tramp steamer,' remarked Edward huffily. 'But I'll see you come to no harm, dress and all.'

He propped the engraved invitation on the mantelpiece.

'There you are. It'll be "Petty Officer Edward DuCane and Mrs DuCane" next time, love. Just think of that.'

Bridie had her head inside the cupboard, stacking bath towels. 'Huh,' she muttered to herself, and pushed the pile of folded cotton angrily.

'I'll leave you, then, because Mum is doing my uniform, and I have to put a bit of spit and polish on it too,' he said.

Bridie turned her head in the cupboard doorway. 'What time's all this happening?' she asked.

Edward peered at the invitation. 'Says two-thirty. Let's say I pick you and the nipper up here at half past ten, to get the twelve fifteen from Waterloo. We'll be in Portsmouth about a quarter past two. That suit you?'

'Yes.'

Edward kissed her upturned cheek, and noting her distracted air, decided to leave it at that. The front door slammed after his departing figure and Bridie was left once more with the rough voices of the work-men downstairs, and a sense of loneliness. Shaking her head slowly to herself, she reached inside another cupboard and pulled out the silken suit in its paper wrapping. It didn't feel right, all this carry on, but if that's what Edward wanted, well, she'd do it. He didn't come back that evening, to look over the day's work on the house and put his strong arms round her with loving kisses. Bridie waited up until she had to admit that it was too late for him to walk over, and as she lay down to try to sleep, a tear trickled its way down her cheek.

Maybe he doesn't love me after all. The treacherous thought gnawed at her heart and she tossed uneasily in a shallow sleep.

Her heart was still heavy when she left David, smartly togged out in a sailor suit, with strict instructions to stay in the front room and look at books. Up in the whorehouse, she put the final touches to her dress. The beautiful, rich silk skirt fell almost to her ankles. Lace frothed at the neck of the long, loose jacket and she'd bought little, lacy gloves to match. Her hair was bundled into a high chignon, on top of which glossy pile perched a dark cream hat with a veil that softened her eyes and just skimmed the bridge of her nose. Downstairs, the workmen leant on their brick hods and stared in admiration.

'Blimey!' one of them was heard to mutter under his breath.

She was just smoothing down David's sailor collar when she heard the sound of a motor car outside. It instantly reminded her of that fateful night when Sam Saul had driven her to Tredegar Square, and involuntarily she shivered. Then, all dark blue worsted and gold buttons, Edward strode into the house.

'Chauffeur is here,' he called.

Bridie emerged from the front room, half puzzled, half excited. 'What are you doing?' she asked.

Edward doffed his white peaked cap. 'If Madam would care to step this way. . . .' He waved a hand towards the door.

Its grey-uniformed driver saluted her as she stood in the doorway and stared.

'Oh, Edward. Whatever are you up to?' she asked in amazement.

'We're going in style to meet the Navy. In you get, my dear.'

With delighted confusion, Bridie stepped into luxury and settled David beside her, who fidgeted and demanded to sit in the front, by the driver. The man grinned cheerfully, and said 'Why not?' So with David transferred to the front passenger seat, Edward swung himself in through the door on the other side, and, like royalty, they drew smoothly away and glided off, heading south down the long, straight road that led to the huge Naval Docks where the great ship *Stalwart* rode motionless on the still waters of the Port.

Edward's hand found Bridie's under the rug that covered their knees, and he held it tightly all the way while David squirmed with excitement and watched every move the chauffeur made, promising himself that one day he'd drive a car like this. One day. . . . The chauffeur drove fast and they drew up on the dockside by early afternoon. Several heads in peaked caps looked down at their arrival, and abruptly vanished. Bridie looked around her.

'I thought there'd be lots of people,' she remarked.

'Oh, there will. I think we're a bit early.'

The reply, along with much else, didn't make sense, but the chauffeur was opening her door and handing her down, and touching his cap respectfully. Bridie gave him a delighted smile, and, taking David's hands, the three of them began to climb the long gangplank. There was silence from the ship. Halfway up, Bridie paused.

'Are you sure we've come on the right day? Is this your ship? You're certain?' she asked uneasily.

'Think I don't know my own vessel?' grinned Edward. 'Carry on up.'

She did as she was told. At the very top there was a step down. She turned to make sure David didn't trip, and suddenly a row of men in brilliant white uniforms appeared at one end of the walkway leading to the front of the great ship. They stood smartly at attention.

A tall, familiar figure rounded the corner of the deck, and against the glare of the light from a late autumn sun, Bridie recognised Jonathan. He smiled broadly and came to meet the little party. Bridie saw in amazement that he was resplendently got up in top hat and tails. As he shook Edward's hand and turned to Bridie, the white-clad sailors moved as one, and suddenly each man had a bugle in his hand. The small, perfectly practised band swung into a spirited rendering of 'Here Comes The Bride'.

Jonathan tucked his hand under Bridie's elbow and gently urged her along the side of the ship. Emerging into full sunlight, she came upon the breathtaking sight of the ship's crew at attention, Ethel, Ted, Susan, Lizzie and her twins, Mrs MacDonald, and any number of DuCane relations and in-laws and second cousins twice removed, and so on and so forth. No-one had been left out, and Ethel was happy and proud fit to burst. Every face broke into a huge smile as Jonathan and Bridie walked, Bridie looking round dazzled, not believing her eyes, towards the white-covered table on the deck, where the Captain stood next to a priest, who wore the robes of a Jesuit over his naval blue.

Jonathan looked down and kissed her cheek, his eyes full of delight. He turned and gestured Edward to stand beside her. The three of them stood before the sailor priest, and as the last notes from the band died away he began to intone the first phrases of the marriage ceremony. Wide-eyed with astonishment, Bridie began to realise that it was really happening. She'd come to be married! She looked up at Edward, who almost laughed aloud at the expression dawning on her face. She shook her head at him, as if to say, 'Oh you. . . .' and then they both turned to attend to the priest's words.

Jonathan produced a plain gold ring from his breast pocket, and in the presence of the crew, the Captain, almost the whole of the DuCane family and her closest friends, Bridie married her Edward, while a gentle onshore breeze cooled her flushed cheeks. David, awed by the occasion, only fidgeted a little bit to go and look over the side of the tall ship, and in any case was taken all over it by a group of enthusiastic sailors when the ceremony was over.

Then there was such a hugging and a kissing, and tears and laughter and excited explanations as you never did see or hear from that day to this. The Captain slapped Edward on the back and told him he was a lucky man indeed. Ethel wept all through the playing of the Guard of Honour that escorted Edward and Bridie down through the small door that led off the deck to a long cabin below, where they drank toasts in white wine and ate little pastries handed round by grinning sailors. Bridie's eyes, brimming with joy, followed her husband everywhere, and when the speeches had been made, and the jokes laughed or groaned at, and the wine all finished up by merry guests, Edward saluted his Captain.

To the sweet high sound of the band playing a farewell, Edward handed his bride over the threshold of the gangplank, and, leaving David to run the length and breadth of the ship as long as he was allowed until Ethel took him home to stay with her and Ted, they rejoined the patient chauffeur on the dockside, and drove the long road back, man and wife, to their now deserted home by the canal.

Ignoring the chaos downstairs, Edward scooped up his wife, carried her over the step, up the stairs and into the whorehouse. Someone had placed a tray, covered with linen and adorned with red roses, on a small table. Cold, pale wine and delicate sandwiches had been placed alongside a small, heartshaped cake whose white icing was decorated with a silver horseshoe and two elegantly piped words: 'Edward. Bridie.'

A candle burned, casting a golden circle into the enchanted place.

The tall officer drew his wife inside. All the world was theirs, in that small candlelit room. Edward and Bridie closed the door. As lovers do.

The Cold Road

Books by Rick Wilber

To Leuchars

Where Garagiola Waits
and Other Baseball Stories

The Cold Road

The Cold Road

RICK WILBER

A Tom Doherty Associates Book
New York

THE COLD ROAD

Edited by James Frenkel

Book design by Michael Collica

A Forge Book
Published by Tom Doherty Associates, LLC
175 Fifth Avenue
New York, NY 10010

www.tor.com

Forge® is a registered trademark of Tom Doherty Associates, LLC.

Library of Congress Cataloging-in-Publication Data

Wilber, Rick.
    The cold road / Rick Wilber.—1st ed.
        p.   cm.
    "A Tom Doherty Associates book."
    ISBN 0-312-86621-6 (acid-free paper)
    1. Women journalists—Fiction.   2. Jamaican Americans—Fiction.   3. Saint
Kitts and Nevis—Fiction.   4. Serial murders—Fiction.   5. Minnesota—Fiction.
6. Resorts—Fiction.   I. Title.

PS3573.I38796C65   2003
813'.54—dc21

                                                                2002045470

First Edition: June 2003

Printed in the United States of America

0   9   8   7   6   5   4   3   2   1

To Robin, Richard, and Samantha—my three favorite people

ACKNOWLEDGMENTS

This novel could not have been written without the generous help of a number of people. First, I owe a special debt to Will Purvis, captain of detectives, Blue Earth County sheriff's department, for his wealth of information on police procedures in the Mankato area and the state of Minnesota. St. Petersburg police patrolman Gary Brainard was also an invaluable source for my understanding of police procedures, as he has been for other novels and short stories.

Kathleen Stauffer of *Catholic Digest* magazine was most helpful in providing details that helped me to appreciate the wonders of a Minnesota winter. Some years ago I was a student at the University of Minnesota, and I later taught journalism at (then) Mankato State University. My memories of life in a hard winter were reinforced by much more recent visits and discussions with colleagues and friends throughout the state. I thank them all for details ranging from the feeling of a barn in winter and the wonders of milking machines to the sights of dancing sun pillars waltzing down the street in north Mankato.

For details of St. Kitts, I thank Selwyn Liburd especially, a Kittitian whose knowledge of his island was both broad and deep, and also my good friend Randy Miller, who accompanied me on a research trip to the island. In addition, other important information about St. Kitts and Jamaica came from a number of my students, most notably the talented Jamaican athlete Rory Marsh. Also, my friend and colleague Dr. Humphrey Regis, originally from St. Lucia, took the time to have a number of discussions with me about Caribbean life and folklore, from Bazeel to obeah. His knowledge was invaluable.

For medical details, I thank my friend and physician Dr. Joe Springle. For the details of sculpting fantastic creations from discarded tractor and automobile parts, I owe a very great debt to the immensely talented St. Petersburg sculptor Paul Eppling, who shared his art and craft with me in some detail. Eppling's welded metal creations can be found throughout Florida and, ironically, Minnesota.

To help me understand the life of a woman athlete, I had numerous conversations with several talented female college athletes, including Alexis Redmond, Rita Arndt, and Cori Kill, all from the University of South Florida.

A special thanks for the sharp eyes and most worthwhile comments from friends and readers Kim Golombisky, Dana Hudepohl, and Diane Pflugrad. And a very special thank-you to my friend and mentor author Ben Bova and to my agent, Barbara Bova, who edited, commented, pushed, pulled, and, ultimately, sold the book.

Editor James Frenkel's patient advice was so insightful that any merits the novel may have surely stem from his guidance. Thank you, Jim, for your help in all matters of this novel ranging from the very particular to the very general.

A book that proved very valuable in explaining the presence of various Irish and Scottish remnant cultures in the Caribbean is *To Hell or Barbados: The Ethnic Cleansing of Ireland* by Sean O'Callaghan (Brandon Books, 2000). I highly recommend the book to those interested in the Irish diaspora.

In all cases, any inaccuracies are mine. I have, of course, altered the details from time to time to suit the needs of the novel. I have, for example, invented Mankato Catholic High School and several parishes in the area. Visitors to St. Kitts will note that I have changed the geography and geology liberally for purposes of plot, including waking up the dormant Mount Liamuiga and moving or inventing from whole cloth several towns on that beautiful and interesting island.

Rick Wilber
St. Petersburg, Florida
January 2003

PROLOGUE

Outside, it's snowing. Again. Eight inches have fallen so far on the southern Minnesota farm fields that surround Mankato and the perky TV weather girl says there's four more inches to come. Moira shivers to hear that and wraps her arms tighter around herself. This will be her sixth Minnesota winter and she's never gotten used to it. She has a bad cold. Again. Her throat is so sore she can hardly speak. She's a long way from home.

By local standards it's a warm day, nearly twenty-five above zero. She stands in the sunroom on the south side of the house and watches as heavy, wet snowflakes hit the outside of the double-glazed windows and melt on the glass, dots of water slowly merging to form tiny rivers that run downstream to the windowsill. Tonight, when the bottom drops out of the temperatures and it falls to fifteen or twenty below, the tiny rivers will freeze solid on the glass. The snowmelt from the gutters will freeze, too, into long, thick icicles that have, at times, reached all the way from the gutters to the ground.

Inside, next to the window, is a crucifix, an eight-inch Christ on the cross, a crown of thorns on His head, a drop of blood dripping from the wound in His side. Below Jesus, on the dressing table beneath the window, stands a small statue of the Virgin Mary, arms outstretched palms up, offering her blessings and her love.

Moira needs the warmth of her Catholicism, the comfort of parish life each Sunday in town at Holy Innocents. They help her survive here.

Bob Marley, a voice from home, spins slowly on the fancy Bang & Olufsen turntable that sits next to Mary on the table below the slain Christ. Melchior bought her the turntable, the receiver, the fancy speakers, and the Marley album last Christmas. Melchior likes to bring her gifts.

"No Woman, No Cry," her favorite from all of Bob's songs, washes through the false tropics of the room. "No cry, little darlin', don't shed no tears," Bob tells her. But she does cry. Sometimes.

Here, in this room, she is surrounded by her ashrubs, the potted medicinal plants from home that she keeps trying to grow here—aloe and blue flowers, some five-fingers, a couple of gale-of-the-winds, some periwinkle, a small salve bush, a small bay geranium that she'll use the leaves from to make tea that will fight her cold.

She'd like to have more plants, but there's no more room and it's a struggle just to keep these alive in the winter when the bitter cold comes seeping through the windows, pushing its way right through the walls and shutters.

She thinks of the cold as an enemy she must fight during the dark months. She uses her prayers and her plants as her weapons in the struggle, both of them reminders of where she's from and who she was, or was planning to be, a teacher of one kind or another, someone loved and needed.

But Moira gave that up to come here; happily at first, and then, as time passed, as her situation has slowly worsened, less so. For the past two years, in fact, she's been writing back and forth with her grandmother, trying to learn more about Gramma's medicinal arts, trying to resurrect at least part of the promise that was buried years ago. It's hard to do at this distance, Gramma doesn't have a telephone and the mail is achingly slow, but Moira's trying to keep alive her sense of herself, of who she was back home in Jamaica, where the heat never faded, where winter never came.

Right now, here, in Minnesota, the locals call it a warm day. If it were a little warmer still, at, say, forty-five or fifty degrees, they'd call it a Chinook wind and marvel at it. Back in Mandeville, in her childhood, it never got so cold as fifty above, not once in the sixteen years she lived there.

But that was then. Here, soon, Moira knows, the wind will shift to the north and west and the temperature will drop, from twenty-five down to ten, then to zero, then to fifteen below, then even colder. She'll shutter the windows tight before she goes to bed tonight, even stuff towels around the edges to hold back the chill, but it won't help.

By tomorrow's dawn the towels around the window's edges will be stiff with frost, and winter, the beast, will continue to press in on her, forcing itself on her, unforgiving and unstoppable—for months and months to come. She feels frozen in place here, trapped by the cold outside.

Today is January 17, Settlement Day for her people back home, the starving Irish who came across to Barbados as indentured servants in the 1840s, during the famine years, and then, long years later after earning or escaping their way to freedom, came to Jamaica to live in the mists of the Blue Mountains and found their own small village near the city of Mandeville.

Back home in Mandeville today the remnant Irish population will hold a parade and listen to a speech or two, celebrating and remembering a shared culture of freedom that they've kept alive for more than a century. Here, trapped, she watches it snow.

There is a child's voice from upstairs. Moira's daughter, Melissa, has been her only joy and salvation in the five years since she was born.

Melchior, normally so quiet and methodical, was a tense, talkative dynamo that day, driving the Ford pickup like a madman to get her to St. Joseph's in time, sliding through the fresh snow on the hospital's entrance drive so quickly that he almost crashed right through the twin doors of the maternity entrance. Twelve hours of labor later little Melissa came into the world, and Melchior, even while he's grown distant from Moira, has doted on his daughter ever since. Sometimes, when the pain of his anger lingers for a day or two, Moira thinks sadly that in Melchior's life there is only enough room for loving one at a time.

Moira turns away from the window and walks into the kitchen, spotless as always, the chicken cooking at 350 above zero, the pot of potatoes ready to boil before she'll mash and whip them the way Melchior loves them, first with the masher and then with the new handheld Black & Decker Spatula Smart six-speed mixer, set on speed number five so that the tiny blades are whirring furiously, smoothing the potatoes into a white softness that reminds her—right in the middle of this awful cold and snow— of the beaches at home on Thompson's Bay, white soft sand stretching for miles in a slow curve looking south. It has been eight years since she's seen that sand, felt it between her toes, watched the clear Caribbean roll in over the reef line while walking along with her mother, her two brothers.

The kitchen has a refrigerator with an ice maker, and over on the corner counter there's a microwave oven, and the dishwasher—a Kenmore—is a marvel. Here she has all the comforts she'd never have back home, all the things her Melchior promised her back in the city of Mandeville, in the parish of Manchester, in the country of Jamaica, when he wooed her and won her heart.

He was a sight for a local girl's eyes back then, wiry and muscular and palely handsome, an Irish-American welder at the Alcan bauxite mine, helping maintain the dragline excavators, the front-end loaders, and, most important, the miles-long cable-belt conveyor that carried the mined ore from the quarry to the plant.

There, at the Kirkvine Works, the raw ore was refined into alumina and sent off on ships to Canada, where it became, finally, aluminum and then automobile bodies or house siding or even, maybe, the whirring blades of her new mixer.

He saw her, that first time, at The Den, the restaurant on Manchester Road where she waited tables, serving ackee and saltfish for breakfast, rice and peas and curry goat with fried bammy for lunch, and then jerk chicken with rice and peas for dinner— all of it washed down with soursop juice or Red Stripe beer.

She was just sixteen; long black hair, green eyes, a beautiful example of the white Jamaicans descended from those Irish indentured workers of more than a century before who found their way to Jamaica to work in their small farms or struggle in the sugarcane fields.

The waitress job was her first, one she happily took despite the warnings of her too-protective mother, who tried for so long to shield her from what she saw as the depredations of the men at the Works, rough men, tough and dark Jamaicans from down in the slums of Kingston, and hard men from Canada and the States here, her mother knew, to escape something awful they'd done back home.

But Mother was wrong, at least about Melchior. He was young, just twenty, and so nice, so soft-spoken and gentle despite the work, despite the ground-in dirt and the hard-worn clothes and the heavy work boots she saw him in at lunch each day. He spoke with that odd northern accent, those odd "o's" and "a's" and the stream of "you knows" and "you bets" in every other sentence.

She laughed at him for that accent, this funny young man from the cold, cold north country where, he said, the lakes froze solid for months on end and the snow got so high that they had to place red metal flags on the fire hydrants so the firefighters could find the hydrants in the drifts in the middle of winter, when home fires raged from wayward fireplaces and wood-burning stoves.

She laughed at all that, too, such utter nonsense. She was a bright girl; she'd been through ninth grade at St. Cecilia's and been at the top of her class. Gramma thought her granddaughter was wise as well as smart, and so was training Moira for the healing arts. Mother, devout in her Catholicism, disagreed strongly with Gramma—thought Gramma's healing arts danced too close to obeah's black magic and the devil—and so they fought over Moira's future, the two of them, struggling to push the girl each where they thought her future lay.

And Melchior, Moira had thought when she first knew him, must have felt she was just a gullible, naive local girl to whom he could tell crazy stories. She wasn't about to fall for tall tales like that—about snow so deep that walking down the plowed street was like being in a gully of snow, the plowed drifts to the side standing ten feet high. Or the one about the sun pillars floating down Main Street, the water in the air quick-frozen in forty-below temperatures so that the ice crystals formed floating, shimmering shafts of light that drifted in the breeze down the street.

He seemed to find her irresistible, starting from day one when he stared at her, trying to figure out the unexpected color of her skin and the way it seemed to clash with her Jamaican accent. Later, when he knew more, he swore he could hear an Irish lilt when she talked about passing the dutchy or how everything today was cool runnings.

He was so outrageous, so utterly outside the boundaries of the local boys with their *irie* talk and their dreadlocks and their ganja-smoking attitude, that she wasn't surprised a bit when he had the nerve to ask her out on a date, despite her fierce mother that he'd met twice at the restaurant. Moira said yes and then Mother, won over by his smile and earnest attitude and his own Catholic up-bringing, grudgingly said yes, too. At the cinema, he held Moira's hand.

And then came another date, and then more, the soft-spoken pale American and his local white girl becoming something of a minor item in Mandeville; not the first time a man from the Works had dated a local, certainly, and wouldn't be the last. Some of the men, a few, even settled down permanently in the town, marrying into the warmth and serenity of Jamaica's high-plateau town, at two thousand feet high the only large town on the whole island with weather that didn't steam year around. Mother hoped for that.

Then came the layoffs when the price of oil shut the Works for two long years and sent the workers home to Canada, the States, other islands in the Caribbean. Came the layoffs and Melchior started thinking of home, of ice fishing on Lake Minnetoksak, of the farm life he'd left behind to weld metal in the tropics, of the clarity, the purity, of winter in the north.

She could see it in his eyes when the layoffs came. He would leave her, go home to the place where he fit in best, the place where he belonged, like she belonged in Mandeville with its palm trees and orchids and green monkeys in the rain forests that ran down the slopes at the edges of town.

She was prepared for him when he came to see her after he

got his notice. She was ready to say good-bye, forget him some-how, get on with her life, go back to school like her mother wanted and become a teacher, or maybe follow Gramma's training and be a healer.

And he asked her to marry him, got down on one foolish knee to say it. He was not an eloquent man or a passionate one; so quiet, so firmly in control, that she sometimes wondered what was going on inside that handsome head of his. But he managed to get it out in that soft-spoken way of his. "Moira," he said so simply. "Will you marry me? Come back to Minnesota? Raise a family?"

She reaches over to the round dials at the back of the stove. Turns one of them to high. She leans down, opens the tall bottom drawer and pulls out her favorite pan, walks over to the sink, fills it with water—so cold!—from the tap, and then puts the pan on the burner, already starting to glow red. She goes to the tall cabinet, lined with oak veneer, and opens it, pulls out the bag of home grown potatoes from the middle drawer, sets the potatoes on the counter next to the sink with its wondrous Disposall and starts to peel the potatoes. By the time the water starts to boil she has five of them peeled and cut and into the water.

She stands there as the steam rises, feels the wet heat rising from the boiling water, lets the dampness wash over her face for a few moments.

She remembers how she felt that day, with that silly boy on one knee asking her to marry him. So unreal, that's how it was—like she was outside some window watching it happen, watching him ask her, watching herself as she took a step back, shocked by the question.

It wasn't as if she hadn't thought about it, Lord knows. Life on a big, prosperous farm in America. Life with all the comforts, all the things he talked about, all the things she'd never had and never would have living in Mandeville waiting on tables and learning her gramma's craft. It was a dangerous dream, one too far from reality to bear the weight of any real thought. But then there he was, on his knees, the moment come alive.

And so she said yes. Her mother wept, her gramma pleaded, but she won them over, finally, and married her cold farmer. Swept up in whole cloth by her dreams and his promises, she said yes, and came north.

Now, while the potatoes start to boil, she looks out the window once more to watch the snow fall while her husband and their daughter play together upstairs.

The Marley album is on "Buffalo Soldier." She listens to the lyrics as she walks from her kitchen back into her sunroom: those buffalo soldiers, dreadlocked rastas, brought to America. She moves with the rhythms she learned as a child as she walks to the windows and pulls tight the shutters.

When did it go bad? The second winter, maybe the third? The baby girl made it all better for a time; Melchior loves her so, spends more time with her than he does with Moira, truth be told. She worries about that.

Gramma's last letter asked her to come home, bring the little girl and come home, the letter said, before it just gets worse, before it gets so bad she can't stand it at all. She wonders how Gramma could know; Moira's unhappiness is not something she's shared in her letters home.

And maybe Gramma is right, Moira thinks. She's a million miles from home, a million miles from herself, lost here in the frozen north. How much more can she take? She doesn't know that, either. How can one know?

She turns up the space heater in the center of the room a few more notches, might as well try to keep things warm. She looks up at the crucifix, reaches out to touch the statue of the Blessed Virgin on the table, whispering a small prayer as she does, asking the Holy Mother for guidance, for help.

Supper is ready. She'd call upstairs to her husband and child, but her throat is too sore, so she sets her washcloth down and leaves the kitchen, heads to the front stairs. She'll walk up to Melissa's room, where they're playing, and get them.

As she moves past the dining-room window the glass rattles. Outside, the wind is shifting to the north.

A SCRAPE AGAINST THE WINDOW

I listened. The darkness deepened.
—*Heart of Darkness,* Joseph Conrad

Melissa O'Malley hated winter, hated it in all its manifestations small and large: the terrible dead stillness that lay over everything; the slush that froze into dirty, ankle-breaking mounds on the sidewalks; the way the snow just lay there, brooding, for month after month; the long hours of darkness that kept even the thin winter sun at bay; the bitter wind that stole your breath and kept you trapped indoors for days on end. And the cold, most of all the Minnesota prairie's penetrating cold, so deep it felt permanent and inescapable, so deep in her bones so that she wondered, sometimes, in January and February, if she'd ever again feel warm.

In her room she covered the walls with posters from Florida and the Caribbean, trying to fool herself into some warmth with pictures of palm trees and white-sand beaches and emerald mountains rising from azure seas. On her tape deck, Bob Marley sang of jammin' and Jimmy Buffett wanted her to come on down to Margaritaville, where the tourists were covered in suntan oil.

She'd lived her whole life here except for one brief trip south when she was so young that now that she could barely remember it—her father taking her out of school for a few days right in the middle of winter. They drove to Minneapolis and then headed out on a long flight south to Jamaica to meet her grandparents and relations. She remembered lush plants everywhere, a hot sun, hushed arguments and slamming doors and a sudden dizzying change in plans that had her back on a plane and heading north with her father.

Other than that she'd never been farther away than the Twin Cities, but she thought she knew from that one short visit to the Caribbean how it must feel to be warm the whole year around— like summer, only forever.

In the summer, on the days when it got really hot, she loved to stand in the sunshine, close her eyes, and look up, letting the warmth wash over her, the beads of sweat breaking out on her forehead. A good game of basketball in the summer, outdoors, was magic. A few miles of jogging in summer's brief heat, too, worked up a soak. Even working in the fields with her father, detasseling the cobs in that little half-acre of sweet corn they grew, even that was worth it when some summer heat was around.

But summer never lasted here, and sometimes it was late coming and early leaving. The standard joke was that summer in Minnesota was great if it fell on a weekend.

She lifted her feet and tucked them under, sitting on them at her study desk to try to warm up cold toes. She was tall for her age, thin and gangly, with green eyes and long dark hair that she put into a ponytail when she played basketball. Her father, when he said much about it at all, told her she was going to be beautiful just like her mother had been, tall and thin and lovely. But Melissa couldn't remember much of her mother; a glimpse in her memory now and then of a smile, a sense of warmth—that was all. And Melissa didn't feel lovely; she felt clumsy, trying to fit those feet under, sitting Indian style on the chair. It didn't seem to help much, either. Even in thick woolen socks the toes still felt numb.

She was wrapped in the comforter from her bed, fighting the cold and the dark with that, the posters, the music, and the bright light from her desk lamp, plus whatever heat she could glean from Conrad's *Heart of Darkness,* which she had to have read by eight-thirty for English 101 at Mankato Catholic High School. She had basketball practice every day after school, so she couldn't get the homework done then. She played point guard for her parish team and it was undefeated, which meant more and more to the girls every time they won one, just adding to the pressure and the busyness of life. And now here it was already nearly 4:00 A.M. and she wasn't more than halfway through the story.

Her father had the oil heater cranked up, he said, about as high as he could afford to set it, trying to keep the drafty old farmhouse warm through this bitter, subzero night. But no amount of warm air oozing from the radiator could cut through this kind of chill. She turned the page and Marlow was talking about choking, stifling tropical heat. Here in Minnesota it was forty below and so cold in her room that she could see her breath.

She heard the rattle of her father's old Ford pickup coming down the unpaved farm road that led in from the highway. The cold road was two bone-rattling miles of dust and dirt in the few warm months and then a frozen, bouncy washboard in the winter, solid as concrete, teeth-rattling with bumps until the snow came and the plows drove down it, their big blades smoothing it out.

Why was he back? He'd left an hour ago for his fishing shack on Lake Minnetoksak, planning on spending the predawn hours ice fishing, dropping his line through the augered hole in the thick ice of the lake and waiting there patiently for that little flag to flip up and let him know he'd caught something, a big northern pike maybe. As often as not, he came home empty.

Melissa put her feet down, immediately feeling the cold floor through the wool against the soles of her feet. She hopped in her socks over to the window, reached out to pull back the lower right corner of the plastic she'd tacked there for extra insulation, and found a spot near the bottom of the window not yet covered by the rime frost. She looked down and saw her father slam the Ford's door shut and then walk to the back of the truck, a cloud of vapor from his breath trailing behind him. There was something there in the bed of the truck. He flipped up the latch, yanked down hard on the tailgate, and brought it down flat. Then he reached in, grabbed at the thing lying there, and pulled on it.

It was a deer. Melissa could see that now as he pulled on it, tugging it along the bed of the truck until it fell, already stiff in this cold, onto the ground. Her father must have hit it with the truck and now had brought it back to dress it and save the meat.

A deer, poor thing, out foraging for something to eat, struggling in the frozen dark to chew some bark off an oak tree, wandering, probably starving, into the path of Melchior's truck, and that was that.

Melissa turned away. Let her father do whatever he was going to do with the deer carcass; she didn't have to watch. She tacked the plastic back in place, shivering with the cold touch of it, then walked back over to her desk, picked up her Conrad, and got back to worrying about Kurtz and the stifling heat that lay at the core of his darkness.

She must have fallen asleep, right there in the middle of the Congo River. One second she was rounding a bend and there was a ramshackle village up ahead, and the next she was hearing something, a creak, a metallic clank from outside.

She sat up, glanced at the small clock on the top of the desk: almost 5:00 A.M. So she'd lost a crucial half hour or more, snoozing away.

She picked up the book, started reading about how he was looking ahead, down the river to the snarled growth of the shoreline where, in that tangled gloom, he could see human limbs in movement and then arrows emerging from the brush and coming toward them in droves.

There was another loud metallic crack from outside, like something—a heavy chain, maybe—swaying in the sharp wind. She shook her head. What was her father up to now? Working away in the dark on some new metal monster? The yard was filling up with them, these half-done welded things he'd been making the last few years, things that looked like giant lizards or enormous insects, all of them made from old farm implements or things salvaged from junkyards. A huge turtle half-made from an upended pig trough and the hood of the old DeSoto sat out at the back of the barn, its long neck out of its shell, and looking up at the sky, as if it expected to see something coming, a giant metal butterfly it could eat, maybe.

Melissa thought she understood why, in the winter especially, her father enjoyed making these things as a kind of stress relief. As far back as she could remember, the farm was in trouble, her father struggling always to keep it going. Spring, summer, and fall the hours were long and the work brutally hard. Only in winter did he get a break. It was such a hard life. She loved him, and understood how he didn't have much time for her, why he was cold and aloof most of the time.

Melissa turned back to the book and read on, scrunching into the comforter, trying to feel some tiny portion of the heat the story was filled with. She was never going to get this read in time, never.

Another creak, a lighter one this time, and then it repeated, and then again. Her father was turning something out there, some crank handle that was unhappy with the cold.

There was a bump against the side of the house, down below her room. Another bump, higher, thumping in a kind of a tympani with the creaking of that handle. Jeez, it was way too much racket. She placed the paperback flat against the table, propped a chemistry textbook over the top edge so it kept the pages flat. There, her hands were free. She blew on them to warm them up again, and then placed them over her ears. Better. Not quiet, really; she could still hear the creak and feel the rising thumps. But better.

Once again into the darkness, arrows flying, a fusillade bursting under his feet. What, she wondered, was a "fusillade"?

More bumps.

She decided she'd had enough. After all, it was five in the morning and way too early for her dad to be banging things around out there. She was simply going to have to go out there and tell him to keep it quiet, if just for another hour while she tried to finish this story. He could wait until later and then make all the contraptions and creations he wanted once she left for practice and school. She shook her head, rolled her eyes. Wait till she told her friend Danny about this one. He already thought her dad was pretty weird—this would clinch it.

Melissa stood up. Problem was, this meant putting on her boots, her long johns over her pajama bottoms, then the bulky

Aran sweater, then wrapping up firmly in the parka, hood up over her hair, scarf across the face to warm the air enough so that she could breathe: the whole nine yards just to go outside in this miserable cold morning and ask her father to keep the racket down for a while.

Still, she had to do it. She walked over to her chest of drawers to pull out the long johns. The rest, boots and parka and scarf, were all downstairs in the snow room.

There was a loud crack right behind her, right at the window. What?

She turned and there, coming into view in that one clear portion of her window, was something.

Oh, my god. She just stared for a few seconds, then took two steps back. Some huge monster was crawling right up the outside of her bedroom window; she could see its shape in the darkness.

No. It was just something her dad was doing. She walked over, slowly, and reached out gingerly to pull back the plastic, finally yanking it clear in one quick tug.

There, clear in the bottom of the window, were the hooves, the back legs and hindquarters of a deer, jerking, rising, moving up past her window.

What in the . . . ?

She had jumped back a step at seeing them. Now, staring at the small, clear portion of the window, she watched in wonder as the rest of the carcass slowly, jerkily, rose by: the haunches, then the slim waist, slit where her father had gutted it; then the barrel of the chest, the front shoulders, and then the back of the head, ears still pointed sharply out as if the deer were still listening to all these goings-on, wondering when it would end.

It paused there, stuck perhaps, or maybe Melchior was just resting below from pulling on the rope to get the carcass up and off the ground. He must have in mind leaving it there while he went back to fish and then coming back later to dress it and store the meat. Venison for dinner tonight, maybe.

There was a quick jerk, the back of the deer's head yanked upward in a short, violent pull, and then it started upward again slowly, rotating as it rose so that the back of the head became a profile through the window and then, just as it moved past the clear portion of the glass and into the area covered with a thick frost, the face edged into view, one dark eye, not clouded, looking for all the world as if the deer still lived. That eye stared at Melissa, stared right through her, and then rose into the white opacity of the frost.

She shivered. What a dumb thing for her father to do, using the block and tackle to hoist the carcass up off the ground. As the snout disappeared upward and the front legs rose into view and continued on, she tacked the cold plastic back, turned away, shivering, and walked back to her desk. An hour left to read, that was all. She'd have to skim it and hope for the best.

The ratcheting stopped suddenly, the quiet seemed loud by comparison. OK, then, she could go back to her reading. She leaned forward, trying to concentrate.

Then came a quiet scritching from the window, a small tapping and scraping against the glass, like a branch against the cold pane. But there were no trees against this southern side of the old frame farmhouse, nothing there to make that scrape.

Except the deer. She looked and couldn't see anything, but that didn't prove much. She groaned, got up from the desk, and walked quickly, ignoring the cold floor now, over to the window.

The front hooves of the deer were tapping against the glass, moving slightly sometimes, just an inch or two in some slight breath of wind, but enough to scrape against the glass and make that scritching sound, almost the sound of chalk against the blackboard at school when Mr. Nordman scribbled his notes about Romantic literature.

She stared at the hooves. Arctic air had come a thousand miles south, all the way from the Yukon, to push the hooves of this poor dead deer back and forth and back and forth, scratching against the glass of her window.

Her father was done. The truck door slammed one final time and with a sharp grind the engine came to life and she could hear him back up, turn the truck around, and head off into the darkness, the lure of the dark, still bottom of Lake Minnetoksak calling to him. So it was up to Melissa to do something on her own about the hooves and their noise.

All right, then; she *would* do something. She walked back across the room to her chest of drawers, pulled out two pairs of mittens, and brought them back to the window. She'd put on one pair, open the window, then reach out there and wrap the other mittens around the hooves of the deer. That should quiet things down.

Easier said than done, of course. First she pulled the plastic loose again. Brittle from the cold, this second tug broke it apart in her hands. She brushed aside the pieces of plastic and pushed against the latch, not surprised to find it frozen shut. Sometimes it's the simplest things that stop you.

OK, then, she'd have to bang it open with a shoe. She went to the closet to find one with a hard heel.

The clogs were perfect for it. She grabbed one, walked back to the window, and got to work.

Whack!

It didn't budge.

Again, then. *Whack!*

Still nothing.

All right. She brought the wooden-soled shoe back, paused for a second, then came at the latch hard, twice. *Whack! Whack!*

And with that last whack she felt the latch finally give a bit. She set the shoe down on the floor and grabbed the latch with her mittened thumb and finger. It was icy cold right through the wool, almost cold enough for her hand to stick to it as she grabbed it hard and twisted. It moved a small fraction of an inch; then, when she twisted again, with an audible crack, it came free.

OK, that was part of it. Now, would the window slide open? She hadn't opened it since October, and it had been sticky then, the wooden frame sliding unevenly up and down in its old grooves.

She put her fingers in the freezing metal thumb hold and tugged up, hard. With a *whoosh*, the window opened, so easily that it banged noisily into the top of the frame.

God, it was cold. It rushed in at her, almost a physical push the way it hit. Forty below bites at you: unprotected skin feels it first as a prickly sensation; then, in seconds, it starts to go numb—a minute or two later, especially if the wind is blowing and the windchill is down around seventy below, you're into the first stages of frostbite. Wait much longer after that and you're losing fingers and toes, then limbs, then life.

Melissa realized she hadn't thought this through all that well. All she had on was her pajamas and these silly thin wool mittens. OK, then, the thing was to get the other mittens onto those hooves as quickly as she could and get the window slammed shut, and quickly.

Up close, the deer carcass was huge. She leaned out the window to grab at the hooves and she could feel the mass of the thing right above her. An hour ago this poor deer was alive in the woods. Now it was hanging here, on the side of her house, while she grabbed at its hooves.

She looked up, and the deer's face turned her way, just a few feet away from her, staring at her. The mouth was slightly open. She could see a small bit of tongue in there, lolling out. And the teeth, surprisingly small. And the nose, black, a thin sheen of moisture frozen on it.

Oh, god. All right, then, get it done. She grabbed at the hooves again, missed. She realized that she was never going to get them both at once and decided on the one closest to her, reached out to grab it with her left hand, felt it in her fingers, then lost it, then grabbed again, with both hands this time, and got it, a good grip, solid.

And felt her heart begin to race, like a switch had turned and suddenly her heart was determined to beat a thousand times a second. It was dizzying, staggering, her heart pounding in her chest madly as she stood there holding the hoof, frozen to the hoof somehow while her chest went wild, went crazy, and then, in an instant, the world fell away and ...

... a hard, erotic pulse washed over her. She felt it travel from her hand to her chest and her stomach and down into her crotch in one quick muscle-tightening spasm.

She thought, with some part of her mind that was watching all this from the outside somehow, that she was falling but was, instead, pawing away at the hard snow to reach the grass beneath it, the edge of the hard path where the man things ran. There was a noise, and lights, bright lights that drew her in to watch them. She stepped toward them, and they were suddenly huge and Man and violent, hitting her in the chest, crushingly hard, and tossing her back onto the drifted snow.

She tried to rise, to run away, but her legs didn't work, though she wanted them to, willed them to bound away, to spring into the underbrush, to safety.

Instead, trying to rise, she stumbled and then fell into the snow and lay there on her side, shallow breathing, quick breathing, and then there was a kind of puzzlement about all this, and the strange running Man things, and then there was darkness, and then there was nothing at all.

HOOPS

For a long time, the vision of the deer's final moments left her terrified. She'd dreamed, again and again, of those seductive lights in the frozen cold, the moment of awful contact, the confusion, the pain, the death. For weeks she avoided touching anything dead, even leather gloves or the pork and beef that her father loved to cook for dinner. She didn't want to see any more visions from other animals, not the final moments of a slaughtered cow or pig. She even worried about picking up a piece of fried chicken.

But there were no more visions, there was no more craziness; and eventually one month became two and two turned to six and then a year went by and she forgot—at least emotionally—about the touch and what it had done. She still recalled it now and then, but with no emotional attachment, no fear of repetition, no sense of the horrible, as life, busier all the time, went on.

Christ wasn't nailed to the fifteen-foot-tall altar cross. Instead of having His wrists and feet firmly attached, the smiling Christ, dressed in flowing taupe robes, seemed to float out in front of the cross, His arms outstretched, His palms up toward heaven.

Melissa, an altar server at Mass most weekday mornings, had first noticed how odd He looked last spring, on Good Friday, when it seemed obvious to her that Christ ought to be up there dying, not smiling. It looked really wrong to see Him with that look on His face; almost a smirk, like He thought He'd really put one over on everybody.

Every Mass she'd served since—and there had been maybe a hundred of them, since she served during the week—she'd looked up there and wondered why He looked like that. She wanted to ask someone about it, but Sister Marie Agnes, Melissa's ninth-grade homeroom teacher last year, was as unapproachable as her nickname, Sister Very Vicious, would suggest, and Father Reskey wasn't exactly the friendly type, either. Father Murphy, who was much more approachable, wasn't getting back from his six months of sabbatical until after the New Year, so it would be another couple of months before she'd finally find out the real story behind Happy Christ, as she thought of Him.

If she leaned back a bit, Melissa could see the thick wooden block that attached Christ at the small of His back to the huge altar cross. That seemed weird, too, to have Him attached at the back to the cross He was supposed to be dying on. All the other crosses she'd seen had Christ bloody, dressed in nothing more than a rag to cover His privates, with the crown of thorns over His head, His face slumped down—His Holy Self in obvious pain. But here, in Holy Innocents, He looked downright joyous.

Melissa wondered if, in an hour, she'd have that joyous look on her own face. Coach Nancy Carlson was posting the cut list for the girls' varsity basketball squad this morning. As soon as Mass was over and she could escape, Melissa planned to run over to Coach's office door and take a look, even before classes started. She thought she was going to make the team this year, maybe even see a lot of playing time, but you never knew. Last year, as a freshman, she'd thought the same thing, but her name hadn't been there on the list when she'd gone by to take a look after Spanish class.

She'd been the last to be cut, and it hurt. A lot. After two hard weeks of playing her heart out every day, diving to the floor for loose balls, always being first up the court on offense and first back on defense, running hard on every wind sprint and working hard on the reaction drills—after all of that—she was still cut.

Coach had been nice enough about it. She'd asked Melissa to come into her office after practice (and Melissa and all the other girls had known what that had to mean) and said, as nicely as she could, "Melissa, you have a lot of talent. I wish we had a freshman team or a JV team, but we don't, and I can only keep twelve players. Five of the girls are seniors, and they've been playing for me for three years now . . ." She'd trailed off with that thought, shrugged her shoulders, added, "So I'm going to have to let you go."

Then she'd smiled. "But I want you to keep playing. I've talked to Father Murphy about you, and he'd love to have you on the CYC team for Holy Innocents Parish. That's pretty competitive ball. Maybe not as competitive as high school, but not too far from it, either. And I think you have a chance to be a starter for him."

Melissa had just stood there, thinking the level of ball couldn't be that good or Coach wouldn't be talking about her starting for the CYC team when she wasn't even good enough to make the high-school squad. She'd seen some church-league games and it wasn't pretty, the parish girls running up and down on that grubby old tile floor in the Holy Innocents gym against a bunch of other girls who couldn't make their high-school teams, either.

But Coach was still talking: "I want you to work on your dribbling skills, Melissa. There's no question about that good outside shot of yours." Then she'd smiled. "And if you can prove to me on that parish team that you can handle the ball for us at point, then we'll have a spot on this team for you next year. That sound all right?"

So, of course, Melissa had said it sounded fine, she understood and all that—though really it hurt like all get-out. She'd promised to work hard on her ball control, her dribbling and her passing, even while thinking to herself that the church team was really just a place for losers. But if it gave her a chance for next year, well then, it was worth it.

And, as it turned out, the girls on the Holy Innocents team hadn't been losers at all. They'd been winners, in fact, ripping through the twelve-game season undefeated and then rolling right through the play-offs to win the whole thing with Melissa leading the way, bringing the ball up the court and then dishing or shooting, whatever was needed. By season's end she'd averaged almost twenty points a game and nearly fifteen assists.

Sure, it was just church ball, and maybe the other players weren't all that hot, but Melissa had found herself enjoying every second of it, loving even the hard work of practice, where Father Murphy had them run wind sprints endlessly, ten times up and down the court to start practice and ten again to end it, with more added in when they made mistakes.

She liked Father Murphy, who worked them hard but gave them all a lot of support, too. He was a little touchy-feely sometimes, putting his arm around you when he gave advice, patting you on the butt when he sent you in to play—stuff like that. But the other girls didn't seem to notice, or mind, and Melissa figured it was just in her head. Heck, Father Murphy coached the boys' parish team, too, and did even more of that stuff with them and no one seemed to mind, least of all the boys, who seemed to think he was a great coach. Melissa tried to just not worry about it. She hadn't been raised that way; but, truth was, she was starting to realize that her own upbringing was a bad way to judge things. Life at home had always been kind of odd, she'd slowly come to realize.

Sometimes, she thought, playing basketball was when she was really her truest self. In one game, against the Queen of Peace team from over in New Ulm, she'd really been in the zone, the rim looking huge, every shot falling from wherever she shot it. Once, trapped in the corner by a double-team, she'd planted her right foot, spun on it, and, falling out-of-bounds, launched a soft turnaround jumper as she faded left. When she'd landed, a full step out-of-bounds, she'd watched through the back of the backboard's glass as the ball slid through, hardly rippling the cords, for a sweet two. The feeling was—what was the term Mr. Dudley used in American history?—"empowering." Yes, that was it; it gave her power, like she had everything under control, like she knew who she was and where she was from and where she was going.

Life, of course, wasn't really like that. Life, as her father liked to point out in those rare times he said much to her at all, was no game.

Melissa hadn't quite realized how odd her relationship with her father was until she'd starting spending some time at her friends' homes, and that hadn't happened, really, until the church-league team. Before that, grade-school friends were school friends and that was that. In grade school, at Holy Innocents, Melissa had come home on the bus every day, gotten her chores done, eaten dinner, then spent the evening with homework and reading, mostly wild fantasies about unicorns and elves and hobbits named Frodo, all while her father worked out in the barn on his own fantasies, those welded-together creatures he made from old scrap parts from tractors and farm implements.

Then one day she went home after basketball practice with a friend she'd made, Summer Arndt, tall and nice and blondly beautiful, a cross-country runner on the high-school team who played church-league basketball to stay in shape in the winter.

Summer was a good rebounder and hard worker on the court, though she didn't have much of an outside shot and couldn't make a free throw to save her life. But she was great to talk to, and then when she brought Melissa home for dinner and some studying one night after practice, Melissa found out that Summer had a dad who actually talked to her, and a mother who hugged her, and a little brother who was an enormous pest.

It was a revelation, that other people, normal people, lived a different kind of life. Other people had mothers, for one thing. Interesting things, mothers, in a lot of odd ways. And other people Had Things and Did Things. That was how Melissa thought of that other life, at first, all capitalized. At Summer's house there were VCRs and Video Games and Cable Television and Aquarium-with-Fish and Pepsi-Cola in the fridge, and Trips to the Mall, and Ice Skating at City Centre, and Little Brother's Hockey Games and on and on and on. Other people had, to Melissa's surprise, parents who hugged them as part of the normal life of a fourteen-year-old girl in Middle America.

Which might as well have been Middle Earth—that was the

year she discovered Tolkien—to Melissa's surprised eyes.

She didn't say anything to her father about it. How could she? He was doing the best he could to provide for her, keep her safe and warm in a place where that was no mean feat. He was trying and, barely, succeeding at keeping their farm afloat in hard times.

But at least she knew, finally, what those others had. And it was a dangerous thing to realize. For the first time in her life she felt trapped, pinned down like a bug on a small farm outside a small city, with no options, nothing to do each day except the same thing she'd done yesterday and would do tomorrow.

Which made basketball all the better, all the more important. When she was on the court, bringing the ball up, looking to see the defensive set she faced, Melissa could Create, could Make Things Happen. She thought of that all capitalized, too: Hoops. Backdoor. Pick and Roll. Drive the Lane and Dish. Kick It Out. Drain the Three.

She felt guilty, sometimes, about how much she loved the escape that came with playing. Time stretched out; worries dried up and blew away. All that mattered was The Game.

She led the Holy Innocents team in scoring and assists, and would have led in rebounds if she hadn't been busy pushing the ball up the court all the time.

Coach Carlson heard about it from Father Murphy, and she started coming to watch the games, smiling at Melissa when she caught her eye, giving her a thumbs-up. That encouragement meant a lot.

Thing was, once tryouts started this year Melissa had discovered that high-school ball was a whole different level of the game and Mankato Catholic was a pretty ambitious team. She wasn't going to be a star, that's for sure. But she thought she was good enough to make the team now, good enough to play.

But the other girls were good, too. Just like her they'd all spent the summer working on their games, shooting a zillion free throws into the rim nailed to the backside of the barn, standing out past the three-point line she'd measured off and painted onto the grass, letting them fly again and again and again, getting into that zone.

✳ ✳ ✳

Mass had reached the homily. Melissa had been so busy day-dreaming about hoops and life that she'd walked through all the server duties like a zombie, only half-aware that she was doing all the things she had to do, holding up the missal for Father Reskey to read, pouring the water and wine, ringing the bells. Time was when she'd been really devout, even thought about becoming a nun, maybe. It seemed like a good life, a holy life serving others.

Now, sitting on the middle of the three wooden chairs to the left of the altar, she was just antsy for Mass to end. Next to her was her friend Danny Finnegan, and next to him was Mrs. Feder, the lector. All three wore vestments, the black cassock covered by the white linen surplice, fringed with lace in fleur-de-lis patterns. And all three held their backs straight, knees in front, eyes to the front, faces impassive, while Father Reskey's sermon talked about this Sunday's First Reading, from the Prophet Isaiah.

"A voice cries out in the desert, prepare the way of the Lord! Make straight in the wasteland a highway for our God!" Reskey said, overly dramatic as usual, arms held out with his palms up, just like the big statue of Christ dangling from that cross behind him over the altar.

It was the seven o'clock Mass—the rock 'n' roll Mass was what Reskey called it, because of Nord Brue and his guitar play-ing that kept the parishioners entertained, and mostly awake, every weekday morning.

That the parishioners were mostly paying even a little attention wasn't bad considering the strangely nice weather outside. It was early November and the sun was dawning on the kind of warmth that would soon have everyone out walking, cycling, playing ten-nis or a round of golf. It was already sixty degrees out, with a light breeze from the south. It might hit seventy before the day was over. Amazing weather, and way too nice to spend too much of it in church listening to Father Reskey go on about making highways in the wasteland.

But go on he did, for another ten minutes. After that the Mass flew by as Reskey hurried to get back on schedule. He had to be done by seven-forty; people had to get to work or, like Melissa, get across the street to school.

And he made it, done at seven-forty on the dot, which gave Melissa twenty minutes to get back into the Sacristy, get out of her vestments, get across the street and down to the gym to check Coach Carlson's door, and then get back to homeroom by the eight o'clock bell.

Danny found it funny, watching her hurry to get her cassock off and hung up in the closet. "You know you're on the team, Melissa. Everyone says you're going to be a starter, for Christ's sake." Danny enjoyed taking the Lord's name in vain.

"Everyone didn't get cut last year, Danny, and then spend the whole season playing for Father Murphy in the church league. I'll believe I'm on the team when I see my name there on that list taped to the door."

He laughed again, shaking his head. He knew how much fun she'd had on the parish team; he'd even gone to some of her games, one friend watching another play. She liked him for that, thought of him, in fact, as her best friend.

They sure had enough in common. Like her, he didn't have a mom; his had been killed in an auto accident when he was seven. He, like Melissa, had been raised since by his dad, who worked for the Blue Earth County Sheriff's Office as a detective. Danny understood what Melissa was talking about when she told him how surprised she'd been to see the home life of some of her friends. Like her, he knew what it was like to fend for yourself.

But he most certainly did not know what it was like to get cut. Danny was the star jock of Mankato Catholic. Small forward on the basketball team, with a nice touch from the three spot. Top receiver on the football team, hauling in touchdown passes like nobody's business. Ace of the pitching staff for the baseball team, winning six games in the short spring season that the weather allowed.

Danny was a star, and getting cut from a team you really, really wanted to play on was something he couldn't possibly understand. Melissa just shook her head at him one last time as he leisurely slipped out of his surplice while she ran for the door, tugging on her coat as she went.

"Good luck!" he managed to yell at her as she left.

She just shook her head. Good luck, she very much hoped, was not something she needed.

DANNY BOY

The Crusaders of Mankato Catholic played in a tough small-school league. All eight schools in the Minnesota River League were private, three of them Catholic and the others either Lutheran or nonreligious. All the schools had the money for decent facilities, reasonably paid teachers and coaches, and an ambitious schedule that included a few games with similar schools from up in the Twin Cities.

And it was Mankato Catholic that had the strongest tradition of winning in the league's twenty-seven years of existence. The Crusaders were the football powerhouse, the soccer stars, the men's basketball team to beat, the baseball league champs four years running, the volleyball defending league champs—the list of athletic excellence covered about everything.

Except women's basketball. There the Crusaders languished at the bottom of the league. Only once in the last ten years had the girls won more than they'd lost. It was not an enviable record, and eventually Sister Rose Patrice, assistant principal and long-time women's coach, had to accept reality and step down from her coaching duties. Within a month, Mankato Catholic hired Nancy Carlson, who'd had success at all-girl St. Joseph's Academy down in St. Louis and wanted to move back to her Minnesota roots.

Carlson was tough, a lot tougher than Sister Rose had ever been. But the payoff for all the conditioning and the long hours of practice and the shouting from the coach was, for the girls, the occasional victory. In Carlson's second season, as Melissa starred for the parish team, the Crusader girls finished third in the league. The next year, with sophomore guard Melissa O'Malley bringing the ball up the court and running the offense, the Crusaders did even better.

"All right, girls, huddle up." Coach had on her game face, tight-lipped, eyes narrowed, that glare in her eyes. "This is it, ladies. These girls from St. Paul think they're better than you. They think they'll win this game. What do you think?"

There was a long moment of silence, then, "No way!" from Trish Coughlin, and it was echoed quickly by the other girls.

"This is what you've worked for, what you've fought for, what you've bled for, since October," Coach said. "You win this game tonight, ladies, and they'll have to respect you. You understand? They'll know all over the state that Mankato Catholic can play basketball. Got it?"

The girls got it. Edgy, bouncy, they looked ready to explode. Coach looked around one more time, looking at each one of her twelve players, then making eye contact with the starters.

"Andrea, are you ready, girl?" Andrea nodded.

"Trish?" Same nod.

"Holly? Samantha?" Nods and narrowed, focused eyes from the shooting forward and the center.

"Melissa?" Yes. Absolutely. Ready.

"All right, then, ladies." And Coach reached in with her hands, palms down, one over the other. "Get it together." The hands came in, one pair on top of another, piling up in the kind of team unity that wins games, that can beat the big-city schools, could maybe win a league championship, maybe even win State.

"Father Murphy?" Coach asked, looking up. The priest smiled, came over to the huddle, leaned in with one hand to put it on top of all the others, and started praying. "Hail Mary, full of grace, the Lord is with thee. Blessed art thou among women and blessed is the fruit of thy womb, Jesus. Holy Mary, Mother of God, pray for us sinners, now and at the hour of our death."

"Amen," the girls shouted back at him.

"Our Lady, Queen of Peace, help us do battle today," he said more firmly, his intensity rising.

"Amen!" the girls shouted.

"Mother of Mercy, help us win!" he shouted. And the girls screamed, "Amen!" And broke the huddle, heading in a pack for the door and the hallway down to the gym.

Melissa, leading the way, wondered briefly once again about exactly why they should expect the Virgin Mary, of all people, to help them get fired up and win basketball games. But then she hit the entrance to the gym, and the roar of the crowd and her focus on the matter at hand—beating Ursuline Academy of St. Paul—took over and she decided that, like the smiling Jesus behind the church altar, the Virgin Mother's school spirit was just another of those unanswerable mysteries that made Catholicism interesting.

"You guys were so great," Danny was saying as they crunched across the hard-packed snow of the backyard and toward the barn. "When that Torensen girl got hot for St. Paul in the third quarter and started hitting all those threes I thought it was all over, but you came back and got 'em."

"I was hoping she couldn't keep it up," Melissa said, walking beside him. "I mean, you can only stay unconsciously hot like that for so long. Everyone cools off sooner or later."

"You didn't."

She smiled. She sure hadn't. Twenty-eight points, eighteen of them on threes, four of them in the fourth quarter when they'd come back and won it. She'd sure had a good game, if she did say so herself.

As she looked back from the cold, clear morning of the next day, it seemed unreal, like it must have been someone else, Melissa "B" or something, who did all that. The real Melissa, the one who lived on the farm outside Mankato and hung out with Danny Finnegan and did her chores and went to school and fixed meals for her dad, that Melissa was watching the whole game from some weird kind of internal distance last night, watching as

Melissa "B" drove the lane and then kicked it out to Sammy for a jumper from the baseline or grabbed a rebound in traffic or drained one of those threes. A triple double, the only one so far this season for anybody on the team: twenty-eight points, twelve rebounds, ten assists.

"Christ almighty, you were just great, Melissa," Danny was saying as he opened the side door to the barn. "I mean, really, Jesus, you were just, just great." He was at a loss for a better way to express it.

They opened the door, walked in. She let Danny go first, watching the way he moved, graceful, almost like a dancer. That was the way he played, too, all catlike and bouncy. He led the league in rebounds, could reverse slam with the best of them even though he was just six-foot-two. He was strong and tough and durable, despite how skinny he looked. He fought his way through bigger, bulkier guys all the time to get those rebounds, sliding past them, ghostlike, like they never even sensed he was there until he was in front of them, soaring higher, sweeping the boards clean, and then flipping it out to Tommy Seals for the fast break that led to another basket, another ten-point run, another win. The boys' team had only lost twice, both during the week in January that Danny was sick with the flu. He was averaging fifteen rebounds a game and almost ten points, pretty amazing for a sophomore, leading his teammates to their big game for the championship next Friday night. It was fun to imagine how great he'd be by his senior year.

And he had a great butt.

He was the talk of the girls. They all thought he was gorgeous and envied Melissa her status as his girlfriend.

She tried, and failed, to explain that she and Danny were just friends like they'd been since third grade, that there wasn't any girlfriend/boyfriend stuff going on, no romance, no sparks.

But Andrea summed up the general feeling the other day when the subject came up yet again. "Listen, girlfriend," she said to Melissa as five of the girls sat at one of the indoor picnic tables at Taco John's and worked their way through some Mucho Grande tacos, "If you really think there's no romance between you two, than you're the only one who does. I mean, look at the way he looks at you, girl. The rest of us have been laughing about his goo-goo eyes since September." She laughed, took a sip on her Diet Coke. "Am I right, girls, or am I right?" And the other girls laughed and agreed.

Melissa shook her head. "It's not like that, Andy. We're just friends. Really."

The other girls laughed again. Trish giggled: "That's why you were holding hands with him during fifth hour yesterday? Because you're just friends? Oh, Melissa, that's so, like, you. Holding hands in the hall." And she giggled again.

Melissa just shook her head. It wasn't like that, but there wasn't anything she could say to her friends that would explain it right. She and Danny were just friends, that was all. They'd never even kissed, not once. And the holding hands thing? Well, that, that was just something that just sort of happened, and only just once or twice in the last week or two. No big deal, probably. She didn't know if Danny even realized it was happening, he seemed to do it so naturally, just taking her hand as they walked along.

When she walked through the barn's side door Danny was standing there, looking up at the creature that dominated the middle of the barn's floor. "You know, Melissa, your dad is *definitely* weird."

Melissa walked up next to him and stared with him at the huge metallic insect that rose on four spindly legs in the middle of the large concrete slab. He took her left hand in his as they stood. She looked at him and he smiled back. Then, still holding her hand, he brought her along as he walked over to the thing and kicked at the right front leg. "Sturdy as hell, I'll give him that. Looks like some kind of big old four-legged spider."

Melissa put her right hand on the leg that Danny had kicked. "I kind of like them. See what they're made out of? He takes old tractor parts and car parts and whatever other junk he can find, and then welds it all together to make these things."

"Yeah, well, I understand *what* he does, Melissa. I just don't understand *why*. What's he get out of this?"

She patted the leg. "Well, money for one thing. He's already sold this one to somebody up in the Twin Cities. People buy them for their office buildings and things, you know. They put them up on the roof or out in front with some fountain."

Danny shook his head. "Weird."

She laughed. "Hey, well, it keeps him busy in the winter. Between this stuff and ice fishing he's always busy."

"Where's he now?"

"Lake Minnetoksak, crouched over a hole in the ice, hoping to catch that monster pike he's been after for the last five years."

She blew out a thin cloud of vapor with her breath. You could barely see it. She loved the barn; somehow she felt warmer in here. You could hear the wind moaning outside, trying to get in, but her memories of childhood summers kept the cold outside, where it belonged.

That's how she thought of the barn, as a summer place where she'd learned how to milk dairy cattle—sloshing on the iodine and then hooking up the suction cups to the Bou-Matic milking machine. In this barn, she could stand in the middle of the floor and look up past the haymow to the slanting light coming through the high windows and pretend she was in some Gothic cathedral in the South of France, dressed in a long gown, waiting for her knight to return from the Crusades.

All that was multiplied somehow, holding hands with Danny. She grinned at him. "You city kids don't know what you've missed, not having a barn to grow up in. You know that?"

"Sure, Melissa. Absolutely. I think about it all the time, how I was cheated out of all sorts of wonderful moments on the farm, growing up in the big city of North Mankato, Minnesota. Hey, I missed out on slogging through muck and ice at four in the morning to milk the cows. I missed out on cleaning out the stalls, and feeding slop to the pigs, and painting the barn, and..."

She punched him in the shoulder. "Creep. You know what I mean."

He looked over at her and grinned. She looked back. He had the most interesting face, those brown eyes, that chipped front tooth, his nose with that wide little flat spot up on the bridge. That smile. They'd been friends since third grade and she'd never noticed all that until just a couple of months ago.

"What are you staring at?" he asked. He reached up to put a fingernail between the top front teeth. "Is there something stuck in my . . ."

"No, Danny. I was just thinking. . . ." She turned to go, pulling him along. "Come on; let's get back to the house."

They ran across the frozen turf of the barnyard, through a light snowfall that meant higher temperatures on the way, maybe up to twenty or twenty-five above zero by tomorrow. At the back of the house they pushed open the door and stepped into the snow room, stomping off the snow and ice, stepping out of their boots, Melissa pulling back her hood and unzipping her parka to hang it on the nail. Then she grabbed Danny's hand and tugged him through the inside door to get into the snug warmth of the kitchen with its stove on.

Melissa had started an apple pie baking just before they walked over to the barn. It smelled glorious. Danny walked over to the stove, pulled open the oven door, and leaned over to take a look inside. "Looks pretty done to me, Melissa. Let's eat."

She peeked over his shoulder, reached in with the oven mitten on, and slid out the pie to take a look, then shook her head. "No way, needs another fifteen minutes." Danny was an eating machine. He could eat three McDonald's double cheeseburgers and two supersized orders of fries at one sitting and not blink an eye over it. She'd seen him do it a hundred times. She might as well make him wait until the pie was really done. Teaching him a little patience when it came to food wasn't a bad idea at all.

He walked away toward the dining room, checking things out while she pushed the pie back into oven. He'd only been in the house a few times, and this was the first time he'd been here when her dad wasn't, so he'd always been careful before, staying in the kitchen and being polite, trying to hold a conversation with Melchior, a pretty painful exercise really, trying to get her dad to open up and talk a little bit. This was really Danny's first chance to check things out.

"Hey, Melissa, what's this?" He sounded farther away.

She walked into the dining room, but he wasn't there. Through that room and into the living room and still he wasn't there. "Danny? Where are you hiding?"

"In here. What a weird room. What's the story in here?"

The sunroom. She shook her head; this would be interesting to try to explain.

The sunroom, as she walked in, was dark and shadowed, the only light coming from the open door into the living room and the dozen or so narrow beams of sunlight that pierced the latticework of the closed interior shutters on the windows.

Danny stood in the middle of the room, hands on hips, shaking his head. "What *is* this?" There were pots everywhere, filled with dirt and dead plants, some of them no more than sticks jutting out from the soil, other dried leaves and twigs covering the pots and dangling over the sides. The air was stale and gone dry, any smells the dying plants might have given off long gone over the years.

On the far wall a crucifix hung, Christ looking over the weird interior desert of the room.

Melissa shivered in the stuffy warmth of the room. "This was my mom's favorite room, Danny. Dad tells me these were all plants from Jamaica that she had growing here. He just closed the door and left it after she disappeared. I don't think he's ever come in here since. I just come in every now and then and dust a little."

"Wow," he said, softly. "You know, I don't think about that much, about how she just left you guys. I don't want to sound . . . but, like, how could she do that? How could a mother just leave her family? Her little girl?"

Melissa folded her arms in front of her chest. "I don't know if that's what happened. I mean, the police never figured it out. Maybe she was kidnapped or something. Maybe she fell into a hole somewhere or just walked off and got lost in the woods. You ought to ask your dad about it. I bet he remembers it."

Danny was running his finger along the edge of a large clay pot. "Yeah, I'm sure he does. He remembers all the cases." He turned to look at Melissa. "How much do you remember about her?"

She shook her head. "Nothing. I was way too young." She hesitated, added, "Well, just a little here and there. I remember her hugging me in bed, I think; you know, tucking me in and giving me a kiss on the cheek. And I remember standing in this room with her in the summer, light just pouring in, and it was so hot in here and she was singing some kid song—something about Bazeel or some other bogeyman going to get you if you don't behave."

She walked over to Danny, stood in front of him. He reached out and took her hands in his and stared at her. She smiled. "What do you remember about your mom?"

"A lot. I was seven when she died. I have tons of memories. I remember her watching me play soccer because Dad was too busy to be there very much. One game I was goalie and gave up, like, ten goals and at the end of the game she just walked over to me and put her arm around me and said it was OK."

Melissa backed up a step, giggled, punched Danny in the chest. "*That's* your best memory of your mother? A hug after a soccer game?"

He grinned. "Hey, the point is she was always there, you know? Always." He looked at Melissa, shrugged his shoulders. "I don't know. There's lots of stuff I remember; that's just one."

"Oh, Danny," she laughed, and came over to give him a hug. For a moment, he stood there, arms at his side as she hugged him. Then, slowly he put his arms around her and hugged back. She liked that; it felt right, felt safe and warm.

She looked up, and there was that face, her Danny's face, looking at her, just inches away. She went up on her tiptoes, kissed him lightly on the lips.

Was this the right thing to do? Did he want this, too? Would this ruin everything, ruin their friendship? Those questions flashed through her mind as their lips touched.

She put her head on his shoulder. She could hear his heart racing along.

"Oh, Melissa," he said, and she looked up at him again. He leaned down and they bumped noses, laughed, embarrassed, then tried again, lips coming together. She realized she really didn't know how she was supposed to do this. Sweet sixteen—well, almost sixteen—and actually never been kissed, she thought. Too much staying home doing the chores, or going to basketball practice, or studying, or just standing around outside in all kinds of weather shooting hoops out at that rim nailed up on the side of the barn. She had a three-point line painted out there, could hit seven out of ten in almost any weather down to about zero, when the ball got so cold and heavy that it wouldn't bounce. Even then she'd try to keep shooting, clumsy mittens and knit cap and bulky parka and all. But eventually, as winter wore on, the net froze solid and the ball wouldn't go through it, and, finally, you just had to stop.

No stopping here. The kiss went on, occasionally the two of them backing away for a second but then back to it. She hadn't realized how soft a man's lips could be. Somehow she'd thought they'd be hard, more forceful. She'd wondered about that, worried about it some, even. How would she handle that, a man forcing his way?

But it turned out to not be a problem. Maybe this kiss wasn't the way it was done in Hollywood, but it was working fine right here, right now.

Finally, years later, they parted, stepped back a foot or so, looked at each other.

"Wow," he said. And then he couldn't say any more, the big lunk. He just stood there. "Melissa, I . . . Was that all right? Did we just . . . ?"

"It was fine, Danny. It was great. Really."

"Man, it sure was. Can we . . . ?" He leaned forward for another kiss. She leaned up to him, more forceful herself this time, stronger, the smell of it, the passion, like she was on fire, like the whole world was in smoke and flames.

Oh, wait. Oh, god. The apple pie. "Danny! The oven!"

He panicked for a brief moment; then, as she turned, grabbing him by the hand again and pulling him along, he laughed, realizing what she was saying.

They ran back out through the sunroom door, through the living room and into the dining room, past the old oak table that was her mother's, the one that her father polished carefully once a week, every Sunday, in a kind of worshipful remembrance of what and who she'd been.

Once a year, right in the depths of January, he liked to tell Melissa stories about her mother, the island girl he'd fallen in love with when he worked for Alcan down in Jamaica. The strange beauty with the long black hair, the surprising pale white skin and the green of her eyes, and that wonderful accent that he'd fallen for right from the start. Melissa had inherited some of that, the soft black hair and the emerald eyes, and skin that never got darker even in summer than a light golden tan.

The way Melchior told the story about her mother's disappearance, he'd been out in the barn for a few hours, and when he'd come back into the house his daughter sat alone on the kitchen floor, banging a wooden spoon against the bottom of a saucepan, and his wife, his lovely perfect wife, was gone. No one ever found a sign of her.

Why was she thinking of this? Melissa's mind was going a thousand miles an hour as she tugged Danny along, unwilling to let go of him even as she raced toward the kitchen and the oven and the burning apple pie.

She pulled him into the kitchen, Danny laughing and now Melissa laughing, too. There was smoke coming from the oven; not much of it but enough to stink up the whole kitchen, that was for sure. She twisted the dial to off and then yanked open the oven door and the smoke roiled out. She started to reach in to grab the pie, remembered she didn't have the oven mittens on. She finally let go of Danny and, tugging up the sleeves of her sweatshirt, grabbed the mittens, slid them on, and reached in to pull out the pie—black along the outer edges of the crust.

Laughing at herself, at her own stupidity for not being able to admit that Danny was right twenty minutes ago about the pie, she pulled it out and was setting the pie on the countertop cutting board just as the kitchen smoke alarm went off, a loud, piercing on-off screech that startled her. She dropped the pie the last few inches and the burnt crust seemed to explode right off the round outer edge of the pie, black crust flying everywhere.

And hot pie from beneath the crust, too. She looked down and saw one great glob of apple pie on her left arm. For a long second, it just seemed silly. Then, with a flash of pain, she realized it was burning her. She raced for the sink.

Danny, bless his heart, had seen it happen and was already there, tugging out the spray nozzle from the top of the sink, turning on the cold water as he did that, and spraying her arm as soon as she was in range.

It worked and the relief was immediate, but there was water everywhere. Her sweatshirt was soaked and water dripped from the front of the refrigerator where the nozzle had sent most of the spray that missed Melissa. Everywhere else in what seemed like the whole kitchen it looked like there'd been a summer rainshower, and all that from just half a minute of spray meant for her left arm. It was a mess, that was for sure.

But it was also hilarious. As she grabbed some ice from the fridge Melissa couldn't help laughing, and when she turned around Danny was laughing so hard he could barely stand up. She walked over to him and there, soaked as she was, he put his arms around her and gave her a hug while she held the ice on the burn spot, the alarm still hooting in the background.

"You're soaked," he said, trying hard to hold in the laughter.

"And the pie is ruined, and the kitchen's a mess, and the place smells like the house burned down. But other than that everything's just fine." She smiled, reached up to touch his lips with her finger. "C'mon; my dad will kill me if we don't get this cleaned up before he gets back."

Danny pulled back, walked over to the smoke alarm, pulled it from the wall, and tugged out the battery. Melissa tried to pull off the sweatshirt but couldn't do that without dropping the ice she held on her arm.

Danny walked over to her, took the ice from her hands, and

tossed it into the sink, then took the ends of the sleeves of the sweatshirt and started tugging. It came off smoothly. Under it, she wore a Mankato Catholic Crusaders T-shirt. She'd never thought of that as a particularly sexy thing to wear, but somehow with Danny helping her get out of the sweatshirt, the T-shirt took on a whole new meaning.

Her arms were pointed straight up and Danny pulling up the sides of the sweatshirt when they looked at each other again, the simple gray T-shirt riding up on her chest, her stomach exposed. Danny leaned down and kissed her again, one that started as a gentle exploration, then grew longer, more passionate until, finally, Danny backed away, looked at this wonderful new girl he'd just found hidden in his old childhood friend, and summed it up with, "Whew."

"I know," she said, and smiled.

Outside, a car door slammed. It took a second to register— everything today seemed to happening in slow motion, Melissa thought—and then it hit her. A car door. Her father. Home from his ice fishing.

"Danny!" She bolted for the door, yanked it open, darted through the small snow room, and rubbed a spot clear in the middle of the frost that covered it in opaque white. Outside, her father was standing there next to the Ford pickup, looking up at the house.

Danny had come up behind her. "Oh, Christ, Melissa. It *is* him."

"And he sees us, or at least me," she said. He was looking right at the door, must have seen her scrape out the clear spot. Danny's Jeep was out in the yard, so he knew Danny was here. She waved at him, but he didn't do anything. So she opened the door, stepped outside in her blue jeans and T-shirt, and, one hand on the door, keeping it open, waved at him from there.

He nodded his head, saying nothing, and then turned to walk away, back toward the barn and his welding.

Melissa turned back to Danny. "I saw," he said, and headed back to the kitchen. They had a few minutes, at least, to try to clean things up. They were lucky as hell that he hadn't seen this mess, hadn't seen them kissing there. Melissa wondered what he would have done if he *had* seen them. Shouted at her?

He hadn't shouted at her in her life. Hadn't touched her, never a single spanking, never a slap, never a heated word. Not much in the way of any words at all, really, and he wasn't much for hugs, either, her father.

Maybe, she thought, he wouldn't have minded seeing her with Danny; maybe he'd have given her one of those rare smiles. Then she laughed to herself as she started cleaning up the mess—sure, and maybe it would be ninety degrees tomorrow, too. Anything was possible if you just believed, right?

In fifteen frantic minutes the kitchen was spotless and most of the smoke aired out. When Melchior never came in from the barn, they finally decided to go out and see him, say hi. There, he was himself. Quiet. Withdrawn. Polite with Danny.

Later, holding hands as they walked out to Danny's Jeep, they were giddy with their escape. What a close call; what an incredibly close call.

TROPHIES

He should be happy, damn it. Last night his boy led all scorers with twenty-six points as Mankato Catholic beat New Ulm Lutheran. Had twelve rebounds, too, so a double-double.

Danny was just a great kid and Detective Dan Finnegan was so proud of the boy that he happily made a fool of himself this morning when he first walked into the office and started bragging on the kid.

But that was hours ago. Now, instead, Finnegan had the Death Investigation Form out, had his pen in his hand, had even filled out the top line where his name went.

But that was it. For the first time in his fifteen years as a detective, the last six as captain, he couldn't bring himself to fill out the form. Jesus, what an awful mess that was.

Who could do such a thing? Maybe the cops in the Twin Cities saw stuff like this, or the guys in Chicago or New York. But not here, not in Blue Earth County in a farmhouse overlooking a bend in the river, with the winter sun bouncing bright reflections off the frozen water and the protective row of cottonwoods standing there, bare branches held out to the pale-blue sky. A perfect winter day. Cold, sharp, clear, innocent.

He thought, when he started to write, that getting it down on paper might help, might soften the brutality of it some, reduce it to hand-written words on paper, harmless things.

He was used to doing that, writing down how two guys in a bar turned their argument deadly, or how, last year, two brothers fighting over one woman managed to kill each other. The woman was still in town, was dating again.

But not now, not with this one. Even just filling in the boxes at the top seemed to be more than he could manage. Day Reported. Time Dispatched. Time Arrived. Time Completed. Weather. Lighting. Location.

Jesus, he wasn't anywhere near to the spot where he had to fill in the narrative and already he couldn't handle it. The blood, the body parts. That little girl and her mother. Sweet Lord in heaven.

He sat back in the wooden chair, tried thinking about how uncomfortable the chair was, how he needed to requisition a new one, how he was tired of wobbling back and forth every time he shifted his weight in the damn thing.

But that didn't help move things along. He needed to get this paperwork done so he could get started on the real job, catching the sick son of a bitch who could do a thing like this. Jesus Christ Almighty, it had been a mess in there.

The two-story frame farmhouse, painted white sometime within the last year or two, sat on a few hundred acres out near Rapidan. Good soil there, a lot of it bottomland along the Maple River. Finnegan had admired the look of the place as they drove up. Well cared for, prosperous. Nice barn, painted a deep burnt-red color; little wooden picket fence around a side yard with a red and white candy-striped swing set in it, covered now with a foot of snow on the seat of the swing and a beautiful swirl of frozen snow coming right down the slide. There were hard, clear beauties to see in a Minnesota winter, if only you looked for them.

Corn and soybean farm, looked like. Miles away from town. Hell, two miles of unpaved road—frozen hard as concrete this time of year—away from the pavement.

The husband and father was in Mankato for the day working out his loans for the seed and fertilizer he'd need once the ground thawed. An older daughter, a teenager, was in school, a sophomore at Rapidan High School.

The uniform guys caught up with the father just as he left the bank, broke the news to him, had to watch him crumble right there, falling to his knees and then just staying like that, dazed, until they took him into the ER at the hospital to get him looked after. Two other officers pulled the high-school daughter out of class and had the tough duty of breaking the horrible news and then taking her to the hospital to see her dad, who by then was in intensive care with what might be a stroke.

Technically speaking, the father, at least, was a suspect for the moment, but that wouldn't hold. He couldn't have done it, time-wise or any other way.

Finnegan had walked in through the front door, pulled off his lined leather gloves, and slipped on the tight latex surgicals while he looked around. Couple of lamps knocked over in the front room, a throw rug in the middle all bunched up where there'd been a scuffle.

You could about follow it from there. He chased her through the dining room, shoving chairs out of his way, bumping up against the dining-room table so that it was turned slightly.

Then he caught up with her in the kitchen. Killed her there, though she must have fought like a demon for a few minutes, from the look of the blood spread around on three walls, hand-prints against one that slid down the wall to where she must have sat back against the wall for a while—dead already, Finnegan hoped—before the guy decided to get artistic with the body. There were puncture wounds in the chest, jagged, from a knife with a serrated edge, maybe. He'd know that for sure when he got the paperwork in from Forensics' mobile crime unit that had driven down from St. Paul and was at the house by now.

And then there was her right hand, hacked off at the wrist. The hand was missing, so the guy was a collector. Great, just great.

The place had reeked of the sharp, acrid bite of bleach mixed with the iron-tinged, back-of-the-throat grab of puddled blood. Veteran detectives don't throw up, but the meticulous cold-bloodedness of it, and the nauseating smell, almost got to him. He had to walk outside for a few minutes in the deep below-zero weather to get a grip on himself.

Finnegan figured the guy was working on the mom when the

little girl showed up. Maybe that surprised him, since it was a
school day and she was only home because she'd come down sick
with a cough and fever. She must have been upstairs, heard the
noise, finally came down to check on things. Saw this strange
man standing over Mommy, saw Mommy lying there, saw the
blood. Maybe he was cutting on Mom when the daughter walked
in.

Jesus. How did she react? Did she scream? Did she just ask
politely what had happened to her mommy? Did she try to run
away? Did she just walk in to get a closer look, rubbing sleep
from those big brown eyes?

Mercifully, it looked like he killed her quickly, with a kind of
awful compassion, her throat sliced wide open. Finnegan couldn't
tell yet if he'd raped her or her mommy. He'd get that news, too,
from Forensics. He hoped the little one, at least, didn't know
much terror, didn't have much time to realize what was going on.

Not like her mommy. Mommy lived long enough to see her
murderer, to struggle with him, fingernails scraping him maybe,
so they might get some DNA from that.

Finnegan spent a couple of hours there, doing all the things
you have to do—not just looking it all over, thinking it through,
but the other stuff, too, like doing a quick interview with the
officer at the scene, making sure he knew what she'd touched and
where she'd been when she first came into the crime scene, then
calling his buddy Jon Hamner from the BCA, the state's Bureau
of Criminal Apprehension, so they could get their crime-scene
team involved.

They didn't have a lot to go on, damn it. The DNA, maybe.
Some bloody partial shoe prints—looked like a woman's shoe,
so maybe from the victim. Some strands of black hair, long. A
handful of tiny black beads on the kitchen floor off a kid's necklace, maybe.

The guy had wiped out most of the rest of what they might
get by pulling out a bottle of bleach from beneath the sink and
rubbing most everything down with it. Very meticulous, this guy.

Finnegan turned back to his report. You're supposed to get

used to it after a while, and if he couldn't stand seeing cases like this, then why was he in the damn business?

He was in it because he could do something, damn it. He could make something better in this job. He could catch the goddamn bad guys. He was smarter than they were; he could outthink them, get inside their perverted little minds and stop them before they could do it again. That's why he had to fill out this damn form. So he could get going on this and stop this son of a bitch before it happened again.

He started writing: "Day Reported: January 17."

A SPECIAL NIGHT

MOTHER, DAUGHTER SLAIN IN RAPIDAN HOME
By Free Press Reporter Michelle Mitchell
RAPIDAN—The bodies of a Rapidan mother and her younger daughter were found today in their farm home near State Route 66, apparent murder victims.

The bodies were found by a postal letter carrier curious about the home's open front door in the sub-zero weather as he delivered the mail shortly before noon. The letter carrier was not available for comment.

Zachary Curlew, the husband and father of the victims, was informed of their deaths shortly after completing a farm-loan application at First National Bank in Mankato. When informed by police officers of the murders, he collapsed and was taken to St. Joseph's Hospital in Mankato for observation.

"Mr. Curlew is not a suspect at this time," said Detective Daniel Finnegan, captain of detectives of the Blue Earth County Sheriff's Department.

Another daughter, Sondra, was not hurt in the crime. She is a student at Rapidan High School and was apparently in class at the time of the murders. She is being cared for by relatives of the Curlew family.

Finnegan said a thorough investigation of the grisly crime scene is under way and it will be some time before police are ready to comment on possible suspects. "It is a very complex crime scene, and we will be there for a while. We have asked for the assistance of the forensics unit of the state Bureau of Criminal Apprehension," he added.

Mrs. Anne Curlew was a volunteer at the St. John Vianney Catholic Church in Rapidan and a lifelong resident of the city. Angela Curlew was seven years old and in the second grade at Rapidan Central Elementary. School officials were informed of her death during the afternoon and have canceled classes for today. "Counseling is available for students," said the school's principal, Sue Klesius.

"They were just the nicest people," neighbor Diane Pflugrad said. "It's hard to imagine this could happen to someone as nice as that mother and her little girl."

The two deaths are the first murders this year in Blue Earth County. Last year there were six murders in the county.

At third-hour chapel, Melissa sat in the tenth pew back on the left side. She'd been there a few hours before to serve the seven o'clock Mass, but Father Murphy hadn't shown up and Father Reskey was busy saying Mass at the hospital chapel, so the morning Mass had been canceled. That was a first.

Now, at eleven o'clock, she was back in the chapel again, this time with the whole school, for a special service to remember the Curlews, mother and daughter. Melissa knelt on the worn padding of the kneeler of her pew and stared up at that smiling Christ on His cross and wondered what He found so funny in the deaths of those two people. Danny was two pews in front of her.

The murders were all anybody could talk about. The mother and daughter who'd been killed so brutally were Catholics over in Rapidan, at St. John's Parish, a little Catholic enclave in the middle of a town full of Lutherans. Their deaths were so shocking, the news so overwhelming, that Melissa's teammates had even quit razzing her about Danny and True Love while they thought about this tragedy that felt so close.

Melissa had played parish basketball against the family's older daughter, Sondra, the one who'd been in school and hadn't been hurt. She recognized Sondra from the picture in the paper, remembered her guiltily as plain-faced and not very talented, all gawky elbows and knees, trying hard but not really getting much done on the court. Melissa and her Holy Innocents team had won that game by at least twenty-five.

After the game they'd all met at the A&W on South Main Street for some root beer and hot dogs, the players from both teams giggling and talking like they were all old friends. Maybe the girl's dad had been there, too. And the mom and the little sister, the murder victims, they'd probably been there, too, smiling and laughing and eating chili dogs and swigging down root beer. Melissa didn't remember that actually happening, but somehow she couldn't get the thought out of her mind, visions of that day coming back to her all last night and now again in the clear, cold light of day.

Rapidan was a nice little town, with a main street that ran along the river, and a hardware store and a feed store and a Dairy Queen and that A&W, and a dozen churches for a few thousand people. And now two of those people were gone, murdered. It was worse, somehow, than if they'd died in some car accident. Worse than disease or a plane crash or a house fire or anything like that. The fact that someone had come in there and murdered them, stared them in the face and tortured them and then killed them, was just so awful that Melissa didn't want to even think about it, but at the same time that she couldn't stop thinking about it.

How could the merciful God she kept hearing about in religion class have allowed something like that to happen? Tonight she had another basketball game, the girls playing at five-thirty and the boys' game at seven, against Gustavus Adolphus Prep from St. Peter. The schools had decided to go ahead and play but dedicate the game to the victims. Melissa didn't know how she'd play, with this on her mind so much. How could you care about your jump shot when all you could think about was murder?

She couldn't talk to her father about it; she hadn't even tried.

This morning at breakfast he'd just read the story in the *Free Press* and then shook his head, muttered something under his breath about what the world was coming to, and then gone on out to the barn to weld. She wanted to tell him that she knew the family, at least a little, but he wasn't listening.

Maybe later, at lunch, she'd be able to talk about it with Danny, who understood this kind of stuff. And his dad was the kind you could talk to, too, though he was the detective in charge of the whole investigation, so he wouldn't say much, even though he'd know if they had a chance of finding the guy who did it. Maybe, she thought, the three of them would have a chance to get sodas and hamburgers after tonight's boys' game if Detective Finnegan wasn't busy at the crime scene or something. She'd like to tell him about how she knew the family some.

He was a great listener, Danny's dad. He was always paying attention to what Danny did: showing up a lot at the football, basketball, and baseball games, checking Danny's homework, setting curfews for him to get home by—all those kinds of things. Danny complained about it, said his dad was way too strict, but Melissa thought it must be great to have a dad who knew what you were doing, a dad who showed up to watch you play a game or came to your seventh-grade science fair.

Thinking about Danny brought her right back to thinking about The Kiss. It was certainly capitalized in her mind, and it changed everything. Little Danny Finnegan, the boy she'd climbed trees with since third grade, the boy she'd been sledding with, ice-skating with, shot hoops with a thousand times. Her buddy Danny, her good pal, her best friend, was suddenly something very different. It was weird and scary and wonderful and exciting all at the same time.

She looked up again at Happy Christ on His cross and felt a quick pang of guilt. She shouldn't be thinking about Danny right now; she should be miserable and sad, thinking about those poor murdered people. And she was sad; she was. It was just that Danny was right there in front of her, maybe fifteen feet away, a free throw's distance, no more than that.

He turned around to look at her once, quickly, before Sister

Rose Patrice, the assistant principal, noticed. Danny smiled. Melissa smiled back.

Detective Finnegan wasn't at the game that night. He was working late on the case, Danny explained, meeting with some kind of team of investigators. Danny didn't mind. He'd been sixteen for almost two months and was the proud possessor of a driver's license. To make up for not being there, his dad gave him the use of the family car, an eight-year-old Toyota Corolla, for the night. Danny and Melissa drove to Vito and Sal's for some pizza and Cokes.

Melissa had played well and her Lady Crusaders had won. Danny, too, had led his team to a win. But that wasn't what they talked about.

"It makes you wonder. I mean, any of us could be murdered," Melissa said over the first slice of pepperoni. "The guy is still out there, you know. He could be anybody. He could be right in this restaurant right now."

"I don't think so," Danny said, looking around. The only other customers were two tables full of high-school kids sitting down to their own after-game pizzas. "And besides, I'd protect you, Melissa; you know I would."

Melissa laughed. "Thanks, Danny, but I'll take your dad when it comes to protection. I mean, like, after all, he's in the business of being fearless. He risks his life to save others. He figures out terrible crimes and catches the bad guys."

Danny was just looking at her, a weird kind of blank expression on his face.

"Oh, Danny," she said, easing off. "You're just like me. You're a high-school sophomore in a small school in Minnesota." She laughed again. "We haven't had a lot of chances to exactly prove our courage, you know."

"Yeah," he said, "I know." And he took a bite of his pizza, sipped on his soft drink. "But, Melissa, Dad doesn't think of himself that way. He thinks what he does is mostly paperwork. He's only fired his gun one time in the last ten years. Hit the guy, too, and stopped him cold."

"Your dad killed someone?" She didn't believe it.

Danny shook his head. "No, but he stopped him. Dad says he was lucky he didn't get killed himself doing it. The guy shot at him five times and missed with them all. It's not like TV, he says. In real life most people are crummy shots with a handgun."

She shuddered. "Boy, good thing." Yesterday, she thought, that would have just been an interesting story. But today, after these murders brought that kind of stuff close to home, it really hit her. People, bad guys, had taken shots at Dan Finnegan. And he shot back.

"Are you cold?" Danny wanted to know. He reached across the table and took her hands from the cold Coke she had them wrapped around. He held them in his. Warm. Safe. "That help?"

She nodded. It helped.

Later, when he drove her home, she spent the entire drive wondering if he was going to kiss her good night when he dropped her off.

He did. Several times.

Her dad, sitting in his favorite chair in the living room watching the tube when she came in, didn't seem to have noticed a thing.

SENIOR YEAR

In the final five seconds of the final game of the first-round regional of the Class A high-school girls' basketball tournament against St. Cloud Cathedral, All-State Senior Guard Melissa O'Malley stood at the free-throw line and dribbled the ball, once, twice, three times. Feet apart about shoulder width, the ball cradled in her fingers, left hand around to the side, right hand nearly straight at the back, she crouched slightly at the knee and stared intently at the front of the rim, fifteen feet away, ten feet high. Her focus narrowed; the crowd disappeared; her teammates melted away. The other team was gone into the gray, the not-real part that didn't matter; everything was gone except that rim, yawning large, wide as a canyon.

She came up from the crouch, raising her elbows from chest high to neck high as she pushed the ball forward with her right wrist. It came off the fingertips of the right hand, a slight backward spin on it as it arced toward the rim. The moment took a month, a year, Melissa not watching the ball at all but just the rim as the ball came swimming down into her field of vision, dropped perfectly through the metal, and swished through the cords.

Made it. Game tied, forty-seven all.

She did the whole routine again, focusing in, getting lost in the mechanics of it. She loved shooting free throws, could routinely hit twenty in a row in practice. It was all mechanics and focus. There was nothing to it. Get set at the line, dribble three times, bend at the knees, rise and release and watch it go through. *Swish.* The Crusaders up one.

There were a frenzied last few seconds as Cathedral, out of time-outs, tried to inbound the ball and get off a shot. But their girls couldn't do it, their best guard dribbling the ball off her foot and out-of-bounds as the horn sounded and the game was over and the Mankato Catholic Crusaders were Section Two champions and headed for the Sweet Sixteen.

Danny had a special night planned for her, and hitting the big free throws just made it all the better. When she came out of the locker room, hair still a little wet as she shoved it up under the bright-blue Crusaders knit cap, he stood there, waiting, smiling. Her Danny.

It hadn't been easy for Danny this year. The boys' team had some talented sophomores and Danny, a senior who'd been a star himself as a sophomore, went from starter to sixth man. As the season wore on, he got less and less playing time, and then last week the boys lost their opening-round game in the regionals and their season was over. That meant it was suddenly baseball season for Danny, and those same sophomores played that sport, too. Even though all they were doing was throwing in the gym to get their arms in shape, Danny said he could see the writing on the wall. More bench time.

But here he was, smiling, putting his arm around his girl to walk her to his car and go get them both a bite to eat before he broke the big news to her. He'd promised her he had something special for her and she thought she knew what that was. She thought she was finally ready for it, too. Danny would propose, and then they'd make love.

Making love with Danny. The thought of that didn't occur to her more than maybe a dozen times a day for the past two years. Some of her girlfriends said they'd done it now, but she didn't know whether to believe them or not. Stacy said she and Greg did it, like, once a week and would do it more if their parents weren't around so much. It was pretty painful the first time, Stacy said, but then absolutely magic after that.

Angela Rasmussen was said to have done it with half the boys in the senior class, and you could just look at her and see that was maybe true; she was so slutty, smoking those Marlboro Ultralights and wearing enough makeup for five girls. She and her little circle of smoker girlfriends, most of them with money, thought they were so fly they could do anything they wanted anytime. They weren't as bad as the druggies, who lately were popping Percodans like they were candy and then heading up to the Twin Cities for raves. The druggies were sort of sad and funny, really. There weren't many of them at Mankato Catholic; most of that type were at Mankato High or North High. But the ones who were at the Catholic high school prided themselves on being different, or as different as you could be in a Catholic high school that kept you in uniforms and wouldn't allow you to pierce your nose or eyebrows or have any tattoos. Deal was, they all worked so hard at being different in the same way that it was pretty comical—all of them exactly different together. Even some of the jocks seemed to set their dials on self-destruct, the football players with their Dianabol steroids and a few of the girls, too, with one called Anadrol.

But most of the better jocks were pretty positive about things. All but a couple were going to college, some to small schools like Gustavus Adolphus over in St. Peter, others aiming at Division II, where they figured they could get some scholarship help and make the team.

With a dozen basketball offers on the table from places like Minnesota, Illinois, and Northwestern and then a bunch of Division II schools, Melissa had decided to take the U.'s offer and head to Minneapolis and be a golden Gopher.

The best thing was that Summer Arndt, a girl she'd known for years and really liked, had a scholarship offer to run cross-country for the Gophers, so the two girls planned to room together at the U.

Melissa's plan was for Danny, who didn't have the grades for the U. right now, to go to Hennepin Community College for a year, get his grades up, and then transfer in—kids did that all the time. HCC was right up the road from the U., so they could see each other all the time and then get an apartment together maybe their sophomore year. HCC had men's and women's basketball, too, so Danny was going to walk-on and see if he could make the team.

If he proposed tonight like she thought he might, that would fit just right with all her plans. They could aim at getting married in a couple of years, maybe over the summer after sophomore year, and then they'd be set, in school and getting their degrees. They could put off starting a family until after they graduated. Then they could get married, move on down to Florida like they always talked about, find jobs down there in the warm sunshine, and live happily ever after. It would be perfect.

The meal was at Donelli's, which was serious Italian and wound up costing Danny a lot of money, twenty-five dollars once he paid that 10 percent tip. Melissa was really hungry, but so curious that she didn't eat nearly as much as she usually did. Eating was not a problem for her; she burned up all the calories with exercise, so she didn't have to worry about her weight. Through the salad and the pasta and the bread dipped in olive oil and the chicken Parmesan and the Italian ices at the end— through it all—she kept waiting for him to pop the big question, but he never did. She thought that was pretty cute, really, and didn't push him. Danny wasn't great with words. Like he was in a lot of things, when he had something important to say he had to kind of plod his way through it. But that meant he was the sort of guy who took his time, thought it all through, and got it done right the first time. Maybe that was his failing in sports, it occurred to her, and that was probably why he did better in football than in basketball or baseball, where reaction times mattered so much. In football he'd wound up playing fullback and done fine there. Take the handoff and go up the middle or block. He wasn't all-conference or anything, but he chewed up yardage, protected his quarterback, opened up the holes for Travis Menken to run through on off-tackle plays, and seemed to have fun.

After dinner, they drove to Danny's house. He still hadn't said whatever it was he was going to say, but Melissa was patient and straight-faced with him since he was so serious about the whole thing.

She wanted to just say, "Danny, this is me, Melissa, remember? It's just me; just say it and I'll say yes and we'll take it from there, OK?" But that would spoil this whole evening he'd worked so hard on, so she kept quiet, acting the part, as he drove her to his house. Was this going to be in front of his dad, then? That'd be kind of strange.

But his dad wasn't home and they had the house to themselves. Danny led the way in, holding her hand and leading her along, into the living room. There he sat her on the couch. She started to say something, but he put his finger to his lip to keep her quiet.

While she sat there at the front of the couch, knees straight out in front, back straight like she was in chapel and Sister Very Vicious was walking by, he walked away, into the kitchen.

She heard the refrigerator door open and the clink of glass and then he walked back in with two wineglasses and a bottle of wine—"Snowy Mountain," it said on the label, and there was a snow-covered peak that rose toward the cork.

"It's Australian wine," he said with a note of pride in his voice. "It's called a Pinot Grigio. Cost me almost ten dollars."

"Wine? How'd you get that?"

"Ron Miller, Randy's older brother, is a junior at Bemidji State and really knows his wines. He got it for me."

"OK, but *why'd* you get that? Since when do you drink wine?" She paused, added, "Since when do *I* drink wine?"

He wrestled with the corkscrew, trying to twist the screw through the metal cap and down into the cork.

"I think you're supposed to take that off first, Danny," she said, and reached out to take the bottle from him. Her father hadn't touched a glass of alcohol in his life, as far as she knew, but you couldn't be a senior girl at Mankato Catholic and not have seen this done plenty of times at parties. Nothing to it. She peeled away the foil, took the corkscrew from Danny's hands—his hands were trembling a little and his knees were doing the same, she noticed—and started winding it into the cork. In about a minute she had the cork pulled.

Danny took the bottle back. Reached for a glass, poured it, handed that to her, and then filled up the other glass. He raised his in a toast. "To us, Melissa."

She raised her glass. God, he was so sweet. "To us," she said, and they clinked the glasses. She took a sip and he did the same.

He grimaced. "I thought this was supposed to be pretty good."

It didn't taste that bad to her. It tasted adult, somehow. "I think it is. I think you have to get used to it." And she took another sip. "Danny, when's your father getting home?"

Danny smiled. "Tomorrow morning. He's at a forensics conference in St. Paul. I'm Home Alone 2," he said, and laughed.

"Well, my dad's not in St. Paul," she reminded him, and then took another sip. It tasted pretty good, actually. Really sweet. When was he going to get around to saying it?

He sat down next to her on the couch. Not on one knee down in front of her? She almost giggled at that thought but caught herself; a giggle would just humiliate him, her sensitive Danny.

He set his glass of wine down on the coffee table, turned sideways to face her. She took another sip. She was feeling light-headed already, surprised that it could happen that quickly. It wasn't a bad feeling at all, maybe made all the more giddy by what was happening, by the way Danny looked at her. She sipped again, finishing off the glass of wine.

She smiled at him, at her lovable Danny. He seemed like he was going to speak, but he couldn't get it out. She leaned forward, poured some more of the sweet Australian wine in her glass, took another sip.

"Melissa," he finally managed to say, his voice hoarse.

"Yes, Danny?"

"Melissa, you know how much I love you."

"Yes, Danny."

"And you tell me that you love me, too, right?"

Another sip. "Yes, Danny. I love you."

"Well, that's good." He took a deep breath. "This is really hard."

No, it wasn't, not really. They'd talked about this all the time, talked about all their plans. "Just say it, Danny."

"OK, then, I will. Melissa, I've been thinking a lot about all our plans, about your being at the U. and me being at the community college and all. About how I'm going to get my grades up and transfer in and then we'll live together and everything. I mean, those are great plans."

Yes, they were great plans, plans they'd talked about a lot, plans she was sure Danny was happy with. And now this? She didn't like what she was hearing. "I hear a 'but' in there, Danny." She couldn't believe it, felt a strange little cold shiver run right down her back. Could she be wrong somehow about Danny, about the whole relationship somehow? She thought she knew exactly where they were, what they were, who they were. And now she heard this "but" in there?

He shifted back a foot on the couch, looked at her as she took a nervous gulp of her wine. "It's just that, well," he hesitated, searched for exactly the right words, "I'm not sure I'm cut out for college right now, even at the community college. You know I'm not that great a student, Melissa. Hell, you're the only reason I passed half my classes. If you hadn't helped me with all those papers . . ."

She looked at him. "So?"

"So here's what I think. I want us to be married. I want us to move to Florida and get great jobs and have a bunch of kids and be happy and everything."

"And?"

"And I'm not sure college is how I'm going to get the kind of job that can support us, you know what I mean?"

"Danny, I'll have a job, too."

He shook his head. "No. See, that's, like, the problem. You're so smart and everything, and you're going to do great in college. You're going to be a basketball star and get all A's in class and all that stuff. And me . . ." he trailed off, took a deep breath, and tried one more time.

"Melissa O'Malley, will you marry me?"

She looked at him, her face puzzled. "Well, yes, Danny Finnegan. Of course. But what are you saying? I thought you were saying you weren't ready or something?"

"No, no, that's not it, Melissa." He was all in a rush now, getting it out in a hurry, getting it said and done. "I want us to get married, you know, in a couple of years. And right now I want us to be engaged while I serve my tour in the Navy. You could stay here in Minnesota, go to the U. and everything, and they say maybe I can get stationed at Great Lakes and be pretty close and we could see each other on weekends and that would be OK, or maybe I'd be in San Diego and you could come visit or even transfer to some school out there and we could be together. Anyway," he took a breath, "in a few years my tour of duty would be up and you'd be done with college and we could move down to Tampa like we've talked about and I'd get a job like my dad's, maybe, and you'd have a job and everything would be great."

She sat there, stunned, staring at him. "Wow," was all she could say. "You want to join the Navy?"

"I've already done it, Melissa. I'm eighteen. I've joined up. I start in six months, after graduation and everything."

"Wait. You're in the Navy?" She couldn't believe it. What was he thinking of? The Navy? "Danny, I don't... I don't..." She couldn't put one word after the next.

He nodded. "I did it, Melissa. I joined up. Just like Dad."

"Your dad joined the Navy?"

He laughed. "He did when he was my age. I told him I wanted to do this and he said if I was sure, it was OK with him."

Danny reached over to her, took the wineglass from her hand, and set the glass on the coffee table, then took both her hands in his. "I love you, Melissa. I always have. Since the third grade at Holy Innocents I've been in love with you. And I want us to be married."

"Me, too, Danny. I mean me, too, that I love you. I mean..."

"And I want us to have that great life we talk about. But this is something I have to do. I have to prove I'm..." he thought that one over, "prove I'm ready, you know?"

She thought maybe she did. And if she didn't, really, well, that didn't matter. This was what Danny wanted to do. He seemed so sure it was the right thing. She scooted over on the couch and hugged him.

"Oh, Melissa, I love you so much."

She didn't say anything, just kept hugging.

He pulled back. Stood up, reached into his blue-jeans pocket, pulled out a small ring case. He knelt down on one knee, opened the case. The most beautiful diamond in the world was in there, shining at her, bright as the stars on a frozen winter night in southern Minnesota. "Melissa. Will you marry me?"

"Oh, Danny." She took the ring from the case. "Oh, Danny, yes, of course I'll marry you. Oh, Danny, sweetheart, yes," she said, and slipped the ring onto her finger.

He took her hands and pulled her up from where she sat on the couch. His face, the most handsome face in the world, studied hers. He leaned toward her. They kissed.

And now, she thought, maybe we'll finally make love. The idea struck her as absolutely perfect. Absolutely, completely perfect.

MINNESOTA ROUSER

Bob Marley was singing about three little birds and their sweet songs of melodies pure and true while Melissa lay on her back on her bed in Room 138 of Frontier Hall at the University of Minnesota and stared at the popcorn plaster of the tiny room's ceiling.

"Don't worry 'bout a thing," Bob was singing. To Melissa's ears, the sounds were pure Jamaica. Palm trees, warm breezes, an azure sea lapping onto white sand, a reef line in the distance with waves breaking over it, white spray blown back by an offshore breeze. Someday, she thought. Someday.

She sighed. Outside, it was October 14 and snowing, the first flakes of the coming winter. She hoped to god the snow wouldn't stick; she wasn't anywhere near ready for winter yet. Yesterday it had been nearly eighty degrees and she'd been in shorts and a T-shirt on her way back from the gym. Then an early-morning front blew through with thunderstorms, strange for October, so strong they knocked out the power and phones for a while. Behind that front came all this cold air and now, hours later, she had to turn on some Marley and live off imagined heat.

Basketball scrimmages were going well, but they were tough as hell even though it wasn't even officially practice yet. For the past month the girls had been playing on their own, with no coaches allowed, according to NCAA rules. Right. Maybe the coaches weren't there, but it sure was curious how they seemed to know how everyone was doing.

Which was OK. As far as Melissa could tell, the so-called

coachless practices had gone well for her. She was relieved, really, to find out she could play at the level of these girls, all of them stars on their high-school teams. Her moves still worked; her shots were falling; her defense was OK. She'd know more in four weeks, for sure, when they started the regular season with a game against the University of Florida, but for the moment she felt pretty good about that side of things.

Tonight was Midnight Madness, when the men's and women's teams kicked off the official start of practice with flashing lights and smoke and a bunch of other splashy stuff to show off for the fans. Melissa was looking forward to that; it sounded like a lot of fun. But she was nervous, too. The school paper, the *Minnesota Daily*, and the local big paper, the *Star-Tribune*, had both made a big deal out of Madness, and both papers gave Melissa a lot of good ink in the season preview stories.

The *Daily* said she was slated to be the starting point guard and raved about her ballhandling and three-point shooting. The *Star-Tribune* said she should solve the point-guard problem that kept the Gophers from making the NCAA Tournament last year, when a late-season collapse—losses at Purdue and Ohio State and a big season-ending home loss by fifteen points against Indiana—turned what had been a pretty good season into a disaster. So Melissa stared at the ceiling and wondered if she could live up to that kind of hype. They were sure asking a lot of her.

She liked college life so far. Her basketball skills were holding up fine, classes were going OK, and she and Summer were getting along as roommates.

It had been a lot of fun, in fact, finally getting to really know Summer. Funny how you could be friends with someone for years but not really know her at all.

Melissa had thought of Summer as a close friend since freshman year of high school. They hung out together some through high school, were on the basketball and track teams together, had classes together in the college prep program at Mankato Catholic.

But, truth was, she'd only been over to Summer's house three or four times total in all those years, and Summer hadn't come to the farm with Mel even once. Somehow it had just worked out that way. Melissa was always busy in school—either in class or at practice for one sport or another or working on the school newspaper as a sportswriter or helping out with the yearbook. School life was pretty busy.

And she spent most of her time outside of school either helping her dad get the basic chores done at the farm or doing things with Danny, and so she hadn't really realized it, but there just hadn't been much time for anyone else. Now, though, off to college and away from the farm, and with Danny in basic training at Great Lakes since Labor Day, Melissa had been forced to restructure her life some. It hadn't been easy, getting used to missing Danny and her dad. The first was obvious—she loved Danny and was used to seeing him all the time, so the letters every few days and the occasional phone call weren't nearly enough to keep her from wanting to be with him. Just the other day she'd been walking on the pedestrian overpass part of the Morris Bridge over the Mississippi with Summer, and when the two of them had looked down on the river to watch the boats go by she'd been thinking how romantic that would have been with Danny. Lost in that thought, she'd reached out to hold Summer's hand, and then the both of them had laughed when she caught herself and jerked it away.

Stuff like that was happening all the time. There were so many couples all over campus, boys and girls—and sometimes boys and boys or girls and girls, too, which had been a shocker the first time, but she was slowly getting used to it—that she kept seeing everyone being in love and wanted that for herself. But her guy was three hundred miles away, learning to be a sailor. It was tough.

To her surprise she missed her father, too. He'd always been such a distant figure that she thought she could just walk away from him and the farm, no problem. But it hadn't been that easy, and she kept missing things that she hadn't even known she'd liked. Like sitting on the edge of the hayloft and watching him down below working on one of his giant sculptures all cobbled together from old tractor and auto parts. She'd watch the sparks fly, her dad bent over at the work of it, the arc welder sparking so painfully blue and white-bright that he'd make her wear the welder's mask if she wanted to watch, even from back up in the loft.

It was amazing how he did that, turning old rusty junk into some new animal, resurrecting the old, dead, and abandoned metal, bringing it back to a new kind of life.

Her favorite from this last summer was a giant twenty-foot-long lizard, the front right leg raised, a dewlap made from a combine's lifting cogs swinging out from the lizard's neck, a giant tongue that used to be a pair of shocks from a semi slashing out from the open mouth to catch a huge moth—wide gray wings from the side panels of an old Ford Falcon frozen in midflutter as the tongue connected and was ready to reel the moth in. She and Danny had watched that lizard rise from a pile of junk to full magnificence, and then came the day the flatbed came to haul it away to a bank in Des Moines, the semishocked tongue of the thing waving at them as the flatbed bounced up and down on the gravel road that ran out to the pavement.

They'd laughed at that, she and Danny, arm in arm. And then she'd turned to see her father, who'd said hardly a word to them the whole six weeks it took to make the thing, give her a slight smile and a nod of the head—like the work was good—before he turned to walk back toward the barn and get started on the next thing: some big northern pike for the front lawn of the Mankato Chamber of Commerce building.

They'd worked out the timing at summer's end. She'd been able to see Danny off at the airport in Minneapolis and then come to school to get into the dorms and go through new-student orientation, which was sometimes silly and sometimes really helpful. For a girl from a small high school in Mankato, the U.'s size had been overwhelming—fifty thousand students in one place and all of them trying to get their paperwork done at the same time. Incredible.

The schoolwork, like everything else here, was a lot harder than she was used to. She was taking five courses and the only easy one was a two-hour blow-off general-ed course called The University Experience. Then on Monday and Wednesday mornings she and Summer were taking an intro to mass comm course together. There were four hundred students in a big lecture hall. On the first day that had been a real shocker—that was as many students as at their whole high school. How could they possibly learn anything in a class like that? But the professor, thank god, was entertaining, and he used a huge screen to show them everything from a video clip of the first moon landing to a half-hour segment of *Citizen Kane*. They'd only had one test so far, and both had aced it. It seemed like the kind of course where if you read the book and took decent notes you'd do well.

Right after that one she was in an English comp course where she couldn't believe that some of the students didn't know the difference between a noun and a verb. As long as you kept up with the writing assignments the course was pretty easy, but she could see already that some of the other students were falling behind. They'd have a rough time by the end of the semester, when they'd be trying to catch up with everything all at once.

Her intro to biology course on Tuesday and Thursday mornings was a challenge not only because it was another big lecture class but also because the professor was this ancient guy with a wheezy cough from too many cigarettes for too many years. He was hard to understand, with all the coughing, and his notes on the blackboard were indecipherable. Summer was in that one, too, and they'd both figured out that the textbook would be their salvation—in the first two tests they'd both managed low A's, which they thought was pretty good under the circumstances.

Melissa's calculus course was the only one she really had to work hard at, not just writing a few essays or reading the textbook and memorizing a few names and dates like in the mass comm course, but actually spending way too much time doing homework assignments. They were tough, but she was scared to death she might get a C if she didn't stay up with things. The teacher was a woman and friendly enough; it was just hard material to get through. There were a lot of nights Melissa spent hours wrestling with quadratic equations, making sure she had it all done right before class the next morning.

Summer ragged on her all the time about it, called her Miss

Study Hall as she headed out for a movie and some pizza—her favorite nighttime activity. But then Summer seemed to be getting good grades without having to study much at all. Summer was one of those lucky ones for whom math was easy, English comp was a breeze; biology was no sweat. All the scholarship athletes had taken a series of tests the first few days of the semester and then been assigned study hall with tutors in areas where they were weak—Melissa's tutor in math was a grad student named, of all things, Candy Kane—but Summer had tested out of the tutor thing completely. No tutoring, no study hall, for her.

It was funny, in fact, that Summer wasn't here now. Her workouts were usually done by five and she was back in the dorm by five-thirty. They ate dinner together over in the caf at six and then came back to the second-floor lounge to share their mutual guilty pleasure—reruns of *Friends*. It was funny how they could remember the whole show once they saw the first few seconds of the rerun, but it didn't matter; they had a blast watching it anyway, sipping on Gatorade and laughing at what a dolt Joey was.

It was five-thirty now. Melissa sat up to look over at the clock—five-forty, in fact. That wasn't like Summer, who had the usual Midwest thing about being on time.

Melissa broke down and took the CD player off the replay of "Don't Worry 'bout a Thing," and let it slide onto the next track, Bob singing now about those buffalo soldiers, dreadlocked rastas. Someday she'd get to the islands, to Jamaica first to see her heritage from her mother's side and then the rest; St. Maarten, Antigua, Barbados, Montserrat, Nevis, St. Kitts, Saba, and Statia, the names ran through her mind with visions of palm trees and blue water and warm, sultry breezes.

She sighed, looked out the window to watch the heavy, wet snowflakes falling. And there, coming up the sidewalk, was Summer, huddled into her lightweight jacket—this weather had caught them all by surprise.

OK, then. To be nice Melissa hit the stop button on Bob Marley, since Summer just didn't get the whole island thing at all, and slid a CD in by a country singer named Tim McGraw. It wasn't the greatest music, Melissa thought, but Summer loved it and McGraw's dad had been a major-league pitcher, so that made him OK in Melissa's book, too.

McGraw was done with the first song, "Memory Lane," before Melissa realized Summer hadn't shown up. Where could she be? She must have stopped to talk with someone on the way. They'd be late for dinner if they didn't get over there soon.

She got up to go search for her roomie but hadn't reached the door yet when the phone rang.

She picked it up, said hi, and it was Dan Finnegan on the other end.

God, he'd been wonderful since Danny left, calling her a couple of times a week to talk about things, not just Danny but how she was doing in school, how basketball was going, if she was making any friends—all of that.

She sure heard a lot more from him than from her dad, who'd only called her once, a few weeks ago, and then just to check on a bill he'd seen on the Visa card for a CD she'd bought at Campus Books in Dinkytown. She'd explained it had been for class—a CD-ROM workbook for the big mass comm lecture class—and he'd been OK with that.

"Hey, how's my girl?" Finnegan wanted to know.

"Hi, Mr. Finnegan. How are you?" She always got formal when she talked with the guy.

"I'm cold," he said, and chuckled a bit. "I'm on the cell phone, out near Good Thunder. Listen, Melissa, I have some news from Danny. He said he tried to reach you this morning, but the phones didn't work."

"There was a big thunderstorm with this front. You know it's snowing here now? Isn't that crazy?"

He chuckled. "Yeah, no snow here, but the wind has sure shifted and the temperature's dropping like a rock."

"I can't believe winter's here already."

"Oh, it'll warm up again at least one more time, Melissa, I think. This is way too early to be the real thing."

He paused. "Listen, there's a couple of important things."

"Important?"

"Yeah. First, Danny called to say he's tested into advanced

training—in electronic countermeasures. If things go right he could wind up an officer."

"Wow, that's great. I bet he's happy. I can't wait to hear the details."

"He said he'd call you again tomorrow, Melissa. I'm really proud of him. This is a lot more than he thought he'd get. It'll be a great thing for his career, and it's a great skill to have. There'll be a ton of good jobs when he gets out."

He paused again. "And there's something else, Melissa. It has to do with your friend Summer, with her family."

"Oh, no. Someone's been hurt. Her brother? Her folks?"

"No. Well, not that we know, at least so far. But there's been a thing with her father. You'll be reading about it in tomorrow's paper."

"A thing?"

"Look, there's no easy way to tell you this, Melissa. There's been another woman murdered, and it looks like the same guy did it. Happened last night sometime, and I've been out here all day looking things over."

"And?"

"And we've found some things that indicate we ought to talk with Walter Arndt, so we're looking for him now."

"Summer's dad?" You're arresting him? For this murder thing?"

"No, no, Melissa, it's not like that. Not yet. It's more," he was being careful how he said things, "more complicated than that. We're looking for him now. And we're talking to his family. So someone will be by there to get Summer and take her for an interview. That's why I called you, to let you know that. They may want to talk to you, too, about Summer and her dad, just to find out anything you might know."

"Talk to me?"

"No, don't worry. It's just that we're trying to get as much information in as we can. I wanted you to know all this from me first, OK? I've already talked to the people there and they know you and Summer are friends of mine, all right? They'll be very nice and polite. They said they'd talk to you right there and

make sure they didn't get in the way of Midnight Madness tonight."

Oh, my god. She'd forgotten about that. She looked at the
clock, sneaking up toward six o'clock. She looked out the window.
A man was walking with Summer toward a squad car. She wasn't
in handcuffs or anything. Summer reached the car and then
turned to look back toward the dorm window. Melissa, still on
the phone, waved to her. Summer waved back, then climbed on
into the squad car.

There was a knock at the door.

GOOD THUNDER

Another ugly damn murder scene. Dan Finnegan hit the end-call button on his new cell phone after he finished talking to Melissa and then shoved its little aerial down into the socket. He'd had the phone for a month now and had finally figured out how to use it some. There was all sorts of programmable stuff he couldn't do with it yet—hell, the thing could probably cook breakfast if you knew how to ask it—but he could at least answer the phone and dial out now, and that was a start.

All this new technology: the new computers in the office, with the way that linked him right up to the BCA in St. Paul; the little computers they were putting in the squad cars so you could punch in a car's tag number and find out if the car was stolen; the cellular telephone—all of this stuff seemed to him sometimes like it was making the job harder, not easier. All he wanted to do was catch the guy who was capable of doing something like this—blood on the walls, pools of it on the polished pinewood floors, the victim's body sitting back against the hallway wall that led from the dining room into the kitchen, her legs straight out in front, arranged neatly so the body wouldn't slump or fall over, very careful and precise, this guy—and instead he spent all his time talking on this phone and worrying about keeping his damn computer happy so it wouldn't keep crashing on him all the time.

He slid the phone into its little holster, right next to his Glock. If he didn't move that holster around some there'd come a day soon when he'd be in a tight spot and pull out the cell phone and try to shoot the perp with it. That'd be something to see.

He was in a sour mood. Nothing had gone right all day. First, it was the car not wanting to start this morning, which had to mean the battery going bad. He'd hauled the charger out of the work shed and gotten the old Pontiac going but wound up getting into the department a good twenty minutes late, which had him backed up all morning, trying to catch up while the computer kept crashing and the phone calls kept coming in, and then, in a wild flurry of activity, the call had come in on this murder in Good Thunder and he'd hurried out here, wondering all the way if it was going to look like the same guy who'd murdered that woman and her little girl in Rapidan three years back.

It did, the only difference being it was just the mother this time, the family's little girl off at school. Everything else looked the same—another isolated farm, another bloody as hell vicious murder where whoever had done this had enjoyed himself while he'd ripped her open and then sliced off the hand at the wrist to take his trophy.

The MO meant this was a serial case now and so now the FBI would get involved. Well, hell, he could use all the help he could get. That first one had been tough, nothing to work with, no suspects, nothing at the scene, no movement at all on it despite all the different things he'd tried—right down to getting the word out on the street, thinking it might be some junkie looking for drug money. It had all come to nothing. He still worked it some every day—looking for something he'd missed, some new angle he could try. Every now and then something came up—the missing priest from Holy Innocents, Father Murphy, was at the top of that list—but nothing solid had come from any of it.

This one, though, was different. With this one there was something to work with at the crime scene, a crumpled-up yellow receipt for two glazed crullers from Dunkin' Donuts in Mankato. Receipt signed by Walter Arndt.

A uniform cop, Gary Brainard, had found it. He'd been the first on the scene after the call came in from the FedEx guy who'd been delivering a box of books and found the door wide open in the cold and shouted out a hello, walked in to see if everything was OK. It wasn't.

Brainard was smart enough not to touch anything once he saw the body. But it was his job, too, to make sure the perp wasn't still around. He'd checked around back, walking through the barn and the toolshed, then come back through the paved concrete at the end of the driveway. There, stuck in the bushes that surrounded the pavement, was the receipt. Brainard had picked it out of the bare twigs, careful with it, thinking maybe fingerprints would be on it, then taken it into the house and set it on the kitchen table for Finnegan to see.

Finnegan, careful with it, too, had opened it up, smoothed it out enough to read it, and just shaken his head. He figured that Arndt had reached into his pocket to get his car keys, pulled out the receipt with the keys, and not noticed when it fell and got blown by this damn cold wind into the bushes.

Damnedest thing. Could Walter Arndt have done something like this?

You wouldn't think so. The guy was well off, maybe one of the three or four richest guys in Mankato—a developer who'd gotten his start with the Oaks Mall out on the outskirts of town, then plowed that money into the downtown redevelopment that had worked so well, putting a roof over Main Street and, in effect, turning the core of downtown into its own indoor mall, complete with that fancy Holiday Inn with its indoor pool and convention hall.

Why would a guy like that be involved in something this terrible?

If there was any one thing Dan Finnegan had learned in twenty years of police work, it was that you just couldn't tell, couldn't always even understand. Something was sick, deadly sick, deep inside some people. They led normal lives on the outside, real upstanding citizens some of them. And then down in there, buried, was the monster, the big ugly, the terrible thing that drove them to do awful things. Maybe Walter Arndt was one of those.

And so now all this bad business had to go on. Finding Arndt's wife at the tennis club, where she was taking lessons on the indoor courts. Finding Arndt's son in class at Mankato Catholic High.

Finding Summer at the U., where she was Melissa's roommate, of all things.

Mainly, of course, finding Walter Arndt himself. Which they hadn't done yet. Had he cut and run? That wouldn't be surprising. They had all the bulletins out already, keeping an eye on the roads for his fancy Lexus, watching the train and bus stations, the airports. With any luck, they'd find him soon enough.

The medical examiner, Joe Springer in from St. Paul, came walking up, pulling off his surgical gloves.

"Nasty business, Joe," Finnegan said to him.

"Yeah. This guy knew what he was doing, Dan. Your guy sound like that? Like somebody who would know where to cut off a hand like that?"

"How do you mean?"

"Look at this," and he pointed at the stump where the wrist ended. "It's a clean job." The blood, puddled beneath the stump, was done running now, the woman's skin a pasty grayish-white.

"Clean? You mean neatly done?"

Springer nodded. "There are really just two ways to take off a hand, Dan. The first is crude but effective—you use a very forceful blow with an ax. Takes a good, strong blow; nothing on the human body comes off easily."

He nodded toward the wrist. "The other way would be with a bit more care and precision. The murderer would need a very sharp blade to get through the soft tissue structures like skin, fat, and blood vessels, and then you need to cut several ligaments which join the carpal bones—that's the wrist. It would take some pulling and tugging, too, like trying to get the leg off the turkey at Thanksgiving."

Good Lord, thought Finnegan, what an image, what a hell of an image. He just stared at that stump, mesmerized by it, wondering at how he was able to do that, thinking of it as clean and tidy and neat, as Springer moved on to the other body.

In 1945, Thomas Finnegan, son of the man who had emigrated from Listowel in County Kerry at age twenty to make his way in America, was top turret gunner in a B-25 Billy Mitchell bomber on the island of Ie Shima, flying missions every few days over Tarawa to strafe the Japanese defenders of that tiny island. They'd come in so low that their props left a wake in the lagoon's calm water, and they'd be firing their front 20mm cannon the whole time and the twin 50-calibers up front, and even Thomas Finnegan would be up in his turret, firing forward hoping to hit a Jap and send him to his final reward. At the last second, Captain Mink would pull up on the stick and the big twin-engined plane would rise as it dropped its load of bombs on the beach and the cave-filled cliff that sat behind rock wall, hiding thousands of soldiers intent on conquering the Pacific for the Greater East Asia Co-Prosperity Sphere. During the low-level attack the flak from the defending Japs was a curtain of red tracers they had to fly through. Each flight their plane was punctured by dozens of holes. It was the kind of mission you wanted to sit on your flak jacket for, hoping some Jap with a rifle wouldn't shoot your balls off or run a round right up your ass.

At night, back safe after another harrowing mission, they all slept under the wings of the plane, where a little bit of breeze seemed to stir and blow off the nighttime sweat.

When Thomas Finnegan was there the island had only been in the hands of the U.S. Marines for a month or so, and there were rumors of Japs hiding up in the hills. The first few nights, the crew was worried about that. Later, they got used to it and quit worrying.

In the predawn mist of June 14, a Thursday, Thomas Finnegan came awake to the sound of movement in the bushes off to the side of the runway. A pig? They'd had a problem with the wild pigs at first, but after ten or twenty were shot and eaten, the others seemed to get the message, and so there hadn't been any for several weeks.

Finnegan sat up to look, started reaching for his side arm, an officer's .45 he'd bought for fifteen dollars, unwilling to count on anyone but himself for his own defense when he was on the ground. It was one thing to trust in your buddies when you were in the air and quite another when you were asleep, on the ground, in the open under nothing on God's earth but the wide wing of a plane.

And there, in the bushes, was someone.

Finnegan stood, and then the man—a skinny, wild-eyed, wild-haired Jap, his uniform in tatters but neatly buttoned where it could be—came jumping out of the bushes, swinging a sword that looked the size of a blade on Finnegan's combine tractor back home.

Finnegan couldn't pull the trigger. The guy was running too fast and right at him, stepping over and around sleeping crewmen of the B-25. He slashed down, and Teddy Brantley, the radio operator, cried out in pain, the blade biting deep into his shoulder.

The guy slashed down again, and then again, and guys were up now, screaming, pulling weapons, afraid to shoot for fear of hitting one of their own, the Jap slashing and running right through them.

He got through them all, turned to stare at them. No one fired at him, another crew jumping to their feet behind him under the wing of another bomber.

He sat down, cross-legged, dropped the sword, and pulled a curved knife from his belt, bowed to them all once with a nod of the head, then disemboweled himself, jabbing the knife in cleanly, then moving it up and around in about an arc. He got damn near two feet along with that, his guts starting to spill out, before he fell backward, not making a sound.

The guy did a lot of damage before he died. Teddy lost his right hand. Joe Stanley's shoulder wound got infected and he wound up in the hospital for more than a month.

But they all lived; all lived through the whole war, in fact. And by the 1980s were starting to get together for reunions, the past far enough back they could remember it for one another, conjuring it up, sharing it again.

Dan Finnegan's father died by age sixty-seven, of prostate cancer. The doc said at first that he'd live for ten years or more with it, but he didn't last two. Nothing helped; the surgery, the chemo, the hormone therapy, something called Lupron that didn't seem to do a damn thing for him. He faded, thinned down, lost interest in it all, lost interest in living through it, and then died.

A few months before he died, only a couple of weeks before he was so deep into the morphine that he couldn't talk, couldn't do anything more than dream, he told his son the story about the Jap and the crew and the sword and the knife.

Finnegan hadn't thought of his father in a long time. But this, this brutal act, brought that memory back. The old man, smoking those hand-rolled cigarettes, drinking a six-pack of beer a night there for a while. Then the cancer. Then dead.

There were puncture wounds in the chest, jagged, from a knife with a serrated edge, maybe. He'd know that for sure when he got the paperwork in from the forensics mobile crime unit that had driven down from St. Paul and was at the house by now.

Dan Finnegan had seen some of the world. He'd joined the Navy after high school, done his duty in Vietnam, and then wound up in Rota, Spain, by his third year in, already finding out that law enforcement, in Shore Patrol, was something he liked, something he felt good at and useful at. It wasn't always fun, too many drunken brawls for that. But when it was good, when he was getting the job done, catching the bad guys and helping the good guys—that simple—it was satisfying as hell.

In the late seventies he'd had two weeks of leave and taken the train and ferry over to London—a thirty-hour sleepless crawl of second-class travel that finally got him there, to the Walsham hotel on Great Russell Street, just down the road from the British Museum.

He'd gotten into his tiny room around noon, washed up a bit down the hall in the shared bathroom, slept until 6:00 P.M., and then gone out to find something to eat, maybe get a pint of ale, check out what was going on. He had a week to spend there, ten days if he really liked it.

Dinner had been ordinary, some bad British beef and pretty good potatoes and an excellent pint. Then he'd started walking, heading up one road and down another until he wound up near King's Cross Station, at the Pint Pot, a bar so loud on a Friday night that he found it irresistible, young English up-and-comers in suits and ties chatting up the office girls as they stood there, packed so tightly into the place that the crowd spilled out onto the sidewalk.

He was no businessman, Lord knows, or ever likely to be a professional anything, but the change from the usual Navy holes he'd been drinking in back in Rota was so welcome he enjoyed the hell out of it.

Into his third pint of Tetley's Bitter he felt a tap on his shoulder and turned to find a dark-haired girl, a little over five feet tall, thin, warm brown eyes, a great smile.

She was Scottish, and proudly so, and he knew all about that a lot more before they closed the place up and she walked him back to his hotel and one great thing led to another until, glory be, they woke up in the morning and went downstairs for breakfast and he discovered the wonders of beans and tomatoes with his eggs in the morning.

Karleen Forsythe.

She was a dizzy blur, the most exciting thing that had ever happened to him. Until he met Karleen, he'd always categorized women into just two categories—the type to marry and, once he'd joined the Navy and discovered they existed, the fun girls.

Karleen, somehow, was both. The sex was the most exhaustingly enjoyable thing he'd ever done—more fun than football, to his amazement. And when they weren't making love they were talking—on a level and about topics that he'd never attempted before. Politics, independence, art, and music—it was an amazing array of things that she seemed able to discuss with anyone anytime.

For a wild week he did his best to keep up on all fronts, listening and reading and watching and learning like he'd never done before in his life. It was exciting, exhilarating, and stimulating as hell. Who'd ever think a small-town boy from southern Minnesota would be faking interest in splashes and swaths of paint over driftwood at a gallery showing in Soho or pretending

to like the music of Ian Dury and the Blockheads and The Tear-
drop Explodes?

But that was the problem. He was pretending. Eventually—
not that first week, certainly, and not even the next leave when
he flew to London to see her again—it began to wear him down,
the pretense of it. He kept searching for himself in all the wild
passion and couldn't find anyone home.

Home. Mankato.

Finally, a wild year later, he had some decisions to make. Re-up
or stay in. London or Minnesota. Pretense or reality.

And he'd headed home to Mankato, where he could know
things; know them deep inside and count on them being real.
Cold winters. The smell of wood smoke. Hockey. People you
could talk to without being on guard. A wide horizon over miles
of white snow, sparkling in the clear cold of a subzero morning.
Clear. Cold. That was what he needed.

And things had worked out fine. He'd met Helen at an evening
class they'd both been taking at Mankato State. They'd gotten
their degrees and then had the wedding a week later. Danny came
two years after that and Finnegan, feeling the pressure of fatherhood and responsibility, had joined the department, worked hard,
risen through the ranks.

As the years slipped by he was certain that he'd done the right
thing with his life. He knew who he was, and where he was, and
what he was doing.

Then death started stealing things from him. First his father,
a good man who ran his own hardware store. Then his mother
a year later. Then Helen's death—wet roads, a divided highway
with nothing but a grass median in the middle; so when the kid
from New Ulm lost control and came spinning and sliding across
on the grass and into Helen's little Toyota she never had the
slightest wisp of a chance.

So nothing was to be trusted after all. He'd learned that. Could
the murderer here be nice-guy Walter Arndt? Sure.

At least he had Danny and that wonderful girlfriend of his—
he already thought of Melissa as a daughter; he wanted to protect
her the way he wanted to protect Danny, his boy now off learning

to be a warrior. Make no mistake about that, he'd told Danny, for all the Navy's talk of careers it was still a job where they taught you how to kill and avoid being killed in return. At least this latest thing should protect him—keep him back behind the lines somewhere if things heated up.

He was still thinking it all through a few hours later when he got home, turned on the TV, and sat down with his fast-food burger and fries to watch the news. There was an attempted coup going on in Saudi Arabia, a country he didn't know much about.

THE KISS

The day they heard the news about Summer's dad, a detective had come by the dorm room and interviewed Melissa, but it hadn't been rough at all, just a half hour's conversation and the guy taking a few notes.

Summer, though, was taken down to the police department building on East Eleventh Street in St. Paul and interviewed there by three different people for four long hours. When was the last time she'd talked to her father? When was the last time she'd been home? How often did she talk with her father? How much did she know about his work? About his free time? About his hobbies? Did she know anyone in the Curlew family in Rapidan? Did her dad? The Branson family in Good Thunder? Did she get to Rapidan very often? Good Thunder? Did she ever go there with her father?

It went on like that, one of the cops being really rough on her and the other two, a man and a woman, she said, really being pretty nice, like they were trying to keep the one guy from getting too rough.

Finally, they let her go home, the two nicer ones even driving her to the dorm, chatting away with her about the Gopher sports and whether or not the Twins were going to be any good this year, stuff like that.

Melissa found out all this when Summer walked into the dorm room, eyes dry, her face set in a determined stare, and told her. She looked good, like she'd gotten mad instead of scared and like she wasn't going to let all this drive her crazy.

Then, ten or fifteen minutes into the conversation, she suddenly sat down on her bed, looked at Melissa, and broke: babbling and crying and ranting all at once, all that bottled-up emotion coming out in a torrent, not just talking and crying and even screaming out in anger once or twice, but also pounding her fists into the pillow, into the bed.

Melissa gave her a few minutes of this and then came over to hug her and listen while Summer, a little calmer, started talking about her dad—about what a great guy he was, how all this couldn't possibly be true, how the police just had to be wrong.

Melissa put her arm around her friend to give her what comfort she could, though it was weird comforting someone whose father was suspected of being a murderer. Melissa just kept her mouth shut and kept her arm around her friend's sobbing shoulders, patting her hair and listening to the outpouring of anger and disbelief.

The two girls had slept together that night, Summer not able to be alone in her bed. Instead, they'd crowded into Melissa's bed and hugged, like a pair of six-year-olds on their first sleepover, until Summer had finally fallen asleep.

In the morning, when Melissa woke up, she saw Summer lying there next to her, face calm, breathing easy, mouth barely open. She was like a painting in her still beauty, the horror of the previous day temporarily gone.

Melissa stared at that mouth, at those lips. She'd held this friend all night long. She leaned in closer to her, her face six inches from Summer's. She leaned down, put her lips to Summer's, lightly, barely touching. She pulled back. The lips were perfect and full and beckoning. She leaned down again, kissed them a second time, feeling the soft pleasure of them against her own.

And Summer was kissing her back. Lips pressing back into hers, wonderful pressure returning, then lips opening, then movement; slow and deliberate and exotic and amazing. More pressure, open wider, a first soft tongue against Melissa's lips, then more, then a lost, long, luscious moment—an hour, a few seconds, a day, a year? She couldn't say—of the two of them lost in The Kiss until, finally, it ended.

Melissa pulled back to look as Summer's eyes slowly opened. Those perfect lips spoke: "Thank you," she said, and then again started to cry, a soft weeping that carried through the morning.

Later, Melissa got out of bed, showered, and went to class and then to basketball practice. When she got back, Summer had gone home to Mankato.

For a week, Melissa was on the periphery of the media attention that swirled around Walter Arndt's family, and especially around Summer, the popular, gorgeous college athlete who was the daughter of a murder suspect. It made for great television, and Summer was on the local news four different times while police hunted for her father. Melissa, her friend and roommate, made the news twice herself as the basketball-playing roommate and friend of the murder suspect's daughter. It was amazing how low local television news could stoop for a story. Both times the local news came up to Melissa after basketball games, the cameras and bright lights and microphone shoved in her face as she walked out from the locker room.

The irony of it was that Melissa was thinking of journalism as a major. After seeing how crazy the media were over this story she had to wonder if she could bear to do that for a living. It'd be less humiliating to sell used cars or something.

Melissa and Summer hadn't talked about The Kiss since it happened, and Melissa liked it just fine that way. She'd never known guilt like she had for a while after that moment. Everything she knew, everything she was, said that was wrong in all sorts of ways. The altar server in her, the girl who'd held the water and the wine out for Father Murphy at Sunday Mass all those times, was shocked and embarrassed by this new Melissa who had— out of nowhere—leaned over and kissed her girlfriend on the lips. How could she do that? God, it was doubly wrong. Kissing *anyone* else while Danny was off in the Navy was terrible enough. And then kissing another girl. It was so terrible a thing she didn't want to remember it happening.

But she couldn't forget it. And eventually, as a week, and then another, and then another went by—the media moving on to new people to bother and new scandals to worry over—she quit worrying about the memory.

She heard a lot from Dan Finnegan, who called at least once a week to chat. Even he didn't talk about the murders anymore. The whole case seemed to be in limbo somewhere. There hadn't been any new murders, Walter Arndt had never turned up and the only real evidence seemed to point toward him, and so as far as the public was concerned, the case had dropped from view.

She still wrote to Danny every day. She still loved Danny, she knew she did, with all her heart. Somehow that love was in a different place—was an entirely different thing—from what was going on with Summer.

If there was something going on at all. Truth was, they hadn't talked about and hadn't pursued it since that day. Whatever that moment might have been, whatever it might have led to, had disappeared in the general crush of things—the media stuff and trying to still have enough mental involvement to go to class and enough energy to keep playing basketball.

That, Melissa thought, was the easy part—playing The Game. Heck, it was the only easy part, bringing the ball up the court and launching a three from beyond the line, getting caught up in the flow of it, getting into the zone, fully involved, time slipping away so that twenty-minute halves were somehow over in seconds and yet took hours, days, to play. All of that took her away from these other issues, took her to some good place where all you had to worry about was beating Northwestern by twenty or, a couple of nights ago, hitting the free throws to get into overtime against Ohio State. Get it done, and while you're getting it done there's nothing else to worry over.

Until after the game. Later. Back in the dorm room, with Summer asleep across the room, breathing, moving on the bed in the middle of the night, legs across the sheets, head against the pillow.

✳   ✳   ✳

But you can get past anything, given enough time. And not only had Melissa and Summer not talked about The Kiss, but the subject of Summer's father hadn't come up in more than two months, either, until Melissa almost found it hard to believe that anything at all had happened back in October.

They were walking home together from Spanky's in Dinkeytown, where they had watched the Timberwolves beat the Orlando Magic on the big-screen TV. The walking was tricky, trudging over the crusted snow that had come with a little bit of warm weather followed by a drop to ten below, so that you could walk on top of the refrozen snow for ten or fifteen steps and then, at a weak spot, you fell through and went down a good couple of feet into the soft snow underneath. The sidewalks had been cleared and it would have made more sense to just stay on them and get home, but it was sure a lot more fun trying to make it over the top of the crusted snow, trying to somehow walk lightly and see who could make it farthest without breaking through. Summer managed thirty-eight steps at one point, and Melissa was determined to beat that record.

She would have, too, if they hadn't decided to cut through Minnehaha Park to save the fifteen minutes it took to walk around the fenced-in park and discovered the gates locked for the night.

They climbed over the fence, giggled their way across the snow-covered softball diamonds, then held hands to slide down the embankment of Minnehaha Creek on their butts. All they had to do was walk across the frozen creek, up the other embankment, past the handball courts, climb the fence, and walk two blocks, and they'd be home.

But the night was beautiful, a big moon over the frozen white of the park. And Minnehaha Waterfall was frozen in place to their right, an incredible sight, really, all that water tumbling over the little fifteen-foot cliff like some tiny glacier up in Greenland or Alaska. The frozen falls were just begging to be climbed, and so they started toward them, got to the base, worked their way around trying to find a place for the first handhold, reaching in the moonlight to find a grip, a step, some way to begin.

And Melissa found, instead, half-buried in snow behind a small boulder to the right of the falls, a body.

At first she thought it was a dead child. She cried out to Summer to come see it, help her pull it from the snow.

They did, Melissa digging away at the snow and hammering with her fist at the ice until it loosened, while Summer used a stick to dislodge the small body.

When it came free they could see, relieved, that it was a cat, wearing a collar and probably dead in the snow for days, maybe weeks, just someone's poor pet that had wandered into the park on a warmer day, stumbled into the still flowing falls maybe, and then gotten trapped, cold, freezing, shivering there and then, finally, when it went down below zero that night, died quietly.

It wasn't a child. Melissa was glad of that, at least. But the poor thing looked so pitiful that they decided to put the body somewhere safe and then tell the SPCA, who had maybe, weeks ago, heard from the owners and could at least pass on the news.

They talked that over for a minute, came up with the right thing to do, putting it behind that same boulder, up a few steps on the ice of the frozen falls and then tucked in behind the rock where they could find it if they needed to for the SPCA. The plan was for Melissa to climb up, get in the right spot, and then Summer would take the cat's body and hand it up to her. Share the duty, that way, they thought, since they were both kind of freaked out about touching the body.

Melissa, carefully, climbed up, slipping twice but grabbing ice or boulder each time to catch herself until she was set, balanced, one leg on the rock, the other on the ice. Holding on with her right hand, she leaned down with the left to take a front leg of the cat's body from Summer, and in grabbing it, holding tight, she felt, as much as remembered, the moment from years before when she'd done that same thing with the deer her father had hit with the Ford. The vision. The weird and awful *seeing* of the deer's death.

This moment, like that one, had her reaching out to touch

death. This moment, like that one, held the promise of knowing too much, feeling too much.

But here, to her relief, there was nothing; no vision, no vision of death, no seeing it through the animal's eyes.

Thank God. She hadn't thought of that moment in years, and that was perfectly fine with her. She certainly didn't want to get lost in that kind of death vision again.

She brought the cat's body up and tucked it behind the rock, like they'd planned.

"You all right?" Summer wanted to know, still holding up the cat's body. "You got weird there for a second."

"Yeah," Melissa said, leaning back against the ice and rock. "Yeah, I'm fine."

And then she took a step back, a very wrong step back, and her left foot went sliding away from her, and, in a moment, no time to think or react, her right knee gave way, and she was flailing, sliding, then tumbling hard from her rocky perch and down onto the ice below.

Later, back in the dorm room and in pain, worried to hell about what she'd done to herself, her right knee packed in snow that she and Summer had brought in from the dorm's open window, Melissa talked it over with Summer after they called it into the SPCA. She tried to explain to Summer how once, years ago, she'd seen this kind of vision thing, how it wasn't like psychic stuff or UFOs or anything like that, really. And how it hadn't happened this time but she thought it was going to and that's what shook her up. And how her knee, frankly, hurt like hell. She wondered whether or not she should go to the ER or if it wasn't serious enough for that. Probably, she thought, it was just banged up some and she was fine, she was perfectly fine.

And then the phone rang. It was Dan Finnegan, and it was the worst news imaginable.

NOT DANNY

She couldn't breathe. Eyes red, Melissa sat in the front pew on the left in Holy Innocents Church, facing the altar, facing that statue of Christ and, at his side, the Holy Mother, staring down benignly at the supplicants.

Melissa had to force herself to take a breath, make the air come in and go out as she fought back the panic that made her want to scream and the guilt, the awful guilt, that made her cry. Her chest, her stomach, her lungs, her heart—all seemed full of her sins, awful and ugly and black, filling her up, overwhelming her so that she could barely function.

Somehow, despite how badly she just wanted to curl up in a little ball in the corner of some small, dark closet, she'd managed to keep it together for the last few days, at least enough to manage to sit quietly in the car that Dan Finnegan had sent for her to bring her down to Mankato for his son's funeral Mass.

Since that afternoon, she'd managed to get up in the mornings, eat a little food here and there through the day, hobble around some in the snow and cold on her bad knee, watch her father work on his grief by welding together this other new life of his, metal monsters on the concrete-slab floor of the barn.

Danny was dead. It was impossible to believe. That couldn't really be her Danny Finnegan up there, not her Danny, lying on his back in that uniform, hands folded on his chest with a rosary clutched in them, staring up at the ceiling.

Her Danny was the boy who scored that touchdown in the state semifinals against Bemidji Central his junior year, the boy who scored twenty-eight points against New Ulm as a sophomore forward on the basketball team, the boy who made the big plays, the boy who had the big plans, the boy who loved her. Her Danny was the boy who called her up every night to get help with his algebra or talk about movies or the Vikings or the Twins or the new CD from Green Day.

Her Danny was alive and laughing and proud that he'd graduated, proud to join the Navy just as his father had done before him, proud to wear that uniform. Her Danny was the boy who laughed for an hour after that day in the kitchen when they'd made that huge mess and her father almost caught them kissing. Her Danny was the man who'd asked her to marry him and to whom she'd said yes. And her Danny was the boy she'd made promises to that she'd broken, and, oh god, not even with some other boy, but with Summer.

And now he was dead.

So Melissa sat, arms folded in her lap, a rosary wound around her fingers, and tried to wrestle her way through all this. Her right knee ached, but that pain was nothing next to the one in her heart, the one in her soul.

Day after tomorrow, at six in the morning, she had to be back in Minneapolis at the Sports Medicine Clinic to have that knee arthroscoped. Ten weeks of rehab would follow that, six if she was lucky. Season over either way. Wait till next year. For Danny, wait forever

She'd tried to go to confession, to see Father Reskey in his little booth and unburden herself from all this, somehow make it better. But she couldn't do it. She'd walked in, sat down, mumbled her way through the opening, "Bless me, Father, for I have sinned," and then, when the moment came, she couldn't do it. That added cowardice to the growing list of horrible things she'd done.

She looked down to see the engagement ring on her finger. Next to her was Danny's father; next to him sat his brother Thomas from New Ulm and Thomas's wife, Kathleen. The church organ was playing some soft, quiet thing in the background. It was not the kind of music that Danny had ever liked.

Two weeks ago. That was all. Two weeks ago she got the latest—she guessed it would be the last—letter from Danny. He talked about how he might see action in the next few days, peace-keeping stuff out in the desert. It was supposed to be pretty minor and he felt ready for it and she shouldn't worry. And he said he loved her and he'd see her soon; just another two months and he'd come home on leave.

He'd really had time now to think things through, he said in that sloppy little-boy handwriting of his, and he'd learned a lot. First, he'd learned what he could learn, and maybe it was more than he had given himself credit for—he thought maybe he'd really be ready for college when this tour was up. So in a few years he'd be home for good and they'd get married. He'd get a degree from the U., not just the community college, and then he'd get a job like his dad's, with some police department, maybe somewhere down south where it was warm. She'd finish school and get her teaching certificate and teach elementary school. It would be perfect.

She should have made love with Danny. How many times had she thought about it? How many times had she almost told him yes? A hundred? A thousand?

Instead, she'd leaned over that time, that one incredible time, and kissed Summer to start all this awfulness and confusion. It was all too much to handle, way too much, and she didn't see any way out of it. And here was the worst part, the most horrible part of all—she thought maybe she wanted to have that kiss again. When she thought of Summer's lips, her mouth slightly open, the perfect fullness of them. Oh, god, the guilt of that was a stone, a boulder, inside her.

Sitting there, staring up at that casket, Melissa forced herself to think of all the times she'd come close to making love with Danny. That day in her house when they stood there and kissed for the first time while the apple pie burned in the oven. She would have then, she wanted to, but her father had come home.

Or the day in Danny's house when he'd asked her to marry him. He'd told her his plans and she'd finally, she thought, begun to understand him. She should have taken him by the hand then and walked him into his bedroom and made love to him. She'd started to do just that. She'd thought she wanted to, thought she'd wanted him inside her, being part of her, the two of them one thing, one wonderful thing. But something stopped her, like it always did, some voice that said it wasn't right, not then, and so she hadn't.

Or the time they'd been at his house, on the couch in the living room, and she'd teased him—first base and second base and thoughts of third and thoughts of, at last, that big home run—and she'd felt ready at last, felt like she could go through with it, like she *should* go through with it. And then his dad came home, unexpected, for lunch, and she and Danny, clothes almost off, everything unbuttoned and shoved down and his hand on her breast, his good warm lips kissing her left breast and it was so delicious that she could feel it again now, right here in church with his casket up there in front, she could feel the caress of those lips on her nipple.

Oh, god. They'd rolled right over the back of the couch and hidden there, quivering with fear and laughter behind the high back of the couch, while his dad walked through the room and on into the kitchen. A few minutes later, dressed, hair brushed back, they'd walked in to join him for lunch.

More times. On Danny's leave after basic, in her dorm room at the U., the two of them fumbling with passion.

But it hadn't happened. Something always stopped her. Something about making love froze her up at the critical moments and now, here she was a virgin, and there he was, lying there, too late for that to change.

It had been funny after a while, her virginity, a kind of shared joke of theirs, Danny laughing it off, telling her he knew how great it would be on their wedding night on some Caribbean island away from the cold and the snow, on their honeymoon. And so she never had, and now never would.

And then had come Summer, and those lips. She shivered. The church was stuffy and hot, the old radiators battling too hard against the subzero cold outside. People were sweating. But not

Melissa. The cold was deeply into her, so much a part of her now that no radiator, no down-filled jacket or warm woolen coat, could possibly do anything about it. She'd always been warm with Danny.

"Dear Melissa," he'd written. "I'll be safe and sound, sweetheart, back behind the lines, sitting in my tent and staring at that radar screen. All I have to do is tell the guys flying the planes where to fire their missiles. It's a piece of cake, so don't worry about me, OK?"

And she'd believed him.

Tommy Seals, the quarterback who'd thrown the ball to Danny for those touchdowns, was speaking, and Melissa thought she really ought to be listening. But it really didn't seem to matter very much.

Tommy was a nice guy, and Danny's father, sitting next to her, was as good as gold, but they couldn't make Danny be alive again; they couldn't make time go backward, rewinding past that moment with Summer. They couldn't warm up the ice in her soul. She stared ahead, trying hard to not-think, to just blank out and get through this whole long thing, this terrible forever thing.

"Melissa?"

It was her father, sitting behind her, leaning forward to whisper in her ear. "Melissa, sweetheart, you're supposed to go up there now with Mr. Finnegan and say a few words."

Her dad had been great this whole awful week. He wasn't usually very demonstrative, god knows, but he'd really come through for her when Detective Finnegan called with the news of Danny's death.

He'd even hugged her, and Melissa couldn't recall the last time her father had done that; back when she was just a little girl, she guessed, back so far she couldn't even remember it.

But he'd hugged her this time, and she'd cried on his shoulder for a good fifteen minutes, just standing there in the barn where she'd run, crying, to tell him, the tears pouring out while he had held her, whispered a few comforting words now and then to her as she sobbed.

He'd been out working on another sculpture, a giant crab thing this time. He smelled of hay and acetylene and molten metal. He smelled warm and comforting. She held on to him for as long as she could before finally releasing him, standing back from him, wiping her eyes, and thanking him.

She thanked him now, nodded her head, stood up alongside Danny's dad, and walked the few paces up to where the podium stood and behind it the open casket, that calm fake version of Danny lying in there, staring nowhere.

She walked over to the casket. Stood there by its side, her hand on the cool metal rail, and looked down on the remains of her best friend, her boyfriend, her lover-to-be, her husband-to-be.

"Oh, Danny," she heard his father say, next to her. "Oh, Son." And he put his right arm around Melissa's shoulders, gave her a comforting squeeze.

She couldn't say anything. She wanted to, wanted to say what they expected her to say: telling Danny good-bye, telling him she loved him and always would—all those things you're supposed to say. But she couldn't speak, was too hurt and angry for that. Why had he done such a stupid thing? Why join up in the first place, and then why volunteer for action in that awful desert? Peacekeeping? That's what he was supposed to be doing there and it sounded harmless enough.

She could only shake her head, close her eyes slowly, and then reopen them, looking down at Danny, poor Danny, that waxy face looking all wrong, all falsely serious. She reached down, finally, to touch it, to lightly stroke his cheek, run the back of her finger alongside that cold, cold cheek.

And her heart took off, zoomed away, her pulse skyrocketing as she stood there, dizzied by the sudden rush, the sudden pounding in her chest. She could hardly breathe, could hardly stand, as her chest seemed ready to burst with the pounding...

...and then, in a wave of emotion, came a convulsive electric shock—a hard, erotic throb that washed through her as he is suddenly terrified, the enemy coming at them, not miles away but here! Now! They're running through the compound, guns blazing and chattering, explosions, screams, curses, chaos everywhere, men running into the comm center yelling about gas, "Get your mask

on! *Get your mask on!" It's been twenty-seven days of boredom and heat in this sweat and stink and now this. Woodenly, mesmerized by all this, slow-motion in the midst of the frenetic action, he stands, walks to the thin metal door, opens it, looks out, and sees the enemy coming his way, running his way, throwing grenades as they come forward.*

His mask, he needs his mask. He walks back to his chair, his screen still cheerily bleeping as it scans the surrounding air and happily reports no missiles have been fired.

The mask isn't there! Oh, Christ. He scrambles to find it, searching under the loose empty bags and crates, under the bundles of wire. But it isn't there. He's heard about the mucous pink death that retches up from the lungs of men who breathed what the enemy brings, and now he can't find the mask, the damn mask! He picks up his weapon, walks to the thin door, opens it, fires one witless burst toward the roiling smoke, and then he discovers he is running, back away from the enemy, running full tilt away from the enemy, from the smoke, the fear, and the coughing death, the blistered skin that falls away to the bone. He hears, distantly, an order to halt. But he can't; he can't stop at all. He feels a slap in his back, a punch, and then warmth, a pleasant glow. His legs give way and he falls onto the sand that is oddly cool and comforting. He tries to look up. He is quite calm. He wonders why he ran as it gets perversely dark around him and then, slow fade, there is nothing.

STRANGE TALENTS

Melissa eased her right knee out of the beat-up old Honda Civic, sliding the metal and plastic supports of the knee brace under the steering wheel and, slowly and carefully, out the door. She stood up, grimacing some with the knee's pain, and then slammed shut the door of her car, the one she'd saved for and bought for $900 last year. It spent most of its time in the stand-alone garage at the farm, since freshmen weren't allowed to have cars at the U. Now, with the special handicap tag on it, she'd get to use it at the university for a while.

The ACL reconstruction had gone fine, the doc told her when she came out of the fog they'd put her under with. With the right attitude, the right rehab regimen, the right this and right that, she'd be back on the court in eight or ten weeks, the doc said, smiling at her, proud of his work. And so they'd only given her a couple of weeks off and then gotten her into the weight room, working her on the double knee bends, lunges, step exercises, lots of reps with it all, lots of energy, lots of work.

She did what they said, working hard on it, ignoring the pain. But the truth of it was she didn't know down deep whether basketball really mattered enough to her anymore. Basketball, in fact, seemed kind of stupid and childish after everything that had happened.

She stepped carefully over the frozen slush in the street to reach the parking meter on Broad Street and shove in a quarter, then trudged through the snow on the sidewalk down toward the Little House restaurant, past the three-story City Hall and the police department building and the public library.

Not caring about basketball had been a revelation to her. She'd realized it during a step exercise, pushing up and down and up and down and up and down, the repetition mind-numbing, the emotional effort of staying on the machine overcoming the ache in her knee, in her soul.

She'd stopped for a long moment. Maybe it was time to hang 'em up? Could that be, at age nineteen? Danny, Summer, the way she somehow managed to ache for both of them in a confusing swamp of uncertainty. It was just all too damn much. She didn't know what to do, couldn't decide, and so had started back into it, stepping, repeating, stepping, up and down and up and down.

She had a lunch date with Danny's father. She didn't have much time; she had a test tomorrow back up at the U. and she needed to study and had two papers due for the journalism class she was taking as kind of a blow-off course since it was so easy. But this was Danny's father and they both needed to talk, so here she was.

A twenty-foot-long northern pike—another in her father's string of successes—arched its metal back to throw a Bunyan-esque hook right over her head as she walked by City Hall. Four inches of fresh snow sat in a narrow line along that arched back, a white line atop the gray metal, with more adding to it as today's snow fell. Built mostly of old tractor parts her father found in a junkyard, the northern's back was made from an old spiral ice auger that Melissa had watched Melchior load into the bed of his pickup for years as he headed out to Lake Minnetoksak to cut some holes in the ice and fish for those pike.

Most times he wound up bringing home a few perch to fry for dinner, but now he'd figured out a way to catch, by god, a real lunker. The city had paid him $5,000 for this sculpture, from some art fund the state government had set up. That had covered the losses from the sugar beet crop for the year and left him with enough for a down payment on Melissa's Civic.

Even Danny had liked the pike. He and Melissa had helped her father make it, standing there in the warmth of the barn on a summer day during Danny's leave after basic, handing her father parts, running errands into town for more acetylene or some compound for the joints or, there at the end, the clear lacquer to coat it with—B-48 from Rohm & Haus.

Melissa reached up to touch the lower lip of the northern, ran her gloved hand along it, thinking of where she'd stood with Danny when they'd watched that mouth come into being, pieces of discarded metal, just junk, slowly taking on this life, successfully throwing off that hook that tried to capture it.

She shook her head. Everything she saw around her connected to Danny one way or another. She kept thinking she'd wake up one day and it would all turn out to be some terrible mistake. Danny would be walking in the door; Summer would be her friend and nothing more. Life would be the way it had been before, understandable, solid, real.

She'd thought, a few times, that she'd heard Danny's voice in the distance, calling to her, yelling her name the way he did, "Hey, Melissa, over here!"

It was just her imagination at work. She knew that; just too much imagination in a tired, beat-up mind, that was all. That must be what her fainting spell was all about at the funeral Mass—just her mind giving up from all this pressure, her heart going crazy for a moment, and then her body calling a time-out right in the middle of some hallucination.

She brushed some of the snow away from the pike's back, then turned to walk on down to the Little House, tugged open the restaurant's outer door, stomped her shoes, and rubbed them over the metal mesh on the floor, then took off her coat and shook it to send the melting snowflakes flying.

Everything in her life had always been planned, and she'd just followed the painted line right through Holy Innocents and Mankato Catholic and the U. and life with Danny and everything else. Look what that had gotten her. Everywhere she looked she saw Danny, and it would always be that way, as long as she was here. In Vito and Sal's for pizza. Driving by Donelli's and remembering the night Danny proposed. Anywhere. Everywhere.

Even in her own house when she was home to visit with her
father, when she walked by the sunroom or stood there by the
stove in the kitchen, it was Danny.

Maybe she just needed to get away from this, maybe take a
semester off, maybe just a two-week vacation. Something. Some
break. Some change. Somewhere warm.

When she walked in through the inner doors she saw Mr. Finnegan right away, waving at her from a corner booth. She loved
the man, had already begun to think of him as another dad before
this terrible thing happened. She'd known him since third grade
when he'd been there at the under-ten soccer games with Danny
and wound up taking her home after every practice, every game.
He'd lost his own wife that year and said he'd known what it
was like for her father, trying to keep the farm going and raise
a daughter, all on his own.

Finnegan was a big man, nearly six-foot-four and carrying too
much weight. But despite his size and his job, he was the sweetest
man she knew, a pussycat underneath all that bulk and all the
tough-guy cop exterior.

They hugged and then sat, Finnegan pulling out her chair for
her and then pushing it back in as she sat. She smiled at that.
Some tough cop.

He stirred a spoonful of sugar into his coffee. "I was trying
to cut back on the sugar, you know, watching my diet and everything. But..." He shrugged his shoulders. "How you doing,
Melissa?"

"OK, I guess."

"Jesus, this is tough, isn't it? I don't know how you can handle
it. I worry about you, Melissa."

"About *me?*"

He smiled at her. "You know, Danny never said one thing
about you that wasn't just glowing." He shook his head slightly.
"He really loved you, Melissa."

She said nothing. The waitress came by with a cup of coffee
for her.

"And he was a brave kid, Melissa. I know he was. The Navy said he died a hero, died to save his friends."

"I know he was a hero, Mr. Finnegan. He was the best." She was absolutely not going to cry, she decided. Absolutely not.

"So when you touched him, Melissa, and there was that, that *thing.*"

Oh, god. Did he see it, too? "What thing?"

"That vision, Melissa. I don't know what else you can call it. I saw it, and you must have seen it, too. It was Danny, and he was afraid. He ran. He ran from his position. He disobeyed a direct order."

She stared at him. He had seen it, too, the same thing she saw.

"He ran, Mel. My Danny ran away from a fight and left his friends behind him."

"Mr. Finnegan, I don't know if that thing we saw was true. I mean, my heart started racing and I felt kind of faint and then I just saw something, that's all, a kind of dream, really. Then I woke up and I was lying there on the floor and you and my dad were standing over me, and you were holding my hand, and then it was over."

He shook his head, slowly. "I didn't want to believe what I saw, Melissa, Lord knows. But now—you know what?—I think maybe it was true. I think maybe what you saw there was what really happened. I think I saw it because I was touching you when you saw it; that's all I can figure."

"But . . ."

"And I think somehow you were inside Danny's head there for the last moments of his life. I could *feel* the damn panic, Melissa. I know that feeling, and I don't think it's anything you could make up."

"Are you OK, Mr. Finnegan?" Melissa asked him, putting her hand over his on the table. His hand felt feverish, hot. She put her other hand on his, too, offering her calming cold.

He took a deep breath. "Yeah, I'm all right." Another deep breath. In the old days, when he still smoked, he'd have lit one up right here. "He ran, Melissa; he did. But I know what happened to him. When you're in battle, when it's all going crazy all around you, you just react. You can't plan it, you don't think about it, everything just happens, and you look up later and see what you did. The right thing. The wrong thing."

He shook his head. "On the Tra Ban River, in 1971, River Assault Squadron 15, I skippered an ATC—an armored troop carrier—ferrying infantry troops up and down the river. We were running some lurps up the river to Quang Tri, routine stuff. It was blazing hot, the humidity unbearable even in the breeze that boat stirred up. Some thunderstorms were building up above us, but it was so hot and languid you just wanted to sit and sweat. There were cattle grazing over to starboard, I remember, and people working in the fields, not even stopping to look up at us."

He paused, took the sugar jar in his hand, poured a little more into his coffee. "And then, hell, it all went bad, light arms in a cross fire from both banks, a mortar zeroing in on us."

He set the sugar down, tilted his head back, eyes closed. "I gave it full throttle, headed upriver to get out of there, but one of those mortar shells found us and we all went flying.

"I remember the sensation, Melissa. I remember flying through the air in slow motion, with plenty of time to think about what had gone wrong, what I could have done differently. How I wasn't paying enough attention to the riverbanks. How I should have seen it coming.

"What I felt bad about was my wife and my boy, back home in Mankato in the middle of winter without me, and here I was flying through the heat, about to die, and I couldn't help them anymore; I couldn't keep them warm and safe and dry, out of the cold."

He stopped, opened his eyes, smiled at her.

She was staring at him, completely caught up in the story. "How'd you live through it? How badly were you hurt?"

"I didn't get anything worse than bumps and bruises. I hit the water, came up gasping for air, found two other guys struggling there in a lot worse shape than me, and pulled them to shore."

"They didn't capture you?"

He shook his head. "I got us into some cover, hiding in the

mangroves and lying low. Ten or fifteen minutes and a couple of our gunboats arrived, but Charlie was gone. I just stood up and waved and that was it, nice and simple."

"But Danny. In that dream thing I had, Danny . . ."

"He ran. But that's the point, Melissa. If I could have run, back then, I would have. Looking back it all seems really clear, like it took days to happen and every moment had all sorts of chances to go differently. But at the time . . ." He paused, thought through how to say it. "At the time, it just happened. You just act and react. I didn't do anything. I didn't make one damn decision that took any thought. I gunned the throttle; we got blown up; I swam; I pulled my buddies in the water; we hid. The gunboats showed up and hauled us out of there. That's it; that was all of it, and all of it on automatic. You know, I got a medal for that, for what I did that day, and it wasn't right. I finished my tour and asked to be reassigned after that. Three of my guys died out there; two were hurt. I was fine. And I got the medal."

He took a sip of his coffee. "Look, Melissa, that's what happened to Danny. All of it was on automatic. He was just reacting, no time to think."

She waved her hand across her face, like waving off some annoying insect. "But it was all just made up anyway. I mean, if it's from my mind it's not what *really* happened. It's just some kind of dream, some hallucination. I don't think you should even think about it."

She paused, launched into her little prepared speech, something she'd thought through on the way here. "Mr. Finnegan, Danny told me a long time ago about what happened to his mother, the automobile accident, the drunk guy going the wrong way on Highway 169, the head-on.

"You had to raise him yourself after that, and it must have been so terrible just getting over your wife's death. I mean, I can't imagine . . ."

"Danny told you this stuff?"

She nodded. "He admired you so much. He wanted to *be* you, to be just like you."

He sat back in his chair. "I know. Sweet Jesus, I know." He

left it unsaid, but she knew where that was going. Danny had joined up to follow in his footsteps and now, instead, Danny was dead.

She reached over to take his hands in hers. So much of her own troubles were of her own making, but this poor man had done nothing wrong, nothing at all, to earn such sadness. "You did so much for him, you meant so much, and this terrible thing has happened. . . ." She paused. "I just wanted to say this. Whatever I can do; however I can help you, please, please let me try, OK? I thought maybe I could come by your house, do some cooking, some cleaning. I mean, at least that would be *something.*"

He shook his head again, smiled at this girl who would have been his daughter-in-law.

"You're really something, Melissa. And thank you. But what we saw *is* what really happened. I'm sure of it. I just wanted to let you know that, and tell you that it doesn't matter. You loved my son, and he was a terrific young man, and you're a terrific young lady. That's all; that's all I wanted to say, really."

He pushed his chair back, planted both shoes square on the floor, put his hands on his knees, elbows out. "There *is* one more thing. Melissa, I've given this a lot of thought. I'm going to call your father this afternoon and talk it over with him. I know you and Danny planned to get away from here, get married one day soon and move down to Florida somewhere after his hitch was up and you finished school. Danny talked about it all the time, about how you couldn't stand the cold and how you wanted to move down there and start a family and everything. He said you two sort of had it all worked out but hadn't dared to tell your dad yet.

"Well, I want to help. I'll go see Melchior and talk it over with him, and then I want to do for you what Danny wanted to do. When you're ready, I'll help you move down there, maybe for the last couple of years of school? Maybe graduate school? Whatever it is, I'll help."

She just looked at him, eyes widening. "What? Move? Oh, Mr. Finnegan, you can't do that. You can't."

"I can. I am. The money's there, and Danny won't be using it.

I can't think of a single better place to spend it than you, Melissa. Danny would approve, Lord knows."

Melissa sat back. Oh, god. Her head was spinning. She looked around once, slowly, taking it all in. The Little House was so warm and humid that the condensation gathered into droplets that ran down the windowpanes, obscuring the view outside of the parking lot and that big neon sign and the snow falling, big, heavy warm-weather flakes building up on top of that northern pike out there. They were going to get dumped on today, no question about it.

But this? No, it was all a dream. It was easy to think all those thoughts about escaping when you knew you wouldn't, knew you couldn't. It was something else again when the offer was out there on the table.

But no, she couldn't do it to her father, didn't have the nerve to go down there on her own.

She looked at Detective Finnegan and opened her mouth to tell him so, to say no with regrets and then to get up, walk out into the snow, and drive home, back to her books and that test and those two stories for journalism class. Back to real life. Back to the cold.

TRITON TIME

Melissa brought the ball up-court, keeping one eye on the clock and the other on the game. Twelve seconds left.

Rakeisha came up to set her pick, and Melissa got her the ball on a bounce pass, then brushed by her. Nine seconds left. She started down the middle, then backed out as Rakeisha spun and took the ball to the hoop.

Too much traffic in there. Five seconds left. Rakeisha stopped, kicked the ball back out to Melissa on the wing. Two seconds left. She stepped back behind the three-point line, set herself, and let the shot go. One second left, then point-five, and then the horn sounding as the ball was in midflight, the small crowd in the Eckerd College gym absolutely quiet, breath held, waiting.

Melissa watched: the ball seemed to be taking an awfully long time to get to the basket. But it did get there, banged once against the back of the rim, rose up a bit, and then settled back through. Three points. Game winner.

There were hugs and screams and cries of joy. Her teammates carried Melissa off the court on their shoulders, screaming at her happily. It was a big win. Melissa, riding her teammates' shoulders, managed a smile. This moment was the closest she'd been to happy in six months.

It had been a rough time, a lot rougher than she'd expected that day in August when Finnegan and her father had driven her to the airport in Minneapolis for the flight south to St. Petersburg. She'd been nervous, sure, then, but she'd been hopeful, too, that this change would work for her, that it would be the start of her new life, a life less confusing. Over the summer she'd managed to transfer to a good college, done the paperwork and chased down all the details—keeping busy doing all that had been a good thing, keeping her mind off other issues.

She'd stayed busy with her rehab, been back on the court, playing pickup games just for fun and working on the stationary bike, the step machine, and all the rest, too. Her knee, at least, felt good.

She'd spent some time with Summer, too. They were both changing their lives, as it turned out; Melissa heading south to a new school in the sunshine, Summer switching her running event from the 5,000-meter to the steeplechase.

They talked about it over lunch at a Wendy's out near Skyline Drive, Summer splurging on a spicy chicken sandwich and fries while Melissa stuck with a salad and a diet cola.

"I mean," Summer said quietly, dipping a French fry into the little paper bowl of ketchup, "you're the only one who could understand, Melissa, the only one I can even talk to about this besides my mom, and I'm not sure she's even listening. The doctor has her on Valium, for Christ's sake, and she's so zoned out she just smiles at me and nods and says everything will be fine.

"But what happens is that every time I run the five-k I wind up thinking about my dad—all those high-school meets where he was there for me, cheering me on; all those early mornings when I was a kid and he'd jog with me, up at dawn before I had school or he had work.

"He schooled me, you know? And he supported me. I just can't believe he . . ." She paused, not even able to say it. ". . . that he could be, you know. . . ."

She took a sip of her root beer. "And so a few weeks ago in practice I tried the steeplechase—you know the event, jumping over the hazards while you race, right?—and I was pretty good at it. And it's so different that Dad wasn't a part of it, really. I felt like I was out there without him, on my own."

"And that felt good?"

Summer nodded. "Yeah, that felt good. Really good." She took a sip on the straw for her drink.

Melissa had watched Summer talk it all through, explaining herself and her changes, watched those lips opening and moving and closing. And she knew, watching Summer, that she wanted more.

But they never talked about it. She'd tried once and Summer had brushed it off, so it was a memory now, nothing more. Something in the past that they'd shared that once, and that was it. Which worked fine most of the time.

Thing was, Eckerd College was a whole world away, it turned out, from Minnesota. It wasn't just the weather—though she'd never been in weather so hot and humid that you sweated just standing outside—it was everything, the people and the way they drove their cars and dressed and talked; the buildings, the air-conditioning everywhere. Everything, all of it, was drastically different and left her feeling very alone, so she had way too much time on her hands, even once classes started, to think about Summer, and about Danny, her hero, running away.

Then, finally, somewhere along the line in the third or fourth week of class, she'd decided she was a fighter, and she reminded herself that her problems were of her own making and so one by one started to conquer them. She'd learned her way around campus, gotten to know some of her classmates. She was still an outsider—a way, way outsider—and felt it, but she thought maybe she wasn't as lonely and homesick as she'd been before.

She'd quite happily adjusted to the hot weather, at least. She'd found you could trust it. Back home, a hot day or two would be followed by cool weather, even in the middle of summer. And back home, every hot summer day would be balanced, she knew, by a week of horrible cold in the winter. In Mankato, out jogging down Cold Road on a blazing hot July day, she'd be thinking about how the road looked in December and January and February and March—deep in snow, the plowed sides going ten or fifteen feet high as the blades from her father's John Deere pushed snow onto snow, day after freezing day.

Here, after a couple of months of nineties and high humidity, she finally started to believe in it, to relax down deep in her bones; for the first time in her life she didn't have a dreadful winter coming at her that she had to fear. She felt like she belonged in the heat.

She'd finally felt good enough about herself and her life that one late September day she'd gone ahead and walked into the office of the women's basketball coach. She had a letter of introduction from the coach of the U. and a few tapes of her games there.

It hadn't been a snap: the Eckerd coach hadn't misled her, warning her that they had a pretty set lineup and this was the top level of the Division II women's game. She was good enough for the team, the coach said, but she might not get a lot of playing time.

But Melissa's knee felt good, the payoff for all the the rehab work, and so she figured she had nothing to lose. She was eligible right away; the NCAA rules allowed a player to move from a Division I school to a Division II school without losing any eligibility. And the challenge had been a good thing, giving her something to think about other than her loneliness. And so she had made the team, sitting on the bench at first, then getting into a few games here and there, and now, in January, coming off the bench a lot, her minutes starting to add up. And she was enjoying herself.

And now this, tonight: a kind of breakthrough game. She liked it, liked being a winner and having things go the way she wanted them to. She'd worked hard for this. She wished like hell that Danny could have been here to see it. He'd have been proud of her.

Straight from the locker room, Melissa and half a dozen teammates walked to the dorms, planning to meet some friends at the dorms and then head over to the Undertow bar on St. Pete Beach to celebrate the victory. They were dressed in baggy shorts, white T-shirts that read "Lady Tritons" in red script across the front, wearing Nike slides: the basic jock look for a warm Florida winter night and the perfect attire for the Undertow, a large wooden shack of a place that sat right on the beach.

When they got to the dorms, they stumbled into a party at

the Pike House. There Melissa got a Pepsi—wishing it was Gatorade since she was still dehydrated from the game—and headed for a corner of the room to talk with Rakeisha and Kathy and some of the other girls and do some serious people watching.

Some of the girls in the crowd were smoking, which she hated. It was hard to believe that the posers who did that could be so stupid, just suckers for advertising. Worse, they made it miserable for everyone else who just wanted to breathe a little normal air.

She wondered, sometimes, why guys didn't smoke as much as the girls—it sure as hell wasn't because guys were any smarter but maybe just because all the ads were aimed at the girls who needed so badly to fit in that they'd do absolutely anything to feel like they were part of the crowd.

She was taking another sip on the Pepsi when she saw him: light-brown hair, about six feet tall, athletic, nice face, wearing tan shorts and a blue knit shirt that he probably bought at Structure, and playing the part of being cool by smoking a Marlboro Light.

He looked up, caught her checking him out. He smiled. She smiled back. The music was cranked up way too loud, as usual, so he'd be hard to talk to.

He walked over, threading his way through the crowd. Well, OK, she'd see what he was like.

"Hi," he yelled, leaning in toward her ear. He took a drag on his cigarette, blew the smoke toward the ceiling, leaned over again. "Nice party, huh?"

She waved her hand to clear the smoke and to see if he got the message, but he just smiled and didn't put out the cigarette. "It's really smoky," she yelled back. "They need to open some windows or something."

"Yeah, it gets pretty bad in here sometimes. I mean, we're used to it, but we *live* here, you know what I mean?"

Typical frat boy. Still, a good-looking typical frat boy. "You're a Pike?"

"Till the day I die. Pledged the first chance I got, spring of my freshman year."

"You're a senior now?"

"Nah, supposed to be, but you know how that goes. I'm a few semesters behind. Switched majors."

"What are you now?"

"Public relations. I was in the Business School, but the math, you know. I mean, Jesus, what was all that math good for anyway? Nothing. So, PR's a lot easier, and it'll do me just as much good."

He paused for a moment, took another dramatic drag on the cigarette, apparently thinking himself very Bogart. "How about you? I'd guess you're an English major."

"English? Why that?"

He smiled. "All the good-looking girls are in either PR or English. I haven't seen you in any of my classes, so that leaves English."

She laughed. "I'm in the J-School."

"Wow, I didn't know they had *any* lookers in journalism. I thought they were all nerdy writer types."

She laughed at him. He was trying too hard, but that was kind of cute, and at least he was willing to pay a compliment now and then. She offered him a smile by way of thanks.

"Hey," he said, "listen, I got an idea. How about we go out on the porch and get some fresh air."

She nodded. "Sure." It wouldn't be a problem, she figured. The teammates all kept an eye out for one another during these parties. She was sure that if she looked around right now she'd see two or three of the other girls watching her as she left to go outside. They'd come out in a few minutes onto the porch themselves, partly to check on her, mostly from curiosity.

And besides, the guy seemed harmless enough. Way too self-assured and cocky, but that's the way some guys were. The way he looked, the girls must be all over him, so he just naturally got to be this way after a while.

And the smoking thing? Well, if they went out somewhere she'd just have to insist that he not smoke around her. Either he'd agree to that or they wouldn't go out: that was all there was to it.

So they worked their way through the crowd and the din, the

music cranked up so loud you could hardly think—some old Smashing Pumpkins mixed in now with Phish and Green Day and even some trustworthy old U2 stuff, Bono screaming that he still hadn't found what he was looking for as she walked by the last big speaker on her way out to the porch.

And it *was* better on the porch. There was a little bit of a breeze taking the edge off the heat and humidity, and the fresh air more than compensated for the lack of cool air from the air conditioner inside. He even stopped smoking for a minute or two, breathing in deeply, making fun of the fresh air.

"Ah, the great outdoors. The clean air, the solitude. Great, huh?"

Melissa grinned, then shook her head. "You're really a smart aleck. Hey, it's better out here than in all that smoke."

"Absolutely right, and we're not the first ones to discover it," he said, waving his hand at the other people, a dozen or more, enjoying the same break from the music and the smoke.

He suddenly wore a look of concern on his face. "Young lady, I can see that you don't have a beer. For shame! Let me get you one. In fact, let me get both of us a beer."

"No thanks, I'm just drinking Pepsi right now," she said, and held up her empty plastic cup, jiggling it a bit so he could hear the ice.

"No problem. Pepsi it is, then. And a beer for me," he added with a wicked grin, and he took the plastic cup from her hand and left her, heading back into the fray and the bar over in the far corner.

In a flash, Rakeisha and Kathy were at her side. Kathy, the short, flirtatious redhead, came up breathless.

"Oh, my god, Mel, do you know who that is?"

She didn't, she realized. They hadn't gotten to names yet.

Rakeisha just shook her head. "Listen, girl, that's Bo Palmer. *The* Bo Palmer."

"*The* Bo Palmer?" She didn't know who they meant.

"Yes!" the two girls squealed together. He was infamous, Melissa managed to get out of them in the next minute or two as they rattled on about Bo before he returned with the drinks.

He was, they said, eyes wide, the biggest womanizer on campus.

"Girl, this guy has had sex with *everyone*. We couldn't believe it was *you* talking to him," Rakeisha said, shaking her head in disbelief.

Melissa didn't know if 'Keisha was praising her or cutting her down. "What's that supposed to mean?"

"Oh, come on, Minnesota girl. You know what I mean. You're the Ice Queen, and that's not his usual type. You're, well, you're too..."

"...nice," Kathy finished. "I mean, really, Melissa, you're just the nicest person, and you're an athlete, and you don't wear any makeup. That's just not his usual type. And he's, he's..."

"I get the picture."

The Ice Queen, eh? Not for the first time, Melissa wondered what the girls thought of her. She hadn't spent much time with the girls socially, other than a few get-togethers after victories, like this one. And while most of the girls on the team knew how to get out there and party, Melissa really hadn't gotten into that much.

There were all sorts of rumors about a few of the girls on the team, that they were gay. The same rumors swirled around the girls' soccer team.

Did the girls think the same thing about Melissa? Did Melissa think the same thing about Melissa? The thought kept occurring to her; the question kept coming up in her own mind. How come she hadn't found another guy who interested her? But then, how come she hadn't found another girl who interested her, either?

All this rolled around in her head as she watched Bo come wandering back with the drinks, one in each hand, stopping along the way to chat—he seemed to know everyone—so that Melissa had plenty of time to watch him make his progress across the room, out the door, and onto the porch at last.

It was like watching a king, the other lords and ladies bowing before him as he walked slowly through the room, taking this kind of adulation as his right, as if he were born to it. He seemed powerful, maybe dangerous, and some new part of her liked that.

He handed her a plastic cup of Pepsi, smiling at her. "Did you miss me?"

She laughed. "Terribly." Then she took a sip of the Pepsi and almost choked on it. "What is this?"

"Oh, I tossed in a little rum, just to spice it up for you. Harmless. Just a splash."

Cautiously, she took another sip. Not too bad. All right, then, she could handle a little rum, certainly.

"So," he said, "you guys win tonight?"

"Yes. By a point, at the buzzer."

"That's great; you're having a great year."

"Do you go to the games?"

"Been to a few. Saw you get into the game against Rollins for a while. You scored some points in that one."

She nodded, said dryly, "I get a few, every now and then."

"Oh, come on, that's not what I meant. I mean you're a really good player. Just a sophomore, right? You'll get a lot of playing time next season, I bet."

She smiled. "I hope so." It was fun not telling him about how she'd won tonight's game. Wait until he heard about it later; he'd be all embarrassed.

They talked for an hour or more, about the Tritons in various sports—it turned out Bo was on the golf team—and about current movies, current bands, the usual conversation.

And then they talked about each other, Melissa going on about life in Minnesota and just how cold cold could really be.

Bo had no idea. He was a rich kid like a lot of Eckerd students were. He was born and mostly raised in St. Kitts in the Caribbean, where his family owned some fancy resort. He'd come up to Florida for high school, a military boarding school in St. Pete called Admiral Farragut where he'd spent four miserable years before finally graduating and coming to Eckerd, he said. Here he'd encountered the coldest weather he'd ever been in when a cold front came through St. Pete and dropped the temperature below the freezing mark. "I thought I'd die," he admitted, talking about that one cold morning. "You know, there was frost on the windshield of my car."

"Frost. Really? Wow," she said dryly.

He laughed. "Sure, doesn't sound like much to you. But it was plenty cold enough for me, thanks very much. After two days of that I begged my family to let me come home to St. Kitts for a few days, just to warm up."

She tried to imagine that, having enough money to get on a plane and go somewhere warm whenever you wanted.

He generally played about fourth- or fifth-best on the golf team, had a good short game, he said, but admitted he didn't try hard enough to do better with the putter. Still, he figured he might try the pro tour after school; take a shot at the qualifying school, maybe get his card, and then try the life of a golf pro, see how that went.

He was, Melissa realized as they chatted, absolutely full of himself. But that sense of absolute confidence was part of being an athlete. He played best, he said, when the pressure was on. When the putt really mattered he knew he would make it.

They had another drink, and another after that, Melissa getting a pleasant buzz going as she told her friends not to worry and then left the party to head over to the Undertow for a little late-night dancing and more, even louder, music. And more drinks. And then a few shooters, the waitress pouring them down, tequila flaming down Melissa's throat, the evening getting more and more surreal as she went along.

It was strange, the way she knew she was drunk and getting drunker even while a part of her, some inner core, was absolutely lucid, coldly clearheaded. And that core was watching the outside of herself get wasted.

By three in the morning that inner self watched in amusement as the outer self, no longer able to stand without swaying, was helped outside and then started the six-block walk with a supportive Bo to his fraternity house, which seemed like a perfectly reasonable place to relax for a while, maybe take a much-needed nap, maybe play a little kissy-face with this incredibly good-looking guy from St. Petersburg and some tiny Caribbean island. The Golfer. With the great hands.

She wasn't sure exactly how it happened, but there they were in his room, and she was lifting the white T-shirt over her head and slipping out of her baggy shorts and collapsing back on the bed, laughing, as she kicked off her Nike slides.

It was all very funny, very sexy.

They were on the bed together. Bo was kissing her, starting at her forehead, lingering on her lips, then her throat, and that was so good she moaned. Then her breasts, Bo sucking on her nipples so that she moaned again. Then farther down, teasing and tickling at the tummy so that, somewhere deep in that alcoholic haze, she heard herself giggling and saying, "No, stop that."

He was kissing her hips, moving down toward her crotch, then onto her there and kissing and then, with his tongue, arousing her. My god, it was fantastic and somehow horrible at the same time.

She put her hands on his head, brought him up from there, said, "No," again as he brought his face up to hers and kissed her on the chin, lightly on the lips, and put himself against her, on top of her so she could feel him down there, urgent, growing.

There was a kind of terror. Something deep and frozen, rising up from within her.

"No, Bo. Please," she said, knowing from that inner core that she was slurring her words, that she never should have been here, that this was horribly wrong somehow. "No. Please," she said again, feeling him against her, feeling the urgency of his wanting her.

"No," she tried, one more time, her voice stronger, and then she started to slip away from this, traveling somewhere in her mind where all this wasn't happening, some dreamtime where she was safe and away from Bo and this bed—some safe, warm, distant place.

SEA TURTLE BLUES

The closing of the bedroom door woke her up, painfully. She opened one eye, looked up to see the boy she'd been with last night standing over her, smiling, holding a drink, something sort of red and with a cucumber stuck in it.

She opened the other eye. She felt awful. "Oh, my god. I couldn't possibly... I feel really sick; you better just stay away from me."

"You're just hungover," he said, and sat down next to her on the bed. "It's no big deal. Here," and he held out the drink, "this will make you feel better—a little Bloody Mary for the morning. Hair of the dog that bit you."

"Bloody Mary?" Oh, god, she could barely focus. Her head pounded; her stomach was in open rebellion; she ached everywhere. She couldn't remember ever feeling this sick.

"Yep. Here, take a sip," and he held it toward her. Shakily, she grabbed it with both hands, took a cautious sip. Not too bad, really. She drank a little more.

And then it dawned on her where she was and what she'd done. She had to get out of there. Now.

"Listen, I have to go." She sat up, covering herself with the blanket. "If you could just give me a minute or two to get dressed and use the bathroom, then I'll get going, OK?"

He smiled at her. "Take another sip. And take your time. It's Saturday morning. Not even noon yet. When you're ready I'll run you back over to your dorm."

Almost noon? Oh, god, what would everyone think? Rakeisha and Kathy would have told everyone by now.

She took another sip. She did feel better; at least her head wasn't pounding quite so much, and her stomach felt a little more settled.

He left, shutting the door, and she shakily got out of his bed. The room was a mixture of college jock, frat boy, and rich kid, with expensive stereo equipment, a bunch of golf trophies, and two street signs nailed to the wall. One said "Christopher Street," the other "Frigate Bay Road."

She walked into the bathroom and splashed some water on her face, wanting her toothbrush in the worst damn way. She looked in the mirror. Her hair was a wreck, all tangled and dirty. She didn't even have a brush with her. She pulled it back into a ponytail, found a rubber band in a little bowl on top of the toilet tank to wrap it with. God, this was embarrassing.

Back in the bedroom, she slipped back into her baggy shorts and her T-shirt, slipped on her slides, took another sip of that drink and then a deep breath, and opened the door. He was standing there in the hallway, talking with two of his frat brothers, smoking a cigarette. He smiled. They smiled. She smiled back; nothing to do but fake it with bravado, right?

His car, good grief, a silver Porsche, was parked right in front of the house. They both climbed in, and he started it up. "Which dorm?"

She told him, and they drove in silence for a few minutes. Then, at the corner of the Bayway and Thirty-fourth Street South, he turned to look at her. "Listen, I had a great time last night."

"Me, too," she said, halfheartedly. "I can't believe I got drunk like that. I *never* get drunk. I'm really sorry, I must have been a real mess by the time we got back to the Pike House."

"You were a little wasted," he said, grinning. "But you were just having fun, and that's cool."

"I guess."

"No. It was great, really. And then later, back in my room ..."

She'd been wondering when he was going to get around to this part. Here she was, in his car, the next morning, on the way back to her dorm. She was another notch on his golf club, that was all. And it was starting to sink in, what she'd done and the implications of it. She'd thought that sometime soon she'd understand herself and maybe then, with someone special, she'd make love for the first time. Last night was not at all how she'd pictured it happening.

He reached across the center console to take her hand. "I just wanted you to know that nothing happened."

She turned sideways in her seat to look at him, try to see if there was truth in those gray eyes of his. "Nothing happened?"

"Well, I thought things *were* going to happen, but then you passed out and everything, so I just put you to bed and that was it."

She sat back in her seat, felt an enormous weight rising and lifting from her. Oh, thank God. He'd saved her. She'd picked the worst guy on campus to put through a test like that, and he'd come through for her. She was lucky, very, very lucky. And she felt better, a lot better, hearing the news. "Thank you," was all she could say to him, but she meant it.

He waved it off. "No, I was just, you know, doing the right thing." He laughed. "That doesn't mean I didn't want to, you know. I mean, you're beautiful."

She laughed, almost giddy with relief. "Yeah, look at me now. Really beautiful, that's me."

They reached the dorm. "That *is* you," he said. He sat back, leaning his head back against the headrest, turning then to look at her. "Listen, Melissa, I have to go down to the family business next weekend for a big birthday party for my stepmom. Would you like to come? You'll have your own room—heck, we'll get you a suite. It's a great island, and the hotel is beautiful. It's right on the beach. There's great snorkeling and scuba, and a terrific restaurant. Do you have a game that Saturday?"

She looked at him and laughed. "You're crazy!"

He grinned, shrugged. "No, I'm serious," he said. "I fly down there all the time for weekends." He looked a little nervous, took the time to pull out and light a cigarette, blew the smoke out the open window.

"Look, it's no big deal; I take friends down there all the time.

And my stepmom's pretty nice, really, under the circumstances. Dad's great. They'll love having you there."

Oh my, it sounded wonderful. But there was no way. She didn't have anything she could possibly wear to such a bash—somehow T-shirts, shorts, and some slides on the feet didn't seem likely to be acceptable. And she hardly knew this guy—all she knew, really, was his reputation. No, she thought, she just couldn't.

"I'd love to. I mean, it sounds really crazy, but I'm sure it would be a lot of fun. But I have basketball practice on Saturday, from ten to about noon. Then another practice on Sunday afternoon at three. I just don't see how..."

He smiled. "No, that'll work. I do this all the time. We'll catch the two P.M. Saturday flight to San Juan, change there, and get the five P.M. to St. Kitts. It's an hour ahead there, so we'll be there about seven, and the party starts at eight. Then Sunday morning we'll have an early breakfast, catch the 9 A.M. flight back, and have you on the court by three."

It was dizzying to think of. And wild. And exciting. "Won't that be incredibly expensive for just one night?" she asked.

He just shook his head, then shrugged his shoulders. "Doesn't matter. Like I said, I fly home for weekends all the time; my folks are used to it. It's really no big deal, honest. And you'll be my guest, of course, so I'll pay for everything."

She just stared at him, trying to think it through by looking at his face, his really very handsome face.

All her life, Melissa had been careful, cautious. Now, here was this rich kid asking her to his folks' resort on some distant Caribbean island for one night for some fancy party. She'd have to get something to wear and get her hair done and buy new shoes. And, most of all, she hardly knew this guy.

But it sounded exotic and fun and risky. She was in the mood for some risk, damn it, just this once. Play-it-safe, play-it-straight Melissa O'Malley was going to be daring this once. Wasn't that was college was all about, taking chances now and then? Learning and growing and all that stuff? Sure it was, she thought. Absolutely. She looked at him and smiled.

✻　　　✻　　　✻

A week later, Palmer's Frigate Bay Resort turned out to be every-thing she'd imagined it might be.

The flight down had been remarkable on its own, the ride, in first class, on the big jet out of Tampa pretty exciting for a girl who'd only flown a few times. And then the flight on the little American Eagle VTR prop plane out of San Juan over to St. Kitts an absolute thrill, the plane flying so low that she could see the houses and fields on the islands that slid by out her win-dow—St. John and St. Croix in the U.S. Virgin Islands, then Saba and Statia, a pair of Dutch islands that seemed to march right on into St. Kitts, which had been British until independence.

Bo kept up a running commentary the whole time, telling her about the islands, describing the resorts on them and which one had great snorkeling or a favorite restaurant—which one was lively and which one quiet.

They were all incredible to see, even out the window, Saba and Statia especially, looking like lush green mountaintops rising from the sea, each fringed by tiny stretches of beach around the edges. It was a fantasy come true, sipping on some rum drink the whole way, slowly drifting in a wonderful, warm alcoholic haze while watching these islands drift by in the turquoise Caribbean.

And St. Kitts, Bo promised as they flew past Saba and Statia, would be the best of them all.

An hour after they landed and were met by the resort's white limousine, she believed him. Her room was a two-bedroom suite on the second floor—it must have cost hundreds of dollars a night, she guessed—with everything done in rattan and bamboo, with blue floral patterns on the couch and the love seats in the parlor and the wide queen-size beds in each bedroom. There were white lamps on the end tables, a glass-topped coffee table and dining room set, and on and on. It was beautiful. Tropical and pastel and just downright beautiful.

And out the picture window as she stood there to look out to the darkening blue of the sunset sea a small freighter went by, its lights small dots of white against the orange and red of the sky behind it, distant thunderheads blocking the sun's final moments.

God, it was heavenly, so radically different from anything she'd ever seen or felt or smelled—it seemed to call to her, some deep part of her that resonated to this beauty, this calm serenity. She stood there for long minutes, transfixed, before finally turning away to unpack and get ready for the party, unpacking the new black dress she'd packed so carefully back in her dorm room at school.

Her friends had helped her find it, in a little shop on Beach Drive downtown, Cecilia's, where the little black dress and matching shoes and purse cost her more money than she'd spent on herself in the past two years—but when she put it on she hardly recognized who that was in the mirror. Staring back at her was a tall, slender woman just a half-inch shy of six-foot, with green eyes and hair so dark that in just the right light there seemed to be purple highlights. The black dress, the shoes, the purse, the way her breasts had magically appeared from the plunge of the dress, the way she looked, standing there in heels, it was like an out-of-body experience, some other person, that other Melissa who was always hidden away, out now for show-and-tell. It was scary, really, and hard to believe that was her at all.

But it was, and she'd been out with Bo every night that week, usually just for dinner but twice for a movie. It had been a struggle, getting her schoolwork done and her basketball in and still seeing Bo, but she'd surprised herself completely by being motivated enough to do it, though she didn't think she could keep up the pace of just five or six hours of sleep a night.

Bo had been a complete gentleman. By the second date he'd talked her into admitting that she was a virgin. Other than Danny, Bo was the first guy who knew that about her, and it didn't seem to bother him. Quite the opposite, in fact. He acted like she was really special, and it was hard to not like that. He held open doors, pulled back her chair in the restaurants, kissed her chastely at just the right times.

She'd had two basketball games that week, both at home, one on Tuesday against St. Leo and then another on Thursday against the University of Tampa. He was at both of them, cheering her on as she led the team in scoring and assists and the Tritons won both games. Then he was waiting for her afterward to drive her out for a late bite to eat.

She found him easy to talk to; that was part of it. When she told him about her mother, the island girl who'd fallen in love with the American farm boy, he clapped his hands in delight. "I knew it," he said, shaking his head and smiling. "There's just something about you. You belong in the sunshine, not up in all that snow."

She couldn't have agreed more, though she hadn't told him yet how her mother had disappeared when Melissa was just five, gone off into a cold Minnesota night, never heard from, never found. That, she thought, she could tell him later.

All in all, it was a whirlwind, and she'd never been caught up in one before. Danny had been the boy she'd grown up with, and there'd been no others. She and Danny had been in class together since third grade at Mary, Queen of Peace School, the old stone Catholic elementary school at the west end of Main Street, built during the postwar baby boom, when there were enough Irish Catholics in southern Minnesota to justify a two-story elementary school. By the time Melissa and Danny went through, there were just enough Kerry Patch kids—descendants of that one wave of Irish immigrants—in Mankato to keep the place open, nine or ten kids in each grade. The few kids there had gotten pretty close with one another—Catholics versus the Lutheran world, it always seemed to them in southern Minnesota.

So she felt like she'd been close to Danny forever, right since Day One in third grade. There'd been no other boy since, with only the enormous confusion of Summer intruding on that history. Coming out of the door of her room when Bo knocked very politely, standing there in front of his admiring gaze, smiling back at him and taking his hand to walk along, she was happy to not worry about Summer at all.

Before heading to the party, they walked out to the beach on a path that wound through dunes covered in sea oats and sea grapes. Melissa struggled to walk in her heels, insecure in shoes like this anyway, and doubly in trouble with the soft sand giving way with each step. Twice she started to stumble and reached out to Bo for support before they finally came out from between the dunes onto the harder sand near the dark Caribbean.

Bo started to pull a cigarette out of a pack of Marlboro Lights, then held back when she looked at him, and shoved them back into his pocket. The sun had set, but the sky still held a tinge of blue with only Venus, in front of them, to light the way.

He reached down and tugged off his shoes and socks, rolled up his trousers, and walked into the water. "It's great," he said. "The water temp is always around eighty here. Not too bad, huh?"

Melissa could only laugh. "You should try swimming in a Minnesota lake sometime, even in August. It's very refreshing."

They walked along, Melissa keeping her feet dry while Bo waded in just a few inches of water, kicking at it some so that a phosphorescent spray rose in the darkness. Melissa had found the Gulf of Mexico to be a revelation when she'd first moved to Florida—water so warm it was like a bath in the summer, the temperature around ninety degrees, the gentle waves a caress compared to the freezing lakes of Minnesota.

But this: wow. It was the most beautiful water she'd ever seen, an eye-opening glimpse of the kind of sea and sky that lured the rich and famous to these tiny islands in the Caribbean.

She stopped to look out toward the sea. "It's beautiful here, Bo. Thanks for inviting me."

"Yeah, my pleasure. I'm here so much that sometimes I forget how nice it is, you know?"

He stopped and started pointing. "Up there," he said, pointing toward the great curve of beach that swept north and west from where they stood, "is Basseterre, the main city. I don't guess we'll get a chance to see it this time. It's pretty nice, as Caribbean towns go. Couple of good restaurants. Some neat history."

He turned and pointed south. "And down there, you can just see it in the dark, is Timothy Hill. The other side of that is the Great Salt Pond. That used to be a big product here, sea salt. I think they still sell some of it."

He turned back again, acting the tour guide, waving north. "Up that way, past the town, is Brimstone Fortress—a cool old fort built in the 1700s, when the British and French were fighting over this island. They called the fort the Gibraltar of the Caribbean back then."

Melissa waved to the west. "And out there is, what, Cuba?"

"Yeah, a little north of that. The Cayman Islands are pretty much straight west of here, I think, but a long way off. Up north and a little west is where we were a couple of hours ago in Puerto Rico."

He pulled a cigarette out after all and lit it. "Just this one, OK? I didn't smoke all the way down in the planes, did I?"

He had a point, though it hadn't been allowed. And he had smoked a couple of cigarettes when they waited while changing planes in San Juan. But Melissa let it go.

They kept walking, chatting about what life was like growing up in the Caribbean. He's spent a lot of time in the States—so much so that his accent was American. But he still thought of this idyllic island as home.

The party itself was magic, held in what Bo called the family's beach house, a three-story home with a good two dozen rooms about two hundred yards up the beach from the resort and a few hundred feet up the side of a hill.

Bo's father was a good-looking man in his late fifties, dressed in a knit shirt, shorts, and loafers with no socks. He chain-smoked and coughed too much, but he was very nice to her and as casual and friendly as you could want. But she could *feel* the money, somehow. Those scuffed-up loafers he wore to knock around the house and the beach in, for instance, were Italian Bottega Venetas and they cost at least $500 a pair. And Bo's stepmother, much younger than his dad at thirty-five or so and a beautiful redhead, wore a pair of Evander Preston earrings that could have bought her a nice automobile if she'd wanted another one of those instead.

It was a strange group of people, more racially mixed than any party Melissa had ever been to, except maybe for just when she hung out with the girls on the basketball team. Difference was, here the black people were as rich as the white ones and they all spoke with a lilting accent that pinned them down as being from one Caribbean island or another.

Some of them, black and white, she found out just listening in to the conversations, were from England and had flown into St. Kitts for the party and a chance for a few days of sunshine and water at the resort. Others, all of them black, seemed to be local government officials, and they dressed and acted with the same sense of confidence as the jetsetters from London—which told Melissa that they, too, had a lot of money.

For a farm girl from Minnesota, it was all pretty incredible, Melissa realized as she took some crabmeat appetizer off a tray that a guy in a tuxedo whisked by. She'd never seen this much jewelry in her life, and she had the distinct feeling that no one here was faking it—the necklaces, the earrings, even the tennis bracelet on the one woman who kept talking about the ladders at her tennis club, were all very real and very expensive.

And they were all so easy with their money. That surprised her. They took all the money, the glamour, their trips to Hong Kong and Paris and Tokyo, this beautiful place and everything in it, absolutely for granted. It all was, as Bo had said to her earlier when she told him how amazing it all was, no big deal.

"Want to go for a walk down there?" Bo asked her hours later, after it was all over, the guests gone, his parents gone to bed, and just the two of them together out by the family pool. They sat under the wide spray of stars, having a drink, looking down the hill to the beach below.

They could hear the surf. Melissa looked at the clock on the wall of the guest bathhouse. It was two in the morning, in the middle of January. It should be forty below. Back in Minnesota it probably was forty below. But here, now, it was warm, the air a gentle kiss against her shoulders, the surf against the beach below a quiet murmur.

She was quiet, sitting back in her chair, sipping on an icy rum punch. He had pegged her right; she *had* been thinking about a walk on that beach—god, it was the single most beautiful sight she'd ever seen, and yet this was, she knew now, just another typical night here.

Her life had sure changed since Danny's death. The plans she'd had with Danny, the person she'd thought she was back then, the person she'd planned to be—that person was miles away from here, from this party, from Bo and his family and friends and this incredible beach house.

Was it gone forever? Was she gone forever, changed forever, from the girl she'd been, the girl she'd planned to be?

"Hey," Bo said, "you all right? You look a million miles away."

"I'm fine," she said, and smiled at him, then took a sip of her drink. For all of the drinking she'd done this evening she didn't feel very drunk; something about the entire evening had been very sobering. "It was a wonderful evening, Bo. The resort, this house, your parents, the whole thing, is really something. But I have to tell you, I feel way out of place here."

"Well, I have news for you, my dear," he said in a mock uppercrust accent, "you are the one who is, as you say, 'really something.' " He leaned toward her, looked her in the eyes. "And you're not out of place here, Melissa, not even a little. I thought you fit in perfectly, and so did my folks. Dad just loved you."

"Really?"

"Really." Bo reached out to take her hands in his, leaned over to kiss her lightly on the lips. She kissed him back.

He sat back, looked at her. "This has been an incredible week, Melissa."

She laughed at the look on his too-serious face. "You mean watching me play basketball was that much fun?"

"You know what I mean. You're incredible. I've never met anybody like you."

"Oh, Bo. Don't be silly. You meet women by the dozens, the hundreds. Beautiful women, dripping with money."

"No, Melissa. I mean it. You're really something."

"You said that."

"I meant it. You are. You're..." He stopped, searching for the word. "Perfect. Innocent. That's what you are."

"Oh, Bo. I'm a Midwest farm girl from Minnesota who can

hit a jump shot and knows how to study. That about sums me up."

He just shook his head. "No. The girls I know, they're all . . ." He just shrugged his shoulders. "They're not like you—beautiful, and smart. Unspoiled."

She laughed out loud. "Oh, please. Unspoiled? Please, Bo."

"No. Really. I mean it."

He reached over to take her hands again. "The stars are beautiful, aren't they?"

She looked up, looked back into his face, and then nodded. They were indeed.

"You know, if we walk down there on that beach now, away from the lights, you'll see more stars than you've ever seen in your life. It's so beautiful here."

"I love the islands, Bo. I've wanted to go to the Caribbean my whole life. See where my mother was from, feel the warm breezes, walk in the soft sand, climb through a rain forest to reach a mountain peak, the whole island thing." She smiled at him. "But you've never been in the middle of nowhere in Minnesota on a clear winter night, Bo Palmer. Stars by the millions, the billions."

"Well, hell," he said with a gentle laugh, "let's get down there and count them and see. I'll bet you there's more here."

She laughed, too, and took his hand, and they headed down the path.

And the beach was—no matter how many stars there were up there—incredible, the great splash of the Milky Way arcing across the sky, the stars so bright and so crowded that, just like at home in the winter, she had a hard time picking out the constellations.

They took off their shoes and walked in the warm water that lapped at the sand. There was no moon, and the stars were so bright and demanding that Melissa kept looking up to see them, trying to figure out a few as she went and point them out to Bo. There, Sirius, the Dog Star. And over there, Polaris, the North Star. And there, the two stars forming the end of the pan pointing at Polaris, was the Big Dipper. Follow that curve around the handle and there, a straight line down from it, was Spica.

It was all too wonderful to believe. Then, as they hit a stretch of beach with hard shells washed up instead of the soft sand, Melissa looked down to see where to place her feet. And there, up ahead ten yards or so, she saw something washed up on the beach; a crab trap, maybe, or a mound of seaweed. They walked closer to it and it took shape as a sea turtle. Not a big one, maybe the size of a hubcap, and long dead, one of its flippers chewed away and nearly gone but the shell looking perfect and unmarked.

"Oh, man," Bo said, shoving at the turtle a bit with his shoe. "Look at this. They lay eggs on this stretch of beach in the summer, but you don't see many this time of year—especially the young ones."

"It's a baby?"

"Well, it's young, just three or four years old, I guess. A green-back, and they get a lot bigger than this when they're adults. Not huge, like the leatherbacks, but plenty bigger than this." He shoved it again, flipped it over. The bottom of the shell was unmarked, too. "Wonder what happened to it?"

He reached down to flip it back over. "Guess I'll have to call the local cops; they keep track of sea turtle deaths and report them to some sea turtle group."

"How come you know so much about sea turtles?" She leaned over herself to get a closer look, then got down on one knee, peered even closer.

He grabbed the turtle by the shell, lifted it free from the sand. "I did a paper on them for class. Real interesting things, really. Tough guys, once they get bigger. Here, feel how hard that shell is?" And he held out the turtle toward her.

Melissa, repulsed and curious both, reached out to touch the shell.

And knew starvation. And pain. What had been serenity, a oneness with the currents, a stroke and steady glide through a warm and perfect world, was now a deep need for food, an eating of jellyfish, but then she was filled with pain, not satisfaction. Forever in such pain, time passing, then, weaker, a sliding down into deeper water, not understanding what was happening but seeing the light at the surface grow dim and then disappear as she headed toward the dark bottom, toward oblivion. . . .

BEGIN AGAIN

Outside, the clarity was blinding, the thin winter sun shining through an achingly clear blue sky to show, in hard outline, the piles of snowdrifts plowed high to the side of the road and the thick tendrils of icicles hanging from the roofs over downtown's buildings. For a week it had been warm, above freezing for a couple of those days, and then this Alberta Clipper had come roaring through, bringing a quick six inches of snow and dropping the temperature some seventy degrees, from thirty above to forty below in one hard night.

Inside the Little House restaurant, Dan Finnegan sat at his favorite table, looking out the window while he sipped on his coffee and waited for his meat loaf and mashed potatoes to arrive.

He unclipped his radio from his belt, set it on the tabletop, and then looked at his watch. Melchior O'Malley was a few minutes late, but that was nothing new. The two men had figured out early on that Finnegan was the early type and Mel the late type, and that was that. Over the past couple of years of their friendship, Finnegan had figured out that the best thing to do was go ahead and order lunch, and when Mel got here he got here. There'd still be time, at least, for a cup of coffee and a chance to get caught up on things, on Melissa and how she was doing down there in Florida.

Finnegan had a letter from Melissa with him; figured he'd compare notes with Melchior when he arrived. She was doing fine, the letter said. The basketball team was winning more than it was losing, her knee felt good, her classwork was hard but pretty interesting, and the weather was hot and humid every day and she loved it.

She also mentioned a boy—very cautiously, just dropping in that she was "hanging out" some with a boy named Bo Palmer, who played on the golf team. His family owned a big resort on the Caribbean island of St. Kitts.

It all sounded very nice, and Finnegan was happy for her. Melissa had always hated the cold, so she'd done the right thing moving down there. He figured he was just making up in his own mind the undercurrent of worry that he felt reading through her letters the last few months. He could ask Melchior what he thought about it—was his daughter happy down there in Florida? But delicate emotional readings were not exactly Mel's strong suit.

Finnegan got the idea, reading through this letter and the others that had come before, that maybe things weren't quite as great in paradise as Melissa seemed to say. He thought maybe he could detect some unhappiness, maybe just homesickness, maybe some worries about this Bo guy, who apparently wanted their relationship to be more than she did.

But it was all pretty subtle. He sipped on the strong, black coffee, liked the heat of it going down: it was a hell of a cold day today. He cared for that girl so much he just might be reading all this worry into it on his own, acting too much like the father he wasn't, being protective where it wasn't his place to be like that.

Oh, hell; who could know? He heard a pickup truck, thought it sounded like Mel's, and glanced outside to watch it go by. No.

Sunshine—that was really her name, poor girl, saddled with that first name by hippie parents two decades ago—came by with his meat loaf. He thanked her, picked up his fork, cut off a big bite of the loaf. He probably ought to not be eating this; his doctor wanted him to lose fifteen or twenty pounds, get more exercise, get that cholesterol level down closer to the 200 mark, raise those HDLs and lower the LDLs and get one up on the triglycerides and drop the blood pressure and all of that: man, middle age was full of worries he hadn't seen coming. No way he should be eating this big hunk of meat loaf smothered in brown gravy. But it sure looked good, big hunks of onion in there like he liked it, some green pepper.

The radio squawked at him. Of course, just when he was ready for that first bite, a burst of static, and then the call: Dispatch sending the nearest unit out to a 911 call near St. Peter. A 10-84, assault in progress. He listened closely, a home invasion, a little girl making the call, someone in the house, downstairs, fighting with Mommy while Daddy wasn't home.

It might just be a domestic violence thing, an angry boyfriend and a missing husband. But no, he could sense this. He hadn't spent the last twenty years of police work for nothing, goddamn it. He could smell it.

The killer was back. The creature who'd done those awful murders before, in Rapidan and Good Thunder, was back for another one, and it was going on right now, still happening. This, maybe, was it, the chance to catch the son of a bitch.

Finnegan had been waiting a very long time to get this chance. He was out the door in a few seconds, in the Pontiac a few seconds after that, tires squealing and slipping on the ice patches that dotted the frozen pavement as he backed up, jammed it into drive, and headed toward St. Peter.

Only when he had the Pontiac under control and headed in the right direction on State Road 66 did he call it in, that he was on the way. Two patrol cars were already responding. The first one would get there in five minutes, maybe in time to stop it, to catch whoever this was. The second was just a few minutes behind. Finnegan figured it would be at least fifteen minutes before he could get there himself. That was too damn long. He floored it, fighting to keep the car under control on the narrow road, patches of frozen snow covering huge sections of it, two tall walls of plowed snow on the sides. Well, hell, at least they'd keep him on the road if he lost control completely.

They really had just two suspects, Walter Arndt and Fr. Jim Murphy from Holy Innocents. Finnegan didn't think it was Murphy, who was missing and had a lot of damn question marks but had probably just left to start over somewhere else, probably with a new name and a whole new life.

But Walter Arndt, now he had to admit that Walter looked pretty damn guilty. They just hadn't been able to track him down, that was all. And now, maybe, just maybe, this was it. After all the bullshit, after how the evidence had stopped the forensic guys cold despite the fingerprints, the DNA, the tire tracks in the snow, the strands of hair. They had all that and more and yet it hadn't added up to a damn thing. Now the guy was back and in the middle of another slaughter.

He slid badly twice, smashed up the right front fender on a snowbank that had been frozen solid for ten weeks, but didn't do any more damage than that and in sixteen minutes by his watch he was roaring along the half-mile of plowed farm road that led from the highway to the farmhouse.

When he pulled in he recognized the first officer he saw, Janie Sweda. Good girl, good cop. She knew him, too, and knew he was coming.

"Dead?" he asked as he opened the door.

She nodded, calm, steady as you go. "Pretty rough in there, Dan. We don't know if the perp is still on the property. Jake Brue and Bob Townsend are checking the house. Jon's out back, looking through the barn and the shed next to it."

"The kid?"

She shook her head; she was a mother herself. "Haven't found her yet. Maybe the guy took her with him."

"Damn." He stood up; the cold wind was needles on his un-protected cheeks—damn, it was cold. "What'd you do in there, Janie? Touch anything?"

"Not much. Walked in, checked on the body to make sure she was dead. No question about that. Then took a quick look around, then came back out here while Jake and Bob went in."

"You know the perp was a guy?" Three years ago, the first time, the footprints were from a woman's shoe, the long strands of black hair a woman's.

Surprise registered on her face. "No. I just figured. You know, the way the mom looks. Jesus."

He nodded. "Yeah, damn it, I know. I better get in there."

"Be careful, Dan."

He nodded again, waved to her, and walked up to the front porch. There were footprints everywhere in the fresh snow; some of them might be from the perp. There'd be a stream of people coming through here soon, the various investigative teams that invaded a crime scene like this. They'd have to get this whole area taped off right away and hope that the fresh snow froze solid for a few days so they could check all the footprints. Probably wouldn't amount to anything useful, but they had to check.

The front door was open, but the second door, inside the little vestibule designed to keep out the cold, was closed. He walked in, slipping off his winter gloves and putting on the latex surgicals he wore at a crime scene. He opened the inside door, a beautiful thing with a stained-glass centerpiece, all flowers and birds and butterflies, permanent summertime, sweetness and light in the middle of this long, dark winter.

Inside, he could smell the blood. One step past the door and he could see a puddle of it, still wet, soaking into the accent rug and spilling over onto the hardwood floor. Someone had put a lot of effort into that floor, polishing and sanding and polishing again. The blood just sat there on it, not sinking at all into that hard varnish.

He stepped around it, walked through the door into the dining room, and there she was, lying on the floor on her face, her left arm stretched out in front of her, the right arm pulled back across her back, the right hand half cut off at the wrist. There were puncture wounds in the chest. He counted them. Seven inch-wide holes, from a knife, then. Two or three had torn right through the heart—the blood was done spurting, but it must have pumped out in a torrent there for a few minutes.

The perp must have killed her first—that was interesting. Knew where to stab, knew how to make it pretty quick. The woman would have lost consciousness in a few seconds with the blood coming out that fast. Then he'd been right in the middle of cutting that hand off when he'd heard the sirens coming. He'd split then, in a hurry. Out the front? Maybe out the back door through the dining room and on into the kitchen and then out that back door, down the steps, and over to the barn?

No, that would get him caught, trapped in the barn. This guy wasn't that stupid. No, probably out toward those woods and then on foot to the road.

Jake Brue, a good cop, came down the steps from the upstairs. Saw Finnegan.

"Job's half-done, Dan, don't you think?"

Finnegan nodded. "You guys checking the woods out there?"

"Yeah. Figured he had to go that way. Six more units coming to close off the road, bring some dogs into the woods. We'll catch the son of a bitch."

"Sure. Nice work. Listen, call and request the State Patrol to get their plane over here from Mankato, all right? You didn't find the child." He said it as fact.

"No. Not upstairs, poor thing. He must have taken her with him. You know how that'll out, damn it."

"Tape all this off, Jake, and be careful with the evidence. Let's make sure on this one. I'm gonna go upstairs and take a look around. I'll get Forensics on the way, but it'll be a couple of hours before they can get here from St. Paul."

"Got it."

Finnegan headed up the wood stairs, beautiful woodwork on the railing. Damn, nice place here, really nice. Goddamn it.

The front bedroom was where the parents slept, king-size bed straightened nicely, a few clothes tossed into a corner, a big chest of drawers with a mirror on top, some jewelry lying there for the taking.

Next was an office, a computer in there, turned on, the screen saver throwing a star pattern at him as he looked at it, like he was moving through the dark night, stars swooshing by.

Next was the upstairs bathroom, nice and clean and tidy. An organized woman had run a tight ship in this big old house.

Then came the kid's room, painted in a light blue, posters of wolves and horses on the wall. He poked around in there a bit, checked the closet, under the bed. Nothing.

He walked back down the hall, stopped for a second, looked at that computer screen, walked over to it, reached down, and grabbed the mouse.

The screen saver disappeared and some kid's game came up, tinny music welling up and a voice asking, "Ready to play? Just click on the frog."

He clicked on the little exit sign, but nothing happened except one of those annoying bell sounds that said you hadn't done it right. Sweet Jesus, he hated computers.

"Daddy?" He heard a voice from somewhere distant. "Daddy, is that you?"

The little girl? Where the hell was she?

"It's a policeman. I'm here to help you, sweetie. Where are you?"

"Are you really a policeman?"

"I am. Just tell me where you are, sweetheart, and we'll get you to your daddy, all right?"

No sound. She was thinking it through. Good girl, careful. That's why she was still alive. Then, "OK, but I have a really big gun, OK? You be very careful coming in here."

It was the closet. He opened the door slowly; she was probably making that up, about the gun, but no use finding out the hard way that she wasn't.

Nothing. He pushed aside a couple of stacked boxes, heavy with papers. Nobody there.

"Up here," a small voice said, and he looked up. Behind some books on a top shelf there was a wide space and a girl crouched in there; a little thing, maybe six or seven, blond hair, blue eyes, cute as a button.

"Do you have proper identification?" she asked. "You're not wearing a uniform."

He smiled, grabbed his badge and ID from his jacket pocket, showed it to her. "I'm Detective Finnegan, sweetheart. We've been looking for you, me and some other police officers."

"Is my mommy OK?"

"Let me help you down from there, sweetheart. C'mon, and we'll get you to your daddy, all right?"

"My daddy's home? That'd be great."

"He'll be here in a minute. What's your name, sweetheart?"

"I'm not supposed to tell strangers that."

"But I'm a police officer, honey. It's OK to tell me."

She wriggled one leg over the shelf, and then the other. He reached up to grab her by the waist and help her down. How the hell had she gotten up there?

She turned to face him when he set her down. "My name is Cynthia Jane, but that's all I'm going to tell you until I see my mommy or daddy."

"All right, sweetheart, if that's what you say." He paused. "Cynthia Jane, did you see anything? You were the one who called 911, right?"

She nodded. "Mommy told me to call when that bad lady broke into the house. So I took the phone from Mommy's room and she helped me climb into my secret clubhouse and then she shut the door so it could stay secret and then I called and then I was really superquiet like I promised Mommy."

"You didn't see anything?"

"No. I told you, I was in my secret clubhouse. Mommy went downstairs and there was yelling like somebody was mad, but that was all I heard. And then a long time went by, hours and hours, I think. And then I heard the computer, making noise like it does at Daddy, so I thought it was him, but it wasn't, it was you, and..."

He raised his hand. "Thanks, Cynthia Jane; I think I understand. Come on, sweetheart; let me take you downstairs and get you some help."

He took her by the hand and led her from the room, wondering how he was going to get her past that scene down there. But Officer Sweda was there at the bottom of the stairs. She almost burst into tears when she saw him come out of the room with the little girl alive and well, and then Sweda took the little girl from him, held her so she couldn't see the carnage, and got her outside, away from the horror.

It couldn't have been more than ten or fifteen minutes he'd been inside, but there was a crowd here now.

He took a few minutes on the radio to call for the Sexual Violence Resource Team from Mankato—that little girl and her dad were going to need all the counseling they could get. And then he checked on the fixed-wing plane from the State Patrol. It was on its way, maybe five or ten more minutes. And the mobile crime unit from St. Paul was on its way, too. And his buddy Jon Hamner from the BCA was on his way, too. He hadn't heard from Robert Andersen from the DBI office in Minneapolis, but he had to be coming, too, all of them heading this way, all these different parts of the team, all aimed toward this farmhouse stuck out in the middle of nowhere. Everyone too late, too damn late, so that all they could do was work on stopping this son of a bitch before he could do this again.

Lying there, next to the body, a handful of those little beads like there'd been at the last place, that farm home in Good Thunder—little bits of polished stone like the last time, tiny cubes of stone with a hole through them. Marble, the forensic guys said, from a necklace of some kind. Real pretty lying there, a little message of some kind that he hadn't figured out yet.

He went back inside, took one more look around. Sure enough, near the kitchen door, another long strand of black hair, just like the last time. From a wig, had to be, since it was woman's hair and nothing else fit the profile for a woman doing this.

Profile. Yeah, that was another call he had to make, get the BCA profilers working on this thing, now. They'd come out here, take a look around, and start to build up their best guess on the person who could do something like this—their childhood, where they were from, how many siblings, damn near how they wore their hair and brushed their teeth. They did good work, those profilers, and Lord knows he needed their help on this. He needed everyone's help.

He came back outside, the black hair and marble beads in plastic Baggies that he put into his car. He started talking to Sweda and the other uniform officers. In five minutes he heard more than he wanted to. The perp had managed to get through the woods and out onto the paved road; they had tracks through the new snow that made that clear. The tracks were from the kind of boot a woman would wear, a high heel on it, so there were two prints at each step, the front part and the heel mark, clear as a bell.

But the trail disappeared at the road. A car parked there? Maybe, though there were no tire tracks on the shoulder—and not much shoulder there anyway, with the piled drifts.

There was one intersection down there, though, another half-mile. If he'd walked that far—Finnegan just couldn't believe it was a woman—in a hurry, there was room there to park a car and get away from the scene. That had to be it.

As he was talking to the officers, taking a few notes down, thinking it all through, another patrol car pulled up. It was the little girl's father, here before the body had been removed. He'd been at a co-op meeting, getting ready to hear the news on price supports this year for corn and soybeans. And now this.

He could barely stand when they helped him out. Staggered by the enormity of what was happening, by the sheer viciousness, the random cruelty of it, he took help from one of the officers to walk over to the van where his daughter sat, keeping warm and out of the weather.

The two of them embraced, a hug that would make you weep to see. Finnegan walked that way; he had a question or two for the guy. He'd go easy, very easy, but, for the record, he had to ask.

As he approached them the little girl pointed to Finnegan and whispered quietly to her dad. He turned to look. "You the one who found my daughter?"

Finnegan nodded. "I'm Detective Finnegan, sir. I have a few questions for you when you're ready?"

"Ready?" The thought was irrelevant, just bounced around there in the rising vapor from their conversation. "Ready? How, how could this happen? What's gone wrong with the world? How could you . . . ?"

"I don't know sir. That's why I have to . . ."

"How?" he asked again. "I mean, why? Who would . . . I mean, why?"

There was no answer to that. Not yet, Finnegan thought. But he was going to find one, though, no matter what it took. Somebody had to stop this monster. For now, all he could do was stare at the man, then turn away to walk back toward the scene.

His cellular phone beeped at him. It was Jim Thompson, a guy who normally didn't get involved in homicide but had been pulled in to help.

Listen, Dan," Thompson said. "We got some interesting information on those pieces of marble, the ones from the Good Thunder crime scene."

"Yeah, Jim, there's more of them here, too. Ten of them."

"That's a decade, then."

"A decade?"

"Yeah. Ten Hail Marys. A decade."

"Hail Marys. What the hell?" Then it hit him. Of course. "They're rosary beads, right?"

"You got it. We got lucky. One of the women in Forensics is Catholic, a serious Catholic, and with a last name of O'Mahoney."

"So?"

"So, she visited Ireland last summer. Went to Galway, she said, and loved the cathedral there. Went to Mass, had her confession heard, the whole Catholic thing?"

"Come on, Jim; just get to it."

"All right. Turns out the cathedral is built of Connemara marble, from a place not too far away, up in the mountains. She went there. They got a gift shop. She bought a rosary. They don't retail them, just special rosaries sold only in that gift shop. She had it in her purse today, saying rosaries for her mom, who's in a bad way."

"And the rosary's got the same damn beads as these we have?"

He could almost hear Thompson nodding his head at the other end. "Exactly the same. Whoever got these beads bought them from that gift shop in Connemara."

"Well, that's something to work on, Jim, thanks. And thank her for noticing."

"I already have," he said, and hung up.

Well, then, Finnegan thought. Walter Arndt was Catholic, or at least had sent his daughter and son to Mankato Catholic High. But had he traveled to Ireland? Ought to be easy enough to find out.

And if he hadn't, that sure pointed the finger in a definite

direction, because there was one guy who Finnegan figured had
to have deep Irish connections. The missing priest. Father Murphy, Fr. James T. Murphy, the one who liked to travel home to
the Auld Sod every few years, connecting with his roots in Ireland. In Connemara, maybe? Finnegan didn't know, but he sure
as hell was going to find out.

ICE MEN

Lake Minnetoksak looked like its own small town in the thin sunlight of morning. A month of hard, cold weather had brought out a couple of hundred ice shacks, the smoke from their stoves and heaters curling up for a hundred feet or so before layering out to form a little roof of smoky air that hovered over the lake.

Finnegan knew he needed the day off. Four weeks since the St. Peter murder of that poor woman, and they hadn't made any progress on it beyond making a firm connection to the previous two murders. The media had finally figured out it was a serial case but hadn't quite settled on a name for it. The *Mankato Free Press* wanted to name them the Intruder Murders. The *Star*, up in Minneapolis, seemed to be lobbying for the Hand Man Murderer, since Pauline Delgado, a good reporter who covered the cops for that paper, had picked up on the right-hand thing. The *Star's* competition, the *Pioneer Press* in St. Paul, seemed content with the vague Southern Minnesota Murderer.

In a few days, Finnegan figured, the FBI would give it a label that would stick—Intruder or Hand Man, one or the other, since the bureau liked the catchy names that grabbed the public's attention. Never doubt the FBI's ability to grab all the publicity it could find, he'd learned over the years—even when that media grab got in the way of good police work.

They did, at least, have another suspect, a transvestite from the Twin Cities gay-bar scene who liked to dress in drag. He had a rap sheet two pages long, mostly for possession—crack and crank and, twice, high-quality heroin. He'd been a suspect in armed robberies—cases where a visiting businessman thought he was a woman, a hooker, and paid to take her up to his room, where things got ugly. An accomplice showed up claiming to be her pimp, and before the john could figure out what was going on he'd be tied up and robbed. Lucky to be alive, really.

They hadn't managed to connect any of the evidence to this guy but were keeping an eye on him. He fit a lot of what the profilers were saying. A few days after the St. Peter murder he'd been in the Lighted Tree bar in St. Paul, bragging about committing it. At the bar he'd been dressed as a woman, wearing bright red lipstick and a wig with long black hair, so maybe this was the guy. The pieces just about fit, and if they could find the guy's wig they could maybe match up the hairs with the ones from the scene. Plus, the guy had disappeared now, and that made sense, too. The bulletins were out, so maybe somebody would find him.

In Finnegan's mind this guy was number two on the list, though, with Father Murphy at number one and, hell, poor old Walter Arndt still in the running. Arndt and Murphy were still missing, but each had a solid connection, the one with the rosary beads, the other with those shoe prints.

In fact, in the back of his mind Finnegan was wondering if maybe old Walter didn't have something to do with the missing priest Father Murphy and the rosary beads were a plant or maybe just of a kind of bragging. Or hell, maybe it was the two of them working together. Outrageous to think that, but this was no time to get caught thinking inside the box—anything was possible.

They'd found out some ugly new things about Father Murphy, most of it rumor about his sexual preferences—men, apparently, and the younger the better. He was no pedophile, apparently, but had a liking for the college boys. No real proof had ever come to light about that, but assume the rumors were true and it threw a whole new look onto everything. Finnegan wondered if Walter Arndt maybe wasn't a real sicko and he'd run into Murphy at just the wrong moment and that was it for the good father. He'd run that one past the profiler from the State guys up in St. Paul and they hadn't gone for it—wrong kind of sexual attraction, they said. Still, it was a thought.

One of many. Way too many. All thoughts and guesses and nothing solid, nothing tangible. It was frustrating as hell, and he'd been at it all day long, every day of the week, until it was starting to go blurry. There'd been stories in the papers talking all about the police frustration, stories full of the usual half-baked guesses by the kid reporters who passed for journalists these days. Finnegan had been quoted in those stories a whole lot more than he liked, and all he could say was that they had some good leads and they were following up on them. The typical bullshit.

So a day off. One day, all day, just sit and drop a line into a hole in the ice and fish. Perfect.

The lake was amazing. There were traffic cones marking off what passed as streets and some of the shacks had TV antennae sprouting from the roof and looked like they had at least three rooms: temporary mansions out here on the ice, all the comforts of home for the man who spends way too much time ice fishing.

Finnegan sat on the passenger side of Melchior's Ford pickup and marveled at the whole frozen little world that existed out here as they drove down onto the plowed roadway and headed toward Mel's shack, over near the southwestern shoreline, a good five hundred yards from where they were now.

"I had no idea that it was like this, Mel. It looks like a whole city out here."

Mel nodded. "Hasn't always been this bad. Used to be, I could come out here and see just another dozen shacks or so. We all knew each other, back then."

"The fishing any good, really, with all these people out here?"

"Not bad. Most of these are weekenders, down from the Cities, so they're not around that much. Plus, to tell you the truth, they're pretty bad fishermen, most of them. Hard-bottom guys."

"Hard-bottom guys?"

"Guys too stupid to realize there ain't any fish over a hard bottom. You got to get your shack on top of a spot with a shelf on the bottom, or a deep hole, or maybe some snag down there—

an old tree or a truck tire—so there's somewhere for the fish to hide or you won't catch a thing. These city guys want it the easy way. I guess they figure you'll never lose a hook over hard bottom. Can't catch a damn thing that way, but maybe catching fish ain't at the top of their list."

Finnegan looked at two guys out in front of a shack sitting on canvas chairs and passing a thermos back and forth—probably Irish coffee in there or maybe just some Jack Daniel's. They wouldn't mind if the fish never bit. He chuckled as they passed by them, said, "See what you mean, Mel."

Melchior looked at them, gave a dismissive grunt as they passed them by, then drove on for another few hundred yards and pulled the Ford up behind a smallish shack, built of plywood. "This one's mine. We call this kind a hard-side. Built her myself, out in the barn, 'bout fifteen years ago. Bring her out in the middle of December, most winters, and set her up here for the season." He shrugged. "Keeps the wind out, mostly."

It did a lot more than that. Finnegan, walking inside, saw that Mel had it divided into two rooms. The larger room was for storage and had a handheld ice auger, an ice spud with a chisel-like blade on the end, a couple of tip-up rigs, a pair of poles with a foot or two of fishing rod attached to a wooden handle, and some neatly stacked rope and small-link chain.

In the other room was a small Coleman heater, a portable radio set on a fold-out table, a large cooler, and two fold-down canvas chairs, opened and ready next to a five-gallon aluminum pail set into the ice.

They got comfortable on the chairs, Melchior opening the large thermos he'd brought along and pouring them out a cup of thick, black coffee, steam billowing out as he poured in the sub-zero cold.

Then, while Finnegan started in on the coffee, wondering where he was going to have to go to relieve himself when the coffee kicked in, Melchior wrestled the bucket back and forth until, with a sharp crack, it broke free. He pulled it up and there was their hole in the ice, almost ready for them.

"Got to open that up some," Mel said, rising to walk into the other room. He came back with the auger and started sawing away at the hole, clearing away the new ice at the bottom, widening the hole as he went. He stopped for a second, looked around the room. "You know, this whole hard-side folds up on these hinges here," he said, pointing out a pair of hinges at the top of each wall. "Ice gets thin and dirty come March, I can have the whole thing folded up and off the ice in half an hour."

Finnegan was looking around in open admiration. "It's really something, Mel. How often you come out here? Melissa made it sound like it was almost every day."

Mel laughed. "That girl always did exaggerate. No, I make it once during the week, usually, sometimes twice. And then sometimes on weekends, though it gets too damn crazy out here for me sometimes on a Saturday, what with all the guys from the Cities showing up all morning long, spooking the fish."

"What do you catch?"

Mel shrugged. "Bluegill, crappie, a lot of perch."

"Good eating?"

He nodded. "And there's a lunker northern pike down there. Bought a license mainly to get him this year. Gonna do it this winter sometime, I swear."

Finnegan laughed. "How big you think he is?"

"Twenty, maybe twenty-five pounds. Hell, maybe more. He broke a twenty-pound test line last winter on me. Ran off with it. I fought him a bit and then, snap, that was that. Broke it right off with one quick twist."

Finnegan watched the expression on Mel's face as he told the story. He was smiling, certainly, and with his eyes almost closed remembering that struggle, picturing it clearly. "Hell, Dan, he might be forty pounds. Do you think?" And then he chuckled, a low, dry rumble. You didn't often hear any kind of laughter from Melchior. Something about being out here on the ice seemed to brighten him up. "Here," he said, and walked over to the cooler, opened it, pulled out a shiner. "Give this a try, maybe you'll catch the son of a bitch on your first try."

He hooked the shiner just beneath the dorsal fin. The pinfish was dead, but the cooler had kept it from freezing—seemed odd to use a cooler to keep things warm, but ice fishing, Finnegan supposed, must be filled with those contradictions.

He scooted his chair over near the hole, dropped the shiner down in, letting fifteen or twenty feet of line go, and sat back to wait. "How deep is it?"

"We're right at the edge of a hole here. Depending on whether you drop it, about thirty feet or, just next to it, a steep drop down to a hundred feet."

"Those big pike like hanging around the edge of a deep hole, right? I read that somewhere."

Melchior nodded. "Yep. Right on the edge, so they can drop down into it if they get spooked." He paused, looked down into the hole. "Water never turns over down there, you know. Cold, just above freezing year-round. And calm. No currents down in that hole, no springs. Just that deep hole gouged out by some glacier a few hundred thousand years back. All that time, since the glaciers melted away, that hole, that water, has just been sitting there."

Finnegan watched his friend say all that, as much as he'd heard him say at one time maybe ever. Hearing it, he thought maybe for the first time he had a little bit of a grip on what Melchior's sculptures were all about. All those weird insects and wild, huge lizards and the enormous skeletal mastodon that he'd built for the science museum up in St. Paul. All of those were getting at that same thing as what he'd just been going on about—the Ice Age and those dinosaurs and lizards and huge insects that had been around here then.

"What are you working on now, Mel? What kind of sculpture?"

"Couple of things for a new office building over in Rochester. Pair of birds, big eagle-looking things, wings outstretched. You know, talons down and all the way out like they were swooping in to catch a mouse or snatch some fish right out of the water." For the second time in ten minutes, he laughed. "Now *there's* a way to catch that damn lunker pike."

Finnegan shifted on his seat, trying to find a way to make it comfortable. "You know, I'd love to see you at work someday, watch how you make those things."

"Hell, just come on by. I'm working on something special when I can these days. Big old thing; be my masterpiece, maybe, if I can get it right. Why don't you come by this weekend, maybe, and take a look at it? I'll show you how it's done, maybe let you do let a little welding yourself."

Finnegan tried shifting again, but it was useless; he wasn't going to get comfortable and that was that. "That'd be great, Mel, thanks."

"And it won't be so cold in there, either, Dan. And if you move around like that so much, it won't matter, won't be any fish to spook."

Finnegan laughed. "Oh, hell, I'm sorry, Mel. Just trying to get comfortable." But comfort, of course, wasn't what it was all about.

After a while, Finnegan did manage to settle in some, but a few hours later they'd given up on the pike, scaled down their bait and their line, and come up with a panful of perch that would make for a good lunch back in town. Finnegan knew Mel was disappointed it had come down to this, but for Finnegan the truth was that he didn't mind at all. At least he was catching something, and the action helped keep him warm. Sitting there on that folding chair he could feel the cold from the ice sneaking right up through the soles of his boots, through both layers of socks and right into his feet. His face was numb, even inside the shack, and that combined with his freezing feet had him ready to quit, though there were hours of fishing left.

When Mel got up and offered to auger out another hole, outside the shack, some twenty yards away, near where he figured the far edge of the deep hole was, Finnegan insisted on helping. A little activity ought to warm him up, and cutting out a hole beat the hell out of sitting still and freezing to death.

But cutting out a hole turned out to be a one-man job, and standing out in the subzero breeze that had picked up with the rising sun just added to his misery. He decided to go for a walk while Mel cut the hole and walked off, stomping his feet to get the blood moving, pounding his arms against his chest, and clapping his gloved hands together.

It helped a little and got him around past some of the other shacks, most of them empty on this Wednesday morning in early January.

In fifteen minutes' time he was clear across to a different shore of the lake and a little warmed up from the walk. He turned to look back and get his bearings. Mel's pickup was hard to miss, so that was where the shack was.

He headed back, cutting off the angle a bit, almost getting to shore near a little peninsula that jutted out into the lake, its bare trees looking like they were marching across the lake on their own, the soil beneath them hidden in snow that blended in with the lake's covering.

He felt pretty good, getting the blood moving as he walked, his boots crunching through the hard snow that sat for a good foot or more on top of the lake's thick ice. It was absolutely quiet except for that steady crunch—a perfect winter day, really, the cloudless pale blue of the morning sky, a light breeze at his back now so his cheeks weren't stinging with it.

He thought about the murders, wondered what it was he was missing, what he hadn't thought about, what it was he'd overlooked. Was this transvestite from the Cities the guy, and it wasn't Walter Arndt or Father Murphy after all? Maybe. But no matter what the profilers from the BCA were saying, this guy just didn't sit right, somehow. What the hell was he doing way down here, and way out on some farm?

The wounds in those women looked like cuts from a deer knife; would that guy have one? Maybe, but he sure didn't sound like the hunting type. Well, hell, if they caught up with the guy they'd know soon enough. The angle of the wounds looked like they'd been done by a left-hander; that was one thing they could check on right away.

He kept thinking it through as he walked, lost in thought. In five minutes he was at the peninsula, rounding its front edge. Across the way he could hear an engine start up. He stopped, looked, and saw Mel's pickup pull away from the shack. What was that about?

He rounded that edge, saw where the snow had drifted differently on the far side, a little deeper here through some vagary of the winter wind, the snow sculpted in a kind of frozen bowl after last week's thaw and this week's plunging temperatures. He took one step that way to take a closer look.

And felt the ice beneath him give, settle a bit. He stopped. There was an audible rumble, a sharp crack. Oh, Jesus, and then the ice gave way beneath him and he was, in an instant, plunging down into the water.

He found bottom almost immediately, just six or seven feet down, muck and silt, sticky on his boots, not frozen hard but clinging, claylike, to his feet.

He kicked against it, kicked again, and then, trying to kick again, suddenly realized how incredibly cold the water was. It felt alive, a monster crushing him in an icy vise, surrounding him, suffocating him, making it impossible to think, to move.

The seconds took forever. He shoved softly with his feet, too tired, too crushed, to do more. He could see the sky above him, the surface of the lake just a foot away.

His feet came free; slowly, achingly slowly, he rose, a few inches, a few inches more, toward that light. And found it, came gasping to the surface, threw his arms out on the ice, broke through, threw them out again, and it held. He was out, and alive.

The shore was just behind him. All he had to do was get there; ten feet away was all. Get there, stagger up on the land, and be alive.

But he couldn't turn, couldn't think, tried to yell for help, but nothing would come out. Sweet Jesus, it was cold.

He heard a voice calling his name. Looked up. It was Melchior, ten yards away, climbing out of the pickup.

"Dan! Can you grab this?" He held the rope, coiled.

Finnegan nodded. Hell, yes, he could grab it, *would* grab it.

Melchior threw it and it uncoiled as it came, the rope spinning out across the ice, skittering toward him, a perfect toss. Just grab it.

It was the hardest physical thing he'd ever done. Harder than football practice at Mankato State all those years ago, taking hits as a tight end coming across the middle on those look-in passes. Harder than boot camp, harder than life in 'Nam, harder than damn anything. Just to reach out a few inches and grab the end of that rope, to hang on to it, took more than he thought he had. But he managed, seconds ticking by as he got it done and Mel pulled him clear, up on the thicker ice, away from the freezing water.

In seconds, Mel had him in the cab of the pickup, was helping him strip out of the cold, wet clothes with the heater cranked up full, and a half hour later he was fine, sipping coffee, wrapped in blankets back at the shack, warmed, laughing about it, thanking Melchior again and again. He owed this man his life.

APPROACHING COLD FRONTS

She was sweating under the long academic gown. To the west, a sharp line of leaden clouds announced the approaching cold front all the weather forecasters were talking about—rain and temperatures dropping into the high thirties overnight, a high no better than fifty-five tomorrow. But Melissa had no complaints; for the moment it was sunshine and seventy-five degrees in the middle of December, and fifty-five above beat Minnesota's forty-five below any old day.

She sat on the final seat of a long, neat row of folding chairs that marched across the crown of Triton Field with forty other ribbons of similar chairs. Three seats away was Bo, who was graduating three semesters late but proud of himself nonetheless. Melissa, graduating a semester early and already admitted to grad school in the English Department, looked his way. He grinned. From his perspective, he'd worked hard to get here and now he could go home to St. Kitts and start working in the family business—the resort would be his someday, he knew, and now it was time to learn the ropes.

Behind Melissa, some ten rows up in the cheering section, sat her father and Dan Finnegan, smiling, proud of her. It was nice to see how they'd become such good friends. Her dad needed a friend. She didn't think he'd ever had one until Finnegan.

She talked on the phone with her father once a month or so, and that seemed often enough for him. When she got him going he seemed to like to share little stories about his latest successes with metal monsters and insects. He'd sold a giant grasshopper to a downtown skyscraper in St. Louis, making more money off that one sale than he'd made in two years of farming sugar beets back in the old days.

She shook her head to think of that. Her father a famous sculptor? Life was weird sometimes, that was the only explanation. At least it gave him something they could share and talk about over the phone.

It was Finnegan who called her every week and kept her up-to-date on Mankato's gossip and the dependably wicked weather. It was always good to hear his voice, and it was interesting how somewhere along the line they'd both gotten past the grief of Danny's death to move toward a different kind of relationship, Finnegan somehow becoming a sort of second father, an odd version of the relationship she might have had with him if Danny hadn't died and all those long-ago plans had fallen into place.

Often when they talked the subject of Danny never came up at all, and Finnegan seemed interested and supportive when she told him about Bo and his ongoing string of proposals.

Bo had asked her half a dozen times again to get married, and always she said no. It had become, over time, a kind of game they played, one that was easy enough for both of them to laugh at a bit. He had his dream of expanding Palmer's to a chain of resorts in the Leeward Islands, first with a new one on Nevis, just to the south of St. Kitts, and then with another on Antigua, and then one on Statia, another on Saba. He talked about it all the time and kept saying how Melissa just had to be part of that warm and sunny future.

But she'd never said yes. She liked Bo Palmer well enough, she supposed. Maybe, in fact, she loved him. It was certainly true that for the past two years she hadn't dated anyone else, and they'd even gone down to St. Kitts a half-dozen times now for long weekends and twice for two-week stays in the summer. She loved it there, loved basking in the heat watching the breakers tumble in over the reef line. The food, the people, the weather, the town of Basseterre, Brimstone Fort and its history, the way the mountain tumbled down into the sea—she loved all of that, felt a deep connection to the Caribbean that must surely have come from her mother.

But still she said no each time he asked her, always putting him off. And they'd never made love—for all this time now he'd never even asked, the two of them in a silent plot to somehow save her virginity.

There were times, too, when she still thought about Summer and The Kiss, though all that took place years ago, almost so distant from the place she was in now that it felt like some other, older, colder world. For a while, she and Summer had talked on the phone some and had written back and forth, just good friends. They'd even both gotten E-mail addresses when that whole thing first hit. But then they'd just sort of slowly stopped communicating, drifting apart, that whole moment of their history slipping away from them, unattended.

Melissa knew girls now who said they were lesbians. Two of the girls on the basketball team admitted they liked girls better, and a few of the other athletes in soccer and in track and field had made it pretty clear that's how they felt, too.

But she didn't feel that way herself, or didn't *think* she did. She didn't, in fact, know exactly how she felt about sex at all. It was really just sort of the strangest distance from it—like it was something that was supposed to matter to her a lot, but it just didn't. Did this mean she was frigid? Some kind of weird asexual creature like they'd talked about in her biology class—reproducing by splitting apart like a cell or something? God, what a thought that was: Melissa O'Malley, practitioner of sexual neurogenesis. Divide and conquer, that was her.

She tried to concentrate a little on the commencement speaker, some politician from Tallahassee who wanted to be governor. It was hopeless, though. The weather was too nice, and with that cold front coming, she and everyone else in the stadium just wanted to savor this moment in the sunshine and get on with things. She wanted to walk up that ramp and across the temporary stage and get that hard-earned diploma before the rains came.

Bo leaned past the people between them to whisper, "Is this guy boring or what?"

She smiled at him. She'd thought about it all, about the whole relationship, while she'd been getting ready this morning, leaning over the bathroom sink to take a good look at herself before starting with the concealer. The old Melissa hadn't bothered with makeup or worried much about her clothes. But a couple of years of dating Bo Palmer had helped to change that. She knew now what money looked like, and that look started with the face and worked its way down.

Her shower was done, her hair dried, sprayed, and ready. She'd turned a bit left and then right, getting the lighting so that she could see her flaws. A few blackheads, but nothing too serious, thank god for small favors. Her period would be back again for another visit next week and her face would make its monthly eruption, blackheads and pimples everywhere. She'd thought that getting into her twenties would put an end to that, but it hadn't. She'd lost a few more pounds and while she wasn't down where she really wanted to be, she knew she looked as good as she ever had—the frumpy jock on the basketball team, the girl who wore T-shirts and baggy shorts and flip-flops, was gone. This was the new Melissa.

She'd started in with the concealer, three or four dots of it under each eye, then rubbing it in with little circles, spreading it out from there, laying down the foundation for a face that could launch, or maybe sink, a thousand ships. It was supposed to prevent wrinkles from forming, too, when she got older. She'd read that in *Cosmo* and liked that thought, keeping her face frozen in its current youth.

After that had come the powder, smoothing everything out. She'd patted it on, then worked to perfect it for a few minutes, blending it in.

Then the eyes: the delicate work of eyeliner first, along the bottom of the eyelid, at the base of the lashes. Then, carefully, a thin layer of eyeliner across the top of the eyelid. This was always tricky, since it meant working with one eye shut. Then came the mascara on both lashes.

She'd stepped back, taken a look. Adequate. She came in closer and looked again: a little blush across the cheekbones would help, bringing them out some. She brushed that on.

She paused in her labors, looked away for a minute, then looked in the mirror again for a fresh perspective. Good. Not great, maybe, but good.

Then the lipstick, Clinique's Rum Raisin, first with some lip liner to define the lips, then filling in from there. A little pat with some tissue, a little moistening, and there it was.

On her bed, laid out, ironed earlier and ready, were the black Gap jeans and a black Gap blouse over the white halter top that looked great with her hair, still long. They were staying in town tonight, eating a late dinner at Gennaro's and then going out, probably to the Undertow.

She put the jeans on, slipping into them easily, standing on one leg and sliding the other in. Last year she'd always had to go through the lie-on-the-bed struggle to get them zipped up, trying to fit into her size 8s. Now, after all the dieting, these same pants even felt a little baggy. She'd have to buy some new ones, tighter, as soon as she could afford them.

She'd thought she would gain weight after basketball season ended and she quit playing every day. Instead, focused on dieting and slimming down, she was losing it—fifteen pounds so far and more yet to come. It felt good to be a little thinner, and Bo made it clear all the time how much he liked it. It was funny to know she wasn't in nearly as good a shape as she'd been, but somehow she looked better, thinner, more attractive.

She walked over to the door to her room, shut it so she could take a look at herself in the full-length mirror on the back of the door. It would do, she'd decided.

At Gennaro's, they'd talked about graduating, about their lives. She'd expected Bo to propose again, and knew she'd laugh with him at it and then put him off once again. Did she love him? She kept asking herself that question, and all she could answer was that she didn't think so, at least not the way she thought love was supposed to be. She liked him all right, liked him a lot. But love? Hard to say.

All through dinner he'd been grinning at her, like he had something up his sleeve. She expected him to ask her again, and she wondered how she'd answer this time. But he hadn't asked. Instead, he'd talked about moving back to St. Kitts to work for the resort with his father. All day, every day, in paradise, he said.

Then he grinned again. "You ready for a big surprise?"

"Depends," she'd said, smiling back.

"Just wait," he said. "Just wait." And that was all he'd say about it. She figured she knew what it was.

The row ahead of her stirred, rose, and then started walking toward the stage. Moments later, Melissa's row did the same. It all happened in a daze. She walked across the stage like it was some out-of-body experience, as if she was watching herself wear a goofy wide grin as she walked toward the university provost and he handed her the scrolled diploma, shook her hand quickly, and got her moving again, off to the other side, down that ramp, and back into the real world, and her folding chair, and a smile a few minutes later from Bo as he walked by, waving his diploma and grinning widely. She grinned back.

Later, she stood outside the stadium with her two father figures, letting them both take pictures.

She was taking a picture of the two of them standing next to a palm tree when someone grabbed her from behind, strong hands gripping her shoulders.

"Hey, Melissa. We did it."

She knew whose hands those had to be to. "Hi, Bo," she said, and turned her head to smile at him. His father and stepmother, Henry and Nancy Palmer, were there with him, reaching out to shake her hand.

Just about every time she met Bo's parents Henry Palmer was busy on the phone, chain-smoking his way through some long-distance business transaction. But today, here, there was no cell phone and, for the moment, no cigarette. He treated her like they were old pals. "Congratulations, Melissa," he said, and then tugged her to him for a hug. He coughed a few times, caught his breath. "We're really proud of you."

She introduced them to her father and Finnegan. "Mr. Palmer, Mrs. Palmer, this is my father, and this is..." She hesitated, wondered how to introduce Finnegan. Her friend? A kind of uncle? Her dead fiancé's father? She chose neutral ground. "This is my father's friend, Dan Finnegan."

There were handshakes all around, and a few minutes of proud conversation from the parents.

Henry Palmer, despite his expensive suit and perfect tan, was friendly and warm with Melchior and Dan Finnegan. If he noticed their clothing, both of them dressed in rumpled JCPenney suits, he certainly didn't seem to care. Instead, he was all smiles and full of praise. Melissa thought he looked thinner, maybe too thin, and that smile looked tired. But then he was *always* working. Bo always said his dad was too cheap to hire the help he needed.

She'd wondered about that over the past couple of years—wondered just how well the resort was doing, how much money the Palmers really had. They *seemed* wealthy and they *acted* wealthy, but every time she visited the resort it looked more run-down than it should, and there was never enough staff, and it looked to her like corners were being cut everywhere, from the restaurant's cutting back its hours to the worn marcite surface in the pool, which looked worse each time she saw it.

From Bo she kept hearing little rumblings about money troubles, kept hearing that tourism on the island was down and so the resort's total number of bed-nights was down, too, for the fifth or sixth year in a row.

Bo seemed to like it that way. He saw it as an opportunity to come in and take over and bring back the family wealth, repeating the way his father had done it—starting without much and working his way up, doing what he had to do to make his millions the hard way. That's why a man born and raised in the Midwest of the U.S. now lived and worked down in the islands where they didn't tax him much, and that's why he worked way too hard himself.

"Mel," Henry said to her dad, "Nancy and I have had the chance to get to know your daughter a bit over the past year or two, and we think she's really something special. You've done a great job with this girl."

Melissa watched her father's face as he went through a complex series of emotions in response to that. On the one hand, he seemed proud of her and happy to hear such praise. On the other hand, though, quiet, careful Melchior clearly heard the unsaid message behind those words. These people wanted to take his daughter away from him.

It wasn't something they'd talked about a lot, Melchior's desire to have his daughter come home after she got her degree. But his hints on the subject had always been there, his assumption clear to Melissa right through the four years she'd been in school. Just a couple of months ago she'd had a long chat in the office of her favorite teacher, Lawrence Morgan, the only published novelist on the faculty, talking about her future now that she was going to graduate, and he'd told her he thought she was grad-student material, that she could handle the work and get a master's in English lit maybe, or even a doctorate, become a teacher, spend her whole life on books and teaching. If she wanted to keep up with basketball she could go into coaching, Morgan said. It might be a perfect fit for someone like her—the academic and athlete's life all rolled into one. It sounded to Melissa like a good way to go.

She'd liked the idea and told her father about it. He'd been quiet, like always, during that phone call, but then, the next time they talked a few weeks later, he'd mentioned that he'd talked to Dan Finnegan about her plans and he'd been talking about the graduate degrees offered right there at home, at Mankato State, up on the hill outside of town.

A few weeks ago she'd gone ahead and sat for the GRE, the big test everyone had to take to get into grad school in English. She'd scored well enough, a 1280, to get into a good grad school somewhere—her grades certainly measured up, too, with a 3.75 out of 4.0.

Grad school was one thing, Melchior's expression seemed to

be saying as Melissa watched his face. But leaving for the Caribbean was something else altogether. He gave Henry Palmer a thin smile, said softly, "I'm real proud of her, that's for sure."

"As you should be; she's really special." Palmer reached out to take Melissa's hand, squeezed it, coughed once or twice, and then smiled. "We've come to think of her almost as part of the family."

Melissa looked at Bo, who rolled his eyes. His dad was putting it on pretty thick.

Palmer turned to face Melchior and Dan Finnegan. "Actually, gentlemen, I have a job offer of my own that I'd like to extend to Melissa, and this would be a perfect time to do that, since she's surrounded here by the people she loves."

Whoa. A job offer? People she loved? Bo? His dad? Wait a minute.

But Henry Palmer went on, unstoppable. "You know I run a business down in the Leeward Islands, on St. Kitts, a little resort there. Bo will be coming to work for me now as vice president for operations."

He coughed, a loose rattle of a cough that seemed to take his breath for a moment before he caught it, smiled, and went on: "I've been thinking for some time that we needed to get rid of our advertising and public relations firm and bring that all in-house. It would save us quite a bit of money, frankly, if we found the right person, someone who could do it all for us, handle the ads and their placement, put out brochures, write press releases, talk to the press and the travel writers who come through—everything.

"It's a job that needs someone with a lot of energy, and a lot of talent. Bo has been telling me for the past year that Melissa is the one for the job, and I think he's right."

He turned to face Melissa, smiled hugely. "Melissa? Are you interested? We can start you at thirty-five thousand a year in U.S. dollars with a nice benefit package."

She looked at Bo. "This is your big surprise?"

He grinned. "Pretty great, huh? Sunshine, beaches; the Caribbean, Melissa, coming back to live in the islands. You know it's paradise, Melissa. You know you love it there."

Paradise. Warm paradise. Oh, my goodness. It was tempting, no doubt about it. "Mr. Palmer, I'm, I'm stunned, really. I don't know what to say."

"Well, of course." He smiled broadly, coughed again. "A simple 'yes' would do nicely."

She turned to look at her father, at Finnegan. She couldn't read anything in their faces beyond surprise and maybe, in her father, a certain dismay.

"We'll fly you home for a couple of weeks twice a year, Melissa, how's that?"

"Really?"

Palmer smiled again. "Really. But not during the winter and spring; that's our high season and we'll need you around then, OK?"

"Daddy? Mr. Finnegan?" But they were no help. Still, she hesitated. What about grad school? She'd told Bo about those plans and he'd seemed to go right along with them—even met her after the GRE to take her out to lunch. Had he known about all this then and just been faking that supportive attitude, or was this as new to him as it was to Melissa?

She turned toward Bo, but his handsome face wore only a grin. He thought he'd done a very funny thing here, springing it on her like this. Just like him, try to change her life as a kind of practical joke.

Still. It *was* the Caribbean, palm trees and beaches and warm breezes all the time. She thought about those posters on her bedroom wall back in Mankato, of pretending she was there, looking at them on a freezing winter night with some Bob Marley on the CD player. She'd never have to be cold again. "Can I think about it overnight?"

The way she phrased that they all knew she'd made up her mind. Palmer smiled, agreed.

A few minutes later, walking with her father and Finnegan toward their rental car and the promised dinner out at Shanahan's, the first spattering of cold rain from the cold front hit them. They didn't have umbrellas ready and started walking fast and then running for the car. There, only a little damp, Melissa looked out the window to see the gray roiling clouds from the cold front as they started to block the sun. It'd be cold tonight after the rain was done. Nothing like Minnesota, but cold enough for jackets, cold enough to see your breath. She shivered in her gown.

Her father put an arm around her. "Never thought you'd wind up back down there where your mother was from, girl. I figured you for a Minnesota girl."

"Me, too, Daddy."

He stopped, held her at arm's length. "But you're a big girl now, Melissa. You got to do what you want. You got to make your own way."

He was, she realized, being brave about this in his own way, giving her permission to go down there or come home and go to grad school—whatever she chose.

She looked at Finnegan. He smiled, shrugged. Her call.

Well, all right then, she'd make the decision on her own. But after dinner. She laughed, tugged on both their arms. "C'mon, you two grumps. This is my Big Day. I graduated! Let's get to that restaurant and enjoy ourselves, OK?"

They both nodded, and so she grinned in return as she led them away to dinner and, later, a few toasts to the new, happy life that was headed her way.

ST. CHRISTOPHER

St. Christopher, long called simply St. Kitts, is aptly known as The
Mother Colony of the West Indies, for this is where European
colonization began in the Indies.
—St. Kitts tourist brochure

The high, rounded bulk of Sir Timothy's Hill separates St.
Kitt's isolated southern peninsula from the fertile, prosperous
northern side of the island.

Melissa stood on her apartment balcony and looked south
toward the hill and beyond, thinking again about graduate school.
To her right, west, was the black sand beach of Frigate Bay. To
her left was North Frigate Bay's white sand on the Atlantic side,
the big combers rolling in as she watched. A salt pond, fed by
the Caribbean at high tide, lay in the middle, barely leaving room
for the lush golf course that Bo's father's money had carved into
the fertile volcanic rock.

A hummingbird, not much bigger than a big bumblebee back
home in Minnesota, zipped Melissa's second-story porch, caught
scent of the bougainvillea and hibiscus she had growing there,
and stopped to hover, a low throb from its wings as it dipped
its long beak down into the bell of the flower and sipped.

It was seven-thirty in the morning: peaceful, quiet, the sun just
coming up over the hills. About four this morning she'd been
awakened by another rumble from Mount Liamuiga, the volcano
that formed the center of the island, but she was getting used to
those, the way, she supposed, people in California must get used
to small earthquakes happening all the time.

The island's beauty was certainly worth the occasional rumble from the old volcano. Even from up here, five hundred feet or more above the water, she could hear the surf coming in, could see the reef she'd snorkeled on once or twice, the black-sand beach where she could lie in the sun and bake, hot right through to the bones, covered in oil like that Jimmy Buffett song.

This was the middle of December and here she was, standing in the morning sun, starting to sweat. God, she loved that, the heat. Back home it was zero and the snow had been on the ground for a month already, with four to go before it melted reluctantly into spring.

Here it was summer. Here it was always summer. The only cold she ever encountered was the office, where the air-conditioning was cranked up so high that she wore a sweater to work. When, that was, they let her work.

The glass door behind her opened. It was Bo, dressed for work in slacks and a blue sport shirt with the Palmer's Resort logo on it. He wore his golf shoes, their metal spikes digging into the carpet as he walked across. They'd had that carpet flown in just for her from North Carolina.

Bo had cared about the carpet back then, a year ago, when he was getting her set up here in this condo, showing her around to everyone, making the situation clear, then introducing her to the public relations staff. Now he wore his golf spikes on that expensive carpet. Another day of doing business on the links.

He was in great shape. He looked better now than when she'd met him, back when he'd swept her off her feet. He'd been a little thin back then, though she hadn't realized it. Now he'd put on weight, most of it muscle. It might go to flab later, but for now his stomach was taut and the outline of his shoulders pushed against the confines of the sport shirt. He'd quit smoking and started lifting weights. Every morning he jogged through the property and every afternoon he played golf with clients and local politicians.

He had two cups of Jamaican Blue Mountain coffee with him, held one out to her, black. His was nearly white with cream and several sugars. She gave him grief about that regularly, about his generally awful diet. He ate too much junk food and counted on all the exercise to burn it off. So far it was working, but still she nagged him.

He smiled at her. "You're up early. Thought I might catch you still in bed."

She smiled at that, at the thought of his catching her in bed. Not all that long ago she thought maybe she wanted to get caught, and by him and in that place. But it hadn't happened, and now she didn't think it would, or should.

She was still a virgin. There'd been some close calls, some times that she thought the moment was right. But it hadn't happened. She wondered, sometimes, if her unwillingness to have sex was part of what kept him attracted to her. He knew she was still a virgin, and how many of those could there be?

She came in from the porch, closed the sliding glass door behind her, and then took the coffee from him, sipped on it as she sat down on the rattan couch with the hibiscus pattern, very tropical, the splash of pinks and reds against the bamboo.

"It's nice here in the mornings. I like to stand here and enjoy it for a while before going in to work."

He shook his head. "Stay here all morning if you want. You know you don't have to work so hard, Melissa. No one's expecting you to work like that, all those hours. Hell, it's been more than a year and you haven't even gone home for a vacation yet."

"I like the work, Bo. I want to do more of it."

He shook his head, offered that pleasant smile that had earned her attention in St. Pete.

"There's a whole staff there for things like brochures and news releases and that sort of shit, Melissa. That's the sort of grunt work Rosemarie is supposed to do. You're the consultant; that's what you get paid for. Consulting. You know, the Big Picture. Not writing copy for brochures."

"That whole staff is two people, Bo. Rosemarie and Sarah. Like everything else at the resort, media relations is understaffed. There's enough work there for five people."

He sighed, forced out that smile one more time.

"I'm not going to argue with you again about this, Melissa.

There isn't any room in the budget for more PR people. Hell, right now there isn't even room in the budget for a manager for the golf course—I'm going to take over that job now, too, until things loosen up some. You know, with Dad's health the way it is, the whole company's on hold."

Bo's father had finally gotten his cough checked out a few months before. Forty years of cigarettes had caught up with him—lung cancer, and caught late. Since then, he'd traveled the route from optimism to despair to acceptance as the cancer spread to the kidneys, the spine, the brain.

It had been tough for Bo, watching his father waste away, trying to do what he could to keep the resort moving forward despite the old man's poor health. Bo, she knew, realized that he had to take over, had to become the man his father had been, come up with financial backing like his father had done back when this all started.

It turned out that wasn't easy, but Bo was trying, bringing in potential partners from the States, from Europe, from the Arab Emirates. It seemed like once a month he had some new possibility on the line.

When, one by one, they didn't quite work out, it just added to Bo's stress level. Watching his father die. Watching the resort die. It was hard, damn hard, and sometimes she thought it was just driving him crazy. At the very least, it made him increasingly difficult to get along with. But she kept trying, kept telling herself that she wanted to help.

"Bo, for just a little bit of money I think we can get the occupancy rate back up to where it belongs. Did you know that the brochure package hasn't been updated in four years? There's nothing in there about the new restaurant, nothing about the children's programs, almost nothing about the snorkeling on the Caribbean side."

He sat down on the rattan chair in the corner. It matched her couch. He sipped on his coffee, ran his hand through his hair. It was starting to thin, and he'd taken to combing it across the top.

"All right, all right," he said, waving at her, asking for mercy. "I just thought I'd mention it, sweetheart, that's all. Look, I've got a round of golf this morning with those investors from South Africa. How about a late lunch. One, maybe one-thirty? Meet you at Cecil's?"

She frowned. "I really shouldn't. I thought if I just made a sandwich here and took it in I could get a few more pages designed."

He shook his head. "I think we should have lunch, Melissa. I think it's important. People are going to start thinking work matters more to you than I do."

"Oh, Bo."

"And I can't afford to have people talking, Melissa. This is a small island; you know how gossip flies around."

"I know, Bo. All right, lunch, at Cecil's. I'll be there for you."

He smiled. "That's my girl. We'll talk about spending some money on improving things, OK? I have a little surprise for you, too. Something I think you'll like."

She nodded, gave him a quick smile back as he stood, walked over to her, leaned down to give her a kiss.

She turned her face up toward him, expecting a quick peck. Instead, he placed his lips to hers, then reached behind her head with his left hand and kissed her with passion, taking her by surprise, holding her to him as his lips, his tongue, claimed her.

It happened so fast, and was so unexpected, that she didn't, she couldn't, react. And then it was over. He pulled back and grinned at her. "Me and you, Melissa. Me and you." And then he gave her a quick peck after all, on her forehead, and walked out, leaving the front door open as he went.

Melissa sat there for a long moment, watching him go. Finally, she stood, shook her head, walked over to shut the door, and then came back inside the living room, sat back down on the small couch, looked out through the porch doors to the scenery beyond.

This was a beautiful place, but she was coming to think that she couldn't stay here. More and more, Bo's behavior was worrying her. It was all little things, like this kiss, but they were adding up. She understood how hard this all was on him, but still, he seemed to be pushing her places she didn't want to go, where she wouldn't go. There was so much tension swirling around that she couldn't stand it.

She loved this island. She felt like she belonged in a place like this, like she could make this home. But that was nonsense if she quit the resort. Without Bo, without his father and the job at the resort, she'd have to leave. Henry Palmer, failing health and troubled finances or not, was too powerful here, knew too many people and pulled too many strings. If she quit his resort she'd find no one else who would hire her.

She felt isolated and knew that was her own fault. It wasn't as if she'd made a lot of friends in her year on the island. Just one, really: Rosemarie, her assistant in media relations for the resort.

Rosie was top-notch. A short, stocky girl with mocha skin and a toothy grin when she smiled, she'd earned her degrees in the States, Rollins College up in Orlando, where she'd done a business bachelor's degree and then followed that with an MBA two years later. Then she'd worked in Orlando in public relations for a few years, even married a guy in the States. When that marriage fell apart, Rosie brought herself back home, where she worked now for a salary that was a fraction of what she was worth. She had the brains and the background to be running this place. Instead, she worked in public relations with the grandiose title of Associate Director of Media Relations.

She was a good writer, and a quick one, and her editing skills were outstanding. Melissa knew that in a fairer world she'd be lucky to be Rosemarie's assistant, not the other way around. But the world wasn't fair, and Melissa was the boss. That much, at least, she had learned from Bo. So, all she could do was try to pay Rosie as much as she could and learn from her while she had the chance.

And Rosie, at least, was willing to talk to her, seemed to understand how things were for Melissa. Several times a week the two of them lunched together.

That was really the extent of their friendship. But a lot of things can get said at lunch, and eventually Melissa came to think of Rosie as a friend, her only friend on St. Kitts, the only person with whom she could have a normal conversation.

One of these days she was going to take Rosie up on her offer of a day sail on her brother Stanley's old schooner. Stanley had come home after years of work in Canada saving up the money to buy the old sailboat and rig it up for the tourist trade, sailing down to Nevis and back, complete with snorkeling, a picnic lunch, and the first rum punch for free.

This was Friday and tomorrow Stanley and Rosie would be out in their boat in the morning, heading down to Nevis and then back on a shakedown cruise after Stanley's rebuilding of the diesel engine. Rosie had asked her along again, tried to talk her into taking a break for a day, meeting Stanley, enjoying the water and wind and the sunshine. But, like she always did, Melissa had turned her down. One of these days, she thought, she'd finally go along, finally meet Stanley, hang out with the two of them for a day of sailing, maybe make it a way to say good-bye to this place before heading back to frozen Minnesota.

No, not there: that thought chilled her. She didn't think she could stand that, despite what her father and Dan Finnegan clearly wanted. No, it would have to be back to Florida, she guessed, and back to graduate school, where she could finally do what Dr. Morgan said she should do, get a master's in English, maybe even a doctorate, and go into teaching and coaching. That would be a good life, a calm life. Nothing at all like this, nothing like with Bo and all his crazy dreams and plans, grandiose schemes right in the middle of the resort's troubles and his father's final, dying months.

She shook her head to think of it. One thing she'd found here was how fake it all was. The family money, the resort, the power and wealth. Most of it wasn't there. There'd been some bad investments with the money that had been there, Bo had told her once. And then, just when things were starting to improve a few years ago, came Hurricane Emily; she slammed the island and the resort hard and then, worse, the pictures in the media of her devastation kept the tourists from the U.S. and U.K. from coming for most of the next year, even when things were rebuilt and ready for them.

So the family's wealth these days was all a facade, an important effort to keep up appearances though it was all a shell, hollow inside. She didn't see, really, how Bo could save it.

But the place, the island. God. She sighed, walked back over to the sliding doors, slid them open, walked back out onto the porch, felt the sun's heat on her face, breathed in deeply the scent of flowers and ocean. She'd miss this when she left.

Cecil's restaurant occupies the second floor of a nineteenth-century building overlooking the Circus Square in Basseterre, St. Kitts's capital. The menu offers smoked salmon and avocado gateau for openers, unless you'd like the escargot and mushroom crepe. For your main course there's veal in pesto sauce, or shrimp and sesame snapper, or fillet of beef with pumpkin and mustard sauce. The vegetables are always fresh, and the white chocolate mousse cake for dessert is delicious. So is the banoffee cheesecake.

Melissa had a love/hate relationship with Cecil's. She loved the food and the service, the white linen tablecloths, the expensive settings, the antique tables and chairs—all of it perfectly preserved examples of the British Empire and its colonial aristocracy at its height.

But the people down in the square, the ones dancing to the soca music coming from the Reef Bar's loudspeakers, looked like they were having a lot more fun. She'd always sworn that she was going in there someday, walk right into the Reef and order a local beer, do some dancing, break out a little bit.

But, of course, she never did. It would be scandalous for Bo Palmer's girlfriend to do something like that, mix with the locals in a run-down bar. Instead, she had to be content with watching, and listening, from her post up above in Cecil's balcony.

She was there early and had ordered a rum punch and then sat alone, looking down over the railing to the good fun below. She looked at her watch. You'd think she'd have gotten used to Bo always being late by now and learned to arrive later herself. But something about her Midwest roots kept her coming on time no matter what, which always meant waiting for at least half an hour. Today was no exception.

Twenty minutes and another rum punch later there was a flurry of activity at the restaurant's front door, and then Bo walked through, a huge grin on his face as he spotted her and walked toward her table.

"Melissa, I have great news, terrific news." He bubbled over with it, grabbed his chair, and tugged it back with a flourish, plopped down onto it, leaving it back from the table, crossing his legs, leaning back and then clapping his hands together once sharply, delighted, before announcing it: "The deal with the Holtzhausen Group looks like it's going to go through."

"The South Africans?"

"Exactly. They loved my proposal. They're ready to take part. My father is overjoyed. Four new major hotel buildings, another golf course, a purpose-built lagoon, two new casinos—the works."

She took a sip of her rum punch, raised it in a toast. "Wow, that's great, Bo. I'm very happy for you."

"Of course there are still a lot of details to be worked out. I'll have to fly up to Miami in a day or two to work on those, but we've agreed in principle. We shook hands on it and the lawyers are drafting a letter of agreement now. This will be the biggest project the island's ever seen, one of the biggest in the Caribbean."

She smiled at him. So he'd done it after all. God knows he'd been working hard on this one. He'd been talking about it for a couple of months or more, about how this one could revive the resort and the family fortune, to boot. She took his hand. All year long she'd watched him try one thing after another, and now he'd finally pulled it off.

"You did it, Bo. You're the one who pulled it all together."

"I don't think Dad thought I could, to tell you the truth. I think he figured he'd have to step in and finish things, or rescue me if it went sour."

"But it didn't go sour, Bo."

He grinned. "Yeah, it didn't."

A waiter came over with a magnum of champagne in an ice-filled silver pail. Bo grabbed the champagne, ripped off the tinfoil, untwisted the wire, and popped the cork, spraying champagne over the railing and onto a strolling couple below. He paid no attention to them when they felt the spray, dancing away from the spot and looking up. Instead, he shook the champagne again and sent another spray out over the railing.

It was the happiest Melissa had seen him in months, all the pressure relieved. Maybe that had been the problem all along. Maybe things hadn't been the way she'd thought them to be. Maybe she'd just been selfish, been feeling sorry for herself when she should have been nicer, kinder, more understanding.

Bo tossed back some champagne with a flourish, then refilled his own glass to the brim and filled another one for Melissa. Well, why not? She knew how these lunches went; there was no way she'd be back to work today anyway. She'd told Rosie what she was doing and Rosie had just nodded, said she'd take care of page 8 of the brochure herself; all it needed was some proofing.

In front of her sat the second rum punch. In her hand the glass of champagne. With the meal would come wine. Melissa smiled at Bo, at the guy who'd gotten the deal done. They clinked their glasses; she sipped from hers while he drank deeper. Below them, down in the Reef, Arrow was singing some soca song and they were dancing in the street. But up here, in the rarer air, life was pretty good, too. She took another sip.

ARC BURN

Dan Finnegan watched Melchior work, bent over the small Niagara of sparks and molten drops that came from the tack weld he was making with the oxyacetylene torch, holding the punch-out in place with a long pair of pliers and using his other hand to guide the work, fixing the small rectangle of metal—a half-inch long and quarter-inch deep with rounded edges—to the larger plate, where it joined the thirty others that were already welded there. A few hundred more and this side of the fish would have scales.

Later, Mel had already explained, he'd polish these scales with the knotted wire wheel. You could look at his hands and see the result of that kind of work—they were beat-up and scarred. He wore work gloves for the welding, he explained, but you needed to feel the work as you went when you were polishing, and gloves got in the way.

After the polishing he'd coat the whole thing with a clear lacquer—B-48 from Rohm & Haus—and that would keep it from rusting. The B-48 didn't get into every crack and crevice and that was good, since it gave a burnished look to the scales of the fish.

Finnegan looked around to see a dozen or more such constructions in various states of completion. Several fish, one huge lizard with one front leg raised and dewlap hanging down, an alligator, two small dogs, and a few pieces that were downright unidentifiable. This menagerie and the equipment that'd made them filled half the floor of the large barn.

The other half, walled off by a pair of sawhorses, was filled to bursting with what Melchior called his palette. Just like a painter—Salvador Dalí came to mind—Mel needed his raw materials right where he could reach them. In this case, that meant things that someone else might call junk. Hell, someone else *had* called it junk, or Mel wouldn't have it here now.

Over by the side of the large front door was a cultivator off a tractor, the small, curved blade meant to plow the good earth of southern Minnesota. It would make, Mel had explained, a perfect head for a bird or maybe legs for a lizard.

Next to that, standing upright, was a wagon hitch, and sitting up against it an old sickle mower and a hay rake. There were parts of bulldozers and push lawn mowers. There were old haying machine tines and the cast-iron leg of a wood-burning stove. The whole place was a junkyard in miniature, full of such stuff, much of it rusting, some of it recently cleaned and out of the dip tank where the rust had been cleaned off chemically.

Mel walked over to the arc welder, flipped a switch to turn it on. "Better wear this," he said, handing Finnegan a beat-up welder's mask and then taking a newer one and putting it on himself. "Stuff's so bright it can hurt your eyes if you don't protect them."

The plan was, Melchior explained, to attach a long, straight piece of metal—an old tie-rod, it looked like—to the back of what was slowly becoming a fish. Mel flipped his helmet down with a quick jerk of the head, struck the starter, and ignited the welding stick, the flame a visible head of yellow, blue, and white through the thick, dark glass of the helmet's faceplate. He touched the tie-rod to the main backbone and put the torch to it for just a few seconds.

The flame went out and Finnegan reached up to shove his helmet up from his face and onto the top of his head, like an odd hat, a sort of face looking up to whatever might be above it in this strange little artistic universe.

"Get it?" he asked.

"Yep," Mel said, looking it over, "but now I got to chip away at this slag some." He picked up a small chipping hammer to tap it against the tiny pieces of metal that had splattered away from the hot point of contact.

"See these little titty bumps?" Mel said. "Got to get them off there so it's smooth. That's important."

"Of course. Then what?"

"Then I get back to work on the next weld with the stick—that's what we call that old arc welder—and get a few more of these fins onto this thing."

"This one sold already?"

"No. This one's just for me, Dan; going to be a monster pike."

"Oh, yeah, this one's your masterpiece, right?"

"That's it. Don't know what I'll do with it yet. Right now, I just want to finish it, and I want it to be perfect."

"Looks great to me so far."

Mel paused from his chipping, turned to look at Finnegan, smiled. "Yeah, it's good. Damn hard work, though, you know? Never thought I'd say it, but I think I got too much of this going on right now. The farm is going to hell without Melissa around to keep things straight. Another five or six weeks and I'll have to decide whether or not to plant that forty acres down the river in sugar beets again or switch back to soybeans. Wasn't going to mess with the beets, but the price is so good right now I just might."

"And that would take time away from the sculpture, right?"

"Yep. It's all about time. Only got so much of it, and I got certain things I need to do."

Finnegan nodded.

"Been thinking, in fact, that when I get this done I ought to take a break, maybe fly on down to that island, see Melissa, relax down there for a week or two, and think it all through."

"Sounds like a good idea, Mel. When's the last time you had a vacation?"

Melchior just laughed, shook his head. "Vacation? One where you go somewhere? Never. Always had too much to do, too much to worry over."

He turned back to try the arc welder again, picking up another long rod. Finnegan, watching, reached up to flip his mask down, saw the bright flash of light in the dark glass as the tip was lit, and then heard Mel scream.

"Damn! Damn it all to hell! Oh, Jesus Christ!"

Finnegan watched as Mel staggered back from the workbench. The point of bright flame died as he extinguished the torch.

Finnegan flipped his mask up. Mel stood there, mask still atop his head, gloves dropped, eyes covered by both hands. He cursed again. "Jesus H. Christ, that hurts. Damn it."

"Mel, what happened?"

"Oh, Christ. I forgot to drop the mask. I was looking right at the weld when I lit the damn stick."

"Oh, sweet Jesus, Mel, let's get you to the hospital, get you taken care of."

Mel was calmer. "No, no. It's happened a couple of times before. Arc burn. It's like a sunburn on the eyeball. Not serious, but, Jesus, it hurts like hell. And it'll be worse tonight. Damn it."

"What can I do?"

He waved Finnegan away. "Nothing, Dan. I just have to . . ." He paused. "Well, you know, you *could* help. I've got to get this all shut down and then get into the house. I'm going to be blind for a day or two until this heals."

"I'll help now, and then get somebody to stay with you. How'd you manage last time?"

"Well, I'm not really blind; it just hurts. Last time the one eye wasn't too bad. I managed."

Finnegan walked over to Melchior, reached his friend's side, grabbed his hands, moved him over toward the bench, and sat him down there. "Now. You tell me what you need me to do here."

"First, get over there," he pointed, "and shut off the stick. Got to turn both of those top valves to the right until they're tight."

Finnegan took two steps over and shut the valves.

"Got it? Good." Melchior put his hands out to feel the top of his workbench, slung the stick over it. "Now, help me get back over to the house."

They walked, the two of them, down a narrow path that

wound its way through the boneyard of old crankcase rods, cultivators, shocks and struts, a snowplow blade—Lord knew how much snow that thing had thrown in its day—and the other rusting parts that lay everywhere on the barn floor. Finnegan went ahead, reaching back to hold Melchior's hand to lead him along step-by-step. When they reached the smaller door cut into the main barn door, Finnegan opened it and started to back through it, still holding Melchior's hand.

The wind was out of the north, a frigid blast from Alberta that slapped the door hard against Finnegan's rear as he backed through. As the door hit him he stumbled forward, falling into Melchior's arms so that the two of them were in an awkward embrace, one they both got disentangled from as quickly as they could before Finnegan again shoved against the door and then, against that warm breeze, backed them both out.

A few minutes later and the screen door of the kitchen was banging shut behind them as they stepped through onto the linoleum flooring. Following Melchior's directions, Finnegan led the strange little parade into the living room, where he helped ease Melchior onto the couch.

"Now, could you get to the upstairs bathroom, do you think, and get into the cabinet? There's some eyewash up there the doc told me to use last time. Ain't been opened in three years, but I guess eyewash ought to hold, don't you think?"

"Suppose so. In the bathroom cabinet over the sink?"

"Yep."

"I'll find it."

"Second door on the right, down that hallway."

"Got it." And Finnegan headed that way.

Oddly, it was his first time past the living room in this house, he realized as he walked toward the bathroom. He caught himself wondering, every now and then, how well his son had known this house. Danny spent a lot of time with Melissa here. Did he walk down this hallway? He must have. Funny how he felt more a presence of his son here in this house than he did at home, in the place where the boy grew up. There, his memory overwhelmed everything; there was no picking out a particular thing as a reminder. Danny was everywhere and so nowhere in particular.

But here. Did Danny walk here? Touch this doorknob?

He walked to the second door on the right. The door opposite had a DO NOT ENTER sign on it and a Mankato Catholic Fightin' Knights basketball banner tacked to it. Melissa's room. Door firmly closed. He left it alone.

The next door on that side wasn't closed tightly. Again, he peeked in. A linen closet. Towels neatly folded and stacked.

On the right, both doors were shut tight. No way to know, and his professional curiosity wasn't strong enough to open a closed door, especially in a friend's house.

He opened the second door and walked in. Your standard farmhouse bathroom, a big porcelain tub with claw feet occupying the left side of the room, twin taps for hot and cold with those old big letters "H" and "C" on them, worn down from a half-century or more of use. There was no shower curtain, so if anyone took showers in this house he did it elsewhere.

There was another door, next to the bathroom sink, that led into the next room. The sink was still wet and with bits of beard stuck to the sides. Mel must have used it not too long ago to shave. It had those same taps and a worn porcelain basin. To the left of that sat the commode. Up above the basin was a newer medicine cabinet—one of those wood ones you could buy at True Value in town.

Finnegan opened the cabinet. It was filled with what you'd expect from a guy living mostly alone these days: an old Gillette razor, a few rusty used blades underneath it and a small, blue pack of new razors next to it; a can of shaving cream; two squeezed-out tubes of Crest toothpaste; a bottle of generic ibuprofen; a few half-filled prescription bottles for antibiotics.

And the eyewash, on the top shelf, in a small, plastic-wrapped box. Great. He reached up to grab it, got his right hand on it, reaching up to that top spot, and then felt his right foot slip on the wet tile of the bathroom floor. As it did, he grabbed for the side of the sink with his left hand to steady himself, felt the foot go a bit more, and then, hanging onto the sink, he spun backward and down, falling hard against the closed door that led to the other room.

He caught himself in time, slipping some against the door but not making a big racket, falling into a kind of catcher's crouch and then pulling from the sink with his left hand, bringing himself back up to stand there, feeling stupid for having been so clumsy.

Still, no harm done and he'd even managed to hang on to the eyewash. He shook his head, started to leave, and then noticed that the door he'd bumped against had popped open a few inches. Close it? Take a look?

He was in the business of taking looks, even just that one quick peek. The door was open six inches or so. Gently, curiously, he pushed it, and it swung away from him, inward, opening wide, into a bedroom, thinly lit by sunlight through an old, thin pull-down window shade.

He took a step in and saw what it was: a shrine, a museum, a time machine to Moira, the wife and mother who'd left Melchior and Melissa when the girl was just five. There one day, the proud, happy mother and dutiful farmwife. Then gone the next day. There'd never been the first inkling of what she'd done, how or why she'd left. She was just gone, and Melchior and his daughter had just finally gone on with their lives without her.

But they hadn't forgotten her, that was clear. This room was hers, frozen in time, waiting for her return.

A crucifix hung on the far wall. He walked that way. Both hands had broken away from the cross. Next to it on the wall was a large framed portrait gallery, a dozen or so pictures of the once-happy family. Melissa at five, a green-eyed beauty. Pictures of Moira, long dark hair, tanned skin, a bit stocky, smiling slightly in a few of the shots. Pictures of Mel with his wife and his beautiful young daughter, out in the yard in the warmth of summer, Mel's arm around Melissa protectively, hugging her to him, she looking up with a five-year-old's adoration to her father's stern face.

A dresser was next to the bed, a foot-tall statue of the Virgin

Mary atop it, gowned in a faded, chipped blue porcelain robe over white robes beneath it. Mary stood atop a globe of Earth, her bare feet crushing a dying serpent that lay atop the globe.

On the wall next to the dresser was a photograph, some scene from the Caribbean: a family, a father and mother and three young girls posed on the front steps of a nice white frame house with bright blue trim, curtains blowing in a breeze, a hillside lush with tropical foliage rising up behind them to a mountain crest with a trail of smoke rising from the peak—a volcano, it must be. The sky was a deep blue with a few puffy white clouds. He could feel the warmth of that. Had Melchior and Moira been to the Caribbean sometime early on in their marriage, for a honeymoon, maybe, and picked this up there? Sure looked like it.

On the wall on the other side of the bed was a calendar. "St. John's Church," it said across the bottom, and it listed Msgr. Peter O'Haloran, Pastor, and the times for Masses and Confessions. Saturday, at 10:00 and 11:00 A.M.; that's when you could go there and confess your sins to the monsignor.

The calendar was turned to the month of January. The year was 1981. It hadn't been turned since that day she left, that day she headed off into the cold, escaping something, maybe just crazy, maybe alive now and with a new life in some warmer place. Maybe dead.

The calendar's picture for the month was of the Three Wise Men, on their way atop camels striding over the dunes, to see the new Baby Jesus.

Wise Men. Finnegan shook his head, headed back downstairs to help his friend. Wise Men indeed.

THE RIGHT TIME

There was a long, slow lunch with more champagne and two bottles of Kanonkop Riesling wine from South Africa and then, about four in the afternoon, they were back at the Palmer house, the villa built into the side of Sir Timothy's Hill near the resort.

At first Melissa had loved the place, but then, slowly, she'd come to see it for what it was—run-down, falling apart, a symbol of the neglect she saw everywhere in the Palmer resort.

She'd seen some of that decay the very first time she'd come here. But back then she guessed it was just part of the island life, the slow pace, the benign neglect she saw everywhere here in the sun and heat.

Now she knew it was just money, the lack of it. The changes in Bo had maybe come from this, too, she thought. The more he saw around him, the more pressure he felt to bring it all back.

But the place still held power. A central atrium had a wide, winding staircase coming down one side, centered with a huge chandelier. The furniture was fabulous, the walls covered with paintings. Henry Palmer, Bo had once explained to Melissa, believed in making a strong impression on the locals. Before ever sinking the pilings for the first building of his resort, twenty years before, he'd built this ostentatious home, making a point about his money. As they drove up, Bo talked about how now he'd be able to fix it up, restore it to its former glory.

She was drunk, the rum punches and the champagne a volatile mix. She giggled at the thought; she hadn't been this drunk since her senior year in college during homecoming, and you sort of *had* to get drunk then.

Bo was unsteady, too, but the two of them managed to find their way into the game room, snickering as they bumped into the pool table and walked on toward the wide, soft couch and the television set hooked up to the satellite dish in the side yard, near the pool.

Bo reached out to Melissa, took her by the shoulders, and brought her over to the couch. "Sit down, sweetheart; I have something I want you to see."

"On the television?"

"Yeah, on the television, sort of. It's a videotape."

She sat, and Bo picked up the remote and sat next to her. He was suddenly very serious. "Melissa, sweetheart. I know it's been a rough year for you. I've been too busy to spend much time with you, and it's a small island, with not much to do, really. But I love you."

He hit the switch, and the TV came to life with a sweeping view of the Eiffel Tower, some spiritual view, from above, that came swooping in and then moved past the tower and on to Notre Dame Cathedral and then past the Île St.-Louis and on down the Seine.

"What are we watching, Bo?"

He knelt down in front of her, reached into his pocket, and brought out a ring case. The video had switched to Rome, hovering over the Colosseum and then Vatican Square before pulling back and zooming over the Italian countryside in a blur to wind up in Venice. "That's our honeymoon, sweetheart."

He opened the ring case. "Melissa. Will you marry me?"

"What?" She suddenly felt very sober.

"Will you marry me?" Behind him they were swooping over the Parthenon, zooming out over the Aegean, heading toward the Sphinx and the Great Pyramid.

"Bo, I didn't expect this."

"You told me, a couple of years ago, that it just wasn't the right time yet, that we should wait awhile before making a decision like this. Well, I've waited. And now it *is* the right time."

There was a hint of steel in his voice. He expected something different from her this time. He expected a yes.

"I'll treat you well, Melissa. We'll see the world; we'll travel whenever you want." Angkor Wat slipped by; junks sailed toward Honk Kong. "And I need you, Melissa. I do. I have plans, great plans, and I need you beside me, helping me get there."

Tokyo, geishas smiling, then Polynesia and hula skirts and Hawaii and volcanoes and the Golden Gate and Yosemite and the Grand Canyon.

"Bo, I can't marry you."

He smiled. "Yes, you can. You will. You have to, Melissa. I've been waiting for years for this, for everything to fall into place. This is it; this is my time; everything starts now. Do you understand? Everything starts now, with you, with the Holtzhausen deal. I've waited and waited for this, Melissa. You know I have."

He knelt there while Chicago rose up from Lake Michigan behind him. "You have to, Melissa."

"I can't."

He leaned forward to kiss her. She pushed him back.

"Melissa," he said, "sweetie," and he leaned toward her again. She pushed, but he kept on coming. He kissed her, hard, and she realized his hand was behind her neck, holding her head there while he kissed her.

She tried to pull away, tried to break the kiss, but couldn't. He was strong, very strong, and pushed down on her, climbing on her, astride her, pushing her back with his hands, reaching to her blouse, pulling it apart, buttons popping.

She wanted very much to stop him, wanted to say something magical that would make him stop, make this all end. But she couldn't speak, could only watch, distanced from it somehow, as he yanked open the blouse, tugged down on her bra to expose her breasts, took them in his hands, grunting something unintelligible, something primal. Then he reached down under her skirt, slipped his hands up to her panties, grabbed them at the sides where they were thin, and ripped them open, pulled them apart, and yanked them from her. Then he sat up, began undoing his own shirt, his belt, his pants, staring at her, saying nothing, as he finished, shoved the pants down, and lay back on top of her, rubbing her, opening her up with his fingers and then quickly, forcefully, putting himself inside her once, twice, and then again and again and again as she drifted off, away from this awful place into some other world, some blank place where nothing was happening to her, nothing at all.

ALBERTA CLIPPER

The world was melting.

Another cold front from Alberta was on the way, but before it could get there it sucked up warm air in front of it, sending the temperature climbing—from twenty below to zero and then to twenty above and then, remarkably for January, above freezing. Warm clouds filled with moisture all the way up from the Caribbean were shooting by overhead.

Dan Finnegan walked down Main Street in Mankato on this warm, breezy Saturday in the dead of winter wearing nothing more than a sweater and marveling that he felt hot with just that on. When you're used to forty below zero, forty above feels pretty damn warm. Incredibly, it even felt like it might rain, of all things.

In his left hand he held a list of things to get, including new light switches for the recently repainted living and dining rooms, a can of paint to finish the job on the basement rec room, some weather-stripping for the bay window that looked out on the cottonwoods of the Minnesota River but faced north and always seemed to let through those Alberta Clipper winter winds, and a new snow shovel to replace the one he'd ruined this morning when he'd tried to take advantage of the thaw to clear the driveway's piles of slush but instead just wound up bending the metal scoop back hopelessly with the wet, heavy slush he'd been plowing through.

He'd been working on the house a lot lately. Something about that dunking in Lake Minnetoksak a couple of weeks ago had reminded him that he had a life and he ought to spend a little time living it. Every now and then you had to put away your worries and think about something else. Like weather-stripping.

He sighed. A beautiful, warm day and he was going to be spending it at the hardware store and then back inside the house working away to finish the paint job. Could be worse, though; could be a lot worse.

It *would* be worse, actually, come tomorrow when that Alberta Clipper arrived. The weatherman was predicting a chance of rain for today—imagine that, rain in January—and then that would slowly get colder and eventually turn into six to ten inches or more of snow from the front's passage before the weather cleared and the temperature fell back to thirty below or so behind the front. Might even get colder than that. He sighed again. What a frozen mess it would be. And only two or three more months of winter to go, too.

It was times like this, with bad weather on the way, that he started thinking about Melissa, down there on that tropical island enjoying herself. Here he was, celebrating a day that reached forty degrees, and down there it was eighty-five every day, year-round. He wondered if it rained much there at all.

He hadn't heard from her in a few weeks. They weren't staying in touch as often as they used to, but that was inevitable, he guessed. She was growing up, all of twenty-three now. Same age Danny would have been if that war over there in that desert hadn't taken the kid.

For a while there he'd begun to think of her as his own child, as if he were sharing parental duty with poor Melchior, who'd had to raise that girl all by himself once Moira disappeared.

Moira O'Malley. He'd been thinking about her lately, since that day a couple of weeks ago when he'd stumbled into Mel's shrine to his absent wife. There was still a file on Moira somewhere. Whatever happened to her? he wondered. At this point, nearly twenty years on down the road from the day she disappeared, they'd probably never find out.

Not finding out was the part of the job he hated most. The whole reason for being a detective was because he liked knowing, liked having answers. Cases like Moira O'Malley's nagged at him, even from the distance of twenty years.

Most of his workload wasn't as frustrating as that; most of it was pretty straightforward, from complaints about crank phone calls to the dozens of mandatory reports that came in from doctors and teachers about kids in trouble, sometimes for something the kid had done and sometimes something that had been done to them, usually at the hands of their parents. It could be a hell of a world sometimes.

But at least those cases had closure, and so they didn't eat at him like the open cases, which sat there reminding him that he couldn't solve them all. Moira O'Malley was one; another was the skeletal remains found in the county last year, probably a murder from up in the Twin Cities and the body was dumped down here.

And these damn Intruder Murders. Above all, these terrible murders.

Twice in the past two weeks they thought maybe they'd had the break they needed—the first time when a traffic cop in Rapid City pulled over a guy named Walter Arndt with a Minnesota driver's license and the second in Bemidji when the transvestite from the Cities showed up in a bar. They had him under surveillance, thought they had him all closed in.

But the Walter Arndt in Rapid City turned out to be a doctor from the Mayo Clinic in Rochester who was visiting his parents, and when they went into the bar to get the transvestite the guy was gone, out through a side door that led into the empty warehouse next door, and then he'd headed out a back alley from there.

Close. But close didn't count, and Dan Finnegan could still see the bodies in those farmhouses, butchered by someone crazy and vicious.

He reached the True Value Hardware Store, its main door hanging wide open to take in the strange and wonderful warmth—it almost felt like summer, and without the mosquitoes. He walked through, headed toward the middle aisle of the small hardware store, where he expected to find the light-switch covers.

What the hell color did he need? Plain white, that was it. Just plain white, easy enough to remember.

He found the aisle, was headed down it when he heard his name called, a raspy voice saying it, ending it with a cough. He turned, smiled to see Mel O'Malley, dressed in blue jeans and a plaid shirt, wearing a DeKalb corn baseball cap, standing there holding a large package.

Finnegan hadn't seen him in more than a week. The last time, the remnants of the arc burn had still been visible on his face—a red sunburn around the eyes and on the cheekbones. Now that was gone.

"You look like you're feeling better, Mel. Enjoying this weather?"

"Just what I needed," Mel said. "Been out in the barn since the Chinook started blowing last night, trying to finish up the big pike, taking advantage of it being so warm out there I could work in my shirtsleeves."

"That masterpiece pike? You almost done with that?" He had been busy. The last time Finnegan had seen the pike it didn't look half-done.

Mel smiled. "Near to finished now that I can see again. Working on the fins now. Might get that last of 'em done today. I'd be done now, but I needed to get some more lacquer before I could finish it up."

"Well, hell, that's great, Mel. Congratulations. Decide what you plan to do with it yet?"

Melchior reached up to take off his ball cap, scratched his head. "You know, I just haven't thought that through yet, Dan. Just keep it in the barn for now, I guess. Then maybe figure out the right place for it. Got to be someplace special, that's for sure."

"The new art museum out at the campus, maybe?"

Mel frowned. "Maybe. Hell, I don't know. Been too busy working on it to give that much thought."

"You mind if I come out in a few days and take a look at it? I'd love to see it all completed."

Melchior nodded, then chuckled loosely, deep. "That'd be

great, Dan. Unless you bring me bad luck and I arc-burn these poor old eyes again."

As the two men talked, Finnegan found his switch plates, and then they stood together in the short checkout line chatting until they could pay. When they walked outside it was even warmer, the bank sign said fifty degrees above, and it was raining, a strangely warm, light drizzle. They both laughed to see it. *Unusual* wasn't the word for it, this surreal bit of tropical weather right in the middle of winter's grip.

"Gonna ruin my ice fishing for a week or two," Melchior groused. "You get a thaw like this, and this warm rain, and it weakens the ice bad."

"It'll refreeze out there just fine, though, right?"

"Nope, different layers of ice, the old stuff weakened by the warm weather and then covered with the new freeze. Weak as hell. There'd be some shacks falling right through Lake Minnetoksak if this kept up for a couple of days. Nobody's used to this."

"Well, it's not supposed to last."

"Yep, back to below zero after tonight's snow is what I hear."

"So tomorrow and Monday are likely a mess. Be a good day on Monday for me to stay in and get some paperwork done if I can."

They stood, the two of them, under the canopy of the hardware store, admiring the warm rain. Finnegan reached out to touch a few drops, watched them bead on his hand. "You know, Mel, that reminds me, I was thinking of getting onto the computer and seeing if I could come up with something on Moira. Been years since we tried any new leads on that. With the new computer systems, the way things are all tied in, I thought I might come up with something."

Melchior looked at him, his expression blank. "You think that will do any good, Dan? That's all a long time ago now."

Finnegan could understand Mel's reluctance. Just thinking about someone checking into it would dredge up old memories that had been away, buried deep, for a long, long time. He'd been wrong, he realized, looking at his friend's face, to say anything about it. Instead, he should have just looked on his own, just to satisfy his curiosity, and kept his mouth shut about it. Still, he was in it, now.

"Oh, hell, I'm sorry, Mel. You know, it was just that I was thinking about some of our open files—the cases we haven't been able to solve—and I thought of Moira, that's all. Look, with all this computerized stuff, it will only take me a few minutes. Probably won't be anything there anyway. I won't bother you unless something turns up."

"Nothing's going to turn up. You know that."

Finnegan nodded. "I realize that. Hell, shouldn't have thought it up."

"Then don't bother with it. Let her be in peace. Let the memory of her be in peace, Dan, all right?" And then, as Finnegan nodded that he'd leave it be, Melchior slipped his old baseball cap onto his balding head and walked off, silent, into the rain, toward his ancient pickup truck.

Later, Monday morning, Finnegan figured a little lie was better than an argument with a friend and checked it out on the databases. There was nothing there, nothing at all. Moira O'Malley remained there two decades back, unchanged, forever lost, frozen in time.

He'd just finished an hour's work on the computer and come to that conclusion when the call came in about what they'd found in an old half-fallen hunting shack out near Norseland: skeletal remains, sitting upright against the one standing wall. There was a wallet, most of it ruined by weather and mice, but with an inside pocket that had a legible plastic credit card, a gold American Express. The name on it was Walter M. Arndt. The remains were mostly whole, and the officer at the scene couldn't tell the cause of the death. Oh, and the right hand was missing. They were checking the rest of the site out now and they'd get back to him.

He hung up the phone. Sat back and thought it through. Well, damn, that sure changed things.

That transvestite from St. Paul? He didn't think so; it just didn't fit in a lot of subtle ways.

Which meant, he thought, Fr. James Murphy, SJ.

A GREEN MONKEY

After Bo was done with her, she sat there on his couch and stared at a painting on the wall of a diver floating over the wreck of some old eighteenth-century ship, an English frigate maybe, or a French caravel. The masts were gone, snapped off centuries before, but the hull sat upright on the bottom, half-covered in coral and sand with parrot fish and huge tarpon hovering around it. You could see mounds of coral where the cannons were on the deck, and a small, dark opening amidships offered the diver a way into the interior.

A large shark, a hammerhead, was behind the diver, swimming toward him. Above, out of reach, was the surface. A trail of bubbles rose from the diver's back.

Melissa had been snorkeling twice with Bo in the year she'd been here, both times during that first month when things were new and exciting. She'd never seen anything like that.

She tried to stand but couldn't. Instead, she sat back down. Something had cracked. She could feel it, somewhere deep inside her; a crevice of some kind had opened up, something in the ice of her soul, something that opened the way down into the darkness, where there was some monstrous object, some terrible and cold and hard creature, trying to break through and rise to where she could see it and know it.

No. Just no.

She took a deep breath. Another. Then she managed to stand, stood there for a moment, then started getting her clothes back together, fighting a zipper some. Bo came over to her. He was smoking a cigarette, the first time he'd smoked since they got the news about his father, months ago.

He smiled, put it out on a small dish on the table, and came over to help her with the zipper. Then he offered her a drink, said something, said something more, all of it dreamy and un-intelligible.

They had dinner, something fish with sauce that she tried to eat one forkful of and then gave up. Instead, she just sat there quietly while Bo talked some more about his plans for the resort, for her, for the future he could see so clearly.

Eventually, he drove her home and she walked in the front door, walked upstairs to her bedroom, opened the door to the bathroom, walked in, slid open the shower-stall door, and stepped in. Clothes still on, she turned the water as hot as she could bear and stood in the hard, cleansing stream for long minutes, until the water cooled, the hot-water heater exhausted. She shut the water off then and slowly stripped off her wet clothes, dropping them, one by one, onto the tile of the shower-stall floor.

Naked, wet, she walked to her chest of drawers and opened the bottom drawer, pulled out a T-shirt, put it on, but it soaked through immediately. OK, then; drier now she went back into the drawers, found a pair of pajamas, slipped them on. She very badly wanted to find her old stuffed Pooh bear in there, the one she'd had when she was just five. She needed him, but he was home, safe, in Minnesota.

She went to bed, tried to sleep but couldn't, and so after an hour or so of staring at the slow circles of the ceiling fan, she got up, walked over to the bathroom, and took another hot shower, draining the water heater once again. Then she tried bed again. Nothing. Blank, but awake.

So she tried the cycle a third time, showering and back to bed. And then a fourth time, and then a fifth, but it was useless, the water cold, the bed hard, the fan turning and turning and turning.

About 4:00 A.M., lying there awake, staring at the ceiling, she felt a rumble from the volcano. It started slow, like a big truck rumbling by outside her window. Then it grew in intensity until her bed shook with it. When she tried to sit up, a final sharp drumbeat of movement sent her onto the floor, landing hard on her side.

She got to her hands and knees, the ground still trembling, and crawled over to the window. There was a wave of motion, then a rumbling she felt more than heard, and there, in the distance, was Mount Liamuiga, a billow of smoke and ash rising from its ancient caldera, lightning flashes in the clouds, a glow from the mountain's heart lighting the clouds from beneath.

Good Lord. She sat back, rubbed her face with her hands, started to cry, sat up to look again.

And the mountain was serene, a black hulk in the darkness, lit only by the river of stars of the Milky Way overhead. Nothing. Quiet. It had all been a dream, some hallucination.

She stood, turned around. The rattan chair was on its side, the love seat fallen onto its back next to the chair, the bamboo and glass-topped table on its side, the glass unbroken.

She shook her head. What was real? She didn't know, so she brushed herself off and went in to take another shower.

Later, finally, it was morning. She walked out on her porch and the sky to the east was lightening up, from black to gray and then some pinks and blues as she stood there, silent, watching. The mountain grew from darkness to shadowed green serenity as she stood there watching. It was all very pretty.

Mechanically, she walked back into her apartment, put on her shoes, a warm pair of blue jeans, an old Mankato Catholic High sweatshirt that she'd bought in town on her last visit there, the day before she'd flown south to this island. She hadn't worn it since the day she arrived.

She walked over to the closet and found a pair of warm gloves and a wool knit cap. Those two had come with her that first day, too.

She came down the stairs of her town house, walked across to the front door, opened it, and stepped outside, leaving the door open behind her since that didn't really matter.

Then she walked on down Dieppe Street to the intersection

with Frigate Bay Road, took a right, and walked east, toward the
sunrise. It felt good, truly cleansing, to be walking hard, working
up a sweat, an angry sweat. She walked harder.

She turned onto the dirt road that ambled over toward Frigate
Bay's Atlantic side. A green monkey, the island was full of them,
sat in the road and watched her approach.

Brazen little thing, used to humans walking along here, hoping
she had a handout for it, some peanuts maybe, or a banana.

She stopped about five feet away, smiled at the monkey. "Good
morning," she said.

The monkey looked at her, looked away, look back to her, its
tail twitching. "Me? Oh, I'm fine," she told it. "Just out for a
little morning stroll, that's all."

She started walking again, and the monkey stepped aside, but
only just. She'd never been this close to one before. They always
hightailed it off into the brush before letting you get this close.

She kept walking, another hundred yards down the dirt road
to the beach. She rounded a final curve and there, past the sand
dunes and the palm trees, was the Atlantic, nothing that way for
four thousand miles until you hit the coast of Africa. There was
a steep beach heading down to it, three-foot waves rolling in from
the east, where the dawn sky was slowly edging into blue. Behind
her, the monkey followed.

She walked on down to the beach, sat down on the black
volcanic sand, and undid her shoelaces and pulled off her shoes.
Then, blue jeans and sweatshirt still on, gloves still warming her
hands, knit cap still on her head, her long, beautiful black hair
shoved up underneath it, hidden, she walked into the water.

It felt cold for some reason, though she knew it was in the
mideighties. It was always in the mideighties here, almost bathtub
warm.

But not this morning, not to her. She waded in and it felt icy,
Minnesota cold. She wondered why, shivering, beating her hands
together to warm them up. She looked back and the monkey was
there on the beach, watching her.

She got past waist deep, fighting through a few waves before
she passed the place where they broke. Then the water deepened

enough to reach the bottom of her breasts beneath the sweatshirt. She stopped then, looked down to see the water touching her breasts. Bo had held them, kissed them briefly right before entering her. She remembered that. She seemed to have forgotten a lot of last night, but she remembered that, the way he'd held them and said something to her—she couldn't remember what it was he'd said—and then he'd mounted her, like some animal, pushing it in, then pulling it back and pushing again, and again, and again. She thought maybe that after a while he'd turned her around so he could come in from behind, like the monkeys did it.

She wondered, as she pushed off and started swimming out to sea, out toward the approaching dawn, what it was he'd been saying. Something about how good it was? Something about love? About marriage and honeymoons and the future?

She was a strong swimmer, but the clothes and the water's strange cold sapped her strength, so the swimming went slowly. She was well past the surf line now, though, and still heading east. If she kept going she'd hit North Africa. She stopped for a moment to look at the morning sky, treading water. The stars were gone; the black had turned to a thin light blue. It was a beautiful morning, really.

She turned to look back at the beach, really not that far away, though she felt like she'd been swimming for hours. The monkey was still there, sitting upright on its haunches, watching her. She waved to it.

And then she turned back to the east and started swimming again. Later, it seemed like forever in the freezing cold of the water, she started getting tired and stopped again. The salt water was very buoyant; it was hard to sink even with these wet, thick clothes. But when you're very tired and very cold, finally you are able to stop thinking, able to stop trying to remember, and able to let go of the surface tension.

Right at the end, hallucinating, she heard what must have been her mother's voice, calling to her in that pleasant, lilting island accent. "Melissa O'Malley. You silly girl, what are you doing out here?"

What was Mom doing out here? And where was her father? He should be here, helping her. And Finnegan, where was he? And Danny, whatever happened to Danny?

She didn't have answers to any of those questions. Instead, she relaxed and let the cold water comfort her, let it reach out and embrace her as she slowly, calmly slipped away.

JACK LONDON WEATHER

Another goddamn double homicide. The call came in at
10:00 A.M., and now, forty minutes later, Finnegan was there,
driving down another cold road to another isolated farm, knowing what he'd see inside, picturing it in his mind.

At least they knew now that it wasn't poor old Walter Arndt
who'd committed these horrors. That had been a painful call he'd
had to make, to Sally Arndt and Summer and Steve—a tragic
good news and bad news thing: "Your husband didn't do it, Sally,
and we've found his body to prove it." He'd gone over there to
visit the next day, been to the funeral two days later. Sally seemed
to understand how he'd just been doing his job, but the kids,
Finnegan thought, would never get over hating him for being the
cop who thought their father was a murderer. He couldn't say he
blamed them much.

That left Fr. Jim Murphy as the best suspect, based mostly on
the rosary beads and not much else. There was James Sibel, the
transvestite from St. Paul whom they'd round up sometime soon,
but that just didn't sit right for a lot of reasons. He wasn't the
guy, despite the match of the hairs from a wig that Sibel had
bought in Minneapolis with hairs at the second and third scenes.
Finnegan's gut told him Sibel wasn't the guy.

So it had to be Murphy, unless something new cropped up.
The forensic guys were working on the evidence from the hunting
shack, but there wasn't much there—just the remains of Walter's
body and the clothes he'd been in. Most likely he'd been murdered right there, they said, since it didn't look like the body had

been moved. Otherwise, there wasn't much to work with except, of course, for the missing right hand, cut off very neatly, some kind of surgical saw most likely.

Finnegan was thinking this all through as he drove up to the farmhouse. The snow was light but steady; tiny flakes in a lazy fall. It was a pretty day for midwinter, but the forecast was ugly. A week before it'd been fifty above, and now it was double digits below zero. It was supposed to warm back up some this afternoon and with the warmth was coming a foot of new snow. Then, after the snow, the real cold would settle in, the fifty-below stuff. Real Jack London weather.

London's "To Build a Fire" was maybe the only piece of fiction that Finnegan had enjoyed reading in high school. In the story, a guy is alone in the Yukon wilderness when it's fifty below. The guy gets wet and knows he has to get a fire started to stay alive. There's some trouble and the guy winds up without a fire, and dead. You grow up in Minnesota and stories like that make great sense to you. Fifty below and cold and wet equals dead. That simple. Minnesota winters don't forgive mistakes.

Finnegan nodded at the patrolman outside the front door and then stepped carefully through the door and into the living room of the farmhouse, taking off his lined gloves and slipping on the latex surgicals. He handed the lined gloves to the patrolman to hang on to for a few minutes, and then he stood there, taking it all in, looking left to right, from the lacy curtains of the dining room window, past the open door to the kitchen, the stairway leading to the second floor, the living room with its couch, television, big glassed-in hutch with photos of the family and a few books in it. It was all very neat and tidy, a good Midwest farm family's well-ordered life on display.

There were no blood-splattered walls this time, no trails of gore on the throw rugs or the stairs, no sign of violence at all, really, except for the main tableau. On a pair of high-backed wooden kitchen chairs set ten feet or so from the front door, the mother and her daughter sat facing the door, great pools of their blood still wet beneath the chairs, the house reeking of the iron-filing smell of it. This must have happened within the last hour or so.

The neighbor had come over with soup from the house across the way, clomping and sliding along on the newly refrozen ice and snow to see her friend and the little girl, home sick with a bad cold. She'd knocked on the door and it had swung open, so she'd walked in. And seen this.

The monster was improving his technique, Finnegan thought, walking carefully over toward the victims. The son of a bitch was getting neater.

The girl, Finnegan guessed, was about ten years old, in fourth or fifth grade. She should be reading some book about unicorns or studying her math or something. Not like this, not dead, a slit across her throat—a kind of awful mercy again for the child, death in a minute or two.

The mother was in her late thirties; slim, blond—good, solid Minnesota Scandinavian stock.

Finnegan walked over to the cabinet, looked in to see the family photographs. The mother had been a knockout, a good-looking woman, probably a cheerleader at St. Peter High School twenty years before and then a beautiful coed who married the best-looking guy on campus. The picture of her had "Karen" in gold lettering across the bottom. Pretty Karen, then, the good-looker who settled down here to run this prosperous farm—maybe it was the old family farmstead—and have two perfect kids. In the family picture there was a son, too, a little older, no doubt off at school right now, not knowing yet the terrible news he'd hear later today. And a handsome father. Damn.

A uniform officer—a new guy with the local department—poked his head in the door, cleared his throat. Finnegan turned to see what was up and could see the look in the guy's eyes as he caught sight of the victims. The officer swallowed hard. "A Jon Hamner from the BCA called in, said he and the mobile crime unit will be here in half an hour, Detective. Thought you'd want to know."

"Thanks. Tell them to find out if the victims were sexually assaulted," Finnegan said, walking past the bodies and on into the kitchen—nice tile floor, new cabinets, a big new Sears Kenmore refrigerator with an ice maker: this farm was doing well.

There were three doors. One led outside through a small snow room. Finnegan could see the barn through the snow room's single window.

Another door opened to a walk-in cupboard, filled with canned vegetables—tomatoes, peas, green beans, Jesus, this woman was a dynamo; there were five rows of the stuff, neatly labeled.

The third door opened to a bathroom. Finnegan walked over and opened the door.

And there was Fr. James Murphy, SJ, sitting on the toilet, his hard, frozen body leaned up against the sidewall, his legs out straight in front of him, his skin a sickly, evil pale white. The eyeballs were missing from the sockets, the skin of the face half eaten away so that clean bone showed through. His hair, black, had been combed forward to cover his bald spot. He was wearing black pants, a white short-sleeved shirt, his priest's collar unbuttoned but still around his neck.

He was dripping, thawing, as a puddle formed on the hardwood floor.

Next to the body was an old bathroom sink with two of the old five-pronged faucets. Above that, a new bathroom cabinet, wooden, its front panel door open wide. Finnegan, trying to capture every detail, forcing himself to see this, not react to it, reached up to close the panel door.

There was a message for him on the cabinet's mirror. Written in lipstick, "Finnegan," it read, scrawled in broad, loopy letters across the top of the mirror. Underneath that, in two lines, lumpy bits of lipstick stuck to the mirror from the force of the writing, "Ego te absolvo."

The lipstick the guy had used to write the little note with was tossed into the sink. Revlon, Ripe Raspberry.

Oh, Jesus. Finnegan could feel his heart rate climb as he stared at Murphy's body, pulled up out of the deep bottom of some lake where it must have been for the past few years.

Finnegan could feel the blood drain from his face, his stomach tightening. Goddamn it. This son of a goddamn bitch. Bastard. Jesus.

He wanted to wipe the message clean, wanted to pound at it with his fist, break the mirror, break the whole damn perfect bathroom apart, screaming and crying as he broke that message to bits, wiped it clean.

But he didn't touch it, of course. And didn't touch the body. Instead, he took a deep breath, backed away from it all, turned his back on it, and walked, slowly, out the door. He yelled at the two uniform officers in the hallway to take a look at it and seal it off, said he'd be back in a moment, and then headed outside for some fresh air, nearly twenty below but the temperature rising now a bit, the air still clean and fresh and biting.

He wanted that, needed it right now, the cold slapping him in the face as he opened the back door and stepped out onto the little porch. In the still air he could hear the murmur of conversation from out front, the uniform guys talking to one another, getting things organized. He'd go out there and talk to them in just a second. Try to pick through what all this meant. How long ago had Murphy been murdered? How in hell did the perpetrator got the body in there after, he supposed, murdering the mother and child? Jesus, what a monster.

For now, Finnegan needed some air, just for a minute or two, something clean to breathe. Jesus, the smell in there, dank and cold and mixing, as he'd stood there, with the gut-grabbing smell of the puddled blood from the other bodies. Christ Almighty.

He looked around. The snowfall was picking up with the rising temps. It'd be up near zero this afternoon, and then would come the heavy snow, ten or twelve new inches of it by tomorrow morning, when the bottom would drop back out of the temperature again.

He looked around. Plenty of footprints and tire tracks all over the backyard, a family's movements over the last few days of thaw and freeze caught there in ice and snow. They'd check it out, and they'd have to be quick before the new snow covered it all, but Finnegan didn't think there'd be much chance of getting anything worthwhile. Never know, though.

It was good to concentrate on something else for a moment or two. The barn was in good shape, painted within the last year or two, he guessed, and standing up straight, without that suspicious lean the older barns got. It was shut up tight, but he'd have to go over there and check that out, too.

Past the barn were the fields, a smooth expanse of snow with a few foot trails cut through them, probably the farm kids or the father, walking on down to the river at the far edge of the fields this past warm weekend. A line of cottonwoods marked the river, the St. Peter, a shallow stream with a few deep pools. It met up with the Minnesota River just a couple of miles from here, and that flowed east until it met the Mississippi in the Twin Cities.

Well, that little girl wouldn't make that walk down to the river anymore, or her mom.

Finnegan took a deep breath. He hated this guy. It was a job, and you couldn't get too caught up in it; get too emotional and you'd go insane. Finnegan had seen that happen, friends of his burned out completely by the work. He didn't want that to happen to himself.

But this guy, and he was sure it was a guy despite the heavy-handed clues about women—the high-heel shoe prints, the lipstick, the hair, and all the rest, even the witness account from that little girl a couple of years back, all of that had to be wrong—this guy had made it personal and, goddamn it, he was a monster that had to be stopped. If he wasn't stopped, he'd do it again and again and again until he *was* stopped.

Finnegan stomped his feet a few times, keeping the circulation going, and beat his arms and hands against his shoulders. His hands, still in the surgicals, were freezing, but he loved the cold, loved the way it hardened all the edges and made things clean and clear. The cold dominated the world here, and he'd long ago learned to appreciate that. Hell, in the middle of winter like this it was hard to even imagine this scene in summer, with those distant cottonwoods leafed out and the field green with sugar beets.

The cottonwoods. Did he see something in there? He stopped moving, froze in place, and looked, hard, down toward the trees and the river, a good four or five hundred yards away.

Probably a deer, but in broad daylight? There was a trail headed down that way, too, footprints in the snow heading down to the river. Could it be?

He started walking that way, was breaking into a trot over the bumpy, slippery frozen slush before he thought that he should've gone out front and told the uniform guys what he was doing, gotten some backup, gotten things organized. But there was no time for that. There was somebody down there, somebody running through the trees, a tiny figure silhouetted against the white expanse of snow, heading through the trees and down to the riverbed. Jesus, the Intruder, the monster, it had to be him.

Finnegan started running, a clumsy slipping run across refrozen snow on a furrowed field, falling, it seemed, every five or six steps, scrambling to get to his feet and run some more, trying to stay upright and get down there.

Time stretched out on him as he struggled through the snow. It was a dream, a bad dream where you run and run and run and can't get anywhere. Jesus, his breath was gone now, too, the air so cold he couldn't bring in enough of it to fill his lungs as he stood there for a moment, halfway to the trees, trying to catch his breath.

He pulled off the surgical gloves, then covered his mouth with his hands, warming the air enough that he could bring it into his mouth and his lungs and warming his hands up some, too. He started running again, was gasping for air as he did it. He could feel himself starting to sweat. Imagine that, twenty damn below, and he was sweating, trying to breathe, trying to run, trying to reach those trees.

He couldn't see the figure anymore by the time he reached the first of the cottonwoods, the river just twenty yards away now, down a gentle slope at first and then in a little gully, the riverbank dropping off a quick ten feet down the riverbed.

Finnegan staggered, dead tired, down that way, slipped on the gentle slope, and went flying, on his back, right over the edge of the embankment and down into the river bottom. *Oomph.* The lights went out.

But only, he thought, for a second. He was on his back, on cold ice, staring up at a gray, snow-filled sky. He sat up, turned to get onto his knees, and then, carefully, stood. Nothing broken. He took a few steps and, yeah, he was fine, just his hands hurting, aching with the cold.

He looked upriver and down, nothing there. The river curved downstream some fifty yards away, a gentle bend that hid everything from view. He started walking that way, then, feeling the footing was OK on the snow-covered ice, started trotting, no falling now with no furrowed fields to struggle through, moving along at a pretty good clip.

There was no sudden rounding of the bend; it was too gentle for that. There was just the realization that he'd gotten into the gentle curve of the riverbed and that if he stopped and looked downstream he could see clearly for a long, long way. He stopped, looked.

And there was a figure trudging along, not looking back, just moving along on the ice steadily, heading downstream, away from him.

Finnegan thought, for a mad moment, about pulling out his Glock from the shoulder holster and firing off a warning round, yelling at the guy to stop. The warning round couldn't hurt anybody out here, so screw department policy.

But he knew that guy wouldn't stop. If Finnegan was going to pull his Glock, he'd better be close enough to use it. OK, then, get close enough, but be quiet about it. See if he could sneak up on the guy some before he noticed. Finnegan started running again on the ice, patches of it clear of snow, but not black ice, not the good ice of a long winter but, instead, a cloudy ice formed over the river from too many thaws and refreezes. What did Melchior call this stuff? Milk ice, that was it. Great plumes of vapor came from Finnegan's breath as he pounded along, trying to be quiet and sneak up on the guy ahead of him, trying to put his feet in the right places on the bad ice and the occasional patches of snow.

He had to stop again. Looked downriver. The guy was

stopped, had turned to look back, clearly saw Finnegan now, Finnegan with his hands on his knees, trying to catch his breath. The guy waved. Waved! Finnegan, absurdly, waved back, having an instant of doubt. It couldn't be the monster, could it? The monster wouldn't wave at him, would he?

Then check it out. He started walking toward the guy, a good hundred yards separating them. The guy backed away. Finnegan walked faster and the guy turned and ran.

OK, then, that settled it. Go get him.

Finnegan ran harder, caution forgotten, catch him now or lose him maybe forever. Catch him, catch him, catch him, the words in a rhythm that matched his steps on the river ice.

There was a loud crack. Oh, sweet Jesus, he'd heard that before, that time with Melchior out on Minnetoksak. Another crack and then, with no other warning, no sense of the ice giving way beneath him, Finnegan was falling, arms thrown wide, into water so cold it was unthinkable, the shock of it knocking his breath from his lungs, knocking him not quite senseless but into a kind of dreamily exterior view of himself, some clear part of his brain watching calmly as he felt himself sinking, unable to do anything about it, weighted down by shoes, his thick woolen coat; dead tired from the run.

Funny how, after a second, it didn't feel cold anymore. Just comforting. His hands didn't hurt anymore.

He was looking up, through the water, through the hole he'd made in the ice, enlarging the thin crust of ice as he'd fallen through. Looking up, and dreaming, he saw the monster there looking down at him, the face a blank mask, shaking its head sadly, watching him fade away into the river's darkness, and then, oddly, reaching down to him.

His last thoughts were of Father Murphy and the poor mother and daughter back in the farmhouse. He could see them clearly somehow: Murphy with his eyes back in his head, and they were open and staring at him, like the mother and daughter were staring, too, questioning him. How come this had happened to them? How come Dan Finnegan couldn't stop it, couldn't catch the guy?

He didn't know. He didn't have an answer to that. Instead, oddly calm as the light above him rippled and shrank, he sank deeper, looking up through the strangely warm water to the figure above him, the one with arms outstretched, Christ-like, peaceful, welcoming.

OVER HER HEAD

There was a long, slow rhythm to the world as Melissa came awake. She was moving back and forth in a bed, a bunk she came to realize as she bumped against its wooden railing.

She was on a boat. What the hell had happened?

Then she remembered, remembered it all, from Bo's raping her to the sleepless night to the showers to the shore and the walk into the cold Atlantic.

She sat up, was dizzy for a second, but then her head cleared. She was wearing a pair of blue sweatpants and a long-sleeved T-shirt, both of them at least two sizes too large. The sweatpants were bright blue, with "Blue Jays" in huge red letters running all the way down the right leg and the head of a bird, a blue jay, inside a maple leaf on the hip. The T-shirt, another maple leaf on it, all blue with white letters in the middle that said: "Toronto Maple Leafs."

She was sweating, was blazing hot actually, dressed for colder weather in these pants and sweatshirt, and crammed into this tiny cabin on some small boat that rolled entirely too much with the waves. She was nauseous, very nauseous. The latticed cabin door, made of lacquered wood, was two steps away. She got to it, twisted the tiny knob, stepped over the steep sill, and headed up the narrow, tiny steps to another door. A quick twist there and she opened it. Four steps up, and then she stepped onto the deck and into the blessed fresh air and the sunlight.

She looked up for a moment, turning her face to the sun and the breeze. It felt wonderful. She shaded her eyes, opened them just as the boat rose on a long swell and St. Kitts, to starboard, seemed to drop from sight. Oh my. Her stomach rebelled, and she headed for the side, the ship's roll almost pitching her back into the sea before she grabbed the rail, hanging on for dear life, and retched over the side.

It was a violent minute or two. She hadn't really eaten anything since lunch with Bo the day before, but her stomach didn't seem to realize that. She retched again.

There was a comforting hand on her shoulder. "It'll pass in a few seconds, Melissa, and then we'll get you ashore inside of an hour. Sooner if Stanley can get the diesel up and running again."

Who was touching her? She jerked away, then turned to see who spoke, and smiled in relief to see it was Rosemarie Edwards, her friend from the media relations office at the resort.

She fell into Rosie's open arms. "Rosie. Oh, Rosie," was all she could manage to say.

Rosemarie held her for a few seconds, squeezing tight, a comforting hug. Then she pushed Melissa back a bit, looked at her face, holding her by her arms, a firm grip. "The things you been going through, girl." She shook her head. "I been watching you all this time, wondering when you would wake up. All this time you been telling yourself it was all right, and now you know different, right?"

Melissa nodded.

"Well, you're the lucky one today, Melissa O'Malley. We're just heading over to Nevis on a little shakedown cruise and I'm looking over the side and there you are, girl, way the hell out to sea and sinking fast."

"You saved me?"

"To be exact, Stanley saved you. He went over the side while I dropped the dinghy. He kept you from going under, girl."

"I should thank him, I guess. He's your brother?"

"That's the one, brother Stanley, back from Canada and that wild life, ready to settle down here."

Melissa nodded; yes, she'd heard of Stanley. Ten years he'd been living in Canada and now he was back, had a taxi he drove, and he'd bought this old sailboat, too, planning to fix it up and run it as a day sail and a charter for the tourists. Rosie planned to help him.

Rosie smiled, joked with Melissa. "Stanley, he finally gets this diesel engine rebuilt, here we are at the crack of dawn on this shakedown cruise, and what happens but we wind up rescuing this silly Midwest girl."

Well, "silly" was a kind way to put it, Melissa thought. "Stupid" would be more accurate. "Cowardly," that was a good one. In way over her head, three thousand miles from home and a good half-mile from shore, heading out to the Atlantic, past Antigua there in the distance, and then nothing but Africa next. A long swim. A long way from home.

Melissa started to say something, to blurt it all out in one long lament to Rosie, admit everything, from last night to this whole lonely year, all the things that had gone wrong. This would be a good time to spew it out, clear it all out. Instead, another wave of nausea hit her and she turned to the railing once again to retch over the side.

When she turned back, Rosie handed her a wet towel. It felt wonderful against her face as she wiped away the mess. Her stomach, for the moment, finally felt better.

"How did you see me, Rosie? Why were you out so early?"

"You're welcome, girl."

"Oh, god. Yes. Thank you, Rosie. And Stanley, too. I don't know what was happening to me. I just started swimming. Got past the surf line and just kept going."

"Wearing blue jeans, and in your knit cap and with your mittens on?"

"Were they? Did I?"

Rosie smiled. "They were. You did. We lost the mittens and cap, though, getting you aboard. Maybe that's a good thing?"

Melissa nodded. Maybe.

Rosie put her arm over Melissa's shoulder. "What happened to you, girl? Yesterday morning you seemed fine. You and Bo have some terrible fight or something?"

Melissa nodded. "Or something. You could say that."

Rosie frowned. "That Bo Palmer do something to you, Melissa? Something you didn't want done?"

There was a metallic whine from below, then a loud mechanical cough and a loud clatter that settled into a steady rumble. The diesel was kicking in.

The latticed door clattered open and a thin guy with smears of black oil on his face and hands started speaking before he cleared the steps and got on deck. "What I tell you, Rosie, eh? Running like a top now, this engine. We'll take her on through the Narrows and back up to town. You call ahead and get the constable to meet us there and . . ."

"Oh." He noticed Melissa. "I'm Stanley. How you feeling, sweetheart? You get that seawater out of that stomach of yours? I think you swallowed most of Frigate Bay before we hauled you out."

She nodded, gave a half-smile. "Yes. I think it's all gone at this point."

"Should be," Rosie laughed. "She's been hanging her head over the rail for ten minutes now. Nothing much come up that last couple a times."

Stanley was walking back toward the wheel. "All right, then, ladies. Let's get this girl to hospital."

Rosie looked hard at Melissa. Turned to speak to Stanley. "I think this girl needs a lawyer, or the police, more than she's needing a doctor, Stanley. That right, Melissa?"

Melissa just stared at her friend. She hadn't begun to think about this, but, "Yes," she said, "yes, that's what I need, I think. A lawyer. Do you know one, a good one?"

Standing behind the wheel, Stanley shaded his eyes with his hand and looked down at Melissa to chuckle. "Yeah, well, this family knows some lawyers, eh, Rosie? She's in that kind of trouble?"

Rosie stood up straight, turned to face her brother, arms on her hips. "Stanley," she said, "no need for any of that. This girl needs our help and she's a friend of mine. You get us to Frigate Bay Harbor and I'll take care of things from there, yeah?"

"But I need you to crew this afternoon, Rosie. You promised. That's why you took the day off, remember?"

She looked at him sternly. "Stanley," she said, only that, but her look said more.

Stanley quit chuckling, just nodded his head. "Yeah, yeah, all right, Rosie, I hear you. Frigate Bay, it is."

"And you get on that fancy radio of yours and call Nicole Percival, too, Stanley. Let her know we got someone needs her help."

"Yeah, no problem, Rosie. You're the boss. Like I always say, the woman knows what's right."

"Damn right, Stanley. Glad you learned something up there in Canada." She laughed then, a little chuckle, while Stanley just smiled.

Melissa watched all this quietly, almost making sense of it. Her friend was going to help her, right? That sounded good. And someone named Nicole would help, too?

She wanted to ask some questions, but truth was she was very tired and her brain was getting foggy again. She felt Rosie helping her down the narrow stairs, could see, through the fog, the in-viting bunk as they walked through the latticed door. Compliant, Melissa raised her arms to help Rosie pull the heavy sweatshirt off and slipped into a T-shirt, much tighter.

Rosie was talking to her as she pulled the sweatshirt off her. "You get some sleep now, girl. We'll get you right up to town and you can meet with Nicole Percival. She'll know what to do about this sort of thing."

"Nicole will know?" That sounded very comforting for some reason.

"Well, yeah, I hope she will." And then there was more, some murmurings about Bo Palmer and his filthy rich father, trying to run the whole damn island. But Melissa wasn't sure she really heard that, thought she might have been dreaming, and somehow it didn't matter anyway. She was safe here and could sleep for just a few minutes. Later, she could go to her apartment. And pack. And head north.

A STUPID TIME OF YEAR

Drifting in:

St. Joseph's Hospital, third floor, Room 308, a uniformed officer at the door. Inside, no longer shivering, Finnegan lay on his back, arms at his side, the wrists and hands covered in gauze; frostbite, they'd told him when he came up out of that dark place his mind had been for a few hours. Outside, the sun was setting at four-thirty on a January day. Inside, everyone was bright and cheery, his pals from the department and a couple of buddies from the BCA here pretending everything was OK.

Half-awake. No, pretty much awake, almost anyway, cobwebby but here, trying to focus on what Jon Hamner, the BCA's best guy, was saying: "The son of a bitch saved your cold, wet ass, Dan."

As Hamner told it, he'd started driving down from St. Paul as soon as he heard about the murders, was just driving up to the farmhouse, in fact, when he heard two shots fired from somewhere down near the cottonwoods and the river, the sound echoing all around, bouncing off the snow and ice, hard to pin down.

Hamner ran down there, others trailing behind when they heard the shots, too, and Hamner's yelling.

Hamner slid down the embankment onto the river ice and ran for fifty yards, slipping and stumbling, trying to keep his feet, before he saw the still form of his friend Dan Finnegan lying there on the ice, five yards from the hole in the ice, a thin layer of new ice already forming on him from the river water as the below-zero air hit it.

Finnegan looked cold. Absolutely still. Dead.

But he wasn't, not yet. When you work in law enforcement or medical services in Minnesota one thing you learn in a hurry is the wonder of hypothermia. The body reacts to the cold by slipping into a kind of suspended animation. Heart rate drops; blood flow shifts away from the extremities and outer skin to the core. Sometimes the body's vital signs disappear entirely. There was a toddler in International Falls who lived through four hours of being frozen alive, the temperature around forty below, the child's body temperature down to half-normal. Another kid, this one in Minneapolis, fell through the ice and had no vital signs for more than two hours after being rescued. He recovered.

What they say in Minnesota in the winter is this: You're not dead until you're warm and dead.

Finnegan heard all this from Hamner, who somehow found it all very funny, especially the part at the end on how they figured out, once they looked around the site where Finnegan had broken through and saw all the footprints in the snow, that it must have been the perpetrator who came back and hauled him out, fired the Glock to get some help, and then got out of there before the cavalry arrived.

Finnegan found out, too, that hypothermia and frostbite are two different things. This he learned from the doctor, a young kid named David Moss who had to be some kind of prodigy to be practicing medicine already—he didn't look more than twenty-five years old.

"Detective Finnegan," the kid doctor had said an hour or so back, right after the nurse had come in, had him swallow a couple of penicillin pills, and then stuck a needle in Finnegan's arm and said, simply, "Tetanus," when Finnegan had asked what it was for. "You were hypothermic, but they brought you through that fine at the site. You also have some first-degree frostbite in your toes and on your cheeks and the bridge of your nose, but I don't see any problems there, really; I think they'll recover nicely."

The kid had paused, tried a thin smile, gone on: "In your fingers, however, the level of injury is a mix of second- and third-degree frostbite. There's some redness, some swelling, a lot of clear blistering, and some blood-filled blisters. These are serious injuries."

"And?" Finnegan had asked.

The kid had tried that smile again, then gone into doctorese, easier to say it in jargon than try to make it clear. "And we're doing what we can for you. We've debrided the clear blisters, but we'll leave the blood blisters alone to heal. The vaccination will head off any tetanus; the intravenous antibiotic should handle any secondary infections. We'll keep cotton pledgets between those digits to decrease tissue maceration. All of that should help immensely."

"I hear a 'but' in there somewhere, Doctor."

The kid took a breath. "But these are serious injuries, especially to the fingers in your right hand. You may lose those fingers."

Jesus. Lose some fingers? The thought that that might happen hadn't even occurred to him.

"You're going to amputate some of my fingers? How many?"

"No, no, we're not certain of that at all, Detective. We may be able to save them all. And perhaps it will only be necessary to take the fingertips of one or two. We can always be optimistic."

"We can?" Jesus, Finnegan didn't feel real optimistic. He needed to get Springer in here, the ME from St. Paul. That guy had seen a lot; he'd have a better idea of what was up, of how serious all this was.

"When will I know something?" he asked the kid.

"Well, that's one of the odd things about frostbite: it may take weeks before we know how well your fingers have healed."

"Weeks? Two weeks? Three?"

"Six or seven, actually, so there's no hurry. We'll continue treatment and keep them free of infection and eventually, we hope, you'll be fine."

"And maybe with all ten fingers?"

The kid doc smiled. "Yes," he said, "maybe." And then he smiled one more time. But Finnegan didn't like the tone of voice. He wanted to argue about it, swear to god he'd be fine, he was a tough cop damn it, and he'd keep his damn fingers, all of them.

But truth was he could feel himself losing it, drifting out. The doc was saying something in the background about how they all had to clear out, give the guy some rest, he needed the sleep now for a while.

Sleep sounded good. Just for an hour or two, maybe. He heard everyone leaving, felt a few touches on his head, his chest, where guys were saying good-bye, wishing him well, touching him but avoiding his arms.

Finally, the door was closing. Eyes closed, tired, he heard the kid doctor saying something to someone who was coming in, telling him to be quiet.

Finnegan opened his eyes to see who the hell this was. Tired, beat, he managed a smile anyway. This was OK; this was Melchior O'Malley, his old buddy, holding a pie, apple, from the Little House. Jesus, that pie smelled good.

NO REGRETS

Nicole Percival, L.D., used the point of her pencil to tick off on her notes, one by one, her reasons for not wanting to take the case. "First [tick], Miss O'Malley, by your own admission you never said no to the young man. Second [tick], you never tried to stop him. Third [tick], he didn't force himself on you."

She frowned at Melissa, raised her pencil from the paper where she'd scribbled down this reasoning, aimed its eraser end at Melissa. "Rape is a crime of violence, Miss O'Malley, not a crime of regret. We simply do not have anything to build a case on. Surely you can see that."

Melissa leaned forward in her chair, angrily shook her head. "But he *raped* me. I didn't say 'yes,' but I didn't want this to happen. I'd had too much to drink, maybe, but that doesn't mean..."

The lawyer sighed, scribbled down another note. "And [tick] you admit to having too much to drink, as well."

She took her glasses off, set them on the paper in front of her. "Now, that doesn't mean that he can force himself on you, and you know and I know that what he did is wrong, and perhaps back home, in," she looked at her notes, "in Minnesota, it might be different. But here," she shook her head, "here, the law does not necessarily *recognize* that it is wrong. Do you see what I mean by that? It is a matter of law, and I am not convinced that there is, under these circumstances, anything that I can do for you."

Melissa sat back against the hard wooden chair in the simple second-floor office on Fort Street, just up from the Circus Square with its Berkeley Memorial clock tower and drinking fountain, built a century ago to commemorate some long-forgotten politician from the glory days of the sugar plantations. Out the window to her right, she could see the people walking up and down the busy street, locals, by and large, with a few tourists mixed in here and there, the tourists all too obvious—white, sometimes rapidly turning red, wearing shorts and flip-flops and T-shirts. They obviously didn't belong, didn't fit in. Today, after living here more than a year, that's how Melissa felt. She'd thought she had her mother's blood, thought she belonged in a place like this, thought she'd gotten to know this island and understood it. She realized now how wrong she was.

"Listen, Miss O'Malley. I know what Stanley and Rosemarie said to you, and Stanley and Rosie are very good friends of mine. But in this case, I must say they're wrong in thinking we can accomplish anything through the legal system. My advice for you is to go down to the Frigate Bay Police Station where you filed the charges and ask to have them removed before the newspapers run a story and you find yourself in the middle of a scandal."

Melissa knew what would happen once the story ran. The Palmers were important on this little island, and island journalism wasn't quite the same thing as the newspaper journalism she'd learned in St. Pete at Eckerd College.

Here the *News-Democrat*—the old, establishment newspaper—would blame the whole thing on her, making sure she looked like a typical money-hungry American gold digger.

What would the other paper, the smaller weekly *Labour News*, do? She didn't know, she had to admit that she'd never read it, but it was hard to imagine it would be any nicer to her than the main paper.

She felt a strange, surreal calm as she walked to her car. Of course it had gone wrong at the lawyer's office. Of course she couldn't possibly win. Of course she'd done it all wrong from the time she'd started drinking with Bo to the moment she'd tried to explain it all to Nicole Percival. Of course, of course, of course.

She'd known, down in her soul, that it had all been her fault from the beginning, from the very first time she'd met Bo, that evening back in college. It had all been a disaster waiting to happen and then she'd taken part in it. God, she was so stupid.

A couple of hours before, she'd been stupid enough to think there might be a way to make it better. After they docked in Frigate Bay, she and Rosie had gone by the local police station and she'd filled out a form, the Initial Filing for an Act of Rape. Rosie, to her surprise, had known everyone in the station, chatting away with them as Melissa sat at a battered old wooden desk and filled out the details of the crime.

Then Rosie had driven her home, waited for her to clean up and change, staying outside, protecting her, while she did that. Melissa had insisted on doing her own driving then, feeling good about having at least that much control, and so Rosie had followed her into Basseterre and Nicole Percival's office.

On that twenty-minute drive Melissa had felt herself recovering some—thinking she was getting things done, slowly building up some heat, stoking it, thinking it all through, and coming to realize what a monster Bo Palmer really was, vowing to stop him, to punish him, to get him to feel something of the horror she'd known. . . .

And now all that was gone, the heat washed away by the impersonal logic of the lawyer's quiet pronouncements.

She'd asked Rosemarie to leave, said she could handle this herself, and so now, alone, she walked to her little Honda and climbed in. What to do next? Just go to the office and pretend it was just another day and she'd missed the morning's work because she was sick?

That wasn't going to work. Once the Palmers heard about the charges being filed she'd be fired on the spot and out the door. It was probably best to just go home and try to relax, now that her head was clearer. Maybe an afternoon of thinking things through some, trying to figure out what was the right thing to do, would help her make some decisions.

And maybe Nicole Percival was right; maybe the best thing to do was just cut her losses here—go back to the station, sign whatever she had to sign to drop the charges, and be done with it. By tonight, tomorrow afternoon at the latest, she could be on a flight back home. The little prop plane back to San Juan and the big jet from there to Minneapolis and she could put this whole Caribbean nightmare behind her.

Back home, back in that awful cold of January, she'd be able to see herself better, understand who she was and why she'd gone through all this. There were good jobs there; she'd work, meet some nice guy named Olsen or Rasmussen, have a nice life, learn once again to put up with winter's demands and enjoy summer's brief appearance. Maybe go ice fishing with her father and to some Timberwolves games with Dan Finnegan. There were worse ways to live.

The police station was back in Frigate Bay, right on the way home. A left turn at that corner instead of a right turn and she'd be there, could drop the charges and be done with it. It made sense.

She sat down in the Honda, buckled her seat belt, turned the key to get it started, and pulled away from the curb, away from the lawyer and Basseterre and these horrible past twenty-four hours. She was heading home.

If she hadn't stopped at her town house to take another shower before going over to the police station to drop the charges, it all would have gone very differently. Stanley, much later, reminded her of that. But she did stop, just for a few minutes, she told herself as she slid the little Honda into the parking space near the front door of her town house on the top of Conaree Hill.

The shower took fifteen minutes, no more, even with drying her hair. She was dressing, nice tan slacks and a white blouse, when the phone rang. She reached to answer it, then realized, oh god, it might be Bo.

It rang again. She let it go, and after four rings the answering machine kicked in. She stood there, trembling, to listen.

And the voice she heard was from a better place, a clearer place, a place more understandable. Oh my, it was good to hear that voice. Happy for the moment, happy for the first time in days, in weeks, longer, she picked up the phone and blurted out his name.

SOME KIND OF SIGN

Dan Finnegan knew he had to give Melissa a call; he owed her that, as deeply connected as she was to all of this. But he'd been putting it off, not only because it would be the first in a long line of tough conversations he was going to have to make but also because it was going to be a hell of a hassle just using the damn phone. So when Mel walked into the room, Finnegan thought to himself that it had to be some kind of sign from above.

"Heard about you on the news," Mel said. "Wanted to come by and see how you're doing." He smiled. "You been in the water a lot the last couple of winters," ribbing him about the time when Finnegan had fallen through on Lake Minnetoksak. That was about as close to joking as Mel was likely to get.

Finnegan smiled back. "Glad you're here, Mel. I have to make some phone calls, and," he held up his bandaged hands, "using the phone's a little tricky. You dial it for me?"

"Sure." He picked up the white hospital phone, hit 9 to get an outside line. "What number?"

Finnegan told him, dialing into the long-distance service the department used, giving him the PIN number and all that, then dictating the area code and the number. Mel just dialed away, not realizing maybe that it was his daughter's number in St. Kitts he was calling, instead just waiting for the call to go through and then putting the phone up to Finnegan's ear, where he could hold it with his bandaged right hand.

"Melissa?"

"Mr. Finnegan? Is that you? Oh, I can't believe it's you." He thought he could hear her crying.

The whole world shifted for a second. Why was she crying? He had other things to worry about, sure, but Melissa was crying.

He could hear her pause and gather herself. "I'm sorry. It's just been a rough couple of days."

Well, he didn't see how far he could dodge getting into things: "Yeah, it's been pretty interesting here, too, Melissa. I don't want to add to your troubles, but there's been a lot going on here lately."

Another pause. She sounded tired but calm. "OK, Mr. Finnegan, what's up?"

"It's Walter Arndt, Melissa. And Father Murphy."

"You found them? You found them both?" He could hear the questions in her voice.

"We found them, Melissa. But it's bad. It's really bad. They're both dead."

Silence on the other end of the line. Finnegan looked up and Mel was looking at him. He sure as hell knew now who Finnegan had dialed. He held out his hand to take the phone. Finnegan nodded and Mel took the phone.

"Melissa? Sweetheart?"

"Daddy?"

"Yeah, Melissa. I'm here in Dan Finnegan's hospital room with him."

"Hospital room? What the hell is going on up there?"

And so they told her, giving the phone back and forth, breaking the news to her about Murphy, about Arndt, about Finnegan's own troubles and the frostbite and all the rest.

It wasn't an easy talk to have, but as Finnegan hung up he was proud of Melissa, who'd been strong about it, hadn't broken down over the phone. She'd check out the airfare and head up their way for the funerals, she said. Said she'd been thinking about coming home for a visit anyway.

It was good talking to her.

BY TOMORROW

The phone call had put things into perspective for Melissa. No question about it now, it was time to go home. That felt right, more right than Minnesota had ever felt to her in her life.

No makeup on, just sliding into some shorts and a bra and T-shirt and some sandals, she headed for the front door. In five minutes she'd be at the police station, where she could tell them to drop the charges. Then she could come back to the town house, call the airlines, and get a one-way ticket for tomorrow afternoon's flight and start to pack. By tomorrow night she'd be back in Minnesota, back in the cold Midwest where she at least knew herself, knew who she'd been and who she could be. She could start over there, and this time she could get it right.

But Stanley was outside, waiting for her, leaning against his taxi, an old Toyota Corolla. He was smiling, dressed in slacks and a short-sleeved white cotton shirt "Hi, girl," he said. "I got some good news for you."

She smiled at him. Goofy-looking guy, really, too thin and couldn't be more than five-eleven, barely taller than she was. He wore the top button on his shirt fastened, had curly short black hair, wire-rimmed glasses. He had to have been the nerd in his high-school class, probably a straight A student. And now here, on this tiny island, he drove a taxi and was trying to start up a charter boat service. He'd been pretty successful in Toronto, Rosie said. Melissa wondered why he'd left Canada to come back home.

"I have news, too, Stanley," she said to him. There was no

reason to get into the mess back home, but he was involved in her stupidity here and deserved to know. "I went to see that lawyer you and Rosie recommended. I told her you sent me and she took the time right on the spot to talk to me."

"And?"

"She doesn't think I have a chance in the world. She recommended I go drop the charges before the newspapers get hold of it and the whole island runs me out, tarred and feathered."

"Nicole said that?"

"That was the gist of it."

He shook his head. "You know, sometimes you have to wonder about this place. You tell her he forced himself on you?"

"I gave her all the details I could." She paused. "That's what ruins the case, those details. There were some things I didn't remember when I told you the story." She looked at him, shook her head. Might as well be honest. "I didn't say 'no' to him. I didn't put up a struggle."

He looked at her, said nothing, his brown eyes just looking into hers, trying to see some truth in there, maybe. She didn't know what that was. Should she have struggled more? Bitten and clawed and scratched? Yelled for help?

Bo would have stopped, she thought. All she'd had to do was say no, like she'd said to him a hundred times before, two hundred. Just push him away, tell him "no, not now, Bo," tell him she still wasn't ready.

But she hadn't done that. She'd put herself in that situation and then hadn't stopped it when she should have. She was pathetic. It was her own damn fault.

"Hey, you know what," Stanley was saying, putting his hands out, palms up as if to catch the sun's light, "I'm no lawyer, but it's a beautiful day here in paradise, trade winds blowing, sun shining down. Let's just go for a little drive, you tell me all about it."

She shook her head. "No, I have to go to the Frigate Bay station and drop the charges. She's right, your lawyer friend; it's the only thing to do.

"And then," she added, thinking it through one more time,

sure of herself, "and then I'm going home, Stanley. Back to Minnesota. I'll get on tomorrow's flight to San Juan and get myself home from there."

"Yeah, well, tell you what, Melissa. We can take care of those charges right here, OK? I'll just make a call there and it's done; you know those boys there know Rosie and me. And then maybe we'll just enjoy this beautiful day for a little while, all right?"

This was Rosie's brother; he could certainly be trusted, couldn't he?

He seemed to read her mind. "Rosie and me and my brother, Joseph, we grew up together in St. John's, up on the north end of the island. I can take you up there, show you the real St. Kitts."

She smiled, the first one of those in a long while. "Near Rawlins Plantation? I had lunch there once and it was delicious. Scenery was really nice, too—sugarcane fields everywhere and then the mountain rising behind it. It was beautiful."

He smiled, looking patient. The plantation was close in some ways to where he'd grown up, terribly far in other ways, she realized.

"Yeah," he said, "that's the place. Near Rawlins, only down the hill from there in St. John's. Rosie still lives there, nice little place right on Courpon's Bay, looking out toward Statia in the distance. You know how that looks?"

She nodded. St. Eustatius, the Dutch island to the north, was only eight miles away from St. Kitts at that point. The views of it from Rawlins Plantation were magnificent.

"OK, here's what we'll do: You call into work and tell them you're taking the day off. Then we'll take a drive up there; you tell me all about this as we go. There's a nice little restaurant there, the Lighthouse. A friend of mine, Reuben Andrews, he runs it. We go up there, meet Rosie; have a bite to eat, look at that view, drink some tea, just relax."

"And the police? We'll do that first?"

He scratched his head. "Well, I think you need to think about this a little before you drop the charges. How about I give them a call and tell them to just sit on that for a while, not put anything through to the Superintendent's Office in Basseterre until they hear from you? That gives you a little time to think it over, right?"

She nodded. Yes, thinking it over might be good. And Stanley knew how things worked here, obviously knew everybody on the whole island. It made sense to listen to him.

"OK, then," he was saying, opening the passenger-side door to his taxi. "You just sit down in here and relax, and Stanley will take of everything, all right?"

She nodded, sat down in the Toyota. He climbed in the driver's side, opened the glove box, and pulled out a cellular phone, handed it to her. She called the office and told Angela, the receptionist, that she didn't feel very good and wouldn't be in. It felt good, safe, saying that, and held its own kind of truth.

Then Stanley took the phone back, hit one button, and put it to his ear and waited for a few seconds.

"Errol, that you? . . . Yeah, man, this is Stanley Edwards." He paused. "Yeah, man, I'm back. . . . That's right, been back for a couple of months now. . . . Yeah, it's good; it's good." He nodded. "Yeah, she's good, too, man; she's fine. . . . At the Palmer House . . . Yeah, they treat her great, there. . . . Yeah, man, thanks for asking."

Another pause. "Listen, Errol, you got charges filed a few hours ago from Melissa O'Malley, that girl from Palmer's, you know? She was in there with Rosie, right? . . . Yeah, man. Well, listen, I'm here talking to her right now, in my official capacity, and she says she wants to hold off on that for a little while, all right? You just hang on to that paper and she'll get back with you tomorrow or the next day on it, right? Don't need to cause anything until then, yeah?"

He listened for a minute, chuckled. "Yeah, man, that's the way it is. You know how that goes. . . . OK, couple of days, right? . . . Yeah, man. I'll tell Rosie that you said hi, OK. You stop by sometime and have dinner with us; she'd love that. Been too long, Errol."

Another pause, then he laughed. "Yeah, man. Thank you," and

hung up. Turned to face her. "All taken care of, then. He'll wait until he hears from you on those charges."

She took a deep breath, the immediate burden lifted some. "Thank you," She paused, added, "And this 'official capacity' that you're in, what's that?"

He put the Toyota into gear and pulled away from the curb. "I thought you knew that. Didn't Rosie tell you that I'm with the *Labour News*?"

Oh, so he was a reporter. So that was what this was all about—a story and maybe a good scandal.

"You're a reporter?" She shook her head. "Please just stop and let me out now, Stanley. I'll walk back. God, that's all I need."

He held up his hand. "No, no. I'm Rosie's brother first, OK? And a reporter second. This is all off the record, all the way, unless and until you tell me otherwise."

He looked over at her, smiled. "I just want to help you, OK? Rosie asked me to help, and so that's what I'm going to do."

She pulled her hand back from the door handle. "Rosie just said that you drive this taxi, that you make a pretty good living at it. And that now you're starting up that charter boat business. And now I find out you work for the paper. How many jobs do you have? Are you a policeman, too? Maybe you're the prime minister?"

He grinned as he made the left onto the Old Bay Road without answering; then, as they approached the roundabout that would lead them eventually to West Coast Road and the drive north up the coast past Sandy Point and on into St. John's, he turned to smile at her. "Listen, girl. I'm about as far from being prime minister of this island as you can get. And for the paper, yeah, I'm a reporter. And I'm the editor, too. And the circulation department. And the advertising staff. And the bookkeeper."

"You run the paper?"

He laughed, nodded. "Run it, own it. Keep it afloat. I *am* the *Labour News*. That's me, Stanley Edwards, media baron, just like Rupert Murdoch."

"And you drive a taxi?"

"And I drive a taxi." He laughed, wheeled the taxi around a slow-moving van. "It's the taxi that pays the bills, girl, so I can keep the paper coming out."

"The paper's a hobby for you?"

"A hobby? Listen, girl, you don't know too much about journalism, I guess. There's a story here, a big one. And the *Labour News* is going to get it—I'm going to get it—someday soon."

"Hey," she said. "I was a journalism major in college, Stanley. I had a piece two years ago in the *Triton* about a developer who wanted to build right next to Fort De Soto Park. He had plans to tear out the mangroves, build a spoil island—all the things you'd think developers weren't allowed to do anymore—but he'd paid the right people.

"I did the story, and it finished fifth in the Hearst Awards. You know about those?"

He grinned. "Never heard of them. But look, Melissa O'Malley, big-time journalist and ex-girlfriend of Bo Palmer, the story I'm working on just might have something to interest you, since it's all about the Palmers. Maybe you want to write it? Win another of those awards?"

She frowned, shook her head. "No, my problem with Bo isn't that kind of story. I'll just leave the island, I think, and that will end it."

Stanley nodded. "Yeah, you could leave. That would be the smart thing to do."

She sensed what was coming. "I hear a 'But.'"

"But if you leave, you'll miss out on this story, and on your chance to find out the truth."

"I know the truth. I know what happened."

"No, no. You know a little bit of the truth, just what happened to you. I'm talking about a lot more, girl. I'm talking about the Palmer family and the whole thing."

She shook her head. "What whole thing?"

"There's things going on here on this island, girl, things that involve that boyfriend of yours, that will interest a lot of people. And I'm going to find the story."

Melissa smiled weakly. Reporters never quit. That's maybe the one thing she learned from all her classes back in college: reporters just don't know when to quit. "I bet you are, Stanley. But not today, all right? I absolutely do not need this today."

He smiled back. "OK, then. Let's just go get that cup of tea with Rosie and let you relax a little, like I promised, all right?"

They were driving along the Bay Road now, the Caribbean a perfect blue to their left, Mount Liamuiga rising to their right. The scenery was so perfect, the weather so perfect, that Melissa had to shake her head to think of what she'd just been through. This whole island was like that—surreal in the way its seeming perfection wrapped up some ugly realities inside that package.

Still, relaxing a little sounded pretty good. Later, at Reuben Andrews' Lighthouse Restaurant—a very fancy name for a place with four wooden tables set on a wood deck behind a small house—they did just that, Melissa and Stanley comparing stories of midwinter misery in the far north, Toronto versus Minnesota, while Rosie listened, shook her head in wonder, and smiled.

Melissa found it very real and comforting. This, she kept telling herself, was the real St. Kitts. These were the real Kittitians. This was reality, and she liked it. For several minutes at a time she could forget what she'd been through the day before, what she'd tried to do this morning. That all seemed very far away, some distant past and some distant place.

Until, exhausted, she finally had to go home.

RUM PUNCH

Rosie drove Melissa home and then stayed with her through the night, sleeping on the fold-out couch bed in the next room and getting up to check on her every hour or so. She said it was just to keep her company, but they all knew it was a suicide watch as well. Melissa knew Rosie was making the bed checks because she was awake each time, convinced as the hours wore on that she never would sleep again. In the morning, when Rosie woke her up with a cup of coffee and some orange juice, that turned out not to be true.

She called in sick again at the resort and no one seemed to question it. Rosie went on into work and called her by ten o'clock to tell her everything seemed normal. Melissa kept expecting Bo's knock on the door or at least a phone call. To keep herself busy she packed and called the airline for a ticket on the afternoon flight to Miami. The price was outrageous. She didn't care.

It wasn't easy, since she didn't think she'd be coming back. She decided she'd pack just enough for a few days up in Minnesota and Rosie could come by and pack up the rest and put it all into storage or keep it or whatever. Trying to figure out exactly how that would work out was just too much to think about at the moment.

While she was packing she kept wondering how she was going to react if Bo called. She found out when it finally happened just before lunch.

She answered and he spoke, without any introduction. "Melissa, you're feeling sick?"

"Yes." She was standing by the phone as she did this, her heart racing, palms sweaty with dread, just hearing his voice.

"Well, listen, sweetheart, like I told you the other night, I've got to get up to Miami for a couple of days on this Holtzhausen thing. Looks like Dad is going to go up there, too, for a checkup—he's not feeling real great lately. So I may have to stay there for a few days. We'll talk more about the wedding when I get back, OK?"

"Sure. When you get back," she managed to say, and then hung up. Could that be, that he thought nothing had really happened, that the wedding plans were on?

Of course it could, she thought. From his perspective it was all entirely possible. That made him all the more a monster.

Was he lying? Telling the truth?

Oh, god, and then it hit her. He'd be on the Miami flight, the same flight she had a ticket for. Oh, great. That was unthinkable. So she'd have to stay for one more day or something, anything to avoid being on that same flight with Bo.

She'd been standing next to the nightstand in her bedroom as she answered the phone. Now she set it back into its cradle and sat on the bed.

She sat there, arms at her sides, palms down to support herself, staring at the bedroom wall where a framed picture of a Caribbean sunset seemed to glow orange and red. She'd bought that the second day here, after seeing a sunset the night before that looked just like it. Bo had kissed her as the sun set and they'd watched for the green flash. She'd kissed him back.

How had it all come to this? Where had things gone so terribly wrong? Had she caused it all to happen? Well, for sure, the Midwest Catholic in her, the old altar server, the True Believer in the words she'd heard from Father Murphy, believed that it was all her fault: Mea culpa, mea culpa, mea maxima culpa.

The phone rang. Startled, she backed away from it. Bo again? Laughing at her this time? Laughing at what she'd become?

She was afraid to pick it up, and when it finished its fourth ring and the answering machine kicked in: "Sorry, I'm not in. Leave a message," whoever it was hung up.

Well, OK then. She stood up, walked out of the bedroom, down the hallway, through the kitchen, and toward the front door. The phone started ringing again. She ignored it, kept walking, out the front door and into the heat for some fresh air.

And there, ten feet away, was Stanley, on his cell phone. He saw her, tapped it off, shut it, and laughed.

"Hey, so you *are* home. How you doing today, girl? Rosie asked me to stop by and check up on you. I tried knocking on the door but got nowhere, so I thought I'd call you before I broke the door down."

She looked at him and was suddenly furious, all the fear and worry and self-loathing coming out at once. "Stanley!" she yelled, and ran at him, fists up, trying to hit him, to hurt him, to get even with him, get even with Bo, get even with everything that had been happening.

But Stanley was tougher than he looked, and more understanding, and the ease with which he stopped her attack turned into a comforting embrace and some murmurings from him as she cried, tears she'd been needing coming out at last as they stood there together in the sun and the heat.

Eventually they walked inside, and, calmer, she told Stanley about Bo's call. Just talking about it exhausted her. She wanted to go lie down and sleep, maybe take another hot shower.

But Stanley had other ideas. "Listen, girl," he said. "I got some things to tell you now, you know? How about I call the airline and change that ticket and then I come by and take you for a drive, maybe we do the tourist thing for the afternoon, OK? Might be good for you, you know?"

"Stanley, I think I just want to take a shower and a long nap."

"Look, girl, Rosie said I needed to be around here today, all right? And I think she's right. You go ahead and take that shower if you want, but I'll just make that phone call and then wait here until you're ready, yeah?"

She sighed. Rosie and Stanley weren't going to leave her alone; they didn't trust her that far. She couldn't blame them, and Stanley was a nice guy. Maybe it was for the best, and she had an afternoon to kill now that she couldn't take today's flight.

Later, as she and Stanley walked down the path to the parking lot, strolling by the Horizons café that sat perched there on the cliff top, Melissa paused for a second to look out toward the sea. She'd always loved this view of the Caribbean, a few puffy clouds riding high out over the blues and greens of the ocean below. Another perfect day.

Two men, one a local and the other a pale white—some British tourist, she guessed—sat at a table, sipping on coffee or tea, watching her and Stanley go by. The white guy wore a beat-up blue baseball cap with a big red "C" on it. A Cubs fan, so an American, then. He smiled at her, nodded slightly. The local, face impassive behind sunglasses, just sat there. Golfers, maybe, getting a late start on the day.

She and Stanley reached the Toyota and he walked to her side of the car to unlock the door. "You know those two?"

She shook her head. "Never saw them before. Golfers, I suppose."

"You think so?"

She looked at him, frowned. "You think they're something else?"

He shrugged, smiled. "Just my paranoia." He opened her door. "OK, Melissa O'Malley from Minnesota, climb in. I'm going to show you some parts of St. Kitts you haven't seen before, all right?"

She tried to smile back, though smiling wasn't easy. OK, then, be a big girl. "That won't be hard to do, but sure, let's enjoy it. You show me the *real* St. Kitts, Stanley."

He started her off by driving south from Frigate Bay down the New Road, which cut through the middle of the island's south-eastern peninsula, a narrow, hilly, thin strip of land between the Atlantic on one side and the Caribbean on the other. It was rough terrain, with no freshwater and almost no one living out there.

Stanley had tried to turn on the car's air conditioner for her, rolling up the windows as he did so. But she'd insisted on welcoming the warm breeze windows down, enjoying the sun and the heat.

The views were great as they rolled over and between the hills, nearly alone on the road except for an occasional tour van and a few other cars here and there. Stanley kept looking in his rearview mirror, watching for something, or someone, back there but apparently not finding them. Melissa could only shake her head at that. He seemed a nice enough guy, but a worrier, too.

Still, the drive was great. For more than a year Melissa had lived on St. Kitts, but not once had she taken this road south out of the main roundabout at Frigate Bay. Always she'd turned left. Always she'd gone to work at the resort, then gone into town with Bo.

Once, in all that time, Bo had taken her to see the sights, but they'd gone straight to the old fort at Brimstone Hill and lunched after that at Rawlins Plantation. That was during her first week on the island, and that was it, just that once. Somehow—and she found this strange, sitting here with Stanley driving along past the salt ponds and weaving around the peninsula's low hills—it hadn't occurred to her to do more. She'd always felt too busy; there'd been a whirl of things to do, from the struggles at work to the dinner parties at the Palmer place. Those parties, several of them a month, always took her hours to get ready for; the clothes, the shoes, the makeup: it all had to be perfect.

Makeup. Oh, good grief, she realized, putting her left hand to her face, she wasn't wearing any. For the first time in a year she was out in public without any makeup on at all. Where had her mind been this morning?

She wanted to glance in a mirror and see just how bad the damage was, but there was no way to do that without Stanley noticing, and she didn't want him to make fun of her. God knows her ego was shattered enough already without adding her looks into the mix, too.

"Over there, that's the Great Salt Pond, the biggest one on the island," he was saying, breaking into her worry and pointing out the right-side window toward the pond. "The seawater comes in there and gets trapped. See the salt around the shoreline? There was a time when the salt from there was used by the Royal Navy to salt down pork for the sailors."

She nodded, thinking that a historical tour of St. Kitts was probably not exactly what she needed today. Still, at least she felt wide awake. Why wasn't she tired? She didn't know. Instead of being sleepy, she felt hyperaware, like everything had sharp edges, nothing fuzzy about it at all. The air was always clear here anyway, but today the clarity was stunning. She could see every leaf on every bush on the hill to the left, every rock outcrop on its side, every mongoose and green monkey scampering up and down its slopes.

"And over there," he said, pointing toward the southeast coast, "that's Sand Bank Bay. Smugglers used to come in there back in the old days." He turned to look at her and smiled slightly. "Some people say the smugglers still come in there."

It went on like that for another half hour, Stanley stopping every now and then to point things out as they drove along the new paved road out to where it ended, then took a dirt road that wound its way past one low hill and then through the scrub to a small bay.

You'd think it would be total isolation out there, she thought, but you'd be wrong. After a half-mile or so on the dirt road they rounded a curve and there, ahead of them, was a picture-perfect tiny bay and a dusty parking lot with several cars and a small tour company van parked in it.

An open-sided bar—the Turtle Bay Club, the beat-up wooden sign on its top said—sat at the back edge of the sandy beach, with a dozen customers or more sitting on the stools drinking tall, thin glasses of orange-and-yellow rum concoctions.

Stanley and Melissa climbed out of his Corolla and walked over to the bar. Stanley ordered a Ting, the local soft drink, and a hamburger. Melissa, from habit, said, "I'll have a rum punch," to the bartender as she sat on the high stool next to Stanley.

The drinks came and they each took a sip, Melissa grateful for the cool calm that came with a long sip of the rum. She'd never been much of a drinker until that last year or two of college.

Something about being a jock on the basketball team and generally staying in shape kept her away from some of the usual college excesses until she started dating Bo. He was a heavy drinker, and that had rubbed off on her some that last year of school, especially after the basketball season ended. Then she came to this island, and there was something about the isolation, the combination of delicious heat and the slow pace of things, that made a cold rum punch seem perfect. Bo liked a few drinks, too, during lunch and at the end of the day, and so she'd gotten used to the idea of getting that slight buzz going over lunch and keeping it going right through the afternoon.

Stanley sat back against the bar and looked toward the parking lot as a black Jeep Cherokee, all shiny gold and chrome over the black paint and tinted windows, pulled into the lot.

He smiled, nodded his head a bit, then turned away from it and looked out toward the sea. "Nice place here, isn't it? I used to come to this bay in the old days, before this bar was built. Took me a couple of hours back then; there was nothing but a dirt road the whole way from Frigate Bay."

"It's beautiful," she said, and meant it. With the rum, she felt calmer, the hard edges on things softening a bit, the sense of hyperreality easing back. This was better, she thought, a little something she could hide behind. She took another long sip.

"It's for sale," he said. "If I had the money I'd buy it, build a little house back behind it there, and put out the paper from here. That'd be nice, wouldn't it?"

She nodded. "*Nice* isn't the word for it. *Fabulous,* maybe. Or how about *perfect?*"

"*Perfect,* yeah, that's the word for it," he said. That's what I think, too. Hey, one of these days."

He looked at Melissa. "So, girl, tell me your story. How'd you meet Bo Palmer? How'd you wind up down here on this little island in the middle of nowhere after getting that expensive education?"

She finished off the rum punch, wagged her finger to the bartender for another one. "Looking back on it, I guess it was a pretty stupid idea, heading down here with a boy I knew I didn't love to do a job that I thought wasn't very important.

"But I'm from Minnesota, and," she laughed, thinking of their arguments from the day before, "and you know how cold it is there. I mean, I went to college in Florida just for that reason, to try and warm myself up some.

"While I was there, I met Bo there and we started dating. It was just...." She paused, searched for the right word. "I don't know, effortless, you know? He was a big man on campus, and he liked showing me off..."

"...and you liked being shown off?"

She nodded, sighed. "Yeah, I did. In high school I was, you know, a jock, on the basketball team, dated a football player. Looks—being attractive—never figured into it."

She took another long drink, finished the rum punch, waved to the bartender for another. She *wanted* to talk about this, she realized. There was something about this moment, this place, this guy she was sitting next to at a bar where you could hear the waves rolling in—it added up to a kind of confessional that she needed. And not for a very pretty confession at that, she thought.

"Anyway, at first it was just kind of a momentum thing. We dated; we sort of got to be an item. I don't know, it was all rather seductive—entrance into a world I'd just dreamed about. People with houses and cars and boats—vacation homes in the islands, trips to Europe, the whole thing. It was just hard to turn down.

"And then when we graduated and his dad offered me a job, all I could think of was sunshine, warm breezes, the water—that's what I wanted, the whole tropical paradise thing."

The bartender came by with the hamburger. Stanley took it from him, set it down on the bar, reached for the ketchup. "And you got what you wanted, right?"

She nodded, sipped again from her rum punch. "Yeah, I guess I did." She looked out to the open Atlantic. It was time to admit some things, to herself as much as to Stanley.

"You know, after a while I came to realize that things weren't how they looked. The resort is understaffed so badly that it's a joke. There's no maintenance, no upkeep, not enough people at the desk, nobody in reservations half the time. The whole place is falling apart if you look at it closely.

"And Bo. Well, it's sort of the same thing. At first glance he looked great, but the closer I looked, the more I knew, the worse it started to look. The other night, I think, was just a kind of awful message for me."

She looked out to the sea. "You know, until a couple of days ago I thought views like this were the most beautiful things I'd ever seen." She shook her head. "But now? I don't know; I think maybe it's just time for this little girl to head on home, get back to Minnesota where I belong."

His face was impassive. "Cold up there this time of year, girl. You remember that?"

She smiled at him, nodding. But then he smiled, added: "But home is a good thing, too. I'd be lying to tell you anything else. Home—that's another reason I came back to St. Kitts."

She nodded, took another sip of the rum punch. "You were gone, what, ten years?"

"Yeah, and that's a long time, ten years. Lots of things change."

"You were in Canada the whole time?"

He nodded. "Went there to be a journalist, like my father. I wanted to do the same thing as him, only not on this little island where nothing ever happened. I wanted to be in London—the center of the universe. Instead, big joke, I wound up in London, Ontario, where we have some family. Meant to stay there for a few months and after I got the job in Toronto, up the road an hour or so, it wound up being ten years."

"And you did OK in Toronto?"

He nodded, smiled. "Yeah, I did fine. Worked for a while on the copy desk. Got a chance to write a few things, too, but editing is where I'm best. I enjoyed it there. Even got used to the weather as the years went by. You can get used to anything, even forty below."

"No, you can't. I never did."

He took a bite of his hamburger, sipped on the Ting, gave

that some thought. "You know, right in the middle of a winter, with the whole city frozen stiff, I could always think about home. That helped."

"And that's really why you came back? To get warm?" It made sense to her.

He didn't answer. Instead, he took another bite from the hamburger, reached into his pocket and grabbed a twenty, slid it onto the bar, stood up from the stool, and held out his hand to help her off hers. She took it, and they walked out toward the water. The sand was loose and gritty at the backside of the beach, spotted with low rocks. He held on to her hand long enough to get her over the loose sand and the rocks and then let go as they walked along the firmer sand near the waterline. They walked along a bit before he spoke.

"My father died when I was eighteen years old. I was just a layabout back then, no education to speak of, no plans, no nothing, just enjoying myself." He chuckled, shook his head. "I was a big local star in cricket. Everyone thought I'd wind up playing for the Leeward Islands against England and score a century. I believed all that myself, so that's what I did—played, drank beer, went limin' on the Bay Road just to hang out there with my friends. Then my father died."

He paused, ran his fingers through his hair, then held both hands out, palms up, in a kind of supplication. "You know how that goes; everything changed."

Melissa reached out to take hold of one hand. "I lost my mother when I was just a child. I don't remember her very much. My father raised me. He never got over her loss, I think."

Stanley nodded. "Those were tough times. Mother tried hard, but eventually she just started to wear down after Father died. She's Jamaican, you know, and she started to believe all that nonsense she'd grown up with—she started thinking of herself as an obeah woman, you know, a kind of witch doctor. She said she had The Eye, could make potions, could see things the rest of us couldn't see. The children, all three of us, did what we could for her. Rosemarie took care of her at first, and then we got her into a good place. She's done fine there, seemed happy and stable.

Then, this last year, after Joseph's death..." He let the thought hang there for a moment. "Well, you know, she's really slipping now.

"Anyway, somewhere along in there I decided I needed to grow up and be a man, make some money for the family, you know? All I knew was what I'd learned from my father about newspapering, so I quit cricket and just left the island, went to Canada, tried to make a decent living. My older brother, Joseph, he took over the business here on the island, and he made a go of it, too, turned it into a money maker after all those years of my father's just getting along, barely staying out of debt."

"The business?"

Stanley smiled. "I told you, girl, it was the *Labour News* that my father ran and then Joseph took it over."

"Oh." It dawned on her. "I didn't realize your family owned the paper all that time."

He laughed dryly. "Yeah, girl, like I said, there's Rupert Murdoch and Ted Turner and then us, the Edwards family of St. Christopher, real media bigwigs, you know. Anyway, Joseph took over the paper after my father, and then Joseph was killed and I came home."

He made it sound simple. And easy. But it couldn't have been. He had a life up there in Canada. He'd had to let all that go to come back here.

She looked at him. "Rosie told me Joseph died. Some car crash, right?"

He shook his head, the smile gone. "No. Listen, Joseph was murdered; *that's* why I came home. Not for the weather, not for the sunshine. I came home to scatter my brother's ashes in Courpon's Bay and then find out who killed him, and why."

"Murdered? When Rosie told me about his death, I thought she said he ran off the road and into the water up near Sandy Point."

Stanley stopped and turned to look at her, shading his eyes from the late-morning sun. "You don't read the papers here, do you? I thought people in your business, in public relations, had to read the newspaper."

"I write—I wrote—brochures. That was it; that was my whole job, producing brochures for the resort."

He nodded, offered a slight smile, and she knew he realized immediately what she now admitted to herself; that her work, the brochures and the meetings and the wrangling with printers and mailing lists and all the rest, had all been just make-work, something to keep her busy while Bo showed her off, his tall, thin, dark-haired trophy from the States.

"No," she admitted, "I didn't read the papers. I've never once read your paper. All I know is what your sister told me."

"And she said it was an accident?"

"That's what she said."

He nodded. "I wish she was right. It would make everything a lot simpler, you know? But no, Joseph was murdered. He was working on some story and got too close to finding out the truth, and he was murdered for it."

"The police, is that what they say about it?"

"No, no. The police here aren't like the police back home in Minnesota. Things don't work that way here, girl. The police say it was an accident, that there was alcohol in his blood, that he hit the turn at Sandy Point and lost control, right off into the bay. They say he drowned."

"But you say that's not how it happened?"

"No, that's not how it happened." He paused. "I have a friend; I grew up with him. He's deputy commissioner now. We talk." He shrugged. "He's honest, and I think he'd do something if I had some proof. But I don't. Yet."

He turned to look out toward the sea. "But I will. I'll find proof of all of this, or part of it. And then I'll go to him, and then, maybe, something good will happen."

The wind was picking up and there were whitecaps over the reef line, a few hundred yards out. "Look, there's something big going on, and it's wrong, wrong as hell. I don't know what it is yet—smuggling, maybe? Cocaine? Heroin? Almost got to be that. This island's always been in the middle of that kind of thing— hell, we got a history of four hundred years of that.

"And then some kind of political payoffs to keep things quiet?

Yeah, got to be something like that, too. Same history, you know? And Joseph, he was getting close to finding it out. He got too close, I know it, and they killed him for it."

She waited for a moment or two for him to continue, but he fell silent instead, and she didn't have the nerve to ask him more about it. He was looking at something back up the beach, back near the bar. She looked that way but couldn't see anything of interest.

They walked back past the Turtle Bay bar and on to the parking lot. There he held open her door for her at the Toyota, then shut it behind her as she sat down, and he walked around to his side.

He started the engine. "You think there's nothing going on here?" he asked her as they pulled back onto the dirt road.

"Did I say that?"

"It's the way you looked when I told you about Joseph."

"You know, Stanley, I have my own problems. I don't know anything about island politics, or who's good and who's bad. I'm sorry about your brother; I really am. And about your father, too. I know how hard it can be when things like that happen. But . . ."

". . . but it's got nothing to do with you, right?" He was driving smoothly down the dirt road, weaving back and forth a bit to avoid the larger holes in the road. Then he took a quick look in the mirror and, without warning, accelerated, rounding a sharp corner and then quickly yanking the car off the dirt road and down a side path hardly wide enough for the Corolla to fit in, cactus, bushes, and low palm trees lining both sides, scratching against the paint, the windows, as they drove down it. "Take a look out the back window," he said, and Melissa turned in her seat to look. There was nothing there. She turned to look back at him.

"Patience, girl," he said. "Wait a few more seconds."

She turned back again to look, and, sure enough, moments later a black Jeep Cherokee drove slowly by. Inside it were two men; one was black, one white. And the white one wore a blue baseball cap. It was the two men from the restaurant this morning. It was eighty-five degrees out, the tropical sun blazing down.

Melissa had a thin sheen of sweat after sitting at the bar, driving along without the air conditioner on. But when those two drove by she felt a cold shiver run through her. My god, what was this about?

They waited a few minutes—it seemed to Melissa like an hour— and then Stanley started backing out of the path and onto the dirt road.

"You know," he said, looking over his left shoulder to keep the Corolla straight in the narrow path, "those two were the ones you smiled at back at the café, when I picked you up."

"I know."

"Yeah, well, now you know what I'm talking about. I got some ideas about what happened to Joseph, and maybe to my father, too, and I know you think those things don't have anything to do with you. But I got to tell you, it's a small island; you know what I mean?"

She nodded. "I think maybe I do. But why would they be after me already? How did they find out?"

"Oh, girl, I'm not the only one with friends in the police department. You stopped in to file those charges and the Palmers and their friends knew about it in five minutes. You get any phone calls about it at home?"

"No. Just a call from Bo saying he was leaving the island for a few days, going up to Miami for a meeting with some developers."

Stanley nodded, thinking it through as he backed them slowly onto the dirt road. They came out slowly, both of them watching for the Jeep, but it was gone. Melissa breathed a sigh of relief. Stanley put the Corolla into gear and headed back toward the main road. "OK," he said, "here's what I think. I don't know if Bo really left or not, but it's clear that they're just keeping an eye on you for now, seeing what you're going to do. Those charges aren't filed yet, so they're thinking maybe you'll be leaving the island and they won't have to do anything."

Melissa shook her head in amazement, listening to him. This started out as one thing and now it was blending into something else, something bigger, wider. She should leave the island. Today. Now. She should put all this behind her and return to the frozen north where in the middle of all that cold, all that ice, she at least knew who she was, where she belonged. There she had a past; she fit in. Here? It was all too crazy.

Stanley was still talking as she thought it through. "Of course, now they know I'm involved, too. Still, all they did was follow us. No threats; they're too smart for that. They know we both get the message just from seeing them."

"What message is that, exactly?"

He just turned to look at her as he stopped at the intersection with the main road. "I don't think you understand what your boyfriend and his father are involved in here, Melissa. This is dangerous business, girl, and if they think you might get in the way of whatever it is they're doing..." He shook his head.

"Dangerous business? Smuggling? Drugs? Why don't we just go right now and tell the police?"

He laughed. "Yeah, girl, the police. I keep telling you, maybe that's how things happen in Minnesota: you just go to the police and they take care of it. But Minnesota's a long, long way from where you are now. No, I don't think the police will help, not unless we have proof of something, good solid proof they can't ignore.

"So, here's a little change of plans. I'm going to call Rosie and get her to meet us somewhere and we'll talk all this through. Maybe she could go with you off the island somewhere, at least over to Antigua, and then I could deal with this alone. I don't want you getting hurt."

He opened the car's center console, picked up the cellular phone, dialed in a number, listened for a few seconds. "Yeah, Rosie, it's me," he said. "Yeah, we're fine, but I think maybe we should meet you."

He listened again. "Yeah, OK, that works fine. Look, we'll meet you at noon at the home, and then after we visit with Mom we can talk this over, all right? We'll see you there."

He hung up, shoved the phone back in the console, and put the Corolla into gear to pull out onto the paved road. "C'mon,

I got something else to show you, up at my end of the island. We'll take the back roads and see if those two can find us again. That will tell me something about whether they're local or hired in from off-island."

"Something to show me?"

"Yeah, girl. My mother. We're going to visit with her—crazy Mom, the obeah woman—at the home, and then maybe get some lunch with Rosie after that, talk things over. That sound all right?"

"You said something about obeah before. It's witch doctor stuff, right?"

"Easier to just show you. Since Joseph's death . . ." He shook his head. "Well, you'll see. For now, just keep an eye out for those two in that Jeep while I drive, OK?"

Doing that—keeping an eye out for that Jeep—was something she was more than willing to do, so for the next half hour or more, bouncing over unpaved back roads, she watched for it. She was very glad, when they turned into the driveway for The Palmer House Convalescent Home, that she hadn't seen it.

ET CUM SPIRITU TUO

In Holy Innocents Church, in the front pew, Dan Finnegan sat and looked up at Christ, arms outstretched reaching out over the altar, welcoming everyone with a small smile on His face despite hanging there on a cross.

Finnegan tried to raise up his own arms like that but couldn't—it hurt too damn much. Underneath the sleeves of his coat his arms were wrapped in gauze from the elbows to the fingertips. The doctor had advised him to stay in the hospital for a few more days, but he was going nuts in there. He needed to do something, take some kind of action, get some damn results. Something, anything, to stop this damn killer before he killed more women and children.

So when he got the phone call from Summer Arndt that she wanted to meet with him at Holy Innocents he thought that sounded good—it would get him out of the hospital room, if nothing else, and he wanted to help out the Arndts if there was something he could do.

Summer had been nice over the phone, said she owed it to him to apologize, said she'd been thinking through a lot of stuff about her dad, about all the things that had happened, about how it all was rolling around on her and she wanted to talk it through and do the right things and at the top of the list was talking with Dan Finnegan. She said, too, that she'd been thinking about the murders and about Melissa and she had some ideas she wanted to talk about. She knew it was crazy, but she wanted to talk them over with him.

It was just a couple of blocks from the hospital, and the sun was out with the temperature all the way up near zero, so Finnegan had bundled up and walked it.

He'd made sure to get here early so he'd have some time to have a little chat with God. Finnegan had come in, genuflecting at the center aisle before crossing over to the left side of the church, then genuflecting again at the side of the pew before he walked in, pulled down the kneeler with his shoe, and got down on his knees to have a word with God about how He could possibly be letting this awful stuff happen.

God, as it turned out, wasn't talking, so after a few painful tries to push off the rail with his hands, Finnegan managed to get up off his knees and sit back on the hard, cold wood of the pew and try to get comfortable. Used to be, a long time ago, he'd spent a lot of time in this church.

He missed the old Latin Mass, the one he'd grown up with back in his altar-boy days. He was sitting in a church he hadn't been to in years except for funerals, trying to get God on his side, or at least maybe get a little help from The Almighty, but what he thought of, instead, was the Latin Mass and how it had been back when he was a kid: memorizing all the responses in Latin, pouring the water and wine from the cruets and ringing the bells when Father Daniels was changing the host into the body and blood of Christ. He had a lot of good memories of those days, back when he'd been a true believer in Holy Mother the Church and when Ike had been threatening the Chinese over Quemoy and Matsu and the Kingston Trio was singing about Tom Dooley and on TV there'd been Davy Crockett and Spin and Marty at the Triple R, with Annette and Cubby and the other Mouseketeers.

He'd been a good Catholic as a kid, had thought for a long time about becoming a priest. If he gave himself a chance, he thought, he could still recite the Confiteor in Latin: "Confiteor Dei omnipotenti, beatae Mariae semper virgini, beato Michaeli Archangelo, beato Joanni Baptistae, sanctis Apostolis Petro et Paulo, omnibus Sanctis..." But he lost it there, somewhere down the list of the saints and apostles. It didn't matter. It hadn't mattered then. Like all the altar boys, he'd known the Latin words, but they never held any meaning: they'd just been words, beautiful but meaningless words recited in a dead language on a cold winter morning when the incense was burning and the candles were all lit for a High Mass and the altar's cold Connemara marble had felt hard and demanding and good beneath his bended knees.

He'd been a Catholic all his life. Still called himself a Catholic if you asked him, though he didn't go to church, didn't practice any of the sacraments, hadn't been to confession in twenty or thirty years. So maybe he wasn't really a Catholic after all anymore. He'd have to find out how that worked.

His kid had been a pretty good Catholic, too, sweet Danny. What a great kid. What a great life that boy would have had, married to a great girl, living in a nice house, getting settled and then making his dad a grandpa—that would have been great.

Oh, hell. What isn't, isn't. Danny was gone, Melissa was down on that island in the sunshine, and Dan Finnegan sat alone in this church with his fingers blackened and frostbit and hurting like hell underneath the gauze wrap.

And his two best suspects were dead while the killer was still alive out there, no doubt planning the next attack. The killer: who'd saved Dan Finnegan's poor pitiful life, pulled him right out of the water, fired off a couple of rounds with the Glock to attract attention, and then gotten away cleanly while everyone attended to the frozen detective.

Finnegan used to love winter. Cold and clear. Dependable. Something you could prepare for and handle. Now, his fingers blackened underneath the gauze, a kind of pins-and-needles pain mingling with a good solid ache in them to remind him of what had happened, he was beginning to hate it. Winter brought death. Winter brought the son-of-a-bitch monster who could do these terrible things.

Wrong way to phrase that question in church, Finnegan supposed, and shook his head. Behind him, from the main entrance, came the squeak of that oversize door. He turned to look, and there was Summer, coming toward him.

OBEAH WOMAN

The Palmer House Convalescent Home rambled along an iron shore on the east side of the island. A two-story frame house, it sat atop a low wall of limestone rock blackened by salt and wind and time that held back the sea near Barker's Point. Its wraparound porch sat over the rocky coast on one side and offered views of the volcano on the other side. There must be ten or twelve bedrooms, Melissa guessed as they drove up the driveway to the small car park.

Rosie was waiting there to meet them, standing next to her own car, a tiny Daihatsu. She walked over and gave Melissa a quick hug, then Stanley. "She's very upset about something, Stanley. She won't sit still, won't eat. Even playing the music doesn't soothe her."

Stanley nodded. "Well, let's see what we can do, eh, Rosie?" he said, taking Melissa by the hand and bringing her along, too, as they came up the walk, flagstones marching toward the wide front porch and the main doors, jacaranda and bougainvillea blossoming all around them.

"This place is beautiful," Melissa said as they stepped up onto the porch. "I had no idea it was even here."

Rosie held open the front door. "Nothing too good for the Palmers, you know, girl. Henry Palmer built this for his first wife, and then turned it into this home when she lost her mind."

"Lost her mind?"

"Alzheimer's, I think we'd say now. She died ten or twelve years ago. Back when she started going, twenty years ago, they just thought she'd grown senile early, in her thirties. Her mother was the same way, and her mother before her."

Rosie waved at the woman behind the front desk, then said, "C'mon, you two; it's this way. Mother's in the East Room, Stanley, the one with the big picture window."

"With that view of Mount Liamuiga," Stanley said, and Rosie nodded, adding, "Yeah, she's walking back and forth, looking at that thing and mumbling."

Stanley just shook his head.

A long, narrow hallway led to the north wing of the house and the East Room. When they got there, Miriam Edwards was alone in the room except for one attendant, a slender, smiling young man in his twenties, who sat alone at a table near her, talking calmly.

"Now, Mrs. Edwards," he was saying, "you know this isn't going to help. You need to calm down, come over here, and sit down for a minute and tell me all about it, all right?"

Miriam was tiny at five-foot-two and terribly thin. But her walk was energetic and she pointed her finger forcefully toward the attendant, wagging it, lecturing him as she spoke back. She wore jangly jewelry everywhere, charm bracelets, several necklaces, anklets.

"Ain't nothin' to tell you, Selwyn Liburd, except you got to get my children here 'cause I got things to tell them, and I got to tell them today, now. That's all, Selwyn Liburd; that's all there is, ain't nothin' else to say."

"We've called them, Mrs. Edwards, and they'll be here soon. So why don't you just sit down..."

He caught sight of them, standing just inside the door. He waved them on in. "Mrs. Edwards, look who's here."

Miriam Edwards turned, caught her breath in delight. "My children! My blessed children. Come in, children, come on in. But where's Joseph?"

Rosie hugged her mother. "Joseph couldn't come, Mother. But he sends his love."

"Couldn't come? Why couldn't that boy come?"

"Joseph died, Mother," Stanley said, and Rosie glared at him. "He died last year, remember? A car wreck."

"Died? Joseph died? Where is that boy? Why didn't he come here with you?"

She caught sight of Melissa. "Who's this?" She walked over toward her. "You're not one of my children."

"No, ma'am. I'm just a friend."

Miriam stood in front of Melissa, dwarfed by Melissa's five-foot-eleven height. "You're huge."

Melissa grinned. "I'm a bit tall."

Miriam turned to Rosie, spoke in a conspiratorial whisper. "This girl's white, Rosie. Where'd you find her?"

Rosie smiled. "Stanley found her, Mother. She lives here, but she's from the United States. Minnesota."

Her mother waved her hand dismissively. "Never heard of it." She turned to Stanley. "You brought this white girl?"

"Yeah, Mom, I did. She's a nice girl, Mom."

"You like this girl?"

"It's not like that, Mom. Me and Rosie, we're just her friends, that's all."

Miriam turned back to Melissa. "You look tired, child. Why's a young girl like you so tired?"

Melissa smiled. "I haven't been sleeping well lately."

Rosie came over. "What's wrong, Mother? Why'd you ask us to come over today?"

Her mother stopped for a second, a puzzled expression on her face—why had she wanted them?

Then it came to her. She grabbed Rosie's hand, reached over to grab Stanley's hand, too. Tugged them toward the large picture window.

"Look, look, look, look, look," she said, excited. "See the smoke coming from the mountain?"

There was no smoke, the mountain's peak serene against a perfect blue sky, a few clouds trailing away thinly from the peak.

"There's no smoke, Mother," Rosie said, Stanley standing there, looking out the window. Melissa had the feeling he wished there *was* smoke.

"No, no, girl. You just can't see it. You just have to know how to look at it. See?" She took another step to the window, put her finger against the glass, pointing. "See that? It's right there, at the top, coming out all brown and gray."

Rosie reached out to take her mother's hand away from the window, held it in her own. "Oh, Mother. We can't see it."

Her mother pulled away, agitated. She waved her arms wildly, shaking her hands and pointing toward the mountain. "You *have* to see it, children; you have to! Your father is there, you know. You have to go help him!"

Selwyn Liburd, the attendant, came over to help, put his arms around the small, frail body to calm her down and pull her away from the window. "Now, now, Mrs. Edwards. You have to calm down."

"No! I don't want to calm down. They have to know this!"

She wrenched herself free from him, started back toward the window. Stanley came over to help, started to grab her, but she stepped aside, waving those arms, dodging furniture, some chairs, a small couch, a lamp table.

Her arms, wild, struck the lamp and sent it spinning. Melissa leaned over to catch it, and at the same time Mrs. Edwards' wildness finally sent her into trouble, tripping over a chair. She started to fall. Melissa, seeing it happen, reached out, caught her by the shoulders to break the fall and ease her down to the carpet.

And there was a brief, electric moment of connection between the two, Melissa feeling it as a spark, a jolt of energy, and then seeing, in a flash, the volcano's peak, ash and smoke rising from it in billowing clouds, blotting out the blue sky, turning the world gray.

Miriam's body jerked once with the force of it, hard, her eyes wide as it stopped. She turned to look at Melissa. "You, girl?

"You saw the mountain, the smoke?"

Melissa nodded.

Miriam turned to her children. "I been waiting for this girl, and now you finally brought her here. And she's white! But this girl is obeah, children. She's the one gonna help you find out about your father, children."

This was what Stanley had talked about, this obeah stuff, Melissa thought. What had he said? Witch doctor stuff. Black magic, white magic? Oh, please, Melissa thought, that was the last thing she needed.

Miriam reached out to touch Melissa's cheek, spoke softly, intimately, to her. "But you so cold, child. How come you so cold?"

What could she say to this crazy woman? How to explain that cold core at the center of her being, the cold that never warmed down there. "I don't know, ma'am. I've just always been that way. That's one of the reasons I came here, to this warm, beautiful island."

Miriam stroked her cheek, whispered to her so softly Melissa could barely hear it, "I can feel your grandmother in you, girl. Your grandmother was obeah, strong obeah. She's from the islands, yeah?"

"Yes, ma'am. From Jamaica."

"Yeah, she off-white girl, Jamaican white. Your mother got some slave blood in her somewhere, but she looked white, like you."

"How do you know this?"

"I can feel her in you, child. You got so much of her in you; you just didn't know, that's all. You see things, like I do, and that ain't even the start of what you can do. You are something special. You get the message she left you? Your mother got something to say to you; she got something for you to do, child."

"Message?" Melissa shook her head. "I don't even remember her. I was only five when she disappeared."

"Yeah, child, I know that. But she left you something, a gift. You going to use that someday, I think."

"A gift?"

Miriam smiled. "You been having some bad times lately, girl, right?" She added a warm smile. "We'll have to see if we can get you warmer here now, girl. My children, they good people, they got hearts of gold. They take care of you."

"Thank you. You're right: they're good people."

Miriam spoke to Rosie and Stanley: "This girl can see things, you two know that?"

Melissa felt Stanley staring at her. He sighed, shook his head. Rosie came over to help her mother to her feet, then hugged her, pulling her slowly away from the overturned lamp. "Yeah, well, if you say so, Mother. She's a nice girl, and you're right, she's had a bad couple of days, and we're helping her out."

Her mother shrugged off the hug, walked back over to Melissa, stared into her eyes, got more agitated again. "No, no. You listen, children; this girl can help you see things. She knows. She knows!"

"Knows what, Mother?" Rosie asked. Selwyn Liburd came over to Melissa, whispered to her that she ought to leave and let the old woman calm down.

"Knows about your father," Mother Miriam said, "and knows about the cave. And that damn money. She does, children. She knows."

Melissa turned to look at Rosie and then to Stanley. She shook her head, mystified by that. Their father? Some money and some cave? She knew nothing about those things.

As Liburd took the old woman by the arm to lead her from the room, she stopped her shouting, smiled instead, then waved at Melissa as she reached the door. "You do what you have to, child, all right?" she said in a normal tone. Then she laughed, a loud, sharp cackle. "You'll see it, child. I know it. You can see what you have to, girl. Now go! Take care of it!"

Melissa waved. "Sure," she said. "Sure, I'll take care of it, ma'am." And then she left the room, walked with Liburd back to the front desk, took a cup of cold water from someone's hands as she sat down there to stop and think. What the hell was that all about? How did that woman know about her mother, about being from the islands?

She shook her head. She had no idea. And doing what she had to do, isn't that what the old woman said? See what's the right thing and then do it? Sure, nothing to that.

She sat back and waited for Stanley and Rosie, shaking her head and taking a sip of the water. She'd lied to Miriam when she said she could see what to do. Truth was, she was lost, wandering around through all this mess completely lost and confused.

She sighed, crumpled up the paper cup and tossed it into the wastebasket, rose, and walked outside. The porch was warm but shaded. She walked to the left, to the edge of the building. From there she could see the mountain.

She looked up and there was the peak, calm, settled. That, she thought, was reality. Right there, rising into that blue tropical sky, that was the real thing.

As she turned to walk back to the front desk, out of sight of the mountain, Rosie and Stanley came out the door.

Stanley smiled. "Melissa, if you're willing to go, I just promised Momma I'd show you something."

"Show me what?"

"The town we grew up in. We'll go take a quick look, and then we'll meet Rosie at her place for lunch."

"This won't take long?"

"No, just a few minutes out of the way. Really, nothing to it; we'll just drive by. It's something you should see, anyway, before you go, OK? Then we'll meet Rosie for lunch at her place."

She nodded. "Sure, OK. And then maybe I think it's time I called home and made some arrangements, you know."

"Time to head north?" Stanley asked with a slow smile. "Yeah, well, safer that way, that's for sure. Oh, and here." He handed her a gold bracelet, solid, a bangle. "My crazy mother says for you to wear this. She says you'll need it when it's cold, that you should hold on tight and learn from it."

He shook his head. "She really believes in this obeah stuff, you know. She thinks she has some special sight—that's what she calls it. And now she's got you thinking you can see things, too. Loony, I swear, the both of you."

Melissa smiled, took it from him, slipped it on her wrist. Perfect fit. All right, then, she'd wear it for a while, and then later she could give it back graciously. Truth was, it looked pretty nice. And it felt warm on her wrist. She liked that, too, the warmth of it, as she opened the car door and climbed in, thinking of home, and cold.

TABERNACLE

They drove north and east around the island, past Cayon and Nicola Town and Ottley's Plantation Inn. Melissa spent the time daydreaming, about Miriam Edwards and her ravings and about just how crazy things were getting here. And about Finnegan and the hard frozen truths of Minnesota. Stanley was right: if she were home she'd just call the police, call Finnegan, and he'd take care of things for her. She missed him. She missed her father, too. She missed the simplicity of the life she'd had up there.

After a while, they stopped at a lay-by on the coast road at the northeast corner of the island. It was as isolated a spot as St. Kitts offered, the main road out of view below them, nothing but sugarcane fields and rain forest above them, climbing the slopes of the mountain.

Melissa had never seen anything like this, the way the rain forest spread around the top half of the volcano that rose to her left or how, halfway down the mountainside, the sugarcane fields abruptly replaced the rain forest with neat patterns of green and gold marching down the slopes.

The worn, bumpy pavement they were on had dipped and circled over a series of deep gulleys—the locals called them guts—that ran down from the mountain's lower slopes, some with occasional higher ridges between the guts. From where they sat she could see one of those guts, a dark, green slash in the earth heading up the low, gradual slope of the mountain.

"Some view, isn't it?" Stanley asked her. He pointed toward a long, wide mound of earth that sat alongside the gut. "See that?"

When she nodded he put the Corolla back into gear and drove across the dirt road toward the gut and the mound. There was a narrow track into the tall underbrush there, and he jammed the Corolla into it, pushing aside the palm fronds and the bushes.

He drove up that a few hundred yards, uphill the whole while, weaving his way past thick hummocks of low palms and a wide tangle of bushes and cacti. When the path ended at a large boulder, he cut the engine, opened his door, and came around to join Melissa as she stepped out, stretching after the long drive.

He pointed to the gut. "Twenty years ago there was a town named Tabernacle there. It ran all along the side of this gut. Maybe two hundred people lived here, all of them dirt-poor. That was before any tourists came to the island with their money, so there was no place to work except the cane fields, and that only for a month or two all year.

"But they did OK. Nobody went hungry, you know? They raised chickens and pigs; they had their own fields for vegetables, and they cut those gardens right into the side of the gut. Good, fertile volcanic soil."

He pointed. "There, if you look close, you can see some of those terraces still, just the ones at the top, the ones that didn't get wiped out by the eruption and that big flow."

"What happened to them?"

"Twenty years ago, when my father was editor of the paper, the volcano, she started getting shaky."

"Like a few nights ago? That rumbling?"

"Oh, yeah, but a lot worse than that. You read about Montserrat in your papers back in Florida? How that volcano blew and the whole island was threatened?"

She nodded. "During my junior in high school. There were pictures in the local paper. But nobody died there, right?"

"Yeah, that's right: nobody died. They had warning, and the government helped them; even the British came, bringing in ships and the Red Cross and all that."

He picked up a dead branch off the ground, etched a pattern into the soil, a big **S** shape, then the line through it—a dollar sign. "Here the government didn't ask for help. They didn't want anyone thinking there was trouble here, you know? The rumbling didn't seem like much at first, just a few little earthquakes here and there, some smoke out the top of Liamuiga. Not much really, so the government played it down. Independence was new, and they were trying to build up some tourist trade—some hotels, resorts, you know. Having a volcano that smokes and shakes a little bit is one thing, no big deal, probably even kind of fun for the tourists. But the threat of a major eruption? No, they didn't want that. Bad for business. Hell, they even changed the name of the mountain. From the time the British came in the seventeenth century until Independence Day it was Mount Misery."

"They didn't want to scare the tourists off with a name like that, I suppose?"

"Well, yeah. Bad PR. But they were more worried about the big developers than the tourists, you know, everyone trying to make deals and all that. All that money coming into the new government, everybody wanting a piece of the new pie, you know. So the government was saying there was nothing to worry about, just a few rumbles here and there.

"But my father, he brought in an expert from the States. This guy, he climbs up to the mountaintop with my father. They check out the caldera for two days, and then they come back down and say it could be big, you know, a major eruption. This expert says we should evacuate the east and north sides of the island, move everyone down to Basseterre."

"And that doesn't fly with the government officials."

He nods. "Yeah, girl, you can see how it all went, right? See, they're busy making those deals—for millions—with developers who want resorts, casinos, you know. Build a new airport, bring in the gamblers, bring in the cash. So they listen to this guy's report and they thank him very much and they send him home. Then, to make sure there's no panic about all this, they shut down my father's paper before he can get out the next issue, the one that would have all this stuff about how she might blow."

"How could they do that? How could they shut it down?"

A deep, hard chuckle. "You been here all this time and you still think things work here the way they do in Minnesota? Maybe up there it's hard to stop the presses, but not here, girl. They just come in one day and say the *Labour News* is not paying all the taxes it owes on its income from the year before and they lock the door and take the case to court."

"And the paper can't publish?"

"Not unless it gets a judge to rule you can keep publishing while you fight with the tax man. And funny how no judge has time on the docket to issue any writs, so the doors stay locked."

Stanley took a breath, looked out over the crowded gut, filled with new growth, with lantana and soursop and coconut palms, with ferns and shrubs and the grass, tall as a man. Hiding in there somewhere, away from these strange people who'd come to visit, were some mongooses probably, some green monkeys certainly, maybe some deer. But no people.

"So, this is what the people say happened. My father, at this big meeting, said he was going to go ahead and print the paper anyway, that they couldn't stop him from printing. And he said he was going to write a story that told the truth—the whole truth—about the government and the developers, especially the developer named Henry Palmer."

It took a second for that to sink in. "Henry Palmer?"

"He was knee-deep in it, girl, the main man down from the States, promising everything he had to, payoffs right and left to the new government for those sweetheart deals that wound up making him millions."

"And your father's paper told the whole story?"

Stanley shrugged. "The paper never came out, and my father, he disappeared."

"My god, Stanley. What happened to him?"

"Don't know. But there's some people say they saw Henry Palmer with a satchel full of cash the day before the volcano blew. Those people, they say Henry Palmer paid my father a lot of money, a *lot* of money for back then, ten thousand dollars, to just leave the island and not say nothing to nobody about it."

"Oh, but you don't think..."

"No, no, not at all. But, you see, my father and my mother, they weren't doing so good back then. Lots of fighting, lots of arguments. My father, he was a drinking man, you know? And my mother, she was always trying to get him to stop, and they would argue." He whistled, remembering, "Man, could they argue."

He shrugged again. "So, he had this reputation, and people, you know, they were ready to believe the worst."

He shook his head. "Anyway, the way the story goes, my father knew from his expert that the volcano would blow, even knew the direction the flow would probably go. He came back from some big meeting at Government House all hot and bothered, got himself into a big fight with Mother, saying he had to do what he had to do, that kind of thing. And then he goes storming out of the house, saying he has to go and warn Tabernacle, get everyone to leave the town because Mount Misery, she could go at any time."

"But he didn't do it?"

Stanley nodded. "That's right; he never got there. People say he left, took the money and ran. I say he was killed and the body buried somewhere."

"But you don't have any proof of that."

"No, nothing. Just like with Joseph's murder, I got no proof at all. I just know what I know, and I'll prove it if it kills me."

Melissa reached out to touch him on the shoulder. "And then the volcano blew. . . ."

"Yeah, that's it. When she went, just like the expert from the States said she would, everyone here, everyone in Tabernacle, died, because my father didn't warn them. Everyone should have been gone, but they weren't. They were there, and the town he lived in most of his life was wiped out. All those people, my aunts and uncles, my friends. All dead."

"You said they never found his body?"

"Nothing, no sign of him. No body, no clothes or his ring he always wore. Nothing. And, I tell you, we looked. See, I thought he was probably here warning them when it blew or something, and he died with them, trying to get people out. I guess I dreamed he was some kind of misunderstood hero, you know, and I was going to be the one to clear his name. But I was fifteen then, full of myself, already a big cricket star with lots of friends. We searched for weeks as soon as things cooled enough. We found a few bodies, frozen in place, up on these ridges, covered in that hard coating—it's like nothing you've ever seen, like rock or concrete. But not him, no sign of him at all. Never found any sign of that damn money, either."

He looked at her. "You know what a pyroclastic flow is?"

She shook her head.

"It's the hot gases and the molten rock that come sliding down the slopes all at once. They said it broke through the side of the crater up there and came down here at one hundred miles an hour. Took just a minute or two from the time it broke through till it filled the whole gut with death. From here, the flow went right out to sea, out that way," he pointed, "took most of the people with it, buried them out there in the ocean. I figure that's where he is."

She shivered, looking at the deep, wet green innocence of the gut. There weren't many signs there'd ever been a town; a few low mounds of foliage-covered rubble were all she could see from those days.

Stanley took her hand. "Follow me; we'll walk down into there a ways. It's tricky now; hang on tight."

Later, she thought about how close she came to saying no, just walking back to the car, turning her back on this whole thing, staying out of trouble that she didn't need to be involved in. It all would have turned out very differently if she had.

Instead, she left her hand in his and followed along, stumbling a bit here and there as they descended the steep side of the gut for about thirty yards.

It was instantly a different world. The slope and the trees blocked the sun, and the sides and the foliage captured the moisture. It was cool, dark, and moist, a slit in the earth that seemed a world away from the ridge above them.

They walked farther into the darkness, letting their eyes adjust, moving slowly. "There'll be a lot of green monkeys in here, you know," Stanley said, "and maybe some deer. The English brought them here a century or more back, toys for the aristocracy, you know? And now they're all over the island. They made St. Kitts their home."

"This is beautiful. And it's so different from the beaches and golf courses."

He laughed. "It *is* that."

She reached out to touch a flower. "These are orchids. My god, they're beautiful, and they're everywhere."

"Yeah, they're all through here, grow like weeds. A lot of bromeliads, too. All the trees are young, of course, but in the older guts, the ones not wiped out by the volcano, there's older, better trees, mahogany, cedar . . ."

"And bamboo," she added, walking over to a tall stand of it. "Look at all these."

But he was walking away, down a worn path. He turned and waved her over. When she got to him she could see he was standing over a small, open square of stone.

"Most of the buildings were wood, and they're gone completely, burned and shoved right out to sea. But this was the town well and it made it through everything somehow."

"But there's nothing down there. No well."

"All filled in. But this is it." He patted the stones. "This is what's left of Tabernacle."

She shook her head. "Why did you bring me here?"

"To show you this. This is where I'm from, this town. I grew up here, in this gut. We had our own store, our own school. I didn't leave here until I was thirteen—two years before the volcano—when we moved to St. John's."

She looked around. "It's beautiful now."

"It was beautiful then, in a different way. But we still had the forest, you know, and the deer and the monkeys, just at the edge of the village. We'd try to trick the monkeys and catch them, but they were too quick." He laughed. "Mean, too. They've got a nasty bite, those monkeys."

"And then the volcano blew."

He nodded. "And then she blew."

"You were lucky you left, I guess."

"Yeah, I guess so. We'd moved to St. John's because Father

wanted us to grow up in a bigger town. He always said he had plans for us, big dreams." He laughed. "And look at all that now: Joseph is dead, Rosie is a secretary for the Palmers, and I drive a taxi."

Melissa sat down on the low stone wall of the old well and took a look around. The quiet beauty of the place, the verdant life of it, was astounding. She put her hands down on the stones to steady herself, then leaned back, face up toward the sun, its brilliance blunted by the canopy of trees. She closed her eyes. It was calm, serene, and heavenly. She could hear parrots screeching in the distance. This was the paradise she'd sought when she first came here.

When she opened her eyes, Stanley stood near her, looking at her. "Nice here, isn't it?"

He walked toward her. She watched him approach, reached out to take his hand when he held it toward her, was ready to rise from the warm stones and come to him, when the earth began to tremble.

He stopped. She sat back, hands down against the stones of the old well, bracing herself, staring at Stanley, her eyes wide. This was what she'd felt the other night in her bed, but it had felt safer there, somehow. More distant. Now, here, it felt terrifying.

"It's a small one," he said, holding out his hands, palms out, to calm her down. "Just sit there for a minute and it will end."

But it didn't. Instead, the trembling grew to a rumble, grew to a distant roar that shook them harder, then seemed to come at them in a wave like a comber at the beach, lifting them up and tossing them, arms flailing for balance, into the air.

They landed in a heap, bruised but otherwise unhurt, and the quake, as quickly as it had risen, died out and it was over.

"My god," Melissa said, first coming shakily to her knees and then, slowly, standing, brushing herself off with her hands, pushing back the hair from her face, blowing away the last few strands that fell in front of her eyes.

Stanley, brushing himself off the same way, was on his feet, too. "That was a good one, girl. That was a *very* good one."

"That was much harder than the other night. I've never felt anything like that before in my life."

"I think maybe this is the epicenter, right here where we are. The rest of the island might not have felt it so much."

"Do you think?"

"Yeah, could be. Maybe this gut is where the action is again these days, eh? We're back to this being the shaky side of the island." And he laughed.

Melissa shook her head. She didn't find this funny; that was for sure. "Listen, let's get back to the car and get out of here before there's an aftershock, all right?"

"Yeah, sure," he said. But he wasn't looking at her as he said it. Instead, he was staring off into the gut.

Melissa looked to see what he was focused on and there, halfway up the far side of the gut, was an open scar on the side of the earth.

"That's the old cave," Stanley said. "I played in there with Joseph and Rosie as kids; that was our pirate cave, where we hid our treasures."

"So?"

"It's been closed since the flow back when Father died. These quakes this past week must have opened it up again."

"That's great, Stanley, but I really think we should get back to the car and get out of here. I mean, what if the volcano's getting ready for another eruption, another flow?"

But he wasn't giving in. "Another quake might close it. No, I have to go check that out," he said. "You don't have to come along. You can just get back to the car and wait there, and if there's another quake, just drive out of here and get away somewhere safe. But I *have* to go check that cave out."

"Stanley." She was sharper now, instantly more confident with him now that she'd used his name. "Stanley, we really should go."

But he was already scrambling down the side of the gut. In another five minutes he'd be down at the bottom and working his way across and then up to the mouth of the cave. Melissa had a choice and she had to make it now. She stood and watched for a few seconds, thinking about where she was, about who she was and who she might want to be.

And then, without saying anything to Stanley, she headed after him.

THE PIRATE'S CAVE

The cave mouth was farther away than it looked, and the terrain was difficult to struggle through. Stanley, pleased that she'd decided to come along, waited for Melissa at the bottom of the gut; then the two of them started across to the far slope so they could make the climb up the other side.

But there were no paths through any of this, no way to get through except to push through the tall grass and bushes, the bromeliads and orchids and the branches of the pepper trees that grew everywhere. There was a strange irony to it as they struggled hard to make their way through entangling beauty.

Halfway across the gut they reached the thin shade of a stand of palm trees, where Stanley stopped, sweating hard, and wiped his brow. He turned to smile at Melissa.

"You know, in most of these guts the older trees have a lot of high branches that shade the place and that helps keep the undergrowth down. It's usually nice and cool down in the guts."

"But not in this one."

"You're right, not in this one. By god, it's hot."

She wiped her forehead, smiled thinly. "I love the heat. You know I spent my whole life trying to get warm. But I have to admit that this is *really* hot."

They moved on, though, and in another fifteen minutes had worked their way to the opposite slope. The foliage thinned as soon as they started to climb, the soil a slippery mix of razor-sharp pumice and windblown sand that had them slipping back a few feet for every step upward. It was painful, sweaty work, but they made progress.

Then, as they neared the cave, the terrain got even worse. A large scree of rock and pumice had come down from the cave mouth and spread out below it, adding a foot of even looser soil to the slope. It was miserable work climbing through it. But they finally reached the cave mouth, Stanley in the lead, grabbing at it with his hands and hauling himself in, then reaching back down to help Melissa up.

She was tired, sweaty, and filthy dirty, covered with sticky fine black pumice sand on her face, her arms and legs, her hands. Every time she reached up to wipe the sweat from her face she put more of the stuff on her cheeks and forehead.

And it was the best she'd felt physically in months, maybe in a couple of years. She'd forgotten how good exercise could feel, how great it felt to sweat, to feel the muscles in the arms and legs tingling with the effort, to breathe hard and deep to catch your breath. She'd taken this feeling for granted for years and then, somehow, let it drift away from her. To have it back, even briefly, was exhilarating.

Stanley was trying to apologize as he hauled her into the cave mouth. "You shouldn't have come, I think. Look what I've put you through."

She was grinning and stood up in the cave mouth to look out toward the gut and the view beyond. "Are you kidding? This is wonderful. Look at that; it's magnificent."

The view was stunning, a broad sweep of terrain that included the gut below and its opposite slope across from them and then, in the middle ground, the island's coast falling away into the sea. To their left, Statia, the next island north just eight miles away across the channel, rose dramatically from the blue and white-capped greens of the Atlantic, its rocky coast holding back the waves she could see crashing against it.

Straight ahead and a little to the east she could see the peaks of another island. She pointed that way and Stanley said, simply, "Antigua."

South from there, and to the east, the view was uninterrupted open water, the deeper blue of the Atlantic mixing with the warmer, greener Caribbean. There were a few puffy white clouds drifting by in an otherwise achingly blue, clear sky.

"Do you ever get used to this?" she asked Stanley, turning to look at him, standing next to her, catching his breath still from the hard climb up the slope.

He laughed. "I grew up with this view, you know, playing with my brother and sister, hiding out from Mother up here, stashing things away in our secret pirate's cave. This opening was blocked by bushes and trees back then, and the slope we just climbed was covered in grass and bushes, with a path that ran right by this cave mouth. It was easy, then. Everything was easy."

She watched his face as he spoke. He was smiling with the memories of those better days as he put his hand up to shade his eyes from the glare while they stood there in the sunshine and looked to the north and east. Behind them, the very heart of darkness in the cave mouth. *Heart of Darkness.* Right. Years ago, she'd read that book by Conrad. She remembered it.

Stanley turned, took her hand. "Come on; let's go take a look in here."

She left her hand in his and followed him as he walked slowly into the shadows of the cave. At the entrance was a ring of stones, and inside it ashes and small bits of burnt wood from a fire two decades old. They walked past that and then, slowly, deeper into the cave, Stanley in front, pulling Melissa along, both of them stumbling some on the uneven cave floor as their eyes slowly adjusted to the dim light.

Stanley was the first to see it, but then he knew what he might be looking for—a low, boxy shape of a thing, a crate, tilted to one side, with two wheels on one side, a third wheel lying next to the other side, and no fourth wheel at all.

"Our prizewinner," he told Melissa as he stood there looking at it. "Come on; let's drag it back where we can see it better."

They each picked up an end and lifted. It was light but so fragile that two of the wood slats cracked as they carried it the thirty feet to the cave entrance where there was light enough to look at it.

When they set it down Stanley stepped back and looked at it, shaking his head. Then he knelt down, brushed off a layer of dirt from the front of it, said, "The name is on it. Here, take a look."

Melissa knelt, too, and read it aloud. "*Stand Up.* Does that mean something?"

"Me and Joseph, we loved Bob Marley back then. That's an old Marley song."

She nodded her head, grinned. "I know it," she said, and started in softly singing it: "Get up, stand up. Stand up for your right. . . ."

Stanley held up his hand to stop her but grinned as he did it. "You just full of surprises, girl. Yeah, that's the one. Me and Joseph planned to win the island cart race with this. We spent weeks on it. Got the crate, scrounged up axles, wheels, that old steering wheel there, got nails, rope for the steering, everything. I remember like it was yesterday, building this."

"What happened?"

"Nothing. We finished it, had it stored in here for the big race in February, but then the eruption came and this old cart didn't matter anymore."

"You had it ready? where'd that fourth wheel go?"

"Must be in there somewhere. I'll come back later with a torch—a flashlight—and find it then." He kicked the wheels on the good side, gently. "This old thing held together pretty good, didn't it?"

"It held together just fine, Stanley. You and your brother did a good job on it."

"Yeah, man, we did; we did a good job." Stanley turned away from her, walked over to the cave mouth to stare out, not showing his face.

Melissa walked over to join him, the glare outside so strong after the cave's interior darkness that she had to squint to see anything. "You all right?" she asked him.

"Sure. Just looking at the scenery, that's all."

"Yeah, it's nice. You going to tell anybody about this? The police, maybe?"

He laughed. "You and always wanting to talk to the police." Then he shrugged. "No, nothing they can do. I'll tell Rosie; she used to come here some as a kid, too. Maybe she'll come back here with me later with some lights to check the whole thing out."

"So what now?"

"We head back, that's what. I get you back to your place, and then you got to make that big decision, stay here and fight this thing or just go home and try to forget about it."

She nodded, wanted to say more but kept it simple instead. "We should move the cart back in where it's out of the weather before we start back, don't you think?"

He agreed, and the two of them walked over to the cart, each grabbing an end to lift, Melissa bending down at the knees to take hold of the cart's good side, with the two wheels on it, and then starting to lift it.

Then, with no warning, the left front wheel came off in her hands. She was leaning back as she stood, and while the front end of the cart fell to the cave floor, Melissa staggered backward from the momentum of her effort, losing her balance, arms flailing, the right hand still holding the old metal wheel with the thin rubber strip around the outside.

Eventually she lost her balance and fell heavily right onto her rear end, dropping the wheel at the last instant and putting both hands down to break her hard fall as she fell back into a small pile of rubbish—old wood and dead plants and a few stones.

It was comical to see, and Stanley couldn't help but laugh at her fall for a moment; then, worried she might have been hurt, he came over quickly to help her up.

But Melissa was laughing, too. It *was* comical. The moment had cut through a tense, difficult day with a pratfall worthy of Chaplin, and they both knew it. Their laughter, infectious, filled the cave for a minute until they both settled down. Then Melissa, still smiling, brushed the debris off her lap, small bits of stone, pumice, and charred wood, even some long, narrow, tubular sticks of congealed lava.

Some of these were a couple of feet long. They were only a

few inches around and surprisingly fragile; two of them broke in her hands as she picked them up to look at them. She handed one to Stanley as she finally climbed to her feet, asking him what they were.

He didn't know. "Lava-encrusted tree branches? I don't know. Take a few with you and I'll have someone look at them back in town."

She shoved several two- or three-inch-long pieces into her pockets. "You have a friend who's a lava expert?"

He laughed again. "I'll find someone who can tell what they are, OK?"

"Sure you will," she said, still brushing herself off as she walked to the mouth of the cave, then shaded her eyes to look out on that terrific view. "This island's just crawling with lava experts. Next thing you know you'll be..."

She stopped in midsentence. "Stanley, come here, quick. I think it's our friends."

Stanley took a glance, then grabbed Melissa's hand and tugged her back into the shadows. There, from the darkness, they both looked across the gut to the opposite slope where two figures stood, outlined against the blue sky.

JAMMING

Stanley looked at the two men who stood on the far side of the deep gut. "Must be them," he agreed. "And they're good, girl, to have found us here."

"Do they know we're in the cave?"

"I don't see how they could." There was a bright glint from the slope. "But I think they have binoculars, so if we're not careful they'll find us soon enough."

"What can we do?" Melissa asked, but her answer came almost as soon as she asked. The two figures started coming down the far side's slope toward the gut.

"We get out of here now, and try to head down the gut toward the sea. Maybe we can get past them and get to the road without them seeing us."

There was no time for hesitation. Melissa nodded at the plan, and the two of them edged toward the cave mouth. As soon as the two men they were watching disappeared down into the gut, Melissa and Stanley moved out of the cave mouth and tried moving down the gut.

But it was impossible. The footing was so treacherous that they could hardly move, and every step sent a small cascade of sand and rock sliding downward. It would give them away, certainly.

Stanley pointed up. "Maybe up on top of this mound we can move faster, and stay out of their view."

That plan worked. In a few minutes' climb they reached the top, and there the soil was more compacted and they could move swiftly. They headed down toward the sea, moving as quickly as they could while trying to stay quiet.

Despite the underbrush, in ten minutes' time they felt they were clear of any immediate danger and slowed their pace, both of them breathing hard and sweating in the hot sun.

"Let's head that way," Stanley said to her, pointing toward a spot where the gut, wider down here and much shallower, looked like it might be crossed easily. She nodded, too tired to say anything, not wanting to waste any energy on conversation.

They scrambled across more loose gravel and sand on the way down, but it was much easier than back by the cave and in a few minutes they were down the slope, across the gut, and headed back up the other side. Another few minutes and they'd reached the relative safety of the far side and were heading off toward the main road.

And then, right in front of them when they hit the dirt path that led down to the road, was the Jeep driven by the men who'd followed them.

Stanley laughed. "Well, this is perfect, girl." He laughed again, enjoying the irony of the moment, then walked over to the Jeep. "While they're up there looking for us, we're down here with their fancy car."

He walked over to the driver-side door and tried it. Locked, but no alarm went off. "OK, then, we'll get in the hard way," he said, looking around on the ground, then walking over to pick up a large rock.

Melissa had walked around to the passenger side. She gave that door a try. It was unlocked, and she swung it open. "A woman's touch, Stanley, that's all you need," she said, climbing in and reaching over to unlock Stanley's side.

He smiled and shook his head as he got in himself, and gave a quick look around for the keys. Nothing.

"OK, then, we'll do *this* the hard way," he said, and started to reach down under the dash to pull wires and try to hot-wire the Jeep.

The jangle of keys stopped him and Melissa chuckled as she

held them out to him. "Under the mat on this side. I'm telling you, Stanley, you need to look before you leap."

He frowned at her, took the keys from her hand, and then reached into his own pocket and grabbed his keys, tossing them to her and then starting the Jeep. "Here's what we'll do. I'll drive you up to my car, you hop in it and drive mine, and we'll leave those guys stranded here. Teach them a lesson, all right?"

She nodded. This was all a lot more action than she'd counted on for today. But she couldn't recall the last time she'd felt this alive. As Stanley dropped the Jeep into first and headed up the path, Melissa felt ready for anything; the excitement, the exhilaration, was intoxicating.

A few seconds later they rounded the corner with the large boulder and saw Stanley's Corolla, its doors and trunk wide open, with the two men standing next to it, looking toward them after hearing the Jeep's engine noise. Both men started reaching into shoulder holsters.

"Shit!" yelled Stanley, and jammed the Jeep into reverse.

One of the men had his weapon out. Melissa watched him like it was in slow motion, his bringing the gun out with his right hand, raising it, bringing the left hand up to help steady his aim, all of this while Stanley got them moving backward, crazily, weaving wildly back and forth over the rough terrain and trying to get back around the corner and that huge boulder.

The guy fired as they got to the boulder. Melissa saw the gun go off, a burst of flame and smoke that came a fraction of a second before she heard the sharp bark of the round going off, heading toward them. A part of the boulder cracked loudly where the slug, hit it, and then they were back past it, out of sight, still careering madly in reverse but at least, for the moment, out of range from those men and their guns.

"Hang on, girl!" Stanley yelled at her as they hit the flat spot at the bottom of the slope a few seconds later. "This might get crazy."

"*Get* crazy?" she yelled back, and then, as he turned hard on the steering wheel and the Jeep started to rise up on its right side, the wheels leaving the ground, she realized what he meant.

Stanley eased off the gas and the Jeep fell back onto all four wheels with a hard thump. As he brought it to a stop and jammed it into first gear, some strangely lucid part of Melissa's mind found that she finally understood what Dan Finnegan had been talking about all those years ago, about Vietnam and friends dying and not being able to see where it was coming from, where the death was hiding.

In another moment, Stanley had the Jeep moving forward, gravel and dirt flying as they roared away, crashing through the underbrush. Melissa looked around quickly when she had the chance, the car sliding around, confusing her vision—where was that path?

They found it, and Stanley got the Jeep cleanly onto it. They were going to make it away then without getting shot. Then, at the very moment she started to relax, Stanley lost control and the Jeep slipped off the dirt road at the first sharp curve, the left front end diving into the ditch next to the road. Melissa, her seat belt not buckled, felt herself go, flying around the passenger side of the car, unable to stop her motion.

She was completely unprepared for it. One second she was just starting to settle into her seat and then next she was flying up toward the roof and crashing forward against the dash and then bouncing back, hard, against her seat.

Then it was over and she was OK, she thought, sitting there checking for pain. She looked at Stanley and he was sitting, moaning quietly, bleeding from a cut on his forehead where it had met the windshield of the Jeep. The windshield was cracked at that spot, a spidery network of fractures held in place by the safety glass layers, but bulging outward from the central depression in the glass where his head had met the windshield.

Melissa reached toward him, then stopped, afraid to touch him or move him. "Stanley? Stanley, are you all right?"

He moaned, sat back, seemed to wake up a bit. "Oh, man, that *really* hurts. I hit my head."

"You sure did. We need to get you to the hospital."

He seemed to wake up more. "Yeah," he said, "to hospital."

He tried shakily to sit up. He reached for the gearshift but couldn't seem to grab hold of it and then sat back. Blood was streaming down from his forehead cut, covering his eyes, his nose. "Melissa, girl. You're going to have to get us out of here."

"Me?"

"You. And now. Those guys won't be far back there."

"I didn't see them after we backed out."

There was a painful chuckle. "I love you for that optimism, girl. But trust me, they're on the way. Now get us out of here." He groaned. "We'll have to change seats. Help me, girl."

And she did, a painful process that took a full minute or more, Melissa helping him out of his side and then helping him stagger around to the passenger side, then Melissa running back to the driver's side, scrambling in, shoving the gearshift into reverse, and flooring it.

The tires just spun, screaming up a cloud of smoke and dust. The Jeep didn't budge.

"Try first gear, and go easy," Stanley offered, wiping off the blood with his shirt.

She did that, and the Jeep moved forward a bit, then settled back.

Stanley groaned, "Oh, hell. What was I thinking of, girl? Shove it into four-wheel drive. That shift there, just pull it back a notch."

She did that, and the Jeep's front wheel grabbed at the loose soil at the front of the ditch while the rear wheels pushed them up it. In seconds, they popped free, the Jeep climbing the far side of the ditch.

She could barely see where she was going through the fractured windshield, and so she leaned left to see around the spidery fracture. That worked, but there was no path there, only scrub brush.

She heard an engine screaming behind them, took a glance back. It was Stanley's Corolla, rounding the corner maybe thirty yards back, dirt and gravel flying.

"Now, now, now, now," Stanley hissed at her hoarsely. "Go, go, go, girl."

And she did, flooring it and flying off through the scrub, the

Jeep bouncing them unmercifully as it rolled over the rough terrain, Stanley moaning in pain as he grappled with the seat belt, finally managed to fasten himself in. Melissa, busy with the gearbox and steering wheel, decided the seat belt was going to have to come later.

But they were moving, at least, and the one glance she could afford into the rearview mirror didn't show the Corolla behind them—it probably couldn't get through that ditch, she realized. So she slowed a bit to gain control and kept them moving.

"That way," Stanley said after another minute or two, pointing toward the right. She went that way, and when they rounded a clump of palm trees they were at the main, paved coastal road. "Go left," he said, and she pulled onto the road and roared away.

Paved it was, but not in great shape, the Jeep still bouncing over ruts and potholes and clumsily patched parts of the road. Melissa pulled it out of four-wheel drive, then tried to go as fast as she could and still keep control. She could see in the rearview mirror clearly now and kept looking for the Corolla, but it wasn't back there.

Then they came into Dieppe Bay Town and she had to slow down and work her way through a pair of roundabouts and the town's traffic, a few cars, two vans, and one agonizingly slow tractor. Peering around the broken windshield, she bumped them over a set of railroad tracks at the far edge of the town, and then the road cleared. It hadn't taken more than five minutes to get through the village.

She took a deep breath, relaxed a bit. Now, where to take Stanley? He was quiet but not moaning anymore, and his breathing sounded all right. "You OK?" she asked.

He waved at her, his eyes closed. "Hurts. But the bleeding's stopped."

"Where should I go, Stanley?"

"In St. John's. I know a doctor there. He'll stitch me up OK."

"OK, how far to St. John's?"

"Just a few miles up this road. Ten minutes maybe. Just keep going."

She nodded, then realized he couldn't see her. "Got it," she added, and sat back, glancing again at the rearview mirror. Oh, my god. It was the Corolla, coming on hard.

"Stanley!"

"The Corolla?"

"Yes. What do I do?"

"Drive. There's a turn up here in a mile or so."

"I don't see it."

"You will. Just drive. Try and get some distance; you've got a lot bigger engine in this than there is in that old Corolla."

He looked at her, grimaced with pain. "I wonder if they're trying to scare us or kill us?"

"Oh, god, Stanley." She pushed the pedal toward the floor and the Jeep surged forward. Melissa was at the very limit of her ability, worried that she could barely keep the car on the road. A quick glance in the mirror, though, showed she was holding her own. The Corolla wasn't gaining on them anymore.

Then came a tight **S** curve, the road winding down and through another shallow gut. There was no traffic coming the other way. She dropped the Jeep down a gear, edged over into the other lane for better entry into the **S**, took it at nearly sixty miles per hour, and wound her way through it cleanly, edging right over onto the shoulder at one point but keeping control as they came out of the curve and she was back in her own lane. She could see an intersection up ahead a few hundred yards.

"Stanley?"

He sat up, opened his eyes, wiping the drying blood from his forehead and eyes with his shirtsleeve. He looked to see where they were. "OK, now, girl, this is your chance to do some fancy driving."

"That wasn't fancy enough for you?" Melissa was terrified, but somehow overriding the fear was a delicious exhilaration. She had just learned that she *could* do the driving that needed to be done. She laughed. "OK, then, Stanley. Lead on, MacDuff. Miss Fancy Driver herself is at the wheel."

He managed a weak smile. "Just take a right at that road up there, all right?"

She took the right, maybe with too much confidence, spinning the Jeep out some on the narrow dirt road but then wrestling it back until they were heading in the right direction. As they drove the few hundred yards down toward the coastline, Statia, the Dutch island just eight miles to the north, rose in front of them from the water. It seemed huge to Melissa, some combination of her own frenetic adrenaline rush and the island's mountainous rise from the blue Caribbean enlarging it for her as she seemed to be driving straight for it, bouncing madly over the rough dirt road.

"How close are they behind us?"

She looked in the mirror. "Oh, god, Stanley, they're coming right up! They must have taken that turn a lot better than I did."

"They're good, but you're doing fine, Melissa. Let them catch up with us. See up there where the road curves left along the beach?"

"Yes."

"Follow that to the left, and then when I say hard left, you do that. This Jeep can do things that old Corolla of mine can't." There was a dry chuckle. "Glad now I didn't fix those brakes. You got it, girl?"

"Got it, Stanley." And she headed for the curve, the ground suddenly rising, the Corolla no more than fifty feet back now and coming hard, banging and flying over the potholes, gaining rapidly. Somewhere in the lucid back of her mind, Melissa realized she was grateful that she was so busy she didn't have time to let the fear overcome her. Instead, strangely calm, she got through the curve and then, when Stanley yelled at her, she turned hard left.

There was no road there. No path. In that instant Melissa could see that the dirt road they'd been on ended at the side of a small inlet cut into the shoreline. To the left, where they were headed, the road ended in a sand dune. Ahead it ended at a low cliff, with a thirty-foot drop-off into the inlet.

The Jeep dived hard down into the sand dune, sending a spray of sand over the hood and windshield, the engine roaring, screaming as it tried to shove them deeper into the sand. Melissa killed the engine and there was a sudden, blessed silence.

She looked over to Stanley, who stared back with a grin. "You go check on them, girl, and I'll see if I'm able to get this thing out of here."

While Stanley hobbled around from his side to the driver's side, Melissa climbed out, then walked back up to the dirt road. There was nothing there. She walked over to the edge of the bluff— a long trail of skid marks led right to it. She reached the edge and looked down. There, thirty feet below, the tail of the Corolla bobbed up and down in the tidal swells. No sign of the occupants.

She heard the Jeep start back, heard the gears screech as Stanley jammed it into reverse, and then heard the engine roar. A few seconds later the Jeep bounced back up the ridge and Stanley, face bloodied but smiling, hit the power window switch to open the window near her.

"You need a lift, girl?"

She managed a laugh, then walked back over to the edge for one more look. The Corolla had disappeared, but then, as she watched, first one and then the next of the two guys popped to the surface. She felt relief—she didn't want to kill anyone, for god's sake—but anger, too. They certainly had seemed willing to kill her.

Then she walked back to the Jeep, climbed in, and managed to back it up and out of the ditch in the four-wheel drive.

As they headed back down the dirt path, to the coast road and into St. John's and its clinic, Stanley looked over her. "I don't think they were really trying to hurt us, girl. They just meant to give us a good scare."

Melissa looked back at him. "It worked," she said, and turned onto the main road and toward St. John's.

CHANGE IN TEMPERATURE

The message on her machine had gone like this:

"Melissa? I haven't heard from you on when you're coming this way and wanted to let you know I'll have you picked up at the airport. Just let me know the flight information and I'll be there, all right?

"And listen, Melissa. I just had a nice talk with Summer Arndt. She says she'd like to see you when you get here. She's sure been through a lot.

"While we were talking about you coming up this way for the funerals she mentioned something to me, Melissa. Remember that thing that happened at Danny's funeral? That funny little—I don't know what you'd call it, a kind of vision or something. Well, Summer told me you talked about it with her. She said it didn't work when she was with you, but then I thought about how it *did* work with me and . . ." He paused.

"Well, listen. I have the craziest damn thing to ask of you. I know it's a lot to ask, and I know it's crazy. But I was wondering if you could maybe try that up here." He paused; she could hear his thinking through how to say this decently. "Maybe with the victims. I know it's a lot to ask of you, but we're just out of information here, Melissa, and this guy is still killing people. I mean, I know it's crazy and the wildest kind of long shot, but, hell, I'll try anything at this point, and since you're coming up anyway I just thought . . ."

There was another pause, punctuated by a ratchety cough. "Listen, Melissa. If you can't do this for me, I understand. It'll be great just to see you anyway. I just wanted to warn you I'd be asking when you get here, OK?"

And that was it.

Melissa had been sitting on the rattan settee at Rosemarie's house when she called home to check her messages. Stanley was back from the doctor's, stitched and bandaged—a minor concussion, eight stitches above the left eye—sitting in the rattan chair opposite her, as anxious as she was to hear whatever messages might be on the machine. Something threatening from the Palmers? Something sweet, an offer, from the Palmers to buy her silence on the rape? Something from the local police? They didn't know.

And there had been just the one message: something from way out in left field, Dan Finnegan, Melissa's cold past, calling again.

But she loved the guy; he was a second father, she explained to Stanley and Rosemarie. So she called him back from Rosie's house and told him yes, told him she was flying up the next day, would get into Minneapolis at 3:00 P.M. on the American flight from San Juan.

He'd laughed on the phone. "It's supposed to get down to forty below tonight, Melissa. Been a long time since you've been in that kind of weather, right?"

She laughed back, thinking it wasn't all that funny, really. "Six years, and I haven't missed it a bit. But it would be great to see you, and Dad, too."

"Oh, yeah, for sure. I thought I'd wait until I got your OK before telling him, though. So you'll come?"

Melissa looked over to Stanley and Rosemarie. Rosie was smiling, happy to see Melissa having a good family conversation with the folks back home.

Stanley, though, was stone-faced, just staring at her. To him it must look like she was escaping, leaving him here alone to fight this strange struggle. Well, she couldn't help that. This was Dan Finnegan calling, and he needed her help, and that was that. She said yes and now, twenty-four hours later, she was coming in for a landing at San Juan, where she would change from the little prop job to the big jumbo jet and head home to Minneapolis and the snow and the unforgiving cold.

At the airport at St. Kitts—everyone still called it Golden Rock though it was now named after the first president following independence, Robert L. Bradshaw International—Stanley had bought her a Walkman and a couple of CDs to listen to on the long trip north.

She had one on now: Marley of course, singing "Jamming," island rhythms running all through the song to remind her of where she lived now, he'd said, not smiling. She'd laughed it off, took it from him there at the gate,

He'd been nervous at the gate, wondering first if anyone was going to walk up and arrest them or, worse, some of the Palmer goons would be hanging around. But there'd been none of that; the strange quiet continued. It was like it hadn't happened. Nothing about it on the radio, nothing in the *News-Democrat*. Nothing at all.

That would end in another two days, when the *Labour News* came out with Stanley's story. Oh, the fur would fly then, he said to her. And he'd seemed nervous, too, just to see Melissa heading north.

She'd hugged him once, careful not to hurt him, and then she'd walked away across the tarmac, turning just once to wave. He'd waved back and then she'd walked up the boarding stairs and on into the plane, found her seat in the hot confines of the plane, and sat back, sweating, liking it, wondering how it would be in Minnesota, trying to conjure up the feeling, the sights and sounds, of forty below. It was hard to do.

As they'd taken off, swinging out over the water and then heading north and west, past Statia's abrupt coast and on toward Puerto Rico, Melissa had turned in her window seat, looked back at the north coast of St. Kitts in the mist and thin light of dawn, and thought that maybe she could see St. John's there. Maybe that was it; maybe that was Rosie's house.

Was this a clean break? Was she coming back? She didn't know. There wasn't anything there in her apartment that she couldn't just leave or have Rosie ship to her. There was nothing, really, to bring her back. Just a couple of hours ago she'd even had Stanley call his friend Errol at the Frigate Bay Police Station from there and told him not to file those charges, just tear up the forms and throw them away.

Stanley hadn't agreed with making that call, but it wasn't Stanley who'd gone through it and would have to go through it all again if the charges were filed. He'd done it, made the call, and then driven her to the airport before dawn for the 7:00 A.M. flight. She knew he didn't think she'd ever come back. He thought she was running away, running back home.

Was she? Looking out the window, she thought the island looked perfect, rising from the sea. Such a beautiful place, a paradise in so many ways. She wondered how long it would be before she came back. A few days? A week? Never? She didn't know.

It was a two-hour layover in San Juan. She got checked in at the gate, then left to walk outside the terminal and stand there in the eighty-five-degree heat, with her face to the sun. She wasn't wearing any makeup. She liked not wearing it; she felt better inside as a result. No more of that, no more false fronts.

Standing there, feeling the warmth, she thought about the north. She hadn't told Finnegan about Bo and the rape, figured she might tell him over the next few days. He'd understand. She'd have to keep it a secret, though, from her father. She didn't like secrets, but there was no way he would be able to handle it.

Five hours later the big jumbo touched down in Minneapolis. The sky was a perfect robin's egg blue as they circled the Twin Cities on their way in, the ground below a dazzling white with browns and blacks mixed in everywhere, roads and paved lots.

And there were thousands of plumes of steam and smoke rising, as if the snow itself were on fire underneath and the smoke and steam were fighting through the cold to emerge and rise and spread. The temperature, the captain said as they started their descent, was thirty-eight below. Melissa, looking down at all that as they came in for their landing, shook her head and smiled. This was a long, long way from St. Kitts.

She could feel the cold right through the skin of the aircraft as she stood there next to her seat, waiting for the passengers to move on ahead of her, snaking their way out of the plane. The cold seeped right through the metal and she shivered. She was back. A minute or two later, the walk down the aisle and then through the connecting jetway was freezing, the blasts of warm air from the heaters just reminding her of how cold it was out there.

Finnegan was waiting for her when she came through the door leading into the gate area. He looked terrible, a knit cap on his gray head, white salve on both his cheeks and ears, large bandages on both hands. He wore a bulky Aran sweater, carried a down parka, and leaned on a cane.

Melissa wanted to hug him and did so, but carefully, putting her arms around him lightly and giving him a slight squeeze. "What's happened to you? You said on the phone that you were OK."

"I *am* OK, I just look like hell, and I didn't want you worrying." He put his bandaged left hand over her shoulder as they walked toward Baggage Claim and added with a wicked grin, "But it was a pain in the butt driving, so you'll be at the wheel on the way back, all right?"

For the next half hour, as they waited for her single bag and then walked through the tunnel to the parking garage, Melissa found herself the one doing all the talking, mostly about how nice St. Kitts was, how the weather was always warm, the rain soft, the coconuts fell off the trees—the standard life-in-paradise conversation. She didn't get into the situation with Bo and his family. She didn't mention Stanley. All of that could come later.

Her bag slung over her shoulder, she took her time, slowing down to keep pace with Finnegan as they made their way through the parking garage to his big Pontiac and then wrestled her bag into the trunk. Soon they were on their way, driving the eighty miles down along Route 169 to Mankato, through Shakopee,

Belle Plaine, Le Sueur, and St. Peter, and then on into town, the sun setting ahead of them, bright but thin.

Melissa played tourist on the drive, Finnegan chatting for a bit about nothing much, then dozing in the seat next to her as she eased the big Pontiac down the highway, the road cleared after the big snow of two days ago, but with huge drifts of plowed snow off to the side here and there, testament to how many inches had fallen.

The road followed the course of the Minnesota River. A century before, riverboats had traveled that route, but a hundred years of farming had silted up the Minnesota so much that nothing much bigger than canoes found most of it navigable. Still, in the summer the views from the road were beautiful, the river to the left, lined with cottonwoods and oaks and glinting in the sun, the low bluff of the river on the right, heading up steeply to the Minnesota prairie, part of the breadbasket that helped feed the world. Up there, rows of corn and wheat, soybeans and sugar beets. Down here, the hidden river valley, lush in the summer, frozen and still in the grip of winter, its beauty now stark, black bare trees against the virginal white snow and ice of the river.

It was four-thirty and already getting dark, the piles of plowed snow on both sides of the highway giving it the feel of a wide tunnel through the darkening night. A bit later, a half-moon started rising in the clear, cold sky, throwing a pale light onto the whiteness. And it was cold, terribly cold. With the heater cranked up, the body lied to the brain on a night like this. Clear sky, pale moon. Once you were outside the cities and couldn't see the rising plumes of vapor and smoke and steam, the countryside looked calm and almost inviting. But forty below was deadly.

The Pontiac needed gas. Melissa figured Le Sueur—the Valley of the Jolly Green Giant, where the sprawling packing plant used to be right there in the heart of town—would be a good place to stop. When she pulled off the highway Finnegan came awake with a moan.

He looked around. "We need gas or something?"

"Yep, down to a quarter of a tank, and in this weather, and in the dark, I didn't want to risk it."

He stretched, carefully. "Good girl, haven't lost that good Minnesotan common sense." He yawned. "I fell asleep? Damn. Sorry, Melissa. I'm still kind of wiped out by all this." He raised his hands.

"Did you get any sleep last night or were you hurting?"

"Not too bad on both counts. I keep taking ibuprofen and that dulls the pain pretty much. But the damn hospital's so busy, you know, with people coming and going . . ."

"You were still in the hospital last night?"

He laughed. "It's a long story, been in and out of there twice this week. This time, they had me in to check on some infection in the left hand's fingers, and then they didn't want to let me go until they were sure there wasn't anything serious going on. I finally convinced them I was OK and they let me go around noon."

"You mean you got home, then turned right around and came to get me?"

"No, didn't have time for that. I just left the hospital, got in the car, and drove to the cities. Made it with a half hour to spare, too."

She shook her head, swung the car around a corner, and headed for the Texaco station. "You're crazy. You shouldn't have done it. I could've taken the airport shuttle bus, you know. Thirty dollars and right to the door."

She pulled into the station, slid into a spot next to the pumps. "I'd forgotten how much I *hate* self-service," she said, pulling on her gloves, jamming her knit cap tight on her head, and then darting out of the car. The ritual of pumping your own gas took on a whole new level of complexity at forty below. She'd forgotten about that and a thousand other subzero things in the years she'd been gone.

Standing there at the pump, hopping back and forth to stay warm as she fed the gas into the tank, she cataloged a few of them: the smell of burning wood everywhere from a thousand stoves and fireplaces; the way the sun pillars danced in the air, shimmery rainbows of frozen moisture that waltzed down the street; the feel of a light breeze against your face that was so cold it felt like needles.

Those things and dozens more flashed by as she stood there pumping, then finished, got the nozzle back into the pumps and the cap back on the gas tank, paid, and got them back on the road.

She was settling back into her seat for the final hour's drive into Mankato when Finnegan, wide awake now, started talking.

"You know, Melissa, this guy has killed eight people now, two of them kids. Last week, when he did it again, I almost caught him. Hell, I was chasing him when I broke through the ice. I thought I was dead when I went in the water."

"And then he was the one who rescued you."

"Yeah. Damnedest thing. Look, will you reach into my right pocket in the parka for me? I have something I want you to see."

They weren't back on 169 yet. She pulled off into a convenience store parking lot, shoved the Pontiac into park, and reached over to pull the folded sheet out of his pocket.

"Open it up. Read it," Finnegan said.

"It's a teletype."

He smiled tiredly. "I know what it is. I wanted you to read it."

She laughed, read it. "It says they found some guy you were looking for. He's dead. He's been dead for weeks, in some building in St. Paul."

"An abandoned building. No heat. The body's been frozen."

"Yeah, I see that."

"He's been our one other good suspect, that guy."

"But this latest murder just happened, right?"

"You got it. And this guy's been dead for weeks."

"So he's not the murderer?"

"Right." He sighed as she folded up the paper, set it on the seat between them, and then got the Pontiac back on the road, back toward Mankato.

"I've been working this thing for six years now, Melissa. I was never convinced it was this guy, anyway; it just didn't quite fit." He was musing out loud, just talking it through. "Oh, we have a lot of things: his handwriting, strands of black hair, probably a woman's, which we figure means he wears a wig, DNA from blood samples, but they were all from the victims, some footprints, a few partial fingerprints, some other bits and pieces here and there. Trouble is, they don't connect up anywhere."

He sighed, shook his head. "Jesus, I'm at the end of my rope, and now the guy is saving my damn life. That's why I'm hoping you can help. If you're willing?"

She nodded. She'd made up her mind about that as she'd flown north, into the cold. "But you know it probably won't work, right?"

He nodded. "But you will try. We'll go to Immanuel St. Joseph's where the county morgue is as soon as we get to town, and you'll try, right?"

She'd known it was coming to this. "Sure," she said, not happy about it, afraid of what it would be like if it did work and how sad it would be if it didn't. Still, for Dan Finnegan she'd do what she could: "Sure," she said again. "Let's go there now and give it a try."

An hour later, Melissa shook her head at her first sight of Mankato again after all these years—clean and white in the throes of winter, ice in the streets and the weird yellow light from the vapor lamps against the snow, with smoke and steam rising everywhere, from car exhausts to homes to faces—vapor everywhere in the cold.

The hospital was on Marsh Street, so she got off 169 and crossed the Veterans' Memorial Bridge, then through residential neighborhoods to get to the hospital, past two-story homes rising above the snowdrifts, then along past Bethany Lutheran College and the Fitzgerald Middle School, and then they were pulling into the doctors' part of the parking lot.

Finnegan laughed at that. He found it funny that they were right back at the same place he'd checked out of a few hours before. She parked the car right in front of the door that said "County Medical Examiner" on it—in the spot marked for official vehicles. Parking there emphasized how real this all was suddenly getting to be. Even as she'd flown north, even as they'd driven down 169 to get here, a part of her hadn't really dealt yet with what she was about to do. Or try to do. Now, here it was, a few minutes away. She took a deep breath after pulling into the parking spot, opened her door, walked around to help Dan Finnegan out. He struggled some, his body not happy about climbing in and out of a car.

The county morgue was in the basement of Immanuel St. Joseph. To get to the room they walked up a steel walkway, crunchy with salt and grit spread to keep the ice off it. Then through an unmarked door and down a long hallway lined by radiators working hard, some old gravity-feed heating system struggling to keep up with the subzero cold, clanking and banging to hold back the hard edge of the bitterness that waited outside, where it was dark and going to get colder—forty-five or even fifty below, down there where everything freezes and stops, the air gets deadly still, engine blocks crack, the tires of parked cars get a hard flat spot where they met the road overnight.

They walked down a flight of stairs into the basement, turned left, and went past the hospital laundry room and then the boiler room and reached a door marked "Morgue," in small letters, inconspicuous.

Finnegan shoved the door open, waved to the young kid behind the counter wearing a lab coat, who smiled at them, waved them in—things were ready for them.

Finnegan walked Melissa back behind the counter, through more doors, and into the walk-in cooler.

The smell was like nothing she'd ever smelled before, sickening, a mix of decay and disinfectant. She almost retched, staggering a bit from it. Finnegan steadied her. "I know; I know. It's awful. And it's going to get worse, Melissa. Just do your best."

There were four hospital gurneys in the middle of the room. On each was a body bag—one of those white disposable bags made from that tough papery fiber material that's impossible to rip.

Finnegan walked over to the first body. Melissa, walking behind him, realized just how hard this was all going to be. Touch what was in that white bag? It didn't seem possible that she could.

Finnegan zipped it back, Melissa watching as he pulled the zipper from top to bottom. At first, all Melissa could see was gray, the poor woman's skin the color of slush on the first day of a thaw, a dirty, sickly gray.

Finnegan turned to look at Melissa. She nodded. Came over to his side, looked down into that awful black plastic, and saw the body there, nothing prettied up here. This was a long way from the only other dead bodies she'd seen, at funeral services, all cleaned up, prepared for a final public showing.

This was Death. Gray lips on the face. Gray torso below it.

Melissa took a deep breath, fighting back a wave of nausea, the smell of the place sharp, biting, reaching to the back of her throat, making her gag.

"The puncture wounds from the knife are farther down on the bodies," Finnegan said, "and there's no right hand on either of the bodies. They've been cut off. The guy takes souvenirs."

She nodded. Get it over with. Finnegan put his arm around her shoulder as she reached down to touch the skin on the poor woman's cheek, expecting that jolt again, that awful vision of final moments, the overwhelming reality that swept over her with that electric pulse, expecting to see things she didn't want to see, things that would help Finnegan.

But there was nothing. A soft give, that was all. Nothing. No vision, no hard pulse, nothing.

She tried touching the shoulder. Nothing.

They zipped the bag, opened the next drawer, the poor little girl. The torso was unmarked, the face strangely peaceful, but the body seemed deflated, pathetic. Melissa touched the cheek, the shoulder. Nothing.

But now it got worse. The next bag was Walter Arndt, a man she'd known and liked years back in high school when she'd been to Summer's house and found out that some of her friends had mothers, and fathers like Walter Arndt, who often showed up at his daughter's basketball games to cheer her on.

But that was years ago, and the face and upper torso she saw when Finnegan opened the bag didn't look much like the man she knew. Thank god.

She reached out to touch the right shoulder, this body dried up and harder than the two females. Nothing came to her.

And then Father Murphy, whose placid face she recognized instantly when Finnegan zipped the bag open. He'd been monstrous to some of the boys, Melissa had been told, but here he looked calm, serene, almost holy. His body, too, was harder than the women. And again, when she touched the skin of the neck this time, there was nothing.

So that was that.

Finnegan, not saying much, walked her back to the car in the cold darkness of early evening. Nothing seemed alive, the world at cessation, still, silent. She felt as if she'd been holding her breath the whole time, holding on to her sanity while she did that. The scrunch of their shoes against the snow and ice seemed deafening.

They climbed in the car. "I got you a room at the Holiday Inn so you could stay in town this evening," Finnegan said. "The funerals are day after tomorrow. I called your dad and he said he'd drive in tomorrow morning and meet you for breakfast. Said he'd leave you a message at the front desk. Hope that's all right."

She nodded. She'd let Finnegan down. She'd warned him it might not work, but she'd thought, really, that it would come through for her, that she'd see what needed to be seen. But there was nothing.

She pulled the Pontiac out of the lot, headed it down Main toward the hotel. Finnegan said, "Maybe it was something you've grown out of, or something that would only happen a few times in a lifetime, and it's gone now. Something like that. It was worth a shot. I'm glad we tried."

"Sure," she said, agreeing. But he'd wanted this one, he'd needed it, and she hadn't come through for him. She wished now that she had been able to—the hell with the horror of it, just helping this man would be worth all that—but it just wasn't there.

"All right," he said as they reached the Holiday Inn, the new one out by the mall at the south edge of town. "Listen, thanks, Melissa. I appreciate it. Say hi to your dad for me."

Melissa opened her door, walked back to the trunk, and pulled out her bag. She looked at Finnegan as he walked around to get into the driver's seat. "You OK to drive this thing home now?"

He laughed. "I got it to the airport to get you, didn't I? Yeah, I'll make it home OK. Got to go into the office first, though."

He sat down, poked his head back out the door, smiled at her tiredly. "Thanks, Melissa. Thanks for trying. Your ticket's good for day after tomorrow, but I bought you one you can change, all right? You can head back anytime you want, get back to that sunshine and warmth."

She nodded, picked up her bag.

"Hey," Finnegan yelled, getting back out of the door to yell it at her as she walked through the double doors of the hotel entrance. "Come to think of it, tell your dad I owe him a lunch. Maybe we can all get together tomorrow, all right?"

She nodded. "Sure, tomorrow. I'll tell him. That sounds really good."

And she walked on into the Holiday Inn while Finnegan, no better off than he was before, pushed the Pontiac into drive with his wrapped hands and, steering mostly with his wrists, headed back to the office.

SCRAPES AGAINST THE WINDOW

Melissa checked in, got to her room, then unpacked, shoving her clothes into the dresser drawers underneath the television console, hanging up her parka and a few blouses.

She turned on the TV to some mindless talk show, and with the sound on, the curtains closed tightly in her second-floor room, and the heater cranked up high, she could almost forget for a moment or two just how bitter it was outside.

She sat on the bed to call her father but for a long moment couldn't recall the phone number. Funny, to have lived there for all those years and then suddenly not be able to remember the number.

When she picked up the phone and hit 9 for an outside line, though, her fingers seemed to remember on their own and the call went through. He answered on the third ring.

"Daddy? It's Melissa. I'm here in town. And, Daddy, I have to tell you, it's incredibly cold."

He laughed on the other end of the line. "You get soft down on that island, Melissa? Of course it's cold; it's January. Dan Finnegan got you at the airport like he said he would, I suppose?"

"Yeah. He was pretty beat up, though. Frostbite on his cheeks, and his hands all bandaged up."

"You know he may lose some fingers, right?"

"No!"

"He didn't tell you? Yeah, the docs say they don't know if they can save 'em—three on his left hand and two on the right."

"He didn't mention that at all."

"He could've died out there, easy, chasing that guy, the one doing the killings."

"It's so awful. And to happen here, of all places."

"Yep, it's a terrible thing," he agreed. "When you going over there to help him out?"

"Oh, we already did it, Daddy."

"What was it you did? He said he couldn't tell me until later, and damned if I can figure it out."

How to explain it? She realized she couldn't think of a way. She'd never told her father about those visions; he wasn't the sort of man who'd listen to any nonsense like that and she'd known that even way back at fourteen. She struggled for an excuse.

"It was just some ID stuff, Daddy. He thought I might recognize some of the victims' clothes." There, that would stall him until she could think of something better. She hesitated, took a breath, remembering how awful that had been in the morgue. "Anyway, it didn't do much good, really. I didn't recognize anything. A waste of time."

Melchior sounded sympathetic. "Dan's been working hard on this one for a long time and getting nowhere—the guy who's doing this is pretty damn smart, tell you that." He paused. "Listen, sweetheart, I know we'd planned to wait until tomorrow to get together and all, but since you're already all checked in there, if you're not too tired I'll come on into town tonight and we'll have dinner, all right?"

She was tired, and some sleep sounded better than dinner. But this was her father, and he was reaching out to her. She could take a nap first for an hour or so and then meet him, right here at the hotel. "Sure, Daddy, that'd be great. Nine-thirty all right, or is that too late?"

"Nope, that's perfect. I'll be there. We got lots to catch up on."

"Sure," she said, and then they said their good-byes and hung up. Melissa sat back against the loose headboard, banging it some against the wall. Losing his fingers? Poor Finnegan, and he hadn't mentioned it at all.

These terrible murders. They made her own troubles look

small by comparison. She shook her head, rose, and headed for the shower, where she turned it as hot as she could bear it and stood there for long minutes, trying to ease the cold that had already settled in deep.

A bit later she lay on the bed, trying to find an hour's sleep. She'd turned the TV off, and the room was quiet, maybe too quiet. Lying on her back, closing her eyes, she tried relaxing, thinking warm thoughts about St. Kitts, pretending she was standing at Turtle Bay with Stanley, staring out toward the sea, sweating in the welcome heat.

There was a faint scritching sound, like fingernails on a chalkboard. What was that?

It came again, louder now that she'd recognized it. And then again, so grating that she flinched to hear it. It was a sound, just a small scratch of a sound, really, and she knew it. But something about it, something malevolent that knifed into her, enlarged it in her mind. She flinched again as she heard it, then put a pillow over her head to muffle the sound.

But that was no way to try to sleep, the pillow over her face. She tossed it aside, sat up, listened. The sound came from the window. She walked over there, tugged on the cord to open the curtains, and saw the monster that was giving her such fits—a tiny branch of an old oak tree outside, the last few inches of it rubbing against her window.

Well, she could stop that. First she unlatched the lock on the inside window and slid it open, the outside cold hitting her as she did it. Then she undid two sets of latches on the outside window and shoved it wide open, the cold taking her breath away for a moment as she reached out, grabbed the offending branch, and snapped it off, taking off more than a foot of it to make sure.

Already her hands felt frozen, her face bitten with the cold, though she stood in a room that was in the midseventies at least. But the branch was gone.

She pulled the outside window shut, latched it. Slid the inside shut, latched that, too. Then, shivering violently, she tugged the thick curtains closed and ran back for the bed. She climbed in underneath the blankets, pulled them over from the other side of the bed to double them up for more warmth, and then, finally, found warmth, and quiet, and some sleep.

Later, dinner went well. Her father seemed warmer, nicer, less stiff and formal than he'd been in a long time. Maybe his friendship with Finnegan had done that for him over the past few years, loosened him up some.

He arrived at nine-thirty on the dot—that solid midwestern on-time thing at work again—wheeling the same old Ford pickup into the parking lot, climbing out stiffly, as if he had a bad back or something, then walking in the main entrance and through the swinging doors into the restaurant.

Melissa watched all this out the window from her little table with the silly red glass candle and checkerboard tablecloth, corny farm implements hung on the walls. She waved at him as he walked into the restaurant.

"Melissa. It's so good to see you, sweetie. I'm so glad you're here." He hugged her, almost picking her up from her chair to do it, crushing her in those strong, wiry arms.

A hug? She couldn't recall the last time he had hugged her, sometime in her childhood, she guessed. There had been some changes in this man, good ones.

"Hi, Daddy," was all she could manage. He looked happy, happier than she'd seen him since as far back as she could remember.

They ordered coffee, went through some perfunctory apologies. She was sorry she hadn't called more, but the island phones weren't that good. He was sorry he hadn't written more often, but he didn't know what to say, how to talk about how much he'd missed having her around. He was not good at putting stuff like that down on paper.

He hit her with questions: How was it down there? Island fever yet? Ready to come home?

She lied to him. "Dad, I'm happy there. The island is just heavenly; you'll have to come and visit. There's a live volcano you can walk down into, and a waterfall that you can stand under, and the sailing is great. You should come visit sometime."

She'd never done any of those things in her two years there, and there was this awful mess with Bo Palmer, and the whole mess with Stanley and his family. There was a lot to talk about, a lot to get off her chest. But this wasn't the place for that, or the time, or maybe the right person.

He shook his head. "I couldn't stand that heat down there. I need the cold, Melissa; I need winter. It's honest, clean. The best time of year. Besides," he added as an afterthought, "someone's got to look after the farm, and then I got my work to do, sold a couple more sculptures, you know."

"You ever get a heater for that barn, Dad? I remember how cold in gets in there when it gets below zero."

He grinned. "Yep, got a couple of space heaters for this sub-zero stuff, so it's not too bad." He switched the conversation. "You're coming out tomorrow, right? I'll show you the latest piece. Sold it to some museum down in St. Louis—big old catfish."

She nodded. Now that she hadn't been able to help Finnegan, she guessed maybe she would go out to the farm and spend some time. Maybe spend tomorrow night out there, see how it went.

Her father was still talking. "I spend most of my time working on the sculptures, that and ice fishing. I've still got that little shack down on Minnetoksak where I drop a line. Hasn't been a great year, too many thaws and freezes on the ice for it to be real safe. But I'm careful.

"Got a lunker pike I'm going to get one of these days soon. Going out there in a few hours, in fact. I don't suppose you want to come along, about three A.M.?"

She laughed. He must really be missing her if he was willing to ask her along to his ice shack—that had always been holy ground out there. She'd never been, not once.

"No, Daddy. I'm really tired. I've been flying all day, and then helping out Dan Finnegan."

"OK, then, maybe the next day, after the funerals. How long you staying?"

Good question, she thought. "A couple of days," she lied, but the truth was she really didn't know. How long *was* she staying? She felt in-between—not belonging here, not there. This, the frozen cold and everything it connected to in Mankato, this was what she'd left behind forever, she thought.

But St. Kitts? She didn't know if she would, or even could, ever go back. She needed to call Stanley. Hear his voice, talk to him, see how he was doing, hear if anything had happened with the strangely quiet police.

Melissa looked at her father, his clean plaid work shirt buttoned to the top, his DeKalb Corn cap covering that every-week haircut right to the trim line, his nails cut and cleaned despite all the dirt they went through every day. He lived a well-ordered life, driving into town every morning for a breakfast of scrambled eggs and hash browns and bacon at the Little House, buying a few supplies, then coming back to the farm to work on his art or, in the summer, maybe plant those last few working acres with some corn or sugar beets.

Melissa wondered if he still kept her mother's room ready for her return, the lace dusted on the top of the old chest of drawers, the bed made with the sheets and comforter cleaned every week, the windows cleaned every Saturday till they squeaked—all of it for poor, missing Moira.

But Melissa didn't ask him anything like that. She just smiled. "I'm glad you could come tonight, Dad. It's good to see you."

He paused, was suddenly serious. "I'm glad you asked me, Melissa. Gives me chance to say something."

He put his rough hands on the table, the hands of a man who'd worked hard for a living all his life, scarred and gnarled. He looked at her. "Things are better now, Melissa. I don't drink much anymore, and I try not to get so mad about things."

What drinking? She had no recollection of him being drunk very often. Once or twice, maybe, when she was in high school, he'd come home late and parked the Ford a little sloppy in the driveway, but that was about it. "Dad. Daddy. You don't have to talk like this. I don't ..."

But he raised his hand to shush her. He was struggling with

this, working hard to admit some things, and he wanted her to listen. "Hell, I know how bad I was, honey. It was awful for you. I'm not surprised you left. I understand all that. Took me a long time to figure all that out, that's all—a long time."

"Daddy, that's not why I left. It was the cold, and this town..."

He brushed her thoughts aside. He had a lot to say here and meant to get it out in the open. He sipped on his coffee. "I know you're not ready for this yet, Melissa. I know you think I'll just go on forever. But the farm is out of debt and when I'm gone it's yours. Jacob Torensen's boys want to buy it; they made me a good offer. But I'd like you to settle on it, find some guy worth spending time with, and make the place really yours.

"I haven't farmed it much the last few years; the art has made me enough money, and I used the set-aside program, let the land lie fallow. But it's a good farm, good soil. You could make a decent life there."

She started to speak, to slow him down. She didn't want to hear this. But he raised his hand to shush her again.

"I know I did a lot of bad things, Melissa. Awful things. Your poor mother. Hell, it was my drinking that drove her off; I'm sure of that now."

He stared right at his daughter, and she could only look back, wondering what he was talking about, why he was saying these things.

"I just want to say I'm sorry for all that. It's different now. I know you don't want to come back yet, but when you do, well, things are different. I'm a better man."

He sat back, smiled again. "There, I've said it, OK?"

"OK, Dad. You've said it." And she smiled back at him, reached across the table to take those huge, rough, gnarled hands into hers. So strong. Kept that farm going all these years.

She looked outside for a moment. A gust of wind stole a thin haze of snow from the frozen drifts the plows had edged around the parking lot. This was a long, long way from Tabernacle, from Stanley and old volcanoes and caves and constant, comforting heat. From up here, all that didn't even seem real.

Dinner was hamburgers done up fancy, and then there was more coffee and more talk. Her dad talked some about the farm, more about his sculptures, which were making real money these days. Then he went on about ice fishing on Minnetoksak, about the weather and the drought and the sugar beets he might plant again this year, just to try the market again. The next couple of hours flowed along nicely.

Eventually it had all pretty much been said. The two of them found themselves just sitting there, staring, and that brought a laugh.

Melchior looked at his watch. "Midnight. OK then, Melissa, I got to go. Couple of hours' sleep for me and then get out to the lake and start working on that damn monster pike."

She just shook her head. Her dad and this ice fishing. It had been the passion of his life for as long as she could remember.

They paid up, arguing over the bill and then agreeing to split it, and then walked outside into the brutal cold, the aurora dancing across the northern horizon in jagged waves of reds and purples as a kind of compensation for the bitter weather.

They stopped to watch for a minute in the parking lot. Melchior pulled out his keys, jangled them in his gloves. "Best lights I seen all winter," he said, and turned to look at his daughter. "None of that down on that island."

"You're right, Dad," Melissa agreed, and then pulled the collar of her coat up tight against the incredible cold as they walked over to Melchior's pickup. Even the slight breeze out of the north was too much to walk into, so she turned sideways, letting the collar and the knit cap on her head stop the wind before its subzero needles bit into her cheeks. Tomorrow she'd have to buy a face mask if she was going to be outside at all in this awful weather.

They reached the pickup truck and there, the truck's cab blocking the wind, she could open her eyes again and take a look around. Same truck he'd had for fifteen years now, beat up plenty, with dents here and there and peeling paint, but it still started and ran. She wasn't at all surprised that he'd kept it.

She started to tell him that, and then she saw, in the bed of the pickup, a deer carcass, a doe, shoved roughly into the bed, one of the legs sticking up against the side of the bed.

"Dad?"

"Found it on the highway on the way here. Broken neck, I think. Still warm when I stopped, so I just put it here to get it off the road, Melissa. I'm thinking I might as well take it on home and dress it. No sense in letting good meat go to waste."

Melissa just shook her head and smiled. Some things don't change. She looked at the deer, dark eyes filmed over in the harsh light from the parking lot. Poor thing. She reached down to give it a pat, express a little sympathy.

And that pulse grabbed her. There was frozen ground beneath her in the moonless dark, then gravel, a smooth, hard surface, sudden lights, horns, screeching noises, huge man thing bearing down, turning its side to her, slamming into her, and she was tossed across the smooth, hard surface to its far side, where she lay for a moment, struggling to rise, but couldn't, trying to move her head but couldn't, trying to see but couldn't as the darkness grew and overwhelmed her until there was nothing.

Melissa jerked her hand back. She saw it, saw the end.

Melchior was talking: "It's been great, Melissa. Thanks, honey, for giving me this chance to say some things I needed to say."

He hugged her one last time, hard, and then, not looking back, climbed into the Ford, slammed the door shut, jammed it into reverse, pulled back, and drove off. He hadn't noticed her shock at the touch of the deer, was too occupied with his own changes, his efforts to put a couple of lives back together.

Melissa watched him drive off, the red taillights shrinking into the cold and then gone. She shook her head. She hadn't imagined that, had she? No. It was back; the thing, whatever it was, was back. She'd have to call Finnegan, get back over to the morgue.

The shock of it, the surprise, was intense; she was still shaking from it, and shivering from the cold. She looked up, tried to draw in a breath of fresh air but couldn't until she held her mittens in front of her mouth to warm the air. Damn place. Damn cold, frozen place.

Overhead, the aurora grew brighter, half the sky now in muted reds and yellows, shattered waves of it moving across the dark dome over her head as she walked quickly back toward the hotel and its warmth and a telephone.

SLOW BREATHING

Finnegan didn't question her 12:30 A.M. call. "It's working? OK, Melissa, I'll be there in thirty minutes. You just wait for me in the lobby, all right?"

She said OK, hung up, and then sat there on the bed for a few minutes, thinking it through. Why had it happened now? She didn't know. Something to do with the temperature, with the northern lights, with Mankato, with her dad? All of the above?

She didn't know and almost didn't want to know. Instead, she figured, she could do this thing for Finnegan, help him out with this—god knows she owed him enough for everything he'd done for her over the years—then stay long enough for the funerals, and then, then what? Go back down to St. Kitts and do what had to be done down there? Stay here, hiding out from all that, here in the deep freeze, where everything could be the way it used to be?

Oh, hell. She didn't know.

She realized, sitting there, that she wanted to call Stanley, tell him the thing had worked, despite how he'd poked fun at it, it had worked, and might work again, might help solve those horrible murders. So there, Stanley Edwards. Take that.

But it was late, even in St. Kitts, and Stanley was still recuperating from that concussion, and she could always call him tomorrow, after she'd touched the bodies and seen what she could see. Maybe that was best.

But she did want to talk to him. She couldn't recall the last time she'd known a guy whom she actually wanted to call and talk to—just chat, about the weather, of course, or something in the news.

Thinking about Stanley, not able to decide whether to call him or not, she walked across the room to her purse, opened it, and reached in to get the lava-encrusted stick she'd found with him in that cave. What a day that had been. It seemed like a year ago, all that excitement, instead of just a few days ago. Crazy how the weather changed everything. It was frozen here, and so that made St. Kitts seem unreal, some fantasy land she'd spent time in before coming back here to reality, frozen hard reality.

But St. Kitts *was* all too real. That cave was real, and the gut they'd climbed through, and that terrible, frightening, exhilarating car chase—she hadn't even told Finnegan about that; he wouldn't believe it of her. She laughed at that thought.

She reached in to pick up the piece of lava, to hold it in her hands and make St. Kitts real again. She reached in, got her fingers around it.

And was there. In that cave, staring at someone, a man with a gun. The gun pointing, the man saying something, angry, shouting. An explosion, slow-motion flame and smoke billowing out, and then she is falling away, falling backward, rolling in pain, writhing, and then just the ceiling, lazy slow breathing, a rattling in the chest, a deep rumbling, the smell of sulfur, but no pain, no pain at all, everything gray and then darker and then black.

Melissa found herself on the floor. She'd lost herself in that scene, the horror of it, the hatred, the fear, the violence.

She knew that smiling face, the man with the gun, the murderer. Henry Palmer. A younger, more vital Henry Palmer, but that was him. Looking at him the way he was back then—this all must have happened twenty years ago—was like looking at Bo today. Bo. That reminded her of things she was trying to keep buried.

She shivered again, then walked to the phone and started dialing, long-distance. Very long-distance. She needed to talk to Stanley, and the sooner the better.

Mankato isn't a big place. Once Finnegan picked her up, right at
1 a.m., it only took them ten minutes of driving over frozen roads
with the crunch of ice and snow beneath the tires sounding loudly
in the dead quiet of the night, to reach the morgue. They didn't
say much as they drove over the flat once-prairie, now housing
tracts and strip malls. "It's worked again, just a few minutes ago.
I don't know why," Melissa said, climbing into the Pontiac.

Stanley hadn't answered, nor Rosemarie. Melissa had left a
message, blurted out everything, not knowing how much room
Rosie's answering machine had on it, how it had happened again
to her and it was real, and this time with the lava from the cave
she knew it was Henry Palmer who'd murdered Stanley and Rosie's father. She knew it. He had to believe her; she knew it: the
piece of lava was a bone from his father's body.

She'd rambled, then, embarrassed by it, had hung up quickly,
asking him to call back and leaving the hotel number at the last
second.

Only after she'd hung up had she thought to ask herself where
Stanley and Rosemarie might be. Were they in jail? They might
be dead. Life was crazy. Life was insane, was chaos. And by then
Finnegan was due to arrive down front and Finnegan needed her
help, and she could do that, at least. One thing at a time.

"That's good to hear, Melissa. I know how tough this must
be on you. Let's go check and get it over with," Finnegan said,
and started driving.

They parked right in front of the building this time, Melissa
surprised to see other cars parked there: a couple of police cruisers
and a little Honda. Busy place for this time of the morning on
a frozen night.

A locked door, a buzzer, a guard, a long walk into the cold
room redolent of formaldehyde. The zippered body bags. First,
the mother, gray and so cold.

Melissa touched her, Finnegan putting his hand on Melissa's
shoulder. Together they were jolted, a spasm in the loins, a surge:
There is a blade, rising, dropping, held by gnarled hands, scarred. Long black

hair flies wildly about a face that flashes by. Splattered blood, droplets of it in the air; she knows it is her own. She knows she's going to die.

Cary, her sweet little girl, is in the other room crying. Cary wants Mommy, but Mommy's busy right now, raising her right hand to ward off that blade and seeing the slash open from the palm down past the wrist so more blood spurts out. There is a certain curious pressure on her chest. She looks and sees the blade, in a horrid kind of forever slow penetration, punch its way through her, then rise for more. There is no pain. There is no feeling. There is the distant cry of Cary as the scene fades, darkens, is black, and then is nothing.

"Oh, Jesus Christ," said Finnegan, taking his hand off Melissa's shoulder. He turned away, walked away from the smell, the touch, the awful reality.

"I couldn't see a face. Just a mouth, and all that hair. But I'm sure it was a man," Melissa said, quite calm now as she stood her ground. This had to be done.

Finnegan walked back, pale, and unzipped the other bag, the one with the daughter, Cary.

Finnegan put his hand on Melissa's shoulder as she reached down to touch the girl's cheek.

She doesn't understand the big woman with the black hair, what she's doing to her and why those rough hands are holding her there on the neck and why Mommy won't help stop it and why is this happening, where is Mommy, when will this stop?

It did stop, mercifully, and Melissa pulled back.

Over to the next bag, Finnegan unzipping it. Father Murphy.

Hands turning the pages of a magazine. A rosary in the hand, "Hail Mary, full of grace, the Lord is with thee. Blessed art thou among women and blessed is the fruit of thy womb, Jesus. Holy Mary, Mother of God, pray for us sinners, now and in the hour of our death. Amen."

Begging forgiveness as the hands turned the pages and there were pictures of boys. Naked boys. And then more. Awful and terrible and excitement and guilt and suppression and a flowering of lust and then a sudden odd pressure from behind, then a terrible hold on the neck and a pain, a sharp pain that grows and grows in an instant to such violence . . . and then nothingness.

Finnegan, too, felt guilty. He had subjected Melissa to this. Poor, sick, awful Father Murphy. The poor, sick, awful Catholic

Church, which hadn't stopped men like him but let that horror grow and left it up to this monster to put a stop to Father Murphy's desires. He wondered if Murphy had done more than look at pictures. Jesus Christ, how could You let this happen?

Oh, hell, then. Quit it. Now. He tried to steer her away from the room, out of the door. But she stopped him, face grim, walked over to the gurney where poor old Walter Arndt lay. Finnegan came over, unzipped the bag, and held her shoulder as she reached in to touch him.

The back of a head, a ball cap, the form leaning over beautiful Karen. A raised hand. A knife. Yelling, grabbing the hand to stop this awfulness he'd stumbled onto. Just came to visit Karen. Full of desire for her, an affair that had been secret and powerful in that secrecy for years. And walked into this, grabbing the hand, watching as the form turned and a knife came at him and a hand at his face, all of this hazy and indistinct in a fury of movement and fear and pain and then one more vision of that cap, then a blade, then a tearing of the heart, of the soul, and then nothing.

She backed away. Finnegan kept his hand on her shoulder, for support now. He should never have asked poor Melissa here for this. It wasn't giving him anything much he could work with and the toll was enormous. He didn't know how she could take it. And all of it came to this: snippets, hints, little bits and pieces of what might be. But nothing definite, nothing certain. Himself, he felt tired, very tired. Melissa must be ready to collapse.

It was over. They left. On the way back to the hotel, nearly two in the morning now, no aurora in the darkness, Finnegan apologized, summing up what they'd learned in one sentence.

"Well, at least we tried, Melissa, and we got a glimpse of him here and there."

"I'm sorry," Melissa said, looking over at him, feeling sorry for him. "I wish I could have helped more."

More than anything now, she wanted to climb into that hard bed at the hotel, put on all the extra blankets she could find or get from the front desk. And then sleep. In the morning she could try to reach Stanley again.

"Listen, Melissa, you going to be OK? You still want that flight on Thursday? I'll change it for you, if you want. Get you back down to the island sooner. This afternoon, if you like. You could get out of here, put all this behind you."

Put it all behind her? This was the right moment to tell Finnegan that she felt trapped, felt she had to put both places behind her, walk away from it all somehow. To go where? She shook her head.

"No, no. I'll stick with Thursday, thanks. Dad and I are going to spend the afternoon together. I may spend the night out there with him, and then there's the funerals." She paused. "That poor little girl, that poor woman."

Melissa knew she'd have this to trouble her forever. That blade, those strong hands, the way the little one couldn't understand the hurt or why Mommy wouldn't come help.

Finnegan dropped her off. "I'll see you later, all right?"

"Right," she said, and smiled at him. "Thanks. I'm sorry it didn't help much."

He smiled back, reached out to touch her shoulder, gave it a squeeze. In the room, a few minutes later, she could barely manage to get out of her clothes. There were no phone messages for her. She lay there, thinking so much had happened, she'd seen so much in the last hour or two, that sleep would never come, but exhaustion outweighed turmoil, and, within a few moments, she slept.

SURPRISES

She was snorkeling the reef line off Frigate Bay, in thirty feet of warm water, looking down on a huge staghorn coral outcrop, a few parrot fish pecking at it while a large devil ray circled the bottom nearby. The afternoon sun sent flickering shafts of cathedral light down to illuminate patches of reef. In one such patch she could see an open tunnel leading down under the coral shelf. A diver's bubbles came up from the tunnel mouth—Stanley was down there, leading the way. He'd come and get her soon; they'd share his air if they needed to, to get to safety down in that tunnel, down deeper into the warm Caribbean where it was safe and comforting.

Alarm bells rang above her, from the surface. She looked up and the sea was covered with blue ice, thick columns of it pushing down toward her, the ice growing and enlarging toward her as she watched. She looked back down, but Stanley wasn't there, the tunnel mouth had disappeared, and the alarm bells still rang up above somewhere. She couldn't breathe, couldn't draw in a single breath, was drowning in the icy water that pushed her toward the bottom, the sharp edges of the coral, the alarm bells ringing.

On the fifth ring she came awake enough to realize where she was, that it was the phone ringing. She glanced at the clock. Five A.M. Good grief.

She reached for the phone, managed to grab it and get it to her ear. "Hello?"

Heavy breathing. For a horrid moment she thought it was some weird crank caller. "Melissa, that you, girl?"

"Stanley?"

"Yeah." His breath came hard. "It's me, and Rosie is here with me. We got your message and came to the cave. We're here now. I knew you'd want to be here, too."

"What? Stanley, you're *at* the cave?"

"Yeah, girl. Technology's great, isn't it? We're using Rosie's new cell phone to call you."

Melissa was waking up, deciding this was real. "Let me do this again, Stanley. You're at the cave now? In the dark? Why?"

"Hey, I had to know, Melissa. I don't know who's the crazier obeah woman, you or my mother, but I *had* to know."

There was a pause; Rosemarie came on the line. "He's the one who's crazy, Melissa, but I told you that, right? We were spending the night with some friends in St. John's, staying out of trouble, worried that trouble might come our way at my place, but then I called from their house to check the messages and there was that long one from you and, well, here we are...."

Another pause, the phone changing hands again, Stanley talking a mile a minute, excited: "And here we are. The sun's just coming up, but we have torches—flashlights. We're tired and dirty as hell, climbing down and then up. You know that climb."

"Hell, yes, I know it."

"And we're at the cave mouth, and I'm looking through the pile of brush you fell in."

There was a long pause. Melissa thought for a moment the line might have gone dead. Then she heard some rustling, some curses from Stanley, some tapping noises, and a loud cry of anguish.

Rosemarie's voice came back on. "Jesus, girl. You did it."

"Did what, Rose?"

"You found our father's body. More than twenty years it's been here, at this cave. And you found it from there, thousands of miles away."

"Where's Stanley? How do you know, Rosie?"

"Stanley's crying right now, Melissa. We found those lava pieces, like you found here. We found more of them, a lot more. Stanley chipped away at one, a small thing, golf ball–sized. He chipped at it with this knife and cracked it wide open. It just fell into pieces."

Another long pause. Melissa didn't say anything.

Rosemarie was crying, too, trying to contain it, but Melissa could hear the tears in her voice. "Inside. It's Daddy's ring, Melissa. My daddy's ring."

Another pause, the phone switching hands. It was Stanley. "Melissa?"

"Yes."

He was crying; she could hear the little intakes of breath as he tried to speak calmly through the tears to her. "You did it. I don't know how that thing you got works, but you did it. Oh, Jesus, Mary, and Joseph. And there's more here," and she could hear his labored breathing, hear the tapping of his knife against the lava. "Oh, hell, a slug, a bullet from a gun."

More breathing, more taps. "Melissa, more bullets here, another one, two more. Oh, sweet Jesus, they *did* shoot him; they murdered him. Melissa, you still there, girl?"

"I hear you, Stanley."

There were three short beeps. "Oh, hell, the battery's running down. Melissa, you did it. Oh, Jesus, you did it, girl. I love you, Melissa. Now we got something to go with here. I'll call you later. After we ..." Three more short beeps and the line went dead, the cellular phone's battery exhausted.

Slowly, Melissa hung up. What a mess. What should she do? Head back down there? Get up, call Finnegan again, and get a ride back into the Twin Cities and the airport, catch a flight south? And what was that Stanley had said, that he loved her? Where the hell had that come from?

She could get there, get to the airport, and by midafternoon be back in St. Kitts, back in the heat, away from this frozen country where life itself came to a standstill when it got to forty below, everyone and everything hiding from the cold.

She turned out the bed lamp, got up, and walked over to the window curtains, tugged on the cords to open them, stood there looking out the window. Thick frost covered the corners and edged inward on the outside window, cold drops of moisture condensed on the inside window. Streetlights illuminated the darkness, and through the clear middle of the window she could see across a small open field deep in snow—a parking lot in better weather maybe, but now so covered by winter that it was unusable. On the far side of the field was an intersection, the light changing from red to green while she watched. There were no cars on the road yet. A bank's temperature sign—First Union of Mankato—was bright in the absolute stillness, blinking back and forth between Farenheit and Celsius. Forty-two below. The same in both readings, the only place the two measurements met.

The northern prairie reclaimed itself in this kind of weather. Humanity's progress stopped in its tracks as the wind died down to a light breeze and the deep cold settled in, feeling permanent and close and personal; even the frozen stars above seemed close enough to touch.

Melissa shivered, looking out on the scene, scatterings of snow undulating across the field, lit by the strange orange glow of the streetlights. She shook her head. She'd left all this behind her years ago. She thought she'd escaped, would never have to be here again for this kind of penetrating cold.

She closed the curtains, turned to look at the clock on the bed stand—five-thirty. All right, then, call the airline, get a ticket, get back down there. Take care of things. Help Stanley and Rosie; help herself. The bullets, maybe that would be proof of something. The bones. Yeah, maybe that would be enough.

She pulled her plane ticket out of her purse, read the number for reservations, picked up the phone, and dialed. Voice mail said nobody was there, that operating hours were from eight in the morning to eight at night to make reservation changes.

Damn. OK, but she couldn't get back to bed now. A cup of coffee would be nice—dark, very hot. Maybe the front desk would have some; the restaurant couldn't be open yet. She'd get a cup, kill an hour or two, and then call, start the process that would have her back in St. Kitts later today. Sometimes you do what you have to do, that's all.

She put the ticket back into her purse, wouldn't want to misplace that. And there, in the purse, was the bracelet Stanley's mother had given her. Pretty little thing, simple, just a simple gold bracelet. What had she said, something about wearing it and learning more? Well, god knows learning more was a good idea. Melissa smiled, put the bracelet on, then slipped her blue jeans on over the long johns she'd worn to bed, tugged a bright orange Florida Gators sweatshirt on over the long-sleeved top she was wearing, tugged on thick socks, boots, and headed for the cup of coffee.

She felt a little warmer just for doing all that, as she headed out the door.

The elevators opened just to the left of the front desk, with the waiting area—couches and overstuffed chairs clustered around a few lamp stands and magazine tables—right in front as the elevator doors opened.

Not paying attention to that waiting area, hardly glancing at it as she came out of the elevator, she took a sharp turn to head toward the front desk and that cup of coffee.

"Mel?"

She turned. It was her father, sitting there reading a magazine in the waiting area, sipping on a steaming cup of coffee.

"Daddy? What are you doing here?"

"I didn't want to ruin your sleep, sweetie. Thought I'd wait here until you got up."

"What?"

"I got a surprise for you, something I got to show you. But I knew how tired you were, sweetie, after all that traveling and helping out Finnegan and everything. So I decided I'd wait here until you came down. Fellow over there behind the desk gave me a nice cup of coffee while I waited."

"How long have you been here, Daddy?"

"Only a little while." He smiled broadly, raised his cup of coffee. "This here's my first cup of coffee."

"And there's a surprise for me?"

"Oh, it's the best, sweetheart. Come on, let's get you a cup of coffee, and then I'll show you this surprise." He was almost chortling with the pleasure of it, certain it would please her.

"What kind of surprise, Daddy? Is it out in the truck?"

"No, no, not in the truck. We got to go there and see it. But I'll get the truck all warmed up for you, sweetheart; I know how you hate the cold. I'll get the heater going, and we'll get you all bundled up in there, and then we'll go see it, all right?"

"And it's a surprise? You can't just tell me?"

He started again, being patient, talking the way a father talks to his little girl. "It's a *surprise*, sweetie. I can't tell you about it, or it won't be a surprise anymore."

She smiled at him, tired, but this was her father, this was the man who raised her all on his own, and it couldn't have been easy, she knew. She owes him. She owes him a lot, owes him everything, really. "All right, Daddy. Sure, let's go see that big surprise."

"Let's get a cup of this good hot coffee in you first, sweetie, get you all warmed up. You sip on that, I'll go out and start the heater cranking in the truck, and then off we go, all right?"

She nodded. "OK, OK. Off we go."

And so, twenty minutes and a couple of cups of coffee later, Melissa carrying a third cup with her that steamed like mad in the subzero air as they walked out front to the truck, the two of them, father and daughter, headed out to see Melchior's big surprise.

WIGS AND PUMPS AND LIPSTICK

Finnegan was up all night, his hands and face aching and itching from the frostbite, his dying fingers, too, aching, and feeling tight so that he wanted to crack his knuckles, loosen them up against the cold. Lost in thought, trying to puzzle through what he'd seen with Melissa there in the morgue, he kept forgetting what had happened to him, worrying instead about what that vision had told him. There was something about what he'd seen that rang a bell, damn it.

He wanted to write it all down, as carefully and exactly as he knew how, using those paperwork skills used hundreds of times on the reports he filled out—the Uniform Crime Reports, Missing Person Reports, Letters of Transmittal, Death Investigation Reports, all of those and more. What did he see, exactly? Details, that's what he wanted to remember, the friggin' details.

But, of course, he couldn't write, not with clumsy wrapped clubs at the ends of his arms instead of hands with fingers.

So all he could do was think about it. Something about the hair—some wig, that's what it had to be. And the hands, maybe that was it, those beat-up hands, bent fingers. He knows those hands, damn it.

The more he thought through what he saw there with Melissa, the more he thought he knew the murderer, but he couldn't quite put two and two together. The wig, the hands: something. He'd been wrestling with it all night.

At three or so in the morning he fell asleep for a bit right there at the dining room table where he was trying to write a few things down, mostly not getting anything done past a sloppy scribble. He woke up with a stiff neck, hurt like hell. He rolled his head, trying to work it out. Got up, tried to start a pot of coffee, couldn't do it, no way to grab things the way he needed to. It was frustrating as hell; the whole damn thing was frustrating as hell.

He took a look at the kitchen clock. Dark outside, but this is midwinter and it's dark till late in the morning, so you really couldn't tell the time from that.

Six A.M. and still no answer; still no way he could figure it out. It was driving him crazy, like the word that's on the tip of your tongue when you can't quite come up with it. Maybe getting out would do it, he thought. A quick walk out to the car in this slap-in-the-face forty-below stuff might do him some good, sharpen him up some, wake up his sleepy subconscious.

It was just a ten-minute drive to the Little House, where he could get a western omelet, hash browns, sausage patties, rye toast, and that scalding coffee. He walked there a lot when it was decent out and he hadn't just lost fingers to frostbite the week before.

The thought of the coffee got him up from his chair, moved him over to the snow room and his snap-tight boots, the new down parka coat that replaced the woolen coat he'd soaked in the St. Peter River. He liked the Little House. It was warm, comfortable, and cheap. This, he thought, was a good idea. Think things through there, drive on back on a full stomach, and go at this again, maybe give Melissa a call about nine or so, just to check in and see if she came up with anything.

He managed to get all his clothes on, no easy task when you're going for a walk in forty below—there's the surgical mask for the face to warm the breath, the muffler for around the neck, the Gore-tex-lined boots, the lined leather cap with the earflaps—all the rig you have to wear if you don't want more damage to your frostbitten body. He struggled with his one open thumb and the wrapped hands to get all this done but did it, got the clothes on, and then walked out to the car. He got in, managed to fumble his way with the keys to the point where the right key was in place, turned it, and, thank god, the car started.

He was almost there—could see the diner down the road—when it hit him.

That black wig, the gnarled fingers and scarred-up back of the hand. Sitting with him at the Little House restaurant, breaking bread with the damn guy. How could it be him?

Melchior. Melissa's dad. Oh, Lord, that couldn't be.

But the wig, that room at his house, probably a whole damn closet full of wigs and pumps and lipstick in there. Old lonely, silent Melchior. Christ.

Melissa. Sweet mother, Finnegan, think. How will he tell her about this, tell her that he thinks her dad may be the murderer, the vicious butcher who could do that to mothers, to their kids?

He was at the Little House. He hit the brakes, turned in to the parking lot, and clumsily tried to pull out his cellphone from his coat pocket. It wasn't easy, or painless, but he got it done.

Here's what he had to do: Get a search warrant signed, check out Mel's house, that special room. See if the wig was there. If it was, see if it matched the hairs from the crime scenes. That would do it. Real evidence.

OK then, he owed Melissa a call. He used his thumb to punch in the number of the Holiday Inn, asked for her room, waited for her to pick up. He'd tell her he had news, something important, and then drive over there and explain it to her face-to-face, tell her what he thought, get it over with.

There was no answer. He let it ring, still no answer. He called back to the front desk. The guy there, a youngster, sounded like, and too damn cheerful for this time of the morning, told him that Melissa left with a man maybe twenty minutes ago. Her father, the kid thought, from what the two were saying to each other.

Damn, she was with Melchior.

Finnegan slammed the phone shut, then cursed at himself for the pain that shot up through his arm as he did that. Damn, it hurt.

He dropped the Pontiac into drive. The farm, that's where Melchior would take her. He wouldn't hurt her, would he? His own daughter?

Finnegan thought maybe he could get there in time to stop things from happening: the farm was only a half hour outside of town; nothing would happen too fast. He could call for assistance, get a patrol car to meet him out on the old farm road, and they could work out their approach from there.

There were complications, he realized as soon he started to make the radio call to Dispatch. What about the search warrant? How could he prove he needed that? He had no evidence at all to point toward Mel except for Melissa's vision thing that he shared with her. He couldn't wait hours for a judge, anyway.

Christ. OK, then, he'd have to do this on his own. Get out there and do it on his own, one way or another. Save Melissa, that was at the top of his list. And then Melchior. Stop him. One way or another. Stop him.

Finnegan slid the radio mike back into its holder, stepped on the gas, and got moving—a predawn phantom sliding too fast down slick streets, sliding around corners, throwing up a spray of snow each time.

About two miles down the road, at the intersection where Highway 169 met Highway 16, a big semi, getting an early start on the day, probably heading up to the Twin Cities, pulled out of the Jackson Yards where all those warehouses sat.

On a good day, with dry roads and hands that worked, no problem. Today, hands aching and wrapped, driving way too fast for the cold road, hitting the brakes in perfect synchronicity with a large patch of ice, Finnegan couldn't react in time and the Pontiac went into a skid.

He did the right things and those maybe saved his life: easy on the brakes, pumping them a little just trying for contact with the road; steering into the skid hoping to get the Pontiac back under control. But the sideways skid turned into a 360 spin, an agonizingly slow revolution that took him all the way around as he sat there, time stretching out so he felt he had all the time in the world to think it through. He thought about his son, about

Melissa and what might happen to her if he died here. Thought about his long-dead wife and how an accident a lot like this had claimed her life way back when.

Thought about all that and then realized, as the Pontiac slowly spun back in the right direction, that if he could just get it under a bit of control here he could move left, avoid the semi after all, spin off into the snowdrifts that covered the left shoulder of the road.

His hands hurt so much. He realized he was gripping the steering wheel hard, and the doc had said he wouldn't be able to grip at all, probably, for a few weeks, maybe a whole lot longer than that if he lost those damn fingers.

He eased the wheel back to the left as he spun right. Felt the tires grab a bit, hold a bit. OK, then, he brought the wheel back a fraction more. Had contact. He could feel the road and was happy about that, at least, as he plowed into the hard snow of the drift, still going at least forty miles an hour, ramming deep into the snow and ice, hearing the air bag explode to protect him, knowing what that impact was going to feel like against his wrecked face, his tortured hands. And then, suddenly, it was over.

WHERE IT BELONGS

Melissa drifted along, snuggled in a parka her father had given her to wear in the truck, the parka's fur-lined hood giving her face some warmth while the truck's heater labored to warm her feet. Despite Melchior's best efforts, the truck was anything but warm inside; even its noisy engine seemed muffled by the snow and cold. Once they were outside Mankato there were no other cars on the road.

Drowsily she watched the intersection approach where they'd turn left to head for the farm so her father could show her whatever this big surprise was.

But they went straight.

"Daddy, wasn't that the turnoff?"

He turned to look at her, grinned. "Yeah, but we're not going to the farm, sweetie; we're heading out this way."

"To?"

"To Lake Minnetoksak. It's out there in my ice shack. You warm enough?"

Melissa groaned. "On the lake? Oh, Daddy, I'm freezing right now; I don't want to go out there on that lake. Can't you just tell me about it or something?"

He chuckled, a deep rumble of delight that she couldn't recall hearing from him before—this was some new version of her father, softened maybe around the edges by all the time he'd spent with Finnegan and working on the sculptures in the barn. The old Melchior, the hardworking farmer who put up with one disaster after another with the sugar beet crop—too much rain or too little, good crops and low prices, high prices and no yield to speak of—had turned, somehow, into this contented man who knew how to smile and chuckle. She liked the improvement, she thought, but it was weird.

He was even downright chatty. "It's been strange, Melissa, really strange since you moved away. After I left tonight I thought about it, about what I'd said, and I thought it was time to show you something. I think you'll understand, honey."

"Understand what, Daddy?"

"Just bear with me for a few more minutes, OK, till we get to the lake."

"Sure, Daddy. But this won't take too long out there, will it?" She hunched down into the parka, trying to make herself smaller, warmer, in the bitter predawn cold.

There was a thin streak of pale gray on the eastern horizon as they drove up the access road to the lake. A right turn past the old oaks, a quick left, and they drove right onto the ice, slowing down to a crawl as they motored out to Mel's shack.

The lake was four miles around, the ice two feet thick or more but a little risky nonetheless after the thaw and refreezes. The surface of the ice was dotted with ice shacks and parked cars. Lights shone from some of the shacks, people up fishing already, some of them even near done for the day after starting at 3:00 A.M.

Melchior drove the old pickup to his shack, over near the southern shore, maybe forty yards out onto the surface of the ice. He slowed the Ford down, stopped, turned off the key, not daring to use the parking brake—no one in their right mind used the parking brake in this kind of weather; it would freeze the shoes right to the drum, given a chance.

They both got out and walked into the shack. Melissa saw it was divided into two rooms. In the one to the left there was a fishing hole cut into the ice over in the far corner. In the near corner an old Coleman catalytic heater labored, already lit so the edge was off the cold just a bit. Next to the doorway an ice auger stood guard duty—the same auger she used to see all summer long in the barn, waiting for its time of year.

There was more: some canvas folding chairs, a Coleman stove

with two burners, a hammer for cracking through the thin layer of ice that formed over an augered hole in just a few hours, two gas lamps, one of them lit, its mantle glowing to throw shadows into the corner of the shack.

Melchior cranked up the stove while Melissa sat on a chair. Then he set an old cast-iron coffeepot on top. "Have you some hot coffee—real good coffee, too—in just a few minutes, sweetie."

Then he stood, walked over to a spot hidden from view behind a few folding chairs and blankets. He nodded, rubbed his hands in glee while Melissa watched him. What was this all about?

He smiled disarmingly at her. "Come here," he said. "Please, Melissa, I want you to see this."

She stood, and he took her by the hand, pulled her to the back of the shack, away from the hole out front that she'd noticed as they walked in.

There was another hole there, a huge one, four or five times as big around as the normal twelve-inch-diameter hole used for fishing. He must have used the auger several times and then pounded away with the hammer to clear a hole this big. A thick rope lay coiled by the side of the hole. One end of it led down into the black water.

"I came out here a couple of hours ago and got the heater started up, hammered open the holes again, sort of got things ready for you," her father said, walking over to the rope and grabbing it where it emerged from the water. "Now help me pull this up and you'll see why, sweetie."

Melissa came over to help, wondering what the hell could be down there. It was heavy, very heavy, whatever it was, and the water so cold she thought she could feel the wet rope right through her lined gloves.

As they pulled together, father and daughter, Melchior started to talk, his speech a rhythmic cadence timed to the pulling motions, a kind of sea chanty.

"I worked for two years on that monster pike. I'd get a chance and weld a fin, get more time, and weld again. It had to be right, you know what I mean. It had to be right, sweetheart."

So, Melissa wondered, was that it? Were they pulling up some sculpture from down there in the cold depths? Why in God's name?

Melchior wasn't done with his chanty. "I finished it, finished it, finished at last. I finished the pike at last."

He looked at Melissa, broke his rhythm, stopped pulling for a second. "And you know what, sweetie? I couldn't think of what to do with it. Two years I'd spent on that thing, getting it right, making it perfect. And when it was done I didn't know what to do with it.

"I couldn't bear to sell it; hell, it was too important for that. But after that, what should I do? I thought about calling you, asking you, but you've got your own life down there on that island now and you hadn't ever seen the thing. I mean, I knew you'd understand if I explained it right. But I wasn't even sure I could do that, you know?"

Melissa was glad they'd stopped tugging for a minute. "Did you talk to Finnegan about it?"

"Thought about it, but couldn't. He's a good man, and he loves you like a daughter, Melissa. I know that, and I don't mind. He misses his boy, and if little Danny hadn't died you'd be his daughter anyway, sort of."

She nodded.

"So then I thought, I know what I'll do with it. I'll put it right where it belongs."

"In the lake? That's what we're pulling up?"

He smiled, giggled. "Almost. You're half-right. That's what I did; I dropped it right into the lake. Right here, too, where I knew it belonged, where I knew she'd appreciate it."

"She'd appreciate it, Daddy?"

"Yep. Where she'd appreciate it. Come on; let's get this up here so you can see the surprise."

They started pulling again, the wet, stiffly cold rope coiling loosely behind them as they tugged. Fifteen, twenty, thirty feet of rope. Fifty. They pulled for a good ten minutes more, the rope cold and hard. The water down at the bottom never got much above freezing year-round, but things lived down there, the rope covered with green slime, tiny snails, and long, stringy plants.

And then it stopped, the thing, whatever it was, bumping against the ice underneath them.

Melissa stopped, thinking through what he'd just said a minute or two before—"where I knew she'd appreciate it." What the hell could that mean? "Daddy, I don't like surprises. Just tell me before we pull this up, all right?"

Melchior turned to stare at his daughter, the old anger showing for just a flash on his face. "Just pull, Melissa. Just do it." He turned back to the task.

So Melissa helped, and the thing bumped again on the bottom of the ice, just a few feet away from the hole. They tugged more slowly.

Melissa couldn't take her eyes off the hole as the rope pulled the thing clear. It was a tarpaulin, wrapped around something and then sewn shut, a concrete block tied to the bottom of it. They pulled the tarp out from the hole and onto the ice. Melchior turned to smile reassuringly at his daughter, took his deer knife, and cut the fishing line that had sewn the thing tight. It parted in a series of precise little pops as he took his time opening things up.

As he cut, Melissa could see inside. There was a piece of worn blue cloth, torn and shredded. There was a body, gray but preserved in the depths of the lake. A crucifix, held in a ghostly gray left hand that lay on the chest. A face. Melissa couldn't turn away. Wanted to, but couldn't.

It was a face from her childhood, a face she only remembered from photographs until that very moment, when she saw it staring up her—frozen, pale, but unmistakable. Moira, long-lost Moira. It was her mother.

DOWN IN THE COLD

There was smoke everywhere—the car on fire? No, it was from the air bag; as he came back to his senses he realized that. He was covered in a white powder, and the limp, deflated air bag sat in his lap. His ears hurt like hell, and his nose felt like somebody had whacked at it with a hammer. Jesus, that hurt.

But he was alive and OK. If he could get the air bag flap shoved back onto the steering wheel and then get the bag itself cut away from the steering wheel, he might be able to keep going.

The trucker he'd just missed was banging on his window, asking if he was OK. Finnegan waved at him to open the door to the Pontiac.

"Jesus Christ! You all right, man?" the guy asked. Then he seemed to notice for the first time the bandages on Finnegan's hands.

Finnegan was definitely a mess, the air bag's powder clinging to the cream on his face, covering his clothes. He ached everywhere. "I'm a police officer," he told the trucker. "I need your help. Can you help me cut this bag away and see if this car'll still run?"

"Sure, man, but you need to see a doctor. Let me get you some help, OK?"

"No, I'm OK; I'm OK. Just help me get this done."

And the trucker did. Together, the trucker supplying the hands, they got the bag cut away, got the air bag panel shoved back onto the steering wheel, got a twenty-foot length of chain from the semi's cab and hooked it to the back of the Pontiac, managed to pull the car back out of the snowbank and on the road. It took a good fifteen minutes and an extraordinary amount of pain.

Finnegan was really beat to hell. The doc had told him his only chance to save his fingers—even parts of his fingers, for that matter—was to keep them warm, wrapped, and safe from infection. And here he was seriously messing up on all three counts.

Christ, it hurt. But he could still function, goddamn it, and the Pontiac, its front end smashed in some with the bumper jammed up in an inverted **V** in front of the hood, still ran, rattling and banging but moving down the road.

So he got back in it and started driving again toward that farm. On the way, he went ahead and called it in to Dispatch, at least telling them where he was going. He called it a routine investigative call. That at least made it official.

He had the car's heater cranked up all the way, trying to warm up his frozen feet, and holding one wrapped hand at a time in front of the upper vent—he'd really like to keep his fingers if he could.

Then, as he neared the intersection with Svensen Road and the highway, the Pontiac's heater conked out and started blowing cold—nasty, vicious cold—outside air at him. He shut it off. And right away the engine heat started climbing. Perfect. Forty below and his engine was going to overheat.

He made it to the farm, easing along the last half-mile of snow-covered dirt road and on into the driveway, pulling in between the house and the barn, out of the breeze, at least.

He climbed out stiffly, wondering if Melchior was watching him from some window in the house. Would Melchior try to kill him? He didn't want to find out the answer to that.

He walked to the back door, the one that led through the snow room and into the kitchen. He started to knock on it and realized he couldn't, not with these hands. Instead, he kicked at it so it banged, hard.

No answer.

He tried looking in the window, but the frost was so thick he couldn't see through any of the kitchen windows.

Knocking his arms against his chest and shoulders, trying to keep the blood moving, he walked around the old house, looking in where he could, kicking at the front, door, too.

Nothing.

He tried the doorknob on the front door and it turned. OK, then, here was a moment. If he walked in here, he might be jeopardizing his whole damn career. He'd called it in, which he now realized was stupid, since that made this official business and not just his visiting a friend. He was entering this house without a search warrant.

Oh, hell. He opened the door, stepped inside the blessed warmth. "Melchior? Mel? You here?"

Nothing.

"Melissa? You here, Melissa?"

Nothing.

He had to check. She could be anywhere; the two of them could be anywhere, hiding maybe. Or right in the middle of things. Jesus.

He checked out the first floor, his hands starting to ache even more as they warmed up, really hurting now. He wished he had some of those pills the doc gave him. Instead, big brave guy, he'd just been taking ibuprofen, which had worked OK until now.

He checked out the basement. First time he'd been down there, and it was nothing much: the old gravity-feed furnace, some shovels and rakes, the storm door leading up to the backyard.

OK, then. Upstairs. He headed that way, up the front stairs by the living room. Hands hurting, he turned the knobs and looked in. Nothing there in Melissa's room, thank Jesus for that. Nothing in Mel's bedroom, the bathrooms.

That left the shrine room, what must have originally been the master bedroom, and then Mel had moved out of it and left it, preserved it, the day his wife disappeared. It occurred to Finnegan that he was probably about to solve that crime, too, after all these years.

There was no one in the room. He walked over to check the closet, a big walk-in country closet filled with clothes. Filled with women's clothes and shoes. And three different black wigs, all sitting there nice and pretty on mannequin heads, Styrofoam heads with eyes, noses, and lips painted in with lipstick.

And there, hanging from a nail, was a rosary. Bits of marble. Connemara marble. One decade of it, ten tiny cubes of marble, stripped from the chain.

Oh, Lord. This was it, then. This was where it all started for Mel, right in this little room. Where the hell was he? Where was Melissa?

He left the wigs there, didn't touch anything, then left the house, back into the cold, walking over to check the barn. Nothing there, either. But the last time he'd been in here, a month or so ago, that big monster metal pike, the thing at least eight feet long and four feet high, had been sitting right there in the middle of the floor, the place of honor. Mel said he'd finished it. Now it was gone.

Finnegan stayed in the barn for a minute to think it through. Jesus Christ, his hands sure ached, right in the middle of the palm for some reason. He thought for a moment that he needed to get the doc to look at them soon or he'd be paying an awful price for this. Then he laughed at himself for that thought—it was way the hell too late for that.

But he had to find Melchior and Melissa. Where could they be?

He stared at where the pike had been, stood there breathing hard into his wrapped hands, trying to warm them a bit with his breath.

The pike. Ice fishing. The lake, of course. That's where they would be. Minnetoksak, out in the fishing shack.

That had to be it. He moved as quickly as he could, out the barn door and over to the battered Pontiac, cranked it up, the engine cooled off and ready to go again. Then he floored it, spinning on the ice-covered gravel of the drive, roaring away toward the lake, another five miles down the road.

ALMOST PERFECT

Melissa dropped the rope, backed away. Her mother. Here. Now.

Her father talked to her, that same tone of voice he always used, like she was still ten years old. "C'mon, sweetie, help me finish this."

She stood there, unable to move. She was starting to remember something, getting little flashes of it as she watched her father pull the tarp away from the top of the body.

"Ah, there, that's got it," Melchior said pleasantly, and he got cleared the tarp from the top of the body, then straightened the body out a bit. He turned to look at his daughter and smiled.

"I thought you'd want to know about this, see her one more time. I found her like this years ago. I just snagged her. It was the luckiest damn thing. So, hell, I brought her up back then, and she was almost perfect. Almost. So all I've been trying to do, sweetie, is fix that, make her perfect. That's all. Just make your mommy perfect after all these years."

Oh, god. Melissa struggled to keep herself sane, to not just scream and run. She looked down at the body, shook her head, shivered, forced herself to look down at her mother's body. The right hand was missing, cut off at the wrist.

"Daddy, do you know what this is? Do you know what you've done? You need help. Let me drive you back to town. We'll get this all taken care of; everything will be fine."

Her father had a puzzled expression on his face. "I just thought you'd want to know that she's been OK, down in the cold. I thought you'd want to know that before you headed back south to that island." His puzzlement turned to a pleasant smile. "You know, she was from the islands. She loved those warm islands, but she loved us more, sweetie. She loved us so much."

His tone of voice was perfectly calm, perfectly reasonable. "But you know, she couldn't go down there this way, down to that island. It's much too hot for her there." He looked down at the body. "Here, in the cold now, she's perfect. I brought her presents to make her that way, to make her perfect."

Melissa tried to stay calm, fought with herself to back slowly away. If she could just get outside the shack and walk calmly over to another ice shack, find someone there with a cellular phone, get some help.

She was thinking very clearly now, seeing it all with crystalline purity. She had to walk out, get away from him, get help somehow.

She took one step back, another, but then Melchior walked over and took her by the shoulders, still smiling at his little girl. "You can't leave just yet, sweetie. We'll go in a minute, but there's one more little thing we have to do, that's all."

She tried to get past him, tried to elbow her way past him and out the door. He quit smiling. They struggled, and Melchior was much the stronger, wiry and quick no matter his age. He stopped her easily, shook her hard, once, by the shoulders. "You sit down, young lady," he said firmly, and then shoved her down firmly, hanging on to her shoulders.

Melissa fell onto her mother, put her hand down to break the fall, and placed it right on her mother's arm. The gray flesh was icy and cold, just a soft give to it as she felt it with the fingers of her left hand and that pulse, that throb, hit her.

She is watching as her husband—a strong young man in his prime, a good man until he drinks, like now—angry, drunk, brutal, holds a knife above her, the knife he uses to gut and dress the deer he kills.

He shoves her around the room, slapping and hitting her with a fist—hard. Waves of pain throb from her jaw, her cheekbone, her eye. Her face is wet from tears and blood. She wipes her eyes and her hands are covered in red. She prays that he'll leave little Melissa alone.

That's what started this fight, her saying he shouldn't be touching their daughter like that, in those places, talking all the time about doing more. She would stop him with her obeah if she could, but her powers are weak here in this icy north. Her potions are all wrong, the ingredients not the same, the power diluted, frozen away from her.

Her daughter, sweet little Melissa, seems born to it, stronger. In time her obeah will be strong enough to stop this brutal man. But now, here, that isn't good enough.

There is a raised hand, that knife, a bright flash of reflected sunlight from the window of her bedroom that bursts off the blade to blind her for a moment. She shuts her eyes, opens them, and sees the final maniacal smile on Melchior's face as the blade goes up and down once.

She thought there would be more pain, but there is none. The blade goes up again, pauses next to that drunken, brutal smile.

Her daughter is all she cares to think of now. The blade comes down again, and there is an odd pressure, a pushing, but still no pain. Then again, and again, and then there is darkness.

All of this flashes by in a second, as it always has. But never like this, never seeing things her mother saw, knowing what her mother knew and feared.

Melchior, holding her, saw all this as well. He shook his head, grimaced. "I had to do that to her, you understand? I just had to stop her, Melissa. She said she was going to go the police about it, about us, sweetie, about how much I loved you.

"I'm not saying it was right, what I did to her. But she just got on me so much about it, about what I was doing to my daughter."

That smile again, as he remembered that day. That old smile. "I was just touching you, that's all. She just didn't understand, sweetie. You were always so pretty. And you liked it, Melissa; you really did. You told me so."

He shook his head. "She pushed and pushed at me until I had to take her up to her room and shut her up. I had to do it to protect you, Melissa.

"I loved her so, sweetie, but I just couldn't stand it when she got like that. I don't know; I just loved you even more, I guess. That's all. I just loved you more."

He was waving the knife around as he explained all this. Melissa sat there, on the ice, next to her mother's frozen gray body, and listened. Water from the hole splashed onto the ice where she was sitting and soaked through her blue jeans. Even in the shelter of the shack, with the heater going, a crust of ice was forming there, her rear and her crotch frozen there behind this new thin layer. The chill soaked all the way through her.

Melissa could only stare at her father. Memories frozen away for twenty years cracked loose and started to climb out of the dark hole where they'd been hiding. She remembered his face above hers, smiling and kissing her cheek. She remembered him touching her, the way it felt so rough.

"It just happened, that's all," he explained again, breaking into her past. "It was some holiday from her hometown that she liked to celebrate. It started out so happy, and then . . . nothing on purpose, Melissa. It just happened. She just egged me on until it happened." He looked at the knife. "I had to punish her. Make her be quiet, make her quit grabbing at me all the time, trying to get in between us, pulling and scratching at me."

He smiled. "So, I took care of that. I made her be quiet. Got her to stop grabbing at me." He got to his knees, tugged on the tarpaulin, pulled it back. "Here, see?" He reached in, felt for a second, pulled up the right arm, the end of the wrist gray and shriveled, only half-closing over the open wound.

Oh, god. Melissa screamed, tried to pull back, to run, to hide somewhere from all of this. But his grip was incredible, the strength of the mad. She collapsed, and the moment stretched on to infinity, would never end. Melissa, half-conscious, remembered bits, fragments. There was more, awful things, important things: noise, shouts and thumps from her mother's room—then silence.

What had happened? It was gone, the memories trailing away into the cold. The bracelet. What had she said, the old woman? Hold it tightly and learn?

Numbly, her father moving away from her now, moving over to pour a kind cup of coffee to warm her up, she took the bracelet from her wrist, held it tightly in her hands, held it in prayer, a supplication.

And remembered a little girl waiting a few minutes, cautiously opening the door to her own room, and looking out. No one there. The back door slamming, her father's heavy footsteps crunching through the old, hard snow as he walked out toward the barn. Quickly then, knowing he might come right back, she ran up the stairs, anxious to comfort Mommy.

Little Melissa knocked on her mother's door. No answer. Knocked again, harder, afraid to bring Daddy back if she was too loud. No answer. She opened the door, peeked in. Mommy was on the bed, sprawled, arms wide. And there was blood everywhere, like when Daddy killed the chickens. Blood on the curtains, even splattered on the window glass.

Little Melissa wondered what this all meant. "Mommy?" She finally got up the nerve to ask, "Mommy, are you all right?"

No answer. Melissa walked over to look at Mommy's face. She loved her mother's smile, that happy laugh. But this was a nothing face: no smile, no laughter.

Melissa turned to leave, and there was Daddy.

He sighed, disappointed. "She had to learn, Melissa, and now look what's happened. She just had to learn."

He reached out to hold his daughter by her shoulders.

"Did you hurt her, Daddy?"

"She made me, sweetie. She was going to tell on us, and we couldn't have that, could we?"

Melissa shook her head no, but it was all so very hard to understand. She turned to look at Mommy, turned back to see Daddy's smile, Daddy's cold, frozen smile.

She wanted to cry, but Daddy shook his head no, shushed her, and moved her over so he could sit next to her on the side of the bed. "Give your mother a kiss, Melissa. Say good-bye to her."

Yes, say good-bye with a kiss. She leaned over Mommy's face. "I love you, Mommy," she said, and leaned down to kiss that quiet mouth, those cold lips. Lips to lips, saying good-bye.

And felt a coldness, a hard, frozen chill that stole its way from Mommy and into Melissa's heart. Hard. Cold. Locked in there. A gift from Mommy. A terrible gift.

Melchior leaned over, too. Melissa felt him, tried to move away as he took her in his strong arms, rolled her over on her back, and started to play.

After a while, little Melissa lay next to her mother's body and pretended to sleep while Daddy did some more things. She didn't watch, couldn't watch, as Daddy took the big knife and did something to Mommy's hand.

After that, Daddy started to clean the room. Melissa listened to the quiet rub and tap of his towel against the bloody windowpane as he cleaned the splattered glass. Melissa tried to think of other places, but it was so hard, so cold, until finally she drifted off.

In the morning, Mommy was gone—Daddy said he had punished her and she wouldn't be back, that she ran away forever—and Melissa believed Daddy's story of how Mommy just walked away. Melissa couldn't remember it any other way.

All this at age five. All of this closed off, sealed off with that frozen gift settled deep into her soul—a whole part of her life that her mind wouldn't let her recall.

She sat there now, coming alive again, coming awake. Where was her early childhood? Where was reality? She'd thought it happy enough—Mommy's smiling face and Daddy's hard work on the farm. There were hazy memories, brief snatches of snowmen, of sleds, of hot chocolate and marshmallows. How much of that was real? How much was blocked off in an icy part of her mind that hid the horror, the pain, of what he'd done?

Now, here, the ice that surrounds those memories is beginning to crack, to break apart. Melissa can see her past—a jolting, horrific reality.

Melchior was very calm. "January seventeenth," he said. "I celebrate it every year. January seventeenth. Oh, it was cold that day, worse than this. Twenty years ago to the day."

He lowered the knife, smiled. "That was the time we finally made love, Melissa, you and me, remember? That time with her, and never again. I stopped everything after that, for the longest time, and you forgot all about it. I stopped just for her, but you know, I wanted us to do more, sweetie. You grew up so beautiful."

He was proud of himself, proud of the self-control he practiced starting twenty years before. "I didn't slip up very much, sweetie, honest. It was just every now and then, in the middle of winter when everything was cold and frozen and perfect. Sometimes, then, I just had to, had to . . ."

His smile broadened. "You came back, too, Melissa. Right on time. So I know things are going to be all right."

Melissa saw it all. January 17. That's why she can do this thing, see these visions, but only on this day, this horrible day. January 17. God, he's a monster.

"Presents, Daddy? Oh, Christ. The women? The little girls?"

"Women? Little girls?" He frowned. "I don't know what you're talking about, sweetie."

"I think you do, Daddy. I think you know."

He shook his head, trying to put it all together, concentrating. "Maybe," he said. "Maybe sometimes things didn't go right, you know? Those girls wouldn't be quiet, Melissa. I had to shush them. It wasn't perfect, like with you and me."

He reached down and tugged some more on the tarp. There were hands there, right hands, women's right hands. "But see," he said, smiling broadly. "I made it better. I fixed things."

Melissa stared at her father. "Daddy. Jesus. You killed them, those poor people." She felt like she was outside herself somehow, talking calmly to this madman. How could he be her father? How could any of this be? "You killed Mom; you raped me." Her voice was rising, near hysteria. She forced herself to calm down, to talk her way out of this, end it. "Dad, you've got to stop. This has all got to stop."

He shook his head. "No, it doesn't. Why should it? You're back, Melissa. You came back to me, back from that island." He paused, said conspiratorially, "You know, your mother was a witch. Did you know that? She thought she had some kind of black magic, that she could stop us, that she could change things."

He started moving toward her, actually putting the knife away in his belt and then unbuckling the brass belt buckle. His Melissa had come back to him. He opened his arms as he came toward her, opened his arms to embrace his daughter. "But I couldn't let her do that, sweetie. I couldn't let her. You can understand that, right? Come on, sweetheart; come to me; come back to your father."

And he reached for her, reached to embrace her, to hold her close.

Melissa bolted, scrambled on all fours, and got by him, made it to the door, crashed through it, and then clambered outside, struggled to her feet to run, slipping badly on the ice. It was light out now; she could see where she was going, headed for the shoreline.

"Melissa, sweetie. Wait!" Her father came out behind her. "You don't understand. Wait a minute!"

She ran, still slipping, falling with every third or fourth frenzied stride. She should have gone to a nearby shack, even if it was farther out on the ice, she realized. She could have gotten help that way. Somebody to stop Melchior.

She heard a car engine behind her, thought it must be him in that damn truck. Angry, blinded by the anger and fear, she turned to see, ready to do battle with him, with the monster she'd thought was her father.

ICE COVERS THE HOLE

The Pontiac kept sliding off the pavement, ricocheting off the frozen drifts that two months of snowplowing had left on the side of the road. It was all Finnegan could do to keep it moving generally forward. His hands didn't hurt as much—that was probably a bad sign and he knew it; they were freezing again. Lord knew how many fingers he would lose from all this.

But he couldn't feel them at all and so had to watch his own hands on the steering wheel, concentrating on willing them to move the car left or right, slipping and sliding down the road to reach the turnoff for Lake Minnetoksak. The engine was starting to overheat again already, too, but that was the least of his worries.

The road he was on was dirt in the summer, frozen hard now and covered in snow, not plowed as often as the paved roads, so it was hell to drive on.

But it was short, only a half-mile or so, and then kept going on, out onto the lake's surface. There, a few hundred yards away, was Mel's shack, the one he'd fished in that day. He shook his head. Mel had saved his life that day, pulling him out of the drink after he'd broken through. And now it turned out there was another Mel, one Finnegan had never known, hadn't seen coming. Goddamn it.

He headed the Pontiac for the shack, struggling with the steering, the cold, his own pain. He peered ahead. It looked like a couple of people were walking away from the shack. That had to be them. He steered right a bit, trying to keep it under control and accelerate on the ice at the same time. Damn, it was cold.

Melissa heard a car engine, looked toward it. A battered wreck of a car was coming toward them, driving like the guy behind the wheel was drunk, twisting the car back and forth like it was waddling out of control toward them.

"Melissa?" Her father was calling to her. "Melissa, sweetie, come on back. You don't understand."

But she did understand. That was it. Now she did finally understand. She turned away from him and started running again, almost to the shoreline now, and from there maybe she could get into the woods and lose him or something. At least she'd be off this ice, away from that shack, from her mother's body, from the monster who chased her.

She heard the car engine roar and she stopped and turned back to look for a second.

Finnegan shook his head to clear it. The two people were Melissa and her father, and she was running away from him, trying to escape. He was in time, then, to stop the monster.

He headed for Melchior, figuring he could hit him, maybe knock him down at least or something. Then he could get to his weapon in the shoulder holster and hold him there until the backup arrived. If he could knock him down. If he could manage to get the damn Glock out of his holster. If he could stay conscious.

Melchior had turned to watch the car's approach as well. The Pontiac was so battered he didn't recognize it as first as Finnegan's. When he did, it was because he could see Finnegan behind the wheel, hands wrapped, face taut. His old friend, Dan Finnegan. He waved to him. Smiled. Now, maybe, the two of them could get Melissa to realize everything was OK, everything would be fine if she would just stop and talk, so they could reason with her.

✳   ✳   ✳

Melissa, too, could see that it was Finnegan in the battered Pontiac, heading it straight toward her father, aiming at him.

It nearly got him, sliding almost sideways toward him and missing him by no more than a couple of feet as he jumped out of the way. Then the Pontiac, continuing the spin it had started, turned all the way around once, then again, and then careened into the lakeshore, coming up on the shore for fifteen feet before running into a stand of young, spindly trees that brought it to a stop. Melissa ran toward it, to help, to get help.

The front door opened as she reached it. Finnegan sat inside, pale, in agony. The wrapping on his hands had come loose; he gripped the steering wheel with black fingers.

"Get in," he said.

"The car's stuck, and you need help."

He looked around, like he was noticing all this for the first time. He nodded. "OK, then get my weapon out from this holster and then help me out of here."

She did that, Finnegan shaky as he stood there, Melissa with the weapon in her hands.

"You have to click off the safety." He pointed. "There, push it forward."

"Melissa? Dan?"

It was her father, walking toward them. Melchior's arms were held out straight at his sides, palms up. Melissa aimed the gun at him as he got closer.

"No. You don't understand; neither one of you understand. It's not like that." He was saying each word slowly, distinctly, trying to make it all clear to them.

"Look," he said, and reached down slowly to his belt, pulled out the knife, tossed it away, skittering across the ice.

"Melissa," he said very calmly. "You don't understand. I'd never hurt you, Melissa. Never."

"Hi, Dan," he added when he got a bit closer, smiling in the cold, vapor rising from that friendly grin. "Maybe you can help me explain things to Melissa. Tell her I love her."

Finnegan walked toward him. "We have to take you in, Mel, clear this all up back at the station, all right?"

Melchior smiled broadly. "Sure, Dan. No problem. Everything's fine now."

He looked at his daughter. "Melissa, sweetie. We'll clear all this up right away. Trust me."

"Sure, Daddy. We'll clear it all up." She kept the gun pointed at him.

They started walking back toward the ice shack and Mel's Ford truck, slipping some on the ice, Melissa helping Finnegan walk. She could see he was dizzy with the pain and the cold, trying to hang on long enough to get the job done.

Melchior nodded toward distant trees. "Right over there's where you fell through that time, Dan."

"I know, Mel. You saved my life."

Melchior chuckled. "And on the river last week, when you fell through again?"

"You saved my life again, right, Mel?"

"You keep falling in, and I keep pulling you out."

"Why did you murder those women, Mel? The children?"

"Didn't want to hurt the kids, but a couple of times they saw, you know? So I had to."

"And the mothers? You murdered those women, Mel."

"You don't understand, Dan. It's not like that. It was because..." He turned to his daughter. "You explain it to him, Melissa."

"In the shack," Melissa said, nodding her head. They were within fifty yards of it now. "He pulled it up from the lake bottom."

Melchior smiled. "Let's go see. Then you'll understand, Dan."

"What's in there, Mel?"

"It's just the best thing, Dan, isn't it, Melissa? Just the best thing."

She wanted to cry, to scream. And she would, as soon as this was over. She just stared at her father, who stared back, smiling. She shook her head.

And suddenly Melchior pushed hard against Finnegan, sent him sprawling onto the ice, and then started running, sprinting toward the shack, scrambling and stumbling along as fast as the slick surface would allow.

She aimed the gun at his back but couldn't pull the trigger. Instead, she helped a groaning Dan Finnegan to his feet and held on to his left arm as they started after Melchior. He was heading toward the old Ford pickup, no doubt. Jesus Christ, he might get away. The thought was unbearable. She might have to shoot after all.

Even with Melissa's help, Finnegan was in no condition to catch anyone. Twice he fell, whimpering in pain. Twice Melissa helped him up and they kept moving, kept trying.

As they watched, Melchior sprinted right past the truck and headed into the shack. Finnegan, seeing his chance to catch him, feeling a final burst of adrenaline, pulled away from Melissa and ran, grunting with the effort, ignoring the pain, scrambling toward the shack while Melissa fell, fell again in her hurry to rise, then followed, watching as Finnegan reached the flimsy door to the ice shack and went in after Melchior.

There was silence from inside as Melissa, moments later, got there. "Dan?" she yelled. "You OK?"

She heard a splash from inside, something into that freezing water. She didn't want to go in there, didn't want to be anywhere near here. She hesitated, terrified by what she might see.

"Melissa!"

She couldn't tell which man it was.

"Melissa, get in here! Now!" Was that her father? Oh, god, in his madness was her father hurting Dan Finnegan, hurting his only friend?

Not thinking, not wanting to think, she kicked open the door and ran in, holding the weapon up with both hands like she'd seen in the movies. She would shoot if she had to.

There, by the large hole in the ice, knelt Dan Finnegan, his arms down into the cold water.

He turned to see her. "Come here, quick, and help me."

She ran to him, looked down into the water, and saw her father there, looking up at them, his left hand held by both of Finnegan's tortured, frostbitten hands. Mel's right hand was wrapped up in a rope that dropped into the depths below. She looked and Moira's body was gone. He'd wrapped his hand in that rope, shoved her body in, and then gotten in with it, tied to his dead wife.

Melissa knelt down and reached into the water—incredible and shocking in its coldness despite her adrenaline—to wrap her fingers around Finnegan's blackened hands and try to help pull her father out.

But he didn't struggle for the surface and the weight of his body and his wife's and the auger was unmovable. Melissa felt his cold fingers through the loose gauze drifting free from Finnegan's wounds. Melchior looked up at her, smiling, serene, and slowly pulled his hand free and then, as she watched, he slipped away, looking up and smiling at first, and then, pulled by the weight of his wife, he turned, facedown, to join her in the depths.

Melissa watched him go, then heard Finnegan moan beside her, pulling his ruined hands from the cold water. They both fell back onto the ice, Finnegan holding out his black, freezing hands in cold supplication.

Mother Moira was gone, back into her grave. Melchior has kicked her in and then, in his madness, grabbed the auger and followed her in, wanting to be with her, preserved with her forever. Finnegan had seen him disappear, had grabbed his hand and hung on, but couldn't do it, those dying fingers giving way. He couldn't hang on to Mel, couldn't bring him back from that deep cold, that perpetual, preserving chill of the bottom of Lake Minnetoksak.

Melissa found a tattered blanket in a corner, wrapped it around Finnegan's arms. The two sat there for a minute; then Melissa thought of the pickup, its heater. They had started to get up, to try to walk out there in the minus-forty frozen perfection of a Minnesota winter day, when they heard a siren. The backup that Finnegan radioed for on his way to the lake was finally arriving. They fell back onto the ice to wait.

It was very cold. Melissa, sitting there, hugging Finnegan, wondered if she'd ever escape this cold.

The next day, when they brought her back to the scene, a thin sheet of ice covered the hole. There was nobody to break it clear until they came in with the equipment to search for the bodies. That took them two days, two very cold days, while Melissa sat next to Finnegan in his room at Mankato Memorial Hospital and hoped he'd heal. She hoped they both would heal.

MOUNT MISERY

The American Eagle VTR prop plane swept south, Statia off to the left, its mountain peak rising abruptly from the sea at the island's north end, then plummeting back into the depths a few miles later to the south as Melissa, in a window seat, watched the north shore of St. Kitts edge into view.

The plane was low enough so that she could see individual houses in the village of St. John's. She even thought, for a moment or two, that she might have picked out Rosie's place. She wondered if Rosie was in there right now, looking out her kitchen window to see the plane, knowing this was about when Melissa would be arriving. But no, she'd probably started her new job already. Rosie wasn't one to waste any time.

The plane dropped lower in its final approach, flying down the west coast of the island. Below, Melissa could see the town of Sandy Point and the huge outcrop of Brimstone Hill with old Fort George perched atop it. The narrow ribbon of the coast road marched along the island's edge, green foliage to one side, a narrow blond strip of sandy beach and then the blue Caribbean on the other. The volcano, Mount Liamuiga—Mount Misery, Stanley had said its name used to be—backed all this up, its bowl-shaped peak cloudless for a change as the plane started to bank left and head for the airport. The vanished town of Tabernacle and the cave—they were out of sight, over on the mountain's eastern slope.

The landing was a double bounce, almost as if the plane didn't want to put its wheels to the runway. But then they finally settled in and the props noisily reversed pitch to slow the plane down and she realized she was truly back. A few days, maybe a week, to pack up her things, go through closing out her lease on the condo, and then she'd be done with St. Kitts and she could get on with her life.

It had been a full day's travel getting here, starting with a couple of hours of driving from Mankato to the Twin Cities, then the five-hour flight from Minneapolis to San Juan, a two-hour wait there, and then the short flight down to St. Kitts.

It was still winter up there, though it had gotten above zero finally and there'd even been a few days above freezing. February, as usual, was filled with snow in Mankato—thirty inches in the first three weeks—but the cold felt less chilling to her now, less oppressive and dark. She'd seen the death it could bring, she'd faced it, and now it held no special threat. These days she didn't shiver so much.

She'd gone to the funerals of Walter Arndt and Father Murphy, then, a few days later buried her father and her mother at two cemeteries, miles apart. Then, for weeks, she'd signed forms, answered a thousand questions from the police, tried to tell the police and the media what she could bear to talk about.

Most of the media, the major newspapers and the magazines, had been pretty good with her, trying hard to be sensitive to what she'd gone through even while they worked hard to get the story.

The television stations and the agents for the TV talk shows, on the other hand, she'd learned to hate them. The lights; the microphones thrust at her face; the slick, pushy women with too much makeup and mock concern, the perfect hair on the men, their vacuous smiles. God, they were awful.

But she'd done what she could, what she felt she had to. Even got a job offer out of it all; the local paper, the *Mankato Free Press,* offering her a spot as a general assignment reporter. She'd said yes but told them she had some things to take care of first and couldn't start for a couple of weeks. Then, that same day, she'd called the airline to finally make her return flight reservation for St. Kitts. Get down there and get it over with.

She still had things to worry about in Minnesota, of course, the farm, for one. She'd decided to go ahead and sell it to the Torensen boys. They'd close on it when she got back up there, and that meant she'd have some money—a lot of money, actually. She had to think about what to do with it.

She'd even spent some time with Summer Arndt. They'd talked at first, then started jogging together some on the cold roads of winter. They didn't mention The Kiss, or those days much at all. There was too much pain back there. Instead, finding again a joy Melissa hadn't known in a long time, they started playing basketball, a little one-on-one, just for fun. Melissa still had her shot.

Dan Finnegan had been wonderful, the father figure she'd needed at a time of crisis for both of them. She'd leaned on him constantly, and he was strong enough to take it. He would have come with her on this trip if the doctors had let him. Instead, minus two fingers on one hand and one on the other, he was still recuperating. When he was better, she'd come back down here with him for a visit, show him what the Caribbean was all about.

The lone flight attendant, a young Latina from Puerto Rico, opened the main fuselage door as the ground crew wheeled up the boarding stairs and Melissa stood in the aisle, collecting her thoughts, wondering if this was the right thing to do.

Stanley had made it clear that she didn't have to come back to help him. His childhood friend the deputy police commissioner had already seen enough evidence to get interested in the old case: slugs from a .38-caliber handgun, the bones of the victim, the ring to show the bones were probably those of Quinton Edwards, Stanley's father. There wasn't much chance of finding the gun that matched the slugs, of course; Henry Palmer must have gotten rid of it years ago. So there didn't seem to be a way to tie Henry Palmer to the murder, except for Melissa's vision of how it had happened. And strange hallucinations, Stanley had pointed out to her over the phone, didn't hold up well under cross-examination.

Finding the gun, finding more evidence in the cave, maybe? That seemed the only option, and Stanley could do those things just fine on his own, thank you; he'd said that to her several times during his long calls. He'd been working on this on his own for a long time, and he was willing to work a lot longer on it. He didn't need her for that.

And he pointed out that with the case in the open and covered now in the *News-Democrat* as well as Stanley's *Labour News*, there was too much publicity for the Palmers to dare attempt anything against Stanley. He was still being followed, he said, by two new guys now. But he just waved at the guys and smiled. They never smiled back, he said.

So Melissa told herself that she was back just to pack up her things and say her good-byes. She'd even had a difficult long-distance call with Bo, telling him she was leaving him, leaving the island. Before the horror of her father's death and the knowledge of what he'd done, the incident with Bo had been, she'd thought, the worst thing in her life. Now it took a backseat to more immediate horrors. She'd needed to make the call and so she'd done it.

He'd been smoothly polite, accepting the resignation she'd faxed him, accepting the news that she was leaving. She'd given him the bare bones of the story, that her father had died awfully, that she'd been there when it happened. He understood, Bo had said, that she'd want to resign and go home, given all the terrible things she'd been through. His own father, he'd said, was still fighting the lung cancer that ate at him. The doctors weren't talking about how long he'd live.

So Bo was sorry it had all worked out this way, but he understood. It felt, to her, like a clean break. Let Stanley worry about the troubles down here; she'd had enough of her own back home in the cold. She didn't say anything to Bo about rape. He didn't mention the marriage proposal. Story over.

How much did Bo know about what his father had done? About the men who'd chased her and Stanley? She didn't know. Someday, maybe, Stanley would find out and let her know.

Stanley. She'd talked to him half a dozen times through the weeks of pain after that awful day on Minnetoksak. He knew how to listen, knew just what to say to her. She looked forward to seeing him again for a few days, and Rosie and their mother,

Miriam, too. They were good people. She'd miss them. She'd miss this island.

She had feelings for Stanley, she'd come to realize, but they were all mixed up with everything they'd gone through and this was certainly not a time to trust her feelings about someone.

She thought about that as the line of people standing in the plane's center aisle started to move toward the open door and she could feel the heat from outside washing into the plane. The heat felt wonderful. She wanted to sweat again, to feel a warm sun against her face, to go stand on a beach somewhere with Stanley and just let the sun, the sand, and the water work on her.

She walked down the steps, followed the line of passengers across the tarmac to the arrivals area, where she worked her way through immigration control and customs, got her passport and her luggage glanced at, and then she was through and into the terminal building.

And there, waiting for her, was Stanley. He gave her a hug as she walked up to him.

"Hey, you looking pale, girl. You been away from this island way too long."

She laughed. "How are you, Stanley?"

"Doing just fine. And you? Other than needing some sunshine, you doing all right?"

He knew the whole story, of course. In those long phone calls she'd told him everything—the horror of her father's madness, the terror of his actions, how she'd touched her mother's body and seen the horrific past, the harrowing way it all had ended.

They walked toward Stanley's new taxi, a Nissan this time, a bright blue Altima. "Couple of years old, but she runs great, got a nice sound system for those tourist tapes. Here, listen," he said, and slid a cassette in as they drove away from the airport.

It was Bob Marley, telling a woman not to cry. Melissa smiled. "Are we going to Rosie's?" she asked.

"Yeah, but we got to stop at Palmer House first and see my mother. She says she wants to see you, and right away."

Melissa smiled at that. Seeing Miriam Edwards sounded like fun; she liked the woman and she had some news for her, too.

As Stanley took the first main turn onto Bay Road, Melissa relaxed, rolling down her window to enjoy the heat, the humid breeze in her face, the smell of the place, alive with morning glory vines, citrus trees bearing their fruit, mango, palm trees. God, it was heavenly.

Stanley shifted gears as he got through the little roundabout at Frigate Road. "Things are spooky calm right now, except for the occasional little earthquake. Ansel Baptiste, my deputy commissioner friend, has some forensics expert from England looking at the bones, just to see if there's a way to make legally certain they're my father's. No word on that yet. Ansel is powerful enough, and honest enough, that no one can get to him, I think. He'll do what he can to help me get some justice, maybe even, someday, connect this all up to Joseph's murder, too."

He looked in his rearview mirror. "And if you look about four cars back you'll see a white Toyota. That's my new friends who follow me around. The two who chased us are gone from the island. You can imagine what must have happened to them."

Melissa reached up to turn the mirror so she could look back. There they were. "I told you I talked to Bo, right? It was like none of this had happened. I said I was quitting and going home, and he said he understood and wished me the very best, and that was that."

Stanley nodded. "I'm not surprised. The Palmers are in trouble and they're trying to lie low. I think they hope it will all just blow over eventually, but with all the newspaper coverage and the radio chatter, they're finding it hard to do business. That business deal of Bo's, the South African deal for the new resort, fell apart. The Holtzhausen Group pulled out and took its money to another developer, over on Nevis."

Stanley smiled, reached down into the side pocket of the door, and pulled out a newspaper, handed it to her. "I ran that yesterday, and the *News-Democrat* ran it today. Here, take a look."

She unfolded the paper and there it was as the main story on page 1: "South Africans Choose Regis Group," the headline read, and the lead paragraph gave the details.

"That was Bo's pet project; he'd been working on it for a

couple of years," she said, folding the paper back up and tucking it into the center console. "He must be furious."

"You sound like you feel sorry for the guy."

She shrugged. "Maybe I do, a little. It was his father who's the murderer, Stanley, right?"

"Yeah, I guess so." He looked at her, shook his head. "But Bo is the one who raped you."

She looked back. "Yes. It seems like a hundred years ago, back when I was young and stupid. But it was only a month or so."

"Long winter, eh?"

"Forever. Stanley, how much do you think Bo knows about all this? Does he know the details? Know about his father?"

It was Stanley's turn to shrug. "Don't know. I hear that your Bo has been taking it all pretty hard, like he was surprised to hear it, and Errol thinks maybe the boy didn't know. But it could all be just an act, just trying to keep himself looking clean. When the old man finally dies, Bo takes over, you know. If there's anything left to take over."

"His father's doing worse again?"

"Yeah, that's what they say. He's up in Miami now, I hear, getting looked at one more time. But he's so far gone..." He shook his head. "He's going to cheat me; I know it. He's going to die before I can nail him."

She looked at him, at the profile of that handsome face, furrowed now in anger, staring ahead at the crowded, narrow road. He wanted some vengeance, and she couldn't blame him.

Fifteen minutes later they pulled into the long driveway at Palmer House. As they drove into the small car park, Melissa could see Rosie and Mother Miriam standing out on the wide wraparound porch.

Rosie came running into the parking lot and threw a huge hug around Melissa as she got out of the Nissan.

"You're back! Hey, we missed you, girl."

"Hi, Rosie. I heard you got a new job with the tourist bureau."

Rosie grinned. "They're even spending money like they should, to get some tourists here. I got the budget I need to print a new brochure in four-color. Can you imagine that?"

Melissa laughed. "No, I can't. And how's your mother doing?"

Stanley came over to them. "Come on; let's go talk to her. She said she had to see you straightaway when you got back."

"So I heard. But why?"

Rosie laughed. "Who knows? But she wants to talk to you right now, and no waiting."

"She's doing all right, then?"

"You'll see," Rosie said as the three of them walked up the wide stairs to the porch.

Miriam Edwards stared off toward the open sea as Melissa approached. Then she turned to see the girl. "Who you?"

"I'm Melissa O'Malley. We met once, a month ago."

"That's right. You a friend of my boy Joseph, right?"

"I'm afraid not, ma'am. I'm a friend of Stanley's, and of Rosie's."

Recognition dawned on that stern face; a smile broke through. She reached out to take Melissa's hand. "Oh, yes. You that obeah girl was here before. I been wanting to see you, girl. We got things to talk about. Important things. What you been up to, girl?"

"I've been home, ma'am, up in Minnesota."

Miriam reached out to touch Melissa's face, let her fingers brush lightly across her cheekbones, her chin. "Oh, girl, you been through cold times, am I right?"

"Oh, yes, ma'am, cold times is right."

Miriam smiled, took Melissa by the hand, and walked with her over to the edge of the porch. She pointed up to the distant peak of Mount Liamuiga. "You and me, we seen that mountain's smoke, right? Just a couple of days ago, right?"

Melissa smiled at her. "A month ago, yes."

"No, couldn't be that long," said Miriam. She pointed again. "Look now; that mountain's still smoking. You don't believe me, you can take a look right here and see for yourself."

Melissa looked. The mountain was clear, one thin stream of white cloud trailing away to the east from its summit. That must be what the old woman meant.

"I believe you, ma'am. Yes, it's smoking."

Miriam grabbed her by the elbow, hard, her grip surprising, demanding. "Don't be saying it if you can't see it, girl."

"I see that cloud. That's all I see."

The old woman sighed. "Well then, you can't see it. But it's there. If you ever do see it, you let me know, girl. You understand?"

Melissa nodded, smiled, humoring her. "Sure, when I see it smoking, I'll let you know."

The old woman seemed to feel something. She looked at Melissa's face and shook her head. "Hard times up there in the cold. I can feel that, girl. Am I right?"

"Yes, ma'am, hard times. But I got through it. When I was here last time, you told me to do what I had to do. You told me to find the truth. And I did it; I did what I had to do. I found the truth."

"It wasn't easy, was it?"

"No, ma'am. It was the hardest thing I've ever done." She reached into her pants pocket and pulled out the bracelet the old woman had given her. No reason not to be nice about this thing. "But this worked fine. I wanted to give it back to you, and say thanks."

Miriam chuckled, tugged Melissa to her for a hug. "Oh, child, that was nothing. I bought that in a shop in Basseterre years ago, cost me a few pennies. I just thought you needed a little something to help you concentrate."

Melissa smiled, shook her head, then reached to put her arms around the old woman and hugged her back for long seconds, the frail body stronger than Melissa would have guessed.

Finally, Miriam stepped back, tilted her head to look at Melissa from a new angle. "You still seeing things, girl?"

"I don't know. Maybe. Something happened up there."

Miriam reached out to take Melissa's hand. She rubbed it. Her eyes widened. "Oh my. You *are* something special. You saw cold things, child. Horrible cold. Frozen. And then you did things, too. Oh my, you got some obeah, child." She said it as a matter of fact.

Mother Miriam kept rubbing Melissa's hand. Gently, she said,

380 . Rick Wilber

"And there's more for you to do, girl, and it's got to do with my children and my husband, Quinton. He was such a good man, a great man, that Quinton. He did important things, you know that?"

Melissa nodded. "Stanley and Rosie told me. He found the truth, right?"

Miriam smiled. "That's right; that's what he found, the truth. They say bad things about him here sometimes. They say he stole some money and left me and the children. But you a smart girl, you an obeah woman, child. You know that can't be so about my Quinton."

"Yes, ma'am, I believe you."

Miriam held her out at arm's length. "Oh, girl. Like I said, you got more things to do."

Melissa stepped back away from her, shook her head. She didn't want to hear that. "More? Oh, ma'am. I've been through so much already."

Miriam frowned. "I am sorry, girl, but there are some things that just got to be, you know what I mean? Some things just got to be, and you the only one who can see the shadow, child. This old woman ain't never seen the likes of you when it comes to seeing the shadow."

Then she smiled again, took Melissa's hand, walked over two steps to Stanley, and took his, put the two together.

She looked at her accomplishment for a moment, the two hands held together. "My Stanley can help you, girl. Ain't my Stanley a nice boy?" she asked Melissa.

Melissa smiled back and turned to look at Stanley, who could only roll his eyes in mock dismay. "Yes, ma'am, he is," she said.

"And you better stop with this ma'am business. You gonna do more things here you got to call me Mother. That all right?"

"Yes, ma'am. Yes, Mother. If that's what you want."

"Ain't what I want, necessarily. Just what's got to be done, I guess. That Stanley, he ain't never going to get it done on his own."

Rosie coughed. "Mother, you've had enough. I think it's time we got you back inside where it's cool."

"I'm cool right here, child. That fan in there gives me the chills."

"Mother," Rosie said firmly. "Let's go inside." And she took her mother by the elbow. But Miriam pulled free and turned to look at Melissa one more time.

"You don't want to hear this, girl. But I think you and Stanley got to be going back to that cave one more time. I wasn't going to say that, but now I know for sure you got the obeah, you have got to be going back there. You hear me?"

"The cave? Oh, Mother, I don't know. I mean, we've been there. And Stanley's been back since, too."

"No. You got to go, the two of you. There's something there you got to find for me."

"What is it we're supposed to find, Mother?" Stanley asked, coming over.

"I don't know exactly, Stanley. But you'll know it when you see it. Got to do with your father, that's all I know."

Stanley sighed. "You haven't been drinking again, have you, Mother?"

"Don't you be poking fun at me, Stanley. You children always thought you were so smart. We always knew about that cave, your father and me." She laughed hard, remembering. "We went up there one day when you were in school, just the two of us, to check the place out, make sure it was safe. It was beautiful up there, and so quiet, just me and my man. Oh, children, that was a good day, for sure. There wasn't no arguing on that day, children."

Rosie wagged her finger at her mother. "Now, Mother, don't you go getting too excited. You know what the doctor said."

"That doctor," Miriam said, "he don't know a thing. He thought I was gone five years ago, and I'm still here."

"And we're glad of it, Mother. But now you have to get some rest."

"Don't need no rest. What I need is for them two to get back to that cave." She turned to face Stanley and Melissa. "You going to do that for me, children?"

"They'll go, Mother," Rosie said, taking her gently by the arm one more time and this time getting her headed in the right direction, toward the double doors.

Miriam turned back one more time. "You heard me, girl, right? You make sure Stanley takes you there. You got to go! You hear me?"

Melissa nodded, waved. "I hear you, ma'am. I'll make sure we go."

And then Mother Miriam was gone, guided on her path back to her room by her good daughter.

Melissa turned back to look at Stanley, who was chuckling. "She's really something, isn't she?" he said.

"Well, she's not afraid to speak her mind."

"That's for sure," he laughed. "She's a strange old thing sometimes, though. And since we found that stuff in the cave she's getting worse."

Melissa looked at him. "But we have to go, right? I mean, we have to go up there and take a look around, don't we?"

Stanley sighed. "Do we?"

Melissa nodded, smiled. "Absolutely."

And so they did.

THE EARTH MOVED

The cave looked the same to Melissa. She couldn't even see where Stanley and Rosie had dug up the bones; the whole area around the mouth of the cave was such a jumble of dirt, plants, and rock that it was impossible to tell if anything had been disturbed or not. There was a slight smell of something decaying, almost a rotten egg smell, like food gone bad. Stanley smelled it, too, and the two of them looked around the cave mouth for anything that might be causing it, but there was nothing.

Melissa had seen what happened to crime scenes back home; how the police got the scene all taped off while teams of investigators crawled around looking for the tiniest clue. Not here. People had been here, sure enough; there were footprints everywhere and it looked like every rock had been checked under, every inch of the cave and its entrance carefully scrutinized. But it wasn't the police who'd done it.

That meant everything had been checked out completely, so there was nothing they could do, really, Melissa thought. It was all a waste of time. But they'd known that coming here. They were just doing a nice thing for Stanley's mother, that was all, so they could report back to her that they'd looked and that nothing was there.

They went ahead and spent a half hour using their flashlights to check all the way to the back of the cave, where it closed off in a pile of rubble from an ancient cave-in. There was nothing there, just rocks piled to the roof. Absentmindedly they both lifted and moved a few, kicked a few of the smaller ones around at the base. Nothing.

Melissa was reaching down with her foot to try to shove aside a large round, flat stone when the earth began to move with another quake. Melissa stumbled backward, her foot caught under the lip of the stone. She lost her shoe and nearly fell flat onto her back before Stanley, right there next to her, reached out to grab her by the waist.

The low rumbling from the quake stopped as they stood there for an awkward moment, inches apart, sweaty faces flushed from the exertion of climbing to the cave and then searching it in the heat and humidity. They stared at each other.

Stanley leaned forward and kissed her on the tip of the nose. She smiled as he backed away for a moment to look at her. Neither of them said a word. He took a step toward her, reached out his arms. She came into them and they embraced, a cautious hug. Melissa wondered if she'd known this was coming and just hadn't admitted it to herself or if it was really the surprise it seemed to be. She stared at his face, his eyes barely visible in the dim light.

He stared back, then spoke softly. "Well, I don't know where that came from, girl. Must be the earthquake got me all shook, you know? Was that OK?"

She nodded slightly, smiled at him. "It was fine, Stanley."

The earth trembled again, dust and shards of rock falling from the walls and roof of the cave. Stanley laughed at it for a moment, "Hey, the earth moved for me."

Then he got deadly serious. "I think we better get out of here. We get another quake as sharp as the one that uncovered this cave and it just might block the opening right back up again, and with us in it."

Another tremble, sharper this time. A burst of smoke and steam came from beneath the pile of rocks they stood next to. The smell of rotten eggs was suddenly overwhelming.

"Oh, Christ," said Stanley. "I should have known. That smell is sulfur, girl. Steam. Smoke. That volcano's acting up and we're right in the middle of it. Grab that shoe and let's go."

Melissa reached down to grab her shoe from where it was wedged into the rock. She tugged on it and it came free, the rock sliding to the side as she tugged.

And there, under the rock, was the edge of a canvas sack.

"My god, Stanley. Look."

"I see it." He reached down and gave the corner of the sack a tug. It came free, sliding out easily, the kind of small sack you'd use to hold your things for an outing to the beach; a drawstring, loose, circled the top of it.

The sack held an oily rag and nothing else. Stanley pulled the rag out, its sharp, greasy smell mixing with the sulfur and smoke in the air. He held it up, shook his head in disappointment. "I think the gun that murdered my father was in here, Melissa. But somebody beat us to it."

He threw the sack and rag to the ground. "Goddamn it. It had to be the Palmers, too. Some of those goons got in here and found the damn thing."

Melissa knew how much this hurt him. He'd spent all these years trying to find proof of what Henry Palmer had done to his father, spent all these years getting this close. And now this.

She walked over to him, gave him a quick hug, sharing in the disappointment. "If the gun was in there, that just means someone on the island has it now, Stanley."

He nodded tiredly. "Sure, but then I'll have..." There came another minor rumble to shake them. He put his arms around Melissa as it grew for a moment. Then when it eased, they stood there in the darkness, the two of them still embracing for one long, delicious moment.

Until a loud bark of laughter and a bright splash of light shone on them from back near the mouth of the cave. They both turned to look but couldn't see anything but that bright source of blinding light.

They heard a voice: "Well, that's just really touching to see. My fiancée and the man who wants to destroy my family getting it on right before my very eyes."

Melissa knew that voice. It was Bo Palmer, walking slowly toward them as they both put their flashlights on him while he aimed his at the pile of rocks behind them.

"I see you've found something there, you two. 'Bout a half hour late, though." And he laughed, a high-pitched giggle. He stood there grinning, drenched in sweat, a baseball cap on his head. In his right hand he held a handgun, a revolver, that he aimed nonchalantly at them. In his other hand he held a handful of money, bills neatly tied together.

"This is *so* perfect. Here I am with a..." He hesitated, held his flashlight to the gun in his hand, read from the gun's grip, "...Colt .45 Defender. The very weapon my father used to solve *his* big problem with the Edwards family. And now, all these years later, I get to use it to solve mine."

He giggled again, waved the gun in the air, looked at Stanley. "It still has some rounds in it, Stanley. You think they'll work?"

"I doubt it."

"I don't know, Stanley. Dad packed it away pretty good. Here, they gave me this note from him this morning. He's dead. Up in Miami, he's dead."

Bo unfolded the piece of paper. "And it tells me everything. How he had everything set up with the new government for the resort. How your goddamn father kept digging up dirt about payoffs, and then the goddamn volcano, anything to stop Dad from getting the permits and getting the resort built.

"Dad came to Tabernacle to try and buy him off. Did you know that? He offered him ten thousand dollars to just shut up. That was a lot of money back then."

He giggled again. "Here's the good part. Let me read this to you, 'I never meant to shoot him, Son. You have to believe that. I just wanted to stop him. But we argued when I tried to give him the money, and then we fought and wound up wrestling for the gun and it went off and he was hit, just outside the cave. I panicked, and wrapped up the gun and the cash and buried it all in the cave. Then I tugged him into the mouth of the cave, too, and left to go for help. I was in the car, a couple of miles away, when the volcano blew, and I knew the help didn't matter.'"

Bo's giggling rose in pitch. He held up the money, his whole body shaking with the hilarity of it all. "You see, it was all an accident! And here's the best part. He says he's sorry! Can you believe that? From my dad? He was very, very sorry."

Melissa watched him squeal in delight. At any moment she expected him to start shooting. Beside her, Stanley stood still, frozen, his eyes narrowed, watching Bo. He was waiting for an opportunity, any chance, and he'd go for him, try to get the gun away from him, get that note. That piece of paper held everything he'd searched for all these years. That note, it admitted it all.

Bo took a deep breath, still smiling. Another deep breath, then, grinning broadly, he aimed the pistol carefully at Melissa. She stared back at him, afraid to move, to think. Another rumble shook them a bit, the series of small quakes continuing, bits of rock falling onto them from the ceiling of the cave. A cloud of sulfurous smoke boiled through the rocks behind them.

Bo slowly moved his aim left, directly at Stanley, then back again to Melissa. He spoke, calmly at first, then rising in tone, the words coming out faster as he said them. "You're fucking terrified, the both of you. Well, you ought to be, 'cause this is it, folks. This is where it all ends!"

There was another rumble, harder, like it was building. "Even the goddamn mountain wants to end it. My father is dead. The goddamn money doesn't matter—ten thousand measly dollars, can you imagine that? Jesus, that's lunch money! Dad was always so fucking cheap."

Bo shook his head, pointed the gun at Stanley. "And now he's gone. Everything's gone. You and your goddamn brother, sticking your noses in where they don't belong, making me do what I don't want to do. Jesus! And now it's all fallen apart. The goddamn South Africans, the fucking resort. Everything!" He cackled. "What a joke! All this goddamn work and now you and your boyfriend fucked it all up for me."

Another rumble, then a sharp crack from outside and a long rumble as a large boulder snapped free from the hillside and tumbled down into the gut.

Bo found it all very funny. He aimed the pistol at Melissa.

"Well, hey, Melissa. Like Dad said, I'm really sorry about this."
Bo squeezed the trigger. There was a loud, dry click. Nothing.
The ground was rolling beneath them now in the cave in a series
of quick, small waves. "Oh, goddamn it," Bo said, and reached
around behind his back, where he must have tucked away another
gun. Stanley, seeing his chance, ran forward, fifteen feet to cover
in a hurry.

The earth's violence rose beneath them all in a larger, more
powerful wave. Melissa felt herself rise toward the roof of the
cave and in that long-drawn-out moment she saw Stanley lose his
footing, too, as if pitched forward off a trampoline, right toward
Bo, who bounced high and backward.

The next few moments seemed to take an hour. The roof gave
way; the walls started collapsing inward: the cave was closing tight
as the earth rolled and heaved. Melissa, rolling back against the
cave wall, felt a hand—Stanley's—reaching for her through a
thick haze of dust and falling rock. She reached up to take it and
Stanley, on his knees, pulled her toward him. There was a dim
light thirty feet away at the cave mouth, light coming through
what was left of the opening and the thick dust.

On their knees they headed for it, scrambling their way over
boulders that seemed determined to keep them trapped in there
to die.

Twenty feet. Ten. They reached the mouth and clawed their
way toward the small opening, the one place left where they might
escape.

Melissa reached the opening first. She couldn't fit through it,
started shoving gravel and rocks out the hole, widening it, as the
earth rumbled again. She was sure it must be building toward
some final shock that would trap them all.

A few larger rocks popped free as she shoved, and the opening
widened, maybe large enough. She put her arms through and tried
to find purchase with her feet. Her head, her shoulders made it
through and then she could feel Stanley shoving her hard from
behind. A second later she popped through, out into the hard
sunshine of the trembling hillside.

She reached back as Stanley's arm came through. She grabbed

it, pulled as hard as she could as another shock hit them, raising the ground a foot and then slamming it down. He wasn't through. She pulled harder, crying out his name, "Stanley! Come on, Stanley," and then the top of his head appeared, his shoulders made it through, and she had him free. They were out, on hands and knees, unable to stand on the trembling earth.

They heard a cry from within. "Melissa!" It was Bo, choking out her name from behind. "Melissa! I need you! Help me!"

She looked at Stanley, who sat there, head hanging down, exhausted. He raised his head to stare back at her, said, "Oh, Jesus, girl. You sure? One more good jolt and this hole's going to close."

They heard him again, closer, coming toward them. "Melissa! I always loved you. My leg's broken. Jesus, I can hardly move. You have to help me! Please, you have to! I love you, Melissa. I love you!"

The earth rumbled again, another violent jolt. Melissa crawled back toward the opening. "Stanley. I have to. We have to."

He moaned. "All right, all right. I'll go back for him." And he crawled back to the opening, put his head and shoulders in, yelled, "Bo! Can you hear me? The opening's this way, over here!"

There was nothing—a long moment of silence. Stanley backed out, then made the commitment, reaching in with his arms and then his head and shoulders, ready to climb back down into the narrow opening. "Bo? This way, Bo!"

There was the loud crack of a gunshot from within, its echoes reverberating through the cave and coming out the hole like a series of cannon shots, one after the other. Stanley cried out and Melissa grabbed him, pulled him back out of the hole. He held his right hand out, blood coming from where a slug had torn through the middle of it, fingers dangling uselessly, blood pulsing out. "Jesus, he shot me!"

The earth seemed to respond with an earsplitting roar of rock torn from rock, of internal violence and heat and death as a huge jolt came from beneath them and sent them tumbling down the hillside. The earth slapped at them as they rolled and slid down the side of the gut.

At the bottom, dazed, they lay next to each other for a long moment, then began to rise as another rumble built up like a freight train bearing down on them. On their knees, trying to ride out the motion, they looked back up toward the cave mouth as a loud whistle screamed at them and then, with an explosive clap of thunder, a yellow cloud of sulfurous smoke and steam burst from the opening, a brown and gray and yellow cloud of boiling heat speckled with a cascade of green—the money, blown out over the hillside, drifting down slowly on Melissa and Stanley as they sat there and watched a final roiling convulsion of the earth send an avalanche of rock and steaming mud over the cave mouth, closing it, filling it, sealing it forever.

Dead calm, a strange quiet. The rock slide rattled to a stop not more than twenty yards from them with the money drifting down, settling onto the pumiced earth. Five-hundreds, one-hundreds, settled onto what once was Tabernacle as Melissa and Stanley struggled to their feet, then stood there in shock and awe, her right arm around his waist, his left over her shoulder as they looked up to where the cave had been, where now, creaking and cracking, the earth settled. It was over.

The cloud slowly drifted away, falling apart, dissipating in the tropical breeze. Melissa lifted her eyes toward the mountain in the strange calm. She smiled. Stanley, next to her, wrapped his hand in cloth torn from his T-shirt and looked toward where she pointed. There, from the top of Mount Misery, a cloud of smoke and steam billowed out. It was over; all of it was over at last. She could go see Mother Miriam and let the old obeah woman know that Melissa O'Malley, that Minnesota girl from the frozen north, had done what she had to do, had seen that mountain smoking, and now she knew the truth of things.

She stood there for a long moment, silent, and watched the billowing smoke rise in the blue tropical sky. She was sweating. It was hot, she realized, steaming hot, and she felt that welcoming warmth clear to her soul as she and Stanley finally turned their backs to the mountain and walked slowly away.

TOO DARK ALTOGETHER

My second self had lowered himself into the water to take his
punishment: a free man, a proud swimmer striking out for a new
destiny.
—"The Secret Sharer," Joseph Conrad

Melissa O'Malley stood at the window of her room in the
old farmhouse outside Mankato and stared out toward the fields
beyond. Soybeans. Sugar beets. An acre of sweet corn. Getting a
jump on things, and with her permission, the Torensen brothers
had planted back in the spring even before the closing, and now,
in July, the farm looked pretty productive.

She was packing. Nearly done, in fact, and that felt good. But
it had been a long, hard couple of weeks. First, all the paperwork
of the closing, struggling over points and payments. Then the
auction for the farm equipment, the things that the Torensen
brothers didn't want or need. Then the yard sale. Then the hard
work of tossing out everything else that she didn't want to keep
and couldn't sell or give away. Then figuring out what to do with
the sculptures, a couple of finished pieces and a half-dozen in
various stages of creation. A collector down in St. Louis had taken
them all finally, and for a song, but what the hell, at least they
were gone.

Through the whole process there'd been a deep, dull background ache, every contract, every phone call, every conversation
a reminder of the monster her father had been, the horrible things
he'd done. Coming back here to do what had to be done had

been harder than she'd imagined from the distance of the Caribbean. There she'd thought she was through with all the horror. Coming back here, she realized there was no escaping it, ever.

For all those years she'd lived with her father and thought of him as a strong, quiet, decent man. How could she not have known or remembered? Each room she walked into in the house held new realities for her now, new terrors cropping up to overwhelm the lifelong lie she'd unknowingly led in this house, growing up the child of a monster. The bedroom where she last saw her mother was terrible, of course. And the sunroom: somehow it was worse seeing it empty now, the dried plants gone, a shadowed cross on the wall where the crucifix had been for decades before it was finally taken down just a couple of weeks ago.

The whole place, all that had happened in it and from it, didn't bear thinking about too much; she wanted to somehow not have it on her mind all the time but, of course, couldn't shake it. A dark horror had started here and rippled outward to become the cold, deep background of her life.

Somehow she was supposed to move on from that. Somehow she was supposed to keep going, despite the violence and trauma of rape, despite the scars that such things left. She was supposed to move on, to stay alive even while knowing that the deaths that centered around her father held a permanence that nothing could change. What he'd done to all those innocents, starting with her mother and then adding, horribly, to the list: there was no moving on from that; no time could heal those wounds.

Dan Finnegan, the tough and hardened detective, seemed to be finding religion a help. He said he'd met Summer at Holy Innocents seven months ago when it was all coming to a head and he'd found something there he felt comfortable with, something he'd ignored for way too long.

He'd offered to take Melissa to Holy Innocents for Mass the past two Sundays and she'd given God a chance, trying to be inconspicuous in a middle aisle, grateful, at least, that everyone— she probably knew half the people there—had pretended not to stare.

Both times she'd spent most of her time not listening to the sermon—given by a new, young African priest with a British accent, of all things—but looking up past the altar to that smiling Christ behind it. Christ on the cross, dying, but smiling and reaching out with those hands to welcome the pain that saved humanity. The Son of man. The Holy Redeemer. Lord, I am not worthy, but can you heal this soul?

She wondered, looking up at Him, how could a merciful God allow such monstrous things as her father to exist? It didn't make any sense to her and she didn't see how it ever could. But Finnegan seemed to be buying into it, and she supposed that was a good thing for him, something he needed: a forgiving, smiling son of man, reaching out through the misery and pain of sacrifice to say it's OK; you can get on with things.

She wondered if she'd ever feel that way herself. Had she ever been a believer? Could she be? It was all so mixed up in this obeah thing and the memories of her mother that she couldn't wrestle it to a stop long enough to think it through.

She'd believed it back when she was a kid; she remembered that. But she wasn't a kid anymore, thank god. She didn't have to live that lie now. She knew what was real, and she'd faced it, up here and down in St. Kitts.

She turned away from the window, walked back toward the middle of the room, turned around to look at what was left of the place, a few bits and pieces of her life still in her own room. A Bob Marley poster hung on her wall, Bob's dreadlocks flying. On the tiny bookshelf that had been over the desk two books still sat, a high-school Spanish textbook, *Lengua viva y gramatica*, and a paperback Joseph Conrad collection, *Heart of Darkness & The Secret Sharer*. They reminded her of simpler times, back when she'd believed life was good, life held promise.

She took the two books, both of them covered in dust, gave them a quick wipe with her hand, and put them into the cardboard box she'd brought.

Then she pulled the Marley poster down carefully, trying not to tear it but ripping the edges anyway. Well, that couldn't be helped. She rolled it up and set it into the box next to the books. That was that. No woman no cry.

She didn't look back as she left the room. She didn't take a final walk-through of the place. Better to leave it and be done.

Outside, walking across the yard toward the rental car, she stopped once to turn around and look back. There, above the window of her room, was the block and tackle her father had once used to hoist the carcass of a deer. That seemed like centuries ago.

She heard the creak of the barn door and turned to look. It was Stanley, who'd come a very long way to help her end things here. He was coming out of the barn, holding a small sculpture, some kind of a bird, no bigger than a mailbox but heavy, the way he struggled to carry it.

"Look at this," he said. "Found it buried under some burlap back in an old stall." He set it on the ground, turning it once to dig the bottom into the soil.

Melissa walked over to look at it. Yes, a bird, a bald eagle maybe, made of four cultivator blades, two haying machine tines, and the bottom ten inches of an ice auger.

"Damn," she said.

"What do you want to do with it?"

She knelt down to touch it. Warm, dirty, rusty metal. Inanimate. Just another piece of junkyard art and nothing more than that.

What should she do with it? Hadn't she done enough? She stood, moved around some to loosen her back, a little stiff after all the heavy lifting of the past two weeks.

"You know, Stanley, let's just leave it right there. I think we've done enough."

"Sounds like a plan to me," he said. Then he looked at his watch and smiled. "We have to get going if we're going to pick up Dan Finnegan and make it to Minneapolis in time for that plane, you know."

"I know," she said, looking around one last time. Summer in Minnesota and they were prying Dan Finnegan away from it for a few weeks in the Caribbean. That was a pretty amazing thing. He was mumbling about retiring, taking the disability money, and moving south himself, buying a condo in Florida, maybe. Somewhere on the beach.

She didn't think he'd do it, but you never knew.

She walked over to the rental car, a Ford, and got in. Stanley did the same. Melissa was doing the driving.

For her, the future wasn't any plainer, but she did, at least, have a plan. She had plenty of money from the sale of the farm, and there was a good little weekly paper that needed a cash infusion and a talented editor to help out the poor publisher, who had to spend as much time working on his charter sailboat as he did reporting and editing.

Melissa O'Malley and the weekly *Labour News.* Melissa O'Malley and Stanley Edwards. How would that all work out? Was she a Minnesota girl or this other girl, the one that Stanley thought she was? Could she ever get past all this terror and bloodshed? Did Jesus on that cross have it right, you could smile through the pain?

She didn't know. But starting later today, at the airport, boarding that flight to San Juan, and on the puddle jumper to St. Kitts, she planned to find out.

ABOUT THE AUTHOR

Rick Wilber is a professor of journalism at the University of South Florida. Wilber has published several dozen short stories in a wide variety of magazines and over 1,000 of his nonfiction essays, reviews, features, and interviews have appeared in the *Boston Globe Sunday Magazine, Sport Magazine,* the *St. Louis Post-Dispatch,* and many other publications. His short fiction has been collected in *To Leuchars* and *Where Garagiola Waits and Other Baseball Stories.* He and his wife, Robin, live in Florida.